PRAISE FOR *BEST NEW HORROR*

"A worthy reflection of the diversity and high quality of contemporary horror and dark fantasy, this annual volume remains an absolute necessity."
— *Publishers Weekly* (starred review)

"Anyone who is interested in the contemporary horror scene should buy a copy of this book and devour it." — *The Times* (London)

"The best horror anthologist in the business is, of course, Stephen Jones."
— *Time Out*

"From its inception, the *Best New Horror* series has been an invaluable resource for all of us who believe in the genre." — Clive Barker

"An essential volume for horror readers." — *Locus*

"The *Best New Horror* series continues to break from the herd, consistently raising the bar of quality and ingenuity." — *Rue Morgue Magazine*

"An essential record, invaluable and irreplaceable, of modern horror fiction in all its range and variousness." — Ramsey Campbell

"All you need to bring you up-to-date with the horror scene." — *SFX*

"No self-respecting relisher of the macabre should ever deny him- or herself a copy." — Gahan Wilson, *Realms of Fantasy*

"Essential reading." — *Hellnotes*

"A real treat for any lover of the genre." — *SF Site*

"*Best New Horror* is a darkly shining beacon of hope in an unimaginative world." — Neil Gaiman

"The most valuable horror book of the year." — *Kirkus Reviews*

"An Ordnance Survey map of the terrain of contemporary horror and dark fantasy." — *Fantazia*

"Stephen Jones' always reliable series remains the key horror anthology of the year." — *Starlog*

"The *definitive* series of Horror 'Bests'." — *Science Fiction Chronicle*

"The collection we'd recommend if you had to make a choice." — *Interzone*

"The sheer range of dark fantasies here is impressive." — *Shivers*

"*Best New Horror* continues to provide a valuable and salutary service for horror." — *Fear*

THE MAMMOTH BOOK OF

The Best of Best New Horror

A TWENTY-YEAR CELEBRATION

Edited by Stephen Jones

With an Introduction by Ramsey Campbell

ROBINSON

RUNNING PRESS
PHILADELPHIA · LONDON

Constable & Robinson Ltd
3 The Lanchesters
162 Fulham Palace Road
London W6 9ER
www.constablerobinson.com

First published in the US as *The Very Best of Best New Horror* by Earthling Publications.

First published in the UK by Robinson,
an imprint of Constable & Robinson, 2010

A copy of the British Library Cataloguing in Publication
Data is available from the British Library

UK ISBN 978-1-84901-304-8

1 3 5 7 9 10 8 6 4 2

First published in the United States in 2010 by Running Press Book Publishers

9   8   7   6   5   4   3   2   1
Digit on the right indicates the number of this printing

US Library of Congress number: 2009929923
US ISBN 978-0-7624-3841-9

Running Press Book Publishers
2300 Chestnut Street
Philadelphia, PA 19103-4371

Visit us on the web!

www.runningpress.com

Printed and bound in the EU

Contents

Acknowledgments

I would like to thank Ramsey Campbell, Paul Miller, Hugh Lamb, Val and Les Edwards, Duncan Proudfoot, Pete Duncan, Dorothy Lumley and all the authors, editors and publishers who have contributed to the series over the past twenty years, for their help and support.

Editor's Foreword

OKAY, LET'S GET SOMETHING absolutely straight from the beginning – despite what the title of this book says, this volume does not necessarily represent the twenty finest stories that have ever appeared in the *Best New Horror* series over the past two decades. For a start, those previous twenty volumes have contained more than 450 stories by almost 200 authors and, given the nature of any "Year's Best" series, *all* the stories in those books can be considered to be the "best" in some form or another – at least according to the criteria of those who compile them.

Back in 1992, in the third volume, my co-editor Ramsey Campbell and I pointed out that: "*Best New Horror* does not purport to be a collection of the year's best horror stories. Instead, we hope to present a varied selection of fiction – loosely connected by various notions of horror – that illustrates the range of themes and ideas currently being explored in the genre, by top names in the field and exciting newcomers."

That policy statement could just as well be applied to this current compilation as well.

We decided very early on that it would be presumptuous to claim that *Best New Horror* contained a definitive selection of the year's best horror stories. After all, such definitions are totally subjective and differ widely between each individual. So instead, as Ramsey and I explained, these anthologies over the years have attempted – based on the material seen – to present an annual "snapshot" of some of the best horror fiction writing to be published in a particular year.

With so many superior stories and talented authors to choose from, and with the number of tales necessarily constrained by the word-length of a single book, I decided to limit my choice for this anniversary edition to what I considered to be one of the best stories from each volume.

When it came to my definition of "best", I considered whether a particular story was the most effective, stylish or simply influential in any individual volume. As a consequence, this led to some juggling of titles and authors until I felt that I had achieved a representative selection of twenty superior horror stories (and don't expect me to define my "various notions" of what constitutes "horror" here – this book speaks for itself).

Unfortunately, because I also decided to allow authors only one story per volume, by necessity some very fine tales and their creators have had to be left out of this anthology.

As a result, many excellent writers who have regularly contributed to the series over the years – including Poppy Z. Brite, Dennis Etchison, Stephen Gallagher, Charles L. Grant, Brian Hodge, Graham Joyce, Joel Lane, Tanith Lee, Thomas Ligotti, Kelly Link, Nicholas Royle, David J. Schow, Steve Rasnic Tem, Karl Edward Wagner, Cherry Wilder and Gene Wolfe, to name only a few – are not represented in this current volume.

There is nothing to say that these and other equally talented writers could not be included in another compilation using the same criteria at a later date. There is certainly a wealth of talent and some extraordinarily powerful material to draw upon throughout the distinguished history of this anthology series. But until then – like the series itself – this current volume should be considered a representative sampling of some of the finest work that has been included in *Best New Horror* over the past twenty years.

Is it actually the *best* of the *Best*? I'm not so sure . . . but I do know that these tales and the authors who crafted them represent the pinnacle of the horror genre from the preceding two decades. And that can't be a bad thing for any "Best of" compilation . . .

Stephen Jones
Costa Dorada, Spain
May 17, 2009

Introduction

Bettering the Best

TWENTY YEARS! We've seen horror dwindle almost to nothing under the pitiless light of the marketplace, tottering away only to grope, however tentatively, back into the open. I'm reminded of the 1950s, when I discovered the field. The great pulps were dead or dying, and almost no horror was being published as such. All horror comics had been banned by the British parliament, and yet two years after the ban came into force, the august Faber & Faber published *Best Horror Stories* with a gleefully lurid cover. The genre was largely being kept alive – underground, if not in its grave – by enterprising small presses and short-lived magazines. In time it struggled to its feet, and by the mid-1970s it was prancing and showing all its many teeth. Like any monster, it was eventually overwhelmed, but we know monsters never really die. Perhaps we're back in that stage of its eternal gestation where I began, with an undead hibernation behind us and an uncertain future to come.

Of course things and even Things have changed. One is the onset of the Internet. Whereas when we began *Best New Horror* our readers were protected from the slush pile, unless they worked in publishing, these days the kind of material that made editors blench can be read online. Just because everybody uses language, that doesn't mean that they can write even tolerable prose. If some of the stuff out there has any merit, it's to show people the kind of thing that editors protect us from.

We begin this *Best of Best* as we mean to continue, with the unexpected. "No Sharks in the Med" is one of Brian Lumley's occasional tales that have no fantastic or supernatural element. Perhaps there's just a hint of revenge from beyond the grave, but the tale draws its power from its vivid evocation of the kind of Greece we tourists seek and from the classically gradual revelation of the dark that lurks beneath it, all this in the kind of Mediterranean sunlight we might think inimical to shadows. It was originally published in *Weird Tales*, a magazine that broke its pact with weirdness by reprinting, in one of its last issues of the 1950s, Merle Constiner's "The Skull of Barnaby Shattuck", a Western novelette first published in *Short Stories*. As a young horror fan I read the tale and waited for the wretched skull to scream or do a jig or put on any kind of a show at all, but no such luck. Brian's story wouldn't have disappointed me, however, in delivering horror.

The year 1990 brought us Michael Marshall Smith, and it's quite an event. You may be reminded here and there of Bradbury's small-town lyricism or Steve King's way with a flavoursome phrase, but Mike's voice is already unmistakeable. Though his prose has grown leaner over the years, it's just as strong when it's well fed, like the tiger in the story. For myself, I wouldn't have less of it, and I'm delighted to renew my acquaintance with his fine first publication. It may owe some of its enviable fluency to having been written in a single day. Sometimes a debut feels as if a flood of talent has been undammed, as here.

Of my own tale, which Steve has been kind enough to include, I've little to say. When I wrote it I'd forgotten that John Ware had written one called "Spinalonga" for the thirteenth *Pan Book of Horror Stories*. That volume was graced by David Case's novella "The Dead End" but also suffered from the rot that had set into the series. Amid the parade of child-burnings and dismemberments and mutilations that the book trots out for its fun-loving customers, Ware's leprous anecdote seems tasteful – sufficiently so to have slipped my mind by the time the family and I went to Crete a decade later.

Ever since the Gothic novel, horror fiction has been inspired by landscapes, and that island off Elounda was too tempting a location to waste. Incidentally, I've just discovered that my yellowing copy of the Pan book contains a souvenir from an earlier owner – the counterfoil of a postal order bought at Bank on December 13, 1977 and sent to Cooking for Outline of Purfleet. On the back the owner has listed the contents of the anthology with an observation about each, including "Sort of comment", "Dead boring!!" and "Whoop-peee?!!" Mysteriously, the only tale not listed is "Spinalonga", which is replaced by something called "Max!" that's summed up as "Rotten!!"

I digress. I do, you know. Perhaps I'm delaying thoughts of Norman Wisdom, though not of Christopher Fowler's tale. In 2007 Sir Norm was rehoused in a nursing home on the Isle of Man. I'm sure his fellow tenants could never have imagined that their last days would be filled with memories of his routines – perhaps some old folks' final moments may consist of them. This fate befalls several of the characters in Christopher's splendid tale, which is both horribly funny and oppressively disturbing. Its portrait of nostalgia turned sour rings all too true, and the narrator is a memorable addition to fiction's gallery of psychotics. One feels one may easily meet him.

Now behold the irrepressible Harlan, a man with a talent so large they might have named a county after him. He dislikes the word horror as applied to fiction, but several of his tales are splendid examples of it: "Shattered Like a Glass Goblin" for certain, and "The Whimper of Whipped Dogs" and "I Have No Mouth and I Must Scream", and equally the novella herein. His stories don't often reach this length, but it sustains the blazing intensity of his best work without faltering. Several decades ago Harlan was kind enough to reminisce about a visit to San Quentin for a novel I was writing. He lent my chapter vividness but by gum, it's nothing compared with his own use of the place. Read his tale, which (in the best sense) reads like the writing of a man possessed.

Even more than Harlan, Paul J. McAuley is more usually associated with science fiction than with horror. The gulf is less wide than it's sometimes perceived to be, however. Where Brian Aldiss cites *Frankenstein* as the first work of modern science fiction, other commentators – Lovecraft, for instance – claim it for horror, and so it's entirely appropriate that Paul's tale should evoke Mary Shelley's seminal novel. He recalls James Whale's gay romp *Bride of Frankenstein* as well (in which, it seems to me, the title applies to Dr Pretorius, who seduces Frankenstein away from an unconsummated marriage to help him give birth to a creature). Paul brings to this story all the attention to detail that makes his science fiction so vivid and convincing. Its terror and pathos are worthy of the original *Frankenstein*. I would happily have helped to choose it for that year's volume of *Best New Horror*, but 1994 was the year I fled as editor, leaving stalwart Steve to sift the mounds of rubbish with which the field was laden. There was plenty of first-rate fiction, but the task of reading the worst of the rest was just too dispiriting. Whose gravestone graces the cover of that year's book? Whose skeletal hand claws at it from the earth?

The year 1995 brought us the fantastic Neil Gaiman – brought him to horror, that is, where he intermittently perches before soaring away on another flight of wonder. Can I take a little credit? Ten years before, as a young journalist he'd interviewed me in the resoundingly empty house to which my family and I were about to move. In "Queen of Knives" he's drawing on much earlier experiences, though. Like his superb work in comics, poetry enables him to say a great deal in enviably few words. What exactly has been said seems to shift and grow with every re-reading. Note the appearance, as in the Fowler tale, of a British comedian from the past. Comedy and horror intersect in many ways.

I can certainly congratulate myself over Terry Lamsley – or over putting out the word about him, at any rate. Having picked up his first collection, *Under the Crust*, at the 1993 Ghost Story Society convention in Chester, I was on the phone days later to Steve Jones, enthusing about a new master of the spectral. Soon I wrote the introduction to Terry's next book, *Conference with the Dead*, from which "The Break" is taken. Like Neil's piece, this story finds weirdness in a family holiday. Not that in many cases it needs much finding; after all, one of the strangest places most of us are likely to end up is our own childhood. Often the point of the child's viewpoint in a horror story is not just to enhance the terror but to remind us what it was like. "The Break" is a fine example of a tradition that began with Machen's masterly "White People".

In his great novel *I Am Legend* (thrice indifferently filmed) Richard Matheson showed us the world overtaken by vampires, and his prophecy has come to pass, at least in terms of copies on the shelves. Series of books proliferate everywhere: erotica (*Muffy the Vampire Layer*), same-sex erotica (*Duffy the Vampire Gayer*), dog stories (*Wuffy the Vampire Bayer*), stories of a seaside donkey (*Gruffy the Vampire Brayer*), a football saga (*Cloughie the Vampire Player*), tales of the priesthood (*Stuffy the Vampire Prayer*), dietary aids (*Puffy the Vampire Weigher*), memoirs of feisty old folk (*Toughie the Vampire Greyer*) . . . Sequels to *Dracula* are a genre in themselves, ranging from the hilarious *Carmel* (written by a bishop, it gives us the tip that vampires don't stutter and includes the line "Imagine my horror when he pulled a decapitated head from the carrier bag he was holding – and asked 'Do you recognize it?'") to Caitlín R. Kiernan's fine tale here. Its poetic compression gives it the substance of a novel in fewer than twenty pages. Like her friend Poppy Z. Brite, she brings lyricism to horror and to the theme of vampirism.

The year 1998 is Peter Straub's year. I'm especially happy to be associated with an anthology in which he appears. Back in the 1970s I did my best to tempt him into *New Terrors* but (like Harlan Ellison and Anthony Burgess, among others) he couldn't be lured. Herman

Melville's "Bartleby the Scrivener: a Story of Wall-street" is central to his tale that follows, "Mr Clubb and Mr Cuff". In 1957 Melville's story appeared in the Faber book I cited at the outset, *Best Horror Stories*, preceded by the editor's admission that many readers might not call it horror. I'd say it was, but all the same, it might lead you to expect Peter's story to be a little staid. You'd be wrong. When he wrote *Floating Dragon* he set out to encompass all horror, but as you'll see, he didn't exhaust his imaginative capacity for it. "Mr Clubb and Mr Cuff" is as intensely grisly as anything he has yet given us.

In 1999 Tim Lebbon ruined the world, in the best sense. The greatest fiction in the field reaches for awe, and "White" certainly delivers that. To combine it with psychological incisiveness and contemporary gruesomeness is a considerable feat, not least of balance and the modulation of prose. It's the work of a writer at the height of his powers (but let me add that Tim is still at that pitch). It also confirms that the novella length is especially hospitable to horror.

And here's another. *The Other Side of Midnight* was previously the title of a mammoth melodrama, dully directed by Charles Jarrott. (Where's Douglas Sirk when you need him?) But 2000 brought us Kim Newman instead, and he's just as subversive. Despite my previous complaint about vampire clones, I'll happily read Kim's vampire fiction. Not only here, he demonstrates that modernism and horror aren't mutually exclusive. He has a good deal of inventive fun with aspects of the text, but despite his witty alternate worldliness, he conveys a real sense of evil. He also summons up a film that this reader would like to see almost as much as a restored *Ambersons*. Perhaps the surviving footage can be found on one of the Criterion editions of Welles.

The year 2001 is the year of Clarke and Kubrick and Elizabeth Hand. Despite its evocative title, "Cleopatra Brimstone" doesn't seem so visionary at first, but it keeps its magic in reserve. In due course it wriggles forth from its pupa of realism to reveal its glorious nature, in explosions of imagery as rich as anything in her more immediately fantastic work (which is fantastic in all the best senses). It's a true and wondrous original, but then so is its author.

In 2002 *Best New Horror* revealed Joe Hill to us. "20th Century Ghost" is simultaneously horrifying and poignant, a combination all too rare in the field. Its ghost is drawn by a love of movies, but equally she's the embodiment of loss and yearning. The final resolution of all the story's themes is as deft as it is very moving. The economy and range of effects are entirely typical of the author, and it lent its title to his first collection. The book was rightly hailed as a major debut and an important contribution to the field, though the odd commentator complained that it had succeeded other than by merit. It had no need.

The year 2003 saw publication of the first collection by Mark Samuels, and about time too. Its title tale, "The White Hands", is here. In my introduction to his later book *Glyphotech* I did my best to celebrate his mastery of the urban weird tale (a form I suggested was distinct from other kinds of urban supernatural horror). He may be described as the British Ligotti, which isn't to imply any imitation. Like that author, the sense of terror in his work is rooted in his philosophy and his aesthetic of horror – indeed, the three elements form a single entity, and an uncommonly disturbing one. If there are faint echoes in "The White Hands" of Lovecraft and more obviously (in a character's name) of M. R. James, they seem to be heard in a nightmare that is all the author's own.

The year 2004 was the year of Lisa Tuttle's great novella "My Death" (or, since it appeared as a book in itself, *My Death*). I'm not alone in playing with the phrase, which means a great deal more in the tale. How disconcertingly personal is this narrative? While there's a faint whiff of *The Aspern Papers* (no, not *The Astern Papers*, despite the prompting of my spellcheck), the story is utterly Tuttle. It epitomizes the kind of subtle disquiet we've rarely seen in fiction since the days of Aickman and Walter de la Mare, but it couldn't have been written by either of them. It's a true tale of unease – the term might have been invented for it – and preserves its profound ambiguity to the end. Like Lisa, I'll take enigma over explanation any time.

The year 2005 brought Clive Barker back to horror, but the process isn't so simple. Long before his *Books of Blood* amazed the world, Clive had been creating fantasy, not least on stage. Many of the tales in the *Books of Blood* are essentially fantastic, but equally some of his later fantasies – *Weaveworld, Coldheart Canyon* – delve into horror. "Haeckel's Tale" couples the two forms in a way that's uniquely Barker: witty, unnervingly erotic, philosophically challenging – altogether an enrichment to the imagination. It's worth noting that despite the vividness of his imagery, Clive is far more restrained than many of his imitators. They should learn that from him.

The year 2006 is represented by Glen Hirshberg. In some ways the tale is typical of him: the immediacy and vividness of the detail, the psychological incisiveness. In my preface to his first collection, *The Two Sams*, I wrote "He brings enviable skills to his work: a stylistic precision that comes of loving language, an unerring eye for character and the moments that define or reveal it, a keen sense not just of place but how light and the time of day transform his settings. It's his sense of the spectral, however, that puts him up there with the best." All this is true of "Devil's Smile", but nothing in his earlier work quite prepares us for the sheer horror it very gradually and insidiously accumulates. Its sense of maritime mystery and terror is worthy of Hodgson, and it has the potency of an actual myth. Davy Jones forbid that the creature is more real than that, but it's certainly unforgettable.

The story for 2007 gives me the chance to reiterate my old saw (not to be confused with *Saw*) that many of the greatest horror stories reach for awe or the numinous: masterpieces by Machen and Blackwood and Lovecraft, among many others, come to mind. With "The Church on the Island" Simon Kurt Unsworth adds a fine tale to this honourable tradition. Over the decades Steve has supported many new writers who have continued to distinguish themselves and their field. I predict Unsworth will be another, and I wish his career all success.

For 2008, we name the man responsible – responsible in large part for the wave of horror fiction from which we fished so many treasures. I recall my agent Kirby McCauley exhorting me in New York at Halloween of 1976 to pick up a novel by a new writer who'd impressed him. I still have that Signet paperback with its mysterious front cover – glossy black without title or author, just an embossed face drooling a single drop of blood – on my shelf. And we all still have Steve King, no longer a young Turk but a grand old (well, elderly) man. (I can say that, being more than a year older.) Let me suggest that his story here epitomizes one of his traits that are too seldom celebrated: his willingness to address themes that are difficult or uncomfortable for the reader (and, I suspect, for the author too). *Pet Sematary* will always come to mind, and even some of his titles – *Misery, Desperation* – are confrontational, challenging his audience to take the risk he's taken. In the present tale he brings an omnipresent contemporary fear out of the depths of our minds and takes on the afterlife with typical bleakness – inimitable, actually, though hordes have tried to copy the easy stuff. All this he achieves in less than four thousand words. And watch out for that title! He's still at the peak of his talent. Long may he tower there.

And long may *Best New Horror* rescue riches for posterity. Meanwhile, there's no better history or treasury of the last twenty years of our field.

Ramsey Campbell
Wallasey, Merseyside
May 4, 2009

1989

"A first-rate collection. Add it to the must-buy list."—*Locus*

BEST NEW HORROR

Stephen Gallagher
Richard Laymon
Thomas Ligotti
Brian Lumley
Robert R. McCammon
Kim Newman
Thomas Tessier
Karl Edward Wagner
Ian Watson
Robert Westall
Cherry Wilder
Ramsey Campbell
and others

Edited by Stephen Jones
& Ramsey Campbell

No Sharks in the Med

Brian Lumley

IN 1989, PUBLISHER Nick Robinson decided to create a companion volume to Gardner Dozois' excellent *The Year's Best Science Fiction* series (retitled *Best New SF* for the UK market).

So when he asked me if I would be interested in editing an annual "Year's Best" horror anthology, containing a selection of stories chosen from those initially published in the preceding year, I immediately agreed. However, I had a couple of stipulations.

The first was that I ask Ramsey Campbell – in my opinion one of the most intelligent and knowledgeable authors in the horror field – to co-edit the book with me. The second was that I check first that it was okay with my old friend Karl Edward Wagner, who was currently editing *The Year's Best Horror Stories* series for DAW Books. (Ellen Datlow and Terri Windling had started *The Year's Best Fantasy and Horror* for St Martin's Press a couple of years previously, but I did not consider that direct competition as half the book was made up of fantasy stories.) Karl graciously gave us his blessing (which is why the first volume was dedicated to him), and Ramsey and I started reading everything we could get our hands on.

That first volume contained twenty stories, and marked the only time we used tales by Robert Westall and Richard Laymon, who both passed away far too early. Our Introduction, which was an overview of horror in 1989, covered just seven pages, and Kim Newman and I carried our Necrology column over from the defunct film magazine *Shock Xpress*. It ran one page longer than the Introduction.

In our summation, Ramsey and I expressed concern that the 1980s horror boom could not be sustained and, to survive, the genre would have to move out of the mid-list category. In retrospect, we were depressingly prescient.

For the cover, the publisher chose Les Edwards' iconic painting of "The Croglin Vampire" (if you want to see where *Buffy the Vampire*

Slayer got its inspiration from for The Gentlemen in the classic "Hush" episode, look no further). The only thing Robinson did not have was a logo, so I quickly knocked up a concept using a sheet of Letraset transfer lettering. To my surprise, they used it on the final book.

In the UK, Robinson Publishing issued that first volume of *Best New Horror* in trade paperback with gold foil on the cover. For the US, Carroll & Graf decided to do it as a hardcover (without the foil), which they then reprinted as a trade paperback the following year.

When it came to selecting a story from that inaugural edition, it was not difficult. For me, Brian Lumley's "No Sharks in the Med" has always been a powerful slice of psychological (as opposed to supernatural) horror, and a perfect example of one of my favourite sub-genres – the "fish out of water" tourist who stumbles into a situation over which they have no control . . .

CUSTOMS WAS NON-EXISTENT; people bring duty frees *out* of Greece, not in. As for passport control: a pair of tanned, hairy, bored-looking characters in stained, too-tight uniforms and peaked caps were in charge. One to take your passport, find the page to be franked, scan photograph and bearer both with a blank gaze that took in absolutely nothing unless you happened to be female and stacked (in which case it took in everything and more), then pass the passport on. Geoff Hammond thought: *I wonder if that's why they call them passports?* The second one took the little black book from the first and hammered down on it with his stamp, impressing several pages but no one else, then handed the important document back to its owner – but grudgingly, as if he didn't believe you could be trusted with it.

This second one, the one with the rubber stamp, had a brother. They could be, probably were, twins. Five-eightish, late twenties, lots of shoulders and no hips; raven hair shiny with grease, so tightly curled it looked permed; brown eyes utterly vacant of expression. The only difference was the uniform: the fact that the brother on the home-and-dry side of the barrier didn't have one. Leaning on the barrier, he twirled cheap, yellow-framed, dark-lensed glasses like glinting propellers, observed almost speculatively the incoming holidaymakers. He wore shorts, frayed where they hugged his thick thighs, barely long enough to be decent. *Hung like a bull!* Geoff thought. It was almost embarrassing. Dressed for the benefit of the single girls, obviously. He'd be hoping they were taking notes for later. His chances might improve if he were two inches taller and had a face. But he didn't; the face was as vacant as the eyes.

Then Geoff saw what it was that was wrong with those eyes: beyond the barrier, the specimen in the bulging shorts was wall-eyed. Likewise his twin punching the passports. Their right eyes had white pupils that stared like dead fish. The one in the booth wore lightly-tinted glasses, so that you didn't notice until he looked up and stared directly at you. Which in Geoff's case he hadn't; but he was certainly looking at Gwen. Then he glanced at Geoff, patiently waiting, and said: "Together, you?" His voice was a shade too loud, making it almost an accusation.

Different names on the passports, obviously! But Geoff wasn't going to stand here and explain how they were just married and Gwen hadn't had time to make the required alterations. That really *would* be embarrassing! In fact (and come to think of it), it might not even be legal. Maybe she should have changed it right away, or got something done with it, anyway, in London. The honeymoon holiday they'd chosen was one of those get-it-while-it's-going deals, a last-minute half-price seat-filler, a gift horse; and they'd been pushed for time. But what the hell – this was 1987, wasn't it?

"Yes," Geoff finally answered. "Together."

"Ah!" the other nodded, grinned, appraised Gwen again with a raised eyebrow, before stamping her passport and handing it over.

Wall-eyed bastard! Geoff thought.

When they passed through the gate in the barrier, the other wall-eyed bastard had disappeared . . .

Stepping through the automatic glass doors from the shade of the airport building into the sunlight of the coach terminus was like opening the door of a furnace; it was a replay of the moment when the plane's air-conditioned passengers trooped out across the tarmac to board the buses waiting to convey them to passport control. You came out into the sun fairly crisp, but by the time you'd trundled your luggage to the kerbside and lifted it off the trolley your armpits were already sticky. One o'clock, and the temperature must have been hovering around eighty-five for hours. It not only beat down on you but, trapped in the concrete, beat up as well. Hammerblows of heat.

A mini-skirted courier, English as a rose and harassed as hell – her white blouse soggy while her blue and white hat still sat jaunty on her head – came fluttering, clutching her millboard with its bulldog clip and thin sheaf of notes. "Mr Hammond and Miss—" she glanced at her notes, "—Pinter?"

"Mr and Mrs Hammond," Geoff answered. He lowered his voice and continued confidentially: "We're all proper, legitimate, and true. Only our identities have been altered in order to protect our passports."

"Um?" she said.

Too deep for her, Geoff thought, sighing inwardly.

"Yes," said Gwen, sweetly. "We're the Hammonds."

"Oh!" the girl looked a little confused. "It's just that—"

"I haven't changed my passport yet," said Gwen, smiling.

"Ah!" Understanding finally dawned. The courier smiled nervously at Geoff, turned again to Gwen. "Is it too late for congratulations?"

"Four days," Gwen answered.

"Well, congratulations anyway."

Geoff was eager to be out of the sun. "Which is our coach?" he wanted to know. "Is it – could it possibly be – air-conditioned?" There were several coaches parked in an untidy cluster a little further up the kerb.

Again the courier's confusion, also something of embarrassment showing in her bright blue eyes. "You're going to – Achladi?"

Geoff sighed again, this time audibly. It was her business to know where they were going. It wasn't a very good start.

"Yes," she cut in quickly, before he or Gwen could comment. "Achladi – but not by coach! You see, your plane was an hour late; the coach for Achladi couldn't be held up for just one couple; but it's okay – you'll have the privacy of your own taxi, and of course Skymed will foot the bill."

She went off to whistle up a taxi and Geoff and Gwen glanced at each other, shrugged, sat down on their cases. But in a moment the courier was back, and behind her a taxi came rolling, nosing into the kerb. Its driver jumped out, whirled about opening doors, the boot, stashing cases while Geoff and Gwen got into the back of the car. Then, throwing his straw hat down beside him as he climbed into the driving seat and slammed his door, the young Greek looked back at his passengers and smiled. A single gold tooth flashed in a bar of white. But the smile was quite dead, like the grin of a shark before he bites, and the voice when it came was phlegmy, like pebbles colliding in mud. "Achladi, yes?"

"Ye—" Geoff began, paused, and finished: "—es! Er, Achladi, right!" Their driver was the wall-eyed passport-stamper's wall-eyed brother.

"I Spiros," he declared, turning the taxi out of the airport. "And you?"

Something warned Geoff against any sort of familiarity with this one. In all this heat, the warning was like a breath of cold air on the back of his neck. "I'm Mr Hammond," he answered, stiffly. "This is my wife." Gwen turned her head a little and frowned at him.

"I'm—" she began.

"My *wife!*" Geoff said again. She looked surprised but kept her peace.

Spiros was watching the road where it narrowed and wound. Already out of the airport, he skirted the island's main town and raced for foothills rising to a spine of half-clad mountains. Achladi was maybe half an hour away, on the other side of the central range. The road soon became a track, a thick layer of dust over pot-holed tarmac and cobbles; in short, a typical Greek road. They slowed down a little through a village where white-walled houses lined the way, with lemon groves set back between and behind the dwellings, and were left with bright flashes of bougainvillea-framed balconies burning like after-images on their retinas. Then Spiros gave it the gun again.

Behind them, all was dust kicked up by the spinning wheels and the suction of the car's passing. Geoff glanced out of the fly-specked rear window. The cloud of brown dust, chasing after them, seemed ominous in the way it obscured the so-recent past. And turning front again, Geoff saw that Spiros kept his strange eye mainly on the road ahead, and the good one on his rearview. But watching what? The dust? No, he was looking at . . .

At Gwen! The interior mirror was angled directly into her cleavage.

They had been married only a very short time. The day when he'd take pride in the jealousy of other men – in their coveting his wife – was still years in the future. Even then, look but don't touch would be the order of the day. Right now it was watch where you're looking, and possession was ninety nine point nine per cent of the law. As for the other point one per cent: well, there was nothing much you could do about what the lecherous bastards were thinking!

Geoff took Gwen's elbow, pulled her close and whispered: "Have you noticed how tight he takes the bends? He does it so we'll bounce about a bit. He's watching how your tits jiggle!"

She'd been delighting in the scenery, hadn't even noticed Spiros, his eyes or anything. For a beautiful girl of twenty-three, she was remarkably naïve, and it wasn't just an act. It was one of the things Geoff loved best about her. Only eighteen months her senior, Geoff hardly considered himself a man of the world; but he did know a rat when he smelled one. In Spiros's case he could smell several sorts.

"He . . . *what*—?" Gwen said out loud, glancing down at herself. One button too many had come open in her blouse, showing the edges of her cups. Green eyes widening, she looked up and spotted Spiros's rearview. He grinned at her through the mirror and licked his lips, but without deliberation. He was naïve, too, in his way. In his different sort of way.

"Sit over here," said Geoff out loud, as she did up the offending button *and* the one above it. "The view is much better on this side." He half-stood, let her slide along the seat behind him. Both of Spiros' eyes were now back on the road . . .

Ten minutes later they were up into a pass through gorgeous pine-clad slopes so steep they came close to sheer. Here and there scree slides showed through the greenery, or a thrusting outcrop of rock. "Mountains," Spiros grunted, without looking back.

"You have an eye for detail," Geoff answered.

Gwen gave his arm a gentle nip, and he knew she was thinking *sarcasm is the lowest form of wit – and it doesn't become you!* Nor cruelty, apparently. Geoff had meant nothing special by his "eye" remark, but Spiros was sensitive. He groped in the glove compartment for his yellow-rimmed sunshades, put them on. And drove in a stony silence for what looked like being the rest of the journey.

Through the mountains they sped, and the west coast of the island opened up like a gigantic travel brochure. The mountains seemed to go right down to the sea, rocks merging with that incredible, aching blue. And they could see the village down there, Achladi, like something out of a dazzling dream perched on both sides of a spur that gentled into the ocean.

"Beautiful!" Gwen breathed.

"Yes," Spiros nodded. "Beautiful, thee village." Like many Greeks speaking English, his definite articles all sounded like *thee*. "For fish, for thee swims, thee sun – is beautiful."

After that it was all downhill; winding, at times precipitous, but the view was never less than stunning. For Geoff, it brought back memories of Cyprus. Good ones, most of them, but one bad one that always made him catch his breath, clench his fists. The reason he hadn't been too keen on coming back to the Med in the first place. He closed his eyes in an attempt to force the memory out of mind, but that only made it worse, the picture springing up that much clearer.

He was a kid again, just five years old, late in the summer of '67. His father was a Staff-Sergeant Medic, his mother with the QARANCs; both of them were stationed at Dhekelia, a Sovereign Base Area garrison just up the coast from Larnaca where they had a married quarter. They'd met and married in Berlin, spent three years there, then got posted out to Cyprus together. With two years done in Cyprus, Geoff's father had a year to go to complete his twenty-two. After that last year in the sun . . . there was a place waiting for him in the ambulance pool of one of London's big hospitals. Geoff's mother had hoped to get on the nursing staff of the same hospital. But before any of that . . .

Geoff had started school in Dhekelia, but on those rare weekends when both of his parents were free of duty, they'd all go off to the beach together. And that had been his favourite thing in all the world: the beach with its golden sand and crystal-clear, safe, shallow water. But sometimes, seeking privacy, they'd take a picnic basket and drive east along the coast until the road became a track, then find a way down the cliffs and swim from the rocks up around Cape Greco. That's where it had happened.

"Geoff!" Gwen tugged at his arm, breaking the spell. He was grateful to be dragged back to reality. "Were you sleeping?"

"Daydreaming," he answered.

"Me, too!" she said. "I think I must be. I mean, just *look* at it!"

They were winding down a steep ribbon of road cut into the mountain's flank, and Achladi was directly below them. A coach coming up squeezed by, its windows full of brown, browned-off faces. Holidaymakers going off to the airport, going home. Their holidays were over but Geoff's and Gwen's was just beginning, and the village they had come to *was* truly beautiful. Especially beautiful because it was unspoiled. This was only Achladi's second season; before they'd built the airport you could only get here by boat. Very few had bothered.

Geoff's vision of Cyprus and his bad time quickly receded; while he didn't consider himself a romantic like Gwen, still he recognized Achladi's magic. And now he supposed he'd have to admit that they'd made the right choice.

White-walled gardens; red tiles, green-framed windows, some flat roofs and some with a gentle pitch; bougainvillea cascading over white, arched balconies; a tiny white church on the point of the spur where broken rocks finally tumbled into the sea; massive ancient olive trees in walled plots at every street junction, and grapevines on trellises giving a little shade and dappling every garden and patio. That, at a glance, was Achladi. A high sea wall kept the sea at bay, not that it could ever be a real threat, for the entire front of the village fell within the harbour's crab's-claw moles. Steps went down here and there from the sea wall to the rocks; a half-dozen towels were spread wherever there was a flat or gently-inclined surface to take them, and the sea bobbed with a half-dozen heads, snorkels and face-masks. Deep water here, but a quarter-mile to the south, beyond the harbour wall, a shingle beach stretched like the webbing between the toes of some great beast for maybe a hundred yards to where a second claw-like spur came down from the mountains. As for the rest of this western coastline: as far as the eye could see both north and south, it looked like sky, cliff and sea to Geoff. Cape Greco all over again. But before he could go back to that:

"Is Villa Eleni, yes?" Spiros's gurgling voice intruded. "Him have no road. No can drive. I carry thee bags."

The road went right down the ridge of the spur to the little church. Half-way, it was crossed at right-angles by a second motor road which contained and serviced a handful of shops. The rest of the place was made up of streets too narrow or too perpendicular for cars. A few ancient scooters put-putted and sputtered about, donkeys clip-clopped here and there, but that was all. Spiros turned his vehicle about at the main junction (the *only* real road junction) and parked in the shade of a giant olive tree. He went to get the luggage. There were two large cases, two small ones. Geoff would have shared the load equally but found himself brushed aside; Spiros took the elephant's share and left him with the small-fry. He wouldn't have minded, but it was obviously the Greek's chance to show off his strength.

Leading the way up a steep cobbled ramp of a street, Spiros's muscular buttocks kept threatening to burst through the thin stuff of his cut-down jeans. And because the holidaymakers followed on a little way behind, Geoff was aware of Gwen's eyes on Spiros's tanned, gleaming thews. There wasn't much of anywhere else to look. "Him Tarzan, you Jane," he commented, but his grin was a shade too dry. "Who you?" she answered, her nose going up in the air. "Cheetah?"

"*Uph, uph!*" said Geoff.

"Anyway," she relented. "Your bottom's nicer. More compact."

He saved his breath, made no further comment. Even the light cases seemed heavy. If he was Cheetah, that must make Spiros Kong! The Greek glanced back once, grinned in his fashion, and kept going. Breathing heavily, Geoff and Gwen made an effort to catch up, failed miserably. Then, toward the top of the way Spiros turned right into an arched alcove, climbed three stone steps, put down his cases and paused at a varnished pine door. He pulled on a string to free the latch, shoved the door open and took up his cases again. As the English couple came round the corner he was stepping inside. "Thee Villa Eleni," he said, as they followed him in.

Beyond the door was a high-walled courtyard of black and white pebbles laid out in octopus and dolphin designs. A split-level patio fronted the "villa", a square box of a house whose one redeeming feature had to be a retractable sun awning shading the windows and most of the patio. It also made an admirable refuge from the dazzling white of everything.

There were whitewashed concrete steps climbing the side of the building to the upper floor, with a landing that opened onto a wooden-railed balcony with its own striped awning. Beach towels and an outsize lady's bathing costume were hanging over the rail, drying, and all the windows were open. Someone was home, maybe. Or maybe sitting in a shady taverna sipping on iced drinks. Downstairs, a key with a label had been left in the keyhole of a louvred, fly-screened door. Geoff read the label, which said simply: "Mr Hammond". The booking had been made in his name.

"This is us," he said to Gwen, turning the key.

They went in, Spiros following with the large cases. Inside, the cool air was a blessing. Now they would like to explore the place on their own, but the Greek was there to do it for them. And he knew his way around. He put the cases down, opened his arms to indicate the central room. "For sit, talk, thee resting." He pointed to a tiled area in one corner, with a refrigerator, sink-unit and two-ring electric cooker. "For thee toast, coffee – thee fish and chips, eh?" He shoved open the door of a tiny room tiled top to bottom, containing a shower, wash-basin and WC. "And this one," he said, without further explanation. Then five strides back across the floor took him to another room, low-ceilinged, pine-beamed, with a Lindean double bed built in under louvred windows. He cocked his head on one side. "And thee bed – just one . . ."

"That's all we'll need," Geoff answered, his annoyance building.

"Yes," Gwen said. "Well, thank you, er, Spiros – you're very kind. And we'll be fine now."

Spiros scratched his chin, went back into the main room and sprawled in an easy chair. "Outside is hot," he said. "Here she is cool – *chrio*, you know?"

Geoff went to him. "It's *very* hot," he agreed, "and we're sticky. Now we want to shower, put our things away, look around. Thanks for your help. You can go now."

Spiros stood up and his face went slack, his expression more blank than before. His wall-eye looked strange through its tinted lens. "Go now?" he repeated.

Geoff sighed. "Yes, go!"

The corner of Spiros's mouth twitched, drew back a little to show his gold tooth. "I fetch from airport, carry cases."

"Ah!" said Geoff, getting out his wallet. "What do I owe you?" He'd bought drachmas at the bank in London.

Spiros sniffed, looked scornful, half-turned away. "One thousand," he finally answered, bluntly.

"That's about four pounds and fifty pence," Gwen said from the bedroom doorway. "Sounds reasonable."

"Except it was supposed to be on Skymed," Geoff scowled. He paid up anyway and saw Spiros to the door. The Greek departed, sauntered indifferently across the patio to pause in the arched doorway and look back across the courtyard. Gwen had come to stand beside Geoff in the double doorway under the awning.

The Greek looked straight at her and licked his fleshy lips. The vacant grin was back on his face. "I see you," he said, nodding with a sort of slow deliberation.

As he closed the door behind him, Gwen muttered, "Not if I see you first! *Ugh!*"

"I am with you," Geoff agreed. "*Not* my favourite local character!"

"Spiros," she said. "Well, and it suits him to a tee. It's about as close as you can get to spider! And that one *is* about as close as you can get!"

They showered, fell exhausted on the bed – but not so exhausted that they could just lie there without making love.

Later – with suitcases emptied and small valuables stashed out of sight, and spare clothes all hung up or tucked away – dressed in light, loose gear, sandals, sunglasses, it was time to explore the village. "And afterwards," Gwen insisted, "we're swimming!" She'd packed their towels and swimwear in a plastic beach bag. She loved to swim, and Geoff might have, too, except . . .

But as they left their rooms and stepped out across the patio, the varnished door in the courtyard wall opened to admit their upstairs neighbours, and for the next hour all thoughts of exploration and a dip in the sea were swept aside. The elderly couple who now introduced themselves gushed, there was no other way to describe it. He was George and she was Petula.

"My *dear*," said George, taking Gwen's hand and kissing it, "such a *stunning* young lady, and how sad that I've only two days left in which to enjoy you!" He was maybe sixty-four or five, ex-handsome but sagging a bit now, tall if a little bent, and brown as a native. With a small grey moustache and faded blue eyes, he looked as if he'd – no, in all probability he *had* – piloted Spitfires in World War II! Alas, he wore the most blindingly colourful shorts and shirt that Gwen had ever seen.

Petula was very large, about as tall as George but two of him in girth. She was just as brown, though, (and so presumably didn't mind exposing it all), seemed equally if not more energetic, and was never at a loss for words. They were a strange, paradoxical pair: very upper-crust, but at the same time very much down to earth. If Petula tended to speak with plums in her mouth, certainly they were of a very tangy variety.

"He'll flatter you to death, my dear," she told Gwen, ushering the newcomers up the steps at the side of the house and onto the high balcony. "But you must *never* take your eyes off his hands! Stage magicians have nothing on George. Forty years ago he magicked himself into my bedroom, and he's been there ever since!"

"She seduced me!" said George, bustling indoors.

"I did not!" Petula was petulant. "What? Why he's quite simply a wolf in . . . in a Joseph suit!"

"A Joseph suit?" George repeated her. He came back out onto the balcony with brandy-sours in a frosted jug, a clattering tray of ice-cubes, slices of sugared lemon and an eggcup of salt for the sours. He put the lot down on a plastic table, said: "Ah! – glasses!" and ducked back inside again.

"Yes," his wife called after him, pointing at his Bermudas and Hawaiian shirt. "Your clothes of many colours!"

It was all good fun and Geoff and Gwen enjoyed it. They sat round the table on plastic chairs, and George and Petula entertained them. It made for a very nice welcome to Achladi indeed.

"Of course," said George after a while, when they'd settled down a little, "we first came here eight years ago, when there were no flights, just boats. Now that people are flying in—" he shrugged, "—two more seasons and there'll be belly-dancers and hotdog stands! But for now it's . . . just perfect. Will you look at that view?"

The view from the balcony was very fetching. "From up here we can see the entire village," said Gwen. "You must point out the best shops, the bank or exchange or whatever, all the places we'll need to know about."

George and Petula looked at each other, smiled knowingly.

"Oh?" said Gwen.

Geoff checked their expressions, nodded, made a guess: "There are no places we need to know about."

"Well, three, actually," said Petula. "Four if you count Dimi's – the taverna. Oh, there are other places to eat, but Dimi's is *the* place. Except I feel I've spoilt it for you now. I mean, that really is something you should have discovered for yourself. It's half the fun, finding the best place to eat!"

"What about the other three places we should know about?" Gwen inquired. "Will knowing those spoil it for us, too? Knowing them in advance, I mean?"

"Good Lord, no!" George shook his head. "Vital knowledge, young lady!"

"The baker's," said Petula. "For fresh rolls – daily." She pointed it out, blue smoke rising from a cluster of chimneypots. "Also the booze shop, for booze—"

"—Also daily," said George, pointing. "Right there on that corner – where the bottles glint. D'you know, they have an *ancient* Metaxa so cheap you wouldn't—"

"*And,*" Petula continued, "the path down to the beach. Which is . . . over there."

"But tell us," said George, changing the subject, "are you married, you two? Or is that too personal?"

"Oh, of *course* they're married!" Petula told him. "But very recently, because they still sit so close together. Touching. You see?"

"Ah!" said George. "Then we shan't have another elopement."

"You know, my dear, you really are an old idiot," said Petula, sighing. "I mean, elopements are for lovers to be together. And these two already *are* together!"

Geoff and Gwen raised their eyebrows. "An elopement?" Gwen said. "Here? When did this happen?"

"Right here, yes," said Petula. "Ten days ago. On our first night we had a young man downstairs, Gordon. On his own. He was supposed to be here with his fiancée but she's jilted him. He went out with us, had a few too many in Dimi's and told us all about it. A Swedish girl – very lovely, blonde creature – was also on her own. She helped steer him back here and, I suppose, tucked him in. She had her own place, mind you, and didn't stay."

"But the next night she did!" George enthused.

"And then they ran off," said Petula, brightly. "Eloped! As simple as that. We saw them once, on the beach, the next morning. Following which —"

"—Gone!" said George.

"Maybe their holidays were over and they just went home," said Gwen, reasonably.

"No," George shook his head. "Gordon had come out on our plane, his holiday was just starting. She'd been here about a week and a half, was due to fly out the day after they made off together."

"They paid for their holidays and then deserted them?" Geoff frowned. "Doesn't make any sense."

"Does anything, when you're in love?" Petula sighed.

"The way I see it," said George, "they fell in love with each other, and with Greece, and went off to explore all the options."

"Love?" Gwen was doubtful. "On the rebound?"

"If she'd been a mousey little thing, I'd quite agree," said Petula. "But no, she really was a beautiful girl."

"And him a nice lad," said George. "A bit sparse but clean, good-looking."

"Indeed, they were much like you two," his wife added. "I mean, not *like* you, but like you."

"Cheers," said Geoff, wryly. "I mean, I know I'm not Mr Universe, but—"

"Tight in the bottom!" said Petula. "That's what the girls like these days. You'll do all right."

"See," said Gwen, nudging him. "Told you so!"

But Geoff was still frowning. "Didn't anyone look for them? What if they'd been involved in an accident or something?"

"No," said Petula. "They were seen boarding a ferry in the main town. Indeed, one of the local taxi drivers took them there. Spiros."

Gwen and Geoff's turn to look at each other. "A strange fish, that one," said Geoff.

George shrugged. "Oh, I don't know. You know him, do you? It's
that eye of his which makes him seem a bit sinister . . ."

Maybe he's right, Geoff thought.

Shortly after that, their drinks finished, they went off to start their
explorations . . .

The village was a maze of cobbled, whitewashed alleys. Even as tiny
as it was you could get lost in it, but never for longer than the length
of a street. Going downhill, no matter the direction, you'd come to the
sea. Uphill you'd come to the main road, or if you didn't, then turn
the next corner and *continue* uphill, and then you would. The most
well-trodden alley, with the shiniest cobbles, was the one that led to
the hard-packed path, which in turn led to the beach. Pass the "booze
shop" on the corner twice, and you'd know where it was always. The
window was plastered with labels, some familiar and others entirely
conjectural; inside, steel shelving went floor to ceiling, stacked with
every conceivable brand; even the more exotic and (back home) wildly
expensive stuffs were on view, often in ridiculously cheap, three-litre,
duty-free bottles with their own chrome taps and display stands.

"Courvoisier!" said Gwen, appreciatively.

"Grand Marnier, surely!" Geoff protested. "What, five pints of
Grand Marnier? At that price? Can you believe it? But that's to take
home. What about while we're here?"

"Coconut liqueur," she said. "Or better still, mint chocolate – to
complement our midnight coffees."

They found several small tavernas, too, with people seated
outdoors at tiny tables under the vines. Chicken portions and slabs
of lamb sputtering on spits; small fishes sizzling over charcoal;
moussaka steaming in long trays . . .

Dimi's was down on the harbour, where a wide, low wall kept
you safe from falling in the sea. They had a Greek salad which they
divided two ways, tiny cubes of lamb roasted on wooden slivers, a
half-bottle of local white wine costing pennies. As they ate and sipped
the wine, so they began to relax; the hot sunlight was tempered by an
almost imperceptible breeze off the sea.

Geoff said: "Do you really feel energetic? Damned if I do."

She didn't feel full of boundless energy, no, but she wasn't going
down without a fight. "If it was up to you," she said, "we'd just sit
here and watch the fishing nets dry, right?"

"Nothing wrong with taking it easy," he answered. "We're on
holiday, remember?"

"Your idea of taking it easy means being bone idle!" she answered. "*I* say we're going for a dip, then back to the villa for siesta and you know, and—"

"Can we have the you know before the siesta?" He kept a straight face.

"—And then we'll be all settled in, recovered from the journey, ready for tonight. Insatiable!"

"Okay," he shrugged. "Anything you say. But we swim from the beach, not from the rocks."

Gwen looked at him suspiciously. "That was almost too easy."

Now he grinned. "It was the thought of, well, you know, that did it," he told her . . .

Lying on the beach, panting from their exertions in the sea, with the sun lifting the moisture off their still-pale bodies, Gwen said: "I don't understand."

"Hmm?"

"You swim very well. I've always thought so. So what is this fear of the water you complain about?"

"First," Geoff answered, "I don't swim very well. Oh, for a hundred yards I'll swim like a dolphin – any more than that and I do it like a brick! I can't float. If I stop swimming I sink."

"So don't stop."

"When you get tired, you stop."

"What was it that made you frightened of the water?" He told her:

"I was a kid in Cyprus. A little kid. My father had taught me how to swim. I used to watch him diving off the rocks, oh, maybe twenty or thirty feet high, into the sea. I thought I could do it, too. So one day when my folks weren't watching, I tried. I must have hit my head on something on the way down. Or maybe I simply struck the water all wrong. When they spotted me floating in the sea, I was just about done for. My father dragged me out. He was a medic – the kiss of life and all that. So now I'm not much for swimming, and I'm absolutely *nothing* for diving! I will swim – for a splash, in shallow water, like today – but that's my limit. And I'll only go in from a beach. I can't stand cliffs, height. It's as simple as that. You married a coward. So there."

"No I didn't," she said. "I married someone with a great bottom. Why didn't you tell me all this before?"

"You didn't ask me. I don't like to talk about it because I don't much care to remember it. I was just a kid, and yet I knew I was going to die. And I knew it wouldn't be nice. I still haven't got it out of my system, not completely. And so the less said about it the better."

A beach ball landed close by, bounced, rolled to a standstill against Gwen's thigh. They looked up. A brown, burly figure came striding. They recognized the frayed, bulging shorts. Spiros.

"Hallo," he said, going down into a crouch close by, forearms resting on his knees. "Thee beach. Thee ball. I swim, play. You swim?" (This to Geoff.) "You come swim, throwing thee ball?"

Geoff sat up. There were half-a-dozen other couples on the beach; why couldn't this jerk pick on them? Geoff thought to himself: *I'm about to get sand kicked in my face!* "No," he said out loud, shaking his head. "I don't swim much."

"No swim? You frighting thee big fish? Thee sharks?"

"Sharks?" Now Gwen sat up. From behind their dark lenses she could feel Spiros's eyes crawling over her.

Geoff shook his head. "There are no sharks in the Med," he said.

"Him right," Spiros laughed high-pitched, like a woman, without his customary gurgling. A weird sound. "No sharks. I make thee jokes!" He stopped laughing and looked straight at Gwen. She couldn't decide if he was looking at her face or her breasts. Those damned sunglasses of his! "You come swim, lady, with Spiros? Play in thee water?"

"My . . . *God!*" Gwen sputtered, glowering at him. She pulled her dress on over her still-damp, very skimpy swimming costume, packed her towel away, picked up her sandals. When she was annoyed, she really *was* annoyed.

Geoff stood up as she made off, turned to Spiros. "Now listen—" he began.

"Ah, you go now! Is Okay. I see you." He took his ball, raced with it down the beach, hurled it out over the sea. Before it splashed down he was diving, low and flat, striking the water like a knife. Unlike Geoff, he swam very well indeed . . .

When Geoff caught up with his wife she was stiff with anger. Mainly angry with herself. "That was *so* rude of me!" she exploded.

"No it wasn't," he said. "I feel exactly the same about it."

"But he's so damned . . . persistent! I mean, he knows we're together, man and wife . . . 'thee bed – just one.' How *dare* he intrude?"

Geoff tried to make light of it. "You're imagining it," he said.

"And you? Doesn't he get on your nerves?"

"Maybe I'm imagining it too. Look, he's Greek – and not an especially attractive specimen. Look at it from his point of view. All of a sudden there's a gaggle of dolly-birds on the beach, dressed in stuff his sister wouldn't wear for undies! So he tries to get closer – for a better view, as it were – so that he can get a wall-eyeful. He's no different to other blokes. Not quite as smooth, that's all."

"Smooth!" she almost spat the word out. "He's about as smooth as a badger's—"

"—Bottom," said Geoff. "Yes, I know. If I'd known you were such a bum-fancier I mightn't have married you."

And at last she laughed, but shakily.

They stopped at the booze shop and bought brandy and a large bottle of Coca-Cola. And mint chocolate liqueur, of course, for their midnight coffees ...

That night Gwen put on a blue and white dress, very Greek if cut a little low in the front, and silver sandals. Tucking a handkerchief into the breast pocket of his white jacket, Geoff thought: *she's beautiful!* With her heart-shaped face and the way her hair framed it, cut in a page-boy style that suited its shiny black sheen – and her green, green eyes – he'd always thought she looked French. But tonight she was definitely Greek. And he was so glad that she was English, and his.

Dimi's was doing a roaring trade. George and Petula had a table in the corner, overlooking the sea. They had spread themselves out in order to occupy all four seats, but when Geoff and Gwen appeared they waved, called them over. "We thought you'd drop in," George said, as they sat down. And to Gwen: "You look charming, my dear."

"Now I feel I'm really on my holidays," Gwen smiled.

"Honeymoon, surely," said Petula.

"*Shh!*" Geoff cautioned her. "In England they throw confetti. Over here it's plates!"

"Your secret is safe with us," said George.

"Holiday, honeymoon, whatever," said Gwen. "Compliments from handsome gentlemen; the stars reflected in the sea; a full moon rising and bouzouki music floating in the air. And—"

"—The mouth-watering smells of good Greek grub!" Geoff cut in. "Have you ordered?" He looked at George and Petula.

"A moment ago," Petula told him. "If you go into the kitchen there, Dimi will show you his menu – live, as it were. Tell him you're with us and he'll make an effort to serve us together. Starter, main course, a pudding – the lot."

"Good!" Geoff said, standing up. "I could eat the saddle off a donkey!"

"Eat the whole donkey," George told him. "The one who's going to wake you up with his racket at six-thirty tomorrow morning."

"You don't know Geoff," said Gwen. "He'd sleep through a Rolling Stones concert."

"And *you* don't know Achladi donkeys!" said Petula.

In the kitchen, the huge, bearded proprietor was busy, fussing over his harassed-looking cooks. As Geoff entered he came over. "Good evenings, sir. You are new in Achladi?"

"Just today," Geoff smiled. "We came here for lunch but missed you."

"Ah!" Dimitrios gasped, shrugged apologetically. "I was sleeps! Every day, for two hours, I sleeps. Where you stay, eh?"

"The Villa Eleni."

"Eleni? Is me!" Dimitrios beamed. "*I* am Villa Eleni. I mean, I owns it. Eleni is thee name my wifes."

"It's a beautiful name," said Geoff, beginning to feel trapped in the conversation. "Er, we're with George and Petula."

"You are eating? Good, good. I show you." Geoff was given a guided tour of the ovens and the sweets trolley. He ordered, keeping it light for Gwen.

"And here," said Dimitrios. "For your lady!" He produced a filigreed silver-metal brooch in the shape of a butterfly, with DIMI'S worked into the metal of the body. Gwen wouldn't like it especially, but politic to accept it. Geoff had noticed several female patrons wearing them, Petula included.

"That's very kind of you," he said.

Making his way back to their table, he saw Spiros was there before him.

Now where the hell had he sprung from? And what the hell was he playing at?

Spiros wore tight blue jeans, (his image, obviously), and a white T-shirt stained down the front. He was standing over the corner table, one hand on the wall where it overlooked the sea, the other on the table itself. Propped up, still he swayed. He was leaning over Gwen. George and Petula had frozen smiles on their faces, looked frankly astonished. Geoff couldn't quite see all of Gwen, for Spiros's bulk was in the way.

What he could see, of the entire mini-tableau, printed itself on his eyes as he drew closer. Adrenalin surged in him and he began to breathe faster. He barely noticed George standing up and sliding out of view. Then as the bouzouki tape came to an end and the taverna's low babble of sound seemed to grow that much louder, Gwen's outraged voice suddenly rose over everything else:

"Get . . . your . . . filthy . . . paws . . . *off* me!" she cried.

Geoff was there. Petula had drawn as far back as possible; no longer smiling, her hand was at her throat, her eyes staring in disbelief. Spiros's left hand had caught up the V of Gwen's dress. His fingers were inside the dress and his thumb outside. In his right hand he clutched a pin like the one Dimitrios had given to Geoff. He was protesting:

"But I giving it! I putting it on your dress! Is nice, this one. We friends. Why you shout? You no like Spiros?" His throaty, gurgling voice was slurred: waves of ouzo fumes literally wafted off him like the stench of a dead fish. Geoff moved in, knocked Spiros's elbow away where it leaned on the wall. Spiros must release Gwen to maintain his balance. He did so, but still crashed half over the wall. For a moment Geoff thought he would go completely over, into the sea. But he just lolled there, shaking his head, and finally turned it to look back at Geoff. There was a look on his face which Geoff couldn't quite describe. Drunken stupidity slowly turning to rage, maybe. Then he pushed himself upright, stood swaying against the wall, his fists knotting and the muscles in his arms bunching.

Hit him now, Geoff's inner man told him. Do it, and he'll go clean over into the sea. It's not high, seven or eight feet, that's all. It'll sober the bastard up, and after that he won't trouble you again.

But what if he couldn't swim? *You know he swims like a fish — like a bloody shark!*

"You think you better than Spiros, eh?" The Greek wobbled dangerously, steadied up and took a step in Geoff's direction.

"No!" the voice of the bearded Dimitrios was shattering in Geoff's ear. Massive, he stepped between them, grabbed Spiros by the hair, half-dragged, half-pushed him toward the exit. "No, everybody thinks he's better!" he cried. "Because everybody *is* better! Out—" he heaved Spiros yelping into the harbour's shadows. "I tell you before, Spiros: drink all the ouzo in Achladi. Is your business. But not let it ruin *my* business. Then comes thee *real* troubles!"

Gwen was naturally upset. It spoiled something of the evening for her. But by the time they had finished eating, things were about back to normal. No one else in the place, other than George and Petula, had seemed especially interested in the incident anyway.

At around eleven, when the taverna had cleared a little, the girl from Skymed came in. She came over.

"Hello, Julie!" said George, finding her a chair. And, flatterer born, he added: "How lovely you're looking tonight – but of course you look lovely all the time."

Petula tut-tutted. "George, if you hadn't met me you'd be a gigolo by now, I'm sure!"

"Mr Hammond," Julie said. "I'm terribly sorry. I should have explained to Spiros that he'd recover the fare for your ride from me. Actually, I believed he understood that but apparently he didn't. I've just seen him in one of the bars and asked him how much I owed him. He was a little upset, wouldn't accept the money, told me I should see you."

"Was he sober yet?" Geoff asked, sourly.

"Er, not very, I'm afraid. Has he been a nuisance?"

Geoff coughed. "Only a *bit* of a one."

"It was a thousand drachmas" said Gwen.

The courier looked a little taken aback. "Well it should only have been seven hundred."

"He did carry our bags, though," said Geoff.

"Ah! Maybe that explains it. Anyway, I'm authorized to pay you seven hundred."

"All donations are welcome," Gwen said, opening her purse and accepting the money. "But if I were you, in future I'd use someone else. This Spiros isn't a particularly pleasant fellow."

"Well he does seem to have a problem with the ouzo," Julie answered. "On the other hand—"

"He has *several* problems!" Geoff was sharper than he meant to be. After all, it wasn't her fault.

"—He also has the best beach," Julie finished.

"Beach?" Geoff raised an eyebrow. "He has a beach?"

"Didn't we tell you?" Petula spoke up. "Two or three of the locals have small boats in the harbour. For a few hundred drachmas they'll take you to one of a handful of private beaches along the coast. They're private because no one lives there, and there's no way in except by boat. The boatmen have their favourite places, which they guard jealously and call 'their' beaches, so that the others don't poach on them. They take you in the morning or whenever, collect you in the evening. Absolutely private . . . ideal for picnics . . . romance!" She sighed.

"What a lovely idea," said Gwen. "To have a beach of your own for the day!"

"Well, as far as I'm concerned," Geoff told her, "Spiros can keep his beach."

"Oh-oh!" said George. "Speak of the devil . . ."

Spiros had returned. He averted his face and made straight for the kitchens in the back. He was noticeably steadier on his feet now. Dimitrios came bowling out to meet him and a few low-muttered words passed between them. Their conversation quickly grew more heated, becoming rapid-fire Greek in moments, and Spiros appeared to be pleading his case. Finally Dimitrios shrugged, came lumbering toward the corner table with Spiros in tow.

"Spiros, he sorry," Dimitrios said. "For tonight. Too much ouzo. He just want be friendly."

"Is right," said Spiros, lifting his head. He shrugged helplessly. "Thee ouzo."

Geoff nodded. "Okay, forget it," he said, but coldly.

"Is . . . okay?" Spiros lifted his head a little more. He looked at Gwen. Gwen forced herself to nod. "It's okay."

Now Spiros beamed, or as close as he was likely to get to it. But still Geoff had this feeling that there was something cold and calculating in his manner.

"I make it good!" Spiros declared, nodding. "One day, I take you thee *best* beach! For thee picnic. Very private. Two peoples, no more. I no take thee money, nothing. Is good?"

"Fine," said Geoff. "That'll be fine."

"Okay," Spiros smiled his unsmile, nodded, turned away. Going out, he looked back. "I sorry," he said again; and again his shrug. "Thee ouzo . . ."

"Hardly eloquent," said Petula, when he'd disappeared.

"But better than nothing," said George.

"Things are looking up!" Gwen was happier now.

Geoff was still unsure how he felt. He said nothing . . .

"Breakfast is on us," George announced the next morning. He smiled down on Geoff and Gwen where they drank coffee and tested the early morning sunlight at a garden table on the patio. They were still in their dressing-gowns, eyes bleary, hair tousled.

Geoff looked up, squinting his eyes against the hurtful blue of the sky, and said: "I see what you mean about that donkey! What the hell time is it, anyway?"

"Eight-fifteen," said George. "You're lucky. Normally he's at it, oh, an hour earlier than this!" From somewhere down in the maze of alleys, as if summoned by their conversation, the hideous braying echoed yet again as the village gradually came awake.

Just before nine they set out, George and Petula guiding them to a little place bearing the paint-daubed legend: BREKFAS BAR. They climbed steps to a pine-railed patio set with pine tables and chairs, under a varnished pine frame supporting a canopy of split bamboo. Service was good; the "English" food hot, tasty, and very cheap; the coffee dreadful!

"*Yechh!*" Gwen commented, understanding now why George and Petula had ordered tea. "Take a note, Mr Hammond," she said. "Tomorrow, no coffee. Just fruit juice."

"We thought maybe it was us being fussy," said Petula. "Else we'd have warned you."

"Anyway," George sighed. "Here's where we have to leave you. For tomorrow we fly – literally. So today we're shopping, picking up our duty-frees, gifts, the postcards we never sent, some Greek cigarettes."

"But we'll see you tonight, if you'd care to?" said Petula.

"Delighted!" Geoff answered. "What, Zorba's Dance, moussaka, and a couple or three of those giant Metaxas that Dimi serves? Who could refuse?"

"Not to mention the company," said Gwen.

"About eight-thirty, then," said Petula. And off they went.

"I shall miss them," said Gwen.

"But it will be nice to be on our own for once," Geoff leaned over to kiss her.

"Hallo!" came a now familiar, gurgling voice from below. Spiros stood in the street beyond the rail, looking up at them, the sun striking sparks from the lenses of his sunglasses. Their faces fell and he couldn't fail to notice it. "Is okay," he quickly held up a hand. "I no stay. I busy. Today I make thee taxi. Later, thee boat."

Gwen gave a little gasp of excitement, clutched Geoff's arm. "The private beach!" she said. "Now that's what I'd call being on our own!" And to Spiros: "If we're ready at one o'clock, will you take us to your beach?"

"Of course!" he answered. "At one o'clock, I near Dimi's. My boat, him called *Spiros* like me. You see him."

Gwen nodded. "We'll see you then."

"Good!" Spiros nodded. He looked up at them a moment longer, and Geoff wished he could fathom where the man's eyes were.

Probably up Gwen's dress. But then he turned and went on his way.

"Now we shop!" Gwen said.

They shopped for picnic items. Nothing gigantic, mainly small things. Slices of salami, hard cheese, two fat tomatoes, fresh bread, a bottle of light white wine, some feta, eggs for boiling, and a litre of crystal-clear bottled water. And as an afterthought: half-a-dozen small pats of butter, a small jar of honey, a sharp knife and a packet of doilies. No wicker basket; their little plastic coolbox would have to do. And one of their pieces of shoulder luggage for the blanket, towels, and swim-things. Geoff was no good for details; Gwen's head, to the contrary, was only happy buzzing with them. He let her get on with it, acted as beast of burden. In fact there was no burden to mention. After all, she was shopping for just the two of them, and it was as good a way as any to explore the village stores and see what was on offer. While she examined this and that, Geoff spent the time comparing the prices of various spirits with those already noted in the booze shop. So the morning passed.

At eleven-thirty they went back to the Villa Eleni for you know and a shower, and afterwards Gwen prepared the foodstuffs while Geoff lazed under the awning. No sign of George and Petula; eighty-four degrees of heat as they idled their way down to the harbour; the village had closed itself down through the hottest part of the day, and they saw no one they knew. Spiros's boat lolled like a mirrored blot on the stirless ocean, and Geoff thought: *even the fish will be finding this a bit much!* Also: *I hope there's some shade on this blasted beach!*

Spiros appeared from behind a tangle of nets. He stood up, yawned, adjusted his straw hat like a sunshade on his head. "Thee boat," he said, in his entirely unnecessary fashion, as he helped them climb aboard. *Spiros* "thee boat" was hardly a hundred per cent seaworthy, Geoff saw that immediately. In fact, in any other ocean in the world she'd be condemned. But this was the Mediterranean in July.

Barely big enough for three adults, the boat rocked a little as Spiros yanked futilely on the starter. Water seeped through boards, rotten and long since sprung, black with constant damp and badly caulked. Spiros saw Geoff's expression where he sat with his sandals in half an inch of water. He shrugged. "Is nothings," he said.

Finally the engine coughed into life, began to purr, and they were off. Spiros had the tiller; Geoff and Gwen faced him from the prow, which now lifted up a little as they left the harbour and cut straight out to sea. It was then, for the first time, that Geoff noticed Spiros's furtiveness: the way he kept glancing back toward Achladi, as if anxious not to be observed. Unlikely that they would be, for the village seemed fast asleep. Or perhaps he was just checking land marks, avoiding rocks or reefs or what have you. Geoff looked overboard. The water seemed deep enough to him. Indeed, it seemed much *too* deep! But at least there were no sharks . . .

Well out to sea, Spiros swung the boat south and followed the coastline for maybe two and a half to three miles. The highest of Achladi's houses and apartments had slipped entirely from view by the time he turned in towards land again and sought a bight in the seemingly unbroken march of cliffs. The place was landmarked: a fang of rock had weathered free, shaping a stack that reared up from the water to form a narrow, deep channel between itself and the cliffs proper. In former times a second, greater stack had crashed oceanward and now lay like a reef just under the water across the entire frontage. In effect, this made the place a lagoon: a sandy beach to the rear, safe water, and the reef of shattered, softly matted rocks where the small waves broke.

There was only one way in. Spiros gentled his boat through the deep water between the crooked outcrop and the overhanging cliff. Clear of the channel, he nosed her into the beach and cut the motor; as the keel grated on grit he stepped nimbly between his passengers and jumped ashore, dragging the boat a few inches up onto the sand. Geoff passed him the picnic things, then steadied the boat while Gwen took off her sandals and made to step down where the water met the sand. But Spiros was quick off the mark.

He stepped forward, caught her up, carried her two paces up the beach and set her down. His left arm had been under her thighs, his right under her back, cradling her. But when he set her upon her own feet his right hand had momentarily cupped her breast, which he'd quite deliberately squeezed.

Gwen opened her mouth, stood gasping her outrage, unable to give it words. Geoff had got out of the boat and was picking up their things to bring them higher up the sand. Spiros, slapping him on the back, stepped round him and shoved the boat off, splashed in shallow water a moment before leaping nimbly aboard. Gwen controlled herself, said nothing. She could feel the blood in her cheeks but hoped Geoff wouldn't notice. Not here, miles from anywhere. Not in this lonely place. No, there must be no trouble here.

For suddenly it had dawned on her just how very lonely it was. Beautiful, unspoiled, a lovers' idyll – but oh so very lonely . . .

"You all right, love?" said Geoff, taking her elbow. She was looking at Spiros standing silent in his boat. Their eyes seemed locked, it was as if she didn't see him but the mind behind the sunglasses, behind those disparate, dispassionate eyes. A message had passed between them. Geoff sensed it but couldn't fathom it. He had almost seemed to hear Spiros say "yes", and Gwen answer "no".

"Gwen?" he said again.

"I see you," Spiros called, grinning. It broke the spell. Gwen looked away, and Geoff called out:

"Six-thirty, right?"

Spiros waggled a hand this way and that palm-down, as if undecided. "Six, six-thirty – something," he said, shrugging. He started his motor, waved once, chugged out of the bay between the jutting sentinel rock and the cliffs. As he passed out of sight the boat's engine roared with life, its throaty growl rapidly fading into the distance . . .

Gwen said nothing about the incident; she felt sure that if she did, then Geoff would make something of it. Their entire holiday could so easily be spoiled. It was bad enough that for her the day had already been ruined. So she kept quiet, and perhaps a little too quiet. When Geoff asked her again if anything was wrong she told him she had a headache. Then, feeling a little unclean, she stripped herself quite naked and swam while he explored the beach.

Not that there was a great deal to explore. He walked the damp sand at the water's rim to the southern extreme and came up against the cliffs where they curved out into the sea. They were quite unscalable, towering maybe eighty or ninety feet to their jagged rim. Walking the hundred or so yards back the other way, the thought came to Geoff that if Spiros didn't come back for them – that is, if anything untoward should happen to him – they'd just have to sit it out until they were found. Which, since Spiros was the only one who knew they were here, might well be a long time. Having thought it, Geoff tried to shake the idea off but it wouldn't go away. The place was quite literally a trap. Even a decent swimmer would have to have at least a couple of miles in him before considering swimming out of here.

Once lodged in Geoff's brain, the concept rapidly expanded itself. Before . . . he had looked at the faded yellow and bone-white facade of the cliffs against the incredible blue of the sky with admiration; the beach had been every man's dream of tranquility, privacy, Eden with its own Eve; the softly lapping ocean had seemed like a warm, soothing bath reaching from horizon to horizon. But now . . . the place was so like Cape Greco. Except at Greco there had always been a way down to the sea – and up from it . . .

The northern end of the beach was much like the southern, the only difference being the great fang of rock protruding from the sea. Geoff stripped, swam out to it, was aware that the water here was a great deal deeper than back along the beach. But the distance was only thirty feet or so, nothing to worry about. And there were hand and footholds galore around the base of the pillar of upthrusting rock. He hauled himself up onto a tiny ledge, climbed higher (not too high), sat on a projecting fist of rock with his feet dangling and called to Gwen. His voice surprised him, for it seemed strangely small and panting. The cliffs took it up, however, amplified and passed it on. His shout reached Gwen where she splashed; she spotted him, stopped swimming and stood up. She waved, and he marvelled at her body, her tip-tilted breasts displayed where she stood like some lovely Mediterranean nymph, all unashamed. *Venus rising from the waves.* Except that here the waves were little more than ripples.

He glanced down at the water and was at once dizzy: the way it lapped at the rock and flowed so gently in the worn hollows of the stone, all fluid and glinting motion; and Geoff's stomach following the same routine, seeming to slosh loosely inside him. *Damn* this terror of his! What was he but eight, nine feet above the sea? God, he might as well feel sick standing on a thick carpet!

He stood up, shouted, jumped outward, toward Gwen.

Down he plunged into cool, liquid blue, and fought his way to the surface, and swam furiously to the beach. There he lay, half-in, half-out of the water, his heart and lungs hammering, blood coursing through his body. It had been such a little thing – something any ten-year-old child could have done – but to him it had been such an effort. And an achievement!

Elated, he stood up, sprinted down the beach, threw himself into the warm, shallow water just as Gwen was emerging. Carried back by him she laughed, splashed him, finally submitted to his hug. They rolled in twelve inches of water and her legs went round him; and there where the water met the sand they grew gentle, then fierce, and when it was done the sea laved their heat and rocked them gently, slowly dispersing their passion . . .

About four o'clock they ate, but very little. They weren't hungry; the sun was too hot; the silence, at first enchanting, had turned to a droning, sun-scorched monotony that beat on the ears worse than a city's roar. And there was a smell. When the light breeze off the sea swung in a certain direction, it brought something unpleasant with it.

To provide shade, Geoff had rigged up his shirt, slacks, and a large beach towel on a frame of drifted bamboo between the brittle, sandpapered branches of an old tree washed halfway up the sand. There in this tatty, makeshift teepee they'd spread their blanket, retreated from the pounding sun. But as the smell came again Geoff crept out of the cramped shade, stood up and shielded his eyes to look along the wall of the cliffs. "It comes . . . from over there," he said, pointing.

Gwen joined him. "I thought you'd explored?" she said.

"Along the tideline," he answered, nodding slowly. "Not along the base of the cliffs. Actually, they don't look too safe, and they overhang a fair bit in places. But if you'll look where I'm pointing – there, where the cliffs are cut back – is that water glinting?"

"A spring?" she looked at him. "A waterfall?"

"Hardly a waterfall," he said. "More a dribble. But what is it that's dribbling? I mean, springs don't stink, do they?"

Gwen wrinkled her nose. "Sewage, do you think?"

"*Yecchh!*" he said. "But at least it would explain why there's no one else here. I'm going to have a look."

She followed him to the place where the cliffs were notched in a V. Out of the sunlight, they both shivered a little. They'd put on swimwear for simple decency's sake, in case a boat should pass by, but now they hugged themselves as the chill of damp stone drew off their stored heat and brought goose-pimples to flesh which sun and sea had already roughened. And there, beneath the overhanging cliff, they found in the shingle a pool formed of a steady flow from on high. Without a shadow of a doubt, the pool was the source of the carrion stench; but here in the shade its water was dark, muddied, rippled, quite opaque. If there was anything in it, then it couldn't be seen.

As for the waterfall: it forked high up in the cliff, fell in twin streams, one of which was a trickle. Leaning out over the pool at its narrowest, shallowest point, Geoff cupped his hand to catch a few droplets. He held them to his nose, shook his head. "Just water," he said. "It's the pool itself that stinks."

"Or something back there?" Gwen looked beyond the pool, into the darkness of the cave formed of the V and the overhang.

Geoff took up a stone, hurled it into the darkness and silence. Clattering echoes sounded, and a moment later—

Flies! A swarm of them, disturbed where they'd been sitting on cool, damp ledges. They came in a cloud out of the cave, sent Geoff and Gwen yelping, fleeing for the sea. Geoff was stung twice, Gwen escaped injury; the ocean was their refuge, shielding them while the flies dispersed or returned to their vile-smelling breeding ground.

After the murky, poisonous pool the sea felt cool and refreshing. Muttering curses, Geoff stood in the shallows while Gwen squeezed the craters of the stings in his right shoulder and bathed them with salt water. When she was done he said, bitterly: "I've *had* it with this place! The sooner the Greek gets back the better."

His words were like an invocation. Towelling themselves dry, they heard the roar of Spiros's motor, heard it throttle back, and a moment later his boat came nosing in through the gap between the rock and the cliffs. But instead of landing he stood off in the shallow water. "Hallo," he called, in his totally unnecessary fashion.

"You're early," Geoff called back. And under his breath: *Thank God!*

"Early, yes," Spiros answered. "But I have thee troubles." He shrugged.

Gwen had pulled her dress on, packed the last of their things away. She walked down to the water's edge with Geoff. "Troubles?" she said, her voice a shade unsteady.

"Thee boat," he said, and pointed into the open, lolling belly of the craft, where they couldn't see. "I hitting thee rock when I leave Achladi. Is okay, but—" And he made his fifty-fifty sign, waggling his hand with the fingers open and the palm down. His face remained impassive, however.

Geoff looked at Gwen, then back to Spiros. "You mean it's unsafe?"

"For three peoples, unsafe – maybe." Again the Greek's shrug. "I thinks, I take thee lady first. Is Okay, I come back. Is bad, I find other boat."

"You can't take both of us?" Geoff's face fell.

Spiros shook his head. "Maybe big problems," he said.

Geoff nodded. "Okay," he said to Gwen. "Go just as you are. Leave all this stuff here and keep the boat light." And to Spiros: "Can you come in a bit more?"

The Greek made a clicking sound with his tongue, shrugged apologetically. "Thee boat is broked. I not want thee more breakings. You swim?" He looked at Gwen, leaned over the side and held out his hand. Keeping her dress on, she waded into the water, made her way to the side of the boat. The water only came up to her breasts, but it turned her dress to a transparent, clinging film. She grasped the upper strake with one hand and made to drag herself aboard. Spiros, leaning backwards, took her free hand.

Watching, Geoff saw her come half out of the water – then saw her freeze. She gasped loudly and twisted her wet hand in Spiros's grasp, tugged free of his grip, flopped back down into the water. And while the Greek regained his balance, she quickly swam back ashore. Geoff helped her from the sea. "Gwen?" he said.

Spiros worked his starter, got the motor going. He commenced a slow, deliberate circling of the small bay.

"Gwen?" Geoff said again. "What is it? What's wrong?" She was pale, shivering.

"He ..." she finally started to speak. "He ... had an erection! Geoff, I could see it bulging in his shorts, throbbing. My God – and I know it was for me! And the boat ..."

"What about the boat?" Anger was building in Geoff's heart and head, starting to run cold in his blood.

"There was no damage – none that I could see, anyway. He ... he just wanted to get me into that boat, on my own!"

Spiros could see them talking together. He came angling close into the beach, called out: "I bring thee better boat. Half-an-hour. Is safer. I see you." He headed for the channel between the rock and the cliff and in another moment passed from sight ...

"Geoff, we're in trouble," Gwen said, as soon as Spiros had left. "We're in serious trouble."

"I know it," he said. "I think I've known it ever since we got here. That bloke's as sinister as they come."

"And it's not just his eye, it's his mind," said Gwen. "He's sick." Finally, she told her husband about the incident when Spiros had carried her ashore from the boat.

"So that's what that was all about," he growled. "Well, something has to be done about him. We'll have to report him."

She clutched his arm. "We have to get back to Achladi before we can do that," she said quietly. "Geoff, I don't think he intends to let us get back!"

That thought had been in his mind, too, but he hadn't wanted her to know it. He felt suddenly helpless. The trap seemed sprung and they were in it. But what did Spiros intend, and how could he possibly hope to get away with it – whatever "it" was? Gwen broke into his thoughts:

"No one knows we're here, just Spiros."

"I know," said Geoff. "And what about that couple who . . ." He let it tail off. It had just slipped from his tongue. It was the last thing he'd wanted to say.

"Do you think I haven't thought of that?" Gwen hissed, gripping his arm more tightly yet. "He was the last one to see them – getting on a ferry, he said. But did they?" She stripped off her dress.

"What are you doing?" he asked, breathlessly.

"We came in from the north," she answered, wading out again into the water. "There were no beaches between here and Achladi. What about to the south? There are other beaches than this one, we know that. Maybe there's one just half a mile away. Maybe even less. If I can find one where there's a path up the cliffs . . ."

"Gwen," he said. "Gwen!" Panic was rising in him to match his impotence, his rage and terror.

She turned and looked at him, looked helpless in her skimpy bikini – and yet determined, too. And to think he'd considered her naïve! Well, maybe she had been. But no more. She managed a small smile, said, "I love you."

"What if you exhaust yourself?" He could think of nothing else to say.

"I'll know when to turn back," she said. Even in the hot sunlight he felt cold, and knew she must, too. He started towards her, but she was already into a controlled crawl, heading south, out across the submerged rocks. He watched her out of sight round the southern extreme of the jutting cliffs, stood knotting and unknotting his fists at the edge of the sea . . .

For long moments Geoff stood there, cold inside and hot out. And at the same time cold all over. Then the sense of time fleeting by overcame him. He ground his teeth, felt his frustration overflow. He wanted to shout but feared Gwen would hear him and turn back.

But there must be something he could do. With his bare hands? Like what? A weapon – he needed a weapon.

There was the knife they'd bought just for their picnic. He went to their things and found it. Only a three-inch blade, but sharp! Hand to hand it must give him something of an advantage. But what if Spiros had a bigger knife? He seemed to have a bigger or better everything else.

One of the drifted tree's branches was long, straight, slender. It pointed like a mocking, sandpapered wooden finger at the unscalable cliffs. Geoff applied his weight close to the main branch. As he lifted his feet from the ground the branch broke, sending him to his knees in the sand. Now he needed some binding material. Taking his unfinished spear with him, he ran to the base of the cliffs. Various odds and ends had been driven back there by past storms. Plastic Coke bottles, fragments of driftwood, pieces of cork ... a nylon fishing net tangled round a broken barrel!

Geoff cut lengths of tough nylon line from the net, bound the knife in position at the end of his spear. Now he felt he had a *real* advantage. He looked around. The sun was sinking leisurely towards the sea, casting his long shadow on the sand. How long since Spiros left? How much time left till he got back? Geoff glanced at the frowning needle of the sentinel rock. A sentinel, yes. A watcher. Or a watchtower!

He put down his spear, ran to the northern point and sprang into the sea. Moments later he was clawing at the rock, dragging himself from the water, climbing. And scarcely a thought of danger, not from the sea or the climb, not from the deep water or the height. At thirty feet the rock narrowed down; he could lean to left or right and scan the sea to the north, in the direction of Achladi. Way out on the blue, sails gleamed white in the brilliant sunlight. On the far horizon, a smudge of smoke. Nothing else.

For a moment – the merest moment – Geoff's old nausea returned. He closed his eyes and flattened himself to the rock, gripped tightly where his fingers were bedded in cracks in the weathered stone. A mass of stone shifted slightly under the pressure of his right hand, almost causing him to lose his balance. He teetered for a second, remembered Gwen ... the nausea passed, and with it all fear. He stepped a little lower, examined the great slab of rock which his hand had tugged loose. And suddenly an idea burned bright in his brain.

Which was when he heard Gwen's cry, thin as a keening wind, shrilling into his bones from along the beach. He jerked his head round, saw her there in the water inside the reef, wearily striking for the shore. She looked all in. His heart leaped into his mouth, and without pause he launched himself from the rock, striking the water feet first and sinking deep. No fear or effort to it this time; no time for any of that; surfacing, he struck for the shore. Then back along the beach, panting his heart out, flinging himself down in the small waves where she kneeled, sobbing, her face covered by her hands.

"Gwen, are you all right? What is it, love? What's happened? I *knew* you'd exhaust yourself!"

She tried to stand up, collapsed into his arms and shivered there; he cradled her where earlier they'd made love. And at last she could tell it.

"I . . . I stayed close to the shore," she gasped, gradually getting her breath. "Or rather, close to the cliffs. I was looking . . . looking for a way up. I'd gone about a third of a mile, I think. Then there was a spot where the water was very deep and the cliffs sheer. Something touched my legs and it was like an electric shock – I mean, it was so unexpected there in that deep water. To feel something slimy touching my legs like that. *Ugh!*" She drew a deep breath.

"I thought: *God, sharks!* But then I remembered: there are no sharks in the Med. Still, I wanted to be sure. So . . . so I turned, made a shallow dive and looked to see what . . . what . . ." She broke down into sobbing again.

Geoff could do nothing but warm her, hug her tighter yet.

"Oh, but there *are* sharks in the Med, Geoff," she finally went on. "One shark, anyway. His name is Spiros! A spider? No, he's a shark! Under the sea there, I saw . . . a girl, naked, tethered to the bottom with a rope round her ankle. And down in the deeps, a stone holding her there."

"My God!" Geoff breathed.

"Her thighs, belly, were covered in those little green swimming crabs. She was all bloated, puffy, floating upright on her own internal gasses. Fish nibbled at her. Her nipples were gone . . ."

"The fish!" Geoff gasped. But Gwen shook her head.

"Not the fish," she rasped. "Her arms and breasts were black with bruises. Her nipples had been bitten through – *right* through! Oh, Geoff, Geoff!" She hugged him harder than ever, shivering hard enough to shake him. "I *know* what happened to her. It was him, Spiros." She paused, tried to control her shivering, which wasn't only the after-effect of the water.

And finally she continued: "After that I had no strength. But somehow I made it back."

"Get dressed," he told her then, his voice colder than she'd ever heard it. "Quickly! No, not your dress — my trousers, shirt. The slacks will be too long for you. Roll up the bottoms. But get dressed, get warm."

She did as he said. The sun, sinking, was still hot. Soon she was warm again, and calmer. Then Geoff gave her the spear he'd made and told her what he was going to do . . .

There were two of them, as like as peas in a pod. Geoff saw them, and the pieces fell into place. Spiros and his brother. The island's codes were tight. These two looked for loose women; loose in their narrow eyes, anyway. And from the passports of the honeymooners it had been plain that they weren't married. Which had made Gwen a whore, in their eyes. Like the Swedish girl, who'd met a man and gone to bed with him. As easy as that. So Spiros had tried it on, the easy way at first. By making it plain that he was on offer. Now that that hadn't worked, now it was time for the hard way.

Geoff saw them coming in the boat and stopped gouging at the rock. His fingernails were cracked and starting to bleed, but the job was as complete as he could wish. He ducked back out of sight, hugged the sentinel rock and thought only of Gwen. He had one chance and mustn't miss it.

He glanced back, over his shoulder. Gwen had heard the boat's engine. She stood halfway between the sea and the waterfall with its foul pool. Her spear was grasped tightly in her hands. *Like a young Amazon*, Geoff thought. But then he heard the boat's motor cut back and concentrated on what he was doing.

The put-put-put of the boat's exhaust came closer. Geoff took a chance, glanced round the rim of the rock. Here they came, gentling into the channel between the rock and the cliffs. Spiros's brother wore slacks; both men were naked from the waist up; Spiros had the tiller. And his brother had a shotgun!

One chance. *Only one chance.*

The boat's nose came inching forward, began to pass directly below. Geoff gave a mad yell, heaved at the loose wedge of rock. For a moment he thought it would stick and put all his weight into it. But then it shifted, toppled.

Below, the two Greeks had looked up, eyes huge in tanned, startled faces. The one with the shotgun was on his feet. He saw the falling rock in the instant before it smashed down on him and drove him through the bottom of the boat. His gun went off, both barrels, and the shimmering air near Geoff's head buzzed like a nest of wasps. Then, while all below was still in a turmoil, he aimed himself at Spiros and jumped.

Thrown about in the stern of his sinking boat, Spiros was making ready to dive overboard when Geoff's feet hit him. He was hurled into the water, Geoff narrowly missing the swamped boat as he, too, crashed down into the sea. And then a mad flurry of water as they both struck out for the shore.

Spiros was there first. Crying out, wild, outraged, frightened, he dragged himself from the sea. He looked round and saw Geoff coming through the water – saw his boat disappear with only ripples to mark its passing, and no sign of his brother – and started at a lopsided run up the beach. Towards Gwen. Geoff swam for all he was worth, flew from the sea up onto the land.

Gwen was running, heading for the V in the cliff under the waterfall. Spiros was right behind her, arms reaching. Geoff came last, the air rasping in his lungs, hell's fires blazing in his heart. He'd drawn blood and found it to his liking. But he stumbled, fell, and when he was up again he saw Spiros closing on his quarry. Gwen was backed up against the cliff, her feet in the water at the shallow end of the vile pool. The Greek made a low, apish lunge at her and she struck at him with her spear.

She gashed his face even as he grabbed her. His hand caught in the loose material of Geoff's shirt, tearing it from her so that her breasts lolled free. Then she stabbed at him again, slicing him across the neck. His hands flew to his face and neck; he staggered back from her, tripped, and sat down in chest-deep water; Geoff arrived panting at the pool and Gwen flew into his arms. He took the spear from her, turned it towards Spiros.

But the Greek was finished. He shrieked and splashed in the pool like the madman he was, seemed incapable of getting to his feet. His wounds weren't bad, but the blood was everywhere. That wasn't the worst of it: the thing he'd tripped on had floated to the surface. It was beginning to rot, but it was – or had been – a young man. Rubbery arms and legs tangled with Spiros's limbs; a ghastly, gaping face tossed with his frantic threshing; a great black hole showed where the bloated corpse had taken a shotgun blast to the chest, the shot that had killed him.

For a little while longer Spiros fought to be rid of the thing – screamed aloud as its gaping, accusing mouth screamed horribly, silently at him – then gave up and flopped back half-in, half-out of the water. One of the corpse's arms was draped across his heaving, shuddering chest. He lay there with his hands over his face and cried, and the flies came swarming like a black, hostile cloud from the cave to settle on him.

Geoff held Gwen close, guided her away from the horror down the beach to a sea which was a deeper blue now. "It's okay," he kept saying, as much for himself as for her. "It's okay. They'll come looking for us, sooner or later."

As it happened, it was sooner . . .

1990

The Man Who Drew Cats

Michael Marshall Smith

THE FIRST VOLUME OF *Best New Horror* won both the British Fantasy Award and the World Fantasy Award. This helped establish the series amongst the readers and some publishers on both sides of the Atlantic, although it has always remained a struggle to convince people to submit material for consideration.

Back in the early days, Ramsey Campbell and I found ourselves spending quite considerable amounts of our own money acquiring books and magazines just so that we could read stories for the anthology. In fact, twenty years later I still have to do the same thing.

This time our Introduction had expanded to nine pages and the Necrology was up to thirteen. Ramsey and I were concerned about the much-hyped recessions in the movie and publishing industries (apparently some things never change), and we warned that the mid-list was under threat. Once again, we were scarily prophetic.

The publishers once again reused my Letraset logo, now embossed and with an added *2*. This time the cover was an original piece by Spanish-Mexican illustrator Luis Rey, who lived in London. As with the first book, Robinson did it in trade paperback and Carroll & Graf went with a hardcover. However, a couple of years later I found an American paperback that neither Robinson nor I had been aware of. G&G claimed it was not a reprint, but a rebinding of their earlier edition, until I pointed out that it was, in fact, a *larger* format than the hardcover . . .!

For this second compilation we found ourselves working with some of the Big Names in genre publishing. Out of the twenty-eight stories in the book, we included work by such established authors as Peter Straub, Jonathan Carroll, Harlan Ellison, F. Paul Wilson, Gene Wolfe and Gahan Wilson.

However, the story I have chosen to represent this particular volume was from a relative newcomer. In fact, it was Michael Marshall Smith's first published story.

One of the most rewarding experiences about being an editor is discovering and nurturing new talent. I have always tried to leave slots for new or upcoming writers in *Best New Horror* and the other anthologies I have edited. Which is why it was such a thrill when David A. Sutton and I plucked "The Man Who Drew Cats" out of the submission pile for *Dark Voices 2: The Pan Book of Horror*.

Rarely have I ever encountered a voice so assured or a writing style so effortless in a first tale. Remarkably, Mike wrote the story in a day. More than anyone else, it reminded me of the work of Stephen King, and given the accolades that both the tale and its author have subsequently received, I can only presume that I was not the only one . . .

TOM WAS A VERY TALL MAN, so tall he didn't even have a nickname for it. Ned Black, who was at least a head shorter, had been "Tower Block" since the sixth grade, and Jack had a sign up over the door saying MIND YOUR HEAD, NED. But Tom was just Tom. It was like he was so tall it didn't bear mentioning even for a joke: be a bit like ragging someone for breathing.

Course there were other reasons too for not ragging Tom about his height or anything else. The guys you'll find perched on stools round Jack's bar watching the game and buying beers, they've known each other forever. Gone to Miss Stadler's school together, gotten under each other's Mom's feet, double-dated right up to giving each other's best man's speech. Kingstown is a small place, you understand, and the old boys who come regular to Jack's mostly spent their childhoods in the same tree-house. Course they'd since gone their separate ways, up to a point: Pete was an accountant now, had a small office down Union Street just off the Square and did pretty good, whereas Ned was still pumping gas and changing oil and after forty years he did that pretty good too. Comes a time when men have known each other so long they forget what they do for a living most the time, because it just don't matter. When you talk there's a little bit of skimming stones down the quarry in second grade, a whisper of dolling up to go to that first dance, a tad of going to the housewarming when they moved ten years back. There's all that, so much more than you can say, and none of it's important except for having happened.

So we'll stop by and have a couple of beers and talk about the town and rag each other, and the pleasure's just in shooting the breeze and it don't really matter what's said, just the fact that we're all still there to say it.

But Tom, he was different. We all remember the first time we saw him. It was a long hot summer like we haven't seen in the ten years since, and we were lolling under the fans at Jack's and complaining about the tourists. Kingstown does get its share in the summer, even though it's not near the sea and we don't have a McDonald's and I'll be damned if I can figure out why folk'll go out of their way to see what's just a quiet little town near some mountains. It was as hot as Hell that afternoon and as much as a man could do to sit in his shirtsleeves and drink the coolest beer he could find, and Jack's is the coolest for us, and always will be, I guess.

Then Tom walked in. His hair was already pretty white back then, and long, and his face was brown and tough with grey eyes like diamonds set in leather. He was dressed mainly in black with a long coat that made you hot just to look at it, but he looked comfortable like he carried his very own weather around with him and he was just fine.

He got a beer, and sat down at a table and read the town *Bugle*, and that was that.

It was special because there wasn't anything special about it. Jack's Bar isn't exactly exclusive and we don't all turn round and stare at anyone new if they come in, but that place is like a monument to shared times. If a tourist couple comes in out of the heat and sits down, nobody says anything – and maybe nobody even notices at the front of their mind – but it's like there's a little island of the alien in the water and the currents just don't ebb and flow the way they usually do, if you get what I mean. Tom just walked in and sat down and it was all right because it was like he was there just like we were, and could've been for thirty years. He sat and read his paper like part of the same river, and everyone just carried on downstream the way they were.

Pretty soon he goes up for another beer and a few of us got talking to him. We got his name and what he did – painting, he said – and after that it was just shooting the breeze. That quick. He came in that summer afternoon and just fell into the conversation like he'd been there all his life, and sometimes it was hard to imagine he hadn't been. Nobody knew where he came from, or where he'd been, and there was something real quiet about him. A stillness, a man in a slightly different world. But he showed enough to get along real well with us, and a bunch of old friends don't often let someone in like that.

Anyway, he stayed that whole summer. Rented himself a place just round the corner from the square, or so he said: I never saw it. I guess no one did. He was a private man, private like a steel door with four bars and a couple of six-inch padlocks, and when he left the square at the end of the day he could have vanished as soon as he turned the corner for all we knew. But he always came from that direction in the morning, with his easel on his back and paint-box under his arm, and he always wore that black coat like it was a part of him. But he always looked cool, and the funny thing was when you stood near him you could swear you felt cooler yourself. I remember Pete saying over a beer that it wouldn't surprise him none if, assuming it ever rained again, Tom would walk round in his own column of dryness. He was just joking, of course, but Tom made you think things like that.

Jack's bar looks right out onto the square, the kind of square towns don't have much anymore: big and dusty with old roads out each corner, tall shops and houses on all the sides and some stone paving in the middle round a fountain that ain't worked in living memory. Well in the summer that old square is just full of out-of-towners in pink towelling jump-suits and nasty jackets standing round saying "Wow" and taking pictures of our quaint old hall and our quaint old stores and even our quaint old selves if we stand still too long. Tom would sit out near the fountain and paint and those people would stand and watch for hours – but he didn't paint the houses or the square or the old Picture House. He painted animals, and painted them like you've never seen. Birds with huge blue speckled wings and cats with cutting green eyes; and whatever he painted it looked like it was just coiled up on the canvas ready to fly away. He didn't do them in their normal colours, they were all reds and purples and deep blues and greens – and yet they fair sparkled with life. It was a wonder to watch: he'd put up a fresh paper, sit looking at nothing in particular, then dip his brush into his paint and draw a line, maybe red, maybe blue. Then he'd add another, maybe the same colour, maybe not. Stroke by stroke you could see the animal build up in front of your eyes and yet when it was finished you couldn't believe it hadn't always been there. When he'd finished he'd spray it with some stuff to fix the paints and put a price on it and you can believe me those paintings were sold before they hit the ground. Spreading businessmen from New Jersey or some such and their bored wives would come alive for maybe the first time in years, and walk away with one of those paintings and their arms round each other, looking like they'd found a bit of something they'd forgotten they'd lost.

Come about six o'clock Tom would finish up and walk across to Jack's, looking like a sailing ship amongst rowing boats and saying yes he'd be back again tomorrow and yes, he'd be happy to do a painting for them. He'd get a beer and sit with us and watch the game and there'd be no paint on his fingers or his clothes, not a spot. I figured he'd got so much control over that paint it went where it was told and nowhere else.

I asked him once how he could bear to let those paintings go. I know if I'd been able to make anything that good in my whole life I couldn't let it out of my sight, I'd want to keep it to look at sometimes. He thought for a moment and then he said he believed it depends how much of yourself you've put into it. If you've gone deep down and pulled up what's inside and put it down, then you don't want to let it go: you want to keep it, so's you can check sometimes that it's still safely tied down. Comes a time when a painting's so right and so good that it's private, and no one'll understand it except the man who put it down. Only he is going to know what he's talking about. But the everyday paintings, well they were mainly just because he liked to paint animals, and liked for people to have them. He could only put a piece of himself into something he was going to sell, but they paid for the beers and I guess it's like us fellows in Jack's Bar: if you like talking, you don't always have to be saying something important.

Why animals? Well if you'd seen him with them I guess you wouldn't have to ask. He loved them, is all, and they loved him right back. The cats were always his favourites. My old Pa used to say that cats weren't nothing but sleeping machines put on the earth to do some of the human's sleeping for them, and whenever Tom worked in the square there'd always be a couple curled up near his feet. And whenever he did a chalk drawing, he'd always do a cat.

Once in a while, you see, Tom seemed to get tired of painting on paper, and he'd get out some chalks and sit down on the baking flagstones and just do a drawing right there on the dusty rock. Now I've told you about his paintings, but these drawings were something else again. It was like because they couldn't be bought but would be washed away, he was putting more of himself into it, doing more than just shooting the breeze. They were just chalk on dusty stone and they were still in these weird colours, but I tell you children wouldn't walk near them because they looked so real, and they weren't the only ones, either. People would stand a few feet back and stare and you could see the wonder in their eyes. If they could've been bought there were people who would have sold their houses. I'm telling you. And it's a funny thing but a couple of times when I walked over to open the store up in the mornings I saw a dead bird or two on top of those drawings, almost like they had landed on it and been so terrified to find themselves right on top of a cat they'd dropped dead of fright. But they must have been dumped there by some real cat, of course, because some of those birds looked like they'd been mauled a bit. I used to throw them in the bushes to tidy up and some of them were pretty broken up.

Old Tom was a godsend to a lot of mothers that summer, who found they could leave their little ones by him, do their shopping in peace and have a soda with their friends and come back to find the kids still sitting quietly watching Tom paint. He didn't mind them at all and would talk to them and make them laugh, and kids of that age laughing is one of the best sounds there is. It's the kind of sound that makes the trees grow. They're young and curious and the world spins round them and when they laugh the world seems a brighter place because it takes you back to the time when you knew no evil and everything was good, or if it wasn't, it would be over by tomorrow.

And here I guess I've finally come down to it, because there was one little boy who didn't laugh much, but just sat quiet and watchful, and I guess he probably understands more of what happened that summer than any of us, though maybe not in words he could tell.

His name was Billy McNeill, and he was Jim Valentine's kid. Jim used to be a mechanic, worked with Ned up at the gas station and raced beat-up cars after hours. Which is why his kid is called McNeill now: one Sunday Jim took a corner a mite too fast and the car rolled and the gas tank caught and they never did find all the wheels. A year later his Mary married again. God alone knows why, her folks warned her, her friends warned her, but I guess love must just have been blind. Sam McNeill's work schedule was at best pretty empty, and mostly he just drank and hung out with friends who maybe weren't always this side of the law. I guess Mary had her own sad little miracle and got her sight back pretty soon, because it wasn't long before Sam got free with his fists when the evenings got too long and he'd had a lot too many. You didn't see Mary around much anymore. In these parts people tend to stare at black eyes on a woman, and a deaf man could hear the whisperings of "We Told Her So".

One morning Tom was sitting painting as usual, and little Billy was sitting watching him. Usually he just wandered off after a while but this morning Mary was at the doctor's and she came over to collect him, walking quickly with her face lowered. But not low enough. I was watching from the store, it was kind of a slow day. Tom's face never showed much. He was a man for a quiet smile and a raised eyebrow, but he looked shocked that morning. Mary's eyes were puffed and purple and there was a cut on her cheek an inch long. I guess we'd sort of gotten used to seeing her like that and if the truth be known some of the wives thought she'd got remarried a bit on the soon side and I suppose we may all have been a bit cold towards her, Jim Valentine having been so well-liked and all.

Tom looked from the little boy who never laughed much, to his mom with her tired unhappy eyes and her beat-up face, and his own face went from shocked to stony and I can't describe it any other way but that I felt a cold chill cross my heart from right across the square.

But then he smiled and ruffled Billy's hair and Mary took Billy's hand and they went off. They turned back once and Tom was still looking after them and he gave Billy a little wave and he waved back and mother and child smiled together.

That night in Jack's Tom put a quiet question about Mary and we told him the story. As he listened his face seemed to harden from within, his eyes growing flat and dead. We told him that old Lou Lachance, who lived next door to the McNeill's, said that sometimes you could hear him shouting and her pleading till three in the morning and on still nights the sound of Billy crying for even longer than that. Told him it was a shame, but what could you do? Folks keep themselves out of other people's faces round here, and I guess Sam and his drinking buddies didn't have much to fear from nearly-retireders like us anyhow. Told him it was a terrible thing, and none of us liked it, but these things happened and what could you do.

Tom listened and didn't say a word. Just sat there in his black coat and listened to us pass the buck. After a while the talk sort of petered out and we all sat and watched the bubbles in our beers. I guess the bottom line was that none of us had really thought about it much except as another chapter of small-town gossip, and Jesus Christ did I feel ashamed about that by the time we'd finished telling it. Sitting there with Tom was no laughs at all. He had a real edge to him, and seemed more unknown than known that night. He stared at his laced fingers for a long time, and then he began, real slow, to talk.

He'd been married once, he said, a long time ago, and he'd lived in a place called Stevensburg with his wife Rachel. When he talked about her the air seemed to go softer and we all sat quiet and supped our beers and remembered how it had been way back when we first loved our own wives. He talked of her smile and the look in her eyes and when we went home that night I guess there were a few wives who were surprised at how tight they got hugged, and who went to sleep in their husband's arms feeling more loved and contented than they had in a long while.

He'd loved her and she him and for a few years they were the happiest people on earth. Then a third party had got involved. Tom didn't say his name, and he spoke real neutrally about him, but it was a gentleness like silk wrapped round a knife. Anyway his wife fell in love with him, or thought she had, or leastways she slept with him. In their bed, the bed they'd come to on their wedding night. As Tom spoke these words some of us looked up at him, startled, like we'd been slapped across the face.

Rachel did what so many do and live to regret till their dying day. She was so mixed up and getting so much pressure from the other guy that she decided to plough on with the one mistake and make it the biggest in the world.

She left Tom. He talked with her, pleaded even. It was almost impossible to imagine Tom ever doing that, but I guess the man we knew was a different guy from the one he was remembering. The pleading made no difference.

And so Tom had to carry on living in Stevensburg, walking the same tracks, seeing them around, wondering if she was as free and easy with him, if the light in her eyes was shining on him now. And each time the man saw Tom he'd look straight at him and crease a little smile, a grin that said he knew about the pleading and he and his cronies had had a good laugh over the wedding bed – and yes, I'm going home with your wife tonight and I know just how she likes it, you want to compare notes?

And then he'd turn and kiss Rachel on the mouth, his eyes on Tom, smiling. And she let him do it.

It had kept stupid old women in stories for weeks, the way Tom kept losing weight and his temper and the will to live. He took three months of it and then left without bothering to sell the house. Stevensburg was where he'd grown up and courted and loved and now wherever he turned the good times had rotted and hung like fly-blown corpses in all the cherished places. He'd never been back.

It took an hour to tell, and then he stopped talking a while and lit a hundredth cigarette and Pete got us all some more beers. We were sitting sad and thoughtful, tired like we'd lived it ourselves. And I guess most of us had, some little bit of it. But had we ever loved anyone the way he'd loved her? I doubt it, not all of us put together. Pete set the beers down and Ned asked Tom why he hadn't just beaten the living shit out of the guy. Now, no one else would have actually asked that, but Ned's a good guy, and I guess we were all with him in feeling a piece of that oldest and most crushing hatred in the world, the hate of a man who's lost the woman he loves to another, and we knew what Ned was saying. I'm not saying it's a good thing and I know you're not supposed to feel like that these days but show me a man who says he doesn't and I'll show you a liar. Love is the only feeling worth a tin shit but you've got to know that it comes from both sides of a man's character and the deeper it runs the darker the pools it draws from.

My guess is he just hated the man too much to hit him. Comes a time when that isn't enough, when nothing is ever going to be enough, and so you can't do anything at all. And as he talked the pain just flowed out like a river that wasn't ever going to be stopped, a river that had cut a channel through every corner of his soul. I learnt something that night that you can go your whole life without realizing: that there are things that can be done that can mess someone up so badly, for so long, that they just cannot be allowed; that there are some kinds of pain that you cannot suffer to be brought into the world.

And then Tom was done telling and he raised a smile and said that in the end he hadn't done anything to the man except paint him a picture, which I didn't understand, but Tom looked like he'd talked all he was going to.

So we got some more beers and shot some quiet pool before going home. But I guess we all knew what he'd been talking about.

Billy McNeill was just a child. He should have been dancing through a world like a big funfair full of sunlight and sounds, and instead he went home at night and saw his mom being beaten up by a man with shit for brains who struck out at a good woman because he was too stupid to deal with the world. Most kids go to sleep thinking about bikes and climbing apple trees and skimming stones, and he was lying there hearing his mom get smashed in the stomach and then hit again as she threw up in the sink. Tom didn't say any of that, but he did. And we knew he was right.

The summer kept up bright and hot, and we all had our businesses to attend to. Jack sold a lot of beer and I sold a lot of ice cream (Sorry ma'am, just the three flavours, and no, Bubblegum Pistachio ain't one of them) and Ned fixed a whole bunch of cracked radiators. Tom sat right out there in the square with a couple of cats by his feet and a crowd around him, magicking up animals in the sun.

And I think that after that night Mary maybe got a few more smiles as she did her shopping, and maybe a few more wives stopped to talk to her. She looked a lot better too: Sam had a job by the sound of it and her face healed up pretty soon. You could often see her standing holding Billy's hand as they watched Tom paint for a while before they went home. I think she realized they had a friend in him. Sometimes Billy was there all afternoon, and he was happy there in the sun by Tom's feet and oftentimes he'd pick up a piece of chalk and sit scrawling on the pavement. Sometimes I'd see Tom lean over and say something to him and he'd look up and smile a simple child's smile that beamed in the sunlight. The tourists kept coming and the sun kept shining and it was one of those summers that go on forever and stick in a child's mind, and tell you what summer should be like for the rest of your life. And I'm damn sure it sticks in Billy's mind, just like it does in all of ours.

Because one morning Mary didn't come into the store, which had gotten to being a regular sort of thing, and Billy wasn't out there in the square. After the way things had been the last few weeks that could only be bad news, and so I left the boy John in charge of the store and hurried over to have a word with Tom. I was kind of worried.

I was no more than halfway across to him when I saw Billy come running from the opposite corner of the square, going straight to Tom. He was crying fit to burst and just leapt up at Tom and clung to him, his arms wrapped tight round his neck. Then his mother came across from the same direction, running as best she could. She got to Tom and they just looked at each other. Mary's a real pretty girl but you wouldn't have believed it then. It looked like he'd actually broken her nose this time, and blood was streaming out of her lip. She started sobbing, saying Sam had lost his job because he was back on the drink and what could she do and then suddenly there was a roar and I was shoved aside and Sam was standing there, still wearing his slippers, weaving back and forth and radiating that aura of violence that keeps men like him safe. He started shouting at Mary to take the kid the fuck back home and she just flinched and cowered closer to Tom like she was huddling round a fire to keep out the cold. This just got Sam even wilder and he staggered forward and told Tom to get the fuck out of it if he knew what was good for him, and grabbed Mary's arm and tried to yank her towards him, his face terrible with rage.

Then Tom stood up. Now Tom was a tall man, but he wasn't a young man, and he was thin. Sam was thirty and built like the town hall. When he did work it usually involved moving heavy things from one place to another, and his strength was supercharged by a whole pile of drunken nastiness.

But at that moment the crowd stepped back as one and I suddenly felt very afraid for Sam McNeill. Tom looked like you could take anything you cared to him and it would just break, like he was a huge spike of granite wrapped in skin with two holes in the face where the rock showed through. And he was mad, not hot and blowing like Sam, but mad and *cold*.

There was a long pause. Then Sam weaved back a step and shouted:

"You just come on home, you hear? Gonna be real trouble if you don't, Mary. Real trouble," and then stormed off across the square the way he came, knocking his way through the tourist vultures soaking up the spicy local colour.

Mary turned to Tom, so afraid it hurt to see, and said she guessed she'd better be going. Tom looked at her for a moment and then spoke for the first time.

"Do you love him?"

Even if you wanted to, you ain't going to lie to eyes like that, for fear something inside you will break.

Real quiet she said: "No," and began crying softly as she took Billy's hand and walked slowly back across the square.

Tom packed up his stuff and walked over to Jack's. I went with him and had a beer but I had to get back to the shop and Tom just sat there like a trigger, silent and strung up tight as a drum. Somewhere down near the bottom of those still waters something was stirring. Something I thought I didn't want to see.

About an hour later it was lunchtime and I'd just left the shop to have a break when suddenly something whacked into the back of my legs and nearly knocked me down. It was Billy. It was Billy and he had a bruise round his eye that was already closing it up.

I knew what the only thing to do was and I did it. I took his hand and led him across to the Bar, feeling a hard anger pushing against my throat. When he saw Tom, Billy ran to him again and Tom took him in his arms and looked over Billy's shoulder at me, and I felt my own anger collapse utterly in the face of a fury I could never have generated. I tried to find a word to describe it but they all just seemed like they were in the wrong language. All I can say is I wanted to be somewhere else and it felt real cold standing there facing that stranger in a black coat.

Then the moment passed and Tom was holding the kid close, ruffling his hair and talking to him in a low voice, murmuring the words I thought only mothers knew. He dried Billy's tears and checked his eye and then he got off his stool, smiled down at him and said:

"I think it's time we did some drawing, what d'you say?" and, taking the kid's hand, he picked up his chalkbox and walked out into the square.

I don't know how many times I looked up and watched them that afternoon. They were sitting side by side on the stone, Billy's little hand wrapped round one of Tom's fingers, and Tom doing one of his chalk drawings. Every now and then Billy would reach across and add a little bit and Tom would smile and say something and Billy's gurgling laugh would float across the square. The store was real busy that afternoon and I was chained to that counter, but I could tell by the size of the crowd that a lot of Tom was going into that picture, and maybe a bit of Billy too.

It was about four o'clock before I could take a break. I walked across the crowded square in the mid-afternoon heat and shouldered my way through to where they sat with a couple of cold Cokes. And when I saw it my mouth just dropped open and took a five-minute vacation while I tried to take it in.

It was a cat all right, but not a normal cat. It was a life-size tiger. I'd never seen Tom do anything near that big before, and as I stood there in the beating sun trying to get my mind round it, it almost seemed to stand in three dimensions, a nearly living thing. Its stomach was very lean and thin, its tail seemed to twitch with colour, and as Tom worked on the eyes and jaws, his face set with a rigid concentration quite unlike his usual calm painting face, the snarling mask of the tiger came to life before my eyes. And I could see that he wasn't just putting a bit of himself in at all. This was a man at full stretch, giving all of himself and reaching down for more, pulling up bloody fistfuls and throwing them down. The tiger was all the rage I'd seen in his eyes, and more, and like his love for Rachel that rage just seemed bigger than any other man could comprehend. He was pouring it out and sculpting it into the lean and ravenous creature coming to pulsating life in front of us on the pavement, and the weird purples and blues and reds just made it seem more vibrant and alive.

I watched him working furiously on it, the boy sometimes helping, adding a tiny bit here and there that strangely seemed to add to it, and thought I understood what he'd meant that evening a few weeks back. He said he'd done a painting for the man who'd given him so much pain. Then, as now, he must have found what I guess you'd call something fancy like "catharsis" through his skill with chalks, had wrenched the pain up from within him and nailed it down onto something solid that he could walk away from. Now he was helping that little boy do the same, and the boy did look better, his bruised eye hardly showing with the wide smile on his face as he watched the big cat conjured up from nowhere in front of him.

We all just stood and watched, like something out of an old story, the simple folk and the magical stranger. It always feels like you're giving a bit of yourself away when you praise someone else's creation, and its often done grudgingly, but you could feel the awe that day like a warm wind. Comes a time when you realize something special is happening, something you're never going to see again, and there isn't anything you can do but watch.

Well I had to go back to the store after a while. I hated to go but, well, John is a good boy, married now of course, but in those days his head was full of girls and it didn't do to leave him alone in a busy shop for too long.

And so the long hot day drew slowly to a close. I kept the store open till eight, when the light began to turn and the square emptied out with all the tourists going away to write postcards and see if we didn't have even just a *little* McDonald's hidden away someplace. I suppose Mary had troubles enough at home, realized where the boy would be and figured he was safer there than anywhere else, and I guess she was right.

Tom and Billy finished up drawing and then Tom sat and talked to him for some time. Then they got up and the kid walked slowly off to the corner of the square, looking back to wave at Tom a couple times. Tom stood and watched him go and when Billy had gone he stayed there a while, head down, like a huge black statue in the gathering dark. He looked kind of creepy out there and I don't mind telling you

I was glad when he finally moved and started walking over towards Jack's. I ran out to catch up with him and drew level just as we passed the drawing. And then I had to stop. I just couldn't look at that and move at the same time.

Finished, the drawing was like nothing on earth, and I suppose that's exactly what it was. I can't hope to describe it to you, although I've seen it in my dreams many times in the last ten years. You had to be there, on that heavy summer night, had to know what was going on. Otherwise it's going to sound like it was just a drawing.

That tiger was out and out terrifying. It looked so mean and hungry, Christ I don't know what: it just looked like the darkest parts of mankind, the pain and the fury and the vengeful hate nailed down in front of you for you to see, and I just stood there and shivered in the humid evening air.

"We did him a picture," Tom said quietly.

"Yeah," I said, and nodded. Like I said, I know what "catharsis" means and I thought I understood what he was saying. But I really didn't want to look at it much longer. "Let's go have a beer, hey?"

The storm in Tom hadn't passed, I could tell, and he still seemed to thrum with crackling emotions looking for an earth, but I thought the clouds might be breaking and I was glad.

And so we walked slowly over to Jack's and had a few beers and watched some pool being played. Tom seemed pretty tired, but still alert, and I relaxed a little. Come eleven most of the guys started going on their way and I was surprised to see Tom get another beer. Pete, Ned and I stayed on, and Jack of course, though we knew our loving wives would have something to say about that. It just didn't seem time to go. Outside it had gotten pretty dark, though the moon was keeping the square in a kind of twilight and the lights in the bar threw a pool of warmth out of the front window.

Then, about twelve o'clock, it happened, and I don't suppose any of us will ever see the same world we grew up in again. I've told this whole thing like it was just me who was there, but we all were, and we remember it together.

Because suddenly there was a wailing sound outside, a thin cutting cry, getting closer. Tom immediately snapped to his feet and stared out the window like he'd been waiting for it. As we looked out across the square we saw little Billy come running and we could see the blood on his face from there. Some of us got to get up but Tom snarled at us to stay there and so I guess we just stayed put, sitting back down like we'd been pushed. He strode out the door and into the square and the boy saw him and ran to him and Tom folded him in his cloak and held him close and warm. But he didn't come back in. He just stood there, and he was waiting for something.

Now there's a lot of crap talked about silences. I read novels when I've the time and you see things like "Time stood still" and so on and you think bullshit it did. So I'll just say I don't think anyone in the world breathed in that next minute. There was no wind, no movement. The stillness and silence were there like you could touch them, but more than that: they were like that's all there was and all there ever had been.

We felt the slow red throb of violence from right across the square before we could even see the man. Then Sam came staggering into view waving a bottle like a flag and cursing his head off. At first he couldn't see Tom and the boy because they were the opposite side of the fountain, and he ground to a wavering halt, but then he started shouting, rough jags of sound that seemed to strike against the silence and die instead of breaking it, and he began charging across the square – and if ever there was a man with murder in his thoughts then it was Sam McNeill. He was like a man who'd given his soul the evening off. I wanted to shout to Tom to get the hell out of the way, to come inside, but the words wouldn't come out of my throat and we all just stood there, knuckles whitening as we clutched the bar and stared, our mouths open like we'd made a pact never to use them again. Tom just stood there, watching Sam come towards him, getting closer, almost as far as the spot where Tom usually painted. It felt like we were looking out of the window at a picture of something that happened long ago in another place and time, and the closer Sam got the more I began to feel very afraid for him.

It was at that moment that Sam stopped dead in his tracks, skidding forward like in some kid's cartoon, his shout dying off in his ragged throat. He was staring at the ground in front of him, his eyes wide and his mouth a stupid circle. Then he began to scream.

It was a high shrill noise like a woman, and coming out of that bull of a man it sent fear racking down my spine. He started making thrashing movements like he was trying to move backwards, but he just stayed where he was.

His movements became unmistakable at about the same time his screams turned from terror to agony. He was trying to get his leg away from something.

Suddenly he seemed to fall forward on one knee, his other leg stuck out behind him, and he raised his head and shrieked at the dark skies and we saw his face then and I'm not going to forget that face so long as I live. It was a face from before there were any words, the face behind our oldest fears and earliest nightmares, the face we're terrified of seeing on ourselves one night when we're alone in the dark and It finally comes out from under the bed to get us, like we always knew it would.

Then Sam fell on his face, his leg buckled up – and still he thrashed and screamed and clawed at the ground with his hands, blood running from his broken fingernails as he twitched and struggled. Maybe the light was playing tricks, and my eyes were sparkling anyway on account of being too paralysed with fear to even blink, but as he thrashed less and less it became harder and harder to see him at all, and as the breeze whipped up stronger his screams began to sound a lot like the wind. But still he writhed and moaned and then suddenly there was the most godawful crunching sound and then there was no movement or sound anymore.

Like they were on a string our heads all turned together and we saw Tom still standing there, his coat flapping in the wind. He had a hand on Billy's shoulder and as we looked we could see that Mary was there too now and he had one arm round her as she sobbed into his coat.

I don't know how long we just sat there staring but then we were ejected off our seats and out of the bar. Pete and Ned ran to Tom but Jack and I went to where Sam had fallen, and we stared down, and I tell you the rest of my life now seems like a build up to and a climb down from that moment.

We were standing in front of a chalk drawing of a tiger. Even now my scalp seems to tighten when I think of it, and my chest feels like someone punched a hole in it and tipped a gallon of ice water inside. I'll just tell you the facts: Jack was there and he knows what we saw and what we didn't see.

What we didn't see was Sam McNeill. He just wasn't there. We saw a drawing of a tiger in purples and greens, a little bit scuffed, and there was a lot more red round the mouth of that tiger than there had been that afternoon and I'm sure that if either of us could have dreamed of reaching out and touching it, it would have been warm too.

And the hardest part to tell is this. I'd seen that drawing in the afternoon, and Jack had too, and we knew that when it was done it was lean and thin.

I swear to God that tiger wasn't thin any more. What Jack and I were looking at was one fat tiger.

After a while I looked up and across at Tom. He was still standing with Mary and Billy, but they weren't crying anymore. Mary was hugging Billy so tight he squawked and Tom's face looked calm and alive and creased with a smile. And as we stood there the skies opened for the first time in months and a cool rain hammered down. At my feet colours began to run and lines became less distinct. Jack and I stood and watched till there was just pools of meaningless colours and then we walked slowly over to the others, not even looking at the bottle lying on the ground, and we all stayed there a long time in the rain, facing each other, not saying a word.

Well that was ten years ago, near enough. After a while Mary took Billy home and they turned to give us a little wave before they turned the corner. The cuts on Billy's face healed real quick, and he's a good looking boy now: he looks a lot like his dad and he's already fooling about in cars. Helps me in the store sometimes. His mom ain't aged a day and looks wonderful. She never married again, but she looks real happy the way she is.

The rest of us just said a simple goodnight. Goodnight was all we could muster and maybe that's all there was to say. Then we walked off home in the directions of our wives. Tom gave me a small smile before he turned and walked off alone. I almost followed him, I wanted to say something, but the end I just stayed where I was and watched him go. And that's how I'll always remember him best, because for a moment there was a spark in his eyes and I knew that some pain had been lifted deep down inside somewhere.

Then he walked and no one has seen him since, and like I said it's been about ten years now. He wasn't there in the square the next morning and he didn't come in for a beer. Like he'd never been, he just wasn't there. Except for the hole in our hearts: it's funny how much you can miss a quiet man.

We're all still here, of course, Jack, Ned, Pete and the boys, and all much the same, though even older and greyer. Pete lost his wife and Ned retired but things go on the same. The tourists come in the summer and we sit on the stools and drink our cold beers and shoot the breeze about ballgames and families and how the world's going to shit, and sometimes we'll draw close and talk about a night a long time ago, and about paintings and cats, and about the quietest man we ever knew, wondering where he is, and what he's doing. And we've had a six-pack in the back of the fridge for ten years now, and the minute he walks through that door and pulls up a stool, that's his.

1991

BEST NEW HORROR 3

EDITED BY
STEPHEN
JONES
AND
RAMSEY
CAMPBELL

Robert R. McCammon

Thomas Ligotti

Nancy A. Collins

William F. Nolan

David J. Schow

Kim Newman

Karl Edward Wagner

and more

The Same in Any Language

Ramsey Campbell

BEST NEW HORROR 2 was the only book I have ever had censored by a publisher.

Ramsey and I had selected and contracted Roberta Lannes' disturbing serial-killer story "Apostate in Denim" (from the first issue of *Iniquities* magazine) for the volume. However, when we delivered the book manuscript to Robinson, certain people in the company vehemently objected to the content of the story and refused to include it. Despite our protestations (how could a horror story be *too* horrific?), we were overruled. At least Roberta was very understanding about the whole matter, and she later included the tale in her 1997 collection *The Mirror of Night*.

For the third volume, Robinson once again used a cover painting by Luis Rey (of a werewolf-like monster crashing through a window) and added a *3* to the embossed Letraset logo. Carroll & Graf went a much classier route, completely redesigning the jacket for its hardcover and subsequent trade paperback editions.

This time our Introduction had crept up to eleven pages, while the Necrology had blossomed to fifteen. In our editorial summation, Ramsey and I took a reviewer for *Locus* magazine to task for his ill-informed assertion that the horror field was "limited in its relevance to anything".

The twenty-nine stories included return appearances by Robert R. McCammon, Thomas Ligotti, Karl Edward Wagner and Kim Newman, amongst others. Rising star Michael Marshall Smith was represented with a second contribution (the British Fantasy Award-winning "The Dark Land"), and we even featured a tale by award-winning Scottish comics writer Grant Morrison ("The Braille Encyclopedia").

However, the story I have chosen from this 1992 volume is by my co-editor, Ramsey Campbell. Over the past twenty years,

Ramsey has been represented in *Best New Horror* more than any other author. In fact, he has had stories in sixteen out of the twenty editions (including two in volume seventeen).

As anyone familiar with my Introductions knows, I usually frown upon editors including their own stories in their anthologies but, in the case of collaborative works, I think it is fine if it is the other editor who makes the selection. Over the five volumes I co-edited with Ramsey, he always disassociated himself when it came to his own work, and it was left up to me to make the final decision.

"The Same in Any Language" is another of those "fish out of water" travelogue tales that I love so dearly. The story was inspired by a visit Ramsey made to the Crete island of Spinalonga, the site of an abandoned leper colony, and the final paragraph is intended as a tribute to Stephen King . . .

THE DAY MY FATHER is to take me where the lepers used to live is hotter than ever. Even the old women with black scarves wrapped around their heads sit inside the bus station instead of on the chairs outside the tavernas. Kate fans herself with her straw hat like a basket someone's sat on and gives my father one of those smiles they've made up between them. She's leaning forwards to see if that's our bus when he says "Why do you think they call them lepers, Hugh?"

I can hear what he's going to say, but I have to humour him. "I don't know."

"Because they never stop leaping up and down."

It takes him much longer to say the first four words than the rest of it. I groan because he expects me to, and Kate lets off one of her giggles I keep hearing whenever they stay in my father's and my room at the hotel and send me down for a swim. "If you can't give a grin, give a groan," my father says for about the millionth time, and Kate pokes him with her freckly elbow as if he's too funny for words. She annoys me so much that I say "Lepers don't rhyme with creepers, dad."

"I never thought they did, son. I was just having a laugh. If we can't laugh we might as well be dead, ain't that straight, Kate?" He winks at her thigh and slaps his own instead, and says to me "Since you're so clever, why don't you find out when our bus is coming."

"That's it now."

"And I'm Hercules." He lifts up his fists to make his muscles bulge for Kate and says "You're telling us that tripe spells A Flounder?"

"Elounda, dad. It does. The letter like a Y upside down is how they write an L."

"About time they learned how to write properly, then," he says, staring around to show he doesn't care who hears. "Well, there it is if you really want to trudge round another old ruin instead of having a swim."

"I expect he'll be able to do both once we get to the village," Kate says, but I can tell she's hoping I'll just swim. "Will you two gentlemen see me across the road?"

My mother used to link arms with me and my father when he was living with us. "I'd better make sure it's the right bus," I say and run out so fast I can pretend I didn't hear my father calling me back.

A man with skin like a boot is walking backwards in the dust behind the bus, shouting "Elounda" and waving his arms as if he's pulling the bus into the space in line. I sit on a seat opposite two Germans who block the aisle until they've taken off their rucksacks, but my father finds three seats together at the rear. "Aren't you with us, Hugh?" he shouts, and everyone on the bus looks at him.

When I see him getting ready to shout again I walk down the aisle. I'm hoping nobody notices me, but Kate says loudly "It's a pity you ran off like that, Hugh. I was going to ask if you'd like an ice cream."

"No thank you," I say, trying to sound like my mother when she was only just speaking to my father, and step over Kate's legs. As the bus rumbles uphill I turn as much of my back on her as I can, and watch the streets.

Aghios Nikolaos looks as if they haven't finished building it. Some of the tavernas are on the bottom floors of blocks with no roofs, and sometimes there are more tables on the pavements outside than in. The bus goes downhill again as if it's hiccuping, and when it reaches the bottomless pool where young people with no children stay in the hotels with discos, it follows the edge of the bay. I watch the white boats on the blue water, but really I'm seeing the conductor coming down the aisle and feeling as if a lump is growing in my stomach from me wondering what my father will say to him.

The bus is climbing beside the sea when he reaches us. "Three for leper land," my father says.

The conductor stares at him and shrugs. "As far as you go," Kate says, and rubs herself against my father. "All the way."

When the conductor pushes his lips forwards out of his moustache and beard my father begins to get angry, unless he's pretending. "Where you kept your lepers. Spiny Lobster or whatever you call the damned place."

"It's Spinalonga, dad, and it's off the coast from where we're going."

"I know that, and he should." My father is really angry now. "Did you get that?" he says to the conductor. "My ten-year-old can speak your lingo, so don't tell me you can't speak ours."

The conductor looks at me, and I'm afraid he wants me to talk Greek. My mother gave me a little computer that translates words into Greek when you type them, but I've left it at the hotel because my father said it sounded like a bird which only knew one note. "We're going to Elounda, please," I stammer.

"Elounda, boss," the conductor says to me. He takes the money from my father without looking at him and gives me the tickets and change. "Fish is good by the harbour in the evening," he says, and goes to sit next to the driver while the bus swings round the zigzags of the hill road.

My father laughs for the whole bus to hear. "They think you're so important, Hugh, you won't be wanting to go home to your mother."

Kate strokes his head as if he's her pet, then she turns to me. "What do you like most about Greece?"

She's trying to make friends with me like when she kept saying I could call her Kate, only now I see it's for my father's sake. All she's done is make me think how the magic places seemed to have lost their magic because my mother wasn't there with me, even Knossos where Theseus killed the Minotaur. There were just a few corridors left that might have been the maze he was supposed to find his way out of, and my father let me stay in them for a while, but then he lost his temper because all the guided tours were in foreign languages and nobody could tell him how to get back to the coach. We nearly got stuck overnight in Heraklion, when he'd promised to take Kate for dinner that night by the bottomless pool. "I don't know," I mumble, and gaze out the window.

"I like the sun, don't you? And the people when they're being nice, and the lovely clear sea."

It sounds to me as if she's getting ready to send me off swimming again. They met while I was, our second morning at the hotel. When I came out of the sea my father had moved his towel next to hers and she was giggling. I watch Spinalonga Island float over the horizon like a ship made of rock and grey towers, and hope she'll think I'm agreeing with her if that means she'll leave me alone. But she says "I suppose most boys are morbid at your age. Let's hope you'll grow up to be like your father."

She's making it sound as if the leper colony is the only place I've wanted to visit, but it's just another old place I can tell my mother I've been. Kate doesn't want to go there because she doesn't like old places – she said if Knossos was a palace she was glad she's not a queen. I don't speak to her again until the bus has stopped by the harbour.

There aren't many tourists, even in the shops and tavernas lined up along the winding pavement. Greek people who look as if they were born in the sun sit drinking at tables under awnings like stalls in a market. Some priests who I think at first are wearing black hatboxes on their heads march by, and fishermen come up from their boats with octopuses on sticks like big kebabs. The bus turns round in a cloud of dust and petrol fumes while Kate hangs onto my father with one hand and flaps the front of her flowery dress with the other. A boatman stares at the tops of her boobs which make me think of spotted fish and shouts "Spinalonga" with both hands round his mouth.

"We've hours yet," Kate says. "Let's have a drink. Hugh may even get that ice cream if he's good."

If she's going to talk about me as though I'm not there I'll do my best not to be. She and my father sit under an awning and I kick dust on the pavement outside until she says "Come under, Hugh. We don't want you with sunstroke."

I don't want her pretending she's my mother, but if I say so I'll only spoil the day more than she already has. I shuffle to the table next to the one she's sharing with my father and throw myself on a chair. "Well, Hugh," she says, "do you want one?"

"No thank you," I say, even though the thought of an ice cream or a drink starts my mouth trying to drool.

"You can have some of my lager if it ever arrives," my father says at the top of his voice, and stares hard at some Greeks sitting at a table. "Anyone here a waiter?" he says, lifting his hand to his mouth as if he's holding a glass.

When all the people at the table smile and raise their glasses and shout cheerily at him, Kate says "I'll find someone and then I'm going to the little girls' room while you men have a talk."

My father watches her crossing the road and gazes at the doorway of the taverna once she's gone in. He's quiet for a while, then he says "Are you going to be able to say you had a good time?"

I know he wants me to enjoy myself when I'm with him, but I also think what my mother stopped herself from saying to me is true – that he booked the holiday in Greece as a way of scoring off her by taking me somewhere she'd always wanted to go. He stares at the taverna as if he can't move until I let him, and I say "I expect so, if we go to the island."

"That's my boy. Never give in too easily." He smiles at me with one side of his face. "You don't mind if I have some fun as well, do you?"

He's making it sound as though he wouldn't have had much fun if it had just been the two of us, and I think that was how he'd started to feel before he met Kate. "It's your holiday," I say.

He's opening his mouth after another long silence when Kate comes out of the taverna with a man carrying two lagers and a lemonade on a tray. "See that you thank her," my father tells me.

I didn't ask for lemonade. He said I could have some lager. I say "Thank you very much," and feel my throat tightening as I gulp the lemonade, because her eyes are saying that she's won.

"That must have been welcome," she says when I put down the empty glass. "Another? Then I should find yourself something to do. Your father and I may be here for a while."

"Have a swim," my father suggests.

"I haven't brought my cossy."

"Neither have those boys," Kate says, pointing at the harbour. "Don't worry, I've seen boys wearing less."

My father smirks behind his hand, and I can't bear it. I run to the jetty the boys are diving off, and drop my T-shirt and shorts on it and my sandals on top of them, and dive in.

The water's cold, but not for long. It's full of little fish that nibble you if you only float, and it's clearer than tap water, so you can see down to the pebbles and the fish pretending to be them. I chase fish and swim underwater and almost catch an octopus before it squirms out to sea. Then three Greek boys about my age swim over, and we're pointing at ourselves and saying our names when I see Kate and my father kissing.

I know their tongues are in each other's mouths – getting some tongue, the kids at my school call it. I feel like swimming away as far as I can go and never coming back. But Stavros and Stathis and Costas are using their hands to tell me we should see who can swim fastest, so I do that instead. Soon I've forgotten my father and Kate, even when we sit on the jetty for a rest before we have more races.

It must be hours later when I realise Kate is calling "Come here a minute."

The sun isn't so hot now. It's reaching under the awning, but she and my father haven't moved back into the shadow. A boatman shouts "Spinalonga" and points at how low the sun is. I don't mind swimming with my new friends instead of going to the island, and I'm about to tell my father so when Kate says "I've been telling your dad he should be proud of you. Come and see what I've got for you."

They've both had a lot to drink. She almost falls across the table as I go to her. Just as I get there I see what she's going to give me, but it's too late. She grabs my head with both hands and sticks a kiss on my mouth.

She tastes of old lager. Her mouth is wet and bigger than mine, and when it squirms it makes me think of an octopus. "Mmm-*mwa*," it says, and then I manage to duck out of her hands, leaving her blinking at me as if her eyes won't quite work. "Nothing wrong with a bit of loving," she says. "You'll find that out when you grow up."

My father knows I don't like to be kissed, but he's frowning at me as if I should have let her. Suddenly I want to get my own back on them in the only way I can think of. "We need to go to the island now."

"Better go to the loo first," my father says. "They wouldn't have one on the island when all their willies had dropped off."

Kate hoots at that while I'm getting dressed, and I feel as if she's laughing at the way my ribs show through my skin however much I eat. I stop myself from shivering in case she or my father makes out that's a reason for us to go back to the hotel. I'm heading for the toilet when my father says "Watch out you don't catch anything in there or we'll have to leave you on the island."

I know there are all sorts of reasons why my parents split up, but just now this is the only one I can think of – my mother not being able to stand his jokes and how the more she told him to finish the more he would do it, as if he couldn't stop himself. I run into the toilet, trying not to look at the pedal bin where you have to drop the used paper, and close my eyes once I've taken aim.

Is today going to be what I remember about Greece? My mother brought me up to believe that even the sunlight here had magic in it, and I expected to feel the ghosts of legends in all the old places. If there isn't any magic in the sunlight, I want there to be some in the dark. The thought seems to make the insides of my eyelids darker, and I can smell the drains. I pull the chain and zip myself up, and then I wonder if my father sent me in here so we'll miss the boat. I nearly break the hook on the door, I'm so desperate to be outside.

The boat is still tied to the harbour, but I can't see the boatman. Kate and my father are holding hands across the table, and my father's looking around as though he means to order another drink. I squeeze my eyes shut so hard that when I open them everything's gone black. The blackness fades along with whatever I wished, and I see the boatman kneeling on the jetty, talking to Stavros. "Spinalonga," I shout.

He looks at me, and I'm afraid he'll say it's too late. I feel tears building up behind my eyes. Then he stands up and holds out a hand towards my father and Kate. "One hour," he says.

Kate's gazing after a bus that has just begun to climb the hill. "We may as well go over as wait for the next bus," my father says, "and then it'll be back to the hotel for dinner."

Kate looks sideways at me. "And after all that he'll be ready for bed," she says like a question she isn't quite admitting to.

"Out like a light, I reckon."

"Fair enough," she says, and uses his arm to get herself up.

The boatman's name is Iannis, and he doesn't speak much English. My father seems to think he's charging too much for the trip until he realises it's that much for all three of us, and then he grins as if he thinks Iannis has cheated himself. "Heave ho then, Janice," he says with a wink at me and Kate.

The boat is about the size of a big rowing-boat. It has a cabin at the front and benches along the sides and a long box in the middle that shakes and smells of petrol. I watch the point of the boat sliding through the water like a knife and feel as if we're on our way to the Greece I've been dreaming of. The white buildings of Elounda shrink until they look like teeth in the mouth of the hills, and then Spinalonga floats up ahead.

It makes me think of an abandoned ship bigger than a liner, a ship so dead that it's standing still in the water without having to be anchored. The evening light seems to shine out of the steep rusty sides and the bony towers and walls high above the sea. I know it was a fort to begin with, but I think it might as well have been built for the lepers. I can imagine them trying to swim to Elounda and drowning because there wasn't enough left of them to swim with, if they didn't just throw themselves off the walls because they couldn't bear what they'd turned into. If I say these things to Kate I bet more than her mouth will squirm – but my father gets in first. "Look, there's the welcoming committee."

Kate gives a shiver that reminds me I'm trying not to feel cold. "Don't say things like that. They're just people like us, probably wishing they hadn't come."

I don't think she can see them any more clearly than I can. Their heads are poking over the wall at the top of the cliff above the little pebbly beach which is the only place a boat can land. There are five or six of them, only I'm not sure they're heads; they might be stones someone has balanced on the wall – they're almost the same colour. I'm wishing I had some binoculars when Kate grabs my father so hard the boat rocks and Iannis waves a finger at her, which doesn't please my father. "You keep your eye on your steering, Janice," he says.

Iannis is already taking the boat towards the beach. He didn't seem to notice the heads on the wall, and when I look again they aren't there. Maybe they belonged to some of the people who are coming down to a boat bigger than Iannis's. That boat chugs away as Iannis's bumps into the jetty. "One hour," he says. "Back here."

He helps Kate onto the jetty while my father glowers at him, then he lifts me out of the boat. As soon as my father steps onto the jetty Iannis pushes the boat out again. "Aren't you staying?" Kate pleads.

He shakes his head and points hard at the beach. "Back here, one hour."

She looks as if she wants to run into the water and climb aboard the boat, but my father shoves his arm round her waist. "Don't worry, you've got two fellers to keep you safe, and neither of them with a girl's name."

The only way up to the fort is through a tunnel that bends in the middle so you can't see the end until you're nearly halfway in. I wonder how long it will take for the rest of the island to be as dark as the middle of the tunnel. When Kate sees the end she runs until she's in the open and stares at the sunlight, which is perched on top of the towers now. "Fancying a climb?" my father says.

She makes a face at him as I walk past her. We're in a kind of street of stone sheds that have mostly caved in. They must be where the lepers lived, but there are only shadows in them now, not even birds. "Don't go too far, Hugh," Kate says.

"I want to go all the way round, otherwise it wasn't worth coming."

"I don't, and I'm sure your father expects you to consider me."

"Now, now, children," my father says. "Hugh can do as he likes as long as he's careful and the same goes for us, eh, Kate?"

I can tell he's surprised when she doesn't laugh. He looks unsure of himself and angry about it, the way he did when he and my mother were getting ready to tell me they were splitting up. I run along the line of huts and think of hiding in one so I can jump out at Kate. Maybe they aren't empty after all; something rattles in one as if bones are crawling about in the dark. It could be a snake under part of the roof that's fallen. I keep running until I come to steps leading up from the street to the top of the island, where most of the light is, and I've started jogging up them when Kate shouts "Stay where we can see you. We don't want you hurting yourself."

"It's all right, Kate, leave him be," my father says. "He's sensible."

"If I'm not allowed to speak to him I don't know why you invited me at all."

I can't help grinning as I sprint to the top of the steps and duck out of sight behind a grassy mound that makes me think of a grave. From up here I can see the whole island, and we aren't alone on it. The path I've run up from leads all round the island, past more huts and towers and a few bigger buildings, and then it goes down to the tunnel. Just before it does it passes the wall above the beach, and between the path and the wall there's a stone yard full of slabs. Some of the slabs have been moved away from holes like long boxes full of soil or darkness. They're by the wall where I thought I saw heads looking over at us. They aren't there now, but I can see heads bobbing down towards the tunnel. Before long they'll be behind Kate and my father.

Iannis is well on his way back to Elounda. His boat is passing one that's heading for the island. Soon the sun will touch the sea. If I went down to the huts I'd see it sink with me and drown. Instead I lie on the mound and look over the island, and see more of the boxy holes hiding behind some of the huts. If I went closer I could see how deep they are, but I quite like not knowing – if I was Greek I expect I'd think they lead to the underworld where all the dead live. Besides, I like being able to look down on my father and Kate and see them trying to see me.

I stay there until Iannis's boat is back at Elounda and the other one has almost reached Spinalonga, and the sun looks as if it's gone down to the sea for a drink. Kate and my father are having an argument. I expect it's about me, though I can't hear what they're saying; the darker it gets between the huts the more Kate waves her arms. I'm getting ready to let my father see me when she screams.

She's jumped back from a hut which has a hole behind it. "Come out, Hugh. I know it's you," she cries.

I can tell what my father's going to say, and I cringe. "Is that you, Hugh? Yoo-hoo," he shouts.

I won't show myself for a joke like that. He leans into the hut through the spiky stone window, then he turns to Kate. "It wasn't Hugh. There's nobody."

I can only just hear him, but I don't have to strain to hear Kate. "Don't tell me that," she cries. "You're both too fond of jokes."

She screams again, because someone's come running up the tunnel. "Everything all right?" this man shouts. "There's a boat about to leave if you've had enough."

"I don't know what you two are doing," Kate says like a duchess to my father, "but I'm going with this gentleman."

My father calls me twice. If I go to him I'll be letting Kate win. "I don't think our man will wait," the new one says.

"It doesn't matter," my father says, so fiercely that I know it does. "We've our own boat coming."

"If there's a bus before you get back I won't be hanging around," Kate warns him.

"Please yourself," my father says, so loud that his voice goes into the tunnel. He stares after her as she marches away; he must be hoping she'll change her mind. But I see her step off the jetty into the boat, and it moves out to sea as if the ripples are pushing it to Elounda.

My father puts a hand to his ear as the sound of the engine fades. "So every bugger's left me now, have they?" he says in a kind of shout at himself. "Well, good riddance."

He's waving his fists as if he wants to punch something, and he sounds as if he's suddenly got drunk. He must have been holding it back while Kate was there. I've never seen him like this. It frightens me, so I stay where I am.

It isn't only my father that frightens me. There's only a little bump of the sun left above the water now, and I'm afraid how dark the island may be once that goes. Bits of sunlight shiver on the water all the way to the island, and I think I see some heads above the wall of the yard full of slabs, against the light. Which side of the wall are they on? The light's too dazzling, it seems to pinch the sides of the heads so they look thinner than any heads I've ever seen. Then I notice a boat setting out from Elounda, and I squint at it until I'm sure it's Iannis's boat.

He's coming early to fetch us. Even that frightens me, because I wonder why he is. Doesn't he want us to be on the island now he realises how dark it's getting? I look at the wall, and the heads have gone. Then the sea puts the sun out, and it feels as if the island is buried in darkness.

I can still see my way down – the steps are paler than the dark – and I don't like being alone now I've started shivering. I back off from the mound, because I don't like to touch it, and almost back into a shape with bits of its head poking out and arms that look as if they've dropped off at the elbows. It's a cactus. I'm just standing up when my father says "There you are, Hugh."

He can't see me yet. He must have heard me gasp. I go to the top of the steps, but I can't see him for the dark. Then his voice moves away. "Don't start hiding again. Looks like we've seen the last of Kate, but we've got each other, haven't we?"

He's still drunk. He sounds as if he's talking to somebody nearer to him than I am. "All right, we'll wait on the beach," he says, and his voice echoes. He's gone into the tunnel, and he thinks he's following me. "I'm here, dad," I shout so loud that I squeak.

"I heard you, Hugh. Wait there. I'm coming." He's walking deeper into the tunnel. While he's in there my voice must seem to be coming from beyond the far end. I'm sucking in a breath that tastes dusty, so I can tell him where I am, when he says "Who's that?" with a laugh that almost shakes his words to pieces.

He's met whoever he thought was me when he was heading for the tunnel. I'm holding my breath – I can't breathe or swallow, and I don't know if I feel hot or frozen. "Let me past," he says as if he's trying to make his voice as big as the tunnel. "My son's waiting for me on the beach."

There are so many echoes in the tunnel I'm not sure what I'm hearing besides him. I think there's a lot of shuffling, and the other noise must be voices, because my father says "What kind of language do you call that? You sound drunker than I am. I said my son's waiting."

He's talking even louder as if that'll make him understood. I'm embarrassed, but I'm more afraid for him. "Dad," I nearly scream, and run down the steps as fast as I can without falling.

"See, I told you. That's my son," he says as if he's talking to a crowd of idiots. The shuffling starts moving like a slow march, and he says "All right, we'll all go to the beach together. What's the matter with your friends, too drunk to walk?"

I reach the bottom of the steps, hurting my ankles, and run along the ruined street because I can't stop myself. The shuffling sounds as though it's growing thinner, as if the people with my father are leaving bits of themselves behind, and the voices are changing too – they're looser. Maybe the mouths are getting bigger somehow. But my father's laughing, so loud that he might be trying to think of a joke. "That's what I call a hug. No harder, love, or I won't have any puff left," he says to someone. "Come on then, give us a kiss. They're the same in any language."

All the voices stop, but the shuffling doesn't. I hear it go out of the tunnel and onto the pebbles, and then my father tries to scream as if he's swallowed something that won't let him. I scream for him and dash into the tunnel, slipping on things that weren't on the floor when we first came through, and fall out onto the beach.

My father's in the sea. He's already so far out that the water is up to his neck. About six people who look stuck together and to him are walking him away as if they don't need to breathe when their heads start to sink. Bits of them float away on the waves my father makes as he throws his arms about and gurgles. I try to run after him, but I've got nowhere when his head goes underwater. The sea pushes me back on the beach, and I run crying up and down it until Iannis comes.

It doesn't take him long to find my father once he understands what I'm saying. Iannis wraps me in a blanket and hugs me all the way to Elounda and the police take me back to the hotel. Kate gets my mother's number and calls her, saying she's someone at the hotel who's looking after me because my father's drowned, and I don't care what she says, I just feel numb. I don't start screaming until I'm on the plane back to England, because then I dream that my father has come back to tell a joke. "That's what I call getting some tongue," he says, leaning his face close to mine and showing me what's in his mouth.

1992

BEST NEW HORROR

EDITED BY STEPHEN JONES AND RAMSEY CAMPBELL

4

Peter Atkins

Clive Barker

Les Daniels

Roberta Lannes

Kim Newman

Peter Straub

Karl Edward Wagner

and many more

Norman Wisdom and the Angel of Death

Christopher Fowler

FOR THE FOURTH EDITION, Robinson Publishing foiled the now-familiar logo for the UK trade paperback. Thankfully, Carroll & Graf adapted the uncredited cover art for another classy-looking hardcover in the US.

Oddly, this time there was no American softcover edition (at least that I am aware of), but *Best New Horror 4* did become the first book in the series to get a foreign reprinting, although translation rights in other individual volumes have been sold to Japan and Russia over the years *Horror: Il Maglio* (a phrase I've always wanted reproduced on a T-shirt) was published in Italy the following year in trade paperback with a dust-jacket painting by my old friend Les Edwards.

At seventeen pages, the Introduction expanded for the first time beyond the eleven pages of the Necrology. Having had a go at a *Locus* reviewer the previous year, Ramsey and I strongly disputed comments made by Paul Brazier in the British SF magazine *Nexus*, in which he claimed that "the abattoir aspect of horror fiction has come to dominate the genre, until it seems we can expect blood to drip from every page . . ."

Roberta Lannes belatedly made it into the series with her tale "Dancing on a Blade of Dreams", and the twenty-four stories included *Hellraiser* alumni Clive Barker and Peter Atkins' first appearances in *Best New Horror*. M. John Harrison was represented with two stories, including a collaboration with Simon Ings.

Ramsey and I have always agreed that humour can be a very important element in horror fiction and, when used well, has the ability to heighten the impact of the most gruesome tale. As an editor, I have also always felt that an anthology should comprise various different types of storytelling – not only to keep the reader off-balance, but also to offer differing moods and styles that hopefully complement each other over the length of the book.

Norman Wisdom may not be all that familiar a name to American readers (he was something of an acquired taste in the UK as well), but for his debut in *Best New Horror*, Christopher Fowler used the British comedian as the inspiration for his tale of maniacal obsession.

Not only did the author watch every single Norman Wisdom movie before writing the story but – perhaps even more disturbingly – Chris admitted that he happened to find the comic really funny. It is unlikely that you will ever hear many people willing to admit to *that . . .!*

Diary Entry #1 Dated 2 July

THE PAST is safe.

The future is unknown.

The present is a bit of a bastard.

Let me explain. I always think of the past as a haven of pleasant recollections. Long ago I perfected the method of siphoning off bad memories to leave only those images I still feel comfortable with. What survives in my mind is a seamless mosaic of faces and places that fill me with warmth when I choose to consider them. Of course, it's as inaccurate as those retouched Stalinist photographs in which comrades who have become an embarrassment have been imperfectly erased so that the corner of a picture still shows a boot or a hand. But it allows me to recall times spent with dear friends in the happy England that existed in the 1950s; the last era of innocence and dignity, when women offered no opinion on sexual matters and men still knew the value of a decent winter overcoat. It was a time that ended with the arrival of the Beatles, when youth replaced experience as a desirable national quality.

I am no fantasist. Quite the reverse; this process has a practical value. Remembering the things that once made me happy helps to keep me sane.

I mean that in *every* sense.

The future, however, is another kettle of fish. What can possibly be in store for us but something worse than the present? An acceleration of the ugly, tasteless, arrogant times in which we live. The Americans have already developed a lifestyle and a moral philosophy entirely modelled on the concept of shopping. What is left but to manufacture more things we don't need, more detritus to be thrown away, more vicarious thrills to be selfishly experienced? For a brief moment the national conscience flickered awake when it seemed that green politics was the only way to stop the planet from becoming a huge concrete turd. And what happened? Conversation was hijacked by the advertising industry and turned into a highly suspect sales concept.

No, it's the past that heals, not the future.

So what about the present? I mean right now.

At this moment, I'm standing in front of a full-length mirror reducing the knot of my tie and contemplating my frail, rather tired appearance. My name is Stanley Morrison, born March 1950, in East Finchley, North London. I'm a senior sales clerk for a large shoe firm, as they say on the quiz programmes. I live alone and have always done so, having never met the right girl. I have a fat cat called Hattie, named after Hattie Jacques, for whom I have a particular fondness in the role of Griselda Pugh in Series Five, Programmes One to Seven of *Hancock's Half Hour*, and a spacious but somewhat cluttered flat situated approximately 150 yards from the house in which I was born. My hobbies include collecting old radio shows and British films, of which I have an extensive collection, as well as a nigh-inexhaustible supply of amusing, detailed anecdotes about the forgotten British stars of the past. There's nothing I enjoy more than to recount these lengthy tales to one of my ailing, lonely patients and slowly destroy his will to live.

I call them my patients, but of course they aren't. I merely bring these poor unfortunates good cheer in my capacity as an official council HVF, that's a Hospital Visiting Friend. I am fully sanctioned by Haringey Council, an organisation filled with people of such astounding narrow-minded stupidity that they cannot see beyond their lesbian support groups to keeping the streets free of dogshit.

But back to the present.

I am rather tired at the moment because I was up half the night removing the remaining precious moments of life from a seventeen-year-old boy named David Banbury who had been in a severe motorcycle accident. Apparently he jumped the lights at the top of Shepherd's Hill and vanished under a truck conveying half-price personal stereos to the Asian shops in Tottenham Court Road. His legs were completely crushed, so much so that the doctor told me they couldn't separate his cycle leathers from his bones, and his spine was broken, but facial damage had been minimal, and the helmet he was wearing at the time of the collision had protected his skull from injury.

He hasn't had much of a life, by all accounts, having spent the last eight years in care, and has no family to visit him.

Nurse Clarke informed me that he might well recover to lead a partially normal life, but would only be able to perform those activities involving a minimal amount of agonisingly slow movement, which would at least qualify him for a job in the Post Office.

Right now he could not talk, of course, but he could see and hear and feel, and I am reliably informed that he could understand every word I said, which was of great advantage as I was able to describe to him in enormous detail the entire plot of Norman Wisdom's 1965 masterpiece *The Early Bird*, his first colour film for the Rank Organisation, and I must say one of the finest examples of post-war British slapstick to be found on the face of this spinning planet we fondly call home.

On my second visit to the boy, my richly delineated account of the backstage problems involved in the production of an early Wisdom vehicle, *Trouble in Store*, in which the Little Comedian Who Won the Hearts of the Nation co-starred for the first time with his erstwhile partner and straight-man Jerry Desmonde, was rudely interrupted by a staff nurse who chose a crucial moment in my narration to empty a urine bag that seemed to be filling with blood. Luckily I was able to exact my revenge by punctuating my description of the film's highlights featuring Moira Lister and Margaret Rutherford with little twists of the boy's drip-feed to make sure that he was paying the fullest attention.

At half-past-seven yesterday evening I received a visit from the mentally disorientated liaison officer in charge of appointing visitors. Miss Chisholm is the kind of woman who has pencils in her hair and NUCLEAR WAR – NO THANKS stickers on her briefcase. She approaches her council tasks with the dispiriting grimness of a sailor attempting to plug leaks in a fast-sinking ship.

"Mr Morrison," she said, trying to peer around the door of my flat, presumably in the vain hope that she might be invited in for a cup of tea, "you are one of our most experienced Hospital Helpers" – this part she had to check in her brimming folder to verify – "so I wonder if we could call upon you for an extracurricular visit at rather short notice." She searched through her notes with the folder wedged under her chin and her case balanced on a raised knee. I did not offer any assistance. "The motorcycle boy . . ." She attempted to locate his name and failed.

"David Banbury," I said, helpfully supplying the information for her.

"He's apparently been telling the doctor that he no longer wishes to live. It's a common problem, but they think his case is particularly serious. He has no relatives." Miss Chisholm – if she has a Christian name I am certainly not privy to it – shifted her weight from one foot to the other as several loose sheets slid from her folder to the floor.

"I understand exactly what is needed," I said, watching as she struggled to reclaim her notes. "An immediate visit is in order."

As I made my way over to the hospital to comfort the poor lad, I thought of the ways in which I could free the boy from his morbid thoughts. First, I would recount all of the plot minutiae, technicalities and trivia I could muster surrounding the big-screen career and off-screen heartache of that Little Man Who Won All Our Hearts, Charlie Drake, climaxing with a detailed description of his 1966 magnum opus *The Cracksman*, in which he starred opposite a superbly erudite George Sanders, a man who had the good sense to kill himself when he grew bored with the world, and then I would encourage the boy to give up the fight, do the decent thing and die in his sleep.

As it happens, the evening turned out quite nicely.

By eleven-thirty I had concluded my description of the film, and detected a distinct lack of concentration on behalf of the boy, whose only response to my description of the frankly hysterical sewer-pipe scene was to blow bubbles of saliva from the corner of his mouth. In my frustration to command his attention, I applied rather more pressure to the sutures on his legs than I intended, causing the crimson blossom of a haemorrhage to appear through the blankets covering his pitifully mangled limbs.

I embarked upon a general plot outline of the classic 1962 Norman Wisdom vehicle *On the Beat*, never shifting my attention from the boy's eyes, which were now swivelling frantically in his waxen grey face, until the ruptured vessels of his leg could no longer be reasonably ignored. Then I summoned the night nurse. David Banbury died a few moments after she arrived at the bedside.

That makes eleven in four years

Some didn't require any tampering with on my part, but simply gave up the ghost, losing the will to go on. I went home and made myself a cup of Horlicks, quietly rejoicing that another young man had gone to meet his maker with a full working knowledge of the later films of Norman Wisdom (not counting *What's Good For the Goose*, a prurient "adult" comedy directed by Menahem Golan which I regard as an offensive, embarrassing travesty unworthy of such a superb family performer).

Now, standing before the mirror attempting to comb the last straggling wisps of hair across my prematurely balding pate, I prepare to leave the house and catch the bus to work, and I do something I imagine most people have done from time to time when faced with their own reflection. I calm myself for the day ahead by remembering the Royal Variety Performance stars of 1952. The familiar faces of Naughton & Gold, Vic Oliver, Jewel & Warriss, Ted Ray, Winifred Atwell, Reg Dixon and the Tiller Girls crowd my mind as I steel myself to confront the self-centred young scum with whom I am forced to work.

It is no secret that I have been passed over for promotion in my job on a number of occasions, but the most terrible slap-in-the-face yet performed by our new (foreign) management was administered last week, when a boy of just twenty-four was appointed as my superior! He likes people to call him Mick, walks around smiling like an idiot, travels to work wearing a Walkman, on which he plays percussive rubbish consisting of black men shouting at each other, and wears tight black jeans which seem specifically designed to reveal the contours of his genitalia. He shows precious little flair for the job, and has virtually no knowledge whatsoever of the pre-1960 British radio comedy scene. Amazingly, everyone seems to like him.

Of course, he will have to go.

Diary Entry #2 Dated 23 August

Mick is a threat no more

I simply waited until the appropriate opportunity arose, as I knew it eventually should. While I watched and listened, patiently enduring the oh-so-clever remarks he made to the office girls (most of whom resemble prostitutes from Michael Powell's excessively vulgar and unnecessary 1960 film *Peeping Tom*) about me, I comforted myself with memories of a happy, sunlit childhood, recalling a row of terraced houses patrolled by smiling policemen, uniformed milkmen and lollipop-ladies, a place in the past where Isobel Barnet was still guessing contestants' professions on *What's My Line*, Alma Cogan was singing "Fly Me to the Moon" on the radio, cornflakes had red plastic guardsmen in their packets and everyone knew his place and damned well stayed in it. Even now when I hear the merry tinkle of

"Greensleeves" heralding the arrival of an ice-cream van beset by clamouring tots I get a painful, thrilling erection.

But I digress.

Last Tuesday, while shifting a wire-meshed crate in the basement workroom, Mick dislocated his little finger, cutting it rather nastily, so naturally I offered to accompany him to the casualty ward. As my flat is conveniently situated on the route to the hospital I was able to stop by for a moment, trotting out some absurd excuse for the detour.

After waiting for over an hour to be seen, my nemesis was finally examined by Dr MacGregor, an elderly physician of passing acquaintance whose name I only remember because it is also that of John Le Mesurier's character in *The Radio Ham*. My experience as an HVF had familiarised me with basic casualty procedures, and I knew that the doctor would most likely inject an antibiotic into the boy's hand to prevent infection.

The needles for the syringes come in paper packets, and are sealed inside little plastic tubes that must be broken only by the attending physician. This is to prevent blood-carried infections from being transmitted.

It was hard to find a way around this, and indeed had taken dozens of attempts over the preceding months. The packets themselves were easy enough to open and reseal, but the tubes were a problem. After a great deal of practice, I found that I was able to melt the end of a tube closed without leaving any traces of tampering. To be on the safe side I had prepared three such needles in this fashion. (You must remember that, as well as having access to basic medical supplies – those items not actually locked away – I also possess an unlimited amount of patience, being willing to wait years if necessary to achieve my goals.)

While we waited for Dr MacGregor to put in an appearance, the boy prattled on to me about work, saying how much he "truly valued my input". While he was thus distracted, it was a simple matter for me to replace the loose needles lying on the doctor's tray with my specially prepared ones.

A little while ago I throttled the life out of a very sick young man whose habit of nightly injecting drugs in the toilet of my local tube station had caused him to become ravaged with terminal disease. I would like to say that he died in order to make the world a safer, cleaner place, but the truth is that we went for a drink together and I killed him in a sudden fit of rage because he had not heard of Joyce Grenfell. How the Woman Who Won the Hearts of the Nation in her thrice-reprised role as Ruby Gates in the celebrated *St Trinians* films could have passed by him unnoticed is still a mystery to me.

Anyway, I strangled the disgusting urchin with his own scarf and removed about a cupful of blood from his arm, into which I dropped a number of needles, filling their capillaries with the poisoned fluid. I then carefully wiped each one clean and inserted it into a tube, neatly resealing the plastic.

Dr MacGregor was talking nineteen to the dozen as he inserted what he thought was a fresh needle into a vein on the back of Mick's hand. He barely even looked down to see what he was doing. Overwork and force of habit had won the day. Thank God for our decaying National Health Service, because I'd never have managed it if the boy had possessed private medical insurance. My unsuspecting adversary maintained an attitude of perky bravery as his finger was stitched up, and I laughed all the way home.

Mick has been feeling unwell for several weeks now. A few days ago he failed to turn up for work. Apparently he has developed a complex and highly dangerous form of Hepatitis B.

As they say, age and treachery will always overcome youth and enthusiasm.

Diary Entry #3 Dated 17 October

The hopeless liaison officer has returned with a new request.

Yesterday evening I opened the door of my flat to find her hovering on the landing uncertainly, as if she could not even decide where she felt comfortable standing.

"Can I help you?" I asked suddenly, knowing that my voice would make her jump. She had not caught me in a good mood. A month ago, Mick had been forced to resign through ill-health, but my promotion had still not been announced for consideration.

"Oh, Mr Morrison, I didn't know if you were in," she said, her free hand rising to her flat chest.

"The best way to find out is by ringing the doorbell, Miss Chisholm." I opened the door wider. "Won't you come in?"

"Thank you." She edged gingerly past me with briefcase and folders, taking in the surroundings. Hattie took one look at her and shot off to her basket. "Oh, what an unusual room," she said, studying the walnut sideboard and armchairs, the matching butter-yellow standard lamps either side of the settee. "Do you collect art deco?"

"No," I said tersely. "This is my furniture. I suppose you'd like a cup of tea." I went to put the kettle on, leaving her hovering uncomfortably in the lounge. When I returned she was still standing, her head tilted on one side as she examined the spines of my post-war *Radio Times* collection.

"Please sit down, Miss Chisholm," I insisted. "I won't bite." And I really don't because teethmarks can be easily traced.

At this instigation she perched herself on the edge of the armchair and nibbled at a bourbon. She had obviously rehearsed the speech that followed.

"Mr Morrison, I'm sure you've read in the papers that the health cuts are leaving hospitals in this area with an acute shortage of beds."

"I fear I haven't read a newspaper since they stopped printing The Flutters on the comic page of the *Daily Mirror*," I admitted, "but I have heard something of the sort."

"Well, it means that some people who are required to attend hospital for tests cannot be admitted as overnight patients any more. As you have been so very helpful in the past, we wondered if you could take in one of these patients."

"For how long?" I asked. "And what sort of patient?"

"It would be for two weeks at the most, and the patient I have in mind for you—" she churned up the contents of her disgusting briefcase trying to locate her poor victim's folder "—is a very nice young lady. She's a severe diabetic, and she's in a wheelchair. Apart from that, she's the same as you or I." She gave me a warm smile, then quickly looked away, sensing perhaps that I was not like other people. She handed me a dog-eared photograph of the patient, attached to a medical history that had more pages than an average weekly script of *The Clitheroe Kid*, a popular BBC radio show which for some reason has never been reissued on audio cassette.

"Her name is Saskia," said Miss Chisholm. "She has no family to speak of, and lives a long way from London. Ours is one of the few hospitals with the necessary equipment to handle complex drug and therapy trials for people like her. She desperately needs a place to stay. We can arrange to have her collected each day. We'd be terribly grateful if you could help. She really has nowhere else to go."

I studied the photograph carefully. The girl was pitifully small-boned, with sallow, almost translucent skin. But she had attractive blonde hair, and well-defined features reminiscent of a young Suzy Kendall in Robert Hartford-Davis' patchy 1966 comedy portmanteau *The Sandwich Man*, in which Our Norman, playing an Irish priest, was not seen to his best advantage. What's more, she fitted in perfectly with my plans. A woman. That would certainly be different.

I returned the photograph with a smile. 'I think we can work something out," I said.

Diary Entry #4 Dated 23 October

Saskia is here, and I must say that for someone so ill she is quite a tonic. The night she arrived, I watched as she struggled to negotiate her wheelchair around the flat without damaging the paintwork on the skirting boards, and despite many setbacks she managed it without a single protestation. Indeed, she has been here for two days now, and never seems to complain about anything or anyone. Apparently all of her life she has been prone to one kind of disease or another, and few doctors expected her to survive her childhood, so she is simply happy to be alive.

I have installed her in the spare room, which she insisted on filling with flowers purchased from the stall outside the hospital. Even Hattie, never the most amenable of cats, seems to have taken to her.

As my flat is on the second floor of a large Victorian house, she is a virtual prisoner within these walls during the hours outside her hospital visits. At those times the ambulance men carry her and the folded wheelchair up and down the stairs.

On her very first night here I entered the lounge to find her going through my catalogued boxes of BBC comedy archive tapes. I was just beginning to grow annoyed when she turned to me and asked if she could play some of them. No one had ever shown the least interest in my collection before. To test her, I asked which shows she would most enjoy hearing.

"I like Leslie Phillips in *The Navy Lark*, and the Fraser Hayes Four playing on *Round the Horne*," she said, running a slim finger across the spines of the tape boxes. "And of course, *Hancock's Half Hour*, although I prefer the shows after Andrée Melly had been replaced by Hattie Jacques."

Suddenly I was suspicious.

This tiny girl could not be more than twenty-two years of age. How could she possibly be so familiar with radio programmes that had scarcely been heard in thirty years?

"My father was a great collector," she explained, as if she had just read my thoughts. "He used to play the old shows nearly every evening after dinner. It's one of the few lasting memories I have of my parents."

Well naturally, my heart went out to the poor girl. "I know exactly how you feel," I said. "I only have to hear Kenneth Williams say '*Good Evening*' and I'm reminded of home and hearth. They were such happy times for me."

For the next hour or so I sounded her out on other favourite film and radio memories of the past, but although there seemed no other common ground between us, she remained willing to listen to my happy tales and learn. At eleven o'clock she yawned and said that she would like to go to bed, and so I let her leave the lounge.

Last night Saskia was kept late at the hospital, and I was in bed by the time the heavy tread of the ambulance man was heard upon the stair. This morning she asked me if I would like her to cook an evening meal. After some initial concern with the hygiene problems involved in allowing one's meal to be cooked by someone else, I agreed. (In restaurants I assiduously question the waitresses about their sanitary arrangements.) Furthermore, I offered to buy produce for the projected feast, but she insisted on stopping by the shops on her way home from the hospital. Although she is frail, she demands independence. I will buy a bottle of wine. After being alone with my memories for so long, it is unnerving to have someone else in the apartment.

And yet it is rather wonderful.

Diary Entry #5 Dated 24 October

What an enthralling evening!

I feel as if I am truly alive for the first time in my life. Saskia returned early tonight – looking drawn and pale, but still vulnerably beautiful, with her blonde hair tied in a smart plait – and headed straight into the kitchen, where she stayed for several hours. I had arranged a ramp of planks by the cooker so that she could reach the hobs without having to rise from her chair.

Hattie, sensing that something tasty was being prepared, hung close to the base of the door, sniffing and licking her chops. To amuse Saskia while she cooked I played dialogue soundtracks which I had recorded in my local cinema as a child during performances of *Passport To Pimlico* and *The Lavender Hill Mob*, but the poor quality of the tapes (from a small reel-to-reel recorder I had smuggled into the auditorium) was such that I imagine the subtleties of these screenplays were rather lost to her, especially as she had the kitchen door shut and was banging saucepans about.

The meal was a complete delight. We had a delicious tomato and basil soup to start with, and a truly spectacular salmon en croute as the main course, followed by cheese and biscuits.

Saskia told me about herself, explaining that her parents had been killed in a car crash when she was young. This tragedy had forced her to live with a succession of distant and ancient relatives. When the one she was staying with died, she was shunted into a foster home. No one was willing to take her, though, as the complications arising from her diabetes would have made enormous demands on any foster-parent.

As she talked she ate very little, really only toying with her food. The diabetes prevents her from enjoying much of anything, but hopefully the tests she is undergoing will reveal new ways of coping with her restricted lifestyle.

The dining table is too low to comfortably incorporate Saskia's wheelchair, so I have promised to raise it for tomorrow's dinner, which I have insisted on cooking. I was rather nervous at the prospect, but then I thought: if a cripple can do it, so can I.

Saskia is so kind and attentive, such a good listener. Perhaps it is time for me to introduce my pet topic into the dinner conversation.

Diary Entry #6 Dated 25 October

Disaster has struck!

Right from the start everything went wrong – and just as we were getting along so well. Let me set it out from the beginning.

The meal. I cooked a meal tonight that was not as elaborate as the one she had prepared, and nothing like as good. This was partly because I was forced to work late (still no news of my promotion), so most of the shops were shut, and partly because I have never cooked for a woman before. The result was a microwaved dinner that was still freezing cold in the centre of the dish, but if Saskia didn't like it she certainly didn't complain. Instead she gave a charming broad smile (one which she is using ever more frequently with me) and slowly chewed as she listened to my detailed description of the indignities daily heaped upon me at the office.

I had bought another bottle of wine, and perhaps had drunk a little too much of it by myself (Saskia being unable to drink for the rest of the week), because I found myself introducing the subject of him, Our Norman, the Little Man Who Won All Our Hearts, before we had even finished the main course. Wishing to present the topic in the correct context I chose to start with a basic chronology of Norman's film appearances, beginning with his thirteen-and-a-half-second appearance in *A Date with a Dream* in 1948. I had made an early decision to omit all but the most essential stage and television appearances of the Little Man for fear of tiring her, and in my description of the films stuck mainly to the classic set pieces, notably the marvellous "Learning to Walk" routine from *On the Beat* and the ten-minute "Teamaking" sequence from the opening of *The Early Bird*.

I was about to mention Norman's 1956 appearance with Ruby Murray at the Palladium in *Painting the Town* when I became distinctly aware of her interest waning. She was fidgeting about in her chair as if anxious to leave the table.

"Anyone would think you didn't like Norman Wisdom," I said, by way of a joke.

"Actually, I'm not much of a fan, no," she said suddenly, then added, "Forgive me, Stanley, but I've suddenly developed a headache." And with that she went to her room, without even offering to do the washing up. Before I went to bed I stood outside her door listening, but could hear nothing.

I have a bad feeling about this.

Diary Entry #7 Dated 27 October

She is avoiding me.

It sounds hard to believe, I know, but there can be no other explanation. Last night she returned to the flat and headed directly to her room. When I put my head around the door to see if she wanted a late-night cup of cocoa (I admit this was at three o'clock in the morning, but I could not sleep for worrying about her), it seemed that she could barely bring herself to be polite. As I stepped into the room, her eyes widened and she pulled the blankets around her in a defensive gesture, which seemed to suggest a fear of my presence. I must confess I am at a loss to understand her.

Could she have led me on, only pretending to share my interests for some secret purpose of her own?

Diary Entry #8 Dated 1 November

At work today we were informed that Mick had died. Complications from the hepatitis, annoyingly unspecified, but I gained the distinct impression that they were unpleasant. When one of the secretaries started crying I made a passing flippant remark that was, I fear, misconstrued, and the girl gave me a look of utter horror. She's a scruffy little tart who was sweet on Mick, and much given to conspiring with him about me. I felt like giving her something to be horrified about, and briefly wondered how she would look tied up with baling wire, hanging in a storm drain. The things we think about to get us through the day.

At home the situation has worsened. Saskia arrived tonight with a male friend, a doctor whom she had invited back for tea. While she was in the kitchen the two of us were left alone in the lounge, and I noticed that he seemed to be studying me from the corner of his eye. It was probably just an occupational habit, but it prompted me to wonder if Saskia had somehow voiced her suspicions to him (assuming she has any, which I consider unlikely).

After he had gone, I explained that it was not at all permissible for her to bring men into the house no matter how well she knew them, and she had the nerve to turn in her chair and accuse me of being old-fashioned!

"What on earth do you mean?" I asked her.

"It's not healthy, Stanley, surrounding yourself with all this," she explained, indicating the alphabetised film and tape cassettes that filled the shelves on the wall behind us. "Most of these people have been dead for years."

"Shakespeare has been dead for years," I replied, "and people still appreciate him."

"But he wrote plays and sonnets of lasting beauty," she persisted. "These people you listen to were just working comics. It's lovely to collect things, Stanley, but this stuff was never meant to be taken so seriously. You can't base your life around it." There was an irritating timbre in her voice that I had not noticed before. She sat smugly back in her wheelchair, and for a moment I wanted to smother her. I could feel my face growing steadily redder with the thought.

"Why shouldn't these people still be admired?" I cried, running to the shelves and pulling out several of my finest tapes. "Most of them had dreary lives filled with hardship and pain, but they made people laugh, right through the war and the years of austerity that followed. They carried on through poverty and ill-health and misery Everyone turned on the radio to hear them. Everyone went to the pictures to see them. It was something to look forward to. They kept people alive. They gave the country happy memories. Why shouldn't someone remember them for what they did?"

"All right, Stanley. I'm sorry – I didn't mean to upset you," she said, reaching out her hand, but I pushed it away. It was then that I realised my cheeks were wet, and I turned aside in shame. To think that I had been brought to this state, forced to defend myself in my own home, by a woman, and a wheelchair-bound one at that.

"This is probably a bad time to mention it," said Saskia, "but I'm going to be leaving London earlier than I first anticipated. In fact, I'll be going home tomorrow. The tests haven't taken as long as the doctors thought."

"But what about the results?" I asked.

"They've already made arrangements to send them to my local GP. He'll decide whether further treatment is necessary."

I hastily pulled myself together and made appropriate polite sounds of disappointment at the idea of her departure, but inside a part of me was rejoicing. You see, I had been watching her hands as they rested on the arms of her wheelchair. They were trembling.

And she was lying.

Diary Entry #9 Dated 2 November

I have much to relate.

After our altercation last night, both of us knew that a new level in our relationship had been reached. The game had begun. Saskia refused my conciliatory offer of tea and went straight to her bedroom, quietly locking the door behind her. I know because I tried to open it at two o'clock this morning, and I heard her breath catch in the darkness as I twisted the knob from side to side.

I returned to my room and forced myself to stay there. The night passed slowly, with both of us remaining uncomfortably awake on our respective beds. In the morning, I left the house early so that I would not be forced to trade insincere pleasantries with her over breakfast. I knew she would be gone by the time I returned, and that, I think, suited both of us. I was under no illusions – she was a dangerous woman, too independent, too free-minded to ever become my friend. We could only be adversaries. And I was dangerous to her. I had enjoyed her company, but now she would only be safe far away from me. Luckily, I would never see her again. Or so I thought. For, fast as the future, everything changed between us.

Oh, how it changed.

This morning, I arrived at work to find a terse note summoning me to my supervisor's office. Naturally I assumed that I was finally being notified of my promotion. You may imagine my shock when, in the five-minute interview that followed, it emerged that far from receiving advancement within the company, I was being fired! I did not "fit in" with the new personnel, and as the department was being "streamlined" they were "letting me go". Depending on my attitude to this news, they were prepared to make me a generous cash settlement if I left at once, so that they could immediately begin "implementing procedural changes".

I did not complain. This sort of thing has happened many times before. I do not fit in. I say this not to gain sympathy, but as a simple statement of fact. Intellect always impedes popularity. I accepted the cash offer. Disheartened, but also glad to be rid of my vile "colleagues", I returned home.

It was raining hard when I arrived at the front gate. I looked up through the dark sycamores and was surprised to find a light burning in the front room. Then I realised that Saskia was reliant on the council for arranging her transport, and as they were never able to specify an exact collection time, she was still in the house. I knew I would have to use every ounce of my control to continue behaving in a correct and civilised manner.

As I turned the key in the lock I heard a sudden scuffle of movement inside the flat. Throwing the door wide, I entered the lounge and found it empty. The sound was coming from my bedroom. A terrible deadness flooded through my chest as I tiptoed along the corridor, carefully avoiding the boards that squeaked.

Slowly, I moved into the doorway. She was on the other side of the room with her back to me. The panels of the wardrobe were folded open, and she had managed to pull one of the heavy-duty bin-liners out on the floor. Somehow she sensed that I was behind her, and the wheelchair spun around. The look on her face was one of profound disturbance.

"What have you done with the rest of them?" she said softly, her voice wavering. She had dislodged a number of air fresheners from the sacks, and the room stank of lavender.

"You're not supposed to be in here," I explained as reasonably as possible. "This is my private room."

I stepped inside and closed the door behind me. She looked up at the pinned pictures surrounding her. The bleak monochrome of a thousand celebrity photographs seemed to absorb the light within the room.

"Saskia. You're an intelligent girl. You're modern. But you have no respect for the past."

"The past?" Her lank hair was falling in her eyes, as she flicked it aside I could see she was close to tears. "What has the past to do with this?" She kicked out uselessly at the plastic sack and it fell to one side, spilling its rotting human contents onto the carpet.

"Everything," I replied, moving forward. I was not advancing on her, I just needed to get to the bedside cabinet. "The past is where everything has its rightful place."

"I know about your past, Stanley," she cried, pushing at the wheels of her chair, backing herself up against the wardrobe, turning her face from the stinking mess. "Nurse Clarke told me all about you."

"What did she say?" I asked, coming to a halt. I was genuinely curious. Nurse Clarke had hardly ever said more than two words to me.

"I know what happened to you. That's why I came here." She started to cry now, and wiped her nose with the back of her hand. Something plopped obscenely onto the floor as the sack settled. "She says you had the worst childhood a boy could ever have. Sexual abuse, violence. You lived in terror every day. Your father nearly killed you before the authorities took charge. Don't you see? That's why you're so obsessed with this stuff, this trivia, it's like a disease. You're just trying to make things all right again."

"That's a damn lie!" I shouted at her. "My childhood was perfect. You're making it up!"

"No," she said, shaking her head, snot flying from her nose. "I saw the marks when you were in the kitchen that first night. Cigarette burns on your arms. Cuts too deep to ever heal. I thought I knew how you must have felt. Like me, always shoved around, always towered over, always scared. I didn't expect anything like this. What were you thinking of?"

"Are you sure you don't know?" I asked, advancing towards the cabinet. "I'm the kind of person nobody notices. I'm invisible until

I'm pointed out. I'm in a private world. I'm not even ordinary. I'm somewhere below that."

I had reached the cabinet, and now slowly pulled open the drawer, groping inside as she tried to conceal her panic, tried to find somewhere to wheel the chair.

"But I'm not alone," I explained. "There are many like me. I see them begging on the streets, soliciting in pubs, injecting themselves in alleyways. For them childhood is a scar that never heals, but still they try to stumble on. I end their stumbling, Saskia. Miss Chisholm ,ays I'm an angel."

My fingers closed around the handle of the carving knife, but the point was stuck in the rear wall of the drawer. I gave it my attention and pulled it free, lowering the blade until it was flat against my leg. A sound from behind made me turn. With a dexterity that amazed me, the infuriating girl had opened the door and slipped through.

I ran into the lounge to find her wheelchair poised before the tape archives and Saskia half out of the seat, one hand pincering a stack of irreplaceable 78s featuring the vocal talents of Flanagan and Allen.

"Leave those alone!" I cried. "You don't understand."

She turned to me with what I felt as a look of deliberate malice on her face and raised the records high above her head. If I attacked her now, she would surely drop them.

"Why did you kill those people?" she asked simply. For a moment I was quite at a loss. She deserved an explanation. I ran my left thumb along the blade of the knife, drawing in my breath as the flesh slowly parted and the pain showed itself.

"I wanted to put their pasts right," I explained. "To give them the things that comfort. Tony Hancock. Sunday roast. Family Favourites. Smiling policemen. Norman Wisdom. To give them the freedom to remember."

I must have allowed the knife to come into view, because her grip on the records faltered and they slid from her hands to the floor. I don't think any smashed, but the wheels of her chair cracked several as she rolled forward.

"I can't give you back the past, Saskia," I said, walking towards her, smearing the knife blade with the blood from my stinging thumb. "I'm sorry, because I would have liked to."

She cried out in alarm, pulling stacks of records and tapes down upon herself, scattering them across the threadbare carpet. Then she grabbed the metal frame of the entire cabinet, as if trying to shake it loose from the wall. I stood and watched, fascinated by her fear.

When I heard the familiar heavy boots quickening on the stairs, I turned the knife over and pushed the blade hard into my chest. It was a reflex action, as if I had been planning to do this all along. Just as I had suspected, there was no pain. To those like us who suffered so long, there is no more pain.

Diary Entry #10 Dated 16 November

And now I am sitting here on a bench with a clean elastic bandage patching up my stomach, facing the bristling cameras and microphones, twenty enquiring faces before me, and the real probing questions have begun.

The bovine policewoman who interrogated me so unimaginatively during my initial detainment period bore an extraordinary resemblance to Shirley Abicair, the Australian zither player who performed superbly as Norman's love interest in Rank's 1954 hit comedy *One Good Turn*, although the *Evening News* critic found their sentimental scenes together an embarrassment.

I think I am going to enjoy my new role here. Newspapers are fighting for my story. They're already comparing me to Nilsen and Sutcliffe, although I would rather be compared to Christie or Crippen. Funny how everyone remembers the name of a murderer, but no one remembers the victim.

If they want to know, I will tell them everything. Just as long as I can tell them about my other pet interests.

My past is safe.

My future is known.

My present belongs to Norman.

1993

HORROR

THE YEAR'S BEST HORROR
STORIES BY SUCH MASTERS
OF TERROR FANTASY AS

POPPY Z. BRITE
HARLAN ELLISON
DENNIS ETCHISON
KATHE KOJA
KIM NEWMAN
and many others

EDITED BY

STEPHEN JONES
AND
RAMSEY CAMPBELL

This collection will at
recommended reading of
mine - I. N. Y.
- INTERZONE

Mefisto in Onyx

Harlan Ellison

BEING AN EDITOR is a tough job, but somebody's got to do it.

Regrettably, as a full-time author, Ramsey decided that he could no longer devote so much of his energy to ploughing through the piles of submissions, and so he reluctantly decided that *The Best New Horror Volume Five* would be his last as co-editor.

I certainly enjoyed our five years of collaboration and, generously, he has remained an unofficial advisor and sounding board for this series over the subsequent years.

With the fifth volume, Robinson decided to give the book a total re-design. And thank goodness that they did. With a new, improved, logo, a split cover design, and Luis Rey's superb artwork now highlighted in spot-varnish, the book finally achieved the impact it deserved. It also resulted in Carroll & Graf dropping its alternative hardcover edition in favour of the new-look trade paperback, finally bringing a sense of cohesion back to the series.

With the book's total extent now more than 500 pages, the Introduction hit its stride at twenty-five pages, and the Necrology expanded to fourteen. For our final editorial together, Ramsey and I went on at some length about the current state of censorship on both sides of the Atlantic.

As we concluded: "So long as such controversy can be fanned by the cynical media, hypocritical politicians and misinformed public opinion, we should all be on our guard. It is all too easy to use horror fiction and films as a scapegoat for economic and social deprivation. As most intelligent people realize, fiction is only a reflection of life. The real problems exist elsewhere . . ."

Over the intervening fifteen years, nothing very much has happened to change that opinion.

Among the twenty-nine contributions was the first appearance in *Best New Horror* of the amazingly talented Terry Lamsley, along with Dennis Etchison's British Fantasy Award-winning story "The Dog Park". In fact, Ramsey and I dedicated the book to Dennis in recognition of our first visit to Mexico with him some years earlier, when he acted as our intrepid guide.

Choosing a representative story from this particular volume was easy.

Harlan Ellison has a reputation of sometimes being difficult to work with. Yet in all my dealings with him over the years, I have never found him to be other than extremely pleasant and accommodating. In fact, when it comes to publishing his work, he is the consummate professional – something an editor always appreciates.

At the time, the Bram Stoker Award-winning novella "Mefisto in Onyx" was one of the longest pieces of fiction Harlan had written in some years. It was also, without any doubt, one of the most powerful . . .

ONCE. I ONLY WENT to bed with her once. Friends for eleven years – before and since – but it was just one of those things, just one of those crazy flings: the two of us alone on a New Year's Eve, watching rented Marx Brothers videos so we wouldn't have to go out with a bunch of idiots and make noise and pretend we were having a good time when all we'd be doing was getting drunk, whooping like morons, vomiting on slow-moving strangers, and spending more money than we had to waste. And we drank a little too much cheap champagne; and we fell off the sofa laughing at Harpo a few times too many; and we wound up on the floor at the same time; and next thing we knew we had our faces plastered together, and my hand up her skirt, and her hand down in my pants . . .

But it was just the *once*, fer chrissakes! Talk about imposing on a cheap sexual liaison! She *knew* I went mixing in other peoples' minds only when I absolutely had no other way to make a buck. Or I forgot myself and did it in a moment of human weakness.

It was always foul.

Slip into the thoughts of the best person who ever lived, even Saint Thomas Aquinas, for instance, just to pick an absolutely terrific person you'd think had a mind so clean you could eat off it (to paraphrase my mother), and when you come out – take my word for it – you'd want to take a long, intense shower in Lysol.

Trust me on this: I go into somebody's landscape when there's nothing else I can do, no other possible solution ... or I forget and do it in a moment of human weakness. Such as, say, the IRS holds my feet to the fire; or I'm about to get myself mugged and robbed and maybe murdered, or I need to find out if some specific she that I'm dating has been using somebody else's dirty needle or has been sleeping around without she's taking some extra-heavy-duty AIDS precautions; or a co-worker's got it in his head to set me up so I make a mistake and look bad to the boss and I find myself in the unemployment line again; or ...

I'm a wreck for weeks after.

Go jaunting through a landscape trying to pick up a little insider arbitrage bric-a-brac, and come away no better heeled, but all muddy with the guy's infidelities, and I can't look a decent woman in the eye for days. Get told by a motel desk clerk that they're all full up and he's sorry as hell but I'll just have to drive on for about another thirty miles to find the next vacancy, jaunt into his landscape and find him lit up with neon signs that got a lot of the word *nigger* in them, and I wind up hitting the sonofabitch so hard his grandmother has a bloody nose, and usually have to hide out for three or four weeks after. Just about to miss a bus, jaunt into the head of the driver to find his name so I can yell for him to hold it a minute Tom or George or Willie, and I get smacked in the mind with all the garlic he's been eating for the past month because his doctor told him it was good for his system, and I start to dry-heave, and I wrench out of the landscape, and not only have I missed the bus, but I'm so sick to my stomach I have to sit down on the filthy curb to get my gorge submerged. Jaunt into a potential employer, to see if he's trying to lowball me, and I learn he's part of a massive cover-up of industrial malfeasance that's caused hundreds of people to die when this or that cheaply-made grommet or tappet or gimbal mounting underperforms and fails, sending the poor souls falling thousands of feet to shrieking destruction. Then just *try* to accept the job, even if you haven't paid your rent in a month. No way.

Absolutely: I listen in on the landscape *only* when my feet are being fried; when the shadow stalking me turns down alley after alley tracking me relentlessly; when the drywall guy I've hired to repair the damage done by my leaky shower presents me with a dopey smile and a bill three hundred and sixty bucks higher than the estimate. Or in a moment of human weakness.

But I'm a wreck for weeks after. For weeks.

Because you can't, you simply can't, you absolutely *cannot* know what people are truly and really like till you jaunt their landscape. If Aquinas had had my ability, he'd have very quickly gone off to be a hermit, only occasionally visiting the mind of a sheep or a hedgehog. In a moment of human weakness.

That's why in my whole life – and, as best I can remember back, I've been doing it since I was five- or six-years-old, maybe even younger – there have only been eleven, maybe twelve people, of all those who know that I can "read minds", that I've permitted myself to get close to. Three of them never used it against me, or tried to exploit me, or tried to kill me when I wasn't looking. Two of those three were my mother and father, a pair of sweet old black folks who'd adopted me, a late-in-life baby, and were now dead (but probably still worried about me, even on the Other Side), and whom I missed very very much, particularly in moments like this. The other eight, nine were either so turned off by the knowledge that they made sure I never came within a mile of them – one moved to another entire country just to be on the safe side, although her thoughts were a helluva lot more boring and innocent than she thought they were – or they tried to brain me with something heavy when I was distracted – I still have a shoulder separation that kills me for two days before it rains – or they tried to use me to make a buck for them. Not having the common sense to figure it out, that if I was *capable* of using the ability to make vast sums of money, why the hell was I living hand-to-mouth like some overaged grad student who was afraid to desert the university and go become an adult?

Now *they* was some dumb-ass muthuhfugguhs.

Of the three who never used it against me – my mom and dad – the last was Allison Roche. Who sat on the stool next to me, in the middle of May, in the middle of a Wednesday afternoon, in the middle of Clanton, Alabama, squeezing ketchup onto her All-American Burger, imposing on the memory of that one damned New Year's Eve sexual interlude, with Harpo and his sibs; the two of us all alone except for the fry-cook; and she waited for my reply.

"I'd sooner have a skunk spray my pants leg," I replied.

She pulled a napkin from the chrome dispenser and swabbed up the red that had overshot the sesame-seed bun and redecorated the Formica countertop. She looked at me from under thick, lustrous eyelashes; a look of impatience and violet eyes that must have been a killer when she unbottled it at some truculent witness for the defence. Allison Roche was a Chief Deputy District Attorney in and for Jefferson County, with her office in Birmingham. Alabama. Where near we sat, in Clanton, having a secret meeting, having All-American Burgers; three years after having had quite a bit of champagne, 1930s black-and-white video rental comedy, and black-and-white sex. One extremely stupid New Year's Eve.

Friends for eleven years. And once, just once; as a prime example of what happens in a moment of human weakness. Which is not to say that it wasn't terrific, because it was; absolutely terrific; but we never did it again; and we never brought it up again after the next morning when we opened our eyes and looked at each other the way you look at an exploding can of sardines, and both of us said *Oh Jeeezus* at the same time. Never brought it up again until this memorable afternoon at the greasy spoon where I'd joined Ally, driving up from Montgomery to meet her halfway, after her peculiar telephone invitation.

Can't say the fry-cook, Mr All-American, was particularly happy at the pigmentation arrangement at his counter. But I stayed out of his head and let him think what he wanted. Times change on the outside, but the inner landscape remains polluted.

"All I'm asking you to do is go have a chat with him," she said. She gave me that look. I have a hard time with that look. It isn't entirely honest, neither is it entirely disingenuous. It plays on my remembrance of that one night we spent in bed. And is just *dis*honest enough to play on the part of that night we spent on the floor, on the sofa, on the coffee counter between the dining room and the kitchenette, in the bathtub, and about nineteen minutes crammed among her endless pairs of shoes in a walk-in clothes closet that smelled strongly of cedar and virginity. She gave me that look, and wasted no part of the memory.

"I don't *want* to go have a chat with him. Apart from he's a piece of human shit, and I have better things to do with my time than to go on down to Atmore and take a jaunt through this crazy sonofabitch's diseased mind, may I remind you that of the hundred and sixty, seventy men who have died in that electric chair, including the original 'Yellow Mama' they scrapped in 1990, about a hundred and thirty of them were gentlemen of colour, and I do not mean you to picture any colour of a shade much lighter than that cuppa coffee you got sittin' by your left hand right this minute, which is to say that I, being an inordinately well-educated African-American who values the full measure of living negritude in his body, am not crazy enough to want to visit a racist '*co*-rectional centre' like Holman Prison, thank you very much."

"Are you finished?" she asked, wiping her mouth.

"Yeah. I'm finished. Case closed. Find somebody else."

She didn't like that. "There *isn't* anybody else."

"There has to be. Somewhere. Go check the research files at Duke University. Call the Fortean Society. Mensa. *Jeopardy.* Some 900 number astrology psychic hotline. Ain't there some semi-senile Senator with a full-time paid assistant who's been trying to get legislation through one of the statehouses for the last five years to fund this kind of bullshit research? What about the Russians . . . now that the Evil Empire's fallen, you ought to be able to get some word about their success with Kirlian auras or whatever those assholes were working at. Or you could—"

She screamed at the top of her lungs. "*Stop it, Rudy!*"

The fry-cook dropped the spatula he'd been using to scrape off the grill. He picked it up, looking at us, and his face (I didn't read his mind) said *If that white bitch makes one more noise I'm callin' the cops.*

I gave him a look he didn't want, and he went back to his chores, getting ready for the after-work crowd. But the stretch of his back and angle of his head told me he wasn't going to let this pass.

I leaned in toward her, got as serious as I could, and just this quietly, just this softly, I said, "Ally, good pal, listen to me. You've been one of the few friends I could count on, for a long time now. We have history between us, and you've *never*, not once, made me feel like a freak. So okay, I trust you. I trust you with something about me that causes immeasurable goddam pain. A thing about me that could get me killed. You've never betrayed me, and you've never tried to use me.

"Till now. This is the first time. And you've got to admit that it's not even as rational as you maybe saying to me that you've gambled away every cent you've got and you owe the mob a million bucks and would I mind taking a trip to Vegas or Atlantic City and taking a jaunt into the minds of some high-pocket poker players so I could win you enough to keep the goons from shooting you. Even *that*, as creepy as it would be if you said it to me, even *that* would be easier to understand than *this*!"

She looked forlorn. "There isn't anybody else, Rudy. *Please.*"

"What the hell is this all about? Come on, tell me. You're hiding something, or holding something back, or lying about—"

"*I'm not lying!*" For the second time she was suddenly, totally, extremely pissed at me. Her voice spattered off the white tile walls. The fry-cook spun around at the sound, took a step toward us, and

I jaunted into his landscape, smoothed down the rippled Astro-Turf, drained away the storm clouds, and suggested in there that he go take a cigarette break out back. Fortunately, there were no other patrons at the elegant All-American Burger that late in the afternoon, and he went.

"Calm fer chrissakes down, will you?" I said.

She had squeezed the paper napkin into a ball.

She was lying, hiding, holding something back. Didn't have to be a telepath to figure *that* out. I waited, looking at her with a slow, careful distrust, and finally she sighed, and I thought, *Here it comes*.

"Are you reading my mind?" she asked.

"Don't insult me. We know each other too long."

She looked chagrined. The violet of her eyes deepened. "Sorry."

But she didn't go on. I wasn't going to be outflanked. I waited.

After a while she said, softly, very softly, "I think I'm in love with him. I *know* I believe him when he says he's innocent."

I never expected that. I couldn't even reply.

It was unbelievable. Unfuckingbelievable. She was the Chief Deputy D.A. who had prosecuted Henry Lake Spanning for murder. Not just one murder, one random slaying, a heat of the moment Saturday night killing regretted deeply on Sunday morning but punishable by electrocution in the Sovereign State of Alabama nonetheless, but a string of the vilest, most sickening serial slaughters in Alabama history, in the history of the Glorious South, in the history of the United States. Maybe even in the history of the entire wretched human universe that went wading hip-deep in the wasted spilled blood of innocent men, women and children.

Henry Lake Spanning was a monster, an ambulatory disease, a killing machine without conscience or any discernible resemblance to a thing we might call decently human. Henry Lake Spanning had butchered his way across a half-dozen states; and they had caught up to him in Huntsville, in a garbage dumpster behind a supermarket, doing something so vile and inhuman to what was left of a sixty-five-year-old cleaning woman that not even the tabloids would get more explicit than *unspeakable*; and somehow he got away from the cops; and somehow he evaded their dragnet; and somehow he found out where the police lieutenant in charge of the manhunt lived; and somehow he slipped into that neighbourhood when the lieutenant was out creating roadblocks – and he gutted the man's wife and two kids. Also the family cat. And then he killed a couple of more times in Birmingham and Decatur, and by then had gone so completely out of his mind that they got him again, and the second time they hung onto him, and they brought him to trial. And Ally had prosecuted this bottom-feeding monstrosity.

And oh, what a circus it had been. Though he'd been *caught*, the second time, and this time for keeps, in Jefferson County, scene of three of his most sickening jobs, he'd murdered (with such a disgustingly similar m.o. that it was obvious he was the perp) in twenty-two of the sixty-seven counties; and every last one of them wanted him to stand trial in that venue. Then there were the other five states in which he had butchered, to a total body-count of fifty-six. Each of *them* wanted him extradited.

So, here's how smart and quick and smooth an attorney Ally is: she somehow managed to coze up to the Attorney General, and somehow managed to unleash those violet eyes on him, and somehow managed to get and keep his ear long enough to con him into setting a legal precedent. Attorney General of the State of Alabama allowed Allison Roche to consolidate, to secure a multiple bill of indictment that forced Spanning to stand trial on all twenty-nine Alabama murder counts at once. She meticulously documented to the state's highest courts that Henry Lake Spanning presented such a clear and present danger to society that the prosecution was willing to take a chance (big chance!) of trying in a winner-take-all consolidation of venues. Then she managed to smooth the feathers of all those other vote-hungry prosecuters in those twenty-one other counties, and she put on a case that dazzled everyone, including Spanning's defence attorney, who had screamed about the legality of the multiple bill from the moment she'd suggested it.

And she won a fast jury verdict on all twenty-nine counts. Then she got *really* fancy in the penalty phase after the jury verdict, and proved up the *other* twenty-seven murders with their flagrantly identical trademarks, from those other five states, and there was nothing left but to sentence Spanning – essentially for all fifty-six – to the replacement for the "Yellow Mama".

Even as pols and power brokers throughout the state were murmuring Ally's name for higher office, Spanning was slated to sit in that new electric chair in Holman Prison, built by the Fred A. Leuchter Associates of Boston, Massachusetts, that delivers 2,640 volts of pure sparklin' death in 1/240th of a second, six times faster than the 1/40th of a second that it takes for the brain to sense it, which is – if you ask me – much too humane an exit line, more than three times the 700 volt jolt lethal dose that destroys a brain, for a pusbag like Henry Lake Spanning.

But if we were lucky – and the scheduled day of departure was very nearly upon us – if we were lucky, if there was a God and Justice and Natural Order and all that good stuff, then Henry Lake Spanning, this foulness, this corruption, this thing that lived only to ruin . . . would end up as a pile of fucking ashes somebody might use to sprinkle over a flower garden, thereby providing this ghoul with his single opportunity to be of some use to the human race.

That was the guy that my pal Allison Roche wanted me to go and "chat" with, down to Holman Prison, in Atmore, Alabama. There, sitting on Death Row, waiting to get his demented head tonsured, his pants legs slit, his tongue fried black as the inside of a sheep's belly . . . down there at Holman my pal Allison wanted me to go "chat" with one of the most awful creatures made for killing this side of a hammerhead shark, which creature had an infinitely greater measure of human decency than Henry Lake Spanning had ever demonstrated. Go chit-chat, and enter his landscape, and read his mind, Mr Telepath, and use the marvellous mythic power of extrasensory perception: this nifty swell ability that has made me a bum all my life, well, not *exactly* a bum: I do have a decent apartment, and I do earn a decent, if sporadic, living; and I try to follow Nelson Algren's warning never to get involved with a woman whose troubles are bigger than my own; and sometimes I even have a car of my own, even though at that moment such was not the case, the Camaro having been repo'd, and not by Harry Dean Stanton or Emilio Estevez, lemme tell you; but a bum in the sense of – how does Ally put it? – oh yeah – I don't "realize my full and forceful potential" – a bum in the sense that I can't hold a job, and I get rotten breaks, and all of this despite a Rhodes scholarly education so far above what a poor nigrahlad such as myself could expect that even Rhodes hisownself would've been chest-out proud as hell of me. A bum, mostly, despite an *outstanding* Rhodes scholar education and a pair of kind, smart, loving parents – even for foster-parents – shit, *especially* for being foster-parents – who died knowing the certain sadness that their only child would spend his life as a wandering freak unable to make a comfortable living or consummate a normal marriage or raise children without the fear of passing on this special personal horror . . . this astonishing ability fabled in song and story that I possess . . . that no one else seems to possess, though I know there must have been others, somewhere, sometime, somehow! Go, Mr Wonder of

Wonders, shining black Cagliostro of the modern world, go with this super nifty swell ability that gullible idiots and flying saucer assholes have been trying to prove exists for at least fifty years, that no one has been able to isolate the way I, me, the only one has been isolated, let me tell you about *isolation*, my brothers; and here I was, here was I, Rudy Pairis . . . just a guy, making a buck every now and then with nifty swell impossible ESP, resident of thirteen states and twice that many cities so far in his mere thirty years of landscape-jaunting life, here was I, Rudy Pairis, Mr I-Can-Read-Your-Mind, being asked to go and walk through the mind of a killer who scared half the people in the world. Being asked by the only living person, probably, to whom I could not say no. And, oh, take me at my word here: I *wanted* to say no. *Was*, in fact, saying no at every breath. What's that? Will I do it? Sure, yeah sure, I'll go on down to Holman and jaunt through this sick bastard's mind landscape. Sure I will. You got two chances: slim, and none.

All of this was going on in the space of one greasy double cheeseburger and two cups of coffee.

The worst part of it was that Ally had somehow gotten involved with him. *Ally!* Not some bimbo bitch . . . but *Ally*. I couldn't believe it.

Not that it was unusual for women to become mixed up with guys in the joint, to fall under their "magic spell", and to start corresponding with them, visiting them, taking them candy and cigarettes, having conjugal visits, playing mule for them and smuggling in dope where the tampon never shine, writing them letters that got steadily more exotic, steadily more intimate, steamier and increasingly dependent emotionally. It wasn't that big a deal; there exist entire psychiatric treatises on the phenomenon; right alongside the papers about women who go stud-crazy for cops. No big deal indeed: hundreds of women every year find themselves writing to these guys, visiting these guys, building dream castles with these guys, fucking these guys, pretending that even the worst of these guys, rapists and woman-beaters and child molesters, repeat paedophiles of the lowest pustule sort, and murderers and stick-up punks who crush old ladies' skulls for food stamps, and terrorists and bunco barons . . . that one sunny might-be, gonna-happen pink cloud day these demented creeps will emerge from behind the walls, get back in the wind, become upstanding nine-to-five Brooks Bros. Galahads. Every year hundreds of women marry these guys, finding themselves in a hot second snookered by the wily, duplicitous, motherfuckin' lying greaseball addictive behaviour of guys who had spent their sporadic years, their intermittent freedom on the outside, doing *just that*: roping people in, ripping people off, bleeding people dry, conning them into being tools, taking them for their every last cent, their happy home, their sanity, their ability to trust or love ever again.

But this wasn't some poor illiterate naïve woman-child. This was *Ally*. She had damned near pulled off a legal impossibility, come *that* close to Bizarro Jurisprudence by putting the Attorneys General of five other states in a maybe frame of mind where she'd have been able to consolidate a multiple bill of indictment *across state lines*! Never been done; and now, probably, never ever would be. But she could have possibly pulled off such a thing. Unless you're a stone court-bird, you can't know what a mountaintop that is!

So, now, here's Ally, saying this shit to me. Ally, my best pal, stood up for me a hundred times; not some dip, but the steely-eyed Sheriff of Suicide Gulch, the over-forty, past the age of innocence, no-nonsense woman who had seen it all and come away tough but not cynical, hard but not mean.

"I think I'm in love with him." She had said.

"I *know* I believe him when he says he's innocent." She had said.

I looked at her. No time had passed. It was still the moment the universe decided to lie down and die. And I said, "So if you're certain this paragon of the virtues *isn't* responsible for fifty-six murders – that we *know* about – and who the hell knows how many more we *don't* know about, since he's apparently been at it since he was twelve years old – remember the couple of nights we sat up and you *told* me all this shit about him, and you said it with your skin crawling, *remember?* – then if you're so damned positive the guy you spent eleven weeks in court sending to the chair is innocent of butchering half the population of the planet – then why do you need me to go to Holman, drive all the way to Atmore, just to take a jaunt in this sweet peach of a guy?

"Doesn't your 'woman's intuition' tell you he's squeaky clean? Don't 'true love' walk yo' sweet young ass down the primrose path with sufficient surefootedness?"

"Don't be a smartass!" she said.

"Say again?" I replied, with disfuckingbelief.

"I said: don't be such a high-verbal goddamned smart aleck!"

Now *I* was steamed. "No, I shouldn't be a smartass: I should be your pony, your show dog, your little trick bag mind-reader freak! Take a drive over to Holman, Pairis; go right on into Rednecks from

Hell; sit your ass down on Death Row with the rest of the niggers and have a chat with the one white boy who's been in a cell up there for the past three years or so; sit down nicely with the king of the fucking vampires, and slide inside his garbage dump of a brain – and what a joy *that's* gonna be, I can't believe you'd ask me to do this – and read whatever piece of boiled shit in there he calls a brain, and see if he's jerking you around. *That's* what I ought to do, am I correct? Instead of being a smartass. Have I got it right? Do I properly pierce your meaning, pal?"

She stood up. She didn't even say *Screw you, Pairis!*

She just slapped me as hard as she could.

She hit me a good one straight across the mouth.

I felt my upper teeth bite my lower lip. I tasted the blood. My head rang like a church bell. I thought I'd fall off the goddam stool.

When I could focus, she was just standing there, looking ashamed of herself, and disappointed, and mad as hell, and worried that she'd brained me. All of that, all at the same time. Plus, she looked as if I'd broken her choo-choo train.

"Okay," I said wearily, and ended the word with a sigh that reached all the way back into my hip pocket. "Okay, calm down. I'll see him. I'll do it. Take it easy."

She didn't sit down. "Did I hurt you?"

"No, of course not," I said, unable to form the smile I was trying to put on my face. "How could you possibly hurt someone by knocking his brains into his lap?"

She stood over me as I clung precariously to the counter, turned halfway around on the stool by the blow. Stood over me, the balled-up paper napkin in her fist, a look on her face that said she was nobody's fool, that we'd known each other a long time, that she hadn't asked this kind of favour before, that if we were buddies and I loved her, that I would see she was in deep pain, that she was conflicted, that she needed to know, *really* needed to know without a doubt, and in the name of God – in which she believed, though I didn't, but either way what the hell – that I do this thing for her, that I just *do it* and not give her any more crap about it.

So I shrugged, and spread my hands like a man with no place to go, and I said, "How'd you get into this?"

She told me the first fifteen minutes of her tragic, heartwarming, never-to-be-ridiculed story still standing. After fifteen minutes I said, "Fer chrissakes, Ally, at least *sit down!* You look like a damned fool standing there with a greasy napkin in your mitt."

A couple of teenagers had come in. The four-star chef had finished his cigarette out back and was reassuringly in place, walking the duckboards and dishing up All-American arterial cloggage.

She picked up her elegant attaché case and without a word, with only a nod that said let's get as far from them as we can, she and I moved to a double against the window to resume our discussion of the varieties of social suicide available to an unwary and foolhardy gentleman of the coloured persuasion if he allowed himself to be swayed by a cagey and cogent, clever and concupiscent female of another colour entirely.

See, what it is, is this:

Look at that attaché case. You want to know what kind of an Ally this Allison Roche is? Pay heed, now.

In New York, when some wannabe junior ad exec has smooched enough butt to get tossed a bone account, and he wants to walk his colours, has a need to signify, has got to demonstrate to everyone that he's got the juice, first thing he does, he hies his ass downtown to Barney's, West 17th and Seventh, buys hisself a Burberry, loops the belt casually *behind*, leaving the coat open to suh*wing*, and he circumnavigates the office.

In Dallas, when the wife of the CEO has those six or eight upper-management husbands and wives over for un *intimo, faux* casual dinner, sans placecards, sans *entrée* fork, *sans cérémonie*, and we're talking the kind of woman who flies Virgin Air instead of the Concorde, she's so in charge she don't got to use the Orrefors, she can put out the Kosta Boda and say *give a fuck*.

What it is, kind of person so in charge, so easy with they own self, they don't *have* to laugh at your poor dumb struttin' Armani suit, or your bedroom done in Laura Ashley, or that you got a gig writing articles for *TV Guide*. You see what I'm sayin' here? The sort of person Ally Roche is, you take a look at that attaché case, and it'll tell you everything you need to know about how strong she is, because it's an Atlas. Not a Hartmann. Understand: she could *afford* a Hartmann, that gorgeous imported Canadian belting leather, top of the line, somewhere around nine hundred and fifty bucks maybe, equivalent of Orrefors, a Burberry, breast of guinea hen and Mouton Rothschild 1492 or 1066 or whatever year is the most expensive, drive a Rolls instead of a Bentley and the only difference is the grille ... but she doesn't *need* to signify, doesn't *need* to suh*wing*, so she gets herself this Atlas. Not some dumb chickenshit Louis Vuitton or Mark Cross all the divorcée real estate ladies carry, but an Atlas. Irish hand leather. Custom tanned cowhide. Hand tanned in Ireland by out of work IRA bombers. Very classy. Just a state understated. See that attaché case? That tell you why I said I'd do it?

She picked it up from where she'd stashed it, right up against the counter wall by her feet, and we went to the double over by the window, away from the chef and the teenagers, and she stared at me till she was sure I was in a right frame of mind, and she picked up where she'd left off.

The next twenty-three minutes by the big greasy clock on the wall she related from a sitting position. Actually, a series of sitting positions. She kept shifting in her chair like someone who didn't appreciate the view of the world from that window, someone hoping for a sweeter horizon. The story started with a gang-rape at the age of thirteen, and moved right along: two broken foster-home families, a little casual fondling by surrogate poppas, intense studying for perfect school grades as a substitute for happiness, working her way through John Jay College of Law, a truncated attempt at wedded bliss in her late twenties, and the long miserable road of legal success that had brought her to Alabama. There could have been worse places.

I'd known Ally for a long time, and we'd spent totals of weeks and months in each other's company. Not to mention the New Year's Eve of the Marx Brothers. But I hadn't heard much of this. Not much at all.

Funny how that goes. Eleven years. You'd think I'd've guessed or suspected or *some*thing. What the hell makes us think we're friends with *any*body, when we don't know the first thing about them, not really?

What are we, walking around in a dream? That is to say: what the fuck are we *thinking*!?!

And there might never have been a reason to hear *any* of it, all this Ally that was the real Ally, but now she was asking me to go somewhere I didn't want to go, to do something that scared the shit out of me; and she wanted me to be as fully informed as possible.

It dawned on me that those same eleven years between us hadn't really given her a full, laser-clean insight into the why and wherefore of Rudy Pairis, either. I hated myself for it. The concealing, the holding-back, the giving up only fragments, the evil misuse of charm when honesty would have hurt. I was facile, and a very quick study; and I had buried all the equivalents to Ally's pains and travails. I could've matched her, in spades; or blacks, or just plain nigras. But I remained frightened of losing her friendship. I've never been able to believe in the myth of unqualified friendship. Too much like standing hip-high in a fast running, freezing river. Standing on slippery stones.

Her story came forward to the point at which she had prosecuted Spanning; had amassed and winnowed and categorized the evidence so thoroughly, so deliberately, so flawlessly; had orchestrated the case so brilliantly; that the jury had come in with guilty on all twenty-nine, soon – in the penalty phase – fifty-six. Murder in the first. Premeditated murder in the first. Premeditated murder with special ugly circumstances in the first. On each and every of the twenty-nine. Less than an hour it took them. There wasn't even time for a lunch break. Fifty-one minutes it took them to come back with the verdict guilty on all charges. Less than a minute per killing. Ally had done that.

His attorney had argued that no direct link had been established between the fifty-sixth killing (actually, only his 29th in Alabama) and Henry Lake Spanning. No, they had not caught him down on his knees eviscerating the shredded body of his final victim – ten-year-old Gunilla Ascher, a parochial school girl who had missed her bus and been picked up by Spanning just about a mile from her home in Decatur – no, not down on his knees with the can opener still in his sticky red hands, but the m.o. was the same, and he was there in Decatur, on the run from what he had done in Huntsville, what they had *caught* him doing in Huntsville, in that dumpster, to that old woman. So they *couldn't* place him with his smooth, slim hands inside dead Gunilla Ascher's still-steaming body. So what? They could not have been surer he was the serial killer, the monster, the ravaging nightmare whose methods were so vile the newspapers hadn't even *tried* to cobble up some smart-aleck name for him like The Strangler or The Backyard Butcher. The jury had come back in fifty-one minutes, looking sick, looking as if they'd try and try to get everything they'd seen and heard out of their minds, but knew they never would, and wishing to God they could've managed to get out of their civic duty on this one.

They came shuffling back in and told the numbed court: hey, put this slimy excuse for a maggot in the chair and cook his ass till he's fit only to be served for breakfast on cinnamon toast. This was the guy my friend Ally told me she had fallen in love with. The guy she now believed to be innocent.

This was seriously crazy stuff.

"So how did you get, er, uh, how did you . . .?"

"How did I fall in love with him?"

"Yeah. That."

She closed her eyes for a moment, and pursed her lips as if she had lost a flock of wayward words and didn't know where to find them. I'd always known she was a private person, kept the really important history to herself – hell, until now I'd never known about the rape, the ice mountain between her mother and father, the specifics of the seven-month marriage – I'd known there'd been a husband briefly; but not what had happened; and I'd known about the foster homes; but again, not how lousy it had been for her – even so, getting *this* slice of steaming craziness out of her was like using your teeth to pry the spikes out of Jesus's wrists.

Finally, she said, "I took over the case when Charlie Whilborg had his stroke . . ."

"I remember."

'He was the best litigator in the office, and if he hadn't gone down two days before they caught . . ." she paused, had trouble with the name, went on, ". . . before they caught Spanning in Decatur, and if Morgan County hadn't been so worried about a case this size, and bound Spanning over to us in Birmingham . . . all of it so fast nobody really had a chance to talk to him . . . I was the first one even got *near* him, everyone was so damned scared of him, of what they *thought* he was . . ."

"Hallucinating, were they?" I said, being a smartass.

"Shut up.

"The office did most of the donkeywork after that first interview I had with him. It was a big break for me in the office; and I got obsessed by it. So after the first interview, I never spent much actual time with Spanky, never got too close, to see what kind of a man he *really* . . ."

I said: "Spanky? Who the hell's 'Spanky'?"

She blushed. It started from the sides of her nostrils and went out both ways toward her ears, then climbed to the hairline. I'd seen that happen only a couple of times in eleven years, and one of those times had been when she'd farted at the opera. *Lucia di Lammermoor.*

I said it again: "Spanky? You're putting me on, right? You call him *Spanky?*" The blush deepened. "Like the fat kid in *The Little Rascals* . . . c'mon, I don't fuckin' be*lieve* this!"

She just glared at me.

I felt the laughter coming.

My face started twitching.

She stood up again. "Forget it. Just forget it, okay?" She took two steps away from the table, toward the street exit. I grabbed her hand and pulled her back, trying not to fall apart with laughter, and I said, "Okay okay okay ... I'm *sorry* ... I'm really and truly, honest to goodness, may I be struck by a falling space lab no kidding 100 per cent absolutely sorry ... but you gotta admit ... catching me unawares like that ... I mean, come *on*, Ally ... *Spanky!?!* You call this guy who murdered at least fifty-six people Spanky? Why not Mickey, or Froggy, or Alfalfa ...? I can understand not calling him Buckwheat, you can save that one for me, but *Spanky*???"

And in a moment *her* face started to twitch; and in another moment she was starting to smile, fighting it every micron of the way; and in another moment she was laughing and swatting at me with her free hand; and then she pulled her hand loose and stood there falling apart with laughter; and in about a minute she was sitting down again. She threw the balled-up napkin at me.

"It's from when he was a kid," she said. "He was a fat kid, and they made fun of him. You know the way kids are ... they corrupted Spanning into 'Spanky' because *The Little Rascals* were on television and ... oh, shut *up*, Rudy!"

I finally quieted down, and made conciliatory gestures.

She watched me with an exasperated wariness till she was sure I wasn't going to run any more dumb gags on her, and then she resumed. "After Judge Fay sentenced him, I handled Spa ... *Henry's* case from our office, all the way up to the appeals stage. I was the one who did the pleading against clemency when Henry's lawyers took their appeal to the Eleventh Circuit in Atlanta.

"When he was denied a stay by the appellate, three-to-nothing, I helped prepare the brief when Henry's counsel went to the Alabama Supreme Court; then when the Supreme Court refused to hear his appeal, I thought it was all over. I knew they'd run out of moves for him, except maybe the Governor; but that wasn't ever going to happen. So I thought: *that's that.*

"When the Supreme Court wouldn't hear it three weeks ago, I got a letter from him. He'd been set for execution next Saturday, and I couldn't figure out why he wanted to see *me.*"

I asked, "The letter ... it got to you how?"

"One of his attorneys."

"I thought they'd given up on him."

"So did I. The evidence was so overwhelming; half a dozen counselors found ways to get themselves excused; it wasn't the kind of case that would bring any litigator good publicity. Just the number of eyewitnesses in the parking lot of that Winn-Dixie in Huntsville . . . must have been fifty of them, Rudy. And they all saw the same thing, and they all identified Henry in lineup after lineup, twenty, thirty, could have been fifty of them if we'd needed that long a parade. And all the rest of it . . ."

I held up a hand. *I know*, the flat hand against the air said. She had told me all of this. Every grisly detail, till I wanted to puke. It was as if I'd done it all myself, she was so vivid in her telling. Made my jaunting nausea pleasurable by comparison. Made me so sick I couldn't even think about it. Not even in a moment of human weakness.

"So the letter comes to you from the attorney . . ."

"I think you know this lawyer. Larry Borlan; used to be with the ACLU; before that he was senior counsel for the Alabama Legislature down to Montgomery; stood up, what was it, twice, three times, before the Supreme Court? Excellent guy. And not easily fooled."

"And what's *he* think about all this?"

"He thinks Henry's absolutely innocent."

"Of all of it?"

"Of everything."

"But there were fifty disinterested random eyewitnesses at one of those slaughters. Fifty, you just said it. Fifty, you could've had a parade. All of them nailed him cold, without a doubt. Same kind of kill as all the other fifty-five, including that schoolkid in Decatur when they finally got him. And Larry Borlan thinks he's not the guy, right?"

She nodded. Made one of those sort of comic pursings of the lips, shrugged, and nodded. "Not the guy."

"So the killer's still out there?"

"That's what Borlan thinks."

"And what do *you* think?"

"I agree with him."

"Oh, jeezus, Ally, my aching boots and saddle! You got to be workin' some kind of off-time! The killer is still out here in the mix, but there hasn't been a killing like those Spanning slaughters for the three years that he's been in the joint. Now *what* do that say to you?"

"It says whoever the guy *is*, the one who killed all those people, he's *days* smarter than all the rest of us, and he set up the perfect freefloater to take the fall for him, and he's either long far gone in some other state, working his way, or he's sitting quietly right here in Alabama, waiting and watching. And smiling." Her face seemed to sag with misery. She started to tear up, and said, "In four days he can stop smiling."

Saturday night.

"Okay, take it easy. Go on, tell me the rest of it. Borlan comes to you, and he begs you to read Spanning's letter and . . .?"

"He didn't beg. He just gave me the letter, told me he had no idea what Henry had written, but he said he'd known me a long time, that he thought I was a decent, fair-minded person, and he'd appreciate it in the name of our friendship if I'd read it."

"So you read it."

"I read it."

"Friendship. Sounds like you an' him was *good* friends. Like maybe you and I were good friends?"

She looked at me with astonishment.

I think *I* looked at me with astonishment.

"Where the hell did *that* come from?" I said.

"Yeah, really," she said, right back at me, "where the hell *did* that come from?" My ears were hot, and I almost started to say something about how if it was okay for *her* to use our Marx Brothers indiscretion for a lever, why wasn't it okay for me to get cranky about it? But I kept my mouth shut; and for once knew enough to move along. "Must've been *some* letter," I said.

There was a long moment of silence during which she weighed the degree of shit she'd put me through for my stupid remark, after all this was settled; and having struck a balance in her head, she told me about the letter.

It was perfect. It was the only sort of come-on that could lure the avenger who'd put you in the chair to pay attention. The letter had said that fifty-six was not the magic number of death. That there were many, *many* more unsolved cases, in many, *many* different states; lost children, runaways, unexplained disappearances, old people, college students hitchhiking to Sarasota for Spring Break, shopkeepers who'd carried their day's take to the night deposit drawer and never gone home for dinner, hookers left in pieces in Hefty bags all over town, and death death death unnumbered and unnamed. Fifty-six, the letter had said, was just the start. And if she, her, no one else, Allison Roche, my pal Ally, would come on down to Holman, and talk to him, Henry Lake Spanning would help her close all those open files. National rep. Avenger of the unsolved. Big time mysteries revealed. "So you read the letter, and you went . . ."

"Not at first. Not immediately. I was sure he was guilty, and I was pretty certain at that moment, three years and more, dealing with the case, I was pretty sure if he said he could fill in all the blank spaces, that he could do it. But I just didn't like the idea. In court, I was always twitchy when I got near him at the defense table. His eyes, he never took them off me. They're blue, Rudy, did I tell you that . . .?"

"Maybe. I don't remember. Go on."

"Bluest blue you've ever seen . . . well, to tell the truth, he just plain *scared* me. I wanted to win that case so badly, Rudy, you can never know . . . not just for me or the career or for the idea of justice or to avenge all those people he'd killed, but just the thought of him out there on the street, with those blue eyes, so blue, never stopped looking at me from the moment the trial began . . . the *thought* of him on the loose drove me to whip that case like a howling dog. I *had* to put him away!"

"But you overcame your fear."

She didn't like the edge of ridicule on the blade of that remark. "That's right. I finally 'overcame my fear' and I agreed to go see him."

"And you saw him."

"Yes."

"And he didn't know shit about no other killings, right?"

"Yes."

"But he talked a good talk. And his eyes was blue, so blue."

"Yes, you asshole."

I chuckled. Everybody is somebody's fool.

"Now let me ask you this – very carefully – so you don't hit me again: the moment you discovered he'd been shuckin' you, lyin', that he *didn't* have this long, unsolved crime roster to tick off, why didn't you get up, load your attaché case, and hit the bricks?"

Her answer was simple. "He begged me to stay a while."

"That's it? He *begged* you?"

"Rudy, he has no one. He's *never* had anyone." She looked at me as if I were made of stone, some basalt thing, an onyx statue, a figure carved out of melanite, soot and ashes fused into a monolith. She feared she could not, in no way, no matter how piteously or bravely she phrased it, penetrate my rocky surface.

Then she said a thing that I never wanted to hear.

"Rudy . . ."

Then she said a thing I could never have imagined she'd say. Never in a million years.

"Rudy . . ."

Then she said the most awful thing she could say to me, even more awful than that she was in love with a serial killer.

"Rudy . . . go inside . . . read my mind . . . I need you to know, I need you to understand . . . Rudy . . ."

The look on her face killed my heart.

I tried to say no, oh god no, not that, please, no, not that, don't ask me to do that, please *please* I don't want to go inside, we mean so much to each other, I don't *want* to know your landscape. Don't make me feel filthy, I'm no peeping-tom, I've *never* spied on you, never stolen a look when you were coming out of the shower, or undressing, or when you were being sexy . . . I never invaded your privacy, I wouldn't *do* a thing like that   we're friends, I don't need to know it all, I don't *want* to go in there. I can go inside anyone, and it's always awful . . . please don't make me see things in there I might not like, you're my friend, please don't steal that from me . . .

"Rudy, *please*. Do it."

Oh jeezusjeezusjeezus, again, she said it again!

We sat there. And we sat there. And we sat there longer. I said, hoarsely, in fear, "Can't you just . . . just *tell* me?"

Her eyes looked at stone. A man of stone. And she tempted me to do what I could do casually, tempted me the way Faust was tempted by Mefisto, Mephistopheles, Mefistofele, Mephostopilis. Black rock Dr Faustus, possessor of magical mind-reading powers, tempted by thick, lustrous eyelashes and violet eyes and a break in the voice and an imploring movement of hand to face and a tilt of the head that was pitiable and the begging word *please* and all the guilt that lay between us that was mine alone. The seven chief demons. Of whom Mefisto was the one "not loving the light".

I knew it was the end of our friendship. But she left me nowhere to run. Mefisto in onyx.

So I jaunted into her landscape.

I stayed in there less than ten seconds. I didn't want to know everything I could know; and I definitely wanted to know *nothing* about how she really thought of me. I couldn't have borne seeing a caricature of a bug-eyed, shuffling, thick-lipped darkie in there. Mandingo man. Steppin Porchmonkey Rudy Pair . . .

Oh god, what was I thinking!

Nothing in there like that. Nothing! Ally wouldn't *have* anything like that in there. I was going nuts, going absolutely fucking crazy, in there, back out in less than ten seconds. I want to block it, kill it, void it, waste it, empty it, reject it, squeeze it, darken it, obscure it, wipe it, do away with it like it never happened. Like the moment you walk in on your momma and poppa and catch them fucking, and you want never to have known that.

But at least I understood.

In there, in Allison Roche's landscape, I saw how her heart had responded to this man she called Spanky, not Henry Lake Spanning. She did not call him, in there, by the name of a monster; she called him a honey's name. I didn't know if he was innocent or not, but *she* knew he was innocent. At first she had responded to just talking with him, about being brought up in an orphanage, and she was able to relate to his stories of being used and treated like chattel, and how they had stripped him of his dignity, and made him afraid all the time. She knew what that was like. And how he'd always been on his own. The running-away. The being captured like a wild thing, and put in this home or that lockup or the orphanage "for his own good". Washing stone steps with a tin bucket full of grey water, with a horsehair brush and a bar of lye soap, till the tender folds of skin between the fingers were furiously red and hurt so much you couldn't make a fist.

She tried to tell me how her heart had responded, with a language that has never been invented to do the job. I saw as much as I needed, there in that secret landscape, to know that Spanning had led a miserable life, but that somehow he'd managed to become a decent human being. And it showed through enough when she was face to face with him, talking to him without the witness box between them, without the adversarial thing, without the tension of the courtroom and the gallery and those parasite creeps from the tabloids sneaking around taking pictures of him, that she identified with his pain. Hers had been not the same, but similar; of a kind, if not of identical intensity.

She came to know him a little.

And came back to see him again. Human compassion. In a moment of human weakness.

Until, finally, she began examining everything she had worked up as evidence, trying to see it from *his* point of view, using *his* explanations of circumstantiality. And there were inconsistencies. Now she saw them. Now she did not turn her prosecuting attorney's mind from them, recasting them in a way that would railroad Spanning; now she gave him just the barest possibility of truth. And the case did not seem as incontestable.

By that time, she had to admit to herself, she had fallen in love with him. The gentle quality could not be faked; she'd known fraudulent kindness in her time.

I left her mind gratefully. But at least I understood.

"Now?" she asked.

Yes, now. Now I understood. And the fractured glass in her voice told me. Her face told me. The way she parted her lips in expectation, waiting for me to reveal what my magic journey had conveyed by way of truth. Her palm against her cheek. All that told me. And I said, "Yes."

Then, silence, between us.

After a while she said, "I didn't feel anything."

I shrugged. "Nothing to feel. I was in for a few seconds, that's all."

"You didn't see everything?"

"No."

"Because you didn't want to?"

"Because . . ."

She smiled. "I understand, Rudy."

Oh, do you? Do you really? That's just fine. And I heard me say, "You made it with him yet?"

I could have torn off her arm; it would've hurt less.

"That's the second time today you've asked me that kind of question. I didn't like it much the first time, and I like it less *this* time."

"You're the one wanted me to go into your head. I didn't buy no ticket for the trip."

"Well, you were in there. Didn't you look around enough to find out?"

"I didn't look for that."

"What a chickenshit, wheedling, lousy and *cowardly* . . ."

"I haven't heard an answer, Counsellor. Kindly restrict your answers to a simple yes or no."

"Don't be ridiculous! He's on Death Row!"

"There are ways."

"How would *you* know?"

"I had a friend. Up at San Rafael. What they call Tamal. Across the bridge from Richmond, a little north of San Francisco."

"That's San Quentin."

"That's what it is, all right."

"I thought that *friend* of yours was at Pelican Bay?"

"Different friend."

"You seem to have a lot of old chums in the joint in California."

"It's a racist nation."

"I've heard that."

"But Q ain't Pelican Bay. Two different states of being. As hard time as they pull at Tamal, it's worse up to Crescent City. In the Shoe."

"You never mentioned 'a friend' at San Quentin."

"I never mentioned a lotta shit. That don't mean I don't know it. I am large, I contain multitudes."

We sat silently, the three of us: me, her, and Walt Whitman. *We're fighting*, I thought. Not make-believe, dissin' some movie we'd seen and disagreed about; this was nasty. Bone nasty and memorable. No one ever forgets this kind of fight. Can turn dirty in a second, say some trash you can never take back, never forgive, put a canker on the rose of friendship for all time, never be the same look again.

I waited. She didn't say anything more; and I got no straight answer; but I was pretty sure Henry Lake Spanning had gone all the way with her. I felt a twinge of emotion I didn't even want to look at, much less analyse, dissect, and name. *Let it be*, I thought. Eleven years. Once, just once. *Let it just lie there and get old and withered and die a proper death like all ugly thoughts.*

"Okay. So I go on down to Atmore," I said. "I suppose you mean in the very near future, since he's supposed to bake in four days. Sometime very soon: like today."

She nodded.

I said, "And how do I get in? Law student? Reporter? Tag along as Larry Borlan's new law clerk? Or do I go in with you? What am I, friend of the family, representative of the Alabama State Department of Corrections; maybe you could set me up as an inmate's rep from 'Project Hope'."

"I can do better than that," she said. The smile. "Much."

"Yeah, I'll just bet you can. Why does that worry me?"

Still with the smile, she hoisted the Atlas onto her lap. She unlocked it, took out a small manila envelope, unsealed but clasped, and slid it across the table to me. I pried open the clasp and shook out the contents.

Clever. Very clever. And already made up, with my photo where necessary, admission dates stamped for tomorrow morning, Thursday, absolutely authentic and foolproof.

"Let me guess," I said, "Thursday mornings, the inmates of Death Row have access to their attorneys?"

"On Death Row, family visitation Monday and Friday. Henry has no family. Attorney visitations Wednesdays and Thursdays, but I couldn't count on today. It took me a couple of days to get through to you . . ."

"I've been busy."

". . . but inmates consult with their counsel on Wednesday and Thursday mornings."

I tapped the papers and plastic cards. "This is very sharp. I notice my name and my handsome visage already here, already sealed in plastic. How long have you had these ready?"

"Couple of days."

"What if I'd continued to say no?"

She didn't answer. She just got that look again.

"One last thing," I said. And I leaned in very close, so she would make no mistake that I was dead serious. "Time grows short. Today's Wednesday. Tomorrow's Thursday. They throw those computer-controlled twin switches Saturday night midnight. What if I jaunt into him and find out you're right, that he's absolutely innocent? What then? They going to listen to me? Fiercely high-verbal black boy with the magic mind-read power?

"I don't think so. Then what happens, Ally?"

"Leave that to me." Her face was hard. "As you said: there are ways. There are roads and routes and even lightning bolts, if you know where to shop. The power of the judiciary. An election year coming up. Favours to be called in."

I said, "And secrets to be wafted under sensitive noses?"

"You just come back and tell me Spanky's telling the truth," and she smiled as I started to laugh, "and I'll worry about the world one minute after midnight Sunday morning."

I got up and slid the papers back into the envelope, and put the envelope under my arm. I looked down at her and I smiled as gently as I could, and I said, "Assure me that you haven't stacked the deck by telling Spanning I can read minds."

"I wouldn't do that."

"Tell me."

"I haven't told him you can read minds."

"You're lying."

"Did you . . . ?"

"Didn't have to. I can see it in your face, Ally."

"Would it matter if he knew?"

"Not a bit. I can read the sonofabitch cold or hot, with or without. Three seconds inside and I'll know if he did it all, if he did part of it, if he did none of it."

"I think I love him, Rudy."

"You told me that."

"But I wouldn't set you up. I need to know . . . that's why I'm asking you to do it."

I didn't answer. I just smiled at her. She'd told him. He'd know I was coming. But that was terrific. If she hadn't alerted him, I'd have asked her to call and let him know. The more aware he'd be, the easier to scorch his landscape.

I'm a fast study, king of the quick learners: vulgate Latin in a week; standard apothecary's pharmacopoeia in three days; Fender bass on a weekend; Atlanta Falcons' play book in an hour; and, in a moment of human weakness, what it feels like to have a very crampy, heavy-flow menstrual period, two minutes flat.

So fast, in fact, that the more somebody tries to hide the boiling pits of guilt and the crucified bodies of shame, the faster I adapt to their landscape. Like a man taking a polygraph test gets nervous, starts to sweat, ups the galvanic skin response, tries to duck and dodge, gets himself hinky and more hinky and hinkyer till his upper lip could water a truck garden, the more he tries to hide from me . . . the more he reveals . . . the deeper inside I can go.

There is an African saying: *Death comes without the thumping of drums.*

I have no idea why that one came back to me just then.

Last thing you expect from a prison administration is a fine sense of humour. But they got one at the Holman facility.

They had the bloody monster dressed like a virgin.

White duck pants, white short sleeve shirt buttoned up to the neck, white socks. Pair of brown ankle-high brogans with crepe soles, probably neoprene, but they didn't clash with the pale, virginal apparition that came through the security door with a large, black brother in Alabama Prison Authority uniform holding onto his right elbow.

Didn't clash, those work shoes, and didn't make much of a tap on the white tile floor. It was as if he floated. Oh yes, I said to myself, oh yes indeed: I could see how this messianic figure could wow even as tough a cookie as Ally. *Oh my, yes.*

Fortunately, it was raining outside.

Otherwise, sunlight streaming through the glass, he'd no doubt have a halo. I'd have lost it. Right there, a laughing jag would *not* have ceased. Fortunately, it was raining like a sonofabitch.

Which hadn't made the drive down from Clanton a possible entry on any deathbed list of Greatest Terrific Moments in My Life. Sheets of aluminum water, thick as misery, like a neverending shower curtain that I could drive through for an eternity and never really penetrate. I went into the ditch off the I-65 half a dozen times. Why I never ploughed down and buried myself up to the axles in the sucking goo running those furrows, never be something I'll understand.

But each time I skidded off the Interstate, even the twice I did a complete three-sixty and nearly rolled the old Fairlane I'd borrowed from John the C Hepworth, even then I just kept digging, slewed like an epileptic seizure, went sideways and climbed right up the slippery grass and weeds and running, sucking red Alabama goo, right back onto that long black anvil pounded by rain as hard as roofing nails. I took it then, as I take it now, to be a sign that Destiny was determined the mere heavens and earth would not be permitted to fuck me around. I had a date to keep, and Destiny was on top of things.

Even so, even living charmed, which was clear to me, even so: when I got about five miles north of Atmore, I took the 57 exit off the I-65 and a left onto 21, and pulled in at the Best Western. It wasn't my intention to stay overnight that far south – though I knew a young woman with excellent teeth down in Mobile – but the rain was just hammering and all I wanted was to get this thing done and go fall asleep. A drive that long, humping something as lame as that Fairlane, hunched forward to scope the rain ... with Spanning in front of me ... all I desired was surcease. A touch of the old oblivion.

I checked in, stood under the shower for half an hour, changed into the three-piece suit I'd brought along, and phoned the front desk for directions to the Holman facility.

Driving there, a sweet moment happened for me. It was the last sweet moment for a long time thereafter, and I remember it now as if it were still happening. I cling to it.

In May, and on into early June, the Yellow Lady's Slipper blossoms. In the forests and the woodland bogs, and often on some otherwise undistinguished slope or hillside, the yellow and purple orchids suddenly appear.

I was driving. There was a brief stop in the rain. Like the eye of the hurricane. One moment sheets of water, and the next, absolute silence before the crickets and frogs and birds started complaining; and darkness on all sides, just the idiot staring beams of my headlights poking into nothingness; and cool as a well between the drops of rain; and I was driving. And suddenly, the window rolled down so I wouldn't fall asleep, so I could stick my head out when my eyes started to close, suddenly I smelled the delicate perfume of the sweet May-blossoming Lady's Slipper. Off to my left, off in the dark somewhere on a patch of hilly ground, or deep in a stand of invisible trees, *Cypripedium calceolus* was making the night world beautiful with its fragrance.

I neither slowed, nor tried to hold back the tears.

I just drove, feeling sorry for myself; for no good reason I could name.

Way, way down – almost to the corner of the Florida Panhandle, about three hours south of the last truly imperial barbeque in that part of the world, in Birmingham – I made my way to Holman. If you've never been inside the joint, what I'm about to say will resonate about as clearly as Chaucer to one of the gentle Tasaday.

The stones call out.

That institution for the betterment of the human race, the Organized Church, has a name for it. From the fine folks at Catholicism, Lutheranism, Baptism, Judaism, Islamism, Druidism . . . Ismism . . . the ones who brought you Torquemada, several spicy varieties of Inquisition, original sin, holy war, sectarian violence, and something called "pro-lifers" who bomb and maim and kill . . . comes the catchy phrase Damned Places.

Rolls off the tongue like *God's On Our Side*, don't it?

Damned Places.

As we say in Latin, the *situs* of malevolent shit. The *venue* of evil happenings. *Locations* forever existing under a black cloud, like residing in a rooming house run by Jesse Helms or Strom Thurmond. The big slams are like that. Joliet, Dannemora, Attica, Rahway State in Jersey, that hellhole down in Louisiana called Angola, old Folsom – not the new one, the old Folsom – Q, and Ossining. Only people who read about it call it "Sing Sing". Inside, the cons call it Ossining. The Ohio State pen in Columbus. Leavenworth, Kansas. The ones they talk about among themselves when they talk about doing hard time. The Shoe at Pelican Bay State Prison. In there, in those ancient structures mortared with guilt and depravity and no respect for human life and just plain meanness on both sides, cons and screws, in there where the walls and floors have absorbed all the pain and loneliness of a million men and women for decades . . . in there, the stones call out.

Damned places. You can feel it when you walk through the gates and go through the metal detectors and empty your pockets on counters and open your briefcase so that thick fingers can rumple the papers. You feel it. The moaning and thrashing, and men biting holes in their own wrists so they'll bleed to death.

And I felt it worse than anyone else.

I blocked out as much as I could. I tried to hold on to the memory of the scent of orchids in the night. The last thing I wanted was to jaunt into somebody's landscape at random. Go inside and find out what he had done, what had *really* put him here, not just what they'd got him for. And I'm not talking about Spanning; I'm talking about every one of them. Every guy who had kicked to death his girl friend because she brought him Bratwurst instead of spicy Cajun sausage. Every pale, wormy Bible-reciting psycho who had stolen, buttfucked, and sliced up an altar boy in the name of secret voices that "tole him to g'wan *do* it!" Every amoral druggie who'd shot a pensioner for her food stamps. If I let down for a second, if I didn't keep that shield up, I'd be tempted to send out a scintilla and touch one of them. In a moment of human weakness.

So I followed the trusty to the Warden's office, where his secretary checked my papers, and the little plastic cards with my face encased in them, and she kept looking down at the face, and up at my face, and down at my face, and up at the face in front of her, and when she couldn't restrain herself a second longer she said, "We've been expecting you, Mr Pairis. Uh. Do you *really* work for the President of the United States?"

I smiled at her. "We go bowling together."

She took that highly, and offered to walk me to the conference room where I'd meet Henry Lake Spanning. I thanked her the way a well-mannered gentleman of colour thanks a Civil Servant who can make life easier or more difficult, and I followed her along corridors and in and out of guarded steel-riveted doorways, through Administration and the segregation room and the main hall to the brown-panelled, stained walnut, white tile over cement floored, roll-out security windowed, white draperied, drop ceiling with 2-inch acoustical Celotex squared conference room, where a Security Officer met us. She bid me fond adieu, not yet fully satisfied that such a one as I had come, that morning, on Air Force One, straight from a 7–10 split with the President of the United States.

It was a big room.

I sat down at the conference table; about twelve feet long and four feet wide; highly polished walnut, maybe oak. Straight back chairs: metal tubing with a light yellow upholstered cushion. Everything quiet, except for the sound of matrimonial rice being dumped on a connubial tin roof. The rain had not slacked off. Out there on the I-65 some luck-lost bastard was being sucked down into red death.

"He'll be here," the Security Officer said.

"That's good," I replied. I had no idea why he'd tell me that, seeing as how it was the reason I was there in the first place. I imagined him to be the kind of guy you dread sitting in front of, at the movies, because he always explains everything to his date. Like a *bracero* labourer with a valid green card interpreting a Woody Allen movie line-by-line to his illegal-alien cousin Humberto, three weeks under the wire from Matamoros. Like one of a pair of Beltone-wearing octogenarians on the loose from a rest home for a wild Saturday afternoon at the mall, plonked down in the third level multiplex, one of them describing whose ass Clint Eastwood is about to kick, and why. All at the top of her voice.

"Seen any good movies lately?" I asked him.

He didn't get a chance to answer, and I didn't jaunt inside to find out, because at that moment the steel door at the far end of the conference room opened, and another Security Officer poked his head in, and called across to Officer Let-Me-State-the-Obvious, "Dead man walking!"

Officer Self-Evident nodded to him, the other head poked back out, the door slammed, and my companion said, "When we bring one down from Death Row, he's gotta walk through the Ad Building and Segregation and the Main Hall. So everything's locked down. Every man's inside. It takes some time, y'know."

I thanked him.

"Is it true you work for the President, yeah?" He asked it so politely, I decided to give him a straight answer; and to hell with all the phony credentials Ally had worked up. "Yeah," I said, "we're on the same *bocce* ball team."

"Izzat so?" he said, fascinated by sports stats.

I was on the verge of explaining that the President was, in actuality, of Italian descent, when I heard the sound of the key turning in the security door, and it opened outward, and in came this messianic apparition in white, being led by a guard who was seven feet in any direction.

Henry Lake Spanning, sans halo, hands and feet shackled, with the chains cold welded into a wide anodized steel belt, shuffled toward me; and his neoprene soles made no disturbing cacophony on the white tiles.

I watched him come the long way across the room, and he watched me right back. I thought to myself, *Yeah, she told him I can read minds. Well, let's see which method you use to try and keep me out of the landscape.* But I couldn't tell from the outside of him, not just by the way he shuffled and looked, if he had fucked Ally. But I knew it had to've been. Somehow. Even in the big lockup. Even here.

He stopped right across from me, with his hands on the back of the chair, and he didn't say a word, just gave me the nicest smile I'd ever gotten from anyone, even my momma. *Oh, yes,* I thought, *oh my goodness, yes.* Henry Lake Spanning was either the most masterfully charismatic person I'd ever met, or so good at the charm con that he could sell a slashed throat to a stranger.

"You can leave him," I said to the great black behemoth brother.

"Can't do that, sir."

"I'll take full responsibility."

"Sorry, sir; I was told someone had to be right here in the room with you and him, all the time."

I looked at the one who had waited with me. "That mean you, too?"

He shook his head. "Just one of us, I guess."

I frowned. "I need absolute privacy. What would happen if I were this man's attorney of record? Wouldn't you have to leave us alone? Privileged communication, right?"

They looked at each other, this pair of Security Officers, and they looked back at me, and they said nothing. All of sudden Mr Plain-as-the-Nose-on-Your-Face had nothing valuable to offer; and the sequoia with biceps "had his orders".

"They tell you who I work for? They tell you who it was sent me here to talk to this man?" Recourse to authority often works. They mumbled yessir yessir a couple of times each, but their faces stayed right on the mark of *sorry, sir, but we're not supposed to leave anybody alone with this man.* It wouldn't have mattered if they'd believed I'd flown in on Jehovah One.

So I said to myself *fuckit* I said to myself, and I slipped into their thoughts, and it didn't take much rearranging to get the phone wires restrung and the underground cables rerouted and the pressure on their bladders something fierce.

"On the other hand . . ." the first one said.

"I suppose we could . . ." the giant said.

And in a matter of maybe a minute and a half one of them was entirely gone, and the great one was standing outside the steel door, his back filling the double-pane chickenwire-imbedded security window. He effectively sealed off the one entrance or exit to or from the conference room; like the three hundred Spartans facing the tens of thousands of Xerxes's army at the Hot Gates.

Henry Lake Spanning stood silently watching me.

"Sit down," I said. "Make yourself comfortable."

He pulled out the chair, came around, and sat down.

"Pull it closer to the table," I said.

He had some difficulty, hands shackled that way, but he grabbed the leading edge of the seat and scraped forward till his stomach was touching the table.

He was a handsome guy, even for a white man. Nice nose, strong cheek-bones, eyes the colour of that water in your toilet when you toss in a tablet of 2000 Flushes. Very nice looking man. He gave me the creeps.

If Dracula had looked like Shirley Temple, no one would've driven a stake through his heart. If Harry Truman had looked like Freddy Krueger, he would never have beaten Tom Dewey at the polls. Joe Stalin and Saddam Hussein looked like sweet, avuncular friends of the family, really nice looking, kindly guys – who just incidentally happened to slaughter millions of men, women, and children. Abe Lincoln looked like an axe murderer, but he had a heart as big as Guatemala.

Henry Lake Spanning had the sort of face you'd trust immediately if you saw it in a TV commercial. Men would like to go fishing with him, women would like to squeeze his buns. Grannies would hug him on sight; kids would follow him straight into the mouth of an open oven. If he could play the piccolo, rats would gavotte around his shoes.

What saps we are. Beauty is only skin deep. You can't judge a book by its cover. Cleanliness is next to godliness. Dress for success. What saps we are.

So what did that make my pal, Allison Roche?

And why the hell didn't I just slip into his thoughts and check out the landscape? Why was I stalling?

Because I was scared of him.

This was fifty-six verified, gruesome, disgusting murders sitting forty-eight inches away from me, looking straight at me with blue eyes and soft, gently blond hair. Neither Harry nor Dewey would've had a prayer.

So why was I scared of him? Because; that's why.

This was damned foolishness. I had all the weaponry, he was shackled, and I didn't for a second believe he was what Ally *thought* he was: innocent. Hell, they'd caught him, literally, redhanded. Bloody to the armpits, fer chrissakes. Innocent, my ass! *Okay, Rudy,* I thought, *get in there and take a look around.* But I didn't. I waited for him to say something.

He smiled tentatively, a gentle and nervous little smile, and he said, "Ally asked me to see you. Thank you for coming."

I looked *at* him, but not *into* him.

He seemed upset that he'd inconvenienced me. "But I don't think you can do me any good, not in just three days."

"You scared, Spanning?"

His lips trembled. "Yes I am, Mr Pairis. I'm about as scared as a man can be." His eyes were moist.

"Probably gives you some insight into how your victims felt, whaddaya think?"

He didn't answer. His eyes were moist.

After a moment just looking at me, he scraped back his chair and stood up. "Thank you for coming, sir. I'm sorry Ally imposed on your time." He turned and started to walk away. I jaunted into his landscape.

Oh my god, I thought. He was innocent.

Never done any of it. None of it. Absolutely no doubt, not a shadow of a doubt. Ally had been right. I saw every bit of that landscape in there, every fold and crease; every bolt hole and rat run; every gully and arroyo; all of his past, back and back and back to his birth in Lewistown, Montana, near Great Falls, thirty-six years ago; every day of his life right up to the minute they arrested him leaning over that disemboweled cleaning woman the real killer had tossed into the dumpster.

I saw every second of his landscape; and I saw him coming out of the Winn-Dixie in Huntsville; pushing a cart filled with grocery bags of food for the weekend. And I saw him wheeling it around the parking lot toward the dumpster area overflowing with broken-down cardboard boxes and fruit crates. And I heard the cry for help from one of those dumpsters; and I saw Henry Lake Spanning stop and look around, not sure he'd heard anything at all. Then I saw him start to go to his car, parked right there at the edge of the lot beside the wall because it was a Friday evening and everyone was stocking up for the weekend, and there weren't any spaces out front; and the cry for help, weaker this time, as pathetic as a crippled kitten; and Henry Lake Spanning stopped cold, and he looked around; and we *both* saw the bloody hand raise itself above the level of the open dumpster's filthy green steel side. And I saw him desert his groceries without a thought to their cost, or that someone might run off with them if he left them unattended, or that he only had eleven dollars left in his checking account, so if those groceries were snagged by someone he wouldn't be eating for the next few days . . . and I watched him rush to the dumpster and look into the crap filling it . . . and I felt his nausea at the sight of that poor old woman, what was left of her . . . and I was with him as he crawled up onto the dumpster and dropped inside to do what he could for that mass of shredded and pulped flesh.

And I cried with him as she gasped, with a bubble of blood that burst in the open ruin of her throat, and she died. But though *I* heard the scream of someone coming around the corner, Spanning did not; and so he was still there, holding the poor mass of stripped skin and black bloody clothing, when the cops screeched into the parking lot. And only *then*, innocent of anything but decency and rare human compassion, did Henry Lake Spanning begin to understand what it must look like to middle-aged *hausfraus*, sneaking around dumpsters to pilfer cardboard boxes, who see what they think is a man murdering an old woman.

I was with him, there in that landscape within his mind, as he ran and ran and dodged and dodged. Until they caught him in Decatur, seven miles from the body of Gunilla Ascher. But they had him, and they had positive identification, from the dumpster in Huntsville; and all the rest of it was circumstantial, gussied up by bedridden, recovering Charlie Whilborg and the staff in Ally's office. It looked good on paper – so good that Ally had brought him down on twenty-nine-*cum*-fifty-six counts of murder in the vilest extreme.

But it was all bullshit.

The killer was still out there.

Henry Lake Spanning, who looked like a nice, decent guy, was exactly that. A nice, decent, goodhearted, but most of all *innocent* guy.

You could fool juries and polygraphs and judges and social workers and psychiatrists and your mommy and your daddy, but you could *not* fool Rudy Pairis, who travels regularly to the place of dark where you can go but not return.

They were going to burn an innocent man in three days.

I had to do something about it.

Not just for Ally, though that was reason enough; but for this man who thought he was doomed, and was frightened, but didn't have to take no shit from a wiseguy like me.

"Mr Spanning," I called after him.

He didn't stop.

"Please," I said. He stopped shuffling, the chains making their little charm bracelet sounds, but he didn't turn around.

"I believe Ally is right, sir," I said. "I believe they caught the wrong man; and I believe all the time you've served is wrong; and I believe you ought not die."

Then he turned slowly, and stared at me with the look of a dog that has been taunted with a bone. His voice was barely a whisper. "And why is that, Mr Pairis? Why is it that you believe me when nobody else but Ally and my attorney believed me?"

I didn't say what I was thinking. What I was thinking was that I'd been *in* there, and I *knew* he was innocent. And more than that, I knew that he truly loved my pal Allison Roche.

And there wasn't much I wouldn't do for Ally.

So what I said was: "I know you're innocent, because I know who's guilty."

His lips parted. It wasn't one of those big moves where someone's mouth flops open in astonishment; it was just a parting of the lips. But he was startled; I knew that as I knew the poor sonofabitch had suffered too long already.

He came shuffling back to me, and sat down.

"Don't make fun, Mr Pairis. Please. I'm what you said, I'm scared. I don't want to die, and I surely don't want to die with the world thinking I did those . . . those things."

"Makin' no fun, captain. I know who ought to burn for all those murders. Not six states, but eleven. Not fifty-six dead, but an even seventy. Three of them little girls in a day nursery, and the woman watching them, too."

He stared at me. There was horror on his face. I know that look real good. I've seen it at least seventy times.

"I know you're innocent, cap'n because *I'm* the man they want. *I'm* the guy who put your ass in here."

*   *   *

In a moment of human weakness. I saw it all. What I had packed off to live in that place of dark where you can go but not return. The wall-safe in my drawing-room. The four-foot-thick walled crypt encased in concrete and sunk a mile deep into solid granite. The vault whose composite laminate walls of judiciously sloped extremely thick blends of steel and plastic, the equivalent of six hundred to seven hundred mm of homogenous depth protection approached the maximum toughness and hardness of crystaliron, that iron grown with perfect crystal structure and carefully controlled quantities of impurities that in a modern combat tank can shrug off a hollow charge warhead like a spaniel shaking himself dry. The Chinese puzzle box. The hidden chamber. The labyrinth. The maze of the mind where I'd sent all seventy to die, over and over and over, so I wouldn't hear their screams, or see the ropes of bloody tendon, or stare into the pulped sockets where their pleading eyes had been.

When I had walked into that prison, I'd been buttoned up totally. I was safe and secure, I knew nothing, remembered nothing, suspected nothing.

But when I walked into Henry Lake Spanning's landscape, and I could not lie to myself that he was the one, I felt the earth crack. I felt the tremors and the upheavals, and the fissures started at my feet and ran to the horizon; and the lava boiled up and began to flow. And the steel walls melted, and the concrete turned to dust, and the barriers dissolved; and I looked at the face of the monster.

No wonder I had such nausea when Ally had told me about this or that slaughter ostensibly perpetrated by Henry Lake Spanning, the man she was prosecuting on twenty-nine counts of murders I had committed. No wonder I could picture all the details when she would talk to me about the barest description of the murder site. No wonder I fought so hard against coming to Holman.

In there, in his mind, his landscape open to me, I saw the love he had for Allison Roche, for my pal and buddy with whom I had once, just once . . .

Don't try tellin' me that the Power of Love can open the fissures. I don't want to hear that shit. I'm telling *you* that it was a combination, a buncha things that split me open, and possibly maybe one of those things was what I saw between them.

I don't know that much. I'm a quick study, but this was in an instant. A crack of fate. A moment of human weakness. That's what I told myself in the part of me that ventured to the place of dark: that I'd done what I'd done in moments of human weakness.

And it was those moments, not my "gift", and not my blackness, that had made me the loser, the monster, the liar that I am.

In the first moment of realization, I couldn't believe it. Not me, not good old Rudy. Not likeable Rudy Pairis never done no one but hisself wrong his whole life.

In the next second I went wild with anger, furious at the disgusting thing that lived on one side of my split brain. Wanted to tear a hole through my face and yank the killing thing out, wet and putrescent, and squeeze it into pulp.

In the next second I was nauseated, actually wanted to fall down and puke, seeing every moment of what I had done, unshaded, unhidden, naked to this Rudy Pairis who was decent and reasonable and law-abiding, even if such a Rudy was little better than a well-educated fuckup. But not a killer . . . I wanted to puke.

Then, finally, I accepted what I could not deny.

For me, never again, would I slide through the night with the scent of the blossoming Yellow Lady's Slipper. I recognized that perfume now.

It was the odour that rises from a human body cut wide open, like a mouth making a big, dark yawn.

The other Rudy Pairis had come home at last.

They didn't have half a minute's worry. I sat down at a little wooden writing table in an interrogation room in the Jefferson County D.A.'s offices, and I made up a graph with the names and dates and locations. Names of as many of the seventy as I actually knew. (A lot of them had just been on the road, or in a men's toilet, or taking a bath, or lounging in the back row of a movie, or getting some cash from an ATM, or just sitting around doing nothing but waiting for me to come along and open them up, and maybe have a drink off them, or maybe just something to snack on . . . down the road.) Dates were easy, because I've got a good memory for dates. And the places where they'd find the ones they didn't know about, the fourteen with exactly the same m.o. as the other fifty-six, not to mention the old-style rip-and-pull can opener I'd used on that little Catholic bead-counter Gunilla Whatsername, who did Hail Mary this and Sweet Blessed Jesus that all the time I was opening her up, even at the last, when I held up parts of her insides for her to look at, and tried to get her to lick them, but she died first. Not half a minute's worry for the State of Alabama. All in one swell foop they corrected a tragic miscarriage of justice, nobbled a maniac killer, solved fourteen more murders than they'd counted on (in five additional states, which made the police departments of those five additional states extremely pleased with the law enforcement agencies of the Sovereign State of Alabama), and made first spot on the evening news on all three major networks, not to mention CNN, for the better part of a week. Knocked the Middle East right out of the box. Neither Harry Truman nor Tom Dewey would've had a prayer.

Ally went into seclusion, of course. Took off and went somewhere down on the Florida coast, I heard. But after the trial, and the verdict, and Spanning being released, and me going inside, and all like that, well, oo-poppadow as they used to say, it was all reordered properly. *Sat cito si sat bene*, in Latin: "It is done quickly enough if it is done well." A favourite saying of Cato. The Elder Cato.

And all I asked, all I begged for, was that Ally and Henry Lake Spanning, who loved each other and deserved each other, and whom I had almost fucked up royally, that the two of them would be there when they jammed my weary black butt into that new electric chair at Holman.

Please come, I begged them.

Don't let me die alone. Not even a shit like me. Don't make me cross over into that place of dark, where you can go, but not return – without the face of a friend. Even a former friend. And as for you, captain, well, hell didn't I save your life so you could enjoy the company of the woman you love? Least you can do. Come on now; be there or be square!

I don't know if Spanning talked her into accepting the invite, or if it was the other way around; but one day about a week prior to the event of cooking up a mess of fried Rudy Pairis, the Warden stopped by my commodious accommodations on Death Row and gave me to understand that it would be SRO for the barbeque, which meant Ally my pal, and her boy friend, the former resident of the Row where now I dwelt in durance vile.

The things a guy'll do for love.

Yeah, that was the key. Why would a very smart operator who had gotten away with it, all the way free and clear, why would such a smart operator suddenly pull one of those hokey courtroom "I did it. I did it!" routines, and as good as strap himself into the electric chair?

Once. I only went to bed with her once.
The things a guy'll do for love.

When they brought me into the death chamber from the holding cell
where I'd spent the night before and all that day, where I'd had my
last meal (which had been a hot roast beef sandwich, double meat,
on white toast, with very crisp french fries, and hot brown country
gravy poured over the whole thing, apple sauce, and a bowl of
Concord grapes), where a representative of the Holy Roman Empire
had tried to make amends for destroying most of the gods, beliefs,
and cultures of my black forebears, they held me between Security
Officers, neither one of whom had been in attendance when I'd
visited Henry Lake Spanning at this very same correctional facility
slightly more than a year before.

It hadn't been a bad year. Lots of rest; caught up on my reading,
finally got around to Proust and Langston Hughes, I'm ashamed to
admit, so late in the game; lost some weight; worked out regularly;
gave up cheese and dropped my cholesterol count. Ain't nothin' to
it, just to do it.

Even took a jaunt or two or ten, every now and awhile. It didn't
matter none. I wasn't going anywhere, neither were they. I'd done
worse than the worst of them; hadn't I confessed to it? So there
wasn't a lot that could ice me, after I'd copped to it and released all
seventy of them out of my unconscious, where they'd been rotting in
shallow graves for years. No big thang, Cuz.

Brought me in, strapped me in, plugged me in.

I looked through the glass at the witnesses.

There sat Ally and Spanning, front row centre. Best seats in the
house. All eyes and crying, watching, not believing everything had
come to this, trying to figure out when and how and in what way it
had all gone down without her knowing anything at all about it. And
Henry Lake Spanning sitting close beside her, their hands locked in
her lap. True love.

I locked eyes with Spanning.

I jaunted into his landscape.

No, I *didn't*.

I *tried* to, and couldn't squirm through. Thirty years, or less, since
I was five or six, I'd been doing it; without hindrance, all alone in the
world the only person who could do this listen in on the landscape
trick; and for the first time I was stopped. Absolutely no fuckin'
entrance. I went wild! I tried running at it full-tilt, and hit something

khaki-coloured, like beach sand, and only slightly giving, not hard, but resilient. Exactly like being inside a ten-foot-high, fifty-foot-diameter paper bag, like a big shopping bag from a supermarket, that stiff butcher's paper kind of bag, and that colour, like being inside a bag that size, running straight at it, thinking you're going to bust through ... and being thrown back. Not hard, not like bouncing on a trampoline, just shunted aside like the fuzz from a dandelion hitting a glass door. Unimportant. Khaki-coloured and not particularly bothered.

I tried hitting it with a bolt of pure blue lightning mental power, like someone out of a Marvel comic, but that wasn't how mixing in other people's minds works. You don't think yourself in with a psychic battering-ram. That's the kind of arrant foolishness you hear spouted by unattractive people on public access cable channels, talking about The Power of Love and The Power of the Mind and the ever-popular toe-tapping Power of a Positive Thought. Bullshit; I don't be home to *that* folly!

I tried picturing myself in there, but that didn't work, either. I tried blanking my mind and drifting across, but it was pointless. And at that moment it occurred to me that I didn't really know *how* I jaunted. I just ... did it. One moment I was snug in the privacy of my own head, and the next I was over there in someone else's landscape. It was instantaneous, like teleportation, which also is an impossibility, like telepathy.

But now, strapped into the chair, and them getting ready to put the leather mask over my face so the witnesses wouldn't have to see the smoke coming out of my eye-sockets and the little sparks as my nose hairs burned, when it was urgent that I get into the thoughts and landscape of Henry Lake Spanning, I was shut out completely. And right *then*, that moment, I was scared!

Presto, without my even opening up to him, there he was: inside my head.

He had jaunted into *my* landscape.

"You had a nice roast beef sandwich, I see."

His voice was a lot stronger than it had been when I'd come down to see him a year ago. A *lot* stronger inside my mind.

"Yes, Rudy, I'm what you knew probably existed somewhere. Another one. A shrike." He paused. "I see you call it 'jaunting in the landscape'. I just called myself a shrike. A butcherbird. One name's as good as another. Strange, isn't it; all these years; and we never met anyone else? There *must* be others, but I think – now I can't prove this, I have no real data, it's just a wild idea I've had for years and years. I think they don't know they can do it."

He stared at me across the landscape, those wonderful blue eyes of his, the ones Ally had fallen in love with, hardly blinking.

"Why didn't you let me know before this?"

He smiled sadly. "Ah, Rudy. Rudy, Rudy, Rudy; you poor benighted pickaninny.

"Because I needed to suck you in, kid. I needed to put out a bear trap, and let it snap closed on your scrawny leg, and send you over. Here, let me clear the atmosphere in here . . ." And he wiped away all the manipulation he had worked on me, way back a year ago, when he had so easily covered his own true thoughts his past, his life, the real panorama of what went on inside his landscape – like bypassing a surveillance camera with a continuous-loop tape that continues to show a placid scene while the joint is being actively burgled – and when he convinced me not only that he was innocent, but that the real killer was someone who had blocked the hideous slaughters from his conscious mind and had lived an otherwise exemplary life. He wandered around my landscape – and all of this in a second or two, because time has no duration in the landscape, like the hours you can spend in a dream that are just thirty seconds long in the real world, just before you wake up – and he swept away all the false memories and suggestions, the logical structure of sequential events that he had planted that would dovetail with my actual existence, my true memories, altered and warped and rearranged so I would believe that I had done all seventy of those ghastly murders . . . so that I'd believe, in a moment of horrible realization, that I was the demented psychopath who had ranged state to state to state, leaving piles of ripped flesh at every stop. Blocked it all, submerged it all, sublimated it all, me. Good old Rudy Pairis, who never killed anybody. I'd been the patsy he was waiting for.

"There, now, kiddo. See what it's really like?

"You didn't do a thing.

"Pure as the driven snow, nigger. That's the truth. And what a find you were. Never even suspected there was another like me, till Ally came to interview me after Decatur. But there you were, big and black as a Great White Hope, right there in her mind. Isn't she fine, Pairis? Isn't she something to take a knife to? Something to split open like a nice piece of fruit warmed in a summer sunshine field, let all the steam rise off her . . . maybe have a picnic . . ."

He stopped.

"I wanted her right from the first moment I saw her.

"Now, you know, I could've done it sloppy, just been a shrike to Ally, that first time she came to the holding cell to interview me; just jump into her, that was my plan. But what a noise that Spanning in the cell would've made, yelling it wasn't a man, it was a woman, not Spanning, but Deputy D.A. Allison Roche . . . too much noise, too many complications. But I *could* have done it, jumped into her. Or a guard, and then slice her at my leisure, stalk her, find her, let her steam . . .

"You look distressed, Mr Rudy Pairis. Why's that? Because you're going to die in my place? Because I could have taken you over at any time, and didn't? Because after all this time of your miserable, wasted, lousy life you finally find someone like you, and we don't even have the convenience of a chat? Well, that's sad, that's really sad, kiddo. But you didn't have a chance."

"You're stronger than me, you kept me out," I said.

He chuckled.

"Stronger? Is that all you think it is? Stronger? You still don't get it, do you?" His face, then, grew terrible. "You don't even understand now, right now that I've cleaned it all away and you can *see* what I did to you, do you?

"Do you think I stayed in a jail cell, and went through that trial, all of that, because I couldn't do anything about it? You poor jig slob. I could have jumped like a shrike any time I wanted to. But the first time I met your Ally I saw *you*."

I cringed. "And you waited . . .? For me, you spent all that time in prison, just to get to me . . .?"

"At the moment when you couldn't do anything about it, at the moment you couldn't shout 'I've been taken over by someone else, I'm Rudy Pairis here inside this Henry Lake Spanning body, help me, help me!' Why stir up noise when all I had to do was bide my time, wait a bit, wait for Ally, and let Ally go for you."

I felt like a drowning turkey, standing idiotically in the rain, head tilted up, mouth open, water pouring in. "You can . . . leave the mind . . . leave the body . . . go out . . . jaunt, jump permanently . . ."

Spanning sniggered like a schoolyard bully.

"You stayed in jail three years just to get *me?*"

He smirked. Smarter than thou.

"Three years? You think that's some big deal to me? You don't think I could have someone like you running around, do you? Someone who can 'jaunt' as I do? The only other shrike I've ever encountered. You think I wouldn't sit in here and wait for you to come to me?"

"But three *years* . . ."

"You're what, Rudy . . . thirty-one, is it? Yes, I can see that. Thirty-one. You've never jumped like a shrike. You've just entered, jaunted, gone into the landscapes, and never understood that it's more than reading minds. You can change domiciles, black boy. You can move out of a house in a bad neighbourhood – such as strapped into the electric chair – and take up residence in a brand, spanking, new housing complex of million-and-a-half-buck condos, like Ally."

"But you have to have a place for the other one to go, don't you?" I said it just flat, no tone, no colour to it at all. I didn't even think of the place of dark, where you can go . . .

"Who do you think I am, Rudy? Just who the hell do you think I was when I started, when I learned to shrike, how to jaunt, what I'm telling you now about changing residences? You wouldn't know my first address. I go a long way back.

"But I can give you a few of my more famous addresses. Gilles de Rais, France, 1440; Vlad Tepes, Romania, 1462; Elizabeth Bathory, Hungary, 1611; Catherine DeShayes, France, 1680; Jack the Ripper, London, 1888; Henri Désiré Landru, France, 1915; Albert Fish, New York City, 1934; Ed Gein, Plainfield, Wisconsin, 1954; Myra Hindley, Manchester, 1963; Albert DeSalvo, Boston, 1964; Charles Manson, Los Angeles, 1969; John Wayne Gacy, Norwood Park Township, Illinois, 1977.

"Oh, but how I do go on. And on. And on and on and on, Rudy, my little porch monkey. That's what I do. I go on. And on and on. Shrike will nest where it chooses. If not in your beloved Allison Roche, then in the cheesy fucked-up black boy, Rudy Pairis. But don't you think that's a waste, kiddo? Spending however much time I might have to spend in your socially unacceptable body, when Henry Lake Spanning is such a handsome devil? Why should I have just switched with you when Ally lured you to me, because all it would've done is get you screeching and howling that you weren't Spanning, you were this nigger son who'd had his head stolen . . . and then you might have manipulated some guards or the Warden . . .

"Well, you see what I mean, don't you?

"But now that the mask is securely in place, and now that the electrodes are attached to your head and your left leg, and now that the Warden has his hand on the switch, well, you'd better get ready to do a lot of drooling."

And he turned around to jaunt back out of me, and I closed the perimeter. He tried to jaunt, tried to leap back to his own mind, but I had him in a fist. Just that easy. Materialized a fist, and turned him to face me.

"Fuck you, Jack the Ripper. And fuck you twice, Bluebeard. And on and on and on fuck you Manson and Boston Strangler and any other dipshit warped piece of sick crap you been in your years. You sure got some muddy-shoes credentials there, boy.

"What I care about all those names, Spanky my brother? You really think I don't know those names? I'm an educated fellah, Mistuh Rippuh, Mistuh Mad Bomber. You missed a few. Were you also, did you inhabit, hast thou possessed Winnie Ruth Judd and Charlie Starkweather and Mad Dog Coll and Richard Speck and Sirhan Sirhan and Jeffrey Dahmer? You the boogieman responsible for *every* bad number the human race ever played? You ruin Sodom and Gomorrah, burned the Great Library of Alexandria, orchestrated the Reign of Terror *dans Paree*, set up the Inquisition, stoned and drowned the Salem witches, slaughtered unarmed women and kids at Wounded Knee, bumped off John Kennedy?

"I don't think so.

"I don't even think you got so close as to share a pint with Jack the Ripper. And even if you did, even if you *were* all those maniacs, you were small potatoes, Spanky. The least of us human beings outdoes you, three times a day. How many lynch ropes you pulled tight, M'sieur Landru?

"What colossal egotism you got, makes you blind, makes you think you're the only one, even when you find out there's someone else, you can't get past it. What makes you think I didn't know what you can do? What makes you think I didn't let you do it, and sit here waiting for you like you sat there waiting for me, till this moment when you can't do shit about it?

"You so goddam stuck on yourself, Spankyhead, you never give it the barest that someone else is a faster draw than you.

"Know what your trouble is, Captain? You're old, you're *real* old, maybe hundreds of years who gives a damn old. That don't count for shit, old man. You're old, but you never got smart. You're just mediocre at what you do.

"You moved from address to address. You didn't have to be Son of Sam or Cain slayin' Abel, or whoever the fuck you been ... you could've been Moses or Galileo or George Washington Carver or Harriet Tubman or Sojourner Truth or Mark Twain or Joe Louis. You could've been Alexander Hamilton and helped found the Manumission Society in New York. You could've discovered radium, carved Mount Rushmore, carried a baby out of a burning building. But you got old real fast, and you never got any smarter. You didn't need to, did you, Spanky? You had it all to yourself, all this 'shrike' shit, just jaunt here and jaunt there, and bite off someone's hand or face like the old, tired, boring, repetitious, no-imagination stupid shit that you are.

"Yeah, you got me good when I came here to see your landscape. You got Ally wired up good. And she suckered me in, probably not even knowing she was doing it . . . you must've looked in her head and found just the right technique to get her to make me come within reach. Good, m'man; you were excellent. But I had a year to torture myself. A year to sit here and think about it. About how many people I'd killed, and how sick it made me, and little by little I found my way through it.

"Because . . . and here's the big difference 'tween us, dummy:

"I unravelled what was going on . . . it took time, but I learned. Understand, asshole? *I* learn! *You* don't.

"There's an old Japanese saying – I got lots of these, Henry m'man – I read a whole lot – and what it says is, 'Do not fall into the error of the artisan who boasts of twenty years experience in his craft while in fact he has had only one year of experience – twenty times'." Then I grinned back at him.

"Fuck you, sucker," I said, just as the Warden threw the switch and I jaunted out of there and into the landscape and mind of Henry Lake Spanning.

I sat there getting oriented for a second; it was the first time I'd done more than a jaunt . . . this was . . . *shrike*; but then Ally beside me gave a little sob for her old pal, Rudy Pairis, who was baking like a Maine lobster, smoke coming out from under the black cloth that covered my, his, face; and I heard the vestigial scream of what had been Henry Lake Spanning and thousands of other monsters, all of them burning, out there on the far horizon of my new landscape; and I put my arm around her, and drew her close, and put my face into her shoulder and hugged her to me; and I heard the scream go on and on for the longest time, I think it was a long time, and finally it was just wind . . . and then gone . . . and I came up from Ally's shoulder, and I could barely speak.

"Shhh, honey, it's okay," I murmured. "He's gone where he can make right for his mistakes. No pain. Quiet, a real quiet place; and all alone forever. And cool there. And dark."

I was ready to stop failing at everything, and blaming everything. Having fessed up to love, having decided it was time to grow up and be an adult – not just a very quick study who learned fast, extremely fast, a lot faster than anybody could imagine an orphan like me could learn, than *any*body could imagine – I hugged her with the intention that Henry Lake Spanning would love Allison Roche more powerfully, more responsibly, than anyone had ever loved anyone in the history of the world. I was ready to stop failing at everything.

And it would be just a whole lot easier as a white boy with great big blue eyes.

Because – get on this now – all my wasted years didn't have as much to do with blackness or racism or being overqualified or being unlucky or being high-verbal or even the curse of my "gift" of jaunting, as they did with one single truth I learned waiting in there, inside my own landscape, waiting for Spanning to come and gloat:

I have always been one of those miserable guys who *couldn't get out of his own way.*

Which meant I could, at last, stop feeling sorry for that poor nigger, Rudy Pairis. Except, maybe, in a moment of human weakness.

This story, for Bob Bloch, because I promised.

1994

HORROR

THE YEAR'S BEST HORROR
STORIES BY SUCH MASTERS
OF DARK FANTASY AS

ROBERT BLOCH
RAMSEY CAMPBELL
HARLAN ELLISON
CHARLES GRANT
KIM NEWMAN
KARL EDWARD WAGNER
and many others

EDITED BY
STEPHEN JONES

"Captures best the range and
breadth of the horror genre"
— *LOCUS*

The Temptation of Dr Stein

Paul J. McAuley

AS A TRIBUTE TO RAMSEY'S inestimable contribution to the series, for the 1994 edition I asked Luis Rey to add a little joke into his atmospheric cover painting.

At a launch party (those were the days!) for the book at the annual British Fantasy Convention, the publisher recreated the cover as, literally, the icing on the cake.

The sixth edition of *The Best New Horror* won the International Horror Guild Award and was the first of two volumes to appear under the Raven Books imprint in the UK. This was a new genre list that I launched and edited for Robinson for a couple of years, until I was reluctantly forced to come to the conclusion that it was not worth all the hard work.

For my first volume as solo editor, the Introduction grew to thirty-one pages and the Necrology was now up to eighteen. In my editorial I warned against the law of diminishing returns as the genre was swamped with " . . . sequels, inferior copies, share-cropped worlds, media novelizations and role-playing tie-ins, most of them written and published with little or no thought given to their intrinsic value of lasting worth."

It was advice that the authors and publishers of many so-called "paranormal romances" would do well to heed today . . .

The twenty-two contributions included the welcome return of Ellison and Lamsley, along with such "regulars" as Charles L. Grant, Joel Lane, Ramsey Campbell, Nicholas Royle, Michael Marshall Smith and Kim Newman (with a marvellous contemporary re imagining of the Zorro mythology that was nominated for a World Fantasy Award).

Esther M. Friesner contributed the only verse we have run in the series so far, but this sixth compilation was also touched with personal sadness.

Also in this edition were stories by two old friends – Karl Edward Wagner's hallucinatory "In the Middle of a Snow Dream" and Robert Bloch's Bram Stoker Award-winning "The Scent of Vinegar". Both authors had died within a month of each other the previous year, and the book was dedicated to their memory.

Paul J. McAuley is another old friend and also one of the UK's most respected science fiction writers. His British Fantasy Award-winning "The Temptation of Dr Stein" may have been set in the same alternate history as his novel *Pasquale's Angel*, but it involved a certain mad scientist memorably portrayed by eccentric English actor Ernest Thesiger in James Whale's classic movie *Bride of Frankenstein*.

In fact, Paul returned to the character with "The True History of Doctor Pretorius", which I selected for the following year's *Best New Horror*, and "Dr Pretorius and the Lost Temple", which appeared in Volume Fourteen.

DR STEIN PRIDED HIMSELF on being a rational man. When, in the months following his arrival in Venice, it became his habit to spend his free time wandering the city, he could not admit that it was because he believed that his daughter might still live, and that he might see her amongst the cosmopolitan throng. For he harboured the small, secret hope that when *Landsknechts* had pillaged the houses of the Jews of Lodz, perhaps his daughter had not been carried off to be despoiled and murdered, but had instead been forced to become a servant of some Prussian family. It was no more impossible that she had been brought here, for the Council of Ten had hired many *Landsknechts* to defend the city and the *terraferma* hinterlands of its empire.

Dr Stein's wife would no longer talk to him about it. Indeed, they hardly talked about anything these days. She had pleaded that the memory of their daughter should be laid to rest in a week of mourning, just as if they had interred her body. They were living in rooms rented from a cousin of Dr Stein's wife, a banker called Abraham Soncino, and Dr Stein was convinced that she had been put up to this by the women of Soncino's family. Who knew what the women talked about when locked in the bathhouse overnight, while they were being purified of their menses? No good, Dr Stein was certain. Even Soncino, a genial, uxorious man, had urged that Dr

Stein mourn his daughter. Soncino had said that his family would bring the requisite food to begin the mourning, after a week all the community would commiserate with Dr Stein and his wife before the main Sabbath service, and with God's help this terrible wound would be healed. It had taken all of Dr Stein's powers to refuse this generous offer courteously. Soncino was a good man, but this was none of his business.

As winter came on, driven out by his wife's silent recriminations, or so he told himself, Dr Stein walked the crowded streets almost every afternoon. Sometimes he was accompanied by an English captain of the Night Guard, Henry Gorrall, to whom Dr Stein had become an unofficial assistant, helping identify the cause of death of one or another of the bodies found floating in the backwaters of the city.

There had been more murders than usual that summer, and several well-bred young women had disappeared. Dr Stein had been urged to help Gorrall by the Elders of the *Beth Din*; already there were rumours that the Jews were murdering Christian virgins and using their blood to animate a Golem. It was good that a Jew – moreover, a Jew who worked at the city hospital, and taught new surgical techniques at the school of medicine – was involved in attempting to solve this mystery.

Besides, Dr Stein enjoyed Gorrall's company. He was sympathetic to Gorrall's belief that everything, no matter how unlikely, had at base a rational explanation. Gorrall was a humanist, and did not mind being seen in the company of a man who must wear a yellow star on his coat. On their walks through the city, they often talked on the new philosophies of nature compounded in the University of Florence's Great Engineer, Leonardo da Vinci, quite oblivious to the brawling bustle all around them.

Ships from twenty nations crowded the quay in the long shadow of the Campanile, and their sailors washed through the streets. Hawkers cried their wares from flotillas of small boats that rocked on the wakes of barges or galleys. Gondoliers shouted vivid curses as skiffs crossing from one side of the Grand Canal to the other got in the way of their long, swift craft. Sometimes a screw-driven Florentine ship made its way up the Grand Canal, its Hero's engine laying a trail of black smoke, and everyone stopped to watch this marvel. Bankers in fur coats and tall felt hats conducted the business of the world in the piazza before San Giacometto, amid the rattle of the new clockwork abacuses and the subdued murmur of transactions.

Gorrall, a bluff muscular man with a bristling black beard and a habit of spitting sideways and often, because of the plug of tobacco he habitually chewed, seemed to know most of the bankers by name, and the most of the merchants, too – the silk and cloth-of-gold mercers and sellers of fustian and velvet along the Mercerie, the druggists, goldsmiths and silversmiths, the makers of white wax, the ironmongers, coopers and perfumers who had stalls and shops in the crowded little streets off the Rialto. He knew the names of many of the yellow-scarved prostitutes, too, although Dr Stein wasn't surprised at this, since he had first met Gorrall when the captain had come to the hospital for mercury treatment of his syphilis. Gorrall even knew, or pretended to know, the names of the cats that stalked between the feet of the crowds or lazed on cold stone in the brittle winter sunshine, the true rulers of Venice.

It was outside the cabinet of one of the perfumers of the Mercerie that Dr Stein for a moment thought he saw his daughter. A grey-haired man was standing in the doorway of the shop, shouting at a younger man who was backing away and protesting that there was no blame that could be fixed to his name.

"You are his friend!"

"Sir, I did not know what it was he wrote, and I do not know and I do not care why your daughter cries so!"

The young man had his hand on his long knife, and Gorrall pushed through the gathering crowd and told both men to calm down. The wronged father dashed inside and came out again, dragging a girl of about fourteen, with the same long black hair, the same white, high forehead, as Dr Stein's daughter.

"Hannah," Dr Stein said helplessly, but then she turned, and it was not her. Not his daughter. The girl was crying, and clasped a sheet of paper to her bosom – wronged by a suitor, Dr Stein supposed, and Gorrall said that it was precisely that. The young man had run off to sea, something so common these days that the Council of Ten had decreed that convicted criminals might be used on the galleys of the navy because of the shortage of free oarsmen. Soon the whole city might be scattered between Corfu and Crete, or even further, now that Florence had destroyed the fleet of Cortés, and opened the American shore.

Dr Stein did not tell his wife what he had seen. He sat in the kitchen long into the evening, and was still there, warmed by the embers of the fire and reading in Leonardo's *Treatise on the Replication of*

Motion by the poor light of a tallow candle, when the knock at the door came. It was just after midnight. Dr Stein picked up the candle and went out, and saw his wife standing in the door to the bedroom.

"Don't answer it," she said. With one hand she clutched her shift to her throat; with the other she held a candle. Her long black hair, streaked with grey, was down to her shoulders.

"This isn't Lodz, Belita," Dr Stein said, perhaps with unnecessary sharpness. "Go back to bed. I will deal with this."

"There are plenty of Prussians here, even so. One spat at me the other day. Abraham says that they blame us for the body-snatching, and it's the doctors they'll come for first."

The knocking started again. Husband and wife both looked at the door. "It may be a patient," Dr Stein said, and pulled back the bolts.

The rooms were on the ground floor of a rambling house that faced onto a narrow canal. An icy wind was blowing along the canal, and it blew out Dr Stein's candle when he opened the heavy door. Two city guards stood there, flanking their captain, Henry Gorrall.

"There's been a body found," Gorrall said in his blunt, direct manner. "A woman we both saw this very day, as it happens. You'll come along and tell me if it's murder."

The woman's body had been found floating in the Rio di Noale. "An hour later," Gorrall said, as they were rowed through the dark city, "and the tide would have turned and taken her out to sea, and neither you or I would have to chill our bones."

It was a cold night indeed, just after St Agnes' Eve. An insistent wind off the land blew a dusting of snow above the roofs and prickly spires of Venice. Fresh ice crackled as the gondola broke through it, and larger pieces knocked against its planking. The few lights showing in the facades of the *palazzi* that lined the Grand Canal seemed bleary and dim. Dr Stein wrapped his ragged loden cloak around himself and asked, "Do you think it murder?"

Gorrall spat into the black, icy water. "She died for love. That part is easy, as we witnessed the quarrel this very afternoon. She wasn't in the water long, and still reeks of booze. Drank to get her courage up, jumped. But we have to be sure. It could be a bungled kidnapping, or some cruel sport gone from bad to worse. There are too many soldiers with nothing to do but patrol the defences and wait for a posting in Cyprus."

The drowned girl had been laid out on the pavement by the canal, and covered with a blanket. Even at this late hour, a small crowd had gathered, and when a guard twitched the blanket aside at Dr Stein's request, some of the watchers gasped.

It was the girl he had seen that afternoon, the perfumer's daughter. The soaked dress which clung to her body was white against the wet flags of the pavement. Her long black hair twisted in ropes about her face. There was a little froth at her mouth, and blue touched her lips. Dead, there was nothing about her that reminded Dr Stein of his daughter.

Dr Stein manipulated the skin over the bones of her hand, pressed one of her fingernails, closed her eyelids with thumb and forefinger. Tenderly, he covered her with the blanket again. "She's been dead less than an hour," he told Gorrall. "There's no sign of a struggle, and from the flux at her mouth I'd say it's clear she drowned."

"Killed herself most likely, unless someone pushed her in. The usual reason, I'd guess, which is why her boyfriend ran off to sea. Care to make a wager?"

"We both know her story. I can find out if she was with child, but not here."

Gorrall smiled. "I forget that you people don't bet."

"On the contrary. But in this case I fear you're right."

Gorrall ordered his men to take the body to the city hospital. As they lifted it into the gondola, he said to Dr Stein, "She drank to get courage, then gave herself to the water, but not in this little canal. Suicides favour places where their last sight is a view, often of a place they love. We'll search the bridge at the Rialto – it is the only bridge crossing the Grand Canal, and the tide is running from that direction – but all the world crosses there, and if we're not quick, some beggar will have carried away her bottle and any note she may have left. Come on, doctor. We need to find out how she died before her parents turn up and start asking questions. I must have something to tell them, or they will go out looking for revenge."

If the girl had jumped from the Rialto bridge, she had left no note there – or it had been stolen, as Gorrall had predicted. Gorrall and Dr Stein hurried on to the city hospital, but the body had not arrived. Nor did it. An hour later, a patrol found the gondola tied up in a backwater. One guard was dead from a single sword-cut to his neck. The other was stunned, and remembered nothing. The drowned girl was gone.

Gorrall was furious, and sent out every man he had to look for the body-snatchers. They had balls to attack two guards of the night watch, he said, but when he had finished with them they'd sing falsetto under the lash on the galleys. Nothing came of his enquiries. The weather turned colder, and an outbreak of pleurisy meant that Dr Stein had much work in the hospital. He thought no more about it until a week later, when Gorrall came to see him.

"She's alive," Gorrall said. "I've seen her."

"A girl like her, perhaps." For a moment, Dr Stein saw his daughter, running towards him, arms widespread. He said, "I don't make mistakes. There was no pulse, her lungs were congested with fluid, and she was as cold as the stones on which she lay."

Gorrall spat. "She's walking around dead, then. Do you remember what she looked like?"

"Vividly."

"She was the daughter of a perfumer, one Filippo Rompiasi. A member of the Great Council, although of the 2,500 who have that honour, I'd say he has about the least influence. A noble family so long fallen on hard times that they have had to learn a trade."

Gorrall had little time for the numerous aristocracy of Venice, who, in his opinion, spent more time scheming to obtain support from the Republic than playing their part in governing it.

"Still," he said, scratching at his beard and looking sidelong at Dr Stein, "it'll look very bad that the daughter of a patrician family walks around after having been pronounced dead by the doctor in charge of her case."

"I don't recall being paid," Dr Stein said.

Gorrall spat again. "Would I pay someone who can't tell the quick from the dead? Come and prove me wrong and I'll pay you from my own pocket. With a distinguished surgeon as witness, I can draw up a docket to end this matter."

The girl was under the spell of a mountebank who called himself Dr Pretorious, although Gorrall was certain that it wasn't the man's real name. "He was thrown out of Padua last year for practising medicine without a licence, and was in jail in Milan before that. I've had my eye on him since he came ashore on a Prussian coal barge this summer. He vanished a month ago, and I thought he'd become some other city's problem. Instead, he went to ground. Now he proclaims this girl to be a miraculous example of a new kind of treatment."

There were many mountebanks in Venice. Every morning and afternoon there were five or six stages erected in the Piazza San Marco for their performances and convoluted orations, in which they praised the virtues of their peculiar instruments, powders, elixirs and other concoctions. Venice tolerated these madmen, in Dr Stein's opinion, because the miasma of the nearby marshes befuddled the minds of her citizens, who besides were the most vain people he had ever met, eager to believe any promise of enhanced beauty and longer life.

Unlike the other mountebanks, Dr Pretorious was holding a secret court. He had rented a disused wine store at the edge of the Prussian *Fondaco*, a quarter of Venice where ships were packed tightly in the narrow canals and every other building was a merchant's warehouse. Even walking beside a captain of the city guard, Dr Stein was deeply uneasy there, feeling that all eyes were drawn to the yellow star he must by law wear, pinned to the breast of his surcoat. There had been an attack on the synagogue just the other day, and pigshit had been smeared on the mezuzah fixed to the doorpost of a prominent Jewish banker. Sooner or later, if the body-snatchers were not caught, a mob would sack the houses of the wealthiest Jews on the excuse of searching out and destroying the fabled Golem which existed nowhere but in their inflamed imaginations.

Along with some fifty others, mostly rich old women and their servants, Gorrall and Dr Stein crossed a high arched bridge over a dark, silently running canal, and, after paying a ruffian a *soldo* each for the privilege, entered through a gate into a courtyard lit by smoky torches. Once the ruffian had closed and locked the gate, two figures appeared at a tall open door that was framed with swags of red cloth.

One was a man dressed all in black, with a mop of white hair. Behind him a woman in white lay half-submerged in a kind of tub packed full of broken ice. Her head was bowed, and her face hidden by a fall of black hair. Gorrall nudged Dr Stein and said that this was the girl.

"She looks dead to me. Anyone who could sit in a tub of ice and not burst to bits through shivering must be dead."

"Let's watch and see," Gorrall said, and lit a foul-smelling cigarillo.

The white-haired man, Dr Pretorious, welcomed his audience, and began a long rambling speech. Dr Stein paid only a little attention, being more interested in the speaker. Dr Pretorious was a gaunt, bird-like man with a clever, lined face and dark eyes under shaggy brows which knitted together when he made a point. He had a habit of stabbing a finger at his audience, of shrugging and laughing immodestly at his own boasts. He did not, Dr Stein was convinced, much believe his speech, a curious failing for a mountebank.

Dr Pretorious had the honour, it appeared, of introducing the true Bride of the Sea, one recently dead but now animated by an ancient Egyptian science. There was much on the long quest he had made in search of the secret of this ancient science, and the dangers he had faced in bringing it here, and in perfecting it. He assured his audience that as it had conquered death, the science he had perfected would also conquer old age, for was that not the slow victory of death over life? He snapped his fingers, and, as the tub seemed to slide forward of its own accord into the torchlight, invited his audience to see for themselves that this Bride of the Sea was not alive.

Strands of kelp had been woven into the drowned girl's thick black hair. Necklaces layered at her breast were of seashells of the kind that anyone could pick from the beach at the mouth of the lagoon.

Dr Pretorious pointed to Dr Stein, called him out. "I see we have here a physician. I recognize you, sir. I know the good work that you do at the Pietà, and the wonderful new surgical techniques you have brought to the city. As a man of science, would you do me the honour of certifying that this poor girl is at present not living?"

"Go on," Gorrall said, and Dr Stein stepped forward, feeling both foolish and eager.

"Please, your opinion," Dr Pretorious said with an ingratiating bow. He added, *sotto voce*, "This is a true marvel, doctor. Believe in me." He held a little mirror before the girl's red lips, and asked Dr Stein if he saw any evidence of breath.

Dr Stein was aware of an intense sweet, cloying odour: a mixture of brandy and attar of roses. He said, "I see none."

"Louder, for the good people here."

Dr Stein repeated his answer.

"A good answer. Now, hold her wrist. Does her heart beat?"

The girl's hand was as cold as the ice from which Dr Pretorious lifted it. If there was a pulse, it was so slow and faint that Dr Stein was not allowed enough time to find it. He was dismissed, and Dr Pretorious held up the girl's arm by the wrist and, with a grimace of effort, pushed a long nail though her hand.

"You see," he said with indecent excitement, giving the wrist a little shake so that the pierced hand flopped to and fro. "You see! No blood! No blood! Eh? What living person could endure such a cruel mutilation?"

He seemed excited by his demonstration. He dashed inside the doorway, and brought forward a curious device, a glass bowl inverted on a stalk of glass almost as tall as he, with a band of red silk twisted inside the bowl and around a spindle at the bottom of the stalk. He began to work a treadle, and the band of silk spun around and around.

"A moment," Dr Pretorious said, as the crowd began to murmur. He glared at them from beneath his shaggy eyebrows as his foot pumped the treadle. "A moment, if you please. The apparatus must receive a sufficient charge."

He sounded flustered and out of breath. Any mountebank worth his salt would have had a naked boy painted in gilt and adorned with cherub wings to work the treadle, Dr Stein reflected, and a drum roll besides. Yet the curious amateurism of this performance was more compelling than the polished theatricality of the mountebanks of the Piazza San Marco.

Gold threads trailed from the top of the glass bowl to a big glass jar half-filled with water and sealed with a cork. At last, Dr Pretorious finished working the treadle, sketched a bow to the audience – his face shiny with sweat – and used a stave to sweep the gold threads from the top of the glass bowl onto the girl's face.

There was a faint snap, as of an old glass broken underfoot at a wedding. The girl's eyes opened and she looked about her, seeming dazed and confused.

"She lives, but only for a few precious minutes," Dr Pretorious said. "Speak to me, my darling. You are a willing bride to the sea, perhaps?"

Gorrall whispered to Dr Stein, "That's definitely the girl who drowned herself?" and Dr Stein nodded. Gorrall drew out a long silver whistle and blew on it, three quick blasts. At once, a full squad of men-at-arms swarmed over the high walls. Some of the old women in the audience started to scream. The ruffian in charge of the gate charged at Gorrall, who drew a repeating pistol with a notched wheel over its stock. He shot three times, the wheel ratcheting around as it delivered fresh charges of powder and shot to the chamber. The ruffian was thrown onto his back, already dead as the noise of the shots echoed in the courtyard. Gorrall turned and levelled the pistol at the red-cloaked doorway, but it was on fire, and Dr Pretorious and the dead girl in her tub of ice were gone.

Gorrall and his troops put out the fire and ransacked the empty wine store. It was Dr Stein who found the only clue, a single broken seashell by a hatch that, when lifted, showed black water a few *braccia* below, a passage that Gorrall soon determined led out into the canal.

*   *   *

Dr Stein could not forget the dead girl, the icy touch of her skin, her sudden start into life, the confusion in her eyes. Gorrall thought that she only seemed alive, that her body had been preserved perhaps by tanning, that the shine in her eyes was glycerine, the bloom on her lips pigment of the kind the apothecaries made of powdered beetles.

"The audience wanted to believe it would see a living woman, and the flickering candles would make her seem to move. You'll be a witness, I hope."

"I touched her," Dr Stein said. "She was not preserved. The process hardens the skin."

"We keep meat by packing it in snow, in winter," Gorrall said. "Also, I have heard that there are magicians in the far Indies who can fall into so deep a trance that they do not need to breathe."

"We know she is not from the Indies. I would ask why so much fuss was made of the apparatus. It was so clumsy that it seemed to me to be real."

"I'll find him," Gorrall said, "and we will have answers to all these questions."

But when Dr Stein saw Gorrall two days later, and asked about his enquiries into the Pretorious affair, the English captain shook his head and said, "I have been told not to pursue the matter. It seems the girl's father wrote too many begging letters to the Great Council, and he has no friends there. Further than that, I'm not allowed to say." Gorrall spat and said with sudden bitterness, "You can work here twenty-five years, Stein, and perhaps they'll make you a citizen, but they will never make you privy to their secrets."

"Someone in power believes Dr Pretorious's claims, then."

"I wish I could say. Do you believe him?"

"Of course not."

But it was not true, and Dr Stein immediately made his own enquiries. He wanted to know the truth, and not, he told himself, because he had mistaken the girl for his daughter. His interest was that of a doctor, for if death could be reversed, then surely that was the greatest gift a doctor could possess. He was not thinking of his daughter at all.

His enquiries were first made amongst his colleagues at the city hospital, and then in the guild hospitals and the new hospital of the Arsenal. Only the director of the last was willing to say anything, and warned Dr Stein that the man he was seeking had powerful allies.

"So I have heard," Dr Stein said. He added recklessly, "I wish I knew who they were."

The director was a pompous man, placed in his position through politics rather than merit. Dr Stein could see that he was tempted to divulge what he knew, but in the end he merely said, "Knowledge is a dangerous thing. If you would know anything, start from a low rather than a high place. Don't overreach yourself, doctor."

Dr Stein bridled at this, but said nothing. He sat up through the night, thinking the matter over. This was a city of secrets, and he was a stranger, and a Jew from Prussia to boot. His actions could easily be mistaken for those of a spy, and he was not sure that Gorrall could help him if he was accused. Gorrall's precipitate attempt to arrest Dr Pretorious had not endeared him to his superiors, after all.

Yet Dr Stein could not get the drowned girl's face from his mind, the way she had given a little start and her eyes had opened under the tangle of gold threads. Tormented by fantasies in which he found his daughter's grave and raised her up, he paced the kitchen, and in the small hours of the night it came to him that the director of the Arsenal hospital had spoken the truth even if he had not known it.

In the morning, Dr Stein set out again, saying nothing to his wife of what he was doing. He had realized that Dr Pretorious must need simples and other necessaries for his trade, and now he went from apothecary to apothecary with the mountebank's description. Dr Stein found his man late in the afternoon, in a mean little shop in a *calle* that led off a square dominated by the brightly painted facade of the new church of Santa Maria de Miracoli.

The apothecary was a young man with a handsome face but small, greedy eyes. He peered at Dr Stein from beneath a fringe of greasy black hair, and denied knowing Dr Pretorious with such vehemence that Dr Stein did not doubt he was lying.

A *soldo* soon loosened his tongue. He admitted that he might have such a customer as Dr Stein described, and Dr Stein asked at once, "Does he buy alum and oil?"

The apothecary expressed surprise. "He is a physician, not a tanner."

"Of course," Dr Stein said, hope rising in him. A second *soldo* bought Dr Stein the privilege of delivering the mountebank's latest order, a jar of sulphuric acid nested in a straw cradle.

The directions given by the apothecary led Dr Stein through an intricate maze of *calli* and squares, ending in a courtyard no bigger than a closet, with tall buildings soaring on either side, and no way out but the narrow passage by which he had entered. Dr Stein knew he was lost, but before he could turn to begin to retrace his steps, someone seized him from behind. An arm clamped across his throat. He struggled and dropped the jar of acid, which by great good luck, and the straw padding, did not break. Then he was on his back, looking up at a patch of grey sky which seemed to rush away from him at great speed, dwindling to a speck no bigger than a star.

Dr Stein was woken by the solemn tolling of the curfew bells. He was lying on a mouldering bed in a room muffled by dusty tapestries and lit by a tall tallow candle. His throat hurt and his head ached. There was a tender swelling above his right ear, but he had no double vision or dizziness. Whoever had hit him had known what they were about.

The door was locked, and the windows were closed by wooden shutters nailed tightly shut. Dr Stein was prying at the shutters when the door was unlocked and an old man came in. He was a shrivelled gnome in a velvet tunic and doublet more suited to a young gallant. His creviced face was drenched with powder, and there were hectic spots of rouge on his sunken cheeks.

"My master will talk with you," this ridiculous creature said.

Dr Stein asked where he was, and the old man said that it was his master's house. "Once it was mine, but I gave it to him. It was his fee."

"Ah. You were sick, and he cured you."

"I was cured of life. He killed me and brought me back, so that I will live forever in the life beyond death. He's a great man."

"What's your name?"

The old man laughed. He had only one tooth in his head, and that a blackened stump. "I've yet to be christened in this new life. Come with me."

Dr Stein followed the old man up a wide marble stair that wound through the middle of what must be a great *palazzo*. Two stories below was a floor tiled black and white like a chessboard; they climbed past two more floors to the top.

The long room had once been a library, but the shelves of the dark bays set off the main passage were empty now; only the chains which had secured the books were left. It was lit by a scattering of candles whose restless flames cast a confusion of flickering light that hid more than it revealed. One bay was penned off with a hurdle, and a pig moved in the shadows there. Dr Stein had enough of a glimpse of it to see that there was something on the pig's back, but it was too dark to be sure quite what it was. Then something the size of a mouse scuttled straight in front of him – Dr Stein saw with a shock that it ran on its hind legs, with a stumbling, crooked gait.

"One of my children," Dr Pretorious said.

He was seated at a plain table scattered with books and papers. Bits of glassware and jars of acids and salts cluttered the shelves that rose behind him. The drowned girl sat beside him in a high-backed chair. Her head was held up by a leather band around her forehead; her eyes were closed and seemed bruised and sunken. Behind the chair was the same apparatus that Dr Stein had seen used in the wine store. The smell of attar of roses was very strong.

Dr Stein said, "It was only a mouse, or a small rat."

"You believe what you must, doctor," Dr Pretorious said, "but I hope to open your eyes to the wonders I have performed." He told the old man, "Fetch food."

The old man started to complain that he wanted to stay, and Dr Pretorious immediately jumped up in a sudden fit of anger and threw a pot of ink at his servant. The old man sputtered, smearing the black ink across his powdered face, and at once Dr Pretorious burst into laughter. "You're a poor book," he said. "Fetch our guest meat and wine. It's the least I can do," he told Dr Stein. "Did you come here of your own will, by the way?"

"I suppose the apothecary told you that I asked for you. That is, if he was an apothecary."

Dr Pretorious said, with a quick smile, "You wanted to see the girl, I suppose, and here she is. I saw the tender look you gave her, before we were interrupted, and see that same look again."

"I knew nothing of my colleague's plans."

Dr Pretorious made a steeple with his hands, touched the tip of the steeple to his bloodless lips. His fingers were long and white, and seemed to have an extra joint in them. He said, "Don't hope he'll find you."

"I'm not afraid. You brought me here because you wanted me here."

"But you should be afraid. I have power of life and death here."

"The old man said you gave him life everlasting."

Dr Pretorious said carelessly, "Oh, so he believes. Perhaps that's enough."

"Did he die? Did you bring him back to life?"

Dr Pretorious said, "That depends what you mean by life. The trick is not raising the dead, but making sure that death does not reclaim them."

Dr Stein had seen a panther two days after he had arrived in Venice, brought from the Friendly Isles along with a great number of parrots. So starved that the bones of its shoulders and pelvis were clearly visible under its sleek black pelt, the panther ceaselessly padded back and forth inside its little cage, its eyes like green lamps. It had been driven mad by the voyage, and Dr Stein thought that Dr Pretorious was as mad as that panther, his sensibility quite lost on the long voyage into the unknown regions which he claimed to have conquered. In truth, they had conquered him.

"I have kept her on ice for much of the time," Dr Pretorious said. "Even so, she is beginning to deteriorate." He twitched the hem of the girl's gown, and Dr Stein saw on her right foot a black mark as big as his hand, like a sunken bruise. Despite the attar of roses, the reek of gangrene was suddenly overpowering.

He said, "The girl is dead. I saw it for myself, when she was pulled from the canal. No wonder she rots."

"It depends what you mean by death. Have you ever seen fish in a pond, under ice? They can become so sluggish that they no longer move. And yet they live, and when warmed will move again. I was once in Gotland. In winter, the nights last all day, and your breath freezes in your beard. A man was found alive after two days lying in a drift of snow. He had drunk too much, and had passed out; the liquor had saved him from freezing to death, although he lost his ears and his fingers and toes. This girl was dead when she was pulled from the icy water, but she had drunk enough to prevent death from placing an irreversible claim on her body. I returned her to life. Would you like to see how it is done?"

"Master?"

It was the old man. With cringing deference, he offered a tray bearing a tarnished silver wine decanter, a plate of beef, heavily salted and greenish at the edges, and a loaf of black bread.

Dr Pretorious was on him in an instant. The food and wine flew into the air; Dr Pretorious lifted the old man by his neck, dropped him to the floor. "We are busy," he said, quite calmly.

Dr Stein started to help the old man to gather the food together, but Dr Pretorious aimed a kick at the old man, who scuttled away on all fours.

"No need for that," Dr Pretorious said impatiently. "I shall show you, doctor, that she lives." The glass bowl sang under his long fingernails; he smoothed the belt of frayed red silk with tender care. He looked sidelong at Dr Stein and said, "There is a tribe in the far south of Egypt who have been metalworkers for three thousand years. They apply a fine coat of silver to ornaments of base metal by immersing the ornaments in a solution of nitrate of silver and connecting them to tanks containing plates of lead and zinc in salt water. Split by the two metals, the opposing essences of the salt water flow in different directions, and when they join in the ornaments draw the silver from solution. I have experimented with that process, and will experiment more, but even when I substitute salt water with acid, the flow of essences is as yet too weak for my purpose. This—" he rapped the glass bowl, which rang like a bell "—is based on a toy that their children played with, harnessing that same essence to give each other little frights. I have greatly enlarged it, and developed a way of storing the essence it generates. For this essence lives within us, too, and is sympathetic to the flow from this apparatus. By its passage through the glass the silk generates that essence, which is stored here, in this jar. Look closely if you will. It is only ordinary glass, and ordinary water, sealed by a cork, but it contains the essence of life."

"What do you want of me?"

"I have done much alone. But, doctor, we can do so much more together. Your reputation is great."

"I have the good fortune to be allowed to teach the physicians here some of the techniques I learned in Prussia. But no surgeon would operate on a corpse."

"You are too modest. I have heard the stories of the man of clay your people can make to defend themselves. I know it is based on truth. Clay cannot live, even if bathed in blood, but a champion buried in the clay of the earth might be made to live again, might he not?"

Dr Stein understood that the mountebank believed his own legerdemain. He said, "I see that you have great need of money. A man of learning would only sell books in the most desperate circumstances, but all the books in this library have gone. Perhaps your sponsors are disappointed, and do not pay what they have promised, but it is no business of mine."

Dr Pretorious said sharply, "The fancies in those books were a thousand years old. I have no need of them. And it might be said that you owe me money. Interruption of my little demonstration cost me at least twenty *soldi*, for there were at least that many dowagers eager to taste the revitalizing essence of life. So I think that you are obliged to help me, eh? Now watch, and wonder."

Dr Pretorious began to work the treadles of his apparatus. The sound of his laboured breathing and the soft tearing sound made by the silk belt as it revolved around and around filled the long room. At last, Dr Pretorious twitched the gold wires from the top of the glass bowl so that they fell across the girl's face. In the dim light, Dr Stein saw the snap of a fat blue flame that for a moment jumped amongst the ends of the wires. The girl's whole body shuddered. Her eyes opened.

"A marvel!" Dr Pretorious said, panting from his exercise. "Each day she dies. Each night I bring her to life."

The girl looked around at his voice. The pupils of her eyes were of different sizes. Dr Pretorious slapped her face until a faint bloom appeared on her cheeks.

"You see! She lives! Ask her a question. Anything. She has returned from death, and there is more in her head than in yours or mine. Ask!"

"I have nothing to ask," Dr Stein said.

"She knows the future. Tell him about the future," he hissed into the girl's ear.

The girl's mouth worked. Her chest heaved as if she was pumping up something inside herself, then she said in a low whisper, "It is the Jews that will be blamed."

Dr Stein said, "That's always been true."

"But that's why you're here, isn't it?"

Dr Stein met Dr Pretorious's black gaze. "How many have you killed, in your studies?"

"Oh, most of them were already dead. They gave themselves for science, just as in the ancient days young girls were sacrificed for the pagan gods."

"Those days are gone."

"Greater days are to come. You will help. I know you will. Let me show you how we will save her. You will save her, won't you?"

The girl's head was beside Dr Pretorious'. They were both looking at Dr Stein. The girl's lips moved, mumbling over two words. A cold mantle crept across Dr Stein's skin. He had picked up a knife when he had stooped to help the old man, and now, if he could, he had a use for it.

Dr Pretorious led Dr Stein to the pen where the pig snuffled in its straw. He held up a candle, and Dr Stein saw clearly, for an instant, the hand on the pig's back. Then the creature bolted into shadow.

It was a human hand, severed at the wrist and poking out of the pink skin of the pig's back as if from a sleeve. It looked alive: the nails were suffused, and the skin was as pink as the pig's skin.

"They don't last long," Dr Pretorious said. He seemed pleased by Dr Stein's shock. "Either the pig dies, or the limb begins to rot. There is some incompatibility between the two kinds of blood. I have tried giving pigs human blood before the operation, but they die even more quickly. Perhaps with your help I can perfect the process. I will perform the operation on the girl, replace her rotten foot with a healthy one. I will not have her imperfect. I will do better. I will improve her, piece by piece. I will make her a true Bride of the Sea, a wonder that all the world will worship. Will you help me, doctor? It is difficult to get bodies. Your friend is causing me a great deal of nuisance . . . but you can bring me bodies, why, almost every day. So many die in winter. A piece here, a piece there. I do not need the whole corpse. What could be simpler?"

He jumped back as Dr Stein grabbed his arm, but Dr Stein was quicker, and knocked the candle into the pen. The straw was aflame in an instant, and the pig charged out as soon as Dr Stein pulled back the hurdle. It barged at Dr Pretorious as if it remembered the torments he had inflicted upon it, and knocked him down. The hand flopped to and fro on its back, as if waving.

The girl could have been asleep, but her eyes opened as soon as Dr Stein touched her cold brow. She tried to speak, but she had very little strength now, and Dr Stein had to lay his head on her cold breast to hear her mumble the two words she had mouthed to him earlier.

"Kill me."

Behind them, the fire had taken hold in the shelving and floor, casting a lurid light down the length of the room. Dr Pretorious ran to and fro, pursued by the pig. He was trying to capture the scampering mice-things which had been driven from their hiding places by the fire, but even with their staggering bipedal gait they were faster than he was. The old man ran into the room, and Dr Pretorious shouted, "Help me, you fool!"

But the old man ran past him, ran through the wall of flames that now divided the room, and jumped onto Dr Stein as he bent over the drowned girl. He was as weak as a child, but when Dr Stein tried to push him away he bit into Dr Stein's wrist and the knife fell to the floor. They reeled backwards and knocked over a jar of acid. Instantly, acrid white fumes rose up as the acid burnt into the wood floor. The old man rolled on the floor, beating at his smoking, acid-drenched costume.

Dr Stein found the knife and drew its sharp point down the length of the blue veins of the drowned girl's forearms. The blood flowed surprisingly quickly. Dr Stein stroked the girl's hair, and her eyes focused on his. For a moment it seemed as if she might say something, but with the heat of the fire beating at his back he could not stay any longer.

Dr Stein knocked out a shutter with a bench, hauled himself onto the window-ledge. As he had hoped, there was black water directly below: like all *palazzi*, this one rose straight up from the Grand Canal. Smoke rolled around him. He heard Dr Pretorious shout at him and he let himself go, and gave himself to air, and then water.

Dr Pretorious was caught at dawn the next day, as he tried to leave the city in a hired skiff. The fire set by Dr Stein had burnt out the top floor of the *palazzo*, no more, but the old man had died there. He had been the last in the line of a patrician family that had fallen on hard times: the *palazzo* and an entry in the *Libro d'Oro* was all that was left of their wealth and fame.

Henry Gorrall told Dr Stein that no mention need be made of his part in this tragedy. "Let the dead lay as they will. There's no need to disturb them with fantastic stories."

"Yes," Dr Stein said, "the dead should stay dead."

He was lying in his own bed, recovering from a rheumatic fever brought about by the cold waters into which he had plunged on his escape. Winter sunlight pried at the shutters of the white bedroom, streaked the fresh rushes on the floor.

"It seems that Pretorious has influential friends," Gorrall said. "There won't be a trial and an execution, much as he deserves both. He's going straight to the galleys, and no doubt after a little while he will contrive, with some help, to escape. That's the way of things here. His name wasn't really Pretorious, of course. I doubt if we'll ever know where he came from. Unless he told you something of himself."

Outside the bedroom there was a clamour of voices as Dr Stein's wife welcomed in Abraham Soncino and his family, and the omelettes and other egg dishes they had brought to begin the week of mourning.

Dr Stein said, "Pretorious claimed that he was in Egypt, before he came here."

"Yes, but what adventurer was not, after the Florentines conquered it and let it go? Besides, I understand that he stole the apparatus not from any savage tribe, but from the Great Engineer of Florence himself. What else did he say? I'd know all, not for the official report, but my peace of mind."

"There aren't always answers to mysteries," Dr Stein told his friend. The dead should stay dead. Yes. He knew now that his daughter had died. He had released her memory when he had released the poor girl that Dr Pretorious had called back from the dead. Tears stood in his eyes, and Gorrall clumsily tried to comfort him, mistaking them for tears of grief.

1995

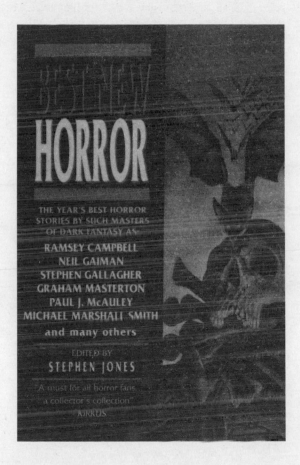

Queen of Knives

Neil Gaiman

FOR THE SEVENTH VOLUME of *The Best New Horror*, Luis Rey contributed, in my opinion, his finest cover to the series, ably showcased by Robinson's classy design.

Once again issued under the soon-to-be-defunct Raven Books imprint, the Introduction leapt to forty-three pages while the Necrology crept up to nineteen. I also added a section of "Useful Addresses", which I thought might function as a helpful reference source for readers and authors alike. At almost 600 pages, this was one of the biggest volumes we have ever published in the series.

This time I got to sound off about a personal irritation at avaricious writers and others who actively solicit awards in our genre. Not only is it debasing to them and their work, but it also dilutes the worth of any prize that is cynically canvassed for in this way. Unfortunately, many of today's awards in the field continue to be diminished by active campaigning and manipulation by those desperate to win them at any price.

Volume Seven contained twenty-six stories, including a posthumously published tale by the great pulp writer Manly Wade Wellman (who died in 1986), and another belated contribution by writer Jane Rice, who regularly appeared in John W. Campbell's pulp magazine *Unknown* in the 1940s.

Brian Stableford's genre-bending novella "The Hunger and Ecstasy of Vampires" was certainly the longest contribution in the book, but this time I've selected one of the shortest – Neil Gaiman's "Queen of Knives".

Neil has never been scared to take chances with his fiction, and this creepy prose poem is another example of one of our most creative writers once again pushing the boundaries of the genre. A view of the adult world as seen through the perspective of a child, like Christopher Fowler's story earlier in this volume, it also stands as a tribute to another almost-forgotten British comedian – Harry Worth.

"The re-appearance of the lady is a matter of individual taste."
—Will Goldston, *Tricks and Illusions*

WHEN I WAS A BOY, from time to time,
   I stayed with my grandparents
   (old people: I knew they were old –
   chocolates in their house
   remained uneaten until I came to stay,
   this, then, was ageing).
My grandfather always made breakfast at sun-up:
   A pot of tea, for her and him and me,
   some toast and marmalade
   (the Silver Shred and the Gold). Lunch and dinner,
those were my grandmother's to make, the kitchen
was again her domain, all the pans and spoons,
the mincer, all the whisks and knives, her loyal subjects.
She would prepare the food with them, singing her little
songs:
   Daisy Daisy give me your answer do,
or sometimes,
   You made me love you, I didn't want to do it,
   I didn't want to do it.
She had no voice, not one to speak of.

Business was very slow.
My grandfather spent his days at the top of the house,
in his tiny darkroom where I was not permitted to go,
bringing out paper faces from the darkness,
the cheerless smiles of other people's holidays.
My grandmother would take me for grey walks along the promenade.
Mostly I would explore
the small wet grassy space behind the house,
the blackberry brambles and the garden shed.

It was a hard week for my grandparents
forced to entertain a wide-eyed boy child, so
one night they took me to the King's Theatre. The King's . . .

Variety!

The lights went down, red curtains rose.
A popular comedian of the day,
came on, stammered out his name (his catchphrase),
pulled out a sheet of glass, and stood half-behind it,
raising the arm and leg that we could see;
reflected
he seemed to fly – it was his trademark,
so we all laughed and cheered. He told a joke or two,
quite badly. His haplessness, his awkwardness,
these were what we had come to see.
Bemused and balding and bespectacled,
he reminded me a little of my grandfather.
And then the comedian was done.
Some ladies danced all legs across the stage.
A singer sang a song I didn't know.

The audience were old people,
like my grandparents, tired and retired,
all of them laughing and applauding.

In the interval my grandfather
queued for a choc ice and a couple of tubs.
We ate our ices as the lights went down.
The "SAFETY CURTAIN" rose, and then the real curtain.

The ladies danced across the stage again,
and then the thunder rolled, the smoke went puff,
a conjurer appeared and bowed. We clapped.

The lady walked on, smiling from the wings:
glittered. Shimmered. Smiled.
We looked at her, and in that moment flowers grew,
and silks and pennants tumbled from his fingertips.

The flags of all nations, said my grandfather, nudging me.
They were up his sleeve.
Since he was a young man,
(I could not imagine him as a child)
my grandfather had been, by his own admission,
one of the people who knew how things worked.
He had built his own television,
my grandmother told me, when they were first married,
it was enormous, though the screen was small.
This was in the days before television programmes;
they watched it, though,
unsure whether it was people or ghosts they were seeing.
He had a patent, too, for something he invented,
but it was never manufactured.
Stood for the local council, but he came in third.
He could repair a shaver or a wireless,
develop your film, or build a house for dolls.
(The doll's house was my mother's. We still had it at my house,
shabby and old it sat out in the grass, all rained-on and forgot.)

The glitter lady wheeled on a box.
The box was tall: grown-up-person-sized, and black.
She opened up the front.
They turned it round and banged upon the back.
The lady stepped inside, still smiling,
The magician closed the door on her.
When it was opened she had gone.
He bowed.

Mirrors, explained my grandfather. *She's really still inside.*
At a gesture, the box collapsed to matchwood.
A trapdoor, assured my grandfather;
Grandma hissed him silent.

The magician smiled, his teeth were small and crowded;
he walked, slowly, out into the audience.
He pointed to my grandmother, he bowed,
a Middle-European bow,
and invited her to join him on the stage.
The other people clapped and cheered.

My grandmother demurred. I was so close
to the magician, that I could smell his aftershave,
and whispered "Me, oh, me . . ." But still,
he reached his long fingers for my grandmother.

Pearl, go on up, said my grandfather. *Go with the man.*

My grandmother must have been, what? Sixty, then?
She had just stopped smoking,
was trying to lose some weight. She was proudest
of her teeth, which, though tobacco-stained were all her own.
My grandfather had lost his, as a youth,
riding his bicycle; he had the bright idea
to hold on to a bus to pick up speed.
The bus had turned,
and Grandpa kissed the road.
She chewed hard liquorice, watching TV at night,
or sucked hard caramels, perhaps to make him wrong.

She stood up, then, a little slowly.
Put down the paper tub half-full of ice cream,
the little wooden spoon—
went down the aisle, and up the steps.
And on the stage.

The conjurer applauded her once more—
A good sport. That was what she was. A sport.
Another glittering woman came from the wings,
bringing another box—
this one was red.

That's her, nodded my grandfather, *the one
who vanished off before. You see? That's her.*
Perhaps it was. All I could see
was a woman who sparkled, standing next to my grandmother,
(who fiddled with her pearls, and looked embarrassed.)
The lady smiled and faced us, then she froze,
a statue, or a window mannequin.
The magician pulled the box,
with ease,
down to the front of stage, where my grandmother waited.

A moment or so of chitchat:
where she was from, her name, that kind of thing.
They'd never met before? She shook her head.

The magician opened the door,
my grandmother stepped in.

Perhaps it's not the same one, admitted my grandfather,
on reflection,
I think she had darker hair, the other girl.
I didn't know.
I was proud of my grandmother, but also embarrassed,
hoping she'd do nothing to make me squirm,
that she wouldn't sing one of her songs.

She walked into the box. They shut the door.
He opened a compartment at the top, a little door. We saw
my grandmother's face. *Pearl? Are you all right Pearl?*
My grandmother smiled and nodded.
The magician closed the door.

The lady gave him a long thin case,
so he opened it. Took out a sword
and rammed it through the box.

And then another, and another
And my grandfather chuckled and explained
*The blade slides in the hilt, and then a fake
slides out the other side.*

Then he produced a sheet of metal, which
he slid into the box half the way up.
It cut the thing in half. The two of them,
the woman and the man, lifted the top
half of the box up and off, and put it on the stage,
with half my grandma in.

The top half.

He opened up the little door again, for a moment,
My grandmother's face beamed at us, trustingly.

When he closed the door before,
she went down a trapdoor,
And now she's standing halfway up,
my grandfather confided.
She'll tell us how it's done, when it's all over.
I wanted him to stop talking: I needed the magic.

Two knives now, through the half-a-box,
at neck-height.
Are you there, Pearl? asked the magician. *Let us know*
– do you know any songs?

My grandmother sang *Daisy Daisy.*
He picked up the part of the box,
with the little door in it – the head part –
and he walked about, and she sang
Daisy Daisy first at one side of the stage,
and at the other.

That's him, said my grandfather, *and he's throwing his voice.*
It sounds like Grandma, I said.
Of course it does, he said. *Of course it does.*
He's good, he said. *He's good. He's very good.*

The conjuror opened up the box again,
now hatbox-sized. My grandmother had finished *Daisy Daisy,*
and was on a song which went
My my here we go the driver's drunk and the horse won't go
now we're going back now we're going back
back back back to London Town.

She had been born in London. Told me ominous tales
from time to time to time
of her childhood. Of the children who ran into her father's shop
shouting *shonky shonky sheeny,* running away;
she would not let me wear a black shirt because,
she said, she remembered the marches through the East End.
Mosley's black-shirts. Her sister got an eye blackened.

The conjurer took a kitchen knife,
pushed it slowly through the red hatbox.

And then the singing stopped.

He put the boxes back together,
pulled out the knives and swords, one by one by one.
He opened the compartment in the top: my grandmother smiled,
embarrassed, at us, displaying her own old teeth.
He closed the compartment, hiding her from view.
Pulled out the last knife.
Opened the main door again,
and she was gone.
A gesture, and the red box vanished too.
It's up his sleeve, my grandfather explained, but seemed unsure.

The conjurer made two doves fly from a burning plate.
A puff of smoke, and he was gone as well.

She'll be under the stage now, or back-stage,
said my grandfather,
having a cup of tea. She'll come back to us with flowers,
or with chocolates. I hoped for chocolates.

The dancing girls again.
The comedian, for the last time.
And all of them came on together at the end.
The grand finale, said my grandfather. *Look sharp,*
perhaps she'll be back on now.

But no. They sang
  when you're riding along
  on the crest of the wave
  and the sun is in the sky.

The curtain went down, and we shuffled out into the lobby.
We loitered for a while.
Then we went down to the stage door,
and waited for my grandmother to come out.
The conjurer came out in street clothes;
the glitter woman looked so different in a mac.

My grandfather went to speak to him. He shrugged,
told us he spoke no English and produced

a half-a-crown from behind my ear,
and vanished off into the dark and rain.

I never saw my grandmother again.

We went back to their house, and carried on.
My grandfather now had to cook for us.
And so for breakfast, dinner, lunch and tea
we had golden toast, and silver marmalade
and cups of tea.
Till I went home.

He got so old after that night
as if the years took him all in a rush.
Daisy Daisy, he'd sing, *give me your answer do.*
If you were the only girl in the world and I were the only boy.
My old man said follow the van.
My grandfather had the voice in the family,
they said he could have been a cantor,
but there were snapshots to develop,
radios and razors to repair . . .
his brothers were a singing duo: the Nightingales,
had been on television in the early days.

He bore it well. Although, quite late one night,
I woke, remembering the liquorice sticks in the pantry,
I walked downstairs:
my grandfather stood there in his bare feet.

And, in the kitchen, all alone,
I saw him stab a knife into a box.
You made me love you.
I didn't want to do it.

1996

MAMMOTH BOOK OF

HORROR

THE YEAR'S BEST HORROR
STORIES BY SUCH MASTERS
OF DARK FANTASY AS,

**POPPY Z. BRITE
STORM CONSTANTINE
CHRISTOPHER FOWLER
IAIN SINCLAIR
MICHAEL MARSHALL SMITH
KARL EDWARD WAGNER**
and many others

EDITED BY
S T E P H E N J O N E S

"The best single horror
collection of the year."
KIRKUS

The Break

Terry Lamsley

LUIS REY'S "EYEBALLS" PAINTING may not have been quite as effective as his previous three contributions, but it ended his association with the series and rounded out a run of four covers that, so far as I am concerned, represent the indisputable high point of *Best New Horror*'s design and packaging.

With an Introduction running to forty-eight pages and a twenty-one page Necrology, the non-fiction elements of the book were finally becoming as important as the fiction. This time I looked at the decline in horror publishing during the second half of the 1990s, and predicted a resurgence in the genre with the new millennium.

In retrospect, horror never did return to the dizzy heights of popularity it achieved in the 1980s, but after the boom-and-bust years it did finally re-establish itself as a viable publishing niche before the next cycle began to decay again.

The twenty-four stories included a final contribution by the late Karl Edward Wagner ("Final Cut") and marked the first of two appearances to date of literary writer Iain Sinclair ("Hardball"). Volume Eight was one of those rare occasions in the series where I didn't use a story by Ramsey Campbell, so the book was – belatedly – dedicated to him instead.

Until then I had succeeded in limiting the contributions (except for collaborations) to one story per author in each volume. However, the publication of Terry Lamsley's second remarkable collection of short stories, *Conference with the Dead: Tales of Supernatural Terror*, forced me to break my own rule and finally accept two stories by a single author. His darkly humorous "Walking the Dog" opened the book, while the even more disturbing story that follows memorably closed the eighth edition of *The Best New Horror* . . .

INSTEAD OF GETTING UNDRESSED straight away, as Gran
had told him to, Danny pulled aside one of the curtains she had
drawn together and peered out again at the jetty, on the edge of
the harbour to the right of him, to see what the men on the boat
were doing. The little craft, a fishing smack, had docked five minutes
earlier, and he had watched with admiration as the men aboard had
manoeuvred it into place as easily as if they were parking a car. The
sky was getting darker and the sea was flat, black and shiny, except
for the white lace of tiny waves tacked along the edge of the beach.
He could no longer make out the shape of the hull of the vessel,
but the jetty was built of pale, slightly yellow stone against which he
could see, in silhouette, the top of the boat and the activities of the
two sailors on board.

They had pulled a cumbersome object, a box of some kind, up
from the deck with a winch operated by a third man, above them on
the jetty. He had been waiting for them, staring out to sea, for some
time before they had arrived. Danny had asked his Gran to open the
top window because it was an oppressively warm evening and the
hotel room had a flat, earthy smell, like the inside of a greenhouse
in winter. Through it he could hear the rattle of the hoist's cranking
chain as the box lurched into the air, and the barking shouts of
the man operating it. He was a very big man, dressed in heavy,
unseasonable garments that made him look like a bear. He moved
like a bear as well, Danny thought, with rolling, lunging motions, and
seemed to have trouble keeping his balance.

When the box rose to the level of his shoulders the man pulled
it around with a rope attached to the top of the hoist, then slowly
lowered it onto the jetty. It must have slipped its chains at the last
moment because Danny saw it suddenly drop a few inches, and
heard it land with a sound that made him think it was very heavy,
and made of wood. The bear-like man walked around it quickly,
inspecting it, then shouted sharply down to the others on the boat.
At once, a light came on in the cabin at the front of the smack. The
engine started clunking, the third man cast off the ropes, and the
vessel curved away out into the bay beyond, leaving a widening ark
of crumpled tin-foil foam in its wake.

"Danny – please. It's *so* late, and you've not even got into your
pyjamas!"

Gran didn't seem at all cross, as his mother would have been,
but she sounded strained and disappointed in him. Danny hadn't
heard her come in, but she always moved like that – so quietly and

carefully, like a phantom. He dropped the edge of the curtain and, feeling slightly ashamed of himself, took the tray bearing a mug of chocolate and some toast she had brought him for supper, and set it down on the table beside his bed.

"I'm not tired, Gran," he lied, then yawned hugely, giving the game away. "I was watching the sea," he explained, somewhat inaccurately.

"You've got all week for that," Gran said, folding a triangle of quilt tidily back away from his pillow to display how temptingly comfortable the bed beneath it looked.

Danny said, "I like the boats. There's hundreds in the harbour. Will we be able to go for a trip on one?"

"I can't take Grandad, and I mustn't leave him behind, but perhaps you could go on your own, if I think it's safe."

"Is Grandad ill?" Danny asked, plugging the sink and twisting the taps to run water for his evening wash. When Gran didn't answer he turned back to her and added, "He looks all right. I can't *see* anything wrong with him."

"He's not exactly ill, like you were last winter, with your chest. It's just that, recently, he's got a bit . . . forgetful."

"Yes," Danny agreed, "I've noticed that," and saw his Gran's face darken. "I mean, sometimes, he looks at me as though he doesn't know who I am. When I met you both at the station, and you left me with him and went to get a magazine, he asked me what my name was."

"Oh dear," said Gran, poking nervously at the grey curl that dangled down over her right eye, "did he really?"

"Then, when I told him, he just shook his head, as though he'd never heard of me."

"I'm sorry."

"It's not your fault," Danny said generously. "He got my name right later." He began to brush his teeth.

Pleased to be presented with this enforced curtailment of the conversation, when she had been thinking how she could change the subject without arousing in Danny an alarming suspicion that her husband was worse than he really was, Gran decided to make an exit.

"Breakfast is at eight-thirty," she said, after kissing Danny goodnight on the top of his head.

"Can I go on my own, or must I wait for you?"

"No, you're big enough now to make your own way down, I think."

"Of course I am," Danny agreed. "I was last year, when we went to Brighton, but you wouldn't believe me."

Gran smiled, but she didn't seem to agree with him. "Into bed now, Danny," she insisted. "I'll look in soon to make sure you're asleep."

When she had gone Danny sipped the chocolate and pulled a face. It didn't taste anything like it did at home, when his mother made it.

He poured the drink down the sink, ate the toast quickly, got into his pyjamas, then could not resist taking one more peep out the window before getting into bed.

The man on the jetty was still there. He was pushing the big heavy box towards the shore with great difficulty. He was bending behind it, almost on all fours, looking more than ever like a fat black bear. Although obviously pushing with all his strength, he was only managing to move it inches at a time. After two or three strenuous efforts he stopped, leaned against the box as though exhausted, then strained to shove it a couple of times more. It made a harsh crunching sound as it moved, as if it was sliding across a surface scattered with broken glass. The box was still only a few feet from where it had landed. At that rate, Danny thought, it would take the man all night to reach the end of the jetty!

He could hear the box sliding and grinding along every now and then as he lay in bed, but it didn't sound as if it was getting any nearer. He felt sorry for the man. Why didn't he get someone to help him? He had looked somehow very lonely out there, and the way he had spoken to the men on the fishing boat, and they to him, had not sounded at all friendly. It occurred to Danny that it was likely that the man was not nice to know, and had no friends.

When Gran peeped in, twenty minutes later, she could tell from his breathing that he was asleep. She was closing the door again when she heard the sound of the huge box being moved outside, and went to the window. By mistake, she had only brought her reading glasses on holiday with her, but was just able to see what Danny had seen and, like him, watched and speculated about the man on the jetty. At that moment he was leaning on the far edge of the box and his white blob of a face was looking up towards the hotel, or seemed to be. He remained in this pose for only a few moments, then suddenly bent down, shuffled his legs back a little, and began to push. His body appeared to compress as he increased his effort then, though Gran's faulty vision could detect no movement, the box grated on the stone surface of the jetty as it jerked a few inches closer, and the figure behind it elongated. This happened three times, then the man stood up, stretched his back, arced his arms above his head, and glanced up towards the hotel again.

Gran stepped away from the window and closed her eyes for a moment as a harsh, cold light shone in on her. She realized it was the headlights of a car turning off the promenade, up into the town. She suddenly felt an unexpected evening breeze from somewhere, that made the edges of the curtains flutter, and caused her to twitch and clench her teeth and shudder.

Because of that, and because she didn't want Danny woken up by any noise, she shut the window before she left the room.

Someone knocked on the door. Danny opened his eyes, registered the dim daylight beyond the curtains, and waited. Gran never needed inviting. When, after a static silence, whoever it was knocked again, Danny sat up and called, "Come in." A young woman in a pale blue overall stepped sideways into the room. Still holding the door handle she showed him a sketch of a smile and said, "G'morning. Tea or coffee?"

Danny had not been expecting this. Hotels he had stayed in in the past had provided equipment for guests to make their own refreshments. He asked for tea and, while the girl was busy at a trolley he could see parked on the corridor outside, hauled himself up out of the last few yards of sleep, feeling obscurely embarrassed and slightly irritated.

The girl placed the tea by his bed and gave it an extra stir. She said, "Sleep well?" in a distant sort of way.

"Mmm, yes. Very, thank you."

"Good," the girl acknowledged, and bent down over him and began fussing with his pillow. Danny made some effort to sit up. The girl must have thought he was having difficulty doing so, as she reached behind his head with her right hand and supported the upper part of his back. It was a gentle, helpful movement, but Danny didn't like it. The girl's fingers were thin and hard against his spine and there was something investigative about the way she touched him that made him uneasy, as though she was literally weighing him up, and testing the quality of the flesh beneath his pyjamas.

He reared up away from her hand and shook his shoulders. The girl's thumb and fingers rested for a moment on the top of his arm, almost squeezing, before she turned away to open the curtains with a flourish, revealing rain-spotted windows and, beyond, the grimy grey sky of the disappointing day outside.

"They say it will clear up later," the girl assured him, and the edgy smile shifted briefly across her face again. Danny couldn't understand why he didn't like her. There was nothing about her looks to upset him. She had a sharp, but almost pretty face, and she was obviously trying to be nice. She couldn't help having hard, bony fingers.

After she had gone Danny snuggled down into the bed again until he remembered the man on the jetty the night before. He played a game in his mind, laying bets with himself about how far the man had moved the box. In the end he decided there would be no sign of it. Someone would have been to collect it, and taken it away.

He hopped out of bed to check, and saw the box still on the jetty, not far from where he had last seen it. A large sheet of dark green tarpaulin, tied in place with a strand of rope, had been draped over it. A puddle of rain had formed on top of it. There was no sign of the man. The jetty was otherwise empty.

Danny found that if he stood on tiptoe he could just see over the roofs of the hotels on the street below him onto the beach to the left of the jetty. It too was deserted now, except for piles of deckchairs and a solitary dog, jumping and jerking in the foam at the waters edge, tugging savagely at something, probably a strand of black seaweed, that glistened like a hank of wet, soapy human hair. From time to time the dog dropped the weed, held up its head, and snapped its jaws open and shut.

Realizing his window had been closed, because he couldn't hear the creature barking, Danny climbed onto the sill and opened it. Cold damp air straight off the sea surged into the room. He could hear the sloshing breakers of the turning tide, slightly baffled by the veils of wind-blown rain that were sweeping across the town, and the urgent, worried yapping of the dog, sounding much further off than it really was.

He washed, dressed quickly in a new T-shirt and jeans, and set out to find the dining room. The hotel was full of the smell of breakfast, and he hoped he could find his food by following his nose. He soon took a wrong turning, however, and wandered into a half-lit, grey painted room full of wheelchairs and pale-blue, uncomfortable looking furniture.

There was a large mural on the wall depicting, in faded primary colours, what he thought must be heaven, with naked sexless angels leading stooping elderly humans, in white togas, through an English rural landscape, drawn in such a way as to suggest a vast perspective.

At the top of the picture other angels, with tiny golden wings, flew through the sky, pulling strings of smiling old people along behind them. Yet more of the heavenly hosts, playing musical instruments, rested on cotton wool clouds beneath a beneficent, smirking sun, while a multitude of ancient mortals hovered around them, listening to their concert with obvious gratitude and appreciation.

At first Danny thought he was alone in the room, then he noticed, scattered along the walls, a number of elderly people, seemingly asleep in their seats and wheelchairs. They were lolling sideways, backwards, or forward, like inanimate puppets. One old man, his liver-spotted head quite bald on top, with an aura of pearly curls of unbrushed hair stretching up from the back of his neck to above his ears like coral or fungus, lay stretched out face down on the table in front of him.

Danny, chilled by the atmosphere of the room, froze on the spot for a few moments. Nobody moved, or showed in any way they were aware he was there, until a voice to his left called out, "Nurse! Is it you? Can you prop me up? My cushion slipped. I've lost it."

Danny turned towards the sound and saw an incredibly thin old lady leaning at a sharp angle out of a wheelchair. She was resting on one arm, with her elbow in her lap, and stretching so far forward, she seemed to defy gravity. Her other arm dangled, limp as a bell rope, by her side. She had had to lift her head right back to see him, and her toothless mouth hung open wide, as dark inside as a railway tunnel. A pair of red-rimmed glasses rested slightly askew on her nose. Behind them, it seemed, her eyes were shut.

At the sound of her voice some of the other old people began to stir. A man's tremulous voice called out insistently, "I'm hungry." Someone started to cough and spit, another to moan, as though suddenly in pain, and a woman protested tiredly, "Mrs Grange has wet herself again. *When* are you going to do something about her?"

Danny stared at the floor below the person closest to the old lady who had spoken last, and saw, under her chair, a dark stain on the carpet.

The woman who had complained that she had lost her cushion repeated her plea for help, now sounding cross. Danny moved towards her and must have stepped into her line of vision because she said fiercely, "Who are you? You're just a boy! Are they sending children, now, to look after us?"

Danny snatched up the cushion and thrust it towards the woman, who whined, "That's no good to me, unless you pick me up and pull me back. Can't you see that if it wasn't for the strap, I'd have fallen on my face? You can't leave me like this . . . I can hardly breathe . . ." and her voice died away, as though she were indeed expiring.

Danny saw she was held in place by a thick white belt tied tight around her waist and the back of her chair. She was so thin, the belt buckle on her stomach was only a couple of inches from the fabric of the chair against her spine.

Danny placed his hand on the top of her chest, that felt like a bird cage under his palms, and tried to push her upright, but he was not tall enough, and must have done something painful, because she gave a shriek and shouted, "What are you doing, child? What are you doing? Let go, for God's sake . . . you're *hurting* me."

Some of the other old people started to shout abuse at him then, and he felt his eyes flood and his throat constrict, and knew he was going to cry.

A man's voice, coming from just behind Danny, said, "What's the matter Betty? You *are* making a fuss. The young gentleman is only trying to help."

The scrawny woman said, "Where have you been Kelvin? Where's our breakfast? You're ever so late."

"No I'm not," the man said. "I'm just on time."

"You're a bloody liar," the woman suggested peevishly. "What do you mean by sending bits of kids to look after us?"

"He's not on the staff, Betty, he's a guest," the man explained, easily hauling the woman upright and adjusting her limbs so she sat in a comfortable, balanced position.

"Then why is he here? This is no place for kids."

"I don't know." The man, who was dressed in a white jacket, like the Chinese who worked in Danny's local chip shop wore, gave him a curious, slightly angry look that was only partly disguised by the shadow of a smile he managed to force across his face. He had a bony, narrow head, with dark hair brushed back tight against his scalp, and a large nose under which sprouted a pencil moustache. His smile reminded Danny of the girl who had brought him tea half an hour earlier, who had also seemed to find it hard to form her features into a good humoured expression for more than a second.

"I expect he's got lost," the man continued. "Is that right, young man?"

Danny, choking back tears, wiped his fingers under his nose and nodded.

"I expect you were looking for the dining room?"

Danny didn't stop nodding.

"This is the Twilight Lounge. The room you want is on the floor below. You should have kept on walking, down another flight of stairs."

The man clasped Danny's shoulder unnecessarily hard and steered him out of the door. Two or three of the old people shouted, "Nurse, *nurse!*" in protest at being left alone again.

"Back in a tick," the man yelled, with an edge of irritation. His voice was so loud, Danny looked up at him, startled. Noticing this the man explained, in a more moderate tone, "They're deaf, sonny. Most of them are deaf," and led Danny to the top of the stairs and pointed the way to the dining room.

Danny, no longer crying, and bursting with curiosity now, said, "Those old people back there . . . they thought you were a nurse, didn't they?"

"That's what I am."

"But this is a hotel, not a hospital!"

"It's a bit of both," the man said, after a short pause.

"Oh," Danny said, totally confused.

Back in the lounge the old people were cackling and calling for Kelvin, who gave Danny a horrible wink that briefly distorted the whole of one side of his face, then retreated to join them.

A portly woman pushed a heated trolley reeking of bacon out of the lift and across the corridor into the Twilight Lounge. She was greeted with a tiny, ironic ovation from the residents.

Danny ran down to the dining room, which was almost empty. He had left his room at exactly eight-thirty, and the incident in the lounge had only lasted two or three minutes.

He sat alone at a table close to a rain-flecked window that looked out to sea. He could see the box on the jetty and, through a gap between two of the buildings below, a slice of the promenade and the beach beyond. The box looked bigger and somehow heavier from the lower level. The wind blew up under the tarpaulin draped across it, causing the hanging sides of the covering to flap mournfully. It looked as though someone inside the box was reaching about through holes in the sides with their hands, trying to find some way out.

When, fifteen minutes later, Gran and Grandad came to join him, Danny had almost finished breakfast. He wondered if he should have waited and eaten with them, but Gran said nothing about that. Perhaps she hadn't noticed. She had a preoccupied, anxious look on her face that Danny was getting used to seeing there. She kept half an eye on Grandad all the time, was aware of every move he made, and turned to give him her full attention whenever he spoke. Something about the way she treated her husband made Danny feel quite grown up, as though he and Grandad had changed places.

The room filled up with old people. Danny looked out for anyone his age, but there was only one girl, a couple of years older and four inches taller than him, who pulled a tight face when he smiled at her, and didn't look up from her plate again.

When Grandad had finished eating he asked Gran what day it was. She told him Sunday, but a little later he asked the same question and, when she tried to get him to remember the answer she had given him earlier, he said he hadn't asked her before, and if she didn't know what day it was, why didn't she just admit it?

Gran put her hand on his arm and, very quietly, said she had told him, and not long ago. Grandad insisted she hadn't, in a high, strange voice, and Danny thought he looked worried, even frightened.

A waitress came to clear the table and Grandad said to her, "My wife has forgotten what day it is. Perhaps you can enlighten her?"

The girl arched her eyebrows, looked from Grandad to Gran and back, and tried to smile.

Why is it nobody at this place can smile for more than a second? Danny thought, and for the first time began to wonder if he was going to enjoy the holiday.

The girl looked unsure of how to respond to Grandad's request for such basic information, hoping, but doubting, it was a joke. To avoid her embarrassment, Danny looked out of the window, towards the box on the jetty.

A big bird was standing on top of it. As Danny, watched the bird started strutting backwards and forwards, half-opening and closing its long, slender wings. It was just some kind of gull, Danny supposed. It was that sort of shape, but he had no idea they could grow so big and he had never seen one that dark before. Perhaps it had been caught in an oil slick? Suddenly, it launched itself off the edge of the box and soared into the sky.

Danny turned back to the table when the waitress said, "It's Sunday, of course. All day."

Grandad said, "Thank you very much", and gave Gran a silly, mocking shake of his head.

Anger, embarrassment, and some other indefinable pain registered on Gran's face. She got to her feet. As she did so, Grandad automatically rose from his chair, only more slowly, with less agility.

Danny jumped up to help him. "What are we going to do today?" he said. "It's raining. Do we have to stay in?"

"*We* will," Gran said, "for now. But you can go for a walk, to explore, if you want to."

"Definitely," Danny said. "It's dead boring here."

Gran gave him the first real smile he had received all day. "Don't catch cold though, and ruin your holiday."

"No problem. I'll be alright."

As Danny moved around the table to follow his grandparents, something moved out of the grey clouds beyond the window next to him, and descended towards him. The oversized gull he had seen landed on the balcony a yard from the window. It folded its wings with an air of deliberation and craned its neck. It turned sideways on awkward, stumbling feet, cocked its head at an angle, and stared at Danny down one side of its beak.

The beak was grimy yellow, like a heavy smoker's teeth. The bird stretched forward and screamed, as though announcing its presence, then stood motionless, watching him. It was at least four times as big as any gull Danny had seen before, and he thought he had been right about the oil slick, because its inky plumage had a glossy sheen, like the wet tarpaulin on the box it had been standing on when he had first noticed it.

"Danny!"

Gran's voice. She and Grandad were waiting for him at the door. Everyone in the room turned towards him.

They're all so old, he thought.

He knew Todley Bay was popular with elderly people, and owed its reputation to what it had to offer that age group. His mother had told him all that weeks ago, and explained that the holiday was intended as a break for Gran and Grandad, and that he had to be on his best behaviour all the time, and not give them any worries.

So he knew the resort would be *their* sort of place, with probably not much going for kids, but he had not expected to see so *many* old people. Most of them looked really ancient. There was hardly anyone in the room under – what? He wildly guessed . . . seventy? Eighty?

Except for the waitresses, and the girl he had noticed, he was the only young person present. He looked for the girl again, and saw she was watching him, like the others. She gave him a withering look that actually made him shudder. There was something about her, he decided, which set her among the old people. She looked used up, done in, worn out. Then he realized she was probably very ill, and felt sorry for her at once.

He hurried to the door, but looked back before stepping out. The gull hadn't moved. It was still there, glaring in through the window.

Danny was keen to get spending. He'd been saving up his pocket money for weeks and couldn't wait to drop some of it into slot-machines, or buy sticks of his favourite pineapple rock and things to play with on the beach.

But the shops were disappointing. They were dingy and dark, with a lot of old stock that no one would ever buy, and the proprietors watched him all the time, as though they thought he were a thief. In one store down near the beach the rock and other sweets were covered in grey dust, and looked shrivelled-up inside their wrappers. Danny bought a stick, because he had to buy something, but it tasted worse than the pencils he was in the habit of chewing at school, so he threw it in a bin.

He wandered into the town, that sprawled almost perpendicularly up the hill behind the bay, in search of anything interesting, but soon got bored with endless rows of cream painted houses advertising BED & BREAKFAST or offering themselves as RESIDENTIAL HOMES FOR THE AGED. He passed a church that was open, with the bell ringing, but nobody went in or out. A gaunt and gloomy vicar with a lead-grey face was standing at the door, stiff as a waxwork, waiting to shake someone's hand.

It got tiring, climbing up the steep streets, so Danny turned back. His feet wanted to run down the sharp incline towards the beach, so he let them. The soles of his trainers slapped like clapping hands on the wet, empty streets, and he began to feel exhilarated, the way you should feel on holiday.

The tide was on its way out and he ran without stopping right down the beach to the water's edge. It was cold down there, and a wind driving off the sea carried a miserable, almost invisible mist with it, but Danny tried not to let that bother him. He threw some pebbles at a jellyfish, played tag with the waves, then trotted along until he was suddenly brought up short by the jetty, half of which still stretched out into the sea. It was about ten feet high, but there were steps up the side, which he climbed without thinking.

As he reached the top, and looked across the harbour beyond, something called out to his right, towards the town. It sounded like the voice of a demented woman screeching his name. He turned and saw, five yards away, the box, and, hovering above it, with its feet stretching down, about to land, the enormous gull. It called again, almost dancing on the tarpaulin with the tips of its claws as it carved at the air with it wings to keep itself just in flight, then settled and became motionless and silent, like a stuffed bird in a museum.

It was staring straight at Danny. There was something threatening about the creature's posture – it looked tense, as though it was ready to burst into furious action any second. Cautiously, Danny took a few paces towards it. It side-stepped once, adjusting its position slightly in a gust of buffeting wind, but showed no fear of him, or any sign that it was about to fly away. Its position on the box put it slightly higher than Danny's head, so its beak was just above his eyes.

The beak resembled a scaled-down sword from a fantasy film. It was at least eight inches long, and the upper section curved sharply down in a cruel, hard, hooked point. Danny thought the bird would have no trouble opening up his skull with a weapon like that on its head.

When he was a few feet away, and still beyond the gull's reach, Danny stopped, worried about his eyes, that suddenly seemed very vulnerable. He saw that the bird had a cold and crazy look in its eyes, which reminded him of snakes and alligators.

Danny blew air out through his pursed lips, and shook his head. He realized he was afraid, and not just of the gull. There was more to it than that. The air around him felt charged and dangerous. Beyond the jetty, the town itself seemed to be watching him, poised and ready to tumble forward on top of him in a huge avalanche if he did the wrong thing. Something, he sensed, was in the balance.

For the first time he took a close look at the box. It was made of wood, bound with strips of greenish metal that could have been brass, and its unpainted surface was mottled with patches of dank, dark-emerald growth. Probably some kind of marine weed. It stood in a puddle of its own making. The wood was waterlogged, which partly explained why the man he had seen pushing it had found the task such heavy going. The lid, if it had a lid, was under the flapping tarpaulin cover, but something about the box gave Danny the impression it was locked up very tight. It looked impenetrable! Briefly he wondered what, if anything, was inside it, then hastily closed his mind to the ugly images that were trying to crawl up out of his imagination.

All at once, Danny wanted to get back into the town. The jetty was narrow, but the box took up less than half its width. He could slip past it easily, but in doing so, he would put himself well within the reach of the gull. If it attacked him, he might fall off the jetty. It was a long way down to the beach, and there were flint rocks sticking out of the sand below. He took another look at the creature's beak. The gull glared back and nodded curtly once, as if to confirm his apprehensions.

"Look," Danny said, without having any idea why, "I don't want anything to do with this. I'm just here on holiday." Then he added, "I'm sorry," in a tone more of confusion than apology, and turned and fled back down the steps.

He didn't stop running when he felt the sand of the beach under his feet, but continued right up to the hotel. When he had almost reached it, just as he was trotting up the drive, the sun slid out from behind the clouds above him and its light blazed down on all the town like a laser beam.

The rest of the day was showery, so the three of them didn't stray far from the TV in the Hotel lounge. When he went to bed Danny thought he could hear the box being pushed along the jetty again, but he was so tired, even though he had done nothing much all day, he fell asleep almost at once.

Next morning, when the girl came into his room, threw back the curtains to reveal a blue, cloudless sky, and came towards him with a cup of tea, he jumped up in bed at once, so she wouldn't have any excuse to touch him. Even so, she put one hand on his head and poked about in his hair while he sipped his drink, as though she was gently feeling for lumps.

It seemed to Danny that her fingertips were like cold, hard marbles rolling about on his scalp. He assumed it was a gesture of affection – he couldn't think what else it could be, and resisted the urge to duck away. But, when she sat down next to him, he jumped out of bed, ran to the sink, and started washing.

In the morning he spent an hour in a drab little seafront cafe with his grandparents drinking banana milkshakes. After lunch the three of them went down to the beach. Grandad, in a boyish mood, led the way. He looked as though he was wearing someone else's clothes, because he had lost so much weight in the last year, but Danny recognized the fawn trousers the old man had worn on the last three of their previous holidays together.

Gran, Danny noticed, seemed more anxious than ever about Grandad when he was at all boisterous, as though she was scared his behaviour might get out of hand. As soon as Grandad had put his cap on backwards, and his face had taken on the now all-too-familiar clown's witless smile that had come to haunt it recently, Gran's features had responded by setting into a rigid, pained expression. She looked as though she had a bad headache.

Grandad had wandered away from her twice, and the second time it had taken her half an hour to locate him. He had been with two men who were leading him away, or seemed to be. They had not spoken to her when she had reclaimed her husband, and she hadn't liked the look of them. They looked like muggers, she said.

Danny, feeling sympathy for both his grandparents, took care to be on his best behaviour when he was with them, but he wished they'd loosen up. He was now definitely beginning to wonder what kind of holiday it was going to be!

Gran decided it was too windy to sit on the beach, so she steered Grandad into a shelter on the promenade from where they could watch Danny doing the things children do on such occasions. He made a cake-like sandcastle without much enthusiasm, because he was beginning to wonder if he was too old for such activities, then stripped down to his trunks and sped towards the sea, now quite a long way out.

In places the surface of the sand had been formed into hard ridges by the action of the out-going tide. They ran along the whole length of the beach. They hurt the soles of his bare feet if he ran, and forced him to slow down and walk carefully. To Danny, it looked as though hundreds of endless fat worms lay paralysed just below the surface.

Old Man Sand's got wrinkles, he said to himself, and laughed at the thought, though there was something not-very-nice about the idea that he found alarming and tried to shove to the back of his mind.

After paddling for a while in the shallow sea, that was starting to warm in the sun, and taking a short, leisurely swim, he noticed he felt constrained and uneasy. Something was missing! Except for the sound of waves breaking on the shore, and the occasional scream of gulls (ordinary sized gulls, that was), the beach was strangely quiet. Conspicuous by its absence, he realized, was hubbub, pandemonium. He missed the voices of children yelling and shouting in excitement to each other, and telling their parents about what they were up to at the tops of their voices. The whole beach, the entire Bay even, though now more populated, was muffled, silent, and somehow static. Like a painting. Danny looked about him at his fellow bathers.

There were not many. Within twenty yards of him half a dozen elderly people, their trousers and skirts rolled or hitched up, wandered about ankle-deep at the water's edge.

A beefy man with bulging eyes and purple skin, looking as though his whole body had been beaten into one huge bruise, occasionally hurled himself into deeper water further out and swam a few stiff, furious strokes.

A woman in a lime-green costume, standing in the sea close to Danny, suddenly stooped, lowered herself to her knees, sat on her heels and bowed her head in a praying attitude. Her flesh oozed out around the edges of her costume like viscous liquid when she moved. Her skin was crinkled, like the monkey's brain in a bottle in the biology lab at Danny's school. She seemed uncomfortable in the position she had adopted and wriggled around so she could lay back on the sand.

A wave breaking over her created the illusion that she was sliding feet first into the sea. Seconds later, when it withdrew, Danny imagined he saw something in the water, clasped around her ankles, tugging her away from the beach.

This impression was so strong he walked closer to get a better look at her. The next wave was bigger, however, and submerged her completely. She did not, as Danny expected, start up when the water covered her face, but her body yawed slightly in the drag of the tide. Her eyes were shut and her mouth was open wide. She could have been shouting, laughing or even yawning.

Baffled and alarmed, Danny thought he ought to try to help the woman, though she gave no indication that she was at all distressed. He wondered if he should ask one of the other old people for their assessment of the situation, then saw that two of them were now also kneeling down. The red-skinned man who had been swimming had vanished, but Danny was sure he had not passed him on his way back to the beach. The last time he had seen him, the man had been in the act of lunging forward in a clumsy dive.

Out in the area where the man had been standing, Danny noticed, for the first time, what looked like dark shadows under the waves. They appeared to be moving. He thought they must be weed-covered rocks, just visible at the bottom of the grey-green water.

One of the two people who were kneeling lay back in the water.

Danny suddenly looked down at his feet. He thought something had touched his right ankle. The sand next to it was disturbed, as though some fast-moving object had hurriedly dug down into it. He turned and ran a few yards out of the water, stood on the nearly dry sand, and looked back. The tide must be coming in fast, he thought, as there was no sign of the woman in the green costume. He could no longer see some of the other people who had been paddling, but a handful more had stumbled forward off the beach into the sea. He realized that none of them had nodded to him, or given him so much as a glance.

He shrugged, and jogged back to where Gran and Grandad were sitting in the shelter. Gran looked more relaxed, perhaps because Grandad was asleep. She held a finger to her lips to warn Danny to keep his voice down, and asked him if he was enjoying himself. Danny didn't want to upset her by telling the truth about how he did feel at that moment, which in any case would be difficult to explain, so he just nodded. He asked for money for an ice cream.

As Gran fumbled in her purse, Danny noticed a man sitting on the bench on the other side of Grandad was watching him. He was heavily built, with a bald head and heavy jowls and was dressed in old, dark, working clothes. He could have been a fisherman. He had one arm along the bench behind Grandad's head. Two fingers of his hand rested on Grandad's shoulder. As Danny looked back at him, he lifted the fingers and curled them back towards his palm.

Danny got ice creams for himself and Gran, and hurried back. The bald man had gone, so Danny sat in the vacant place.

"Who was that man, Gran?" he asked.

"Which man?"

"The one who had his arm around Grandad."

"Danny, what do you mean? I'm sure he wasn't doing anything of the kind."

"He was," Danny insisted. "I think he wanted Grandad to go with him."

Gran, hearing the conviction in his voice, leaned forward and turned to look at him.

"This is a funny place, isn't it?" Danny continued.

"Todley Bay? Don't you like it here?"

"Not as much as Brighton."

"I think it's very nice."

"There's no kids."

Gran smiled. "There must be some."

"I can't see any."

Gran pushed her glasses up her nose and looked around. "Not here, at the moment, perhaps," she conceded, "but on the beach . . ."

Danny swallowed the last of his ice cream and wiped his mouth. "No. It's all old people, everywhere."

"You're exaggerating. What about that girl who's staying at our hotel. She's about your age. Why don't you try to get to know her?"

"She's sick. I bet she never leaves the hotel."

"Um," Gran agreed thoughtfully, "she doesn't look well. I expect she's convalescing."

"I think she's dying," Danny said, matter-of-factly.

"Danny!" Gran said loudly, causing Grandad to twitch out of his doze, "I'm sure that's not true. What *has* got into you?"

"What's the trouble?" Grandad demanded. "What's got into who?"

"Danny, Harry. I don't think he's enjoying himself. He's in a very strange mood."

"Danny?" said Grandad, looking at his grandson as though he were a total stranger.

The grim look returned to Gran's face. She glanced at her watch. "Good heavens, look at the time. We'd better start back for the evening meal," she said, rising from her seat. Grandad rose up with her, like a Siamese twin joined to her at the shoulder.

Danny was surprised how easy it was to get lost in the hotel. The corridors and public rooms were decorated uniformly throughout, which made it hard to get your bearings, but even so, it didn't explain why he lost his way quite so often. He kept finding himself on the wrong floor! He'd carefully count the turns in the flights of stairs, so he was sure he knew exactly where he was, only to discover he was one, or even two, floors out.

He noticed quite a few of the old people wandering around in even deeper bafflement than usual from time to time, which made him feel better, because it suggested he wasn't the only one experiencing this peculiar disorientation.

A couple of times Danny bumped into Kelvin, the nurse with the thin pencil moustache, who told him how to get to where he wanted to go. He wasn't exactly unfriendly, but he must have been a very busy man, because he hardly stopped long enough to give the necessary directions before he blustered off again.

On the third night of the holiday, after leaving his grandparents in the TV Lounge, Danny searched about down wrong corridors for ten minutes before he found his room. He complimented himself – he was getting better. The night before it had taken twice that long to get his bearings.

As he was putting on his pyjamas, he heard the big box being shoved along the jetty. A shining mist that had crawled up off the sea with the onset of darkness had vanished when he looked out of the window. The air was clear, and he could see the man had nearly got the box to the end of the jetty. Danny was very interested to see what would happen next, because he knew there were two steps up from the jetty to the promenade and the street beyond, and he couldn't see how one man could possibly get the box up them without help.

He got into bed and pretended to be asleep when Gran came, so she only stayed a moment. (He felt bad about it, but he had become fed-up with her company that evening, because she was wearing herself out fussing over Grandad, who was definitely going ga-ga. They were both getting visibly worse daily. A lot of the time it was a *pain* being with them.)

When Gran had gone, Danny got up again and looked out the window. The box was about a foot from the steps, and the man had gone. He watched for a while, but nothing happened, so he slid back between the sheets, feeling let-down and disappointed, and fell asleep. Later, something woke him up. Noises, coming from the direction of the jetty. Different noises! He trotted to the window and looked out.

The man was back. He had set a lantern on the edge of the top step, and had placed a long metal tube or roller, four or five inches in diameter, at the base of the box, on the side closest to the steps. He was lifting the box with a jack.

When it was the right height he kicked the roller under it on one side, let the box drop, then went around to the far side to repeat the process. When the roller was under the full length of the leading edge of the box, he went behind it and began to push. After a struggle, it moved a short distance towards the steps, and the side of the box above the roller rose a little higher. After giving three huge shoves the man got another, thicker roller from somewhere and laid it in front of the first one he had positioned. Then he went behind the box, and pushed and pushed.

The front edge of the thing was soon higher than the bottom step and, in twenty minutes, after the man had put more rollers in place and done a lot more heaving, it was hovering a good distance above and beyond the top of the second. Then the man hit a problem.

Because it was inclined at an angle, he was finding it increasingly difficult to move the box. He was having to push it up, as well as forward. He seemed to give up then, and went and sat on the top step and stared down at the box.

Danny watched the slumped figure for a while until he got bored. He thought the man might have gone to sleep. He was just about ready to return to bed when he saw movements on the beach below him. The tide was almost in, and a man was walking off the narrow strip of sand, diagonally out into the sea.

The small, thin, stooping figure, dressed in dark clothes, was just visible against the inky water, moving slowly and regularly, as though setting out for a stroll on the ocean bed. When the sea was in up to his waist he stopped, sank back into the water and disappeared from sight. Danny thought – no, he knew – the person, whoever he was, had stretched out on the sand, like the woman in the green costume he had seen the day before.

There were a few deckchairs left out on the beach, Danny noticed, spread about near where the now presumably drowning man had been when he'd first sighted him. To his amazement he could see shapes that could only be people, sprawling in some of the chairs. Danny peered at his watch. It was almost midnight – it had been dark for almost two hours!

They're moon-bathing, he thought, and smiled uneasily in the dark, aware that the people didn't look at all funny.

As he looked back out the window he saw something scuttle up out of the sea, across the beach, in among the parked deckchairs. It moved like a spider. It clung close to the sand, had no definite shape, and at first Danny thought it was dead seaweed, broken loose from its roots, washed ashore, dried in the sun, and blowing in the wind. Until he realized there was no wind to speak of, certainly not enough to set in motion anything more substantial than a scrap of paper.

What he could see was moving of its own volition, and soon demonstrated that it had considerable strength! A section of its edge blended with the outline of one of the occupied chairs, which lifted and tumbled over on its side, tipping the person seated on it onto the sand. The figure lay motionless for as long as it took the mobile shape to dart around and attach itself to an outstretched arm, the part of the body closest to the sea. The body twitched once, then slid smoothly to the tide line and into the waves beyond, where it, and the thing pulling it, sank out of sight. Then, for a time, nothing moved on the beach that Danny could see, though his eyes were alert for the slightest motion.

It was a sound from the end of the jetty that grabbed his attention next – a loud grunt of pain or effort, or both. He turned just in time to see the bear-like man heave the box almost into the air and up onto the edge of the promenade. The action seemed to have spent the last of his energy. He flopped around picking up the rollers and tucking them under his arm like a man at the last extreme of exhaustion, then staggered off towards the harbour. Danny watched him shrink away into the darkness, then realized he was stiff with standing still, and crawled into bed.

He fell asleep wondering what the man, who was awake most nights, did in the daytime.

It was very hot next day. So much so that Gran and Grandad sat on the beach for the first time. They couldn't walk far in the sand, because of Gran's feet, so Danny put up deckchairs for them at the bottom of the steps that led to the promenade. He sat with them for a while, watching the beach fill with elderly holidaymakers then, for something to say, because the old pair were not inclined to talk in the heat, he mentioned that he had seen people on the sands late at night.

"I expect they were workmen tidying up all the litter," Gran said.

"The tide does that," Danny said, "when it goes in and out. No, they were sitting in chairs, like we are, or walking into the sea."

"Danny, you were dreaming. They'd have caught their deaths of cold."

Danny wanted to say he thought they were dead, or looked it, but knew that Gran would say he was talking nonsense and get cross with him.

Even so, he couldn't help saying, "I wish we *had* gone to Brighton. This place is *weird*."

"I think it's very pleasant," Gran said, "and restful. There's none of the noise and fuss you get at so many holiday places nowadays. And people are so nice and polite."

"You didn't like those men who tried to walk off with Grandad," Danny observed.

"You were probably wrong about them. Perhaps they thought Grandad was lost and they were taking him to a policeman."

Danny didn't answer, because he had just spotted, not far away along the beach, one of the deckchairs he had seen someone slumped in last night. He knew it was the same one, because it was in exactly the same position in relation to a stack of chairs next to it as it had been when he had seen it from his bedroom window.

It was facing away from him but he could tell it was occupied because the canvas seat was bulging down and back. He was about to go and take a look at it and its occupant when something made him change his mind. There was a cloud of flies swarming above the chair, dozens of them, big black ones, he thought he could almost hear them buzzing. No one else had set up their deckchairs for a good distance all around that particular one, Danny noticed.

"Look at all those flies, Gran," he said.

"What?"

"Over there – look." He pointed. "Above that chair."

"I can't see *flies*, Danny, if they land on me. My eyes aren't good enough. I can only just see the chair."

For some reason this remark made Danny rather anxious. He felt suddenly isolated and vulnerable. Looking around he discovered he was, as far as he could see, the only child on the beach.

He shut his eyes then, and pretended to sunbathe, but he couldn't settle. His mind was swirling with vague apprehensions.

For the first time all week he found he was missing his parents. At first, he had been relieved to get away from them. They had been so grumpy and depressing recently, though they had continued to treat him as kindly as they had always done. Nevertheless, life at home had been different since his father had received the letter telling him his job would no longer exist in ten weeks, and his parents had taken to endless grinding arguments about money. Danny heard them late at night in the room below his, their voices rasping on like two blunt saws taking turns to cut through a particularly thick, hard log.

They were worried about Gran and Grandad too, and Danny could understand why now. He realized that the whole family had problems. He had problems! Suddenly he wanted to talk to his parents very badly, but he knew he wouldn't see them until the end of the week.

After half-an-hour he went and got some drinks. Grandad insisted on coming with him, somewhat to Danny's relief. He tried not to listen to Grandad's talk, because he seemed to think Danny was someone he had worked with years ago in Canada. That was unnerving, but he felt glad he was not walking alone.

The way to the cafe took them past the huge, brass-bound box parked on the promenade. Even in bright sunlight it looked sinister

Danny thought, though other passers-by seemed unawed by it. The wood had dried out a lot, and was beginning to crack, and the mossy weed clinging to it had turned grey and ash-like. A heat-haze shimmered over the tarpaulin.

There was no sign of the great gull but, when Danny looked up into the sky, he saw, very high up, a black dot that was growing larger as it descended fast towards the ground. Danny grabbed Grandad's hand to hurry him along. He had a vision of what the bird could do with its beak if it hit someone after descending at that speed from that height.

He made sure, when they returned to Gran with their drinks, they went by a roundabout way along the beach, keeping well clear of the box. The route took them past the deckchair that had been shrouded with flies. It was empty now. Danny got the impression that a small group of youngish men in overalls, moving down the beach towards the sea, were carrying something they had lifted from the chair but, in the confusion of people, it was hard to be sure. He went quite near the chair and saw there were still a few flies on duty there, hovering over a wet, red-brown stain on the canvas seat.

It seemed to be a bad day for insects. Early in the afternoon millions of tiny silver and brown flies with thin bodies and long legs appeared from nowhere on the beach. They hopped rather than flew, and got all over Danny's bare legs and arms. They were strangely dry and weightless, like the congregations of corpses that gather on window ledges in empty houses in the summer, and seemed almost without substance. They didn't bite or sting. They were just disgusting. Danny had soon had enough of them. He asked Gran if he could go for a boat trip around the bay.

"You said I could, and if I don't go soon, the holiday will be over," he pleaded.

"There's still three more whole days," Gran said, but she agreed he could do as he had asked. They left their beach-bag and Danny's towels on their chairs because Gran said she was sure there were no thieves about, and the three of them made their way to the harbour.

One of the two boats that did trips was out beyond the headland, just visible in the distance, and the second was almost full and ready to go. It was a big, wide boat that Gran declared quite safe, so she gave Danny some money and told him to get on board. He found a seat at the front and waved at his grandparents with his handkerchief for a joke. Gran waved back, and Grandad copied her movements exactly, a sight that made Danny laugh aloud.

A teenage boy in sun-bleached denim jumped onto the boat and began collecting money and handing out tickets, then a man stepped quickly down from the harbour, started the engine, and grasped hold of the wheel.

It was the bear-like man who Danny had seen moving the box. There was no mistaking his rolling movements, and he was wearing the same clothes as he had been the night before. Danny could tell by the shape of him. The only difference was that at night the man wore a cap and now had nothing on his bald head. Danny got a good look at his face, and not for the first time. He was sure the man had been sitting next to Grandad the day before, with his arm around the back of Grandad's chair and his fingers on the old man's shoulder.

Danny jumped up to get off the boat just as, with a grinding growl of the engine that echoed off the hill behind the town, it cut away from the harbour wall. The man glanced sharply at him and the teenager asked him to get back in his seat. Danny did so at once, and tried to make himself small and inconspicuous.

The man, at the front of the boat, was facing away from Danny. He made an announcement about safety procedures as he steered the vessel out through the maze of moored pleasure-craft to the harbour mouth, then handed the wheel over to his young mate when they reached the open sea. He turned around, sat down, and lit a little cigar. As he blew out smoke he raised his head and glanced quickly around at his passengers. When he saw Danny, he took another sharp drag at his cigar and seemed to shake his head slightly. The gesture had no clear meaning that Danny could interpret, but it frightened him because he felt he had been singled out, perhaps even recognized.

He remembered when he had been watching the man pushing the box along the jetty he had got the impression that the fellow had looked back up at him on a number of occasions, though there was no chance he could really have seen a small boy standing some considerable distance away in the dark, half-hidden behind a curtain. Unless he had remarkable eyesight! He certainly had remarkable eyes, which stared through Danny as though they were focused on a point a million miles behind his head.

Danny thought of the huge black seagull then, that had been so high in the sky above the box when he had passed close to it with Grandad just a couple of hours earlier. The bird must have good eyesight too – it had dropped down at once when it had seen him approach, or so it had appeared to Danny.

Why? Did it think he was going to do some harm to the box, that it seemed to be guarding? Danny couldn't believe that. He hadn't the means or strength to damage it, even if, for some crazy reason, he'd had the inclination to do so. He wasn't bothered about the box – he wanted nothing to do with it, as he had told the bird when he had come close to it on the jetty two days ago. At the time it he had felt foolish talking to a seagull, but not so now. He just wished he had said more. He was afraid he had not made himself understood.

When, after a quarter of an hour, the boat turned its prow into the Bay again for the return trip, Danny was glad the ride was half over. He'd been too confused and anxious to enjoy himself and imagined he was seasick, his stomach felt so queasy. He was very glad when the man, whose hard, unfriendly gaze had returned to him every few minutes, got up to take over the wheel again as they approached the harbour.

Gran was waiting for him on the promenade, holding onto a railing at the very edge of the harbour. Danny waved, but he knew she wouldn't see him. He doubted if she could even see the boat, but she knew what time he was due to return, and was just being there for him.

Grandad sat on a bench a few feet behind her, talking to a man seated next to him. His conversation was animated – he waved his arms and at one point stood up and made a gesture, incomprehensible to Danny, to illustrate some point he was making. Danny guessed he thought his companion was someone from years back in his past, when his life had been exciting, and that they were sharing some adventure together.

As Grandad, in his enthusiasm, took a few steps away from the bench, another man, who Danny had not noticed, but who must have been standing near by, screwed up some paper he had been eating out of and tossed it into a bin. Then he sidled closer to Grandad as though he were on wheels, in a sliding, gliding movement that arrested Danny's attention completely, and totally altered his understanding of the scene he was witnessing.

The man on the bench got up, stood next to Grandad, and pointed inland to somewhere in the town. When Grandad turned to look, the man took his arm, and began, with a certain amount of force, Danny thought, to lead him away. The second man, moving as though he were sliding on ice, fell in behind them.

Gran, still peering myopically out to sea, was obviously unaware of what was going on behind her. The boat was coming in to dock now, and Danny could see her bland, smiling face staring out at the blur of the world in front of her.

He half stood up and shouted at her, and made jerking movements with his hand intended to make her look behind. As he rose to his feet some of the other passengers thought he was getting ready to disembark and also started to get up off their seats. Perceiving this, the man who was steering the boat turned and yelled something to his mate, who jumped onto a chair and called to everyone to be seated. In the confusion of people bobbing up and down Danny lost sight of Gran, but he was careful to keep an eye on Grandad, who was being led slowly uphill into the town.

Not a purposeful walker at the best of times, Grandad liked to stop and start when the urge took him, and the two men were plainly having trouble getting him to go where they wanted him to, and were making slow progress.

The boat bumped against the harbour wall and the teenager skipped ashore to fasten the ropes. The bear-like man took his place next to the couple of steps up the side of the vessel and helped his frail, nervous passengers onto dry land by steering them across the short gangplank, whether they wanted him to or not.

Danny tried to squeeze forward in the queue, getting a few sharp comments from some old ladies as he did so. When his turn to disembark came he tried to avoid the hands of the man by almost running off the boat, but without success. He felt fingers like tentacles curl around his upper arm to stop him in mid-stride.

The man lifted him effortlessly and half-turned him so they were face to face. Danny could smell cigar smoke on his breath, and other more strange odours that he had never come across before. There was a scrap of tobacco on the man's lip that must have irritated him, as he flicked it with his tongue, and spat it out over Danny's shoulder with a toss of his head. The action reminded Danny of squirrels he had seen in the park at home, standing on their hind legs and spitting out indigestible fragments of nuts they were eating.

Not that there was anything cute or squirrel-like about the man's appearance. His heavily-featured face with its sharp, down-curving nose, and receding, almost horizontal forehead was set hard in an ambiguous mask of contempt and vague curiosity, as though Danny were a not-very-fine example of something that, had it been of better or different quality, would perhaps have interested him. Either his head was unusually small, or it seemed so in proportion to the bulk of his vast, barrel-like body. His little gimlet eyes bore in on

Danny's like nails. In the irises of each of them Danny could see tiny reflections of his own frightened face.

The man loosened his grip on Danny's arms and ran his hands down them to the wrists, pressing with his finger tips, feeling for the bones beneath the flesh. He held the joints of Danny's wrists between his thumbs and fingers and lifted them to the height of his shoulders, so the boy's hands hung in front of him like a half-animated puppet's.

Danny squirmed and looked back over his shoulder. Gran was just behind him on the promenade. He could tell from the confusion and apprehension on her face that she was close enough to see what was happening to him.

He tried to get away from the man's grasp, and yelled out, "Grandad's gone. They've taken him away again. Get after him. He's gone up into the town."

The man moved then, and held Danny out so he was hanging by his wrists over the side of the boat next to the little gangplank. The vessel was about twelve inches from the harbour wall and rocking slightly, up and down and from side to side, in the wake of other boats passing beyond. Danny thought if the man let go and he fell he might be crushed between the wall and the side of the boat.

The water below his feet, the colour of boiled cabbage, and marbled with rainbow-tinted whorls of diesel fuel, looked deep, thick and viscous, like glue. Darker shapes moved below its surface. It somehow looked hungry too. Danny imagined his broken body being sucked down into it, dragged under the keel, and pulled out to sea by swirling undercurrents.

He was only suspended thus for a few seconds before the man stretched out over the side of the boat and lowered him slowly onto the edge of the harbour and released him, but they were long seconds, and terrible while they lasted. Some of the elderly people waiting their turn to go ashore thought the man had played an amusing joke on Danny, and squawked with laughter as he ran shouting to his grandmother.

By this time she had discovered her husband's absence, and, as soon as Danny's toes touched the ground, went stumbling away on her arthritic feet to look for him.

"Up the hill," Danny yelled, "they've taken him up the hill."

Gran turned to him with a hopeless look, already out of breath and concerned about her hammering heart.

"Don't worry," Danny said as he overtook her. "Wait here. I'll get him back."

The streets were full of old people drifting back and forth from the beach. They reacted too slowly to get out of Danny's way so he had to run a zig-zag course around them. He lost sight of Grandad from time to time but knew he must soon catch up with him because the trio had come to a stop halfway up the hill.

They seemed to be arguing. They were standing just inside an alleyway between two decrepit-looking red-brick Victorian hotels. The man who had been seated on the bench next to Grandad had had hold of his sleeve. He wasn't actually tugging at it, but was making it impossible for the old man to retreat.

The other would-be abductor, with the smooth, oily movements, was gliding around the pair of them, talking all the while, and making calming gestures with his outstretched hands. Danny could hear Grandad's voice. He was bellowing at the two men that he had had enough of their nonsense. He was going to arrest them. Didn't they know he was a member of the Mounted Police? He was back in the past in Canada again. His face looked more worried than he sounded, but brightened when he saw Danny, who assumed he had been recognized for once.

The two men, following the old man's gaze, turned to see Danny running towards them. The one with peculiar movements detached himself from the tableau and slid towards Danny like a skater. He was dressed in a tight black jacket and shiny trousers, like a waiter's. Danny couldn't be sure, but it seemed that the man's feet, encased in narrow patent-leather shoes, hardly moved, and never quite touched the floor – as though he were suspended a fraction of an inch above the pavement. Perhaps because he was, nevertheless, coming at Danny fast, his form seemed slightly blurred, his features indistinct. When they were almost touching they both side-stepped to avoid each other in the same direction, and collided.

Danny expected to get hurt. He heard himself shout to Grandad to get away as he made contact, then automatically shut his eyes to protect them. He felt a sensation as though he had run into a large, soft mattress that gave to the slightest pressure. There was no indication that what he had hit was anything like a human body that contained flesh and bones, and whatever it was gave way on contact and spread out alarmingly, as though it had come apart. Danny thought he had run right through it and somehow come out the other side.

He opened his eyes and saw what looked like a two-dimensional drawing of a bloated human figure expanding above and in front of him. It was floating away, and waving its flattened arms and legs slowly, like someone drowning in a dream, and clawing desperately at the air with its hands. Almost at once its finger tips appeared to grasp onto something invisible – a hard thin edge of reality, perhaps – and dug in and held on. Then, with an obviously painful effort, it pulled itself back together, contracted, shrunk into itself, and reformed.

All this happened very quickly and, almost before Danny had time to think, the man was hovering in front of him again, with a mildly expectant look on his bland, undistinguished face, exactly like a waiter lingering at a table in expectation of an order. It was as though he were silently challenging Danny to believe that the astonishing metamorphosis he had just observed had indeed happened, and was trying to suggest, by his unconcerned expression and the shear ordinariness of his appearance, that it could not have done.

But Danny *knew*. He knew what he had seen. He knew a great deal all of a sudden, and what he didn't know he guessed.

He flung himself at Grandad, latched onto his arm, and pulled the old man sideways down the hill with all his strength. They tottered along like the contestants in a three-legged race, barging into a number of ancient holidaymakers who they were not able to brush aside, and stumbling and almost falling on the steep incline.

Gran was waiting for them on the promenade. She looked as though she was going to cry when she saw Grandad's face. It was blank and empty, like a paper mask before the features have been painted on it.

Gran said, "Where were they taking him, Danny? What did they want him for?"

Danny couldn't bring himself to say what he thought he knew. He pretended to be more out of breath than he was, and stammered something about muggers. He could see Gran was terribly distraught, but knew this was because of the state her husband was in, and because he had nearly been stolen from her. Thankfully, she could not have seen what occurred when he, Danny, collided with the man in the waiter's outfit, so he wouldn't be called upon to give an explanation of that. On the other hand, he realized, if she had seen, she would at least be more aware of what they were up against.

He looked back up the hill to see if the men had followed him, but there was no sign of them. Suddenly his stomach lurched, and he felt a surge of dizzying nausea, a return of the seasickness that had started half an hour earlier when he had been on the boat, now exacerbated by his recent experiences.

"Gran," he said, "I'm ill. Let's get away from here. This is a terrible place."

Misunderstanding him, thinking he merely wanted to return to the hotel, Gran nodded emphatically. She put her arm around her husband's shoulder and steered him away. The old man walked like an automaton, staring down at the pavement just in front of his dragging feet and saying nothing. Danny dawdled behind all the way to the hotel, to keep the couple in his sight.

Danny looked even worse than he felt when the three of them got together in the dining room for their evening meal. Gran led Grandad in by the elbow. His walk had developed an aimless, twisting tendency that had to be corrected every few steps, and his eyes looked empty and uncomprehending, like a blind man's, or someone concussed. The old man would eat nothing, and Danny couldn't.

Gran stuffed some meat into her mouth and made a show of chewing it to encourage him to do the same, but the smell and appearance of what was on his plate convulsed his stomach and he had to get up and away. Gran's face took on an even more concerned expression when he explained how sick he was. He hated to put this extra burden on her, but he had no alternative. She dug in her bag for some pills, instructed him on the dosage, and told him to get to bed. Danny said "Good night" to Grandad, who made no response at all.

"He's lost his tongue," Gran said, trying to make a half-angry, desperate joke of it, but sounding instead, strangely, much younger than her years, and on the edge of tears again.

Danny dragged himself up the wide blue-carpeted stairs feeling dizzy and disorientated. The spaces around him seemed much wider than he knew they were, as though the hotel had expanded in all directions – a process that appeared to be obscurely continuing out at the edge of his vision. He counted flights from floor to floor grimly, passing hand-over-hand on the stair rail like a man hauling himself along a rope to safety. It occurred to him to take the lift, but he knew his stomach wouldn't stand for that.

On the second floor corridor he heard a confusion of hushed sounds behind him, and somebody called out sharply for him to step aside.

Two men in white jackets were approaching him, pushing a grey painted metal stretcher-bearer. On it was a slender human form half wrapped in a loose-knit white blanket. The lower part of the face of this person was encased in a plastic mask attached by a tube to a cylinder slung below the stretcher. A pink tube curled up from the blanket to what looked like a brown bladder on a stick one of the men was holding above his head.

Danny realized the figure on the stretcher was the young girl he had seen in the dining room a few times. She was lying on her side with her eyes wide open. The transparent mask had a black rim that underlined and isolated her eyes. They looked like two shiny purple holes drilled into her almost bald head. Her little white ears stuck out like toadstools from the sides of her scalp that looked as though it was made of scrubbed white wood. Danny realized that normally she must wear some kind of wig.

She stared at him hard as she passed, giving him an even worse version of the withering look he was used to seeing on her face, and rose up and turned as she passed to keep him in view. Danny found he was pressing his back against the wall to get away from her.

The power of her gaze had a negative force strong enough to repel him physically. It felt like a protracted bomb blast.

She struggled to keep her eyes on him, to keep up the pressure, and tried to sit up. As she did so the blanket slid down from her shoulders to her waist and Danny saw what looked like black shadows, just beneath the skin, sliding down over the ribs of her flat white chest to take shelter under the blanket over her belly. It was as though they were afraid of the light.

The shapes moved hastily, but with purposeful, controlled caution, like fish seeking the safety of deeper, darker waters. The girl kept her purple-black eyes on Danny until one of the men pressed her back down and pulled the blanket up to her chin. They stopped the stretcher at the service lift and Danny, released from the repulsive attraction of the girl, turned his back on them and staggered away.

He found his room at last, wriggled clumsily out of his clothes, pulled the curtains across the open window to hold back the early evening sunlight, clambered into bed and fell, sweating and squirming, into feverish sleep.

Suddenly, Danny was staring into the dark. His eyes had clicked open with a snap that was almost audible. His whole body was rigid with tension. His senses were as alert as a hunter's and, when at last he moved, he moved stealthily. He peeled the quilt smoothly back off the bed and stood up. As he did so the sound that had woken him was repeated somewhere out beyond his window. It was a sliding sound similar to the noises he had heard earlier in the week, but not quite the same. It was a lighter, easier sound. The box was moving faster.

Danny crept to the window and edged the curtain to one side just far enough to give him a view of the section of the street visible between two hotels at the lower level. The sound seemed to be coming from down there.

Seconds later he heard it again, as a long corner of shadow stretched out to his left along the street below. It was followed by the blunt black end of the box, which slid swiftly into full view and came to rest at a point halfway between the hotels. But only for a moment – the bear-like man behind it hardly paused for rest before pushing it on out of sight. The box was only briefly visible, but Danny noticed that the tarpaulin had been removed from the top, and that an upper section seemed to be slightly askew, as though the lid had been lifted and not properly replaced.

Something has been taken out, or has come out, Danny thought. Either that or the box has been opened in preparation for something that was going to be put into it. Or was going to get into it . . . For a second Danny had a dim vision of something huge and dark clambering out to make way for something frail and white that was desperate to clamber in. He shut his eyes and shook his head to shatter the fantasy, and went and sat on his bed.

He almost went back to the window to take a look at what, if anything, was going on on the beach, but decided against it. He was still feeling ill. He was weak and cold, though his skin was damp with sweat. The pills Gran had given him had helped, but their effect had worn off. But he knew she had more in her bag.

He went into the corridor, and tapped on the door of his grandparents' room. No answer. He tapped again, louder, then tried the handle. The door wouldn't move when he pushed it. It must be earlier than he thought, he decided, if it is locked. Gran and Grandad always went to bed at ten. They must be somewhere down stairs, probably in the television lounge.

He set off at a trot along the corridor and ran down the stairs. It wasn't so easy to get lost going down into the hotel because you just kept on going until you reached the bottom, then you stopped. Or so he had assumed. It had worked before.

Nevertheless, he misjudged where he was, and found he had wandered into the Twilight Lounge. It was pitch-dark in there, but he knew where he was, because of the sharp, faint smell of urine. He stood for a moment just inside the door and heard a rustling noise, like paper being slowly crumpled, then someone sighed, and he thought he heard liquid dripping. A wheelchair creaked. *They're waking up!* Danny thought, and hurtled off without bothering to shut the door behind him.

When he found the Television Lounge it was unoccupied. The big set in the corner was still on, filling the room with jumpy silver light and swirls of romantic music from the ancient black and white costume drama that was showing. Danny noticed the clock on the video player below the TV said 01:47. In the morning, that was. He'd never been awake at that time before that he could remember. It wasn't surprising there was nobody about, but why weren't his grandparents in their room? In the past Danny had often had a feeling that grownups did things after their children had gone to bed that they never talked about. It had only ever been a vague suspicion before, but now the idea played on his mind. Where were the adults . . . what were they up to? He would have to find out.

Whenever he had gone in and out of the hotel before there had always been someone at the reception desk, but now even that post was deserted. It seemed that the only people other than himself in the building were the ancient residents in the Twilight Lounge and, young as he was, Danny knew he couldn't expect help or advice from them. They had their own problems.

His only hope of finding his Gran and her medication was to contact a member of staff, and ask them to take him to her. Then he remembered he had seen a big sign that said

STAFF QUARTERS
Staff Only Beyond This Point
PLEASE

on a door at the rear of the hotel. Surely, he would find assistance there!

He ran down the silent corridor towards the kitchens, found the door, and saw with relief that it was half-open. Beyond it, grey-carpeted stairs led down to the basement. He could her music thumping somewhere below, so someone must be awake down there. He glanced again at the off-putting sign on the door, then ventured cautiously onto the stairs. He felt that what he was doing was probably wrong, but guessed that if people were cross with him for venturing where he should not go, they wouldn't do him any harm, and would take him to his grandparents just to get rid of him.

Everything in the staff quarters was smaller and shabbier than on the floors above. The corridors were narrow, illuminated by dim, unshaded yellow bulbs, and the drab carpets were worn and hard. He passed lots of numbered doors, some of them split and cracked, as though the locks had been forced, or they had been punched or kicked. He kept walking, without trying to rouse anyone who might be beyond them, because he could tell, from the increasing volume of the music, he was getting closer to its source. In fact, when he turned the first corner, he walked right into it. Two doors, one marked STAFF and the other RECREATION, stood open wide and he found he had gatecrashed a party in full swing.

There were about two dozen people in the long, low-ceilinged room, and most of them were sitting at a couple of trestle tables covered by white paper tablecloths. The air was murky with what at first he thought was smoke, then realized was a thin damp mist, like fog.

A couple were dancing, away to one side, and a girl in a black, tight, silky outfit twirled somewhat awkwardly to the music, alone in the centre of the available space. She stopped when she saw Danny, and stared at him as though he were an apparition. He recognized her as the girl who had brought him tea in bed each morning, and at once began to feel uneasy.

The girl came and crouched down in front of him, on tiptoes, with her knees bent. She stayed like that for a while, without speaking or moving, weighing him up with her eyes. The calculating quality of her gaze chilled Danny's blood. He wanted to speak, but his lips had gone stiff and his tongue felt like leather. He was aware that other people in the room beyond had become aware of his presence, and were also watching him. Someone with an old man's voice gave a creaky laugh that was echoed by a woman's shrill, mirthless cackle. A man, shouting over the music, said something he didn't catch, then most of them laughed. Danny was just thinking of running off when the girl reached out and took his left elbow in her hand. Then she said sharply, "What are *you* doing here?"

As she waited for his answer her thin fingers massaged the bones of his elbow and her thumb pressed painfully into his inner arm. He mumbled something about his grandparents that was inaudible to the girl, who shook her head to indicate she could not hear him.

Then, desperately, he shouted, "I've lost my Gran. I want someone to help me find her."

As he did so, the rock music tape that had been playing ended abruptly, and he found himself shouting into total silence. His voice sounded like a scream. It frightened him.

The girl moved her head back slightly under the impact of it. She rose up again, still holding Danny's arm, and pulled him further into the room towards the tables. A man on a bench moved to one side to make way for him. The girl, by manipulating his arm, forced him to sit in the vacant space. The man next to him gave him a toothy smile. It was Kelvin, the moustachioed nurse who had rescued him from the people in the Twilight Lounge at the start of the holiday. He still looked reasonably friendly.

Danny recognized a few of the faces of the people seated around him. To his horror, he saw, opposite him across the table, the man in a waiter's uniform – the one with the strange, sliding locomotion, who had tried to lure his grandfather away, and who Danny had run literally right into. The man looked very solid now however, and seemed amused to find Danny in his present predicament.

Danny licked his dry lips and tried to avoid looking anyone in the eye by looking down at the paper cloth on the table in front of him. It was bare except for dishes of nuts and crisps, a couple of big cut-glass decanters almost full of what looked like tomato juice, and a quantity of glasses containing drinks of this liquid. The people around him lifted these glasses to their mouths from time to take a sip, then their eyes would roll and they pursed and smacked their lips with almost ecstatic satisfaction. It was obvious they relished their refreshments.

Danny liked tomato juice himself, but he couldn't understand why anyone should make such a fuss about it. It was nothing special. Last Christmas his father had drunk lots of it with vodka, and there had been a row between his parents when his Dad had fallen from his chair when they had guests round, but there was no sign of any vodka on the tables now. Yet the people at the party, if that was what it was, seemed to think tomato juice was the finest drink in the world!

The man opposite him, the one dressed like a waiter, poured a fresh glass of the liquid and handed it to Danny. The drink had a funny smell, not a bit like tomato juice, that Danny detected as soon as he had taken the glass, and he looked at it suspiciously. He raised it to his lips and sniffed. As he did so, the girl, who still had hold of his arm, increased the pressure of her grasp on his elbow.

Danny saw, out of the corner of his eye, that the girl's face was flushed and excited and . . . hungry-looking. The tip of her tongue appeared briefly against her upper lip, and her brow arched up as her eyes stretched wide. He could tell she wanted him to try the drink. She wanted him to try it very much. And so did all the other people. They were all watching him with sharp, intense anticipation.

Danny held the glass a couple of inches from his mouth. His hand was not quite steady.

"What is this?" he asked. "It's not tomato juice, is it?"

"Did we say it was?" someone said. "Did *anyone* say it was?"

Everybody shook their heads.

"It's a fine drink," the girl said softly. "A rare old vintage. Something you won't have tasted before. But once you've tried it, you'll want more of it. There's no doubt about that."

"I don't like the smell," Danny said nervously.

"Never mind that. It's not the taste or the smell that matters, it's what it does for you," the girl insisted.

Danny said nothing.

"It won't harm you," someone said. "We drink it all the time, and look at us. We're lucky here, we get plenty of it."

"The fine old stuff," the girl repeated, almost singing, as though she was quoting a popular song, "the rare old vintage."

Danny lowered his mouth to the glass and took a sip. The drink was thick and flat and metallic and slightly warm. It was neither good nor bad. He drank some more, and found he was suddenly thirsty. He emptied the glass slowly and put it down.

"Well?" asked the girl.

"It's okay," Danny said, unenthusiastically.

"Would you like some more?"

Danny was a polite boy. "Not at the moment, thank you," he said, and for some reason most of the people seated around him started to laugh. It was relaxed, good-humoured laughter. Danny noticed the girl had released her hold on his arm at last and, when the laughter had subsided, he repeated his request to be taken to his Gran. Someone made a joke that made no sense, about taking Gran to Danny, then Kelvin got up and told Danny it was too late to disturb Gran now, but he would take him back up to his room in the service lift. Danny would have to sort his other problems out in the morning.

To Danny's surprise, the entrance to the lift was at the back of the room they were in. Kelvin went and leaned on the button and, high up in the hotel, the lift lurched and groaned as it begun unsteadily to descend. When it arrived Kelvin had trouble pulling the slightly rusty, cage-like bars of the metal outer door open, then cursed as he bent to tug up the inner door that rose and slid back somewhere at the top of the lift. A cloud of the cold, steamy looking mist Danny had noticed earlier wafted out of the lift shaft, surged across the floor, then floated up towards the ceiling on a cushion of warm air.

Danny saw at once that the lift was not empty. The huge brass-bound box he had seen so many times before was in there, taking up most of the space.

It had been pushed up tight against one wall and there was just a narrow gap vacant to one side of it. Kelvin motioned to Danny to get in beside it. Danny shook his head and backed off a little way. He saw that the lid of the box was now in place, but could tell it was loose, unsealed. The dry wooden structure had finger-wide splits in it, and its sides were warped and slightly concave. In places, the wood had sunk away from the brass to reveal sections of the ancient, primitive nails that held it together. The seaweed that had been growing on it had shrunk, withered and turned colourless, like old wreathes in a graveyard.

Kelvin gave Danny a look that the boy recognized as the expression Todley Bay people sometimes put on their faces when they wanted to smile. It was probably meant to be encouraging, but Danny thought it had an impatient edge to it. Kelvin was in a hurry. Probably he wanted to get back for more of the red juice before the others drank it all.

Kelvin said, "What's the matter? Get in. I'll get you to your room in no time."

Danny pointed to the box. "What's that?"

"This?" Kelvin stepped forward and thumped the lid of the box with his fist. "Nothing for you to worry about, anyway. Not for a long time, I shouldn't think. You needn't trouble yourself about that."

"Is it empty?"

"I expect so." To placate Danny, Kelvin lifted the lid slightly, and peered inside. He took a long, hard look.

"Are you sure," Danny insisted nervously.

"Well," Kevin said, lowering the lid, "it's not quite empty, but don't go bothering yourself about that."

"What's in there?"

"If you really want to know, sonny, I'll show you. I'll lift you up so you can take a look inside, if you think it'll make you happy. But I wouldn't recommend it."

"I don't want to see inside. I don't want to go near it. I don't want anything to do with it."

"You don't have to like it, son," Kevin said, now definitely irritable, "but if you want me to show you to your room, you're going to have to ride up with it. So get in."

Danny waited for a long moment, and stared at the box. Something could be hiding in there, observing him, staring back at him through the cracks in the sides. But, if there was, he didn't feel it was necessarily out to harm him, it could be that it was just . . . curious about him. If there *was* anything in there, it wasn't him, Danny, it was after – or so, for no clear reason, he began to believe.

He decided to test his theory, since he could see no other option, and stepped quickly into the lift before he could think about his situation any more. He suddenly wanted to get to bed more than anything else he could think of.

Kelvin followed Danny onto the floor of the lift, shut the outer gates, pulled down the inner door, squeezed in along the side of the box beside the boy, and pushed a button. A stump of fluorescent tube set in the roof flickered and almost died. Something high in the building squealed as it took the strain. The sheet metal panels on the walls creaked all around them, and the lift juddered – hesitated – lurched – then began to rise slowly, swinging slightly from side to side because it was out of balance.

Danny kept as far away from the box as he could in yellow-green gloom that was almost darkness, and gulped to relieve his dry throat and mouth, that now seemed to be full of imaginary dust.

Kelvin saw him swallowing air, and said, "What's the trouble?"

"I'm very thirsty," Danny admitted.

"Well, yes, you will be. It's only to be expected. But you'll get used to it. That's the way it is."

"I don't understand," Danny complained.

The lift shuddered to a halt.

"You will," Kelvin said, and stooped to pull up the door. He said something else as he tugged aside the doors of the metal cage, but Danny couldn't hear him over the clanging of the iron bars. Kelvin stepped onto the corridor and pointed to a door a little way away that Danny recognized at once as his own, leading to his room.

"You get to bed now," Kelvin ordered, "and don't go looking for your Gran any more tonight."

In his room Danny drank at least a pint of water out of the tap at the washbasin. It was warm, and tasted slightly ferric, like the drink he had been given in the basement. He realized then that he hadn't felt at all ill since he had taken that crimson drink. In fact, it had made him feel very good – he was almost glowing with health inside. But he was tired out.

He flung himself into bed and slept at once.

Someone was moving quietly about in his room. Danny knew from the quality of the light it was early morning, so assumed the girl had let herself in to deliver his tea. Good, because he still had a thirst like an ache in the back of his throat. He didn't want to talk to her, however, for obvious reasons, so kept his face under the quilt.

Then, whoever was in the room sat down on his bed. Someone big and heavy. He knew this, because the whole bed sank in the middle, whereas it had only dipped slightly when the girl had perched on it on previous occasions.

A big person had come into his room, uninvited, and was sitting on his bed! An image of the bear-like man carved into his mind and filled him with fear. *He's come for me, or he's come for the box, or he's come for both*, Danny thought, and he nearly stopped breathing.

Then the someone cleared his throat and said, "Danny, I know you're awake. It's me, don't worry." It was his father's voice.

Danny sat up with a jerk. "Dad! What are you doing here? What's wrong?"

His father's face was crumpled and tired, and his usually immaculately combed hair stuck up in bristles in a dozen places. His eyes looked sore and the flesh below them was flaky and grey. He was wearing his best suit over a white shirt that looked grimy at the collar, as though he'd worn it one day too many, and his tie was loose and askew.

"Danny, I'm sorry, but the holiday's over. Something's happened, so your mother and I came down here overnight. The car broke down. It's been very difficult, but we're here now, so . . ."

"Has something happened to Grandad?" Danny asked, thinking he could see the light. "Have they got him then? Has he disappeared?" He jumped out of bed, went to the sink, and drank more warm washing water from his tooth-mug.

His father looked confused. "No, he's okay. Your mother is with him now. It's Gran, I'm afraid. You're going to have to know . . . I'm sorry Danny, but she passed away, during the night."

"Passed away?"

Realizing the euphemism was above and beyond Danny, his father explained that Gran was dead.

*　　*　　*

Three hours later Danny, his parents, and Grandad were waiting in the hotel foyer for a taxi to take them to the station. The manager of the establishment, a razor-thin, crop-haired woman in a black and white check blouse and grey suit, was commiserating with his mother, who was crying softly all the time that she was speaking. Danny heard part of the conversation, but didn't understand much of what was said.

"—terribly sad time – everything done that could be done – first-rate staff who are used to dealing with death – see it all the time – we've taken care of the body – leave everything to us – unfortunately, another guest *in extremis*, even now, as I speak – and so young, just a girl – but of course, we prefer to deal with older people – the more mature person – ripe old age is our speciality – you understand?"

The manageress sounded as though she had been reading from a publicity handout and had suddenly discovered that the last page was missing. She took a dive into sudden silence. Her sympathetic expression, set in stone, seemed only to affect her face below her eyes, which were empty and uninvolved. She and Danny's mother were seated on two gold-painted chairs, facing each other almost knee to knee.

"It was meant to be a break for them both," Danny's mother said, glad of a silence to break. She pushed her nose into her handkerchief and wiped her eyes. "She only had six months to live. That's what they told her, and she was so worried about leaving my father behind. He has Alzheimer's disease, so she was hoping to find somewhere here in Todley Bay where he could spend what time he has left in comfort. He could last years. She wanted to leave him in good hands."

The manageress nodded and clucked her tongue.

"She insisted on bringing the boy, because it would be their last chance of a holiday together, though I didn't think it was right. But you can't argue with someone who's going to die soon, can you? Especially if it's your own mother, so I let him come."

The manageress nodded and looked about her for some excuse to get away. No obvious opportunity presented itself.

"It's so terribly sad, that she should be denied those last few months they promised her," Danny's mother said, and hid her face in her hands.

Danny was keeping an eye on Grandad. The old man was quite oblivious to his wife's death. He had a loopy half-smile on his face, and was rubbing his hands together a lot, as though they were cold, or he were washing them. He kept strolling off, and Danny kept leading him back to his parents.

Danny used these opportunities to buy soft drinks from a machine in the bar. He could feel them all sloshing about in his stomach, but he still wanted more. Or perhaps he wanted something else. It was a funny kind of thirst he had, that would not be quenched, and there didn't seem to be anything he could do about it.

He had tried to explain his other worry to his father and mother, about the people who had attempted to lure Grandad away, but his mother had started to get angry with him, and told him that this was no time for him to talk rubbish.

It was obvious his father thought he was fantasizing too. He had shaken his head at Danny when the boy had mentioned the man who travelled across the ground without moving his feet, like a skater. So Danny shut up. He realized there was no point in trying to get through to his parents, who were both up to their ears in troubles of their own, so he gave himself the job of protecting Grandad. He was delighted when his father told him the four of them were returning home by train at once, that very morning.

When the taxi came Danny sat in the back with Grandad and his mother, who was now overwhelmed with grief. He held her hand, but got the impression she was unaware that he was there. Strangely, he had no feelings at all about Gran's death. It meant nothing to him yet. He was more concerned with the torrent of weeping beside him, and alarmed at his mother's inconsolable condition. He felt Grandad was safe now.

As the taxi drove along the seafront Danny saw the great bulk of the box ahead of them on the edge of the promenade. Someone had started to push it back towards the jetty, but hadn't got very far. The oily-black, overgrown gull was perched on top of it, standing in perfect balance on one leg. Its head was set at an angle. It seemed to be carefully scrutinizing the traffic moving towards it.

The taxi, travelling slowly because a number of elderly people were dawdling and doddering across the road to get to the beach, came almost to a stop less than ten feet from the box. Danny slid down in his seat and turned away, trying to make himself invisible, just as the driver saw a gap ahead and accelerated into it, taking the vehicle some way beyond the box and the bird. Danny, thinking and hoping he had got by unobserved, couldn't resist turning around and sticking his head up over the top of the back seat to take one last look out the rear window at the gull.

The bird was riding the air a few inches above the boot of the taxi. Its beak dipped down towards the glass of the rear window, and it stared with one dead-reptile eye straight into both of Danny's. It retained this pose for a moment, then broke away from the taxi with a single tug of its wings that took it soaring into the air.

Danny expected it to follow the vehicle, but it didn't. It climbed up to a vast height at incredible speed, as though it had seen a hole in the sky it was afraid was due to close. Then it seemed to change its mind. It plummeted back towards the town and disappeared behind the roofs to the right, ahead of the taxi.

Danny's father, sitting next to the driver, looked at his watch and remarked that they might miss the train. The driver shrugged, indicated towards the clutter of old people crossing the road ahead, and said he was doing his best.

When they got to the station there was no queue at the ticket office. Even so, Danny's father had to write a cheque, and seemed to take an age doing so.

Danny bought a tin of Coke, gulped it down, then stood with the other two and a little heap of luggage at the ticket barrier, ready to assault the platform to get to the train the instant they were free to do so.

When his father emerged running with the tickets Danny grabbed some of the baggage and shot past the ticket inspector right behind him. His father, with one arm around his still distraught wife, scuttled awkwardly alongside the train looking for an empty compartment. They were halfway along the platform before Danny thought to look back to see where Grandad was. There was no sign of him.

Danny stopped and looked all around. Except for himself and his parents, the platform was empty. He shouted to his father, and felt the eyes of dozens of passengers on the train turn to stare at him curiously from behind the dusty carriage windows. His father understood what had happened at once.

"We've got to find him Danny. Go back. You take the right and I'll go left. He can't be far."

Danny shed his baggage and pelted back through the barrier again. He saw Grandad almost at once, standing by a newspaper kiosk, talking to the man in waiter's uniform. The man was half-hidden in a doorway. His face was just visible, and only his arms protruded. They undulated in beckoning, luring movements, like the tentacles of an octopus. Grandad, shifting from foot to foot, was rubbing his hands and smacking his forehead in gestures of wild indecision. He also seemed to be laughing anxiously, like a donkey, with his mouth wide open. The man in the doorway slid back a few inches, like a man on roller skates, and Danny could see his feet were definitely not touching the ground. His body even seemed to float up a little way as he receded, and Danny remembered that he had no bones, no *substance*.

Danny shouted wordlessly at Grandad, who froze. The man in the doorway glanced at Danny, sneered, and vanished. He went out in an instant, like a fused light.

Danny grabbed Grandad's arm and yanked him away, almost pulling the old man off his feet. He seemed to get the idea for once, however, and, to Danny's surprise, started running quite fast. So fast in fact, the boy found it hard to steer him. He urged him in the right direction by pushing and pulling, a procedure that constantly threatened to entangle their legs and trip them both.

The man at the barrier, who had watched the whole performance with some amusement, let them through and signalled to the guard at the far end of the station that the train could go.

It started moving almost at once, sending Danny into a panic. There was no sign of his parents or the luggage, so he assumed that they had got on board. One of the doors of the nearest carriage was hanging invitingly open. Danny urged Grandad towards it, then trotted alongside as the old man climbed up the step to the corridor. As he did so he glanced back and saw his mother struggling towards him clutching the luggage. Behind her, running desperately through the ticket barrier, was his father, his face purple with unaccustomed effort. Both his parents looked very angry.

For a moment Danny thought he was going to start to scream and cry in protest against the waves of confusion and frustration that were sweeping over him.

He turned to pull Grandad back. It was obvious that his parents would not reach the train in time to get aboard, since the carriage next to him was now moving at running speed. He shouted to Grandad to get down, then realized that it would be very dangerous if he did try to disembark. Nevertheless, the old man turned and appeared to make some confident attempt to get back off the step.

As he did so an arm reached out from the carriage door and the big hand at the end of it took firm hold of Grandad's shoulder and started to pull him in. A second hand emerged to take a grip on the other shoulder and Grandad was lifted up off his feet altogether and hauled into the darkness beyond the door. Then a figure leaned out for the handle of the door and quickly pulled it shut. Danny saw the hawk-like nose and receding forehead of the bear-like man for just a second, peering out at him from behind the window at the upper part of the door, then the train gathered speed, retreated along the line, and snaked away out of the platform.

Then Danny did begin to scream and cry. He cried even louder when his mother caught up with him and started to blame him for what had occurred. Her face was a damp, white puffy blotch of grief and anger. His father, when he joined them, tried to calm things down.

"We can phone ahead, down the line, and get someone to go on the train at the next stop and bring him off," he said, but his wife didn't seem to hear him.

"He's senile," she protested. "He doesn't know where he is or what he's doing. He might just open a door and walk out while the train is moving. Anything could happen."

"It's not just that," Danny yelled, now quite beside himself. "One of those men was in the carriage. They've got him now. They've been trying to get him all week."

"What men, Danny?" his father said, trying to conceal his impatience.

"The ones I told you about," Danny said, "but you wouldn't listen."

On the very edge of anger, his father said, "And why would these men want an old man like Grandad, for God's sake?"

"For his blood," said Danny, "and some of them want his bones."

Then his mother dropped all the luggage that she was carrying and stepped very close to Danny. "How could you talk such rubbish?" she yelled. "At a time like this . . . on the day of my mother's death?"

She spluttered to a halt, overwhelmed with indignation and rage.

A surge of intense and actually painful thirst, a craving for a drink that was not available, a liquid he could not obtain, cut into Danny, and made him gag. He put his fingers into his mouth to touch his tongue to see if it was as dry as it seemed to be. It was.

His father, alarmed by the expression on Danny's face, asked him what was wrong.

"I'm drying up inside Dad," Danny said, suddenly afraid to hear his own words. "I've got a terrible . . ." his tongue clicked against his palate, ". . . a terrible, awful thirst."

His mother regained her voice then. Her face was wet, wild, and dangerous, like a storm at sea. She howled at Danny wordlessly, and held her shaking hands, half-clenched like claws, in front of her face. "What are you trying to do to me?" she screamed at last. "How can you stand there and . . . *talk* . . . *such* . . . *nonsense*? After all that's happened, at a time like this, *you stand there whining about your thirst!*"

Danny, shattered, feeling quite alone, stood grey-faced and devastated by the injustice of it all. Something in his expression must have pushed his mother over the edge of her patience at that moment, because, for the first time in her life, she slapped Danny hard across the face. Her ring cut the flesh of his cheek.

Danny broke away and ran. His mouth gaped open in a scream that only he could hear. Warm blood trickled down his cheek and into his mouth. The taste of it was at once familiar. It was like, but not quite the same as, what he was seeking. What he needed to quench his thirst.

Thinking about the dying girl back at the hotel, Danny ran right out of the station into the slowly moving holiday crowds passing back and forth along the front of Todley Bay. He darted through them like a wraith. Nobody seemed to notice him. He moved so fast, he thought he might be invisible.

He hoped the staff back at the hotel would understand, and be kind to him.

When he got there he found they were only too happy to receive him. They took him in, concealed him, and urged him to be patient.

The feast, they told him, though not of the rare old vintage of the night before, was almost ready. It would soon be served.

So, for the present, Danny had to content himself with that.

1997

THE
MAMMOTH BOOK OF

BEST NEW
HORROR

THE YEAR'S BEST HORROR
STORIES BY SUCH MASTERS
OF DARK FANTASY AS:

RAMSEY CAMPBELL
DENNIS ETCHISON
CHRISTOPHER FOWLER
DAVID J. SCHOW
MICHAEL MARSHALL-SMITH
KIM NEWMAN
and many others

EDITED BY
STEPHEN JONES

"A superb range of
mature, challenging tales."
— *TIME OUT*

Emptiness Spoke Eloquent

Caitlín R. Kiernan

WITH VOLUME NINE the publisher decided that *Best New Horror* needed a new look. Unfortunately, it got one. But at least the trite Photoshopped image that finally appeared on the cover was not as garish as the version they originally wanted to use.

They also decided that, in the UK at least, the series should be folded into Robinson's very successful series of "Mammoth Book" titles, which they (not unreasonably) believed would give the volume a higher profile amongst booksellers and readers. Carroll & Graf obviously needed a bit more persuading and, as a result, only the British edition was retitled *The Mammoth Book of Best New Horror*.

By now the Introduction had reached sixty two pages and the Necrology was hovering around twenty-eight. For the ninth volume I concentrated my ire on those practitioners of so-called "extreme horror".

I find most literary "movements" slightly incestuous and cliquey anyway, but this loosely connected band of misogynistic and gratuitous horror writers belonged to a club that I certainly had no interest in joining. Like the "Splatterpunks" a decade before them, I predicted that they were destined to end up as a marginal footnote in the history of the genre. I'm delighted to say that it looks as if I was correct.

Champions of the equally pointless "New Weird" please take note . . .

The book featured just nineteen stories – the lowest number since the series began. However, this was partially due to the inclusion of Douglas E. Winter's satirical novella "The Zombies of Madison County".

Veteran 1960s author John Burke was also represented, as was David Langford, a former contributor to the Fontana and Armada horror anthologies who is better known for his multiple Hugo Award-winning non-fiction.

Every year I read countless vampire or Cthulhu Mythos stories for possible inclusion in *Best New Horror*. Rarely do they achieve anything new or different within their respective sub-genres (this statement obviously excludes Kim Newman's ongoing *Anno Dracula* series, about which more later). There usually has to be something very special about such stories for me to even consider including them in the anthology.

With Caitlín R. Kiernan it is all about the language. "Emptiness Spoke Eloquent" is a sequel to Bram Stoker's *Dracula* (or, as the author readily admits, Francis Ford Coppola's uneven 1992 movie adaptation). "Eloquent" is the right word to describe Caitlín's first contribution to *Best New Horror*, which supplies an answer for those readers who – like the author – ever wondered what happened next to Mina Harker . . .

LUCY HAS BEEN AT the window again, her sharp nails tap-tapping on the glass, scratching out there in the rain like an animal begging to be let in. Poor Lucy, alone in the storm. Mina reaches to ring for the nurse, but stops halfway, forcing herself to believe all she's hearing is the rasping limbs of the Crape Myrtle, whipped by the wind, winter-bare twigs scritching like fingernails on the rain-slick glass. She forces her hand back down onto the warm blanket. And, she knows well enough, that this simple action says so much. Retreat, pulling back from the cold risks; windows kept shut against night and chill and the thunder.

There was so much of windows.

On the colour television bolted high to the wall, tanks and soldiers in the Asian jungle and that bastard Nixon, soundless.

Electric-white flash and almost at once, a thunderclap that rattles the sky, and sends a shudder through the concrete and steel skeleton of the hospital and the windows and old Mina, safe and warm, in her blanket.

Old Mina.

She keeps her eyes open, avoiding sleep, and memories of other storms.

And Lucy at her window.

Again she considers the nurse, that pale angel to bring pills to grant her mercy, blackness and nothingness, the dreamless space between hurtful wakings. Oh, if dear Dr Jack, with his pitiful morphine, his chloral and laudanum, could see the marvels that men have devised to unleash numbness, the flat calm of mind and body and soul. And she *is* reaching then, for the call button and for Jonathan's hand, that he should call Seward, anything against the dreams and the scritching at the window.

This time she won't look, eyes safe on the evening news, and the buzzer makes no sound in her room. This time she will wait for the soft rubber-soled footsteps, she will wait for the door to open and Andrea or Neufield or whoever is on duty to bring oblivion in a tiny paper cup.

But after a minute, a minute-and-a-half, and no response, Mina turns her head, giving in by turtle-slow degrees, and she watches the rain streaking the dark glass, the restless shadows of the Crape Myrtle.

June 1904

The survivors of the Company of Light stood in the rubble at the base of the castle on the Arges and looked past iron and vines, at the empty, soulless casements. It seemed very little changed, framed now in the green froth of the Carpathian summer instead of snow, ice, and bare grey stone.

The trip had been Jonathan's idea, had become an obsession, despite her protests and Arthur's and in the end, seeing how much the journey would cost her, even Van Helsing's. Jack Seward, whose moods had grown increasingly black since their steamer had docked in Varna, had refused to enter the castle grounds and stood alone outside the gates. Mina held little Quincey's hand perhaps too tightly and stared silently up at the moss-chewed battlements.

There was a storm building in the east, over the mountains. Thunder rumbled like far-off cannon, and the warm air smelled of rain and ozone and the heavy purplish blooms hanging from the creepers. Mina closed her eyes and listened, or *tried* to listen the way she had that November day years before. Quincey squirmed, restless six, by her side. The gurgle and splash of the swollen river, rushing unseen below them, and the raucous calls of birds, birds she didn't recognize. But nothing else.

And Van Helsing arguing with Jonathan.

". . . now, Jonathan, now you are satisfied?"

"Shut up. Just shut the bloody hell up."

What are you listening for, Mina?

Lord Godalming lit his pipe, some Turkish blend, exotic spice and smoke, sulphur from his match. He broke into the argument, something about the approaching storm, about turning back.

What do you expect you'll hear?

The thunder answered her, much closer this time, and a sudden, cold gust was blown out before the storm.

He's not here, Mina. He's not here.

Off in the mountains, drifting down through passes and trees, a wild animal cried out, just once, in pain or fear or maybe anger. And Mina opened her eyes, blinked, waiting for the cry to come again, but then the thunder cracked like green wood overhead and the first drops of rain, fat and cold, began to fall. The Professor took her arm, leading her away, mumbling Dutch under his breath, and they left Jonathan standing there, staring blankly up at the castle. Lord Godalming waited, helpless, at his side.

And in the falling rain, her tears lost themselves, and no one saw them.

November 1919

Fleeing garish victory, Mina had come back to Whitby hardly two weeks after the armistice. Weary homecomings for the living and maimed and flag-draped caskets. She'd left Quincey behind to settle up his father's affairs.

From the train, the lorry from the station, her bags carried off to a room she hadn't seen yet; she would not sleep at the Westenra house at the Crescent, although it was among the portion of the Godalming estate left to her after Arthur Holmwood's death. She took her tea in the inn's tiny dining room, sitting before the bay windows. From there she could see down the valley, past red roofs and whitewash to the harbour pilings and the sea. The water glittered, sullen under the low sky. She shivered and pulled her coat tighter, sipped at the Earl Gray and lemon in cracked china, the cup glazed as dark as the brooding sky. And if she looked back the other way, towards East Cliff, she might glimpse the ruined abbey, the parish church, and the old graveyard.

Mina refilled her cup from the mismatched teapot on the table, stirred at the peat-coloured water, watching the bits of lemon pulp swirl in the little maelstrom.

She'd go to the graveyard later, maybe tomorrow.

And again the fact, the cold candour of her situation, washed over and through her; she had begun to feel like a lump of gravel polished smooth by a brook. That they were all dead now, and she'd not attended even a single funeral. Arthur first, almost four years back now, and then Jack Seward, lost at Suvla Bay. The news about Jonathan hadn't reached her until two days after the drunken cacophony of victory had erupted in Trafalgar Square and had finally seemed to engulf the whole of London. He'd died in some unnamed village along the Belgian border, a little east of Valenciennes, a senseless German ambush only hours before the cease-fire.

She laid her spoon aside, watched the spreading stain it made on her napkin. The sky was ugly, bruised.

A man named MacDonnell, a grey-bearded Scotsman, had come to her house, bearing Jonathan's personal things – his pipe, the brass-framed daguerreotype of her, an unfinished letter. The silver crucifix he'd worn like a scar the last twenty years. The man had tried to comfort her, offering half-heard reassurances that her husband had been as fine a corporal as any on the Front. She thought sometimes that she might have been more grateful to him for his trouble.

She still had the unfinished letter, carried with her from London, and she might look at it again later, though she knew it almost by heart now. Scribblings she could hardly recognize as his, mad and rambling words about something trailing his battalion through the fields and muddy trenches.

Mina sipped her tea, barely noticing that it had gone cold, and watched the clouds outside as they swept in from the sea and rushed across the rocky headland.

A soupy fog in the morning, misty ghosts of ships and men torn apart on the reef, and Mina Harker followed the curve of stairs up from the town, past the ruined Abbey, and into the old East Cliff churchyard. It seemed that even more of the tombstones had tumbled over, and she remembered the elderly sailors and fishermen and whalers that had come here before, Mr Swales and the others, and wondered if anyone ever came here now. She found a bench and sat, looking back down to where Whitby lay hidden from view. The yellow lantern eyes of the lighthouses winked in the distance, bookending the invisible town below.

She unfolded Jonathan's letter and the chilling breeze fingered the edges of the paper.

The foghorns sounded, that throaty bellow, perplexed and lonesome.

Before leaving London, she'd taken all the papers, the typed pages and old notebooks, the impossible testament of the Company, from the wall safe where Jonathan had kept them. Now they were tucked carefully inside the brocade canvas satchel resting on the sandy cobbles at her feet.

"*. . . and burn them, Mina, burn every trace of what we have seen,*" scrawled in that handwriting that was Jonathan's, and also surely no one's she'd ever met.

And so she had sat at the hearth, these records in her lap, watching the flames, feeling the heat on her face. Had lifted a letter to Lucy from the stack, held the envelope a moment, teasing the fire as a child might tease a cat with table scraps.

"No," she whispered, closing her eyes against the hungry orange glow, and putting the letter back with the rest. *It's all I have left, and I'm not that strong.*

Far out at sea, she thought she heard bells, and down near Tate Hill Pier, a dog barking. But the fog made a game of sound and she couldn't be sure she'd heard anything but the surf and her own breathing. Mina lifted the satchel and set it on the bench beside her.

Earlier that morning she'd stood before the looking glass in her room at the inn, staring into the soft eyes of a young woman, not someone who had seen almost forty-two years and the horrors of her twentieth. As she had so often done before her own mirrors, she'd looked for the age that should have begun to crease and ruin her face and found only the faintest crow's feet.

"*. . . every trace, Mina, if we are ever to be truly free of this terrible damnation.*"

She opened the satchel and laid Jonathan's letter inside, pressed it between the pages of his old diary, then snapped the clasp shut again. *Now*, she thought, filled suddenly with the old anger, black and acid, *I might fling it into the sea, lose these memories here, where it started.*

Instead, she hugged the bag tightly to her and watched the light-houses as the day began to burn the mist away.

Before dusk, the high clouds had stacked themselves out beyond Kettleness, filling the eastern sky with thunderheads, their bruise-black underbellies already dumping sheets of rain on a foamy white sea. Before midnight, the storm had reared above Whitby Harbour and made landfall. In her narrow room above the kitchen, framed in wood and plaster and faded gingham wallpaper haunted by a hundred thousand boiled cabbages, Mina dreamed.

She was sitting at the small window, shutters thrown back, watching the storm walk the streets, feeling the icy salt spray and rain on her face. Jonathan's gold pocket watch lay open on the writing desk, ticking loud above the crash and boom outside. MacDonnell had not brought the watch back from Belgium, and she'd not asked him about it.

Quick and palsied fingers of lightning forked above the rooftops and washed the world in an instant of daylight.

On the bed behind her, Lucy said something about Churchill and the cold wind and laughed. Chandelier diamond tinkling and asylum snigger between velvet and gossamer and rust-scabbed iron bars.

And still laughing, "Bitch . . . apostate, Wilhelmina coward."

Mina looked down, watching the hands, hour, minute, second, racing themselves around the dial. The fob was twisted and crusted with something dark.

"Lucy, please . . ." and her voice came from very far away, and it sounded like a child asking to be allowed up past her bedtime.

Groan and bedspring creak, linen rustle and a sound wetter than the pounding rain. Lucy Westenra's footsteps moved across the bare floor, her heels clocking, ticking off the shortening distance.

Mina looked back down, and Drawbridge Road was absurdly crowded with bleating sheep, soppy wool in the downpour, and the gangling shepherd, a scarecrow blown from the wheat fields west of Whitby. Twiggy fingers beneath his burlap sleeve, driving his flock towards the harbour.

Lucy was standing very close now. Stronger than the rain and the old cabbage stink, anger that smelled like blood and garlic bulbs and dust. Mina watched the sheep and the storm.

"Turn *around*, Mina. Turn around and look at me and tell me that you even loved Jonathan."

Turn around Mina and tell

"Please, Lucy, don't leave me here."

and tell me that you even loved

And the sheep were turning, their short necks craning upwards and she saw they had red little rat eyes, and then the scarecrow howled.

Lucy's hands were cool silk on Mina's fevered shoulders.

"Don't leave, not yet . . ."

And Lucy's fingers, like hairless spider legs, had crawled around Mina's cheeks, and seized her jaw. Something brittle and dry, something crackling papery against her teeth, was forced past her lips.

On the street, the sheep were coming apart in the storm, reduced to yellowed fleece and fat-marbled mutton; a river of crimson sluicing between paving stones. Grinning skulls and polished white ribs, and the scarecrow had turned away, and broken up in the gale.

Lucy's fingers pushed the first clove of garlic over Mina's tongue, then shoved another into her mouth.

And she felt the cold steel at her throat.

We loved you, Mina, loved you as much as the blood and the night and even as much as

Mina Harker woke up in the hollow space between lightning and thunderclap.

Until dawn, when the storm tapered off to gentle drizzle and distant echoes, she sat alone on the edge of the bed, shaking uncontrollably and tasting bile and remembered garlic.

January 1922

Mina held the soup to the Professor's lips, chicken steam curling in the cold air. Abraham Van Helsing, eighty-seven and so much more dead than alive, tried to accept a little of the thin, piss-yellow broth. He took a clumsy sip, and the soup spilled from his mouth, dribbling down his chin into his beard. Mina wiped his lips with the stained napkin lying across her lap.

He closed his grey-lashed eyes and she set the bowl aside. Outside, the snow was falling again, and the wind yowled wolf noises around the corners of his old house. She shivered, trying to listen, instead, to the warm crackle from the fireplace, and the Professor's laboured breath. In a moment, he was coughing again, and she was helping him sit up, holding his handkerchief.

"Tonight, Madam Mina, tonight . . ." and he smiled, wan smile, and his words collapsing into another fit, the wet consumptive rattle. When it passed, she eased him back into the pillows, and noticed a little more blood on the ruined handkerchief.

Yes, she thought, *perhaps*. And once she would have tried to assure him that he would live to see spring and his damned tulips and another spring after that, but she only wiped the sweaty strands of hair from his forehead, and pulled the moth-gnawed quilt back around his bony shoulders.

Because there was no one else and nothing to keep her in England, she'd made the crossing to Amsterdam the week before Christmas; Quincey had been taken away by the influenza epidemic after the war. Just Mina now, and this daft old bastard. And soon enough, there would be only her.

"Shall I read for a bit, Professor?" They were almost halfway through Mr Conrad's *The Arrow of Gold*. She was reaching for the book on the nightstand (and saw that she'd set the soup bowl on it) when his hand, dry and hot, closed softly around her wrist.

"Madam Mina," and already he was releasing her, his parchment touch withdrawn and there was something in his eyes now besides cataracts and the glassy fever flatness. His breath wheezed in, then forced itself harshly out again.

"I am *afraid*," he said, his voice barely a rasping whisper slipped into and between the weave of the night.

"You should rest now, Professor," she told him, wishing against anything he might say.

"So much a fraud I was, Madam Mina."

Did you ever even love?

"It was *my* hand that sent her, by my *hand*."

"Please, Professor. Let me call for a priest. I cannot..."

The glare that flashed then behind his eyes – something wild and bitter, a vicious humour – made her look away, scissoring her fraying resolve.

"Ah," he sighed, and "Yes," and something strangled that might have been laughter. "So, I confess my guilt. So, I scrub the blood from my hands with that other blood?"

The wind banged and clattered at the shuttered windows, looking for a way inside. And for a moment, the empty space filled with mantel-clock ticking and the wind and his ragged breathing, there was nothing more.

Then he said, "Please, Madam Mina, I am thirsty."

She reached for the pitcher and the chipped drinking glass.

"Forgive me, sweet Mina . . ."

The glass was spotty, and she wiped roughly at its rim with her blue skirt.

". . . had it been hers to choose . . ." and he coughed again, once, a harsh and broken sound, and Mina wiped at the glass harder.

Abraham Van Helsing sighed gently, and she was alone.

When she was done, Mina carefully returned the glass to the table with the crystal pitcher, the unfinished book, and the cold soup. When she turned to the bed, she caught her reflection in the tall dressing mirror across the room. The woman staring back could easily have passed for a young thirty. Only her eyes, hollow, bottomless things, betrayed her.

May 1930

As twilight faded from the narrow rue de l'Odéon, Mina Murray sipped her glass of Chardonnay and roamed the busy shelves of Shakespeare and Company. The reading would begin soon, some passages from Colette's new novel. Mina's fingers absently traced the spines of the assembled works of Hemingway and Glenway Wescott and D. H. Lawrence, titles and authors gold or crimson or flat-black pressed into cloth. Someone she half-recognized from a café or party or some other reading passed close, whispering a greeting, and she smiled in response, then went back to the books.

And then Mlle Beach was asking everyone to please take their seats, a few straight-backed chairs scattered among the shelves and bins. Mina found a place close to the door and watched as the others took their time, quietly talking among themselves, laughing at unheard jokes. Most of them she knew by sight, a few by name and casual conversation, one or two by reputation only. Messieurs Pound and Joyce, and Radclyffe Hall in her tailored English suit and sapphire cuff links. There was an unruly handful of minor Surrealists she recognized from the rue Jacob bistro where she often took her evening meals. And at first unnoticed, a tallish young woman, un-accompanied, choosing a chair off to one side.

Mina's hands trembled, and she spilled a few drops of the wine on her blouse.

The woman sat down, turning her back to Mina. Beneath the yellowish glow of the bookstore's lamps, the woman's long hair blazed red-gold. The murmuring pack of Surrealists seated themselves in the crooked row directly in front of Mina, and she quickly looked away. Sudden sweat and her mouth gone dry, a dull undercurrent of nausea, and she hastily, clumsily, set her wine glass on the floor.

That name, held so long at bay, spoken in a voice she thought she'd forgotten.

Lucy.

Mina's heart, an arrhythmic drum, raced inside her chest like a frightened child's.

Sylvia Beach was speaking again, gently hushing the murmuring crowd, introducing Colette. There was measured applause as the writer stepped forward, and something sarcastic mumbled by one of the Surrealists. Mina closed her eyes tightly, cold and breathing much too fast, sweaty fingers gripping at the edges of her chair. Someone touched her arm and she jumped, almost cried out, gasping loud enough to draw attention.

"Mademoiselle Murray, *êtes-vous bon?*"

She blinked, dazed, recognizing the boy's unshaven face as one of the shop's clerks, but unable to negotiate his name.

"*Oui, je vais bien.*" And she tried to smile, blinking back sucking in vertigo and dismay. "*Merci . . . je suis désolé.*"

He nodded, doubtful, reluctantly returning to his windowsill behind her.

At the front of the gathering, Colette had begun to read, softly relinquishing her words. Mina glanced to where the red-haired woman had sat down, half expecting to find the chair empty, or occupied by someone else entirely. She whispered a faithless prayer that she'd merely hallucinated, or suffered some trick of light and shadow. But the woman was still there, though turned slightly in her seat so that Mina could now see her profile, her full lips and familiar cheekbones. The smallest sound, a bated moan, escaped from Mina's pale lips, and she saw an image of herself, rising, pushing past bodies and through the bookstore's doors, fleeing headlong through the dark Paris streets to her tiny flat on Saint-Germain.

Instead, Mina Murray sat perfectly still, watching, in turn, the reader's restless lips and the delicate features of the nameless red-haired woman wearing Lucy Westenra's face.

After the reading, as the others milled and mingled, spinning respectful pretensions about *Sido* (and Madame Colette in general), Mina inched towards the door. The crowd seemed to have doubled during the half hour, and she squeezed, abruptly claustrophobic, between shoulders and cigarette smoke. But four or five of the rue Jacob Surrealists were planted solidly – typically confrontational – in the shop's doorway, muttering loudly among themselves, the novelist already forgotten in their own banter.

"*Pardon,*" she said, speaking just loudly enough to be heard above their conversation. "*Puis-je . . .*" Mina pointed past the men, to the door.

The one closest to her, gaunt and unwashed, almost pale enough to pass for an albino, turned towards her. Mina remembered his face, its crooked nose. She'd once seen him spit at a nun outside the Deux Magots. He gave no sign that he intended to let her pass, and she thought that even his eyes looked unclean. *Carrion eyes,* she thought.

"Mademoiselle Murray. Please, one moment."

Mina matched the man's glare a second longer, and then, slowly, turned, recognizing Adrienne Monnier; her own shop, the Maison des Amis des Livres, stood, dark-windowed tonight, across the street. It was generally acknowledged that Mlle Monnier shared considerable responsibility for the success of Shakespeare and Company.

"I have here someone who would very much like to meet you." The red-haired woman was standing at Adrienne's side, sipping dark wine. She smiled, and Mina saw that she had hazel-green eyes.

"This is Mademoiselle Carmichael from New York. She says that she is a great admirer of your work, Mina. I was just telling her that you've recently placed another story with the *Little Review*."

"*Anna* Carmichael," the woman said, eager and silken-voiced, offering Mina her hand. Detached, drifting, Mina watched herself accept it.

Anna Carmichael, from New York. Not Lucy.

"Thank you," Mina said, her voice gone the same dead calm as the sea before a squall.

"Oh, Christ no, thank *you*, Miss Murray."

Not Lucy, not Lucy at all, and Mina noticed how much taller than Lucy Westenra this woman was, her hands more slender, and there was a small mole at the corner of her rouged lips.

Then Adrienne Monnier was gone, pulled back into the crowd by a fat woman in an ugly ostrich-plumed hat, leaving Mina alone with Anna Carmichael. Behind her, the divided Surrealists argued, a threadbare quarrel and wearisome zeal.

"I've been reading you since 'The White Angel of Carfax', and last year, my God, last year I read 'Canto Babel' in *Harper's*. In America, Miss Murray, they're saying that you're the new Poe, that you make Le Fanu and all those silly Victorians look—"

"Yes, well," Mina began, uncertain what she meant to say, only meaning to interrupt. The dizziness, sharpening unreality, was rushing back, and she leaned against a shelf for support.

"Miss Murray?" And a move, then, as if to catch someone who had stumbled, long fingers alert. Anna Carmichael took a cautious step forward, closing the space between them.

"Mina, please. Just Mina."

"Are you—?"

"Yes," but she was sweating again. "Forgive me, Anna. Just a little too much wine on an empty stomach."

"Then please, let me take you to dinner."

Lips pursed, Mina bit the tip of her tongue, biting hard enough to bring a salted hint of blood, and the world began to tilt back into focus, the syrupy blackness at the edges of her vision withdrawing by degrees.

"Oh, no. I couldn't," she managed. "Really, it's not . . ."

But the woman was taking her by the arm, her crescent-moon smile baring teeth like perfectly spaced pearls, every bit the forceful American. She thought of Quincey Morris, and wondered if this woman had ever been to Texas.

"But I insist, Mina. It'll be an honour, and in return, well, I won't feel so guilty if I talk too much."

Together, arm in arm, they elbowed their way through the Surrealist blockade, the men choosing to ignore them. Except her gaunt albino, and Mina imagined something passing between him and Anna Carmichael, unspoken, or simply unspeakable.

"I hate those idiot bastards," Anna whispered, as the door jangled shut behind them. She held Mina's hand tightly, squeezing warmth into her clammy palm, and surprising herself, Mina squeezed back.

Out on the gaslit rue de l'Odéon, a warm spring breeze was blowing, and the night air smelled like coming rain.

The meal had been good, though Mina had hardly tasted the little she'd eaten. Cold chicken and bread, salad with wild thyme and goat cheese, chewed and swallowed indifferently. And more than her share from a large carafe of some anonymous red Bordeaux. She'd listened to the woman who was not Lucy talk, endless talk of Anna Carmichael's copious ideas on the macabre and of Mina's writing.

"I actually went to the Carfax estate," she'd said, and then paused, as if she had expected some particular reaction. "Just last summer. There's some restoration underway now, you know."

"No," Mina answered, sipping her wine, and picking apart a strip of breast meat with her fork. "No, I wasn't aware of that."

Finally, the waitress had brought their bill, and Anna had grudgingly allowed Mina to leave the tip. While they'd eaten, the shower had come and gone, leaving the night dank and chilly and unusually quiet. Their heels sounded like passing time on the wet cobblestones. Anna Carmichael had a room in one of the less expensive Left Bank hotels, but they walked together back to Mina's flat.

When Mina woke, it was raining again, and for a few uncounted minutes she lay still, listening, smelling the sweat and incense, a hint of rose and lilac in the sheets. Finally, there was only a steady drip, falling perhaps from the leaky gutters of the old building, and maybe from the eaves, striking the flagstones in the little garden. She could still smell Anna Carmichael on her skin. Mina closed her eyes, and thought about going back to sleep, realizing only very slowly that she was now alone in the bed.

The rain was over and the drip – the minute and measured splash of water on water, that clockwork cadence – *wasn't* coming from outside. She opened her eyes and rolled over, into the cold and hollow place made by Anna's absence. The lavatory light was burning; Mina blinked and called out her name, calling

Lucy

"Anna?"

drip and drip and drip and

"Anna?" and her throat tightened, whatever peace she'd awakened with suddenly leached away by fear and adrenaline. "Anna, are you all right?"

did you call for Lucy, at first, did I

drip and drip and

The floor was cold against her feet. Mina stepped past the chiffonier, bare floorboards giving way to a time- and mildew- and foot-dulled mosaic of ceramic polygons. Some of the tiles were missing, leaving dirty liver-coloured cavities in the design. The big tub, chipped alabaster enamel and the black cast iron showing through, lion's feet claws frozen in moulded rictus, grappling for some hold on the slick tiles.

Lucy Westenra lay, empty again, in the tub filled almost to overflowing. Each drop of water swelled like an abscess until its own weight tore it free of the brass faucet, and so it fell, losing itself in the crimson water. The suicide's wrists hung limply over the sides, hands open; her head tilted back at a broken angle. And there were three bright smiles carved into her flesh, all of them offered to heaven, or only to Mina.

The straight razor lay, wet and its blade glinting sticky scarlet, on the floor where it had fallen from Lucy's hand. And, like the dripping water, Mina stood until gravity pulled her free, and she fell.

October 1946

After the war and the ammonia antiseptic rooms where electrodes bridged the writhing space between her eyes with their deadening quick sizzle, after the long years that she was kept safe from herself and the suicidal world kept safe from her, Mina Murray came back to London.

A new city to embrace the mop-water grey Thames, changed utterly, scarred by the Luftwaffe's firestorms and aged by the twenty-four years of her absence. She spent three days walking the streets, destruction like a maze for her to solve or discard in frustration. At Aldermanbury, she stood before the ruins of St Mary's and imagined – no, *wished* – her hands around Van Helsing's neck. His brittle, old bones to break apart like charred timbers and shattered pews. *Is* this *it, you old bastard? Is this what we saved England for?*

And the question, recognizing its own intrinsic senselessness, its inherent futility, had hung nowhere, like all those blown-out windows framing the autumn-blue sky, the hallways ending only in rubble. Or her reflection, the woman a year from seventy looking back from a windowpane that seemed to have somehow escaped destruction especially for this purpose, for this moment. Mina Murray was a year from seventy, and she almost looked it.

The boy sitting on the wall watched the woman get out of the taxi, an old woman in black stockings and a black dress with a high collar, her eyes hidden behind dark spectacles. He absently released the small brown lizard he'd been tormenting, and it skittered gratefully away into some crack or crevice in the tumbledown masonry. The boy thought the woman looked like a widow, but better to pretend she was a spy for the Jerries on a clandestine rendezvous, secrets to be exchanged for better secrets. She walked in short steps that seemed like maybe she was counting off the distance between them. In the cool, bright morning, her shoes clicked, a coded signal click, possibly, Morse-code click, and he thought perhaps he should quickly hide himself behind the crumbling wall, but then she saw him, and it was too late. She paused, then waved hesitantly as the taxi pulled away. Too late, so he waved back, and, there. She was just an old woman again.

"Hello," she said, fishing about for something in her handbag. She took out a cigarette out, and when he asked, the widow gave him one, also. She lit it for him with a silver lighter and turned to stare at the gutted ruins of Carfax Abbey, at the broken, precarious walls braced against their inevitable collapse. Noisy larks and sparrows sang to themselves in the limbs of the blasted trees, and further on, the duck pond glinted in the sun.

The woman leaned against the wall and sighed out smoke. "They didn't leave much, did they?" she asked him.

"No, Ma'am," he said. "It was one of them doodlebugs last year that got it," and he rocket-whistled for her, descending octaves and sticking a big rumbling boom stuck on the end. The woman nodded and crushed her cigarette out against a raw edge of mortar, ground it back and forth, the black ash smear against oatmeal grey, and she dropped the butt at her feet.

"It's haunted, you know," the boy told her, "Mostly at night, though," and she smiled, and he glimpsed her nicotine-stained teeth past the lipstick bruise of her lips. She nodded again.

"Yes," she said. "Yes. I guess that it is, isn't it?"

Mina killed the boy well back from the road, the straight razor she'd bought in Cheapside slipped out of her purse while he was digging about for bits of shrapnel to show her, jagged souvenirs of a pleasant autumn afternoon in Purfleet. One gloved hand fast over his mouth and only the smallest muffled sound of surprise before she drew the blade quick across his throat, and the boy's life sprayed out dark and wet against the flagstones. He was the first murder she'd done since returning to England, and so she sat with him a while in the chilly shade of the tilted wall, his blood drying to a crust around her mouth.

Once, she heard a dog barking excitedly off towards the wreck that had been Jack Seward's asylum such a long time ago. There was a shiver of adrenaline, and her heart skipped a beat and raced for a moment because she thought maybe someone was coming, that she'd been discovered. But no one came, and so she sat with the boy and wondered at the winding knot of emptiness still inside her, unchanged and, evidently, unchangeable.

An hour later, she'd left the boy beneath a scraggly hedgerow and went to wash her hands and face in the sparkling pool. If there *were* ghosts at Carfax, they kept their distance.

August 1955

The cramped and cluttered office on West Houston was even hotter than usual, the venetian blinds drawn shut to keep the sun out, so only the soft glow from Audry Cavanaugh's brass desk lamp, a gentle incandescence through the green glass shade. But the dimness went unheeded by the sticky, resolute Manhattan summer. The office was sweltering, and Mina had to piss again. Her bladder ached, and she sweated and wrinkled her nose at the stale, heavy smell of the expensive English cigarettes the psychoanalyst chain-smoked. A framed and faded photograph of Carl Jung dangled on its hook behind the desk, and Mina felt his grey and knowing eyes, wanting inside her, wanting to see and know and draw reason from insanity.

"You're looking well today, Wilhelmina," Dr Cavanaugh said, then offered a terse smile. She lit another cigarette, and exhaled a great cloud into the torpid air of the office. The smoke settled about her head like a shroud. "Sleeping any better?"

"No," Mina told her, which was true. "Not really." Not with the nightmares and the traffic sounds all night outside her SoHo apartment, and not with the restless voices from the street that she could never be sure weren't meant for her. And not the heat, either. The heat like a living thing to smother her, to hold the world perpetually at the edge of conflagration.

"I'm very sorry," and Dr Cavanaugh was squinting at her through the gauze of smoke, her stingy smile already traded for familiar concern. Audry Cavanaugh never seemed to sweat, always so cool in her mannish suits, her hair pulled back in its neat, tight bun.

"Did you speak with your friend in London?" Mina asked. "You *said* that you would . . ." and maybe the psychoanalyst heard the strain in Mina's voice because she sighed a loud, impatient sigh and tilted her head backwards, gazing up at the ceiling,

"Yes," she answered. "I've talked with Dr Beecher. Just yesterday, actually."

Mina licked her lips, her dry tongue across drier lips, the parched skin of dead fruit. There was a pause, a moment if silence, and then Audry Cavanaugh said, "He was able to find a number of references to attacks on children by a 'bloofer lady', some articles dating from late in September, 1897, in *The Westminster Gazette* and a few other papers. A couple of pieces on the wreck at Whitby, also. But, Mina, I never *said* I doubted you. You didn't have to prove anything."

"I *had* those clippings," Mina mumbled around her dry tongue. "I used to have *all* the clippings."

"I always believed that you did."

There was more silence, then, and only street sounds ten storeys down to fill the void, Dr Cavanaugh put on her reading glasses and opened her yellow stenographer's pad. Her pencil scritched across the paper to record the date. "The dreams, are they still about Lucy? Or is it the asylum again?"

And a drop of sweat ran slowly down Mina's rouged cheek, pooling at the corner of her mouth, offering an abrupt tang of salt and cosmetics to tease her thirst. She looked away, at the worn and dusty rug under her shoes, at the barrister shelves stuffed with medical books and psychological journals. The framed diplomas and, almost whispering, she said, "I had a dream about the world."

"Yes?" and Audry Cavanaugh sounded a little eager, because here was something new, perhaps, something novel in old Mina Murray's tiresome parade of delusions. "What did you dream about the world, Wilhelmina?"

Another drop of sweat dissolved on the tip of Mina's tongue, leaving behind the musky, fleeting taste of herself and fading too soon. "I dreamed that the world was dead," she said. "That the world ended a long, long time ago. But it doesn't know it's dead, and all that's left of the world is the dream of a ghost."

For a few minutes, neither of them said anything more, and so there was only the sound of the psychoanalyst's pencil, and then not even that. Mina listened to the street, the cars and trucks, the city. The sun made blazing slashes through the aluminium blinds, and Audry Cavanaugh struck a match, lighting another cigarette. The stink of sulphur made the insides of Mina's nostrils burn.

"Do you think that's true, Mina?"

And Mina closed her eyes, wanting to be alone with the weary, constant rhythm of her heart, the afterimages like burn-scar slashes in the dark behind her vellum eyelids. She was too tired for confession or memory today, too uncertain to commit her scattered thoughts to words; she drifted, and there was no intrusion from patient Cavanaugh, and in a few minutes she was asleep.

April 1969

After she's swallowed the capsules and a mouthful of plastic-flavoured water from the blue pitcher on her nightstand, after Brenda Neufield and her white shoes have left the hospital room, Mina sits up. She wrestles the safety bar down and her legs swing slowly, painfully, over and off the edge of the bed. She watches her bare feet dangling above the linoleum floor, her ugly yellowed toenails, age spots and skin parchment-stretched too tightly over kite-frame bones.

A week ago, after her heart attack and the ambulance ride from her shitty little apartment, there was the emergency room and the doctor who smiled at her and said, "You're a pip, Miss Murray. I have sixty-year old patients who should be glad to look half so good as you."

She waits, counting the nurse's footsteps – twelve, thirteen, fourteen, and surely Neufield's at the desk by now, going back to her magazines. And Mina sits, staring across the room, her back to the window, cowardice to pass for defiance. If she had a razor, or a kitchen knife, or a few more of Neufield's tranquillizer pills.

If she had the courage.

Later, when the rain has stopped and the Crape Myrtle has settled down for the night, the nurse comes back and finds her dozing, still perched upright on the edge of her bed, like some silly parakeet or geriatric gargoyle. She eases Mina back, and there's a dull click as the safety bar locks again. The nurse mumbles something so low Mina can't make out the words. So, she lies very still, instead, lies on those starch-stiff sheets and her pillowcase and listens to the drip and patter from the street outside, the velvet sounds after the storm almost enough to smooth the edges off Manhattan for a few hours. The blanket tucked rough beneath her chin and taxi wheels on the street, the honk of a car horn, a police siren blocks away. And footsteps on the sidewalk below her window, and, then, the soft and unmistakable pad of wolf paws on asphalt.

"The blood-dimmed tide is loosed, and everywhere
The ceremony of innocence is drowned . . ."
— W. B. Yeats, "The Second Coming"

1998

THE MAMMOTH BOOK OF

BEST NEW HORROR

THE YEAR'S BEST HORROR
STORIES BY SUCH MASTERS
OF DARK FANTASY AS:
RAMSEY CAMPBELL
HARLAN ELLISON
CHRISTOPHER FOWLER
NEIL GAIMAN
TANITH LEE
PETER STRAUB
and many others

EDITED BY
STEPHEN JONES

"A must-have, must-read
anthology for horror buffs."
~ PUBLISHERS WEEKLY

TENTH
ANNIVERSARY
EDITION

Mr Clubb and Mr Cuff

Peter Straub

JUST BECAUSE *I* THOUGHT vampires had become a cliché did not mean that the publisher was in any way averse to putting them on the cover. However, it was perhaps unfortunate that they chose to do so with the Tenth Anniversary edition which, unlike the previous volume, did not actually contain any stories featuring the undead.

At least the British Fantasy Award-winning anthology kicked off with four pages of testimonials by the likes of Clive Barker, Peter Straub, Brian Lumley, Neil Gaiman, Ellen Datlow and others, including the redoubtable Ramsey Campbell.

This time I managed to rein the Introduction back to just over sixty pages, while the Necrology held fast at twenty-eight. With the twenty-first century just around the corner, I predictably looked back over the first decade of *The Mammoth Book of Best New Horror* (as the series was now entitled on both sides of the Atlantic).

Once again featuring just nineteen stories, the tenth volume introduced the incomparable Tanith Lee and astonishing newcomer Kelly Link to the series, and included the novella "The Boss in the Wall: A Treatise on the House Devil", the last major work by the late Avram Davidson (who died in 1993), completed by Grania Davis.

However, I have chosen another powerful novella to represent this edition. Peter Straub had previously made two appearances in *Best New Horror*, but neither could have prepared us for his International Horror Guild Award-winning revenge tale "Mr Clubb and Mr Cuff". Loosely inspired by Herman Melville's story "Bartleby the Scrivener", this is just about as dark and funny as horror can get . . .

I

I NEVER INTENDED TO GO astray, nor did I know what that meant. My journey began in an isolated hamlet notable for the piety of its inhabitants, and when I vowed to escape New Covenant I assumed that the values instilled within me there would forever be my guide. And so, with a depth of paradox I still only begin to comprehend, they have been. My journey, so triumphant, also so excruciating, is both *from* my native village and *of* it. For all its splendour, my life has been that of a child of New Covenant.

When in my limousine I scanned *The Wall Street Journal*, when in the private elevator I ascended to the rosewood-panelled office with harbour views, when in the partners' dining room I ordered squab on a mesclun bed from a prison-rescued waiter known to me alone as Charlie-Charlie, also when I navigated for my clients the complex waters of financial planning, above all when before her seduction by my enemy Graham Lesson I returned homeward to luxuriate in the attentions of my stunning Marguerite, when transported within the embraces of my wife, even then I carried within the frame houses dropped like afterthoughts down the streets of New Covenant, the stiff faces and suspicious eyes, the stony cordialities before and after services in the grim great Temple, the blank storefronts along Harmony Street – tattooed within me was the ugly, enigmatic beauty of my birthplace. Therefore I believe that when I strayed, and stray I did, make no mistake, it was but to come home, for I claim that the two strange gentlemen who beckoned me into error were the night of its night, the dust of its dust. In the period of my life's greatest turmoil – the month of my exposure to Mr Clubb and Mr Cuff, "Private Detectives Extraordinaire," as their business card described them – in the midst of the uproar I felt that I saw *the contradictory dimensions of . . .*

of . . .

I felt I saw . . . had seen, had at least glimpsed . . . what a wiser man might call . . . try to imagine the sheer difficulty of actually writing these words . . . the Meaning of Tragedy. You smirk; I don't blame you: in your place I'd do the same, but I assure you I saw *something*.

I must sketch in the few details necessary for you to understand my story. A day's walk from New York State's Canadian border, New Covenant was (and still is, still is) a town of just under a thousand inhabitants united by the puritanical Protestantism of the Church of the New Covenant, whose founders had broken away from the even more puritanical Saints of the Covenant. (The Saints had proscribed sexual congress in the hope of hastening the Second Coming.) The village flourished during the end of the nineteenth century and settled into its permanent form around 1920.

To wit: Temple Square, where the Temple of the New Covenant and its bell tower, flanked left and right by the Youth Bible Study Centre and the Combined Boys and Girls Elementary and Middle School, dominate a modest greensward. Southerly stand the shop fronts of Harmony Street, the bank, also the modest placards indicating the locations of New Covenant's doctor, lawyer, and dentist; south of Harmony Street lie the two streets of frame houses sheltering the town's clerks and artisans, beyond these the farms of the rural faithful, beyond the farmland deep forest. North of Temple Square is Scripture Street, two blocks lined with the residences of the reverend and his Board of Brethren, the aforementioned doctor, dentist, and lawyer, the president and vice president of the bank, also the families of some few wealthy converts devoted to Temple affairs. North of Scripture Street are more farms, then the resumption of the great forest, in which our village described a sort of clearing.

My father was New Covenant's lawyer, and to Scripture Street was I born. Sundays I spent in the Youth Bible Study Centre, weekdays in the Combined Boys and Girls Elementary and Middle School. New Covenant was my world, its people all I knew of the world. Three-fourths of all mankind consisted of gaunt, bony, blond-haired individuals with chiselled features and blazing blue eyes, the men six feet or taller in height, the women some inches shorter – the remaining fourth being the Racketts, Mudges and Blunts, our farm families, who after generations of intermarriage had coalesced into a tribe of squat, black-haired, gap-toothed, moon-faced males and females seldom taller than five feet, four or five inches. Until I went to college I thought that all people were divided into the races of town and barn, fair and dark, the spotless and the mud-spattered, the reverential and the sly.

Though Racketts, Mudges and Blunts attended our school and worshipped in our Temple, though they were at least as prosperous as we in town, we knew them tainted with an essential inferiority. Rather than intelligent they seemed *crafty*, rather than spiritual, *animal*. Both in classrooms and Temple, they sat together, watchful as dogs compelled for the nonce to be "good", now and again tilting their heads to pass a whispered comment. Despite Sunday baths and Sunday clothes, they bore an unerasable odour redolent of the barnyard. Their public self-effacement seemed to mask a peasant amusement, and when they separated into their wagons and other vehicles, they could be heard to share a peasant laughter.

I found this mysterious race unsettling, in fact profoundly annoying. At some level they frightened me – I found them compelling. Oppressed from my earliest days by life in New Covenant, I felt an inadmissible fascination for this secretive brood. Despite their inferiority, I wished to know what they knew. Locked deep within their shabbiness and shame I sensed the presence of a freedom I did not understand but found *thrilling*.

Because town never socialized with barn, our contacts were restricted to places of education, worship, and commerce. It would have been as unthinkable for me to take a seat beside Delbert Mudge or Charlie-Charlie Rackett in our fourth-grade classroom as for Delbert or Charlie-Charlie to invite me for an overnight in their farmhouse bedrooms. Did Delbert and Charlie-Charlie actually have bedrooms, where they slept alone in their own beds? I recall mornings when the atmosphere about Delbert and Charlie-Charlie suggested nights spent in close proximity to the pigpen, others when their worn dungarees exuded a freshness redolent of sunshine, wildflowers and raspberries.

During recess an inviolable border separated the townies at the northern end of our play area from the barnies at the southern. Our play, superficially similar, demonstrated our essential differences, for we could not cast off the unconscious stiffness resulting from constant adult measurement of our spiritual worthiness. In contrast, the barnies did not play at playing but actually *played*, plunging back and forth across the grass, chortling over victories, grinning as they muttered what must have been jokes. (We were not adept at jokes.) When school closed at end of day, I tracked the homebound progress of Delbert, Charlie-Charlie, and clan with envious eyes and a divided heart.

Why should they have seemed in possession of a liberty I desired? After graduation from Middle School, we townies progressed to Shady Glen's Consolidated High, there to monitor ourselves and our fellows while encountering the temptations of the wider world, in some cases then advancing into colleges and universities. Having concluded their educations with the seventh grade's long division and "Hiawatha" recitations, the barnies one and all returned to their barns. Some few, some very few of *us*, among whom I had determined early on to be numbered, left for good, thereafter to be celebrated, denounced, or mourned. One of *us*, Caleb Thurlow, violated every standard of caste and morality by marrying Munna Blunt and vanishing into barnie-dom. A disgraced, disinherited pariah during my childhood, Thurlow's increasingly pronounced stoop and decreasing teeth terrifyingly mutated him into a blond, wasted barnic-parody on his furtive annual Christmas appearances at Temple. One of *them*, one only, my old classmate Charlie-Charlie Rackett, escaped his ordained destiny in our twentieth year by liberating a plough horse and Webley-Vickers pistol from the family farm to commit serial armed robbery upon Shady Glen's George Washington Inn, Town Square Feed & Grain, and Allsorts Emporium. Every witness to his crimes recognized what, if not who, he was, and Charlie-Charlie was apprehended while boarding the Albany train in the next village west. During the course of my own journey from and of New Covenant, I tracked Charlie-Charlie's gloomy progress through the way stations of the penal system until at last I could secure his release at a parole hearing with the offer of a respectable job in the financial-planning industry.

I had by then established myself as absolute monarch of three floors in a Wall Street monolith. With my two junior partners, I enjoyed the services of a fleet of paralegals, interns, analysts, investigators, and secretaries. I had chosen these partners carefully, for as well as the usual expertise, skill and dedication, I required other, less conventional qualities.

I had sniffed out intelligent but unimaginative men of some slight moral laziness; capable of cutting corners when they thought no one would notice; controlled drinkers and secret drug takers: juniors with reason to be grateful for their positions. I wanted no *zealousness*. My employees were to be steadfastly incurious and able enough to handle their clients satisfactorily, at least with my paternal assistance.

My growing prominence had attracted the famous, the established, the notorious. Film stars and athletes, civic leaders, corporate pashas, and heirs to long-standing family fortunes regularly visited our offices, as did a number of conspicuously well-tailored gentlemen who had accumulated their wealth in a more colourful fashion. To these clients I suggested financial stratagems responsive to their labyrinthine needs. I had not schemed for their business. It simply *came to me*, willy-nilly, as our Temple held that salvation came to the elect. One May morning, a cryptic fellow in a pin-striped suit appeared in my office to pose a series of delicate questions. As soon as he opened his mouth, the cryptic fellow summoned irresistibly from memory a dour, squinting member of the Board of Brethren of New Covenant's Temple. I *knew* this man, and instantly I found the tone most acceptable to him. Tone is all to such people. After our interview he directed others of his kind to my office, and by December my business had tripled. Individually and universally these gentlemen pungently reminded me of the village I had long ago escaped, and I cherished my suspicious buccaneers even as I celebrated the distance between my moral life and theirs. While sheltering these self-justifying figures within elaborate trusts, while legitimizing subterranean floods of cash, I immersed myself within a familiar atmosphere of pious denial. Rebuking home, I *was* home.

Life had not yet taught me that revenge inexorably exacts its own revenge.

My researches eventually resulted in the hiring of the two junior partners known privately to me as Gilligan and the Skipper. The first, a short, trim fellow with a comedian's rubber face and dishevelled hair, brilliant with mutual funds but an ignoramus at estate planning, each morning worked so quietly as to become invisible. To Gilligan I had referred many of our actors and musicians, and those whose schedules permitted them to attend meetings before the lunch hour met their soft-spoken adviser in a dimly lighted office with curtained windows. After lunch, Gilligan tended toward the vibrant, the effusive, the extrovert. Red-faced and sweating, he loosened his tie, turned on a powerful sound system, and ushered emaciated musicians with haystack hair into the atmosphere of a backstage party. Morning Gilligan spoke in whispers; Afternoon Gilligan batted our secretaries' shoulders as he bounced officeward down the corridors. I snapped him up as soon as one of my competitors let him go, and he proved a perfect complement to the Skipper. Tall, plump, silver-haired, this gentleman had come to me from a specialist in estates and trusts discomfited by his tendency to become pugnacious when outraged by a client's foul language, improper dress, or other offenses against good taste. Our tycoons and inheritors of family fortunes were in no danger of arousing the Skipper's ire, and I myself handled the unshaven film stars' and heavy metallists' estate planning. Neither Gilligan nor the Skipper had any contact with the cryptic gentlemen. Our office was an organism balanced in all its parts. Should any mutinous notions occur to my partners, my spy the devoted Charlie-Charlie Rackett, known to them as Charles the Perfect Waiter, every noon silently monitored their every utterance while replenishing Gilligan's wine glass. My marriage of two years seemed blissfully happy, my reputation and bank account flourished alike, and I anticipated perhaps another decade of labour followed by luxurious retirement. I could not have been less prepared for the disaster to come.

Mine, as disasters do, began at home. I admit my contribution to the difficulties. While immersed in the demands of my profession, I had married a beautiful woman twenty years my junior. It was my understanding that Marguerite had knowingly entered into a contract under which she enjoyed the fruits of income and social position while postponing a deeper marital communication until I cashed in and quit the game, at which point she and I could travel at will, occupying grand hotel suites and staterooms while acquiring every adornment that struck her eye. How could an arrangement so harmonious have failed to satisfy her? Even now I feel the old rancour. Marguerite had come into our office as a faded singer who wished to invest the remaining proceeds from a five- or six-year-old "hit", and after an initial consultation Morning Gilligan whispered her down the corridor for my customary lecture on estate tax, trusts, so forth and so on, in her case due to the modesty of the funds in question mere show. (Since during their preliminary discussion she had casually employed the Anglo-Saxon monosyllable for excrement, Gilligan dared not subject her to the Skipper.) He escorted her into my chambers, and I glanced up with the customary show of interest. You may imagine a thick bolt of lightning slicing through a double-glazed office window, sizzling across the width of a polished teak desk, and striking me in the heart.

Already I was lost. Thirty minutes later I violated my most sacred edict by inviting a female client to a dinner date. She accepted, damn her. Six months later, Marguerite and I were married, damn us both. I had attained everything for which I had abandoned New Covenant, and for twenty-three months I inhabited the paradise of fools.

I need say only that the usual dreary signals, matters like unexplained absences, mysterious telephone calls abruptly terminated upon my appearance, and visitations of a melancholic, distracted *daemon* forced me to set one of our investigators on Marguerite's trail, resulting in the discovery that my wife had been two-backed-beasting it with my sole professional equal, the slick, the smooth Graham Leeson, to whom I, swollen with uxorious pride a year after our wedding day, had introduced her during a function at the Waldorf-Astoria hotel. I know what happened. I don't need a map. Exactly as I had decided to win her at our first meeting, Graham Leeson vowed to steal Marguerite from me the instant he set his handsome blue eyes on her between the fifty-thousand-dollar tables on the Starlight Roof.

My enemy enjoyed a number of natural advantages. Older than she by but ten years to my twenty, at six-four three inches taller than I, this reptile had been blessed with a misleadingly winning Irish countenance and a full head of crinkly red-blond hair. (In contrast, my white tonsure accentuated the severity of the all-too-Cromwellian townie face.) I assumed her immune to such obvious charms, and I was wrong. I thought Marguerite could not fail to see the meagreness of Leeson's inner life, and I was wrong again. I suppose he exploited the inevitable temporary isolation of any spouse to a man in my position. He must have played upon her grudges, spoken to her secret vanities. Cynically, I am sure, he encouraged the illusion that she was an "artist". He flattered, he very likely wheedled. By every shabby means at his disposal he had overwhelmed her, most crucially by screwing her brains out three times a week in a corporate suite at a Park Avenue hotel.

After I had examined the photographs and other records arrayed before me by the investigator, an attack of nausea brought my dizzied head to the edge of my desk; then rage stiffened my backbone and induced a moment of hysterical blindness. My marriage was dead, my wife a repulsive stranger. Vision returned a second or two later. The chequebook floated from the desk drawer, the Waterman pen glided into position between thumb and forefinger, and while a shadow's efficient hand inscribed a cheque for ten thousand dollars, a disembodied voice informed the hapless investigator that the only service required of him henceforth would be eternal silence.

For perhaps an hour I sat alone in my office, postponing appointments and refusing telephone calls. In the moments when I had tried to envision my rival, what came to mind was some surly drummer or guitarist from her past, easily intimidated and readily bought off. In such a case, I should have inclined toward mercy. Had Marguerite offered a sufficiently self-abasing apology, I would have slashed her clothing allowance in half, restricted her public appearances to the two or three most crucial charity events of the year and perhaps as many dinners at my side in the restaurants where one is "seen", and ensured that the resultant mood of sackcloth and ashes prohibited any reversion to bad behaviour by intermittent use of another investigator.

No question of mercy, now. Staring at the photographs of my life's former partner entangled with the man I detested most in the world, I shuddered with a combination of horror, despair, loathing, and – appallingly – an urgent spasm of sexual arousal. I unbuttoned my trousers, groaned in ecstatic torment, and helplessly ejaculated over the images on my desk. When I had recovered, weak-kneed and trembling, I wiped away the evidence, closed the hateful folders, and picked up the telephone to request Charlie-Charlie Rackett's immediate presence in my office.

The cryptic gentlemen, experts in the nuances of retribution, might have seemed more obvious sources of assistance, but I could not afford obligations in that direction. Nor did I wish to expose my humiliation to clients for whom the issue of respect was all-important. Devoted Charlie-Charlie's years in the jug had given him an extensive acquaintanceship among the dubious and irregular, and I had from time to time commandeered the services of one or another of his fellow yardbirds. My old companion sidled around my door and posted himself before me, all dignity on the outside, all curiosity within.

"I have been dealt a horrendous blow, Charlie-Charlie," I said, "and as soon as possible I wish to see one or two of the best."

Charlie-Charlie glanced at the folders. "You want serious people," he said, speaking in code. "Right?"

"I must have men who can be serious when seriousness is necessary," I said, replying in the same code.

While my lone surviving link to New Covenant struggled to understand this directive, it came to me that Charlie-Charlie had now become my only true confidant, and I bit down on an upwelling of fury. I realized that I had clamped shut my eyes, and opened them upon an uneasy Charlie-Charlie.

"You're sure," he said.

"Find them," I said. Then, to restore some semblance of our conventional atmosphere, I asked, "The boys still okay?"

Telling me that the juniors remained content, he said, "Fat and happy. I'll find what you want, but it'll take a couple of days."

I nodded, and he was gone.

For the remainder of the day I turned in an inadequate impersonation of the executive who usually sat behind my desk and, after putting off the moment as long as reasonably possible, buried the awful files in a bottom drawer and returned to the town house I had purchased for my bride-to-be and which, I remembered with an unhappy pang, she had once in an uncharacteristic moment of cuteness called "our town home".

Since I had been too preoccupied to telephone wife, cook, or butler with the information that I would be staying late at the office, when I walked into our dining room the table had been laid with our china and silver, flowers arranged in the centre-piece, and, in what I took to be a new dress, Marguerite glanced mildly up from her end of the table and murmured a greeting. Scarcely able to meet her eyes, I bent to bestow the usual homecoming kiss with a mixture of feelings more painful than I previously would have imagined myself capable. Some despicable portion of my being responded to her beauty with the old husbandly appreciation even as I went cold with the loathing I could not permit myself to show. I hated Marguerite for her treachery, her beauty for its falsity, myself for my susceptibility to what I knew was treacherous and false. Clumsily, my lips brushed the edge of an azure eye, and it came to me that she may well have been with Leeson while the investigator was displaying the images of her degradation. Through me coursed an involuntary tremor of revulsion with, strange to say, at its centre a molten erotic core. Part of my extraordinary pain was the sense that I too had been contaminated: a layer of illusion had been peeled away, revealing monstrous blind groping slugs and maggots.

Having heard voices, Mr Moncrieff, the butler I had employed upon the abrupt decision of the Duke of Denbigh to cast off worldly ways and enter an order of Anglican monks, came through from the kitchen and awaited orders. His bland, courteous manner suggested as usual that he was making the best of having been shipwrecked on an island populated by illiterate savages. Marguerite said that she had been worried when I had not returned home at the customary time.

"I'm fine," I said. "No, I'm not fine. I feel unwell. Distinctly unwell. Grave difficulties at the office." With that I managed to make my way up the table to my chair, along the way signaling to Mr Moncrieff that the Lord of the Savages wished him to bring in the pre-dinner martini and then immediately begin serving whatever the cook had prepared. I took my seat at the head of the table, and Mr Moncrieff removed the floral centrepiece to the sideboard. Marguerite regarded me with the appearance of probing concern. This was false, false, false. Unable to meet her eyes, I raised mine to the row of Canalettos along the wall, then the intricacies of the plaster moulding above the paintings, at last to the chandelier depending from the central rosette on the ceiling. More had changed than my relationship with my wife. The moulding, the blossoming chandelier, even Canaletto's Venice resounded with a cold, selfish lovelessness.

Marguerite remarked that I seemed agitated.

"No, I am not," I said. The butler placed the ice-cold drink before me, and I snatched up the glass and drained half its contents. "Yes, I am agitated, terribly," I said. "The difficulties at the office are more far reaching than I intimated." I polished off the martini and tasted only glycerine. "It is a matter of betrayal and treachery made all the more wounding by the closeness of my relationship with the traitor."

I lowered my eyes to measure the effect of this thrust to the vitals on the traitor in question. She was looking back at me with a flawless imitation of wifely concern. For a moment I doubted her unfaithfulness. Then the memory of the photographs in my bottom drawer once again brought crawling into view the slugs and maggots. "I am sickened unto rage," I said, "and my rage demands vengeance. Can you understand this?"

Mr Moncrieff carried into the dining room the tureens or serving dishes containing whatever it was we were to eat that night, and my wife and I honoured the silence that had become conventional during the presentation of our evening meal. When we were alone again, she nodded in affirmation.

I said, "I am grateful, for I value your opinions. I should like you to help me reach a difficult decision."

She thanked me in the simplest of terms.

"Consider this puzzle," I said. "Famously, vengeance is the Lord's, and therefore it is often imagined that vengeance exacted by anyone other is immoral. Yet if vengeance is the Lord's, then a mortal being who seeks it on his own behalf has engaged in a form of worship, even an alternate version of prayer. Many good Christians regularly pray for the establishment of justice, and what lies behind an act of vengeance but a desire for justice? God tells us that eternal torment awaits the wicked. He also demonstrates a pronounced affection for those who prove unwilling to let Him do all the work."

Marguerite expressed the opinion that justice was a fine thing indeed, and that a man such as myself would always labour on its behalf. She fell silent and regarded me with what on any night previous I would have seen as tender concern. Though I had not yet so informed her, she declared, the Benedict Arnold must have been one of my juniors, for no other employee could injure me so greatly. Which was the traitor?

"As yet I do not know," I said. "But once again I must be grateful for your grasp of my concerns. Soon I will put into position the bear-traps that will result in the fiend's exposure. Unfortunately, my dear, this task will demand all of my energy over at least the next several days. Until the task is accomplished, it will be necessary for me to camp out in the —Hotel." I named the site of her assignations with Graham Leeson.

A subtle, momentary darkening of the eyes, her first genuine response of the evening, froze my heart as I set the bear-trap into place. "I know, the —'s vulgarity deepens with every passing week, but Gilligan's apartment is only a few doors north, the Skipper's one block south. Once my investigators have installed their electronic devices, I shall be privy to every secret they possess. Would you enjoy spending several days at Green Chimneys? The servants have the month off, but you might enjoy the solitude there more than you would being alone in town."

Green Chimneys, our country estate on a bluff above the Hudson River, lay two hours away. Marguerite's delight in the house had inspired me to construct on the grounds a fully equipped recording studio, where she typically spent days on end, trying out new "songs".

Charmingly, she thanked me for my consideration and said that she would enjoy a few days in seclusion at Green Chimneys. After I had exposed the traitor, I was to telephone her with the summons home. Accommodating on the surface, vile beneath, these words brought an anticipatory tinge of pleasure to her face, a delicate heightening of her beauty I would have, very likely *had*, misconstrued on earlier occasions. Any appetite I might have had disappeared before a visitation of nausea, and I announced myself exhausted. Marguerite intensified my discomfort by calling me her poor darling. I staggered to my bedroom, locked the door, threw off my clothes, and dropped into bed to endure a sleepless night. I would never see my wife again.

II

Sometime after first light I had attained an uneasy slumber; finding it impossible to will myself out of bed on awakening, I relapsed into the same restless sleep. By the time I appeared within the dining room, Mr Moncrieff, as well-chilled as a good Chardonnay, informed me that Madame had departed for the country some twenty minutes before. Despite the hour, did Sir wish to breakfast? I consulted, trepidatiously, my wristwatch. It was ten-thirty: my unvarying practice was to arise at six, breakfast soon after, and arrive in my office well before seven. I rushed downstairs, and as soon as I slid into the back seat of the limousine forbade awkward queries by pressing the button to raise the window between the driver and myself.

No such mechanism could shield me from Mrs Rampage, my secretary, who thrust her head around the door a moment after I had expressed my desire for a hearty breakfast of poached eggs, bacon, and whole-wheat toast from the executive dining room. All calls and appointments were to be postponed or otherwise put off until the completion of my repast. Mrs Rampage had informed me that two men without appointments had been awaiting my arrival since 8:00 a.m. and asked if I would consent to see them immediately. I told her not to be absurd. The door to the outer world swung to admit her beseeching head. "Please," she said. "I don't know who they are, but they're *frightening* everybody."

This remark clarified all. Earlier than anticipated, Charlie-Charlie Rackett had deputized two men capable of seriousness when seriousness was called for. "I beg your pardon," I said. "Send them in."

Mrs Rampage withdrew to lead into my chambers two stout, stocky, short, dark-haired men. My spirits had taken wing the moment I beheld these fellows shouldering through the door, and I rose smiling to my feet. My secretary muttered an introduction, baffled as much by my cordiality as by her ignorance of my visitors' names.

"It is quite all right," I said. "All is in order, all is in train." New Covenant had just entered the sanctum.

Barnie-slyness, barnie-freedom shone from their great, round gap-toothed faces: in precisely the manner I remembered, these two suggested mocking peasant violence scantily disguised by an equally mocking impersonation of convention. Small wonder that they had intimidated Mrs Rampage and her underlings, for their nearest exposure to a like phenomenon had been with our musicians, and when offstage they were pale, emaciated fellows of little physical vitality. Clothed in black suits, white shirts, and black neckties, holding their black derbies by their brims and turning their gappy smiles back and forth between Mrs Rampage and myself, these barnies had evidently been loose in the world for some time. They were perfect for my task. *You will be irritated by their country manners, you will be annoyed by their native insubordination,* I told myself, *but you will never find men more suitable, so grant them what latitude they need.* I directed Mrs Rampage to cancel all telephone calls and appointments for the next hour.

The door closed, and we were alone. Each of the black-suited darlings snapped a business card from his right jacket pocket and extended it to me with a twirl of the fingers. One card read:

MR CLUBB AND MR CUFF
Private Detectives Extraordinaire
MR CLUBB

and the other:

MR CLUBB AND MR CUFF
Private Detectives Extraordinaire
MR CUFF

I inserted the cards into a pocket and expressed my delight at making their acquaintance.

"Becoming aware of your situation," said Mr Clubb, "we preferred to report as quickly as we could."

"Entirely commendable," I said. "Will you gentlemen please sit down?"

"We prefer to stand," said Mr Clubb.

"I trust you will not object if I again take my chair," I said, and did so. "To be honest, I am reluctant to describe the whole of my problem. It is a personal matter, therefore painful."

"It is a domestic matter," said Mr Cuff.

I stared at him. He stared back with the sly imperturbability of his kind.

"Mr Cuff," I said, "you have made a reasonable and, as it happens, an accurate supposition, but in the future you will please refrain from speculation."

"Pardon my plain way of speaking, sir, but I was not speculating," he said. "Marital disturbances are domestic by nature."

"All too domestic, one might say," put in Mr Clubb. "In the sense of pertaining to the home. As we have so often observed, you find your greatest pain right smack-dab in the living room, as it were."

"Which is a somewhat politer fashion of naming another room altogether." Mr Cuff appeared to suppress a surge of barnie-glee.

Alarmingly, Charlie-Charlie had passed along altogether too much information, especially since the information in question should not have been in his possession. For an awful moment I imagined that the dismissed investigator had spoken to Charlie-Charlie. The man may have broadcast my disgrace to every person encountered on his final journey out of my office, inside the public elevator, thereafter even to the shoeshine "boys" and cup-rattling vermin lining the streets. It occurred to me that I might be forced to have the man silenced. Symmetry would then demand the silencing of valuable Charlie-Charlie. The inevitable next step would resemble a full-scale massacre.

My faith in Charlie-Charlie banished these fantasies by suggesting an alternate scenario and enabled me to endure the next utterance.

Mr Clubb said, "Which in plainer terms would be to say the bedroom."

After speaking to my faithful spy, the Private Detectives Extraordinaire had taken the initiative by acting as if *already employed* and following Marguerite to her afternoon assignation at the — Hotel. Here, already, was the insubordination I had foreseen, but instead of the expected annoyance I felt a thoroughgoing gratitude for the two men leaning slightly toward me, their animal senses alert to every nuance of my response. That they had come to my office armed with the essential secret absolved me from embarrassing explanations; blessedly, the hideous photographs would remain concealed in the bottom drawer.

"Gentlemen," I said, "I applaud your initiative."

They stood at ease. "Then we have an understanding," said Mr Clubb. "At various times, various matters come to our attention. At these times we prefer to conduct ourselves according to the wishes of our employer, regardless of difficulty."

"Agreed," I said. "However, from this point forward I must insist—"

A rap at the door cut short my admonition. Mrs Rampage brought in a coffeepot and cup, a plate beneath a silver cover, a rack with four slices of toast, two jam pots, silverware, a linen napkin, and a glass of water, and came to a halt some five or six feet short of the barnies. A sinfully arousing smell of butter and bacon emanated from the tray. Mrs Rampage deliberated between placing my breakfast on the table to her left or venturing into proximity to my guests by bringing the tray to my desk. I gestured her forward, and she tacked wide to port and homed in on the desk. "All is in order, all is in train," I said. She nodded and backed out – literally walked backward until she reached the door, groped for the knob, and vanished.

I removed the cover from the plate containing two poached eggs in a cup-sized bowl, four crisp rashers of bacon, and a mound of

home fried potatoes all the more welcome for being a surprise gift
from our chef.

"And now, fellows, with your leave I shall—"

For the second time my sentence was cut off in midflow. A thick
barnie-hand closed upon the handle of the coffeepot and proceeded
to fill the cup. Mr Clubb transported my coffee to his lips, smacked
appreciatively at the taste, then took up a toast slice and plunged it
like a dagger into my egg cup, releasing a thick yellow suppuration.
He crunched the dripping toast between his teeth.

At that moment, when mere annoyance passed into dumb-
founded ire, I might have sent them packing despite my earlier
resolution, for Mr Clubb's violation of my breakfast was as good
as an announcement that he and his partner respected none of
the conventional boundaries and would indulge in boorish, even
disgusting behaviour. I very nearly did send them packing, and both
of them knew it. They awaited my reaction, whatever it should be.
Then I understood that I was being tested, and half of my insight was
that ordering them off would be a failure of imagination. I had asked
Charlie-Charlie to send me serious men, not Boy Scouts, and in the
rape of my breakfast were depths and dimensions of seriousness I
had never suspected. In that instant of comprehension, I believe,
I virtually knew all that was to come, down to the last detail, and
gave a silent assent. My next insight was that the moment when
I might have dismissed these fellows with a conviction of perfect
rectitude had just passed, and with the sense of opening myself to
unpredictable adventures I turned to Mr Cuff. He lifted a rasher
from my plate, folded it within a slice of toast, and displayed the
result.

"Here are our methods in action," he said. "We prefer not to go
hungry while you gorge yourself, speaking freely, for the one reason
that all of this stuff represents what you ate every morning when you
were a kid." Leaving me to digest this shapeless utterance, he bit into
his impromptu sandwich and sent golden-brown crumbs showering
to the carpet.

"For as the important, abstemious man you are now," said Mr
Clubb, "what do you eat in the mornings?"

"Toast and coffee," I said. "That's about it."

"But in childhood?"

"Eggs," I said. "Scrambled or fried, mainly. And bacon. Home
fries, too." Every fatty, cholesterol-crammed ounce of which, I
forbore to add, had been delivered by barnie-hands directly from

barnie-farms. I looked at the rigid bacon, the glistening potatoes, the mess in the egg cup. My stomach lurched.

"We prefer," Mr Clubb said, "that you follow your true preferences instead of muddying mind and stomach by gobbling this crap in search of an inner peace that never existed in the first place, if you can be honest with yourself." He leaned over the desk and picked up the plate. His partner snatched a second piece of bacon and wrapped it within a second slice of toast. Mr Clubb began working on the eggs, and Mr Cuff grabbed a handful of home fried potatoes. Mr Clubb dropped the empty egg cup, finished his coffee, refilled the cup, and handed it to Mr Cuff, who had just finished licking the residue of fried potato from his free hand.

I removed the third slice of toast from the rack. Forking home fries into his mouth, Mr Clubb winked at me. I bit into the toast and considered the two little pots of jam, greengage, I think, and rosehip. Mr Clubb waggled a finger. I contented myself with the last of the toast. After a while I drank from the glass of water. All in all I felt reasonably satisfied and, but for the deprivation of my customary cup of coffee, content with my decision. I glanced in some irritation at Mr Cuff. He drained his cup, then tilted into it the third and final measure from the pot and offered it to me. "Thank you," I said. Mr Cuff picked up the pot of greengage jam and sucked out its contents, loudly. Mr Clubb did the same with the roschip. They sent their tongues into the corners of the jam pots and cleaned out whatever adhered to the sides. Mr Cuff burped. Overlappingly, Mr Clubb burped.

"Now, that is what I call by the name of breakfast, Mr Clubb," said Mr Cuff. "Are we in agreement?"

"Deeply," said Mr Clubb. "That is what I call by the name of breakfast now, what I have called by the name of breakfast in the past, and what I shall continue to call by that sweet name on every morning in the future." He turned to me and took his time, sucking first one tooth, then another. "Our morning meal, sir, consists of that simple fare with which we begin the day, except when in all good faith we wind up sitting in a waiting room with our stomachs growling because our future client has chosen to skulk in late for work." He inhaled. "Which was for the same exact reason that brought him to our attention in the first place and for which we went without in order to offer him our assistance. Which is, begging your pardon, sir, the other reason for which you ordered a breakfast you would ordinarily rather starve than eat, and all I ask before we get down to the business at hand is that you might begin to entertain the possibility that simple men like ourselves might possibly understand a thing or two."

"I see that you are faithful fellows," I began.

"Faithful as dogs," broke in Mr Clubb.

"And that you understand my position," I continued.

"Down to its smallest particulars," he interrupted again. "We are on a long journey."

"And so it follows," I pressed on, "that you must also understand that no further initiatives may be taken without my express consent."

These last words seemed to raise a disturbing echo – of what I could not say, but an echo nonetheless, and my ultimatum failed to achieve the desired effect. Mr Clubb smiled and said, "We intend to follow your inmost desires with the faithfulness, as I have said, of trusted dogs, for one of our sacred duties is that of bringing these to fulfilment, as evidenced, begging your pardon, sir, in the matter of the breakfast our actions spared you from gobbling up and sickening yourself with. Before you protest, sir, please let me put to you the question of how you think you would be feeling right now if you had eaten that greasy stuff all by yourself?"

The straightforward truth announced itself and demanded utterance. "Poisoned," I said. After a second's pause, I added, "Disgusted."

"Yes, for you are a better man than you know. Imagine the situation. Allow yourself to picture what would have transpired had Mr Cuff and myself not acted on your behalf. As your heart throbbed and your veins groaned, you would have taken in that while you were stuffing yourself the two of us stood hungry before you. You would have remembered that good woman informing you that we had patiently awaited your arrival since eight this morning, and at that point, sir, you would have experienced a self-disgust which would forever have tainted our relationship. From that point forth, sir, you would have been incapable of receiving the full benefits of our services."

I stared at the twinkling barnie. "Are you saying that if I had eaten my breakfast you would have refused to work for me?"

"You did eat your breakfast. The rest was ours."

This statement was so literally true that I burst into laughter. "Then I must thank you for saving me from myself. Now that you may accept employment, please inform me of the rates for your services."

"We have no rates," said Mr Clubb.

"We prefer to leave compensation to the client," said Mr Cuff.

This was crafty even by barnie-standards, but I knew a counter-move. "What is the greatest sum you have ever been awarded for a single job?"

"Six hundred thousand dollars," said Mr Clubb.

"And the smallest?"

"Nothing, zero, nada, zilch," said the same gentleman.

"And your feelings as to the disparity?"

"None," said Mr Clubb. "What we are given is the correct amount. When the time comes, you shall know the sum to the penny."

To myself I said, *So I shall, and it shall be nothing*; to them, "We must devise a method by which I may pass along suggestions as I monitor your ongoing progress. Our future consultations should take place in anonymous public places on the order of street corners, public parks, diners, and the like. I must never be seen in your office."

"You must not, you could not," said Mr Clubb. "We would prefer to instal ourselves here within the privacy and seclusion of your own beautiful office."

"Here?" He had once again succeeded in dumbfounding me.

"Our installation within the client's work space proves so advantageous as to overcome all initial objections," said Mr Cuff. "And in this case, sir, we would occupy but the single corner behind me where the table stands against the window. We would come and go by means of your private elevator, exercise our natural functions in your private bathroom, and have our simple meals sent in from your kitchen. You would suffer no interference or awkwardness in the course of your business. So we prefer to do our job here, where we can do it best."

"You prefer," I said, giving equal weight to every word, "to move in with me."

"Prefer it to declining the offer of our help, thereby forcing you, sir, to seek the aid of less reliable individuals."

Several factors, first among them being the combination of delay, difficulty, and risk involved in finding replacements for the pair before me, led me to give further thought to this absurdity. Charlie-Charlie, a fellow of wide acquaintance among society's shadow side, had sent me his best. Any others would be inferior. It was true that Mr Clubb and Mr Cuff could enter and leave my office unseen, granting us a greater degree of security than possible in diners and public parks. There remained an insuperable problem.

"All you say may be true, but my partners and clients alike enter this office daily. How do I explain the presence of two strangers?"

"That is easily done, Mr Cuff, is it not?" said Mr Clubb.

"Indeed it is," said his partner. "Our experience has given us two infallible and complementary methods. The first of these is the installation of a screen to shield us from the view of those who visit this office."

I said, "You intend to hide behind a screen."

"During those periods when it is necessary for us to be on-site."

"Are you and Mr Clubb capable of perfect silence? Do you never shuffle your feet, do you never cough?"

"You could justify our presence within these sacrosanct confines by the single manner most calculated to draw over Mr Clubb and myself a blanket of respectable, anonymous impersonality."

"You wish to be introduced as my lawyers?" I asked.

"I invite you to consider a word," said Mr Cuff. "Hold it steadily in your mind. Remark the inviolability that distinguishes those it identifies, measure its effect upon those who hear it. The word of which I speak, sir, is this: Consultant."

I opened my mouth to object and found I could not.

Every profession occasionally must draw upon the resources of impartial experts – consultants. Every institution of every kind has known the visitations of persons answerable only to the top and given access to all departments – consultants. Consultants are *supposed* to be invisible. Again I opened my mouth, this time to say, "Gentlemen, we are in business." I picked up my telephone and asked Mrs Rampage to order immediate delivery from Bloomingdale's of an ornamental screen and then to remove the breakfast tray.

Eyes agleam with approval, Mr Clubb and Mr Cuff stepped forward to clasp my hand.

"We are in business," said Mr Clubb.

"Which is by way of saying," said Mr Cuff, "jointly dedicated to a sacred purpose."

Mrs Rampage entered, circled to the side of my desk, and gave my visitors a glance of deep-dyed wariness. Mr Clubb and Mr Cuff looked heavenward. "About the screen," she said. "Bloomingdale's wants to know if you would prefer one six feet high in a black and red Chinese pattern or one ten feet high, Art Deco, in ochres, teals and taupes."

My barnies nodded together at the heavens. "The latter, please, Mrs Rampage," I said. "Have it delivered this afternoon, regardless of cost, and place it beside the table for the use of these gentlemen, Mr Clubb and Mr Cuff, highly regarded consultants to the financial industry. That table shall be their command post."

"Consultants," she said. "Oh."

The barnies dipped their heads. Much relaxed, Mrs Rampage asked if I expected great changes in the future.

"We shall see," I said. "I wish you to extend every co-operation to these gentlemen. I need not remind you, I know, that change is the first law of life."

She disappeared, no doubt on a beeline for her telephone.

Mr Clubb stretched his arms above his head. "The preliminaries are out of the way, and we can move to the job at hand. You, sir, have been most *exceedingly*, most *grievously* wronged. Do I over-state?"

"You do not," I said.

"Would I overstate to assert that you have been injured, that you have suffered a devastating wound?"

"No, you would not," I responded, with some heat.

Mr Clubb settled a broad haunch upon the surface of my desk. His face had taken on a grave, sweet serenity. "You seek redress. Redress, sir, is a *correction*, but it is nothing more. You imagine that it restores a lost balance, but it does nothing of the kind. A crack has appeared on the earth's surface, causing widespread loss of life. From all sides are heard the cries of the wounded and dying. It is as though the earth itself has suffered an injury akin to yours, is it not?"

He had expressed a feeling I had not known to be mine until that moment, and my voice trembled as I said, "It is exactly."

"Exactly," he said. "For that reason I said *correction* rather than *restoration*. Restoration is never possible. Change is the first law of life."

"Yes, of course," I said, trying to get down to brass tacks.

Mr Clubb hitched his buttock more comprehensively onto the desk. "What will happen will indeed happen, but we prefer our clients to acknowledge from the first that, apart from human desires being a messy business, outcomes are full of surprises. If you choose to repay one disaster with an equal and opposite disaster, we would reply, in our country fashion, There's a calf that won't suck milk."

I said, "I know I can't pay my wife back in kind, how could I?"

"Once we begin," he said, "we cannot undo our actions."

"Why should I want them undone?" I asked.

Mr Clubb drew up his legs and sat cross-legged before me. Mr Cuff placed a meaty hand on my shoulder. "I suppose there is no dispute," said Mr Clubb, "that the injury you seek to redress is the adulterous behaviour of your spouse."

Mr Cuff's hand tightened on my shoulder.

"You wish that my partner and myself punish your spouse."

"I didn't hire you to read her bedtime stories," I said.

Mr Cuff twice smacked my shoulder, painfully, in what I took to be approval.

"Are we assuming that her punishment is to be of a physical nature?" asked Mr Clubb. His partner gave my shoulder another all-too-hearty squeeze.

"What other kind is there?" I asked, pulling away from Mr Cuff's hand.

The hand closed on me again, and Mr Clubb said, "Punishment of a mental or psychological nature. We could, for example, torment her with mysterious telephone calls and anonymous letters. We could use any of a hundred devices to make it impossible for her to sleep. Threatening incidents could be staged so often as to put her in a permanent state of terror."

"I want physical punishment," I said.

"That is our constant preference," he said. "Results are swifter and more conclusive when physical punishment is used. But again, we have a wide spectrum from which to choose. Are we looking for mild physical pain, real suffering, or something in between, on the order of, say, broken arms or legs?"

I thought of the change in Marguerite's eyes when I named the —Hotel. "Real suffering."

Another bone-crunching blow to my shoulder from Mr Cuff and a wide, gappy smile from Mr Clubb greeted this remark. "You, sir, are our favourite type of client," said Mr Clubb. "A fellow who knows what he wants and is unafraid to put it into words. This suffering, now, did you wish it in brief or extended form?"

"Extended," I said. "I must say that I appreciate your thoughtfulness in consulting with me like this. I was not quite sure what I wanted of you when first I requested your services, but you have helped me become perfectly clear about it."

"That is our function," he said. "Now, sir. The extended form of real suffering permits two different conclusions, gradual cessation or termination. Which is your preference?"

I opened my mouth and closed it. I opened it again and stared at the ceiling. Did I want these men to murder my wife? No. Yes. No. Yes, but only after making sure that the unfaithful trollop understood exactly why she had to die. No, surely an extended term of excruciating torture would restore the world to proper balance. Yet I wanted the witch dead. But then I would be ordering these barnies to kill her. "At the moment I cannot make that decision," I said. Irresistibly, my eyes found the bottom drawer containing the files of obscene photographs. "I'll let you know my decision after we have begun."

Mr Cuff dropped his hand, and Mr Clubb nodded with exaggerated, perhaps ironic slowness. "And what of your rival, the seducer, sir? Do we have any wishes in regard to that gentleman, sir?"

The way these fellows could sharpen one's thinking was truly remarkable. "I most certainly do," I said. "What she gets, he gets. Fair is fair."

"Indeed, sir," said Mr Clubb, "and, if you will permit me, sir, only fair is fair. And fairness demands that before we go any deeper into the particulars of the case we must examine the evidence as presented to yourself, and when I speak of fairness, sir, I refer to fairness particularly to yourself, for only the evidence seen by your own eyes can permit us to view this matter through them."

Again, I looked helplessly down at the bottom drawer. "That will not be necessary. You will find my wife at our country estate, Green . . ."

My voice trailed off as Mr Cuff's hand ground into my shoulder while he bent down and opened the drawer.

"Begging to differ," said Mr Clubb, "but we are now and again in a better position than the client to determine what is necessary. Remember, sir, that while shame unshared is toxic to the soul, shame shared is the beginning of health. Besides, it only hurts for a little while."

Mr Cuff drew the files from the drawer.

"My partner will concur that your inmost wish is that we examine the evidence," said Mr Clubb. "Else you would not have signaled its location. We would prefer to have your explicit command to do so, but in the absence of explicit, implicit serves just about as well."

I gave an impatient, ambiguous wave of the hand, a gesture they cheerfully misunderstood.

"Then all is . . . how do you put it, sir? 'All is . . .'"

"All is in order, all is in train," I muttered.

"Just so. We have ever found it beneficial to establish a common language with our clients, in order to conduct ourselves within terms enhanced by their constant usage in the dialogue between us." He took the files from Mr Cuff's hands. "We shall examine the contents of these folders at the table across the room. After the examination has been completed, my partner and I shall deliberate. And then, sir, we shall return for further instructions."

They strolled across the office and took adjoining chairs on the near side of the table, presenting me with two identical wide, black-clothed backs. Their hats went to either side, the files between them. Attempting unsuccessfully to look away, I lifted my receiver and asked my secretary who, if anyone, had called in the interim and what appointments had been made for the morning.

Mr Clubb opened a folder and learned forward to inspect the topmost photograph.

My secretary informed me that Marguerite had telephoned from the road with an inquiry concerning my health. Mr Clubb's back and shoulders trembled with what I assumed was the shock of disgust. One of the scions was due at 2.00 p.m., and at four a cryptic gentleman would arrive. By their works shall ye know them, and Mrs Rampage proved herself a diligent soul by asking if I wished her to place a call to Green Chimneys at three o'clock. Mr Clubb thrust a photograph in front of Mr Cuff. "I think not," I said. "Anything else?" She told me that Gilligan had expressed a desire to see me privately – meaning, without the Skipper – sometime during the morning. A murmur came from the table. "Gilligan can wait," I said, and the murmur, expressive, I had thought, of dismay and sympathy, rose in volume and revealed itself as amusement.

They were chuckling – even chortling!

I replaced the telephone and said, "Gentlemen, your laughter is insupportable." The potential effect of this remark was undone by its being lost within a surge of coarse laughter. I believe that something else was at that moment lost . . . some dimension of my soul . . . an element akin to pride . . . akin to dignity . . . but whether the loss was for good or ill, then I could not say. For some time, in fact an impossibly lengthy time, they found cause for laughter in the wretched photographs. My occasional attempts to silence them went unheard as they passed the dread images back and forth, discarding some instantly and to others returning for a second, a third, even a fourth and fifth perusal.

At last the barnies reared back, uttered a few nostalgic chirrups of laughter, and returned the photographs to the folders. They were still twitching with remembered laughter, still flicking happy tears from their eyes, as they sauntered, grinning, back across the office and tossed the files onto my desk. "Ah me, sir, a delightful experience," said Mr Clubb. "Nature in all her lusty romantic splendour, one might say. Remarkably stimulating, I could add. Correct, sir?"

"I hadn't expected you fellows to be stimulated to mirth," I grumbled, ramming the foul things into the drawer and out of view.

"Laughter is merely a portion of the stimulation to which I refer," he said. "Unless my sense of smell has led me astray, a thing I fancy it has yet to do, you could not but feel another sort of arousal altogether before these pictures, am I right?"

I refused to respond to this sally but felt the blood rising to my cheeks. Here they were again, the slugs and maggots.

"We are all brothers under the skin," said Mr Clubb. "Remember my words. Shame unshared poisons the soul. And besides, it only hurts for a little while."

Now I could not respond. What was the "it" that hurt only for a little while – the pain of cuckoldry, the mystery of my shameful response to the photographs, or the horror of the barnies knowing what I had done?

"You will find it helpful, sir, to repeat after me: *It only hurts for a little while.*"

"It only hurts for a little while," I said, and the naïve phrase reminded me that they were only barnies after all.

"Spoken like a child," Mr Clubb most annoyingly said, "in, as it were, the tones and accents of purest innocence," and then righted matters by asking where Marguerite might be found. Had I not mentioned a country place named Green . . .?

"Green Chimneys," I said, shaking off the unpleasant impression that the preceding few seconds had made upon me. "You will find it at the end of —Lane, turning right off —Street just north of the town of—. The four green chimneys easily visible above the hedge along —Lane are your landmark, though as it is the only building in sight you can hardly mistake it for another. My wife left our place in the city just after ten this morning, so she should be getting there. . ." I looked at my watch. ". . . in thirty to forty-five minutes. She will unlock the front gate, but she will not relock it once she has passed through, for she never does. The woman does not have the self-preservation of a sparrow. Once she has entered the estate, she will travel up the drive and open the door of the garage with an electronic device. This door, I assure you, will remain open, and the door she will take into the house will not be locked."

"But there are maids and cooks and laundresses and bootboys and suchlike to consider," said Mr Cuff. "Plus a majordomo to conduct the entire orchestra and go around rattling the doors to make sure they're locked. Unless all of these parties are to be absent on account of the annual holiday."

"My servants have the month off," I said.

"A most suggestive consideration," said Mr Clubb. "You possess a devilish clever mind, sir."

"Perhaps," I said, grateful for the restoration of the proper balance. "Marguerite will have stopped along the way for groceries and other essentials, so she will first carry the bags into the kitchen, which is the first room to the right off the corridor from the garage. Then I suppose she will take the staircase upstairs and air out her bedroom." I took pen and paper from my topmost drawer and sketched the layout of the house. "She may go around to the library, the morning room, and the drawing room, opening the shutters and a few windows. Somewhere during this process, she is likely to use the telephone. After that, she will leave the house by the rear entrance and take the path along the top of the bluff to a long, low building that looks like this."

I drew in the outlines of the studio in its nest of trees above the Hudson. "It is a recording studio I had built for her convenience. She may well plan to spend the entire afternoon inside it. You will know if she is there by the lights." I saw Marguerite smiling to herself as she fit her key into the lock on the studio door, saw her let herself in and reach for the light switch. A wave of emotion rendered me speechless.

Mr Clubb rescued me by asking, "It is your feeling, sir, that when the lady stops to use the telephone she will be placing a call to that energetic gentleman?"

"Yes, of course," I said, only barely refraining from adding *you dolt*. "She will seize the earliest opportunity to inform him of their good fortune."

He nodded with an extravagant caution I recognized from my own dealings with backward clients. "Let us pause to see all 'round the matter, sir. Would the lady wish to leave a suspicious entry in your telephone records? Isn't it more likely that the person she telephones will be you, sir? The call to the athletic gentleman will already have been placed, according to my way of seeing things, either from the roadside or the telephone in the grocery where you have her stop to pick up her essentials."

Though disliking these references to Leeson's physical condition, I admitted that he might have a point.

"In that case, sir, and I know that a mind as quick as yours has already overtaken mine, you would want to express yourself with the utmost cordiality when the missus calls again, so as not to tip your hand in even the slightest way. But that, I'm sure, goes without saying, after all you have been through, sir."

Without bothering to acknowledge this, I said, "Shouldn't you fellows be leaving? No sense in wasting time, after all."

"Precisely why we shall wait here until the end of the day," said Mr Clubb. "In cases of this unhappy sort, we find it more effective to deal with both parties at once, acting in concert when they are in prime condition to be taken by surprise. The gentleman is liable to leave his place of work at the end of the day, which implies to me that he is unlikely to appear at your lovely country place at any time before seven this evening or, which is more likely, eight. At this time of the year, there is still enough light at nine o'clock to enable us to conceal our vehicle on the grounds, enter the house, and begin our business. At eleven o'clock, sir, we shall call with our initial report and request additional instructions."

I asked the fellow if he meant to idle away the entire afternoon in my office while I conducted my business.

"Mr Cuff and I are never idle, sir. While you conduct your business, we will be doing the same, laying out our plans, refining our strategies, choosing our methods and the order of their use."

"Oh, all right," I said, "but I trust you'll be quiet about it."

At that moment, Mrs Rampage buzzed to say that Gilligan was before her, requesting to see me immediately, proof that bush telegraph is a more efficient means of spreading information than any newspaper. I told her to send him in, and a second later Morning Gilligan, pale of face, dark hair tousled but not as yet completely wild, came treading softly toward my desk. He pretended to be surprised that I had visitors and pantomimed an apology which incorporated the suggestion that he depart and return later. "No, no," I said, "I am delighted to see you, for this gives me the opportunity to introduce you to our new consultants, who will be working closely with me for a time."

Gilligan swallowed, glanced at me with the deepest suspicion, and extended his hand as I made the introductions. "I regret that I am unfamiliar with your work, gentlemen," he said. "Might I ask the name of your firm? Is it Locust, Bleaney, Burns or Charter, Carter, Maxton, and Coltrane?"

By naming the two most prominent consultancies in our industry, Gilligan was assessing the thinness of the ice beneath his feet: LBB specialized in investments, CCM&C in estates and trusts. If my visitors worked for the former, he would suspect that a guillotine hung above his neck; if the latter, the Skipper was liable for the chop. "Neither," I said. "Mr Clubb and Mr Cuff are the directors of their own concern, which covers every aspect of the trade with such tactful professionalism that it is known to but the few for whom they will consent to work."

"Excellent," Gilligan whispered, gazing in some puzzlement at the map and floor plan atop my desk. "Tip-top."

"When their findings are given to me, they shall be given to all. In the meantime, I would prefer that you say as little as possible about the matter. Though change is a law of life, we wish to avoid unnecessary alarm."

"You know that you can depend on my silence," said Morning Gilligan, and it was true, I did know that. I also knew that his alter ego, Afternoon Gilligan, would babble the news to everyone who had not already heard it from Mrs Rampage. By 6.00 p.m., our entire industry would be pondering the information that I had called in a consultancy team of such rarified accomplishments *that they chose to remain unknown but to the very few*. None of my colleagues could dare admit to an ignorance of Clubb & Cuff, and my reputation, already great, would increase exponentially.

To distract him from the floor plan of Green Chimneys and the rough map of my estate, I said, "I assume some business brought you here, Gilligan."

"Oh! Yes – yes – of course," he said, and with a trace of embarrassment brought to my attention the pretext for his being there, the ominous plunge in value of an overseas fund in which we had advised one of his musicians to invest. Should we recommend selling the fund before more money was lost, or was it wisest to hold on? Only a minute was required to decide that the musician should retain his share of the fund until next quarter, when we anticipated a general improvement, but both Gilligan and I were aware that this recommendation call could easily have been handled by telephone. Soon he was moving toward the door, smiling at the barnies in a pathetic display of false confidence.

The telephone rang a moment after the detectives had returned to the table. Mr Clubb said, "Your wife, sir. Remember: the utmost cordiality." Here was false confidence, I thought, of an entirely different sort. I picked up the receiver to hear Mrs Rampage tell me that my wife was on the line.

What followed was a banal conversation of the utmost *duplicity*. Marguerite pretended that my sudden departure from the dinner table and my late arrival at the office had caused her to fear for my health. I pretended that all was well, apart from a slight indigestion. Had the drive up been peaceful? Yes. How was the house? A little musty, but otherwise fine. She had never quite realized, she said, how very large Green Chimneys was until she walked around in it, knowing she was going to be there alone. Had she been out to the studio? No, but she was looking forward to getting a lot of work done over the next three or four days and thought she would be working every night, as well. (Implicit in this remark was the information that I should be unable to reach her, the studio being without a telephone.) After a moment of awkward silence, she said, "I suppose it is too early for you to have identified your traitor." It was, I said, but the process would begin that evening. "I'm so sorry you have to go through this," she said. "I know how painful the discovery was for you, and I can only begin to imagine how angry you must be, but I hope you will be merciful. No amount of punishment can undo the damage, and if you try to exact retribution you will only injure yourself. The man is going to lose his job and his reputation. Isn't that punishment enough?" After a few meaningless pleasantries the conversation had clearly come to an end, although we still had yet to say good-bye. Then an odd thing happened to me. I nearly said, *Lock all the doors and windows tonight and let no one in.* I nearly said, *You are in grave danger and must come home.* With these words rising in my throat, I looked across the room at Mr Clubb and Mr Cuff. Mr Clubb winked at me. I heard myself bidding Marguerite farewell, and then heard her hang up her telephone.

"Well done, sir," said Mr Clubb. "To aid Mr Cuff and myself in the preparation of our inventory, can you tell us if you keep certain staples at Green Chimneys?"

"Staples?" I said, thinking he was referring to foodstuffs.

"Rope?" he asked. "Tools, especially pliers, hammers, and screwdrivers? A good saw? A variety of knives? Are there by any chance firearms?"

"No firearms," I said. "I believe all the other items you mention can be found in the house."

"Rope and tool chest in the basement, knives in the kitchen?"

"Yes," I said, "precisely." I had not ordered these barnies to murder my wife, I reminded myself; I had drawn back from that precipice. By the time I went into the executive dining room for my luncheon, I felt sufficiently restored to give Charlie-Charlie that ancient symbol of approval, the thumbs-up sign.

III

When I returned to my office the screen had been set in place, shielding from view the detectives in their preparations but in no way muffling the rumble of comments and laughter they brought to the task. "Gentlemen," I said in a voice loud enough to be heard behind the screen – a most unsuitable affair decorated with a pattern of ocean liners, martini glasses, champagne bottles, and cigarettes – "you must modulate your voices, as I have business to conduct here as well as you." There came a somewhat softer rumble of acquiescence. I took my seat to discover my bottom desk drawer pulled out, the folders absent. Another roar of laughter jerked me once again to my feet.

I came around the side of the screen and stopped short. The table lay concealed beneath drifts and mounds of yellow legal paper covered with lists of words and drawings of stick figures in varying stages of dismemberment. Strewn through the yellow pages were the photographs, loosely divided into those in which either Marguerite or Graham Leeson provided the principal focus. Crude genitalia had been drawn, without reference to either party's actual gender, over and atop both of them. Aghast, I began gathering up the defaced photographs. "I must insist . . ." I said. "I really must insist, you know . . ."

Mr Clubb immobilized my wrist with one hand and extracted the photographs with the other. "We prefer to work in our time-honoured fashion," he said. "Our methods may be unusual, but they are ours. But before you take up the afternoon's occupations, sir, can you tell us if items on the handcuff order might be found in the house?"

"No," I said. Mr Cuff pulled a yellow page before him and wrote *handcuffs*.

"Chains?" asked Mr Clubb.

"No chains," I said, and Mr Cuff added *chains* to his list.

"That is all for the moment," said Mr Clubb, and released me.

I took a step backward and massaged my wrist, which stung as if from rope burn. "You speak of your methods," I said, "and I understand that you have them. But what can be the purpose of defacing my photographs in this grotesque fashion?"

"Sir," said Mr Clubb in a stern, teacherly voice, "where you speak of defacing, we use the term *enhancement*. Enhancement is a tool we find vital to the method known by the name of Visualization."

I retired defeated to my desk. At five minutes before two, Mrs Rampage informed me that the Skipper and our scion, a thirty-year-old inheritor of a great family fortune named Mr Chester Montfort de M—, awaited my pleasure. Putting Mrs Rampage on hold, I called out, "Please do give me absolute quiet, now. A client is on his way in."

First to appear was the Skipper, his tall, rotund form as alert as a pointer's in a grouse field as he led in the taller, inexpressibly languid figure of Mr Chester Montfort de M—, a person marked in every inch of his being by great ease, humour, and stupidity. The Skipper froze to gape horrified at the screen, but Montfort de M— continued around him to shake my hand and say, "Have to tell you, I like that thingamabob over there immensely. Reminds me of a similar thingamabob at the Beeswax Club a few years ago, whole flocks of girls used to come tumbling out. Don't suppose we're in for any unicycles and trumpets today, eh?"

The combination of the raffish screen and our client's unbridled memories brought a dangerous flush to the Skipper's face, and I hastened to explain the presence of top-level consultants who preferred to pitch tent on-site, as it were, hence the installation of a screen, all the above in the service of, well, *service*, an all-important quality we . . .

"By Kitchener's mustache," said the Skipper. "I remember the Beeswax Club. Don't suppose I'll ever forget the night Little Billy Pegleg jumped up and . . ." The colour darkened on his cheeks, and he closed his mouth.

From behind the screen, I heard Mr Clubb say, "Visualize *this*." Mr Cuff chuckled.

The Skipper recovered himself and turned his sternest glare up on me. "Superb idea, consultants. A white-glove inspection tightens up any ship." His veiled glance toward the screen indicated that he had known of the presence of our "consultants" but, unlike Gilligan, had restrained himself from thrusting into my office until given legitimate reason. "That being the case, is it still quite proper that these people remain while we discuss Mr Montfort de M—'s confidential affairs?"

"Quite proper, I assure you," I said. "The consultants and I prefer to work in an atmosphere of complete co-operation. Indeed, this arrangement is a condition of their accepting our firm as their client."

"Indeed," said the Skipper.

"Top of the tree, are they?" said Mr Montfort de M——. "Expect no less of you fellows. Fearful competence. *Terrifying* competence."

Mr Cuff's voice could be heard saying, "Okay, visualize *this*." Mr Clubb uttered a high-pitched giggle.

"Enjoy their work," said Mr Montfort de M——.

"Shall we?" I gestured to their chairs. As a young man whose assets equaled two to three billion dollars (depending on the condition of the stock market, the value of real estate in half a dozen cities around the world, global warming, forest fires, and the like), our client was as catnip to the ladies, three of whom he had previously married and divorced after siring a child upon each, resulting in a great interlocking complexity of trusts, agreements, and contracts, all of which had to be re-examined on the occasion of his forthcoming wedding to a fourth young woman, named like her predecessors after a semiprecious stone. Due to the perspicacity of the Skipper and myself, each new nuptial altered the terms of those previous so as to maintain our client's liability at an unvarying level. Our computers had enabled us to generate the documents well before his arrival, and all Mr Montfort de M—— had to do was listen to the revised terms and sign the papers, a task that generally induced a slumberous state except for those moments when a prized asset was in transition.

"Hold on, boys," he said ten minutes into our explanations, "you mean Opal has to give the racehorses to Garnet, and in return she gets the teak plantation from Turquoise, who gets Garnet's ski resort in Aspen? Opal is crazy about those horses."

I explained that his second wife could easily afford the purchase of a new stable with the income from the plantation. He bent to the task of scratching his signature on the form. A roar of laughter erupted behind the screen. The Skipper glanced sideways in displeasure, and our client looked at me blinking. "Now to the secondary trusts," I said. "As you will recall, three years ago——"

My words were cut short by the appearance of a chuckling Mr Clubb clamping an unlighted cigar in his mouth, a legal pad in his hand, as he came toward us. The Skipper and Mr Montfort de M—— goggled at him, and Mr Clubb nodded. "Begging your pardon, sir, but some queries cannot wait. Pickaxe, sir? Dental floss? Awl?"

"No, yes, no," I said, and then introduced him to the other two men. The Skipper appeared stunned, Mr Montfort de M— cheerfully puzzled.

"We would prefer the existence of an attic," said Mr Clubb.

"An attic exists," I said.

"I must admit my confusion," said the Skipper. "Why is a consultant asking about awls and attics? What is dental floss to a consultant?"

"For the nonce, Skipper," I said, "these gentlemen and I must communicate in a form of cipher or code, of which these are examples, but soon—"

"Plug your blowhole, Skipper," broke in Mr Clubb. "At the moment you are as useful as wind in an outhouse, always hoping you will excuse my simple way of expressing myself."

Spluttering, the Skipper rose to his feet, his face rosier by far than during his involuntary reminiscence of what Little Billy Pegleg had done one night at the Beeswax Club.

"Steady on," I said, fearful of the heights of choler to which indignation could bring my portly, white-haired, but still powerful junior.

"Not on your life," bellowed the Skipper. "I cannot brook . . . cannot tolerate. . . . If this ill mannered dwarf imagines excuse is possible after . . ." He raised a fist. Mr Clubb said, "Pish tosh," and placed a hand on the nape of the Skipper's neck. Instantly, the Skipper's eyes rolled up, the colour drained from his face, and he dropped like a sack into his chair.

"Hole in one," marvelled Mr Montfort de M—. "Old boy isn't dead, is he?"

The Skipper exhaled uncertainly and licked his lips.

"With my apologies for the unpleasantness," said Mr Clubb, "I have only two more queries at this juncture. Might we locate bedding in the aforesaid attic, and have you an implement such as a match or a lighter?"

"There are several old mattresses and bed frames in the attic," I said, "but as to matches, surely you do not . . ."

Understanding the request better than I, Mr Montfort de M— extended a golden lighter and applied an inch of flame to the tip of Mr Clubb's cigar. "Didn't think that part was code," he said. "Rules have changed? Smoking allowed?"

"From time to time during the workday my colleague and I prefer to smoke," said Mr Clubb, expelling a reeking miasma across the desk. I had always found tobacco nauseating in its every form, and in all parts of our building smoking had, of course, long been prohibited.

"Three cheers, my man, plus three more after that," said Mr Montfort de M—, extracting a ridged case from an inside pocket, an absurdly phallic cigar from the case. "I prefer to smoke, too, you know, especially during these deadly conferences about who gets the pincushions and who gets the snuffboxes." He submitted the object to a circumcision, *snick-snick*, and to my horror set it alight. "Ashtray?" I dumped paper clips from a crystal oyster shell and slid it toward him. "Mr Clubb, is it? Mr Clubb, you are a fellow of wonderful accomplishments, still can't get over that marvellous whopbopaloobop on the Skipper, and I'd like to ask if we could get together some evening, cigars and cognac kind of thing."

"We prefer to undertake one matter at a time," said Mr Clubb. Mr Cuff appeared beside the screen. He, too, was lighting up eight or nine inches of brown rope. "However, we welcome your appreciation and would be delighted to swap tales of derring-do at a later date."

"Very, very cool," said Mr Montfort de M—, "especially if you could teach me how to do the whopbopaloobop."

"This is a world full of hidden knowledge," Mr Clubb said. "My partner and I have chosen as our sacred task the transmission of that knowledge."

"Amen," said Mr Cuff.

Mr Clubb bowed to my awed client and sauntered off. The Skipper shook himself, rubbed his eyes, and took in the client's cigar. "My goodness," he said. "I believe . . . I can't imagine . . . heavens, is smoking permitted again? What a blessing." With that, he fumbled a cigarette from his shirt pocket, accepted a light from Mr Montfort de M—, and sucked in the fumes. Until that moment I had not known that the Skipper was an addict of nicotine.

For the remainder of the hour a coiling layer of smoke like a low-lying cloud established itself beneath the ceiling and increased in density as it grew toward the floor while we extracted Mr Montfort de M—'s careless signature on the transfers and assignments. Now and again the Skipper displaced one of a perpetual chain of cigarettes from his mouth to remark upon the peculiar pain in his neck. Finally I was able to send client and junior partner on their way with those words of final benediction, "All is in order, all is in train", freeing me at last to stride about my office flapping a copy of *Institutional Investor* at the cloud, a remedy our fixed windows made more symbolic than actual. The barnies further defeated the effort by wafting senseless billows of cigar effluvia over the screen, but as they seemed to be conducting their business in a conventionally businesslike manner I made no objection and retired in defeat to my desk for the preparations necessitated by the arrival in an hour of my next client, Mr Arthur "This Building is Condemned" C—, the most cryptic of all the cryptic gentlemen.

So deeply was I immersed in these preparations that only a polite cough and the supplication of "Begging your pardon, sir" brought to my awareness the presence of Mr Clubb and Mr Cuff before my desk. "What is it now?" I asked.

"We are, sir, in need of creature comforts," said Mr Clubb. "Long hours of work have left us exceeding dry in the region of the mouth and throat, and the pressing sensation of thirst has made it impossible for us to maintain the concentration required to do our best."

"Meaning a drink would be greatly appreciated, sir," said Mr Cuff.

"Of course, of course," I said. "I'll have Mrs Rampage bring in a couple of bottles of water. We have San Pellegrino and Evian. Which would you prefer?"

With a smile almost menacing in its intensity, Mr Cuff said, "We prefer drinks when we drink. *Drink* drinks, if you take my meaning."

"For the sake of the refreshment found in them," said Mr Clubb, ignoring my obvious dismay. "I speak of refreshment in its every aspect, from relief to the parched tongue, taste to the ready palate, warmth to the inner man, and to the highest of refreshments, that of the mind and soul. We prefer bottles of gin and bourbon, and while any decent gargle would be gratefully received, we have, like all men who partake of grape and grain, our favourite tipples. Mr Cuff is partial to J. W. Dant bourbon, and I enjoy a drop of Bombay gin. A bucket of ice would not go amiss, and I could say the same for a case of ice-cold Old Bohemia beer. As a chaser."

"You consider it a good idea to consume alcohol before embarking on . . ." I sought for the correct phrase. "A mission so delicate?"

"We consider it an essential prelude. Alcohol inspires the mind and awakens the imagination. A fool dulls both by overindulgence, but up to that point, which is a highly individual matter, there is only enhancement. Through history, alcohol has been known for its sacred properties, and the both of us know that during the sacrament of Holy Communion, priests and reverends happily serve as bartenders, passing out free drinks to all comers, children included."

"Besides that," I said after a pause, "I suppose you would prefer not to be compelled to quit my employment after we have made such strides together."

"We are on a great journey," he said.

I placed the order with Mrs Rampage, and fifteen minutes later into my domain entered two ill-dressed youths laden with the requested liquors and a metal bucket, in which the necks of beer bottles protruded from a bed of ice. I tipped the louts a dollar apiece, which they accepted with a boorish lack of grace. Mrs Rampage took in this activity with none of the revulsion for the polluted air and spirituous liquids I had anticipated.

The louts slouched away; the chuckling barnies disappeared from view with their refreshments; and, after fixing me for a moment of silence, her eyes alight with an expression I had never before observed in them, Mrs Rampage ventured the amazing opinion that the recent relaxation of formalities should prove beneficial to the firm as a whole and added that, were Mr Clubb and Mr Cuff responsible for the reformation, they had already justified their reputation and would assuredly enhance my own.

"You believe so," I said, noting with momentarily delayed satisfaction that the effects of Afternoon Gilligan's indiscretions had already begun to declare themselves.

Employing the tactful verbal formula for *I wish to speak exactly half my mind and no more*, Mrs Rampage said, "May I be frank, sir?"

"I depend on you to do no less," I said.

Her carriage and face became what I can only describe as girlish – years seemed to drop away from her. "I don't want to say too much, sir, and I hope you know how much everyone understands what a privilege it is to be a part of this firm." Like the Skipper but more attractively, she blushed. "Honest, I really mean that. Everybody knows that we're one of the two or three companies best at what we do."

"Thank you," I said.

"That's why I feel I can talk like this," said my ever-less-recognizable Mrs Rampage. "Until today, everybody thought if they acted like themselves, the way they really were, you'd fire them right away. Because, and maybe I shouldn't say this, maybe I'm way out of line, sir, but it's because you always seem, well, so proper you could never forgive a person for not being as dignified as you are. Like the Skipper is a heavy smoker and everybody knows it's not supposed to be permitted in this building, but a lot

of companies here let their top people smoke in their offices as long
as they're discreet because it shows they appreciate those people,
and that's nice because it shows that if you get to the top you can be
appreciated, too, but here the Skipper has to go all the way to the
elevator and stand outside with the file clerks if he wants a cigarette.
And in every other company I know the partners and important
clients sometimes have a drink together and nobody thinks they're
committing a terrible sin. You're a religious man, sir, we look up
to you so much, but I think you're going to find that people will
respect you even more once it gets out that you've loosened the
rules a little bit." She gave me a look in which I read that she feared
having spoken too freely. "I just wanted to say that I think you're
doing the right thing, sir."

What she was saying, of course, was that I was widely regarded
as pompous, remote, and out of touch. "I had not known that my
employees regarded me as a religious man," I said.

"Oh, we all do," she said with almost touching earnestness.
"Because of the hymns."

"The hymns?"

"The ones you hum to yourself when you're working."

"Do I, indeed? Which ones?"

" 'Jesus Loves Me', 'The Old Rugged Cross', 'Abide with Me', and
'Amazing Grace', mostly. Sometimes 'Onward, Christian Soldiers'."

Here, with a vengeance, were Temple Square and Scripture
Street! Here was the Youth Bible Study Centre, where the child-
me had hours on end sung these same hymns during our Sunday
school sessions! I did not know what to make of the knowledge that
I hummed them to myself at my desk, but it was some consolation
that this unconscious habit had at least partially humanized me to
my staff.

"You didn't know you did that? Oh, sir, that's so *cute!*"

Sounds of merriment from the far side of the office rescued Mrs
Rampage from the fear that this time she had truly overstepped the
bounds, and she made a rapid exit. I stared after her for a moment,
at first unsure how deeply I ought to regret a situation in which my
secretary found it possible to describe myself and my habits as *cute*,
then resolved that it probably was, or eventually would be, for the
best. "All is in order, all is in train," I said to myself. "It only hurts
for a little while." With that, I took my seat once more to continue
delving into the elaborations of Mr "This Building is Condemned"
C—'s financial life.

Another clink of bottle against glass and ripple of laughter brought with them the recognition that this particular client would never consent to the presence of unknown "consultants". Unless the barnies could be removed for at least an hour, I should face the immediate loss of a substantial portion of my business.

"Fellows," I cried, "come up here now. We must address a serious problem."

Glasses in hand, cigars nestled into the corners of their mouths, Mr Clubb and Mr Cuff sauntered into view. Once I had explained the issue in the most general terms, the detectives readily agreed to absent themselves for the required period. Where might they install themselves? "My bathroom," I said. "It has a small library attached, with a desk, a worktable, leather chairs and sofa, a billiard table, a large-screen cable television set, and a bar. Since you have not yet had your luncheon, you may wish to order whatever you like from the kitchen."

Five minutes later, bottles, glasses, hats, and mounds of paper arranged on the bathroom table, the bucket of beer beside it, I exited through the concealed door as Mr Clubb ordered up from my doubtless astounded chef a meal of chicken wings, french fries, onion rings, and T-bone steaks, medium well. With plenty of time to spare, I immersed myself again in details, only to be brought up short by the recognition that I was humming, none too quietly, that most innocent of hymns, "Jesus Loves Me". Then, precisely at the appointed hour, Mrs Rampage informed me of the arrival of my client and his associates, and I bade her bring them through.

A sly, slow-moving whale encased in an exquisite double-breasted black pinstripe, Mr "This Building is Condemned" C— advanced into my office with his customary hauteur and offered me the customary nod of the head while his three "associates" formed a human breakwater in the centre of the room. Regal to the core, he affected not to notice Mrs Rampage sliding a black leather chair out of the middle distance and around the side of the desk until it was in position, at which point he sat himself in it without looking down. Then he inclined his slablike head and raised a small, pallid hand. One of the "associates" promptly moved to hold the door for Mrs Rampage's departure. At this signal, I sat down, and the two remaining henchmen separated themselves by a distance of perhaps eight feet. The third closed the door and stationed himself by his general's right shoulder. These formalities completed, my client shifted his close-set obsidian eyes to mine and said, "You well?"

"Very well, thank you," I replied, according to ancient formula. "And you?"

"Good," he said. "But things could be better." This, too, followed long-established formula. His next words were a startling deviation. He took in the stationary cloud and the corpse of Montfort de M—'s cigar rising like a monolith from the reef of cigarette butts in the crystal shell and, with the first genuine smile I had ever seen on his pockmarked, small-featured face, said, "I can't believe it, but one thing just got better already. You eased up on the stupid no-smoking rule which is poisoning this city, good for you."

"It seemed," I said, "a concrete way in which to demonstrate our appreciation for the smokers among those clients we most respect." When dealing with the cryptic gentlemen, one must not fail to offer intervallic allusions to the spontaneous respect in which they are held.

"Deacon," he said, employing the sobriquet he had given me on our first meeting, "you being one of a kind at your job, the respect you speak of is mutual, and besides that, all surprises should be as pleasant as this here." With that, he snapped his fingers at the laden shell, and as he produced a ridged case similar to but more capacious than Mr Montfort de M—'s, the man at his shoulder whisked the impromptu ashtray from the desk, deposited its contents in the *poubelle*, and repositioned it at a point on the desk precisely equidistant from us. My client opened the case to expose the six cylinders contained within, removed one, and proffered the remaining five to me. "Be my guest, Deacon," he said. "Money can't buy better Havanas."

"Your gesture is much appreciated," I said. "However, with all due respect, at the moment I shall choose not to partake."

Distinct as a scar, a vertical crease of displeasure appeared on my client's forehead, and the ridged case and its five inhabitants advanced an inch toward my nose. "Deacon, you want me to smoke alone?" asked Mr "This Building is Condemned" C—. "This stuff, if you were ever lucky enough to find it at your local cigar store, which that lucky believe me you wouldn't be, is the best of the best, straight from me to you as what you could term a symbol of the co-operation and respect between us, and at the commencement of our business today it would please me greatly if you would do me the honour of joining me in a smoke."

As they say or, more accurately, as they used to say, needs must when the devil drives, or words to that effect. "Forgive me," I said, and drew one of the fecal things from the case. "I assure you, the honour is all mine."

Mr "This Building is Condemned" C— snipped the rounded end from his cigar, plugged the remainder in the centre of his mouth, then subjected mine to the same operation. His henchman proffered a lighter, and Mr "This Building is Condemned" C— bent forward and surrounded himself with clouds of smoke, in the manner of Bela Lugosi materializing before the brides of Dracula. The henchmen moved the flame toward me, and for the first time in my life I inserted into my mouth an object that seemed as large around as the handle of a baseball bat, brought it to the dancing flame, and drew in that burning smoke from which so many other men before me had derived pleasure.

Legend and common sense alike dictated that I should sputter and cough in an attempt to rid myself of the noxious substance. Nausea was in the cards, also dizziness. It is true that I suffered a degree of initial discomfort, as if my tongue had been lightly singed or seared, and the sheer unfamiliarity of the experience – the thickness of the tobacco tube, the texture of the smoke, as dense as chocolate – led me to fear for my well-being. Yet, despite the not altogether unpleasant tingling on the upper surface of my tongue, I expelled my first mouthful of cigar smoke with the sense of having sampled a taste every bit as delightful as the first sip of a properly made martini. The thug whisked away the flame, and I drew in another mouthful, leaned back, and released a wondrous quantity of smoke. Of a surprising smoothness, in some sense almost cool rather than hot, the delightful taste defined itself as heather, loam, morel mushrooms, venison, and some distinctive spice akin to coriander. I repeated the process, with results even more pleasurable – this time I tasted a hint of black butter sauce. "I can truthfully say," I told my client, "that never have I met a cigar as fine as this one."

"You bet you haven't," said Mr "This Building is Condemned" C—, and on the spot presented me with three more of the precious objects. With that, we turned to the tidal waves of cash and the interlocking corporate shells, each protecting another series of inter-connected shells that concealed yet another, like Chinese boxes.

The cryptic gentlemen one and all appreciated certain ceremonies, such as the appearance of espresso coffee in thimble-sized porcelain cups and an accompanying assortment of *biscotti* at the halfway point of our meditations. Matters of business being forbidden while coffee and cookies were dispatched, the conversation generally turned to the conundrums posed by family life. Since I had no family to speak of, and, like most of his kind, Mr "This Building is Condemned" C— was richly endowed with grandparents, parents, uncles, aunts, sons, daughters, nephews, nieces, and grandchildren, these remarks on the genealogical tapestry tended to be monologic in nature, my role in them limited to nods and grunts. Required as they were more often by the business of the cryptic gentlemen than was the case in other trades or professions, funerals were also an ongoing topic. Taking tiny sips of his espresso and equally maidenish nibbles from his favourite sweetmeats (Hydrox and Milano), my client favoured me with the expected praises of his son, Arthur Jr (Harvard graduate school, English lit.), lamentations over his daughter, Fidelia (thrice-married, never wisely), hymns to his grandchildren (Cyrus, Thor, and Hermione, respectively the genius, the dreamer, and the despot), and then proceeded to link his two unfailing themes by recalling the unhappy behaviour of Arthur Jr at the funeral of my client's uncle and a principal figure in his family's rise to an imperial eminence, Mr Vincente "Waffles" C—.

The anecdote called for the beheading and ignition of another magnificent stogie, and I greedily followed suit.

"Arthur Jr's got his head screwed on right, and he's got the right kinda family values," said my client. "Straight A's all through school, married a stand-up dame with money of her own, three great kids, makes a man proud. Hard worker. Got his head in a book morning to night, human-encyclopedia-type guy, up there at Harvard, those professors, they love him. Kid knows how you're supposed to act, right?"

I nodded and filled my mouth with another fragrant draft.

"So he comes to my uncle Vincente's funeral all by himself, which troubles me. On top of it doesn't show the proper respect to old Waffles, who was one hell of a man, there's guys still pissing blood on account of they looked at him wrong forty years ago, on top of that, I don't have the good feeling I get from taking his family around to my friends and associates and saying, So look here, this here is Arthur Jr, my Harvard guy, plus his wife, Hunter, whose ancestors I think got here even before that rabble on the *Mayflower*, plus his three kids – Cyrus, little bastard's even smarter than his dad, Thor, the one's got his head in the clouds, which is okay because we need people like that, too, and Hermione, who you can tell just by looking at her she's mean as a snake and is gonna wind up running the world someday. So I say, Arthur Jr, what the hell happened, everybody else get killed in a train wreck or something? He says, No, Dad, they just didn't wanna come, these big family funerals, they make 'em feel funny, they don't like having their pictures taken so they show up on the six o'clock news. Didn't wanna come, I say back, what kinda shit is that, you shoulda made 'em come, and if anyone took their pictures when they didn't want, we can take care of that, no trouble at all. I go on like this, I even say, What good is Harvard and all those books if they don't make you any smarter than this, and finally Arthur Jr's mother tells me, Put a cork in it, you're not exactly helping the situation here.

"So what happens then? Insteada being smart like I should, I go nuts on account of I'm the guy who pays the bills, that Harvard up there pulls in the money better than any casino I ever saw, and you wanna find a real good criminal, get some Boston WASP in a bow tie, and all of a sudden nobody listens to me! I'm seeing red in a big way here, Deacon, this is my uncle Vincente's funeral, and insteada backing me up his mother is telling me I'm not *helping*. I yell, You wanna help? Go up there and bring back his wife and kids, or I'll send Carlo and Tommy to do it. All of a sudden I'm so mad I'm thinking these people are insulting me, how can they think they can get away with that, people who insult me don't do it twice – and then I hear what I'm thinking, and I do what she said and put a cork in it, but it's too late, I went way over the top and we all know it.

"Arthur Jr takes off, and his mother won't talk to me for the whole rest of the day. Only thing I'm happy about is I didn't blow up where anyone else could see it. Deacon, I know you're the type guy wouldn't dream of threatening his family, but if the time ever comes, do yourself a favour and light up a Havana instead."

"I'm sure that is excellent advice," I said.

"Anyhow, you know what they say, it only hurts for a little while, which is true as far as it goes, and I calmed down. Uncle Vincente's funeral was beautiful. You woulda thought the Pope died. When the people are going out to the limousines, Arthur Jr is sitting in a chair at the back of the church reading a book. Put that in your pocket, I say, wanna do homework, do it in the car. He tells me it isn't homework, but he puts it in his pocket and we go out to the cemetery. His mother looks out the window the whole time we're driving to the cemetery, and the kid starts reading again. So I ask what the hell is it, this book he can't put down? He tells me but it's like he's speaking some foreign language, only word I understand is 'the', which happens a lot when your kid reads a lot of fancy books, half the titles make no sense to an ordinary person. Okay, we're out there in Queens, goddamn graveyard the size of Newark, FBI and reporters all over the place, and I'm thinking maybe Arthur Jr wasn't so wrong after all, Hunter probably hates having the FBI take her picture, and besides that little Hermione probably woulda mugged one of 'em and stole his wallet. So I tell Arthur Jr I'm sorry about what happened. I didn't really think you were going to put me in the same grave as Uncle Waffles, he says, the Harvard smart-ass. When it's all over, we get back in the car, and out comes the book again. We get home, and he disappears. We have a lot of people over, food, wine, politicians, old-timers from Brooklyn, Chicago people, Detroit people, L.A. people, movie directors, cops, actors I never heard of, priests, bishops, the guy from the Cardinal. Everybody's asking me, Where's Arthur Jr? I go upstairs to find out. He's in his old room, and he's still reading that book. I say, Arthur Jr, people are asking about you, I think it would be nice if you mingled with our guests. I'll be right down, he says, I just finished what I was reading. Here, take a look, you might enjoy it. He gives me the book and goes out of the room. So I'm wondering – what the hell *is* this, anyhow? I take it into the bedroom, toss it on the table. About ten-thirty, eleven, everybody's gone, kid's on the shuttle back to Boston, house is cleaned up, enough food in the refrigerator to feed the whole bunch all over again, I go up to bed. Arthur Jr's mother still isn't talking to me, so I get in and pick up the book. Herman Melville is the name of the guy who wrote it. The story the kid was reading is called 'Bartleby the Scrivener'. I decide I'll try it. What the hell, right? You're an educated guy, you ever read that story?"

"A long time ago," I said. "A bit . . . *odd*, isn't it?"

"Odd? That's the most terrible story I ever read in my whole life! This dud gets a job in a law office and decides he doesn't want to work. Does he get fired? He does not. This is a story? You hire a guy who won't do the job, what do you do, pamper the asshole? At the end, the dud ups and disappears and you find out he used to work in the dead-letter office. Is there a point here? The next day I call up Arthur Jr, say could he explain to me please what the hell that story is supposed to mean? Dad, he says, it means what it says. Deacon, I just about pulled the plug on Harvard right then and there. I never went to any college, but I do know that nothing means what it says, not on this planet."

This reflection was accurate when applied to the documents on my desk, for each had been encoded in a systematic fashion that rendered their literal contents deliberately misleading. Another code had informed both of my recent conversations with Marguerite. "Fiction is best left to real life," I said.

"Someone shoulda told that to Herman Melville," said Mr Arthur "This Building is Condemned" C—.

Mrs Rampage buzzed me to advise that I was running behind schedule and inquire about removing the coffee things. I invited her to gather up the debris. A door behind me opened, and I assumed that my secretary had responded to my request with an alacrity remarkable even in her. The first sign of my error was the behaviour of the three other men in the room, until this moment no more animated than marble statues. The thug at my client's side stepped forward to stand behind me, and his fellows moved to the front of my desk. "What the hell is this shit?" said the client, unable, because of the man in front of him, to see Mr Clubb and Mr Cuff. Holding a pad bearing one of his many lists, Mr Clubb gazed in mild surprise at the giants flanking my desk and said, "I apologise for the intrusion, sir, but our understanding was that your appointment would be over in an hour, and by my simple way of reckoning you should be free to answer a query as to steam irons."

"What the hell *is* this shit?" said my client repeating his original question with a slight tonal variation expressive of gathering dismay.

I attempted to salvage matters. "Please allow me to explain the interruption. I have employed these men as consultants, and as they prefer to work in my office, a condition I of course could not permit during our business meeting, I temporarily relocated them in my washroom, outfitted with a library adequate to thier needs."

"Fit for a king, in my opinion," said Mr Clubb.

At that moment the other door into my office, to the left of my desk, opened to admit Mrs Rampage, and my client's guardians inserted their hands into their suit jackets and separated with the speed and precision of a dance team.

"Oh, my," said Mrs Rampage. "*Excuse* me. Should I come back later?"

"Not on your life, my darling," said Mr Clubb. "Temporary misunderstanding of the false-alarm sort. Please allow us to enjoy the delightful spectacle of your feminine charms."

Before my wondering eyes, Mrs Rampage curtsied and hastened to my desk to gather up the wreckage.

I looked toward my client and observed a detail of striking peculiarity, that although his half-consumed cigar remained between his lips, four inches of cylindrical ash had deposited a grey smear on his necktie before coming to rest on the shelf of his belly. He was staring straight ahead with eyes grown to the size of quarters. His face had become the colour of raw piecrust.

Mr Clubb said, "Respectful greetings, sir."

The client gargled and turned upon me a look of unvarnished horror.

Mr Clubb said, "Apologies to all." Mrs Rampage had already bolted. From unseen regions came the sound of a closing door.

Mr "This Building is Condemned" C— blinked twice, bringing his eyes to something like their normal dimensions. With an uncertain hand but gently, as if it were a tiny but much-loved baby, he placed his cigar in the crystal shell. He cleared his throat; he looked at the ceiling. "Deacon," he said, gazing upward. "Gotta run. My next appointment musta slipped my mind. What happens when you start to gab. I'll be in touch." He stood, dislodging the ashen cylinder to the carpet, and motioned his goons to the outer office.

IV

Of course at the earliest opportunity I interrogated my detectives about this turn of events, and while they moved their mountains of paper, bottles, buckets, glasses, hand-drawn maps, and other impedimenta back behind the screen, I continued the questioning. No, they averred, the gentleman at my desk was not a gentleman whom previously they had been privileged to look upon, acquaint themselves with, or encounter in any way whatsoever. They had never been employed in any capacity by the gentleman. Mr Clubb observed that the unknown gentleman had been wearing a conspicuously handsome and well-tailored suit.

"That is his custom," I said.

"And I believe he smokes, sir, a noble high order of cigar," said Mr Clubb with a glance at my breast pocket. "Which would be the sort of item customarily beyond the dreams of honest labourers such is ourselves."

"I trust that you will permit me," I said with a sigh, "to offer you the pleasure of two of the same." No sooner had the offer been accepted, the barnies back behind their screen, than I buzzed Mrs Rampage with the request to summon by instant delivery from the most distinguished cigar merchant in the city a box of his finest. "Good for you, boss!" whooped the new Mrs Rampage.

I spent the remainder of the afternoon brooding upon the reaction of Mr Arthur "This Building is Condemned" C— to my "consultants". I could not but imagine that his hasty departure boded ill for our relationship. I had seen terror on his face, and he knew that *I* knew what I had seen. An understanding of this sort is fatal to that nuance-play critical alike to high-level churchmen and their outlaw counterparts, and I had to confront the possibility that my client's departure had been of a permanent nature. Where Mr "This Building is Condemned" C— went, his colleagues of lesser rank, Mr Tommy "I Believe in Rainbows" B—, Mr Anthony "Moonlight Becomes You" M—, Mr Bobby "Total Eclipse" G—, and their fellow archbishops, cardinals, and papal nuncios would assuredly follow. Before the close of the day, I would send a comforting fax informing Mr "This Building is Condemned" C— that the consultants had been summarily released from employment. I would be telling only a "white" or provisional untruth, for Mr Clubb and Mr Cuff's task would surely be completed long before my client's return. All was in order, all was in train, and as if to put the seal upon the matter, Mrs Rampage buzzed to inquire if she might come through with the box of cigars. Speaking in a breathy timbre I had never before heard from anyone save Marguerite in the earliest, most blissful days of our marriage, Mrs Rampage added that she had some surprises for me, too. "By this point," I said, "I expect no less." Mrs Rampage *giggled*.

The surprises, in the event, were of a reassuring practicality. The good woman had wisely sought the advice of Mr Montfort de M—, who, after recommending a suitably aristocratic cigar emporium and a favourite cigar, had purchased for me a rosewood humidor, a double-bladed cigar cutter, and a lighter of antique design. As soon as Mrs Rampage had been instructed to compose a note of gratitude embellished in whatever fashion she saw fit, I arrayed all but one of the cigars in the humidor, decapitated that one, and set it alight. Beneath a faint touch of fruitiness like the aroma of a blossoming pear tree, I met in successive layers the tastes of black olives, aged Gouda cheese, pine needles, new leather, miso soup, either sorghum or brown sugar, burning peat, library paste, and myrtle leaves. The long finish intriguingly combined Bible paper and sunflower seeds. Mr Montfort de M— had chosen well, though I regretted the absence of black butter sauce.

Feeling comradely, I strolled across my office toward the merriment emanating from the far side of the screen. A superior cigar should be complemented by a worthy liquor, and in the light of what was to transpire during the evening I considered a snifter of Mr

Clubb's Bombay gin not inappropriate. "Fellows," I said, tactfully announcing my presence, "are preparations nearly completed?"

"That, sir, they are," said one or the other of the pair.

"Welcome news," I said, and stepped around the screen. "But I must be assured—"

It was as if the detritus of New York City's half dozen filthiest living quarters had been scooped up, shaken, and dumped into my office. Heaps of ash, bottles, shoals of papers, books with stained covers and broken spines, battered furniture, broken glass, refuse I could not identify, refuse I could not even *see*, undulated from the base of the screen, around and over the table, heaping itself into landfill-like piles here and there, and washed against the plate-glass windows. A jagged, five-foot opening gaped in a smashed pane. Their derbies perched on their heads, islanded in their chairs, Mr Clubb and Mr Cuff leaned back, feet up on what must have been the table.

"You'll join us in a drink, sir," said Mr Clubb, "by way of wishing us success and adding to the pleasure of that handsome smoke." He extended a stout leg and kicked rubble from a chair. I sat down. Mr Clubb plucked an unclean glass from the morass and filled it with Dutch gin, or *jenever*, from one of the minaret-shaped stone flagons I had observed upon my infrequent layovers in Amsterdam, the Netherlands. Mrs Rampage had been variously employed during the barnies' sequestration. Then I wondered if Mrs Rampage might not have shown signs of intoxication during our last encounter.

"I thought you drank Bombay," I said.

"Variety is, as they say, life's condiment," said Mr Clubb, and handed me the glass.

I said, "You have made yourselves quite at home."

"I thank you for your restraint," said Mr Clubb. "In which sentiment my partner agrees, am I correct, Mr Cuff?"

"Entirely," said Mr Cuff. "But I wager you a C-note to a see-gar that a word or two of explanation is in order."

"How right that man is," said Mr Clubb. "He has a genius for the truth I have never known to fail him. Sir, you enter our work space to come upon the slovenly, the careless, the unseemly, and your response, which we comprehend in every particular, is to recoil. My wish is that you take a moment to remember these two essentials: one, we have, as aforesaid, our methods, which are ours alone, and two, having appeared fresh on the scene, you see it worse than it is. By morning tomorrow, the cleaning staff shall have done its work."

"I suppose you have been Visualizing." I quaffed *jenever*.

"Mr Cuff and I," he said, "prefer to minimize the risk of accidents, surprises, and such by the method of rehearsing our, as you might say, performances. These poor sticks, sir, are easily replaced, but our work once under way demands completion and cannot be duplicated, redone, or undone."

I recalled the all-important guarantee. "I remember your words," I said, "and I must be assured that you remember mine. I did not request termination. During the course of the day my feelings on the matter have intensified. Termination, if by that term you meant—"

"Termination is termination," said Mr Clubb.

"*Ex*termination," I said. "Cessation of life due to external forces. It is not my wish, it is unacceptable, and I have even been thinking that I overstated the degree of physical punishment appropriate in this matter."

"'Appropriate'?" said Mr Clubb. "When it comes to desire, 'appropriate' is a concept without meaning. In the sacred realm of desire, 'appropriate', being meaningless, does not exist. We speak of your inmost wishes, sir, and desire is an extremely *thingy* sort of thing."

I looked at the hole in the window, the broken bits of furniture and ruined books. "I think," I said, "that permanent injury is all I wish. Something on the order of blindness or the loss of a hand."

Mr Clubb favoured me with a glance of humorous irony. "It goes, sir, as it goes, which brings to mind that we have but an hour more, a period of time to be splendidly improved by a superior Double Corona such as the fine example in your hand."

"Forgive me," I said. "And might I then request . . .?" I extended the nearly empty glass, and Mr Clubb refilled it. Each received a cigar, and I lingered at my desk for the required term, sipping *jenever* and pretending to work until I heard sounds of movement. Mr Clubb and Mr Cuff approached. "So you are off," I said.

"It is, sir, to be a long and busy night," said Mr Clubb. "If you take my meaning."

With a sigh I opened the humidor. They reached in, snatched a handful of cigars apiece, and deployed them into various pockets. "Details at eleven," said Mr Clubb.

A few seconds after their departure, Mrs Rampage informed me that she would be bringing through a fax communication just received.

The fax had been sent me by Chartwell, Munster, and Stout, a legal firm with but a single client, Mr Arthur "This Building is

Condemned" C—. Chartwell, Munster, and Stout regretted the necessity to inform me that their client wished to seek advice other than my own in his financial affairs. A sheaf of documents binding me to silence as to all matters concerning the client would arrive for my signature the following day. All records, papers, computer disks, and other data were to be referred posthaste to their offices. I had forgotten to send my intended note of client-saving reassurance.

V

What an abyss of shame I must now describe, at every turn what humiliation. It was at most five minutes past 6:00 p.m. when I learned of the desertion of my most valuable client, a turn of events certain to lead to the loss of his cryptic fellows and some forty per cent of our annual business. Gloomily I consumed my glass of Dutch gin without noticing that I had already far exceeded my tolerance. I ventured behind the screen and succeeded in unearthing another stone flagon, poured another measure, and gulped it down while attempting to demonstrate numerically that (a) the anticipated drop in annual profit could not be as severe as feared and (b) if it were, the business could continue as before, without reductions in salary, staff, or benefits. Despite ingenious feats of juggling, the numbers denied (a) and mocked (b), suggesting that I should be fortunate to retain, not lose, forty per cent of present business. I lowered my head to the desk and tried to regulate my breathing. When I heard myself rendering an off-key version of "Abide with Me", I acknowledged that it was time to go home, got to my feet, and made the unfortunate decision to exit through the general offices on the theory that a survey of my presumably empty realm might suggest the sites of pending amputations.

I tucked the flagon under my elbow, pocketed the five or six cigars remaining in the humidor, and passed through Mrs Rampage's chamber. Hearing the abrasive music of the cleaners' radios, I moved with exaggerated care down the corridor, darkened but for the light spilling from an open door thirty feet before me. Now and again, finding myself unable to avoid striking my shoulder against the wall, I took a medicinal swallow of *jenever*. I drew up to the open door and realized that I had come to Gilligan's quarters. The abrasive music emanated from his sound system. *We'll get rid of that, for starters,* I said to myself, and straightened up for a dignified navigation past his doorway. At the crucial moment I glanced within to observe my jacketless junior partner sprawled, tie undone, on his sofa beside a scrawny ruffian with a quiff of lime-green hair and attired for some reason in a skintight costume involving zebra stripes and many chains and zippers. Disreputable creatures male and female occupied themselves in the background. Gilligan shifted his head, began to smile, and at the sight of me turned to stone.

"Calm down, Gilligan," I said, striving for an impression of sober paternal authority. I had recalled that my junior had scheduled a late appointment with his most successful musician, a singer whose band sold millions of records year in and year out despite the absurdity of their name, the Dog Turds or the Rectal Valves, something of that sort. My calculations had indicated that Gilligan's client, whose name I recalled as Cyril Futch, would soon become crucial to the maintenance of my firm, and as the beaky little rooster coldly took me in I thought to impress upon him the regard in which he was held by his chosen financial planning institution. "There is, I assure you, no need for alarm, no, certainly not, and in fact, Gilligan, you know, I should be honoured to seize this opportunity of making the acquaintance of your guest, whom it is our pleasure to assist and advise and whatever."

Gilligan reverted to flesh and blood during the course of this utterance, which I delivered gravely, taking care to enunciate each syllable clearly in spite of the difficulty I was having with my tongue. He noted the bottle nestled into my elbow and the lighted cigar in the fingers of my right hand, a matter of which until that moment I had been imperfectly aware. "Hey, I guess the smoking lamp is lit," I said. "Stupid rule anyhow. How about a little drink on the boss?"

Gilligan lurched to his feet and came reeling toward me.

All that followed is a montage of discontinuous imagery. I recall Cyril Futch propping me up as I communicated our devotion to the safeguarding of his wealth, also his dogged insistence that his name was actually Simon Gulch or Sidney Much or something similar before he sent me toppling onto the sofa; I see an odd little fellow with a tattooed head and a name like Pus (there was a person named Pus in attendance, though he may not have been the one) accepting one of my cigars and eating it; I remember inhaling from smirking Gilligan's cigarette and drinking from a bottle with a small white worm lying dead at its bottom and snuffling up a white powder recommended by a female Turd or Valve; I remember singing "The Old Rugged Cross" in a state of partial undress. I told a face brilliantly lacquered with makeup that I was "getting a feel" for "this music". A female Turd or Valve, not the one who had recommended the powder but one in a permanent state of hilarity I found endearing, ushered me into my limousine and on the homeward journey experimented with its many buttons and controls. Atop the town-house steps, she removed the key from my fumbling hand gleefully to insert it into the lock. The rest is welcome darkness.

VI

A form of consciousness returned with a slap to my face, the muffled screams of the woman beside me, a bowler-hatted head thrusting into view and growling, "The shower for you, you damned idiot." As a second assailant whisked her away, the woman, whom I thought to be Marguerite, wailed. I struggled against the man gripping my shoulders, and he squeezed the nape of my neck.

When next I opened my eyes, I was naked and quivering beneath an onslaught of cold water within the marble confines of my shower cabinet. Charlie-Charlie Rackett leaned against the open door of the cabinet and regarded me with ill-disguised impatience. "I'm freezing, Charlie-Charlie," I said. "Turn off the water."

Charlie-Charlie thrust an arm into the cabinet and became Mr Clubb. "I'll warm it up, but I want you sober," he said. I drew myself up into a ball.

Then I was on my feet and moaning while I massaged my forehead. "Bath time all done now," called Mr Clubb. "Turn off the wa-wa." I did as instructed. The door opened, and a bath towel unfurled over my left shoulder.

Side by side on the bedroom sofa and dimly illuminated by the lamp, Mr Clubb and Mr Cuff observed my progress toward the bed. A black leather satchel stood on the floor between them. "Gentlemen," I said, "although I cannot presently find words to account for the condition in which you found me, I trust that your good nature will enable you to overlook ... or ignore ... whatever it was that I must have done. . . . I cannot quite recall the circumstances."

"The young woman has been dispatched," said Mr Clubb, "and you need never fear any trouble from that direction, sir."

"The young woman?" I remembered a hyperactive figure playing with the controls in the back of the limousine. A fragmentary memory of the scene in Gilligan's office returned to me, and I moaned aloud.

"None too clean, but pretty enough in a ragamuffin way," said Mr Clubb. "The type denied a proper education in social graces. Rough about the edges. Intemperate in language. A stranger to discipline."

I groaned – to have introduced such a creature to my house!

"A stranger to honesty, too, sir, if you'll permit me," said Mr Cuff. "It's addiction turns them into thieves. Give them half a chance, they'll steal the brass handles off their mothers' coffins."

"Addiction?" I said. "Addiction to what?"

"Everything, from the look of the bint," said Mr Cuff. "Before Mr Clubb and I sent her on her way, we retrieved these items doubtless belonging to you, sir." While walking toward me he removed from his pockets the following articles: my wristwatch, gold cuff links, wallet, the lighter of antique design given me by Mr Montfort de M—, likewise the cigar cutter and the last of the cigars I had purchased that day. "I thank you most gratefully," I said, slipping the watch on my wrist and all else save the cigar into the pockets of my robe. It was, I noted, just past four o'clock in the morning. The cigar I handed back to him with the words, "Please accept this as a token of my gratitude."

"Gratefully accepted," he said. Mr Cuff bit off the end, spat it onto the carpet, and set the cigar alight, producing a nauseating quantity of fumes.

"Perhaps," I said, "we might postpone our discussion until I have had time to recover from my ill-advised behaviour. Let us reconvene at . . ." A short period was spent pressing my hands to my eyes while rocking back and forth. "Four this afternoon?"

"Everything in its own time is a principle we hold dear," said Mr Clubb. "And this is the time for you to down aspirin and Alka-Seltzer, and for your loyal assistants to relish the hearty breakfasts the thought of which sets our stomachs to growling. A man of stature and accomplishment like yourself ought to be able to overcome the effects of too much booze and attend to business, on top of the simple matter of getting his flunkies out of bed so they can whip up the bacon and eggs."

"Because a man such as that, sir, keeps ever in mind that business faces the task at hand, no matter how lousy it may be," said Mr Cuff.

"The old world is in flames," said Mr Clubb, "and the new one is just being born. Pick up the phone."

"All right," I said, "but Mr Moncrieff is going to *hate* this. He worked for the Duke of Denbigh, and he's a terrible snob."

"All butlers are snobs," said Mr Clubb. "Three fried eggs apiece, likewise six rashers of bacon, home fries, toast, hot coffee, and for the sake of digestion a bottle of your best cognac."

Mr Moncrieff picked up his telephone, listened to my orders, and informed me in a small, cold voice that he would speak to the cook. "Would this repast be for the young lady and yourself, sir?"

With a wave of guilty shame that intensified my nausea, I realized that Mr Moncrieff had observed my unsuitable young companion accompanying me upstairs to the bedroom. "No, it would not," I said. "The young lady, a client of mine, was kind enough to assist me when I was taken ill. The meal is for two male guests." Unwelcome memory returned the spectacle of a scrawny girl pulling my ears and screeching that a useless old fart like me didn't deserve her band's business.

"The phone," said Mr Clubb. Dazedly I extended the receiver.

"Moncrieff, old man," he said, "amazing good luck, running into you again. Do you remember that trouble the Duke had with Colonel Fletcher and the diary? . . . Yes, this is Mr Clubb, and it's delightful to hear your voice again. . . . He's here, too, couldn't do anything without him. . . . I'll tell him. . . . Much the way things went with the Duke, yes, and we'll need the usual supplies. . . . Glad to hear it. . . . The dining room in half an hour." He handed the telephone back to me and said to Mr Cuff, "He's looking forward to the pinochle, and there's a first-rate Pétrus in the cellar he knows you're going to enjoy."

I had purchased six cases of 1928 Château Pétrus at an auction some years before and was holding it while its already immense value doubled, then tripled, until perhaps a decade hence, when I would sell it for ten times its original cost.

"A good drop of wine sets a man right up," said Mr Cuff. "Stuff was meant to be drunk, wasn't it?"

"You know Mr Moncrieff?" I asked. "You worked for the Duke?"

"We ply our humble trade irrespective of nationality and borders," said Mr Clubb. "Go where we are needed, is our motto. We have fond memories of the good old Duke, who showed himself to be quite a fun-loving, spirited fellow, sir, once you got past the crust, as it were. Generous, too."

"He gave until it hurt," said Mr Cuff. "The old gentleman cried like a baby when we left."

"Cried a good deal before that, too," said Mr Clubb. "In our experience, high-spirited fellows spend a deal more tears than your gloomy customers."

"I do not suppose you shall see any tears from me," I said. The brief look that passed between them reminded me of the complicitous glance I had once seen fly like a live spark between two of their New Covenant forebears, one gripping the hind legs of a pig, the other its front legs and a knife, in the moment before the knife opened the pig's throat and an arc of blood threw itself high into the air. "I shall heed your advice," I said, "and locate my analgesics." I got on my feet and moved slowly to the bathroom. "As a matter of curiosity," I said, "might I ask if you have classified me into the high-spirited category, or into the other?"

"You are a man of middling spirit," said Mr Clubb. I opened my mouth to protest, and he went on, "But something may be made of you yet."

I disappeared into the bathroom. *I have endured these moon-faced yokels long enough,* I told myself. *Hear their story, feed the bastards, then kick them out.*

In a condition more nearly approaching my usual self, I brushed my teeth and splashed water on my face before returning to the bedroom. I placed myself with a reasonable degree of executive command in a wing chair, folded my pin-striped robe about me, inserted my feet into velvet slippers, and said, "Things got a bit out of hand, and I thank you for dealing with my young client, a person with whom in spite of appearances I have a professional relationship only. Now let us turn to our real business. I trust you found my wife and Leeson at Green Chimneys. Please give me an account of what followed."

"Things got a bit out of hand," said Mr Clubb. "Which is a way of describing something that can happen to us all, and for which no one can be blamed. Especially Mr Cuff and myself, who are always careful to say right smack at the beginning, as we did with you, sir, what ought to be so obvious as to not need saying at all, that our work brings about permanent changes which can never be undone. Especially in the cases when we specify a time to make our initial report and the client disappoints us at the said time. When we are let down by our client, we must go forward and complete the job to our highest standards with no rancour or ill will, knowing that there are many reasonable explanations of a man's inability to get to a telephone."

"I don't know what you mean by this self-serving double-talk," I said. "We had no arrangement of that sort, and your effrontery forces me to conclude that you failed in your task."

Mr Clubb gave me the grimmest possible suggestion of a smile. "One of the reasons for a man's failure to get to a telephone is a lapse of memory. You have forgotten my informing you that I would give you my initial report at eleven. At precisely eleven o'clock I called, to no avail. I waited through twenty rings, sir, before I abandoned the effort. If I had waited through a hundred, sir, the result would have been the same, on account of your decision to put yourself into a state where you would have had trouble remembering your own name."

"That is a blatant lie," I said, then remembered. The fellow had in fact mentioned in passing something about reporting to me at that hour, which must have been approximately the time when I was regaling the Turds or Valves with "The Old Rugged Cross". My face grew pink. "Forgive me," I said. "I am in error, it is just as you say."

"A manly admission, sir, but as for forgiveness, we extended that quantity from the git-go," said Mr Clubb. "We are your servants, and your wishes are our sacred charge."

"That's the whole ball of wax in a nutshell," said Mr Cuff, giving a fond glance to the final inch of his cigar. He dropped the stub onto my carpet and ground it beneath his shoe. "Food and drink to the fibres, sir," he said.

"Speaking of which," said Mr Clubb. "We will continue our report in the dining room, so as to dig into the feast ordered up by that wondrous villain Reggie Moncrieff."

Until that moment it had never quite occurred to me that my butler possessed, like other men, a Christian name.

VII

"A great design directs us," said Mr Clubb, expelling morsels of his cud. "We poor wanderers, you and me and Mr Cuff and the milkman too, only see the little portion right in front of us. Half the time we don't even see that in the right way. For sure we don't have a Chinaman's chance of understanding it. But the design is ever-present, sir, a truth I bring to your attention for the sake of the comfort in it. Toast, Mr Cuff."

"Comfort is a matter cherished by all parts of a man," said Mr Cuff, handing his partner the toast rack. "Most particularly that part known as his soul, which feeds upon the nutrient adversity."

I was seated at the head of the table, flanked by Mr Clubb and Mr Cuff. The salvers and tureens before us overflowed, for Mr

Moncrieff, who after embracing each barnie in turn and entering into a kind of conference or huddle, had summoned from the kitchen a banquet far surpassing their requests. Besides several dozen eggs and perhaps two packages of bacon, he had arranged a mixed grill of kidneys, lambs' livers and lamb chops, and strip steaks, as well as vats of oatmeal and a pasty concoction he described as "kedgeree – as the old Duke fancied it."

Sickened by the odours of the food, also by the mush visible in my companions' mouths, I tried again to extract their report. "I don't believe in the grand design," I said, "and I already face more adversity than my soul finds useful. Tell me what happened at the house."

"No mere house, sir," said Mr Clubb. "Even as we approached along —Lane, Mr Cuff and I could not fail to respond to its magnificence."

"Were my drawings of use?" I asked.

"Invaluable." Mr Clubb speared a lamb chop and raised it to his mouth. "We proceeded through the rear door into your spacious kitchen or scullery. Wherein we observed evidence of two persons having enjoyed a dinner enhanced by a fine wine and finished with a noble champagne."

"Aha," I said.

"By means of your guidance, Mr Cuff and I located the lovely staircase and made our way to the lady's chamber. We effected an entry of the most praiseworthy silence, if I may say so."

"That entry was worth a medal," said Mr Cuff.

"Two figures lay slumbering upon the bed. In a blamelessly professional manner we approached, Mr Cuff on one side, I on the other. In the fashion your client of this morning called the whopbopaloobop, we rendered the parties in question even more unconscious than previous, thereby giving ourselves a good fifteen minutes for the disposition of instruments. We take pride in being careful workers, sir, and like all honest craftsmen we respect our tools. We bound and gagged both parties in timely fashion. Is the male party distinguished by an athletic past?" Alight with barnieish glee, Mr Clubb raised his eyebrows and washed down the last of his chop with a mouthful of cognac.

"Not to my knowledge," I said. "I believe he plays a little racquetball and squash, that kind of thing."

He and Mr Cuff experienced a moment of mirth. "More like weightlifting or football, is my guess," he said. "Strength and stamina. To a remarkable degree."

"Not to mention considerable speed," said Mr Cuff with the air of one indulging a tender reminiscence.

"Are you telling me that he got away?" I asked.

"No one gets away," said Mr Clubb. "That, sir, is gospel. But you may imagine our surprise when for the first time in the history of our *consultancy*" – and here he chuckled – "a gentleman of the civilian persuasion managed to break his bonds and free himself of his ropes whilst Mr Cuff and I were engaged in the preliminaries."

"Naked as jaybirds," said Mr Cuff, wiping with a greasy hand a tear of amusement from one eye. "Bare as newborn lambie-pies. There I was, heating up the steam iron I'd just fetched from the kitchen, sir, along with a selection of knives I came across in exactly the spot you described, most grateful I was, too, squatting on my haunches without a care in the world and feeling the first merry tingle of excitement in my little soldier—"

"What?" I said. "You were naked? And what's this about your little soldier?"

"Hush," said Mr Clubb, his eyes glittering. "Nakedness is a precaution against fouling our clothing with blood and other bodily products, and men like Mr Cuff and myself take pleasure in the exercise of our skills. In us, the inner and the outer man are one and the same."

"Are they, now?" I said, marvelling at the irrelevance of this last remark. It then occurred to me that the remark might have been relevant after all – most unhappily so.

"At all times," said Mr Cuff, amused by my having missed the point. "If you wish to hear our report, sir, reticence will be helpful."

I gestured for him to go on.

"As said before, I was squatting in my birthday suit by the knives and the steam iron, not a care in the world, when I heard from behind me the patter of little feet. *Hello*, I say to myself, *what's this?* and when I look over my shoulder here is your man, bearing down on me like a steam engine. Being as he is one of your big, strapping fellows, sir, it was a sight to behold, not to mention the unexpected circumstances. I took a moment to glance in the direction of Mr Clubb, who was busily occupied in another quarter, which was, to put it plain and simple, the bed."

Mr Clubb chortled and said, "By way of being in the line of duty."

"So in a way of speaking I was in the position of having to settle this fellow before he became a trial to us in the performance of our duties. He was getting ready to tackle me, sir, which was what put us in mind of football being in his previous life, tackle the life out of me before he rescued the lady, and I got hold of one of the knives. Then, you see, when he came flying at me that way all I had to do was give him a good jab in the bottom of the throat, a matter which puts the fear of God into the bravest fellow. It concentrates all their attention, and after that they might as well be little puppies for all the harm they're likely to do. Well, this boy was one for the books, because for the first time in I don't know how many similar efforts, a hundred—"

"I'd say double at least, to be accurate," said Mr Clubb.

"—in at least a hundred, anyhow, avoiding immodesty, I underestimated the speed and agility of the lad, and instead of planting my weapon at the base of his neck stuck him in the side, a manner of wound which in the case of your really *aggressive* attacker, who you come across in about one out of twenty, is about as effective as a slap with a powder puff. Still, I put him off his stride, a welcome sign to me that he had gone a bit loosey-goosey over the years. Then, sir, the advantage was mine, and I seized it with a grateful heart. I spun him over, dumped him on the floor, and straddled his chest. At which point I thought to settle him down for the evening by taking hold of a cleaver and cutting off his right hand with one good blow.

"Ninety-nine times out of a hundred, sir, chopping off a hand will take the starch right out of a man. He settled down pretty well. It's the shock, you see, shock takes the mind that way, and because the stump was bleeding like a bastard, excuse the language, I did him the favour of cauterizing the wound with the steam iron because it was good and hot, and if you sear a wound there's no way that bugger can bleed anymore. I mean, the *problem* is *solved*, and that's a fact."

"It has been proved a thousand times over," said Mr Clubb.

"Shock being a healer," said Mr Cuff. "Shock being a balm like salt water to the human body, yet if you have too much of shock or salt water, the body gives up the ghost. After I seared the wound, it looked to me like he and his body got together and voted to take the next bus to what is generally considered a better world." He held up an index finger and stared into my eyes while forking kidneys into his mouth. "This, sir, is a *process*. A *process* can't happen all at once, and every reasonable precaution was taken. Mr Clubb and I do not have, nor ever have had, the reputation for carelessness in our undertakings."

"And never shall." Mr Clubb washed down whatever was in his mouth with half a glass of cognac.

"Despite the *process* under way," said Mr Cuff, "the gentleman's left wrist was bound tightly to the stump. Rope was again attached to the areas of the chest and legs, a gag went back into his mouth, and besides all that I had the pleasure of whapping my hammer once and once only on the region of his temple, for the purpose of keeping him out of action until we were ready for him in case he was not boarding the bus. I took a moment to turn him over and gratify my little soldier, which I trust was in no way exceeding our agreement, sir." He granted me a look of the purest innocence.

"Continue," I said, "although you must grant that your tale is utterly without verification."

"Sir," said Mr Clubb, "we know one another better than that." He bent over so far that his head disappeared beneath the table, and I heard the undoing of a clasp. Resurfacing, he placed between us on the table an object wrapped in one of the towels Marguerite had purchased for Green Chimneys. "If verification is your desire, and I intend no reflection, sir, for a man in your line of business has grown out of the habit of taking a fellow at his word, here you have wrapped up like a birthday present the finest verification of this portion of our tale to be found in all the world."

"And yours to keep, if you're taken that way," said Mr Cuff.

I had no doubts whatsoever concerning the nature of the trophy set before me, and therefore I deliberately composed myself before pulling away the folds of towelling. Yet for all my preparations the spectacle of the actual trophy itself affected me more greatly than I would have thought possible, and at the very centre of the nausea rising within me I experienced the first faint stirrings of enlightenment. *Poor man*, I thought, *poor mankind*.

I refolded the material over the crablike thing and said, "Thank you. I meant to imply no reservations concerning your veracity."

"Beautifully said, sir, and much appreciated. Men like ourselves, honest at every point, have found that persons in the habit of duplicity often cannot understand the truth. Liars are the bane of our existence. And yet, such is the nature of this funny old world, we'd be out of business without them."

Mr Cuff smiled up at the chandelier in rueful appreciation of the world's contradictions. "When I replaced him on the bed, Mr Clubb went hither and yon, collecting the remainder of the tools for the job at hand."

"When you say you replaced him on the bed," I broke in, "is it your meaning—"

"Your meaning might differ from mine, sir, and mine, being that of a fellow raised without the benefits of a literary education, may be simpler than yours. But bear in mind that every guild has its legacy of customs and traditions which no serious practitioner can ignore without thumbling his nose at all he holds dear. For those brought up into our trade, physical punishment of a female subject invariably begins with the act most associated in the feminine mind with humiliation of the most rigorous sort. With males the same is generally true. Neglect this step, and you lose an advantage which can never be regained. It is the foundation without which the structure cannot stand, and the foundation must be set in place even when conditions make the job distasteful, which is no picnic, take my word for it." He shook his head and fell silent.

"We could tell you stories to curl your hair," said Mr Clubb. "Matter for another day. It was on the order of nine-thirty when our materials had been assembled, the preliminaries taken care of, and business could begin in earnest. This is a moment, sir, ever cherished by professionals such as ourselves. It is of an eternal freshness. You are on the brink of testing yourself against your past achievements and those of masters gone before. Your skill, your imagination, your timing and resolve will be called upon to work together with your hard-earned knowledge of the human body, because it is a question of being able to sense when to press on and when to hold back, of, I can say, having that instinct for the right technique at the right time you can acquire only through experience. During this moment you hope that the subject, your partner in the most intimate relationship which can exist between two people, owns the spiritual resolve and physical capacity to inspire your best work. The subject is our instrument, and the nature of the instrument is vital. Faced with an out-of-tune, broken-down piano, even the greatest virtuoso is up Shit Creek without a paddle. Sometimes, sir, our work has left us tasting ashes for weeks on end, and when you're tasting ashes in your mouth you have trouble remembering the grand design and your wee part in that majestical pattern."

As if to supplant the taste in question and without benefit of knife and fork, Mr Clubb bit off a generous portion of steak and moistened it with a gulp of cognac. Chewing with loud smacks of the lips and tongue, he thrust a spoon into the kedgeree and began moodily slapping it onto his plate while seeming for the first time to notice the Canalettos on the walls.

"We started off, sir, as well as we ever have," said Mr Cuff, "and better than most times. The fingernails was a thing of rare beauty, sir, the fingernails was prime. And the hair was on the same transcendent level."

"The fingernails?" I asked. "The hair?"

"Prime," said Mr. Clubb with a melancholy spray of food. "If they could be done better, which they could not, I should like to be there as to applaud with my own hands."

I looked at Mr Cuff, and he said, "The fingernails and the hair might appear to be your traditional steps two and three, but they are in actual fact steps one and two, the first procedure being more like basic groundwork than part of the performance work itself. Doing the fingernails and the hair tells you an immense quantity about the subject's pain level, style of resistance, and aggression/passivity balance, and that information, sir, is your virtual bible once you go past step four or five."

"How many steps are there?" I asked.

"A novice would tell you fifteen," said Mr Cuff. "A competent journeyman would say twenty. Men such as us know there to be at least a hundred, but in their various combinations and refinements they come out into the thousands. At the basic or kindergarten level, they are, after the first two: foot soles; teeth; fingers and toes; tongue; nipples; rectum; genital area; electrification; general piercing; specific piercing; small amputation; damage to inner organs; eyes, minor; eyes, major; large amputation; local flaying; and so forth."

At mention of "tongue", Mr Clubb had shoved a spoonful of kedgeree into his mouth and scowled at the paintings directly across from him. At "electrification", he had thrust himself out of his chair and crossed behind me to scrutinise them more closely. While Mr Cuff continued my education, he twisted in his chair to observe his partner's actions, and I did the same.

After "and so forth", Mr Cuff fell silent. The two of us watched Mr Clubb moving back and forth in evident agitation before the paintings. He settled at last before a depiction of a regatta on the Grand Canal and took two deep breaths. Then he raised his spoon like a dagger and drove it into the painting to slice beneath a handsome ship, come up at its bow, and continue cutting until he had deleted the ship from the painting. "Now that, sir, is local flaying," he said. He moved to the next picture, which gave a view of the Piazzetta. In seconds he had sliced all the canvas from the frame. "And that, sir, is what is meant by general flaying." He crumpled the canvas in his hands, threw it to the ground, and stamped on it.

"He is not quite himself," said Mr Cuff.

"Oh, but I am, I am myself to an alarming degree, I am," said Mr Clubb. He tromped back to the table and bent beneath it. Instead of the second folded towel I had anticipated, he produced his satchel and used it to sweep away the plates and serving dishes in front of him. He reached within and slapped down beside me the towel I had expected. "Open it," he said. I unfolded the towel. "Are these not, to the last particular, what you requested, sir?"

It was, to the last particular, what I had requested. Marguerite had not thought to remove her wedding band before her assignation, and her . . . I cannot describe the other but to say that it lay like the egg perhaps of some small shore bird in the familiar palm. Another portion of my eventual enlightenment moved into place within me, and I thought: *Here we are, this is all of us, this crab and this egg.* I bent over and vomited beside my chair. When I had finished, I grabbed the cognac bottle and swallowed greedily, twice. The liquor burned down my throat, struck my stomach like a branding iron, and rebounded. I leaned sideways and, with a dizzied spasm of throat and guts, expelled another reeking contribution to the mess on the carpet.

"It is a Roman conclusion to a meal, sir," said Mr Cuff.

Mr Moncrieff opened the kitchen door and peeked in. He observed the mutilated paintings and the objects nested in the striped towel and watched me wipe a string of vomit from my mouth. He withdrew for a moment and reappeared holding a tall can of ground coffee, wordlessly sprinkled its contents over the evidence of my distress, and vanished back into the kitchen. From the depths of my wretchedness, I marvelled at the perfection of this display of butler decorum.

I draped the towelling over the crab and the egg. "You are conscientious fellows," I said.

"Conscientious to a fault, sir," said Mr Cuff, not without a touch of kindness. "For a person in the normal way of living cannot begin to comprehend the actual meaning of that term, nor is he liable to understand the fierce requirements it puts on a man's head. And so it comes about that persons in the normal way of living try to back out long after backing out is possible, even though we explain exactly what is going to happen at the very beginning. They listen, but they do not hear, and it's the rare civilian who has the common sense to know that if you stand in a fire you must be burned. And if you turn the world upside down, you're standing on your head with everybody else."

"Or," said Mr Clubb, calming his own fires with another deep draft of cognac, "as the Golden Rule has it, what you do is sooner or later done back to you."

Although I was still one who listened but could not hear, a tingle of premonition went up my spine. "Please go on with your report," I said.

"The responses of the subject were all one could wish," said Mr Clubb. "I could go so far as to say that her responses were a thing of beauty. A subject who can render you one magnificent scream after another while maintaining a basic self-possession and not breaking down is a subject highly attuned to her own pain, sir, and one to be cherished. You see, there comes a moment when they understand that they are changed for good, they have passed over the border into another realm, from which there is no return, and some of them can't handle it and turn, you might say, sir, to mush. With some it happens right at the foundation stage, a sad disappointment because thereafter all the rest of the work could be done by the crudest apprentice. It takes some at the nipples stage, and at the genital stage quite a few more. Most of them comprehend irreversibility during the piercings, and by the stage of small amputation ninety per cent have shown you what they are made of. The lady did not come to the point until we had begun the eye work, and she passed with flying colours, sir. But it was then the male upped and put his foot in it."

"And eye work is delicate going," said Mr Cuff. "Requiring two men, if you want it done even close to right. But I couldn't have turned my back on the fellow for more than a minute and a half."

"Less," said Mr Clubb. "And him lying there in the corner meek as a baby. No fight left in him at all, you would have said. You would have said, that fellow there is not going to risk so much as opening his eyes until his eyes are opened for him."

"But up he gets, without a rope on him, sir," said Mr Cuff, "which you would have said was beyond the powers of a fellow who had recently lost a hand."

"Up he gets and on he comes," said Mr Clubb. "In defiance of all of Nature's mighty laws. Before I know what's what, he has his good arm around Mr Cuff's neck and is earnestly trying to snap that neck while beating Mr Cuff about the head with his stump, a situation which compels me to set aside the task at hand and take up a knife and ram it into his back a fair old number of times. The next thing I know, he's on *me*, and it's up to Mr Cuff to peel him off and set him on the floor."

"And then, you see, your concentration is gone," said Mr Cuff. "After something like that, you might as well be starting all over again at the beginning. Imagine if you are playing a piano about as well as ever you did in your life, and along comes another piano with blood in its eye and jumps on your back. It was pitiful, that's all I can say about it. But I got the fellow down and jabbed him here and there until he was still, and then I got the one item we count on as a surefire last resort for incapacitation."

"What is that item?" I asked.

"Dental floss," said Mr Clubb. "Dental floss cannot be overestimated in our line of work. It is the razor wire of everyday life, and fishing line cannot hold a candle to it, for fishing line is dull, but dental floss is both *dull* and *sharp*. It has a hundred uses, and a book should be written on the subject."

"What do you do with it?" I asked.

"It is applied to a male subject," he said. "Applied artfully and in a manner perfected only over years of experience. The application is of a lovely *subtlety*. During the process, the subject must be in a helpless, preferably an unconscious, position. When the subject regains the first fuzzy inklings of consciousness, he is aware of no more than a vague discomfort like unto a form of tingling, similar to when a foot has gone to sleep. In a wonderfully short period of time, that discomfort builds itself up, ascending to mild pain, *severe* pain, and outright agony. Then it goes past agony. The final stage is a mystical condition I don't think there is a word for which, but it closely resembles ecstasy. Hallucinations are common. Out-of-body experiences are common. We have seen men speak in tongues, even when tongues were, strictly speaking, organs they no longer possessed. We have seen wonders, Mr Cuff and I."

"That we have," said Mr Cuff. "The ordinary civilian sort of fellow can be a miracle, sir."

"Of which the person in question was one, to be sure," said Mr Clubb. "But he has to be said to be in a category all by himself, a man in a million you could put it, which is the cause of my mentioning the grand design ever a mystery to us who glimpse but a part of the whole. You see, the fellow refused to play by the time-honoured rules. He was in an awesome degree of suffering and torment, sir, but he would not do us the favour to lie down and quit."

"The mind was not right," said Mr Cuff. "Where the proper mind goes to the spiritual, sir, as just described, this was that one mind in *ten* million, I'd estimate, which moves to the animal at the reptile level. If you cut off the head of a venomous reptile and detach it from the body, that head will still attempt to strike. So it was with our boy. Bleeding from a dozen wounds. Minus one hand. Seriously concussed. The dental floss murdering all possibility of thought. Every nerve in his body howling like a banshee. Yet up he comes with his eyes red and the foam dripping from his mouth. We put him down again, and I did what I hate, because it takes all feeling away from the body along with the motor capacity, and cracked his spine right at the base of the head. Or would have, if his spine had been a normal thing instead of solid steel in a thick india-rubber cone. Which is what put us in mind of weightlifting, sir, an activity resulting in such development about the top of the spine you need a hacksaw to get even close to it."

"We were already behind schedule," said Mr Clubb, "and with the time required to get back into the proper frame of mind, we had at least seven or eight hours of work ahead of us. And you had to double that, because while we could knock the fellow out, he wouldn't have the decency to *stay* out more than a few minutes at a time. The natural thing, him being only the secondary subject, would have been to kill him outright so we could get on with the real job, but improving our working conditions by that fashion would require an amendment to our contract. Which comes under the heading of Instructions from the Client."

"And it was eleven o'clock," said Mr Cuff.

"The exact time scheduled for our conference," said Mr Clubb. "My partner was forced to clobber the fellow into senselessness, how many times was it, Mr Cuff, while I prayed for our client to do us the grace of answering his phone during twenty rings?"

"Three times, Mr Clubb, three times exactly," said Mr Cuff. "The blow each time more powerful than the last, which, combined with his having a skull made of granite, led to a painful swelling of my hand."

"The dilemma stared us in the face," said Mr Clubb. "Client unreachable. Impeded in the performance of our duties. State of mind, very foul. In such a pickle, we could do naught but obey the instructions given us by our hearts. *Remove the gentleman's head*, I told my partner, *and take care not to be bitten once it's off*. Mr Cuff took up an axe. Some haste was called for, the fellow just beginning to stir again. Mr Cuff moved into position. Then from the bed, where all had been lovely silence but for soft moans and whimpers, we hear a god-awful yowling ruckus of the most desperate and importunate protest. It was of a sort to melt the heart, sir. Were we not experienced professionals who enjoy pride in our work, I believe we might have been persuaded almost to grant the fellow mercy, despite his being a pest of the first water. But now those heart-melting screeches reach the ears of the pest and rouse him into movement just at the moment Mr Cuff lowers the boom, so to speak."

"Which was an unfortunate bit of business," said Mr Cuff. "Causing me to catch him in the shoulder, causing him to rear up, causing me to lose my footing what with all the blood on the floor, then causing a tussle for possession of the axe and myself suffering several kicks to the breadbasket. I'll tell you, sir, we did a good piece of work when we took off his hand, for without the nuisance of a stump really being useful only for leverage, there's no telling what that fellow might have done. As it was, I had the devil's own time getting the axe free and clear, and once I had done, any chance of making a neat, clean job of it was long gone. It was a slaughter and an act of butchery with not a bit of finesse or sophistication to it, and I have to tell you, such a thing is both an embarrassment and an outrage to men like ourselves. Turning a subject into hamburger by means of an axe is a violation of all our training, and it is not why we went into this business."

"No, of course not, you are more like artists than I had imagined," I said. "But in spite of your embarrassment, I suppose you went back to work on . . . on the female subject."

"We are not *like* artists," said Mr Clubb, "we *are* artists, and we know how to set our feelings aside and address our chosen medium of expression with a pure and patient attention. In spite of which we discovered the final and insurmountable frustration of the evening, and that discovery put paid to all our hopes."

"If you discovered that Marguerite had escaped," I said, "I believe I might almost, after all you have said, be—"

Glowering, Mr Clubb held up his hand. "I beg you not to insult us, sir, as we have endured enough misery for one day. The subject had escaped, all right, but not in the simple sense of your meaning. She had escaped for all eternity, in the sense that her soul had taken leave of her body and flown to those realms at whose nature we can only make our poor, ignorant guesses."

"She died?" I asked. "In other words, in direct contradiction of my instructions, you two fools killed her. You love to talk about your expertise, but you went too far, and she died at your hands. I want you incompetents out of my house immediately. Begone. Depart. This minute."

Mr Clubb and Mr Cuff looked into each other's eyes, and in that moment of private communication I saw an encompassing sorrow that utterly turned the tables on me: before I was made to understand how it was possible, I saw that the only fool present was myself. And yet the sorrow included all three of us, and more besides.

"The subject died, but we did not kill her," said Mr Clubb. "We did not go, nor have we ever gone, too far. The subject chose to die. The subject's death was an act of suicidal will. While you are listening, sir, is it possible, sir, for you to open your ears and hear what I am saying? She who might have been in all of our long experience the noblest, most courageous subject we ever will have the good fortune to be given witnessed the clumsy murder of her lover and decided to surrender her life."

"Quick as a shot," said Mr Cuff. "The simple truth, sir, is that otherwise we could have kept her alive for about a year."

"And it would have been a rare privilege to do so," said Mr Clubb. "It is time for you to face facts, sir."

"I am facing them about as well as one could," I said. "Please tell me where you disposed of the bodies."

"Within the house," said Mr Clubb. Before I could protest, he said, "Under the wretched circumstances, sir, including the continuing unavailability of the client and the enormity of the personal and professional letdown felt by my partner and myself, we saw no choice but to dispose of the house along with the telltale remains."

"Dispose of Green Chimneys?" I said, aghast. "How could you dispose of Green Chimneys?"

"Reluctantly, sir," said Mr Clubb. "With heavy hearts and an equal anger. With the same degree of professional unhappiness experienced previous. In workaday terms, by means of combustion. Fire, sir, is a substance like shock and salt water, a healer and a cleanser, though more drastic."

"But Green Chimneys has not been healed," I said. "Nor has my wife."

"You are a man of wit, sir, and have provided Mr Cuff and myself many moments of precious amusement. True, Green Chimneys has not been healed, but cleansed it has been, root and branch. And you hired us to punish your wife, not heal her, and punish her we did, as well as possible under very trying circumstances indeed."

"Which circumstances include our feeling that the job ended before its time," said Mr Cuff. "Which circumstance is one we cannot bear."

"I regret your disappointment," I said, "but I cannot accept that it was necessary to burn down my magnificent house."

"Twenty, even fifteen years ago, it would not have been," said Mr Clubb. "Nowadays, however, that contemptible alchemy known as Police Science has fattened itself up into such a gross and distorted breed of sorcery that a single drop of blood can be detected even after you scrub and scour until your arms hurt. It has reached the hideous point that if a constable without a thing in his head but the desire to imprison honest fellows employed in an ancient trade finds two hairs at what is supposed to be a crime scene, he waddles along to the laboratory and instantly a loathsome sort of wizard is popping out to tell him that those same two hairs are from the heads of Mr Clubb and Mr Cuff, and I exaggerate, I know, sir, but not by much."

"And if they do not have our names, sir," said Mr Cuff, "which they do not and I pray never will, they ever after have our particulars, to be placed in a great universal file against the day when they *might* have our names, so as to look back into that cruel file and commit the monstrosity of unfairly increasing the charges against us. It is a malignant business, and all sensible precautions must be taken."

"A thousand times I have expressed the conviction," said Mr Clubb, "that an ancient art ought not be against the law, nor its practitioners described as criminals. Is there a name for our so-called crime? There is not. GBH they call it, sir, for Grievous Bodily Harm, or, even worse, Assault. We do not Assault. We induce, we instruct, we instill. Properly speaking, these cannot be crimes, and those who do them cannot be criminals. Now I have said it a thousand times and one."

"All right," I said, attempting to speed this appalling conference to its end, "you have described the evening's unhappy events. I appreciate your reasons for burning down my splendid property. You have enjoyed a lavish meal. All remaining is the matter of your remuneration, which demands considerable thought. This night has left me exhausted, and after all your efforts, you, too, must be in need of rest. Communicate with me, please, in a day or two, gentlemen, by whatever means you choose. I wish to be alone with my thoughts. Mr Moncrieff will show you out."

The maddening barnies met this plea with impassive stares and stoic silence, and I renewed my silent vow to give them nothing – not a penny. For all their pretensions, they had accomplished naught but the death of my wife and the destruction of my country house. Rising to my feet with more difficulty than anticipated, I said, "Thank you for your efforts on my behalf."

Once again, the glance that passed between them implied that I had failed to grasp the essentials of our situation.

"Your thanks are gratefully accepted," said Mr Cuff, "though, dispute it as you may, they are premature, as you know in your soul. Yesterday morning we embarked upon a journey of which we have yet more miles to go. In consequence, we prefer not to leave. Also, setting aside the question of your continuing education, which if we do not address will haunt us all forever, residing here with you for a sensible period out of sight is the best protection from law enforcement we three could ask for."

"No," I said, "I have had enough of your education, and I need no protection from officers of the law. Please, gentlemen, allow me to return to my bed. You may take the rest of the cognac with you as a token of my regard."

"Give it a moment's reflection, sir," said Mr Clubb. "You have announced the presence of high-grade consultants and introduced these same to staff and clients both. Hours later, your spouse meets her tragic end in a conflagration destroying your upstate manor. On the very same night also occurs the disappearance of your greatest competitor, a person certain to be identified before long by a hotel employee as a fellow not unknown to the late spouse. Can you think it wise to have the high-grade consultants vanish right away?"

I did reflect, then said, "You have a point. It will be best if you continue to make an appearance in the office for a time. However, the proposal that you stay here is ridiculous." A wild hope, utterly irrational in the face of the grisly evidence, came to me in the guise of doubt. "If Green Chimneys has been destroyed by fire, I should have been informed long ago. I am a respected figure in the town of —, personally acquainted with its chief of police, Wendall Nash. Why has he not called me?"

"Oh, sir, my goodness," said Mr Clubb, shaking his head and smiling inwardly at my folly, "for many reasons. A small town is a beast slow to move. The available men have been struggling throughout the night to rescue even a jot or tittle portion of your house. They will fail, they have failed already, but the effort will keep them busy past dawn. Wendall Nash will not wish to ruin your night's sleep until he can make a full report." He glanced at his wristwatch. "In fact, if I am not mistaken . . ." He tilted his head, closed his eyes, and raised an index finger. The telephone in the kitchen began to trill.

"He has done it a thousand times, sir," said Mr Cuff, "and I have yet to see him strike out."

Mr Moncrieff brought the instrument through from the kitchen, said, "For you, sir," and placed the receiver in my waiting hand. I uttered the conventional greeting, longing to hear the voice of anyone but . . .

"Wendall Nash, sir," came the chief's raspy, high-pitched drawl. "Calling from up here in —. I hate to tell you this, but I have some awful bad news. Your place Green Chimneys started burning sometime around midnight last night, and every man jack we had got put on the job and the boys worked like dogs to save what they could, but sometimes you can't win no matter what you do. Me personally, I feel terrible about this, but, tell you the truth, I never saw a fire like it. We nearly lost two men, but it looks like they're going to come out of it okay. The rest of our boys are still out there trying to save the few trees you got left."

"Dreadful," I said. "Please permit me to speak to my wife."

A speaking silence followed. "The missus is not with you, sir? You're saying she was inside there?"

"My wife left for Green Chimneys yesterday morning. I spoke to her there in the afternoon. She intended to work in her studio, a separate building at some distance from the house, and it is her custom to sleep in the studio when working late." Saying these things to Wendall Nash, I felt almost as though I were creating an alternative world, another town of— and another Green Chimneys, where another Marguerite had busied herself in the studio, and there gone to bed to sleep through the commotion. "Have you checked the studio? You are certain to find her there."

"Well, I have to say we didn't, sir," he said. "The fire took that little building pretty good, too, but the walls are still standing and you can tell what used to be what, furnishingwise and equipmentwise. If she was inside it, we'd of found her."

"Then she got out in time," I said, and instantly it was the truth: the other Marguerite had escaped the blaze and now stood, numb with shock and wrapped in a blanket, unrecognized amidst the voyeuristic crowd always drawn to disasters.

"It's possible, but she hasn't turned up yet, and we've been talking to everybody at the site. Could she have left with one of the staff?"

"All the help is on vacation," I said. "She was alone."

"Uh-huh," he said. "Can you think of anyone with a serious grudge against you? Any enemies? Because this was not a natural-type fire, sir. Someone set it, and he knew what he was doing. Anyone come to mind?"

"No," I said. "I have rivals, but no enemies. Check the hospitals and anything else you can think of, Wendall, and I'll be there as soon as I can."

"You can take your time, sir," he said. "I sure hope we find her, and by late this afternoon we'll be able to go through the ashes." He said he would give me a call if anything turned up in the meantime.

"Please, Wendall," I said, and began to cry. Muttering a consolation I did not quite catch, Mr Moncrieff vanished with the telephone in another matchless display of butler politesse.

"The practice of hoping for what you know you cannot have is a worthy spiritual exercise," said Mr Clubb. "It brings home the vanity of vanity."

"I beg you, leave me," I said, still crying. "In all decency."

"Decency lays heavy obligations on us all," said Mr Clubb. "And no job is decently done until it is done completely. Would you care for help in getting back to the bedroom? We are ready to proceed."

I extended a shaky arm, and he assisted me through the corridors. Two cots had been set up in my room, and a neat array of instruments – "staples" – formed two rows across the bottom of the bed. Mr Clubb and Mr Cuff positioned my head on the pillows and began to disrobe.

VIII

Ten hours later, the silent chauffeur aided me in my exit from the limousine and clasped my left arm as I limped toward the uniformed men and official vehicles on the far side of the open gate. Blackened sticks that had been trees protruded from the blasted earth, and the stench of wet ash saturated the air. Wendall Nash separated from the other men, approached, and noted without comment my garb of grey homburg hat, pearl-grey cashmere topcoat, heavy gloves, woolen charcoal-grey pin-striped suit, sunglasses, and malacca walking stick. It was the afternoon of a midsummer day in the upper eighties. Then he looked more closely at my face. "Are you, uh, are you sure you're all right, sir?"

"In a manner of speaking," I said, and saw him blink at the oozing gap left in the wake of an incisor. "I slipped at the top of a marble staircase and tumbled down all forty-six steps, resulting in massive bangs and bruises, considerable physical weakness, and the persistent sensation of being uncomfortably cold. No broken bones, at least nothing major." Over his shoulder I stared at four isolated brick towers rising from an immense black hole in the ground, all that remained of Green Chimneys. "Is there news of my wife?"

"I'm afraid, sir, that—" Nash placed a hand on my shoulder, causing me to stifle a sharp outcry. "I'm sorry, sir. Shouldn't you be in the hospital? Did your doctors say you could come all this way?"

"Knowing my feelings in this matter, the doctors insisted I make the journey." Deep within the black cavity, men in bulky orange space suits and space helmets were sifting through the sodden ashes, now and then dropping unrecognizable nuggets into heavy bags of the same colour. "I gather that you have news for me, Wendall," I said.

"Unhappy news, sir," he said.."The garage went up with the rest of the house, but we found some bits and pieces of your wife's little car. This here was one incredible hot fire, sir, and by hot I mean *hot*, and whoever set it was no garden-variety firebug."

"You found evidence of the automobile," I said. "I assume you also found evidence of the woman who owned it."

"They came across some bone fragments, plus a small portion of a skeleton," he said. "This whole big house came down on her, sir. These boys are experts at their job, and they don't hold out hope for finding a whole lot more. So if your wife was the only person inside . . ."

"I see, yes, I understand," I said, staying on my feet only with the support of the malacca cane. "How horrid, how hideous that it should all be true, that our lives should prove such a *littleness* . . ."

"I'm sure that's true, sir, and that wife of yours was a, was what I have to call a special kind of person who gave pleasure to us all, and I hope you know that we all wish things could of turned out different, the same as you."

For a moment I imagined that he was talking about her recordings. Then I understood that he was labouring to express the pleasure he and the others had taken in what they, no less than Mr Clubb and Mr Cuff but much, much more than I, had perceived as her essential character.

"Oh, Wendall," I said into the teeth of my sorrow, "it is not possible, not ever, for things to turn out different."

He refrained from patting my shoulder and sent me back to the rigours of my education.

IX

A month – four weeks – thirty days – seven hundred and twenty hours – forty-three thousand, two hundred minutes – two million, five hundred and ninety-two thousand seconds – did I spend under the care of Mr Clubb and Mr Cuff, and I believe I proved in the end to be a modestly, moderately, middlingly satisfying subject, a matter in which I take an immodest and immoderate pride. "You are little in comparison to the lady, sir," Mr Clubb once told me while deep in his ministrations, "but no one could say that you are nothing." I, who had countless times put the lie to the declaration that they should never see me cry, wept tears of gratitude. We ascended through the fifteen stages known to the novice, the journeyman's further five, and passed, with the frequent repetitions and backward glances appropriate for the slower pupil, into the artist's upper eighty, infinitely expandable by grace of the refinements of his art. We had the little soldiers. We had *dental floss*. During each of those forty-three thousand, two hundred minutes, throughout all two million and nearly six hundred thousand seconds, it was always deepest night. We made our way through perpetual darkness, and the utmost darkness of the utmost night yielded an infinity of textural variation, cold, slick dampness to velvety softness to leaping flame, for it was true that no one could say I was nothing.

Because I was not nothing, I glimpsed the Meaning of Tragedy.

Each Tuesday and Friday of these four sunless weeks, my consultants and guides lovingly bathed and dressed my wounds, arrayed me in my warmest clothes (for I never after ceased to feel the blast of arctic wind against my flesh), and escorted me to my office, where I was presumed much reduced by grief as well as by certain household accidents attributed to grief.

On the first of these Tuesdays, a flushed-looking Mrs Rampage offered her consolations and presented me with the morning newspapers, an inch-thick pile of faxes, two inches of legal documents, and a tray filled with official-looking letters. The newspapers described the fire and eulogized Marguerite; the increasingly threatening faxes declared Chartwell, Munster, and Stout's intention to ruin me professionally and personally in the face of my continuing refusal to return the accompanying documents along with all records having reference to their client; the documents were those in question; the letters, produced by the various legal firms representing all my other cryptic gentlemen, deplored the (unspecified) circumstances necessitating their clients' universal desire for change in re financial management. These lawyers also desired all relevant records, disks, etc., etc., urgently. Mr Clubb and Mr Cuff roistered behind their screen. I signed the documents in a shaky hand and requested Mrs Rampage to have these shipped with the desired records to Chartwell, Munster, and Stout. "And dispatch all these other records, too," I said, handing her the letters. "I am now going in for my lunch."

Tottering toward the executive dining room, now and then I glanced into smoke-filled offices to observe my much-altered underlings. Some of them appeared, after a fashion, to be working. Several were reading paperback novels, which might be construed as work of a kind. One of the Skipper's assistants was unsuccessfully lofting paper airplanes toward his wastepaper basket. Gilligan's secretary lay asleep on her office couch, and a records clerk lay sleeping on the file room floor. In the dining room, Charlie-Charlie Rackett hurried forward to assist me to my accustomed chair. Gilligan and the Skipper gave me sullen looks from their usual lunch-time station, an unaccustomed bottle of Scotch whisky between them. Charlie-Charlie lowered me into my seat and said, "Terrible news about your wife, sir."

"More terrible than you know," I said.

Gilligan took a gulp of whisky and displayed his middle finger, I gathered to me rather than Charlie-Charlie.

"Afternoonish," I said.

"Very much so, sir," said Charlie-Charlie, and bent closer to the brim of the homburg and my ear. "About that little request you made the other day. The right men aren't nearly so easy to find as they used to be, sir, but I'm still on the job."

My laughter startled him. "No squab today, Charlie-Charlie. Just bring me a bowl of tomato soup."

I had partaken of no more than two or three delicious mouthfuls when Gilligan lurched up beside me. "Look here," he said, "it's too bad about your wife and everything, I really mean it, honest, but that drunken act you put on in my office cost me my biggest client, not to forget that you took his girlfriend home with you."

"In that case," I said, "I have no further need of your services. Pack your things and be out of here by three o'clock."

He listed to one side and straightened himself up. "You can't mean that."

"I can and do," I said. "Your part in the grand design at work in the universe no longer has any connection with my own."

"You must be as crazy as you look," he said, and unsteadily departed.

I returned to my office and gently lowered myself into my seat. After I had removed my gloves and accomplished some minor repair work to the tips of my fingers with the tape and gauze pads thoughtfully inserted by the detectives into the pockets of my coat, I slowly drew the left glove over my fingers and became aware of feminine giggles amid the coarser sounds of male amusement behind the screen. I coughed into the glove and heard a tiny shriek. Soon, though not immediately, a blushing Mrs Rampage emerged from cover, patting her hair and adjusting her skirt. "Sir, I'm so sorry, I didn't expect . . ." She was staring at my right hand, which had not as yet been inserted into its glove.

"Lawn-mower accident," I said. "Mr Gilligan has been released, and I should like you to prepare the necessary papers. Also, I want to see all of our operating figures for the past year, as significant changes have been dictated by the grand design at work in the universe."

Mrs Rampage flew from the room. For the next several hours, as for nearly every remaining hour I spent at my desk on the Tuesdays and Fridays thereafter, I addressed with a carefree spirit the details involved in shrinking the staff to the smallest number possible and turning the entire business over to the Skipper. Graham Leeson's abrupt disappearance greatly occupied the newspapers, and when not occupied as described I read that my arch rival and competitor had been a notorious Don Juan, i.e., a compulsive womanizer, a flaw in his otherwise immaculate character held by some to have played a substantive role in his sudden absence. As Mr Clubb had predicted, a clerk at the —Hotel revealed Leeson's sessions with my late wife, and for a time professional and amateur gossipmongers alike speculated that he had caused the disastrous fire. This came to nothing. Before the month had ended, Leeson sightings were reported in Monaco, the Swiss Alps, and Argentina, locations accommodating to sportsmen – after four years of varsity football at the University of Southern California, Leeson had won an Olympic silver medal in weightlifting while earning his MBA at Wharton.

In the limousine at the end of each day, Mr Clubb and Mr Cuff braced me in happy anticipation of the lessons to come as we sped back through illusory sunlight toward the real darkness.

X The Meaning of Tragedy

Everything, from the designs of the laughing gods down to the lowliest cells in the human digestive tract, is changing all the time, every particle of being large and small is eternally in motion, but this simple truism, so transparent on its surface, evokes immediate headache and stupefaction when applied to itself, not unlike the sentence "Every word that comes out of my mouth is a bald-faced lie". The gods are ever laughing while we are always clutching our heads and looking for a soft place to lie down, and what I beheld in my momentary glimpses of the meaning of tragedy preceding, during, and after the experience of *dental floss* was so composed of paradox that I can state it only in cloud or vapour form, as:

The meaning of tragedy is: *All is in order, all is in train.*
The meaning of tragedy is: *It only hurts for a little while.*
The meaning of tragedy is: *Change is the first law of life.*

XI

So it took place that one day their task was done, their lives and mine were to move forward into separate areas of the grand design, and all that was left before preparing my own departure was to stand, bundled up against the non-existent arctic wind, on the bottom step and wave farewell with my remaining hand while shedding buckets and bathtubs of tears with my remaining eye. Chaplinesque in their black suits and bowlers, Mr Clubb and Mr Cuff ambled cheerily toward the glittering avenue and my bank, where arrangements had been made for the transfer into their hands of all but a small portion of my private fortune by my private banker, virtually his final act in that capacity. At the distant corner, Mr Clubb and Mr Cuff, by then only tiny figures blurred by my tears, turned, ostensibly to bid farewell, actually, as I knew, to watch as I mounted my steps and went back within the house, and with a salute I honoured this last painful agreement between us.

A more pronounced version of the office's metamorphosis had taken place inside my town house, but with the relative ease practice gives even to one whose step is halting, whose progress is interrupted by frequent pauses for breath and the passing of certain shooting pains, I skirted the mounds of rubble, the dangerous loose tiles, more dangerous open holes in the floor, and the regions submerged under water and toiled up the resilient staircase, moved with infinite care across the boards bridging the former landing, and made my way into the former kitchen, where broken pipes and limp wires protruding from the lathe marked the sites of those appliances rendered pointless by the gradual disappearance of the household staff. (In a voice choked with feeling, Mr Moncrieff, Reggie Moncrieff, Reggie, the last to go, had informed me that his final month in my service had been "as fine as my days with the Duke, sir, every bit as noble as ever it was with that excellent old gentleman.") The remaining cupboard yielded a flagon of *jenever*, a tumbler, and a Monte Cristo torpedo, and with the tumbler filled and the cigar alight I hobbled through the devastated corridors toward my bed, there to gather my strength for the ardours of the coming day.

In good time, I arose to observe the final appointments of the life soon to be abandoned. It is possible to do up one's shoelaces and knot one's necktie as neatly with a single hand as with two, and shirt buttons eventually become a breeze. Into my travelling bag I folded a few modest essentials atop the flagon and the cigar box, and into a pad of shirts nestled the black lucite cube prepared at my request by my instructor-guides and containing, mingled with the ashes of the satchel and its contents, the few bony nuggets rescued from Green Chimneys. The travelling bag accompanied me first to my lawyer's office, where I signed papers making over the wreckage of the town house to the European gentleman who had purchased it sight unseen as a "fixer upper" for a fraction of its (considerably reduced) value. Next I visited the melancholy banker and withdrew the pittance remaining in my accounts. And then, glad of heart and free of all unnecessary encumbrance, I took my place in the sidewalk queue to await transportation by means of a kindly kneeling bus to the great terminus where I should employ the ticket reassuringly lodged within my breast pocket.

Long before the arrival of the bus, a handsome limousine crawled past in the traffic, and glancing idly within, I observed Mr Chester Montfort de M— smoothing the air with a languid gesture while in conversation with the two stout, bowler-hatted men on his either side. Soon, doubtless, he would begin his instructions in the whop-bopaloobop.

XII

What is a pittance in a great city may be a modest fortune in a hamlet, and a returned prodigal might be welcomed far in excess of his true deserts. I entered New Covenant quietly, unobtrusively, with the humility of a new convert uncertain of his station, inwardly rejoicing to see all unchanged from the days of my youth. When I purchased a dignified but unshowy house on Scripture Street, I announced only that I had known the village in my childhood, had travelled far, and now in my retirement wished no more than to immerse myself in the life of the community, exercising my skills only inasmuch as they might be requested of an elderly invalid. How well the aged invalid had known the village, how far and to what end had he travelled, and the nature of his skills remained unspecified. Had I not attended daily services at the Temple, the rest of my days might have passed in pleasant anonymity and frequent perusals of a little book I had obtained at the terminus, for while my surname was so deeply of New Covenant that it could be read on a dozen headstones in the Temple graveyard, I had fled so early in life and so long ago that my individual identity had been entirely forgotten. New Covenant is curious – intensely curious – but it does not wish to pry. One fact and one only led to the metaphoric slaughter of the fatted calf and the prodigal's elevation. On the day when, some five or six months after his installation on Scripture Street, the afflicted newcomer's faithful Temple attendance was rewarded with an invitation to read the Lesson for the Day, Matthew 5:43–48, seated amid numerous offspring and offspring's offspring in the barnie-pews for the first time since an unhappy tumble from a hayloft was Delbert Mudge.

My old classmate had weathered into a white-haired, sturdy replica of his own grandfather, and although his hips still gave him considerable difficulty his mind had suffered no comparable stiffening. Delbert knew my name as well as his own, and though he could not connect it to the wizened old party counselling him from the lectern to embrace his enemies, the old party's face and voice so clearly evoked the deceased lawyer who had been my father that he recognized me before I had spoken the whole of the initial verse. The grand design at work in the universe once again could be seen at its mysterious business: unknown to me, my entirely selfish efforts on behalf of Charlie-Charlie Rackett, my representation to his parole board and his subsequent hiring as my spy, had been noted by all of barnie-world. I, a child of Scripture Street, had become a hero to generations of barnies! After hugging me at the conclusion of the fateful service, Delbert Mudge implored my assistance in the resolution of a fiscal imbroglio that threatened his family's cohesion. I of course assented, with the condition that my services should be free of charge. The Mudge imbroglio proved elementary, and soon I was performing similar services for other barnie-clans. After listening to a half dozen accounts of my miracles while setting broken barnie-bones, New Covenant's physician visited my Scripture Street habitation under cover of night, was prescribed the solution to his uncomplicated problem, and sang my praises to his fellow townies. Within a year, by which time all New Covenant had become aware of my "tragedy" and consequent "reawakening", I was managing the Temple's funds as well as those of barn and town. Three years later, our reverend having in his ninety-first year, as the Racketts and Mudges put it, "woke up dead", I submitted by popular acclaim to appointment in his place.

Daily, I assume the honoured place assigned me. Ceremonious vestments assure that my patchwork scars remain unseen. The lucite box and its relics are interred deep within the sacred ground beneath the Temple where I must one day join my predecessors – some bony fragments of Graham Leeson reside there, too, mingled with Marguerite's more numerous specks and nuggets. Eye patch elegantly in place, I lean forward upon the malacca cane and, while flourishing the stump of my right hand as if in demonstration, with my ruined tongue whisper what I know none shall understand, the homily beginning, *It only* . To this I append in silent exhalation the two words concluding that little book brought to my attention by an agreeable murderer and purchased at the great grand station long ago, these: *Ah, humanity!*

1999

THE MAMMOTH BOOK OF

BEST NEW HORROR

THE YEAR'S BEST HORROR STORIES BY SUCH MASTERS OF DARK SUSPENSE AS

RAMSEY CAMPBELL, NEIL GAIMAN,
JAMES HERBERT, PETER STRAUB,
F. PAUL WILSON, GENE WOLFE
and many others

EDITED BY
STEPHEN JONES

"Outstanding . . . indispensable reading
for horror lovers." *PUBLISHERS WEEKLY*

White

Tim Lebbon

DESPITE FEATURING A SOMEWHAT muddy painting by renowned illustrator Julek Heller, the re-design of the cover continued apace with a new layout and a blood-red logo for *The Mammoth Book of Best New Horror Volume Eleven*.

The Introduction covered the last year of the twentieth century and grew to sixty-seven pages, while the Necrology blossomed to thirty-eight. I devoted almost five pages to discussing alternative forms of publishing, including the proliferation of overpriced small press editions and the burgeoning electronic book formats.

I finally got bestselling British author James Herbert into the book with an extract from his novel *Others*, and the remaining twenty stories featured a strong line-up of recognizable names that included Neil Gaiman, Peter Straub, Ramsey Campbell, Kim Newman, Michael Marshall Smith, F. Paul Wilson, Gene Wolfe, Graham Masterton, Thomas Tessier, Terry Lamsley, T.E.D. Klein and David J. Schow, to name only a few. Steve Rasnic Tem was represented with two stories set in the same haunted milieu, and I was also delighted to include a new novella, "Jimmy", by veteran Arkham House writer David Case.

But the story that made the most impact on me was by a relative newcomer to the genre. Tim Lebbon has gone on to forge an impressive career with a string of commercial books to his name, but back at the end of the 1990s he was still honing his craft in the small press. I had been following his career for some time, but when I read his apocalyptic novella "White", which subsequently won the British Fantasy Award, I was totally captivated by his command of character development and the claustrophobic setting. It was then that I knew that he had truly made it as a writer.

I: The Colour of Blood

WE FOUND THE FIRST BODY two days before Christmas.

Charley had been out gathering sticks to dry for tinder. She had worked her way through the wild garden and down toward the cliffs, scooping snow from beneath and around bushes and bagging whatever dead twigs she found there. There were no signs, she said. No disturbances in the virgin surface of the snow; no tracks; no warning. Nothing to prepare her for the scene of bloody devastation she stumbled across.

She had rounded a big boulder and seen the red splash in the snow which was all that remained of a human being. The shock froze her comprehension. The reality of the scene struggled to imprint itself on her mind. Then, slowly, what she was looking at finally registered.

She ran back screaming. She'd only recognized her boyfriend by what was left of his shoes.

We were in the dining room trying to make sense of the last few weeks when Charley came bursting in. We spent a lot of time doing that: talking together in the big living rooms of the manor; in pairs, crying and sharing warmth; or alone, staring into darkening skies and struggling to discern a meaning in the infinite. I was one of those more usually alone. I'd been an only child and contrary to popular belief, my upbringing had been a nightmare. I always thought my parents blamed me for the fact that they could not have any more children, and instead of enjoying and revelling in my own childhood, I spent those years watching my mother and father mourn the ghosts of unborn offspring. It would have been funny if it were not so sad.

Charley opened the door by falling into it. She slumped to the floor, hair plastered across her forehead, her eyes two bright sparks peering between the knotted strands. Caked snow fell from her boots and speckled the timber floor, dirtied into slush. The first thing I noticed was its pinkish tinge.

The second thing I saw was the blood covering Charley's hands.

"Charley!" Hayden jumped to his feet and almost caught the frantic woman before she hit the deck. He went down with her, sprawling in a sudden puddle of dirt and tears. He saw the blood then and backed away automatically. "Charley?"

"Get some towels," Ellie said, always the pragmatist, "and a fucking gun."

I'd seen people screaming – all my life I'd never forgotten Jayne's final hours – but I had never seen someone actually *beyond* the point of screaming. Charley gasped and clawed at her throat, trying to open it up and let out the pain and the shock trapped within. It was not exertion that had stolen her breath; it was whatever she had seen.

She told us what that was.

I went with Ellie and Brand. Ellie had a shotgun cradled in the crook of her arm, a bobble hat hiding her severely short hair, her face all hard. There was no room in her life for compliments, but right now she was the one person in the manor I'd choose to be with. She'd been all for trying to make it out alone on foot; I was so glad that she eventually decided to stay.

Brand muttered all the way. "Oh fuck, oh shit, what are we doing coming out here? Like those crazy girls in slasher movies, you know? Always chasing the bad guys instead of running from them? Asking to get their throats cut? Oh man . . ."

In many ways I agreed with him. According to Charley there was little left of Boris to recover, but she could have been wrong. We owed it to him to find out. However harsh the conditions, whatever the likelihood of his murderer – animal or human – still being out here, we could not leave Boris lying dead in the snow. Apply whatever levels of civilization, foolish custom or superiority complex you like, it just wasn't done.

Ellie led the way across the manor's front garden and out onto the coastal road. The whole landscape was hidden beneath snow, like old sheet-covered furniture awaiting the homecoming of long-gone owners. I wondered who would ever make use of this land again – who would be left to bother when the snow did finally melt – but that train of thought led only to depression.

We crossed the flat area of the road, following Charley's earlier footprints in the deep snow; even and distinct on the way out, chaotic on the return journey. As if she'd had something following her.

She had. We all saw what had been chasing her when we slid and clambered down toward the cliffs, veering behind the big rock that signified the beginning of the coastal path. The sight of Boris opened up and spread across the snow had pursued her all the way, and was probably still snapping at her heels now. The smell of his insides slowly cooling under an indifferent sky. The sound of his frozen blood crackling under foot.

Ellie hefted the gun, holding it waist-high, ready to fire in an instant. Her breath condensed in the air before her, coming slightly faster than moments before. She glanced at the torn-up Boris, then surveyed our surroundings, looking for whoever had done this. East and west along the coast, down toward the cliff edge, up to the lip of rock above us, east and west again; Ellie never looked back down at Boris.

I did. I couldn't keep my eyes off what was left of him. It looked as though something big and powerful had held him up to the rock, scraped and twisted him there for a while, and then calmly taken him apart across the snow-covered path. Spray patterns of blood stood out brighter than their surroundings. Every speck was visible and there were many specks, thousands of them spread across a ten-metre area. I tried to find a recognizable part of him, but all that was even vaguely identifiable as human was a hand, stuck to the rock in a mess of frosty blood, fingers curled in like the legs of a dead spider. The wrist was tattered, the bone splintered. It had been snapped, not cut.

Brand pointed out a shoe on its side in the snow. "Fuck, Charley was right. Just his shoes left. Miserable bastard always wore the same shoes."

I'd already seen the shoe. It was still mostly full. Boris had not been a miserable bastard. He was introspective, thoughtful, sensitive, sincere, qualities which Brand would never recognize as anything other than sourness. Brand was as thick as shit and twice as unpleasant.

The silence seemed to press in around me. Silence, and cold, and a raw smell of meat, and the sea chanting from below. I was surrounded by everything.

"Let's get back," I said. Ellie glanced at me and nodded.

"But what about—" Brand started, but Ellie cut in without even looking at him.

"You want to make bloody snowballs, go ahead. There's not much to take back. We'll maybe come again later. Maybe."

"What did this?" I said, feeling reality start to shimmy past the shock I'd been gripped by for the last couple of minutes. "Just what the hell?"

Ellie backed up to me and glanced at the rock, then both ways along the path. "I don't want to find out just yet," she said.

Later, alone in my room, I would think about exactly what Ellie had meant. *I don't want to find out just yet*, she had said, implying that the perpetrator of Boris's demise would be revealed to us soon. I'd hardly known Boris, quiet guy that he was, and his fate was just another line in the strange composition of death that had overcome the whole country during the last few weeks.

Charley and I were here in the employment of the Department of the Environment. Our brief was to keep a check on the radiation levels in the Atlantic Drift, since things had gone to shit in South America and the dirty reactors began to melt down in Brazil. It was a bad job with hardly any pay, but it gave us somewhere to live. The others had tagged along for differing reasons; friends and lovers of friends, all taking the opportunity to get away from things for a while and chill out in the wilds of Cornwall.

But then things went to shit here as well. On TV, minutes before it had ceased broadcasting for good, someone called it the ruin.

Then it had started to snow.

Hayden had taken Charley upstairs, still trying to quell her hysteria. We had no medicines other than aspirin and cough mixtures, but there were a hundred bottles of wine in the cellar. It seemed that Hayden had already poured most of a bottle down Charley's throat by the time the three of us arrived back at the manor. Not a good idea, I thought – I could hardly imagine what ghosts a drunken Charley would see, what terrors her alcohol-induced dreams held in store for her once she was finally left on her own – but it was not my place to say.

Brand stormed in and with his usual subtlety painted a picture of what we'd seen. "Boris' guts were just everywhere, hanging on the rock, spread over the snow. Melted in, like they were still hot when he was being cut up. What the fuck would do that? Eh? Just what the fuck?"

"Who did it?" Rosalie, our resident paranoid, asked.

I shrugged. "Can't say."

"Why not?"

"Not won't," I said, "can't. Can't tell. There's not too much left to tell by, as Brand has so eloquently revealed."

Ellie stood before the open fire and held out her hands, palms up, as if asking for something. A touch of emotion, I mused, but then my thoughts were often cruel.

"Ellie?" Rosalie demanded an answer.

Ellie shrugged. "We can rule out suicide." Nobody responded.

I went through to the kitchen and opened the back door. We were keeping our beers on a shelf in the rear conservatory now that the electricity had gone off. There was a generator, but not enough fuel to run it for more than an hour every day. We agreed that hot water was a priority for that meagre time, so the fridge was now extinct.

I surveyed my choice: Stella; a few final cans of Caffreys; Boddingtons. That had been Jayne's favourite. She'd drunk it in pints, inevitably doing a bad impression of some moustachioed actor after the first creamy sip. I could still see her sparkling eyes as she tried to think of someone new . . . I grabbed a Caffreys and shut the back door, and it was as the latch clicked home that I started to shake.

I'd seen a dead man five minutes ago, a man I'd been talking to the previous evening, drinking with, chatting about what the hell had happened to the world, making inebriated plans of escape, knowing all the time that the snow had us trapped here like chickens surrounded by a fiery moat. Boris had been quiet but thoughtful, the most intelligent person here at the manor. It had been his idea to lock the doors to many of the rooms because we never used them, and any heat we managed to generate should be kept in the rooms we did use. He had suggested a long walk as the snow had begun in earnest and it had been our prevarication and, I admit, our arguing that had kept us here long enough for it to matter. By the time Boris had persuaded us to make a go of it, the snow was three feet deep. Five miles and we'd be dead. Maximum. The nearest village was ten miles away.

He was dead. Something had taken him apart, torn him up, ripped him to pieces. I was certain that there had been no cutting involved as Brand had suggested. And yes, his bits did look melted into the snow. Still hot when they struck the surface, blooding it in death. Still alive and beating as they were taken out.

I sat at the kitchen table and held my head in my hands. Jayne had said that this would hold all the good thoughts in and let the bad ones seep through your fingers, and sometimes it seemed to work. Now it was just a comfort, like the hands of a lover kneading hope into flaccid muscles, or fear from tense ones.

It could not work this time. I had seen a dead man. And there was nothing we could do about it. We should be telling someone, but over the past few months any sense of "relevant authorities" had fast faded away, just as Jayne had two years before; faded away to agony, then confusion, and then to nothing. Nobody knew what had killed her. Growths on her chest and stomach. Bad blood. Life.

I tried to open the can but my fingers were too cold to slip under the ring-pull. I became frustrated, then angry, and eventually my temper threw the can to the floor. It struck the flagstones and one edge split, sending a fine yellowish spray of beer across the old kitchen cupboards. I cried out at the waste. It was a feeling I was becoming more than used to.

"Hey," Ellie said. She put one hand on my shoulder and removed it before I could shrug her away. "They're saying we should tell someone."

"Who?" I turned to look at her, unashamed of my tears. Ellie was a hard bitch. Maybe they made me more of a person than she.

She raised one eyebrow and pursed her lips. "Brand thinks the army. Rosalie thinks the Fairy Underground."

I scoffed. "Fairy-fucking-Underground. Stupid cow."

"She can't help being like that. You ask me, it makes her more suited to how it's all turning out."

"And how's that, exactly?" I hated Ellie sometimes, all her stronger-than-thou talk and steely eyes. But she was also the person I respected the most in out pathetic little group. Now that Boris had gone.

"Well," she said, "for a start, take a look at how we're all reacting to this. Shocked, maybe. Horrified. But it's almost like it was expected."

"It's all been going to shit . . ." I said, but I did not need to continue. We had all known that we were not immune to the rot settling across society, nature, the world. Eventually it would find us. We just had not known when.

"There is the question of who did it," she said quietly.

"Or what."

She nodded. "Or what."

For now, we left it at that.

"How's Charley?"

"I was just going to see," Ellie said. "Coming?"

I nodded and followed her from the room. The beer had stopped spraying and now fizzled into sticky rivulets where the flags joined. I was still thirsty.

Charley looked bad. She was drunk, that was obvious, and she had been sick down herself, and she had wet herself. Hayden was in the process of trying to mop up the mess when we knocked and entered.

"How is she?" Ellie asked pointlessly.

"How do you think?" He did not even glance at us as he tried to hold onto the babbling, crying, laughing and puking Charley.

"Maybe you shouldn't have given her so much to drink," Ellie said. Hayden sent her daggers but did not reply.

Charley struggled suddenly in his arms, ranting and shouting at the shaded candles in the corners of the room.

"What's that?" I said. "What's she saying?" For some reason it sounded important, like a solution to a problem encoded by grief.

"She's been saying some stuff," Hayden said loudly, so we could hear above Charley's slurred cries. "Stuff about Boris. Seeing angels in the snow. She says his angels came to get him."

"Some angels," Ellie muttered.

"You go down," Hayden said, "I'll stay here with her." He wanted us gone, that much was obvious, so we did not disappoint him.

Downstairs, Brand and Rosalie were hanging around the mobile phone. It had sat on the mantelpiece for the last three weeks like a gun without bullets, ugly and useless. Every now and then someone would try it, receiving only a crackling nothing in response. Random numbers, recalled numbers, numbers held in the 'phone's memory, all came to naught. Gradually it was tried less – every unsuccessful attempt had been more depressing.

"What?" I said.

"Trying to call someone," Brand said. "Police. Someone."

"So they can come to take fingerprints?" Ellie flopped into one of the old armchairs and began picking at its upholstery, widening a hole she'd been plucking at for days. "Any replies?"

Brand shook his head.

"We've got to do something," Rosalie said, "we can't just sit here while Boris is lying dead out there."

Ellie said nothing. The telephone hissed its amusement. Rosalie looked to me. "There's nothing we can do," I said. "Really, there's not much to collect up. If we did bring his . . . bits . . . back here, what would we do?"

"Bury . . ." Rosalie began.

"Three feet of snow? Frozen ground?"

"And the things," Brand said. The phone cackled again and he turned it off.

"What things?"

Brand looked around our small group. "The things Boris said he'd seen."

Boris had mentioned nothing to me. In our long, drunken talks, he had never talked of any angels in the snow. Upstairs, I'd thought that it was simply Charley drunk and mad with grief, but now Brand had said it too I had the distinct feeling I was missing out on something. I was irked, and upset at feeling irked.

"Things?" Rosalie said, and I closed my eyes. *Oh fuck, don't tell her*, I willed at Brand. She'd regale us with stories of secret societies and messages in the clouds, disease-makers who were wiping out the inept and the crippled, the barren and the intellectually inadequate. Jayne had been sterile, so we'd never had kids. The last thing I needed was another one of Rosalie's mad ravings about how my wife had died, why she'd died, who had killed her.

Luckily, Brand seemed of like mind. Maybe the joint he'd lit up had stewed him into silence at last. He turned to the fire and stared into its dying depths, sitting on the edge of the seat as if wondering whether or not to feed it some more. The stack of logs was running low.

"Things?" Rosalie said again, nothing if not persistent.

"No things," I said. "Nothing." I left the room before it all flared up.

In the kitchen I opened another can, carefully this time, and poured it into a tall glass. I stared into creamy depths as bubbles passed up and down. It took a couple of minutes for the drink to settle, and in that time I had recalled Jayne's face, her body, the best times we'd had together. At my first sip, a tear replenished the glass.

That night I heard doors opening and closing as someone wandered between beds. I was too tired to care who.

The next morning I half-expected it to be all better. I had the bitter taste of dread in my mouth when I woke up, but also a vague idea that all the bad stuff could only have happened in nightmares. As I dressed – two shirts, a heavy pullover, a jacket – I wondered what awaited me beyond my bedroom door.

In the kitchen Charley was swigging from a fat mug of tea. It steamed so much, it seemed liable to burn whatever it touched. Her lips were red-raw, as were her eyes. She clutched the cup tightly, knuckles white, thumbs twisted into the handle. She looked as though she wanted to never let it go.

I had a sinking feeling in my stomach when I saw her. I glanced out of the window and saw the landscape of snow, added to yet again the previous night, bloated flakes still fluttering down to reinforce the barricade against our escape. Somewhere out there, Boris's parts were frozen memories hidden under a new layer.

"Okay?" I said quietly.

Charley looked up at me as if I'd farted at her mother's funeral.

"Of course I'm not okay," she said, enunciating each word carefully. "And what do you care?"

I sat at the table opposite her, yawning, rubbing hands through my greasy hair, generally trying to disperse the remnants of sleep. There was a pot of tea on the table and I took a spare mug and poured a steaming brew. Charley watched my every move. I was aware of her eyes upon me, but I tried not to let it show. The cup shook, I could barely grab a spoon. I'd seen her boyfriend splashed across the snow, I felt terrible about it, but then I realized that she'd seen the same scene. How bad must she be feeling?

"We have to do something," she said.

"Charley—"

"We can't just sit here. We have to go. Boris needs a funeral. We have to go and find someone, get out of this God-forsaken place. There must be someone near, able to help, someone to look after us? I need someone to look after me."

The statement was phrased as a question, but I ventured no answer.

"Look," she said, "we have to get out. Don't you see?" She let go of her mug and clasped my hands; hers were hot and sweaty. "The village, we can get there, I know we can."

"No, Charley," I said, but I did not have a chance to finish my sentence (*there's no way out, we tried, and didn't you see the television reports weeks ago?*) before Ellie marched into the room. She paused when she saw Charley, then went to the cupboard and poured herself a bowl of cereal. She used water. We'd run out of milk a week ago.

"There's no telephone," she said, spooning some soggy corn flakes into her mouth. "No television, save some flickering pictures most of us don't want to see. Or believe. There's no radio, other than the occasional foreign channel. Rosie says she speaks French. She's heard them talking of 'the doom'. That's how she translates it, though I think it sounds more like 'the ruin'. The nearest village is ten miles away. We have no motorized transport that will even get out of the garage. To walk it would be suicide." She crunched her limp breakfast, mixing in more sugar to give some taste.

Charley did not reply. She knew what Ellie was saying, but tears were her only answer.

"So we're here until the snow melts," I said. Ellie really was a straight bitch. Not a glimmer of concern for Charley, not a word of comfort.

Ellie looked at me and stopped chewing for a moment. "I think until it does melt, we're protected." She had a way of coming out with ideas that both enraged me, and scared the living shit out of me at the same time.

Charley could only cry.

Later, three of us decided to try to get out. In moments of stress, panic and mourning, logic holds no sway.

I said I'd go with Brand and Charley. It was one of the most foolish decisions I've ever made, but seeing Charley's eyes as she sat in the kitchen on her own, thinking about her slaughtered boyfriend, listening to Ellie go on about how hopeless it all was . . . I could not say no. And in truth, I was as desperate to leave as anyone.

It was almost ten in the morning when we set out.

Ellie was right, I knew that even then. Her face as she watched us struggle across the garden should have brought me back straight away: she thought I was a fool. She was the last person in the world I wanted to appear foolish in front of, but still there was that nagging feeling in my heart that pushed me on – a mixture of desire to help Charley and a hopeless feeling that by staying here, we were simply waiting for death to catch us up.

It seemed to have laid its shroud over the rest of the world already. Weeks ago the television had shown some dreadful sights: people falling ill and dying in their thousands; food riots in London; a nuclear exchange between Greece and Turkey. More, lots more, all of it bad. We'd known something was coming – things had been falling apart for years – but once it began it was a cumulative effect, speeding from a steady trickle toward decline, to a raging torrent. *We're better off where we are*, Boris had said to me. It was ironic that because of him, we were leaving.

I carried the shotgun. Brand had an air pistol, though I'd barely trust him with a sharpened stick. As well as being loud and brash, he spent most of his time doped to the eyeballs. If there was any trouble, I'd be watching out for him as much as anything else.

Something had killed Boris and whatever it was, animal or human, it was still out there in the snow. Moved on, hopefully, now it had fed. But then again perhaps not. It did not dissuade us from trying.

The snow in the manor garden was almost a metre deep. The three of us had botched together snowshoes of varying effectiveness. Brand wore two snapped-off lengths of picture frame on each foot, which seemed to act more as knives to slice down through the snow than anything else. He was tenaciously pompous; he struggled with his mistake rather than admitting it. Charley had used two frying pans with their handles snapped off, and she seemed to be making good headway. My own creations consisted of circles of mounted canvas cut from the redundant artwork in the manor. Old owners of the estate stared up at me through the snow as I repeatedly stepped on their faces.

By the time we reached the end of the driveway and turned to see Ellie and Hayden watching us, I was sweating and exhausted. We had travelled about fifty metres.

Across the road lay the cliff path leading to Boris's dismembered corpse. Charley glanced that way, perhaps wishing to look down upon her boyfriend one more time.

"Come on," I said, clasping her elbow and heading away. She offered no resistance.

The road was apparent as a slightly lower, smoother plain of snow between the two hedged banks on either side. Everything was glaring white, and we were all wearing sunglasses to prevent snow-blindness. We could see far along the coast from here as the bay swept around toward the east, the craggy cliffs spotted white where snow had drifted onto ledges, an occasional lonely seabird diving to the sea and returning empty-beaked to sing a mournful song for company. In places the snow was cantilevered out over the edge of the cliff, a deadly trap should any of us stray that way. The sea itself surged against the rocks below, but it broke no spray. The usual roar of the waters crashing into the earth, slowly eroding it away and reclaiming it, had changed. It was now more of a grind as tonnes of slushy ice replaced the usual white horses, not yet forming a solid barrier over the water but still thick enough to temper the waves. In a way it was sad; a huge beast winding down in old age.

I watched as a cormorant plunged down through the chunky ice and failed to break surface again. It was as if it were committing suicide. Who was I to say it was not?

"How far?" Brand asked yet again.

"Ten miles," I said.

"I'm knackered." He had already lit up a joint and he took long, hard pulls on it. I could hear its tip sizzling in the crisp morning air.

"We've come about three hundred metres," I said, and Brand shut up.

It was difficult to talk; we needed all our breath for the effort of walking. Sometimes the snowshoes worked, especially where the surface of the snow had frozen the previous night. Other times we plunged straight in up to our thighs and we had to hold our arms out for balance as we hauled our leg out, just to let it sink in again a step along. The rucksacks did not help. We each carried food, water and dry clothing, and Brand especially seemed to be having trouble with his.

The sky was a clear blue. The sun rose ahead of us as if mocking the frozen landscape. Some days it started like this, but the snow never seemed to melt. I had almost forgotten what the ground below it looked like; it seemed that the snow had been here forever. When it began our spirits had soared, like a bunch of school-kids waking to find the landscape had changed overnight. Charley and I had still gone down to the sea to take our readings, and when we returned there was a snowman in the garden wearing one of her bras and a pair of my briefs. A snowball fight had ensued, during which Brand became a little too aggressive for his own good. We'd ganged up on him and pelted him with snow compacted to ice until he shouted and yelped. We were cold and wet and bruised, but we did not stop laughing for hours.

We'd all dried out in front of the open fire in the huge living room. Rosalie had stripped to her knickers and danced to music on the radio. She was a bit of a sixties throwback, Rosalie, and she didn't seem to realize what her little display did to cosseted people like me. I watched happily enough.

Later, we sat around the fire and told ghost stories. Boris was still with us then, of course, and he came up with the best one which had us all cowering behind casual expressions. He told us of a man who could not see, hear or speak, but who knew of the ghosts around him. His life was silent and senseless save for the day his mother died. Then he cried and shouted and raged at the darkness, before curling up and dying himself. His world opened up then, and he no longer felt alone, but whoever he tried to speak to could only fear or loathe him. The living could never make friends with the dead. And death had made him more silent than ever.

None of us would admit it, but we were all scared shitless as we went to bed that night. As usual, doors opened and footsteps padded along corridors. And, as usual, my door remained shut and I slept alone.

Days later the snow was too thick to be enjoyable. It became risky to go outside, and as the woodpile started to dwindle and the radio and television broadcasts turned more grim, we realized that we were becoming trapped. A few of us had tried to get to the village, but it was a half-hearted attempt and we'd returned once we were tired. We figured we'd travelled about two miles along the coast. We had seen no one.

As the days passed and the snow thickened, the atmosphere did likewise with a palpable sense of panic. A week ago, Boris had pointed out that there were no 'plane trails anymore.

This, our second attempt to reach the village, felt more like life and death. Before Boris had been killed we'd felt confined, but it also gave a sense of protection from the things going on in the world. Now there was a feeling that if we could not get out, worse things would happen to us where we were.

I remembered Jayne as she lay dying from the unknown disease. I had been useless, helpless, hopeless, praying to a God I had long ignored to grant us a kind fate. I refused to sit back and go the same way. I would not go gentle. Fuck fate.

"What was that?"

Brand stopped and tugged the little pistol from his belt. It was stark black against the pure white snow.

"What?"

He nodded. "Over there." I followed his gaze and looked up the sloping hillside. To our right the sea sighed against the base of the cliffs. To our left – the direction Brand was now facing – snowfields led up a gentle slope towards the moors several miles inland. It was a rocky, craggy landscape, and some rocks had managed to hold off the drifts. They peered out darkly here and there, like the faces of drowning men going under for the final time.

"What?" I said again, exasperated. I'd slipped the shotgun off my shoulder and held it waist-high. My finger twitched on the trigger guard. Images of Boris's remains sharpened my senses. I did not want to end up like that.

"I saw something moving. Something white."

"Some snow, perhaps?" Charley said bitterly.

"Something running across the snow," he said, frowning as he concentrated on the middle-distance. The smoke from his joint mingled with his condensing breath.

We stood that way for a minute or two, steaming sweat like smoke signals of exhaustion. I tried taking off my glasses to look, but the glare was too much. I glanced sideways at Charley. She'd pulled a big old revolver from her rucksack and held it with both hands. Her lips were pulled back from her teeth in a feral grimace. She really wanted to use that gun.

I saw nothing. "Could have been a cat. Or a seagull flying low."

"Could have been." Brand shoved the pistol back into his belt and reached around for his water canteen. He tipped it to his lips and cursed. "Frozen!"

"Give it a shake," I said. I knew it would do no good but it may shut him up for a while. "Charley, what's the time?" I had a watch but I wanted to talk to Charley, keep her involved with the present, keep her here. I had started to realize not only what a stupid idea this was, but what an even more idiotic step it had been letting Charley come along. If she wasn't here for revenge, she was blind with grief. I could not see her eyes behind her sunglasses.

"Nearly midday." She was hoisting her rucksack back onto her shoulders, never taking her eyes from the snowscape sloping slowly up and away from us. "What do you think it was?"

I shrugged. "Brand seeing things. Too much wacky baccy."

We set off again. Charley was in the lead, I followed close behind and Brand stumbled along at the rear. It was eerily silent around us, the snow muffling our gasps and puffs, the constant grumble of the sea soon blending into the background as much as it ever did. There was a sort of white noise in my ears: blood pumping; breath ebbing and flowing; snow crunching underfoot. They merged into one whisper, eschewing all outside noise, almost soporific in rhythm. I coughed to break the spell.

"What the hell do we do when we get to the village?" Brand said.

"Send back help," Charley stated slowly, enunciating each word as if to a naïve young child.

"But what if the village is like everywhere else we've seen or heard about on TV?"

Charley was silent for a while. So was I. A collage of images tumbled through my mind, hateful and hurtful and sharper because of that. Hazy scenes from the last day of television broadcasts we had watched: loaded ships leaving docks and sailing off to some nebulous sanctuary abroad; shootings in the streets, bodies in the gutters, dogs sniffing at open wounds; an airship, drifting over the hills in some vague attempt to offer hope.

"Don't be stupid," I said.

"Even if it is, there will be help there," Charley said quietly.

"Like hell." Brand lit up another joint. It was cold, we were risking our lives, there may very well be something in the snow itching to attack us . . . but at that moment I wanted nothing more than to take a long haul on Brand's pot, and let casual oblivion anaesthetise my fears.

An hour later we found the car.

By my figuring we had come about three miles. We were all but exhausted. My legs ached, knee joints stiff and hot as if on fire.

The road had started a slow curve to the left, heading inland from the coast toward the distant village. Its path had become less distinct, the hedges having sunk slowly into the ground until there was really nothing to distinguish it from the fields of snow on either side. We had been walking the last half-hour on memory alone.

The car was almost completely buried by snow, only one side of the windscreen and the iced-up aerial still visible. There was no sign of the route it had taken; whatever tracks it had made were long-since obliterated by the blizzards. As we approached the snow started again, fat flakes drifting lazily down and landing on the icy surface of last night's fall.

"Do not drive unless absolutely necessary," Brand said. Charley and I ignored him. We unslung our rucksacks and approached the buried shape, all of us keeping hold of our weapons. I meant to ask Charley where she'd got hold of the revolver – whether she'd had it with her when we both came here to test the sea and write environmental reports which would never be read – but now did not seem the time. I had no wish to seem judgmental or patronizing.

As I reached out to knock some of the frozen snow from the windscreen a flight of seagulls cawed and took off from nearby. They had been all but invisible against the snow, but there were at least thirty of them lifting as one, calling loudly as they twirled over our heads and then headed out to sea.

We all shouted out in shock. Charley stumbled sideways as she tried to bring her gun to bear and fell on her back. Brand screeched like a kid, then let off a pop with his air pistol to hide his embarrassment. The pellet found no target. The birds ignored us after the initial fly-past, and they slowly merged with the hazy distance. The new snow shower brought the horizon in close.

"Shit," Charley muttered.

"Yeah." Brand reloaded his pistol without looking at either of us, then rooted around for the joint he'd dropped when he screamed.

Charley and I went back to knocking the snow away, using our gloved hands to make tracks down the windscreen and across the

bonnet. "I think it's a Ford," I said uselessly. "Maybe an old Mondeo."
Jayne and I had owned a Mondeo when we'd been courting. Many
was the time we had parked in some shaded woodland or beside
units on the local industrial estate, wound down the windows and
made love as the cool night air looked on. We'd broken down once
while I was driving her home; it had made us two hours late and her
father had come close to beating me senseless. It was only the oil on
my hands that had convinced him of our story.

I closed my eyes.

"Can't see anything," Charley said, jerking me back to cold reality.
"Windscreen's frozen up on the inside."

"Take us ages to clear the doors."

"What do you want to do that for?" Brand said. "Dead car,
probably full of dead people."

"Dead people may have guns and food and fuel," I said. "Going
to give us a hand?"

Brand glanced at the dark windshield, the contents of the car
hidden by ice and shadowed by the weight of snow surrounding it.
He sat gently on his rucksack, and when he saw it would take his
weight without sinking in the snow, he re-lit his joint and stared out
to sea. I wondered whether he'd even notice if we left him there.

"We could uncover the passenger door," Charley said. "Driver's
side is stuck fast in the drift, take us hours."

We both set about trying to shift snow away from the car. "Keep
your eyes open," I said to Brand. He just nodded and watched the
sea lift and drop its thickening ice-flows. I used the shotgun as a
crutch to lift myself onto the bonnet, and from there to the covered
roof.

"What?" Charley said. I ignored her, turning a slow circle, trying
to pick out any movement against the fields of white. To the west
lay the manor, a couple of miles away and long since hidden by
creases in the landscape. To the north the ground still rose steadily
away from the sea, rocks protruding here and there along with an
occasional clump of trees hardy enough to survive Atlantic storms.
Nothing moved. The shower was turning quickly into a storm and
I felt suddenly afraid. The manor was at least three miles behind
us; the village seven miles ahead. We were in the middle, three weak
humans slowly freezing as nature freaked out and threw weeks of
snow and ice at us. And here we were, convinced we could defeat
it, certain in our own puny minds that we were the rulers here, we
called the shots. However much we polluted and contaminated, I

knew, we would never call the shots. Nature may let us live within it, but in the end it would purge and clean itself. And whether there would be room for us in the new world . . .

Perhaps this was the first stage of that cleansing. While civilization slaughtered itself, disease and extremes of weather took advantage of our distraction to pick off the weak.

"We should get back," I said.

"But the village—"

"Charley, it's almost two. It'll start getting dark in two hours, maximum. We can't travel in the dark; we might walk right by the village, or stumble onto one of those ice overhangs at the cliff edge. Brand here may get so doped he thinks we're ghosts and shoot us with his pop-gun."

"Hey!"

"But Boris . . ." Charley said. "He's . . . we need help. To bury him. We need to tell someone."

I climbed carefully down from the car roof and landed in the snow beside her. "We'll take a look in the car. Then we should get back. It'll help no one if we freeze to death out here."

"I'm not cold," she said defiantly.

"That's because you're moving, you're working. When you walk you sweat and you'll stay warm. When we have to stop – and eventually we will – you'll stop moving. Your sweat will freeze, and so will you. We'll all freeze. They'll find us in the thaw, you and me huddled up for warmth, Brand with a frozen reefer still in his gob."

Charley smiled, Brand scowled. Both expressions pleased me.

"The door's frozen shut," she said.

"I'll use my key." I punched at the glass with the butt of the shotgun. After three attempts the glass shattered and I used my gloved hands to clear it all away. I caught a waft of something foul and stale. Charley stepped back with a slight groan. Brand was oblivious.

We peered inside the car, leaning forward so that the weak light could filter in around us.

There was a dead man in the driver's seat. He was frozen solid, hunched up under several blankets, only his eyes and nose visible. Icicles hung from both. His eyelids were still open. On the dashboard a candle had burnt down to nothing more than a puddle of wax, imitating the ice as it dripped forever toward the floor. The scene was so still it was eerie, like a painting so life-like that textures and shapes could be felt. I noticed the driver's door handle was jammed open, though the door had not budged against the snowdrift burying that side of the car. At the end he had obviously attempted to get out. I shuddered as I tried to imagine this man's lonely death. It was the second body I'd seen in two days.

"Well?" Brand called from behind us.

"Your drug supplier," Charley said. "Car's full of snow."

I snorted, pleased to hear the humour, but when I looked at her she seemed as sad and forlorn as ever. "Maybe we should see if he brought us anything useful," she said, and I nodded.

Charley was smaller than me so she said she'd go. I went to protest but she was already wriggling through the shattered window, and a minute later she'd thrown out everything loose she could find. She came back out without looking at me.

There was a rucksack half full of canned foods; a petrol can with a swill of fuel in the bottom; a novel frozen at page ninety; some plastic bottles filled with piss and split by the ice; a rifle, but no ammunition; a smaller rucksack with wallet, some papers, an electronic credit card; a photo wallet frozen shut; a plastic bag full of shit; a screwed-up newspaper as hard as wood.

Everything was frozen.

"Let's go," I said. Brand and Charley took a couple of items each and shouldered their rucksacks. I picked up the rifle. We took everything except the shit and piss.

It took us four hours to get back to the manor. Three times on the way Brand said he'd seen something bounding through the snow – a stag, he said, big and white with sparkling antlers – and we dropped everything and went into a defensive huddle. But nothing ever materialized from the worsening storm, even though our imaginations painted all sorts of horrors behind and beyond the snowflakes. If there was anything out there, it kept itself well hidden.

The light was fast fading as we arrived back. Our tracks had been all but covered, and it was only later that I realized how staggeringly lucky we'd been to even find our way home. Perhaps something was on our side, guiding us, steering us back to the manor. Perhaps it was the change in nature taking us home, preparing us for what was to come next.

It was the last favour we were granted.

Hayden cooked us some soup as the others huddled around the fire, listening to our story and trying so hard not to show their disappointment. Brand kept chiming in about the things he'd seen in the snow. Even Ellie's face held the taint of fading hope.

"Boris's angels?" Rosalie suggested. "He *may* have seen angels, you know. They're not averse to steering things their way, when it suits them." Nobody answered.

Charley was crying again, shivering by the fire. Rosalie had wrapped her in blankets and now hugged her close.

"The gun looks okay." Ellie said. She'd sat at the table and stripped and oiled the rifle, listening to us all as we talked. She illustrated the fact by pointing it at the wall and squeezing the trigger a few times. *Click click click.* There was no ammunition for it.

"What about the body?" Rosalie asked. "Did you see who it was?"

I frowned. "What do you mean?"

"Well, if it was someone coming along the road toward the manor, maybe one of us knew him." We were all motionless save for Ellie, who still rooted through the contents of the car. She'd already put the newspaper on the floor so that it could dry out, in the hope of being able to read at least some of it. We'd made out the date: one week ago. The television had stopped showing pictures two weeks ago. There was a week of history in there, if only we could save it.

"He was frozen stiff," I said. "We didn't get a good look . . . and anyway, who'd be coming here? And why? Maybe it was a good job—"

Ellie gasped. There was a tearing sound as she peeled apart more pages of the photo wallet and gasped again, this time struggling to draw in a breath afterwards.

"Ellie?"

She did not answer. The others had turned to her but she seemed not to notice. She saw nothing, other than the photographs in her hand. She stared at them for an endless few seconds, eyes moist yet unreadable in the glittering firelight. Then she scraped the chair back across the polished floor, crumpled the photos into her back pocket and walked quickly from the room.

I followed, glancing at the others to indicate that they should stay where they were. None of them argued. Ellie was already halfway up the long staircase by the time I entered the hallway, but it was not until the final stair that she stopped, turned and answered my soft calling.

"My husband," she said, "Jack. I haven't seen him for two years." A tear ran icily down her cheek. "We never really made it, you know?" She looked at the wall beside her, as though she could stare straight through and discern logic and truth in the blanked-out landscape beyond. "He was coming here. For me. To find me."

There was nothing I could say. Ellie seemed to forget I was there and she mumbled the next few words to herself. Then she turned and disappeared from view along the upstairs corridor, shadow dancing in the light of disturbed candles.

Back in the living room I told the others that Ellie was all right, she had gone to bed, she was tired and cold and as human as the rest of us. I did not let on about her dead husband, I figured it was really none of their business. Charley glared at me with bloodshot eyes, and I was sure she'd figured it out. Brand flicked bits of carrot from his soup into the fire and watched them sizzle to nothing.

We went to bed soon after. Alone in my room I sat at the window for a long time, huddled in clothes and blankets, staring out at the moonlit brightness of the snowdrifts and the fat flakes still falling. I tried to imagine Ellie's estranged husband struggling to steer the car through deepening snow, the radiator clogging in the drift it had buried its nose in, splitting, gushing boiling water and steaming instantly into an ice-trap. Sitting there, perhaps not knowing just how near he was, thinking of his wife and how much he needed to see her. And I tried to imagine what desperate events must have driven him to do such a thing, though I did not think too hard.

A door opened and closed quietly, footsteps, another door slipped open to allow a guest entry. I wondered who was sharing a bed tonight.

I saw Jayne, naked and beautiful in the snow, bearing no sign of the illness that had killed her. She beckoned me, drawing me nearer, and at last a door was opening for me as well, a shape coming into the room, white material floating around its hips, or perhaps they were limbs, membranous and thin . . .

My eyes snapped open and I sat up on the bed. I was still dressed from the night before. Dawn streamed in the window and my candle had burnt down to nothing.

Ellie stood next to the bed. Her eyes were red-rimmed and swollen. I tried to pretend I had not noticed.

"Happy Christmas," she said. "Come on. Brand's dead."

Brand was lying just beyond the smashed conservatory doors behind the kitchen. There was a small courtyard area here, protected somewhat by an overhanging roof so that the snow was only about knee-deep. Most of it was red. A drift had already edged its way into the conservatory, and the beer cans on the shelf had frozen and split. No more beer.

He had been punctured by countless holes, each the width of a thumb, all of them clogged with hardened blood. One eye stared hopefully out to the hidden horizon, the other was absent. His hair was also missing; it looked like he'd been scalped. There were bits of him all around – a finger here, a splash of brain there – but he was less mutilated than Boris had been. At least we could see that this smudge in the snow had once been Brand.

Hayden was standing next to him, posing daintily in an effort to avoid stepping in the blood. It was a lost cause. "What the hell was he doing out here?" he asked in disgust.

"I heard doors opening last night," I said. "Maybe he came for a walk. Or a smoke."

"The door was mine," Rosalie said softly. She had appeared behind us and nudged in between Ellie and me. She wore a long, creased shirt. Brand's shirt, I noticed. "Brand was with me until three o'clock this morning. Then he left to go back to his own room, said he was feeling ill. We thought perhaps you shouldn't know about us." Her eyes were wide in an effort not to cry. "We thought everyone would laugh."

Nobody answered. Nobody laughed. Rosalie looked at Brand with more shock than sadness, and I wondered just how often he'd opened her door in the night. The insane, unfair notion that she may even be relieved flashed across my mind, one of those awful thoughts you try to expunge but which hangs around like a guilty secret.

"Maybe we should go inside," I said to Rosalie, but she gave me such an icy glare that I turned away, looking at Brand's shattered body rather than her piercing eyes.

"I'm a big girl now," she said. I could hear her rapid breathing as she tried to contain the disgust and shock at what she saw. I wondered if she'd ever seen a dead body. Most people had, nowadays.

Charley was nowhere to be seen. "I didn't wake her," Ellie said when I queried. "She had enough to handle yesterday. I thought she shouldn't really see this. No need."

And you? I thought, noticing Ellie's puffy eyes, the gauntness of her face, her hands fisting open and closed at her sides. *Are you all right? Did you have enough to handle yesterday?*

"What the hell do we do with him?" Hayden asked. He was still standing closer to Brand than the rest of us, hugging himself to try to preserve some of the warmth from sleep. "I mean, Boris was all over the place, from what I hear. But Brand . . . we have to do something. Bury him, or something. It's Christmas, for God's sake."

"The ground's like iron," I protested.

"So we take it in turns digging," Rosalie said quietly.

"It'll take us—"

"Then I'll do it myself." She walked out into the blooded snow and shattered glass in bare feet, bent over Brand's body and grabbed under each armpit as if to lift him. She was naked beneath the shirt. Hayden stared in frank fascination. I turned away, embarrassed for myself more than for Rosalie.

"Wait," Ellie sighed. "Rosalie, wait. Let's all dress properly, then we'll come and bury him. Rosalie." The girl stood and smoothed Brand's shirt down over her thighs, perhaps realizing what she had put on display. She looked up at the sky and caught the morning's first snowflake on her nose.

"Snowing," she said. "Just for a fucking change."

We went inside. Hayden remained in the kitchen with the outside door shut and bolted while the rest of us went upstairs to dress, wake Charley and tell her the grim Yule tidings. Once Rosalie's door had closed I followed Ellie along to her room. She opened her door for me and invited me in, obviously knowing I needed to talk.

Her place was a mess. Perhaps, I thought, she was so busy being strong and mysterious that she had no time for tidying up. Clothes were strewn across the floor, a false covering like the snow outside. Used plates were piled next to her bed, those at the bottom already blurred with mould, the uppermost still showing the remains of the meal we'd had before Boris had been killed. Spaghetti Bolognese, I recalled, to Hayden's own recipe, rich and tangy with tinned tomatoes, strong with garlic, the helpings massive. Somewhere out there Boris's last meal lay frozen in the snow, half digested, torn from his guts—

I snorted and closed my eyes. Another terrible thought that wouldn't go away.

"Brand really saw things in the snow, didn't he?" Ellie asked.

"Yes, he was pretty sure. At least, *a* thing. He said it was like a stag, except white. It was bounding along next to us, he said. We stopped a few times but I'm certain I never saw anything. Don't think Charley did, either." I made space on Ellie's bed and sat down. "Why?"

Ellie walked to the window and opened the curtains. The snowstorm had started in earnest, and although her window faced the Atlantic all we could see was a sea of white. She rested her forehead on the cold glass, her breath misting, fading, misting again. "I've seen something too," she said.

Ellie. Seeing things in the snow. Ellie was the nearest we had to a leader, though none of us had ever wanted one. She was strong, if distant. Intelligent, if a little straight with it. She'd never been much of a laugh, even before things had turned to shit, and her dogged conservatism in someone so young annoyed me no end.

Ellie, seeing things in the snow.

I could not bring myself to believe it. I did not want to. If I did accept it then there really were things out there, because Ellie did not lie, and she was not prone to fanciful journeys of the imagination.

"What something?" I asked at last, fearing it a question I would never wish to be answered. But I could not simply ignore it. I could not sit here and listen to Ellie opening up, then stand and walk away. Not with Boris frozen out there, not with Brand still cooling into the landscape.

She rocked her head against the glass. "Don't know. Something white. So how did I see it?" She turned from the window, stared at me, crossed her arms. "From this window," she said. "Two days ago. Just before Charley found Boris. Something flitting across the snow like a bird, except it left faint tracks. As big as a fox, perhaps, but it had more legs. Certainly not a deer."

"Or one of Boris's angels?"

She shook her head and smiled, but there was no humour there. There rarely was. "Don't tell anyone," she said. "I don't want anyone to know. But! We will have to be careful. Take the guns when we try to bury Brand. A couple of us keep a look-out while the others dig. Though I doubt we'll even get through the snow."

"You and guns," I said perplexed. I didn't know how to word what I was trying to ask.

Ellie smiled wryly. "Me and guns. I hate guns."

I stared at her, saying nothing, using silence to pose the next question.

"I have a history," she said. And that was all.

Later, downstairs in the kitchen, Charley told us what she'd managed to read in the paper from the frozen car. In the week since we'd picked up the last TV signal and the paper was printed, things had gone from bad to worse. The illness that had killed my Jayne was claiming millions across the globe. The USA blamed Iraq. Russia blamed China. Blame continued to waste lives. There was civil unrest and shootings in the streets, mass-burials at sea, martial law, air strikes, food shortages . . . the words melded into one another as Rosalie recited the reports.

Hayden was trying to cook mince pies without the mince. He was using stewed apples instead, and the kitchen stank sickeningly sweet. None of us felt particularly festive.

Outside, in the heavy snow that even now was attempting to drift in and cover Brand, we were all twitchy. Whoever or – now more likely – whatever had done this could still be around. Guns were held at the ready.

We wrapped him in an old sheet and enclosed this in torn black plastic bags until there was no white or red showing. Ellie and I dragged him around the corner of the house to where there were some old flowerbeds. We stared to dig where we remembered them to be, but when we got through the snow the ground was too hard. In the end we left him on the surface of the frozen earth and covered the hole back in with snow, mumbling about burying him when the thaw came. The whole process had an unsettling sense of permanence.

As if the snow would never melt.

Later, staring from the dining room window as Hayden brought in a platter of old vegetables as our Christmas feast, I saw something big and white skimming across the surface of the snow. It moved too quickly for me to make it out properly, but I was certain I saw wings.

I turned away from the window, glanced at Ellie and said nothing.

II: The Colour of Fear

During the final few days of Jayne's life I had felt completely hemmed in. Not only physically trapped within our home – and more often the bedroom where she lay – but also mentally hindered. It was a feeling I hated, felt guilty about and tried desperately to relieve, but it was always there.

I stayed, holding her hand for hour after terrible hour, our palms fused by sweat, her face pasty and contorted by agonies I could barely imagine. Sometimes she would be conscious and alert, sitting up in bed and listening as I read to her, smiling at the humorous parts, trying to ignore the sad ones. She would ask me questions about how things were in the outside world, and I would lie and tell her they were getting better. There was no need to add to her misery. Other times she would be a shadow of her old self, a grey stain on the bed with liquid limbs and weak bowels, a screaming thing with bloody growths sprouting across her skin and pumping their venom inward with uncontrollable, unstoppable tenacity. At these times I would talk truthfully and tell her the reality of things – that the world was going to shit and she would be much better off when she left it.

Even then I did not tell her the complete truth: that I wished I were going with her. Just in case she could still hear.

Wherever I went during those final few days I was under assault, besieged by images of Jayne, thoughts of her impending death, vague ideas of what would happen after she had gone. I tried to fill the landscape of time laid out before me, but Jayne never figured and so the landscape was bare. She was my whole world; without her I could picture nothing to live for. My mind was never free although sometimes, when a doctor found time to visit our house and *tut* and sigh over Jayne's wasting body, I would go for a walk. Mostly she barely knew the doctor was there, for which I was grateful. There was nothing he could. I would not be able to bear even the faintest glimmer of hope in her eyes.

I strolled through the park opposite our house, staying to the paths so that I did not risk stepping on discarded needles or stumbling across suicides decaying slowly back to nature. The trees were as beautiful as ever, huge emeralds against the grimly polluted sky. Somehow they bled the taint of humanity from their systems. They adapted, changed, and our arrival had really done little to halt their progress. A few years of poisons and disease, perhaps. A shaping of the landscape upon which we projected an idea of control. But when we were all dead and gone our industrial disease on the planet would be little more than a few twisted, corrupted rings in the lifetime of the oldest trees. I wished we could adapt so well.

When Jayne died there was no sense of release. My grief was as great as if she'd been killed at the height of health, her slow decline doing nothing to prepare me for the dread that enveloped me at the moment of her last strangled sigh. Still I was under siege, this time by death. The certainty of its black fingers rested on my shoulders day and night, long past the hour of Jayne's hurried burial in a local football ground alongside a thousand others. I would turn around sometimes and try to see past it, make out some ray of hope in a stranger's gaze. But there was always the blackness bearing down on me, clouding my vision and the gaze of others, promising doom soon.

It's ironic that it was not death that truly scared me, but living. Without Jayne the world was nothing but an empty, dying place.

Then I had come here, an old manor on the rugged South West coast. I'd thought that solitude – a distance between me and the terrible place the world was slowly becoming – would be a balm to my suffering. In reality it was little more than a placebo and realizing that negated it. I felt more trapped than ever.

The morning after Brand's death and botched burial – Boxing Day – I sat at my bedroom window and watched nature laying siege. The snow hugged the landscape like a funeral shroud in negative. The coast was hidden by the cliffs, but I could see the sea further out. There was something that I thought at first to be an iceberg and it took me a few minutes to figure out what it really was; the upturned hull of a big boat. A ferry, perhaps, or one of the huge cruise liners being used to ship people south, away from blighted Britain to the false promise of Australia. I was glad I could not see any more detail. I wondered what we would find washed up in the rock pools that morning, were Charley and I to venture down to the sea.

If I stared hard at the snowbanks, the fields of virgin white, the humped shadows that were our ruined and hidden cars, I could see no sign of movement. An occasional shadow passed across the snow, though it could have been from a bird flying in front of the sun. But if I relaxed my gaze, tried not to concentrate too hard, lowered my eyelids, then I could see them. Sometimes they skimmed low and fast over the snow, twisting like sea-serpents or Chinese dragons and throwing up a fine mist of flakes behind them. At other times they lay still and watchful, fading into the background if I looked directly at them until one shadow looked much like the next, but could be so different.

I wanted to talk about them. I wanted to ask Ellie just what the hell they were, because I knew that she had seen them too. I wanted to know what was happening and why it was happening to us. But I had some mad idea that to mention them would make them real, like ghosts in the cupboard and slithering wet things beneath the bed. Best ignore them and they would go away.

I counted a dozen white shapes that morning.

"Anyone dead today?" Rosalie asked.

The statement shocked me, made me wonder just what sort of relationship she and Brand had had, but we all ignored her. No need to aggravate an argument.

Charley sat close to Rosalie, as if a sharing of grief would halve it. Hayden was cooking up bacon and bagels long past their sell-by date. Ellie had not yet come downstairs. She'd been stalking the manor all night, and now we were up she was washing and changing.

"What do we do today?" Charley asked. "Are we going to try to get away again? Get to the village for help?"

I sighed and went to say something, but the thought of those things out in the snow kept me quiet. Nobody else spoke, and the silence was the only answer required.

We ate our stale breakfast, drank tea clotted with powdered milk, listened to the silence outside. It had snowed again in the night and our tracks from the day before had been obliterated. Standing at the sink to wash up I stared through the window, and it was like looking upon the same day as yesterday, the day before, and the day before that; no signs of our presence existed. All footprints had vanished, all echoes of voices swallowed by the snow, shadows covered with another six inches and frozen like corpses in a glacier. I wondered what patterns and traces the snow would hold this evening, when darkness closed in to wipe us away once more.

"We have to tell someone," Charley said. "Something's happening, we should tell someone. We have to do something, we can't just . . ." She trailed off, staring into a cooling cup of tea, perhaps remembering a time before all this had begun, or imagining she could remember. "This is crazy."

"It's God," Rosalie said.

"Huh?" Hayden was already peeling wrinkled old vegetables ready for lunch, constantly busy, always doing something to keep his mind off everything else. I wondered how much really went on behind his fringed brow, how much theorizing he did while he was boiling, how much nostalgia he wallowed in as familiar cooking smells settled into his clothes.

"It's God, fucking us over one more time. Crazy, as Charley says. God and crazy are synonymous."

"Rosie," I said, knowing she hated the shortened name, "if it's not constructive, don't bother. None of this will bring—"

"Anything is more constructive than sod-all, which is what you lot have got to say this morning. We wake up one morning without one of us dead, and you're all tongue-tied. Bored? Is that it?"

"Rosalie, why—"

"Shut it, Charley. You more than anyone should be thinking about all this. Wondering why the hell we came here a few weeks ago to escape all the shit, and now we've landed right in the middle of it.

Right up to our armpits. Drowning in it. Maybe one of us is a Jonah and it's followed—"

"And you think it's God?" I said. I knew that asking the question would give her open opportunity to rant, but in a way I felt she was right, we did need to talk. Sitting here stewing in our own thoughts could not help anyone.

"Oh yes, it's His Holiness," she nodded, "sitting on his pedestal of lost souls, playing around one day and deciding, hmm, maybe I'll have some fun today, been a year since a decent earthquake, a few months since the last big volcano eruption. Soooo, what can I do?"

Ellie appeared then, sat at the table and poured a cup of cold tea that looked like sewer water. Her appearance did nothing to mar Rosalie's flow.

"I know, he says, I'll nudge things to one side, turn them slightly askew, give the world a gasp before I've cleaned my teeth. Just a little, not so that anyone will notice for a while. Get them paranoid. Get them looking over their shoulders at each other. See how the wrinkly pink bastards deal with that one!"

"Why would He do that?" Hayden said.

Rosalie stood and put on a deep voice. "Forget me, will they? I'll show them. Turn over and open your legs, humanity, for I shall root you up the arse."

"Just shut up!" Charley screeched. The kitchen went ringingly quiet, even Rosalie sitting slowly down. "You're full of this sort of shit, Rosie. Always telling us how we're being controlled, manipulated. Who by? Ever seen anyone? There's a hidden agenda behind everything for you, isn't there? If there's no toilet paper after you've had a crap you'd blame it on the global dirty-arse conspiracy!"

Hysteria hung silently in the room. The urge to cry grabbed me, but also a yearning to laugh out loud. The air was heavy with held breaths and barely restrained comments, thick with the potential for violence.

"So," Ellie said at last, her voice little more than a whisper, "let's hear some truths."

"What?" Rosalie obviously expected an extension of her foolish monologue. Ellie, however, cut her down.

"Well, for starters has anyone else seen things in the snow?" Heads shook. My own shook as well. I wondered who else was lying with me. "Anyone seen anything strange out there at all?" she continued. "Maybe not the things Brand and Boris saw, but something else?" Again, shaken heads. An uncomfortable shuffling from Hayden as he stirred something on the gas cooker.

"I saw God looking down on us," Rosalie said quietly, "with blood in his eyes." She did not continue or elaborate, did not go off on one of her rants. I think that's why her strange comment stayed with me.

"Right," said Ellie, "then may I make a suggestion. Firstly, there's no point trying to get to the village. The snow's even deeper than it was yesterday, it's colder and freezing to death for the sake of it will achieve nothing. If we did manage to find help, Boris and Brand are long past it." She paused, waiting for assent.

"Fair enough," Charley said quietly. "Yeah, you're right."

"Secondly, we need to make sure the manor is secure. We need to protect ourselves from whatever got at Brand and Boris. There are a dozen rooms on the ground floor, we only use two or three of them. Check the others. Make sure windows are locked and storm shutters are bolted. Make sure French doors aren't loose or liable to break open at the slightest . . . breeze, or whatever."

"What do you think the things out there are?" Hayden asked. "Lock pickers?"

Ellie glanced at his back, looked at me, shrugged. "No," she said, "I don't think so. But there's no use being complacent. We can't try to make it out, so we should do the most we can here. The snow can't last forever, and when it finally melts we'll go to the village then. Agreed?"

Heads nodded.

"If the village is still there," Rosalie cut in. "If everyone isn't dead. If the disease hasn't wiped out most of the country. If a war doesn't start somewhere in the meantime."

"Yes," Ellie sighed impatiently, "if all those things don't happen." She nodded at me. "We'll do the two rooms at the back. The rest of you check the others. There are some tools in the big cupboard under the stairs, some nails and hammers if you need them, a crowbar too. And if you think you need timber to nail across windows . . . if it'll make you feel any better . . . tear up some floorboards in the dining room. They're hardwood, they're strong."

"Oh, let battle commence!" Rosalie cried. She stood quickly, her chair falling onto its back, and stalked from the room with a swish of her long skirts. Charley followed.

Ellie and I went to the rear of the manor. In the first of the large rooms the snow had drifted up against the windows to cut out any view or light from outside. For an instant it seemed as if nothing existed beyond the glass and I wondered if that was the case, then why were we trying to protect ourselves?

Against nothing.

"What do you think is out there?" I asked.

"Have you seen anything?"

I paused. There was something, but nothing I could easily identify or put a name to. What I had seen had been way beyond my ken, white shadows apparent against whiteness. "No," I said, "nothing."

Ellie turned from the window and looked at me in the half-light, and it was obvious that she knew I was lying. "Well, if you do see something, don't tell."

"Why?"

"Boris and Brand told," she said. She did not say any more. They'd seen angels and stags in the snow and they'd talked about it, and now they were dead.

She pushed at one of the window frames. Although the damp timber fragmented at her touch, the snowdrift behind it was as effective as a vault door. We moved on to the next window. The room was noisy with unspoken thoughts, and it was only a matter of time before they made themselves heard.

"You think someone in here has something to do with Brand and Boris," I said.

Ellie sat on one of the wide windowsills and sighed deeply. She ran a hand through her spiky hair and rubbed at her neck. I wondered whether she'd had any sleep at all last night. I wondered whose door had been opening and closing; the prickle of jealousy was crazy under the circumstances. I realized all of a sudden how much Ellie reminded me of Jayne, and I swayed under the sudden barrage of memory.

"Who?" she said. "Rosie? Hayden? Don't be soft."

"But you do, don't you?" I said again.

She nodded. Then shook her head. Shrugged. "I don't bloody know, I'm not Sherlock Holmes. It's just strange that Brand and Boris . . ." She trailed off, avoiding my eyes.

"I have seen something out there," I said to break the awkward silence. "Something in the snow. Can't say what. Shadows. Fleeting glimpses. Like everything I see is from the corner of my eye."

Ellie stared at me for so long that I thought she'd died there on the windowsill, a victim of my admission, another dead person to throw outside and let freeze until the thaw came and we could do our burying.

"You've seen what I've seen," she said eventually, verbalizing the trust between us. It felt good, but it also felt a little dangerous. A trust like that could alienate the others, not consciously but in our mind's eye. By working and thinking closer together, perhaps we would drive them further away.

We moved to the next window.

"I've known there was something since you found Jack in his car," Ellie said. "He'd never have just sat there and waited to die. He'd have tried to get out, to get here, no matter how dangerous. He wouldn't have sat watching the candle burn down, listening to the wind, feeling his eyes freeze over. It's just not like him to give in."

"So why did he? Why didn't he get out?"

"There was something waiting for him outside the car. Something he was trying to keep away from." She rattled a window, stared at the snow pressed up against the glass. "Something that would make him rather freeze to death than face it."

We moved on to the last window, Ellie reached out to touch the rusted clasp and there was a loud crash. Glass broke, wood struck wood, someone screamed, all from a distance.

We spun around and ran from the room, listening to the shrieks. Two voices now, a man and a woman, the woman's muffled. Somewhere in the manor, someone else was dying.

The reaction to death is sometimes as violent as death itself. Shock throws a cautious coolness over the senses, but your stomach still knots, your skin stings as if the Reaper is glaring at you as well. For a second you live that death, and then shameful relief floods in when you see it's someone else.

Such were my thoughts as we turned a corner into the main hallway of the manor. Hayden was hammering at the library door, crashing his fists into the wood hard enough to draw blood. "Charley!" he shouted, again and again. "Charley!" The door shook under his assault but it did not budge. Tears streaked his face, dribble strung from chin to chest. The dark old wood of the door sucked up the blood from his split knuckles. "Charley!"

Ellie and I arrived just ahead of Rosalie.

"Hayden!" Rosalie shouted.

"Charley! In there! She went in and locked the door, and there was a crash and she was screaming!"

"Why did she—?" Rosalie began, but Ellie shushed us all with one wave of her hand.

Silence. "No screaming now," she said.

Then we heard other noises through the door, faint and tremulous as if picked up from a distance along a bad telephone line. They sounded like chewing; bone snapping; flesh ripping. I could not believe what I was hearing, but at the same time I remembered the bodies of Boris and Brand. Suddenly I did not want to open the door. I wanted to defy whatever it was laying siege to us here by ignoring the results of its actions. Forget Charley, continue checking the windows and doors, deny whoever or whatever it was the satisfaction—

"Charley," I said quietly. She was a small woman, fragile, strong but sensitive. She'd told me once, sitting at the base of the cliffs before it had begun to snow, how she loved to sit and watch the sea. It made her feel safe. It made her feel a part of nature. She'd never hurt anyone. "Charley."

Hayden kicked at the door again and I added my weight, shouldering into the tough old wood, jarring my body painfully with each impact. Ellie did the same and soon we were taking it in turns. The noises continued between each impact – increased in volume if anything – and our assault became more frantic to cover them up.

If the manor had not been so old and decrepit we would never have broken in. The door was probably as old as all of us put together, but its surround had been replaced some time in the past. Softwood painted as hardwood had slowly crumbled in the damp atmosphere and after a minute the door burst in, frame splintering into the coldness of the library.

One of the three big windows had been smashed. Shattered glass and snapped mullions hung crazily from the frame. The cold had already made the room its home, laying a fine sheen of frost across the thousands of books, hiding some of their titles from view as if to conceal whatever tumultuous history they contained. Snow flurried in, hung around for a while then chose somewhere to settle. It did not melt. Once on the inside, this room was now a part of the outside.

As was Charley.

The area around the broken window was red and Charley had spread. Bits of her hung on the glass like hellish party streamers. Other parts had melted into the snow outside and turned it pink. Some of her was recognizable – her hair splayed out across the soft whiteness, a hand fisted around a melting clump of ice – other parts had never been seen before, because they'd always been inside.

I leaned over and puked. My vomit cleared a space of frost on the floor so I did it again, moving into the room. My stomach was in agonized spasms but I enjoyed seeing the white sheen vanish, as if I were claiming the room back for a time. Then I went to my knees and tried to forget what I'd seen, shake it from my head, pound it from my temples. I felt hands close around my wrists to stop me from punching myself, but I fell forward and struck my forehead on the cold timber floor. If I could forget, if I could drive the image away, perhaps it would no longer be true.

But there was the smell. And the steam, rising from the open body and misting what glass remained. Charley's last breath.

"Shut the door!" I shouted. "Nail it shut! Quickly!"

Ellie had helped me from the room, and now Hayden was pulling on the broken-in door to try to close it again. Rosalie came back from the dining room with a few splintered floorboards, her face pale, eyes staring somewhere no one else could see.

"Hurry!" I shouted. I felt a distance pressing in around me; the walls receding; the ceiling rising. Voices turned slow and deep, movement became stilted. My stomach heaved again but there was nothing left to bring up. I was the centre of everything but it was all leaving me, all sight and sound and scent fleeing my faint. And then, clear and bright, Jayne's laugh broke through. Only once, but I knew it was her.

Something brushed my cheek and gave warmth to my face. My jaw clicked and my head turned to one side, slowly but inexorably. Something white blurred across my vision and my other cheek burst into warmth, and I was glad, the cold was the enemy, the cold brought the snow, which brought the fleeting things I had seen outside, things without a name or, perhaps, things with a million names. Or things with a name I already knew.

The warmth was good.

Ellie's mouth moved slowly and watery rumbles tumbled forth. Her words took shape in my mind, hauling themselves together just as events took on their own speed once more.

"Snap out of it," Ellie said, and slapped me across the face again.

Another sound dragged itself together. I could not identify it, but I knew where it was coming from. The others were staring fearfully at the door, Hayden was still leaning back with both hands around the handle, straining to get as far away as possible without letting go.

Scratching. Sniffing. Something rifling through books, snuffling in long-forgotten corners at dust from long-dead people. A slow regular beat, which could have been footfalls or a heartbeat. I realized it was my own and another sound took its place.

"What . . .?"

Ellie grabbed the tops of my arms and shook me harshly. "You with us? You back with us now?"

I nodded, closing my eyes at the swimming sensation in my head. Vertical fought with horizontal and won out this time. "Yeah."

"Rosalie," Ellie whispered. "Get more boards. Hayden, keep hold of that handle. Just keep hold." She looked at me. "Hand me the nails as I hold my hand out. Now listen. Once I start banging, it may attract—"

"What are you doing?" I said.

"Nailing the bastards in."

I thought of the shapes I had watched from my bedroom window, the shadows flowing through other shadows, the ease with which they moved, the strength and beauty they exuded as they passed from drift to drift without leaving any trace behind. I laughed. "You think you can keep them in?"

Rosalie turned a fearful face my way. Her eyes were wide, her mouth hanging open as if readying for a scream.

"You think a few nails will stop them—?"

"Just shut up," Ellie hissed, and she slapped me around the face once more. This time I was all there, and the slap was a burning sting rather than a warm caress. My head whipped around and by the time I looked up again Ellie was heaving a board against the doors, steadying it with one elbow and weighing a hammer in the other hand.

Only Rosalie looked at me. What I'd said was still plain on her face – the chance that whatever had done these foul things would find their way in, take us apart as it had done to Boris, to Brand and now to Charley. And I could say nothing to comfort her. I shook my head, though I had no idea what message I was trying to convey.

Ellie held out her hand and clicked her fingers. Rosalie passed her a nail.

I stepped forward and pressed the board across the door. We had to tilt it so that each end rested across the frame. There were still secretive sounds from inside, like a fox rummaging through a bin late at night. I tried to imagine the scene in the room now but I could not. My mind would not place what I had seen outside into the library, could not stretch to that feat of imagination. I was glad.

For one terrible second I wanted to see. It would only take a kick at the door, a single heave and the whole room would be open to view, and then I would know whatever was in there for the second before it hit me. Jayne perhaps, a white Jayne from elsewhere, holding out her hands so that I could join her once more, just as she had promised on her death bed. *I'll be with you again,* she had said, and the words had terrified me and comforted me and kept me going ever since. Sometimes I thought they were all that kept me alive *I'll be with you again.*

"Jayne . . ."

Ellie brought the hammer down. The sound was explosive and I felt the impact transmitted through the wood and into my arms. I expected another impact a second later from the opposite way, but instead we heard the sound of something scampering through the already shattered window.

Ellie kept hammering until the board held firm, then she started another, and another. She did not stop until most of the door was covered, nails protruding at crazy angles, splinters under her fingernails, sweat running across her face and staining her armpits.

"Has it gone?" Rosalie asked. "Is it still in there?"

"Is what still in there, precisely?" I muttered.

We all stood that way for a while, panting with exertion, adrenaline priming us for the chase.

"I think," Ellie said after a while, "we should make some plans."

"What about Charley?" I asked. They all knew what I meant: *we can't just leave her there; we have to do something; she'd do the same for us.*

"Charley's dead," Ellie said, without looking at anyone. "Come on." She headed for the kitchen.

"What happened?" Ellie asked.

Hayden was shaking. "I told you. We were checking the rooms, Charley ran in before me and locked the door, I heard glass breaking and . . ." He trailed off

"And?"

"Screams. I heard her screaming. I heard her dying."

The kitchen fell silent as we all recalled the cries, as if they were still echoing around the manor. They meant different things to each of us. For me death always meant Jayne.

"Okay, this is how I see things," Ellie said. "There's a wild animal, or wild animals, out there now."

"What wild animals!" Rosalie scoffed. "Mutant badgers come to eat us up? Hedgehogs gone bad?"

"I don't know, but pray it is animals. If a person has done all this, then they'll be able to get in to us. However fucking goofy crazy, they'll have the intelligence to get in. No way to stop them. Nothing we could do." She patted the shotgun resting across her thighs as if to reassure herself of its presence.

"But what animals—?"

"Do you know what's happening everywhere?" Ellie shouted, not just at doubting Rosie but at us all. "Do you realize that the world's changing? Every day we wake up there's a new world facing us. And every day there're fewer of us left. I mean the big us, the world-wide us, us humans." Her voice became quieter. "How long before one morning, no one wakes up?"

"What has what's happening elsewhere got to do with all this?" I asked, although inside I already had an idea of what Ellie meant. I think maybe I'd known for a while, but now my mind was opening up, my beliefs stretching, levering fantastic truths into place. They fitted; that terrified me.

"I mean, it's all changing. A disease is wiping out millions and no one knows where it came from. Unrest everywhere, shootings, bombings. Nuclear bombs in the Med, for Christ's sake. You've heard what people have called it; it's the Ruin. Capital R, people. The world's gone bad. Maybe what's happening here is just not that unusual any more."

"That doesn't tell us what they are," Rosalie said. "Doesn't explain why they're here, or where they come from. Doesn't tell us why Charley did what she did."

"Maybe she wanted to be with Boris again," Hayden said.

I simply stared at him. "I've seen them," I said, and Ellie sighed. "I saw them outside last night."

The others looked at me, Rosalie's eyes still full of the fear I had planted there and was even now propagating.

"So what were they?" Rosalie asked. "Ninja seabirds?"

"I don't know." I ignored her sarcasm. "They were white, but they hid in shadows. Animals, they must have been. There are no people like that. But they were canny. They moved only when I wasn't looking straight at them, otherwise they stayed still and . . . blended in with the snow." Rosalie, I could see, was terrified. The sarcasm was a front. Everything I said scared her more.

"Camouflaged," Hayden said.

"No. They blended in. As if they melted in, but they didn't. I can't really . . ."

"In China," Rosalie said, "white is the colour of death. It's the colour of happiness and joy. They wear white at funerals."

Ellie spoke quickly, trying to grab back the conversation. "Right. Let's think of what we're going to do. First, no use trying to get out. Agreed? Good. Second, we limit ourselves to a couple of rooms downstairs, the hallway and staircase area and upstairs. Third, do what we can to block up, nail up, glue up the doors to the other rooms and corridors."

"And then?" Rosalie asked quietly. "Charades?"

Ellie shrugged and smiled. "Why not? It is Christmas time."

I'd never dreamt of a white Christmas. I was cursing Bing fucking Crosby with every gasped breath I could spare.

The air sang with echoing hammer-blows, dropped boards and groans as hammers crunched fingernails. I was working with Ellie to board up the rest of the downstairs rooms while Hayden and Rosalie tried to lever up the remaining boards in the dining room. We did the windows first, Ellie standing to one side with the shotgun aiming out while I hammered. It was snowing again and I could see vague shapes hiding behind flakes, dipping in and out of the snow like larking dolphins. I think we all saw them, but none of us ventured to say for sure that they were there. Our imagination was pumped up on what had happened and it had started to paint its own pictures.

We finished one of the living rooms and locked the door behind us. There was an awful sense of finality in the heavy *thunk* of the tumblers clicking in, a feeling that perhaps we would never go into that room again. I'd lived the last few years telling myself that there was no such thing as never – Jayne was dead and I would certainly see her again, after all – but there was nothing in these rooms that I could ever imagine us needing again. They were mostly designed for luxury, and luxury was a conceit of the contented mind. Over the past few weeks, I had seen contentment vanish forever under the grey cloud of humankind's fall from grace.

None of this seemed to matter now as we closed it all in. I thought I should feel sad, for the symbolism of what we were doing if not for the loss itself. Jayne had told me we would be together again, and then she had died and I had felt trapped ever since by her death and the promise of her final words. If nailing up doors would take me closer to her, then so be it.

In the next room I looked out of the window and saw Jayne striding naked towards me through the snow. Fat flakes landed on her shoulders and did not melt, and by the time she was near enough for me to see the look in her eyes she had collapsed down into a drift, leaving a memory there in her place. Something flitted past the window, sending flakes flying against the wind, bristly fur spiking dead white leaves.

I blinked hard and the snow was just snow once more. I turned and looked at Ellie, but she was concentrating too hard to return my stare. For the first time I could see how scared she was – how her hand clasped so tightly around the shotgun barrel that her knuckles were pearly white, her nails a shiny pink – and I wondered exactly what *she* was seeing out there in the white storm.

By midday we had done what we could. The kitchen, one of the living rooms and the hall and staircase were left open; every other room downstairs was boarded up from the outside in. We'd also covered the windows in those rooms left open, but we left thin viewing ports like horizontal arrow slits in the walls of an old castle. And like the weary defenders of those ancient citadels, we were under siege.

"So what did you all see?" I said as we sat in the kitchen. Nobody denied anything.

"Badgers," Rosalie said. "Big, white, fast. Sliding over the snow like they were on skis. Demon badgers from hell!" She joked, but it was obvious that she was terrified.

"Not badgers," Ellie cut in. "Deer. But wrong. Deer with scales. Or something. All wrong."

"Hayden, what did you see?"

He remained hunched over the cooker, stirring a weak stew of old vegetable and stringy beef. "I didn't see anything."

I went to argue with him but realized he was probably telling the truth. We had all seen something different, why not see nothing at all? Just as unlikely.

"You know," said Ellie, standing at a viewing slot with the snow reflecting sunlight in a band across her face, "we're all seeing white animals. White animals in the snow. So maybe we're seeing nothing at all. Maybe it's our imaginations. Perhaps Hayden is nearer the truth than all of us."

"Boris and the others had pretty strong imaginations, then," said Rosalie, bitter tears animating her eyes.

We were silent once again, stirring our weak milk-less tea, all thinking our own thoughts about what was out in the snow. Nobody had asked me what I had seen and I was glad. Last night they were fleeting white shadows, but today I had seen Jayne as well. A Jayne I had known was not really there, even as I watched her coming at me through the snow. *I'll be with you again.*

"In China, white is the colour of death," Ellie said. She spoke at the boarded window, never for an instant glancing away. Her hands held onto the shotgun as if it had become one with her body. I wondered what she had been in the past: *I have a history*, she'd said. "White. Happiness and joy."

"It was also the colour of mourning for the Victorians," I added.

"And we're in a Victorian manor." Hayden did not turn around as he spoke, but his words sent our imaginations scurrying.

"We're all seeing white animals," Ellie said quietly. "Like white noise. All tones, all frequencies. We're all seeing different things as one."

"Oh," Rosalie whispered, "well that explains a lot."

I thought I could see where Ellie was coming from; at least, I was looking in the right direction. "White noise is used to mask other sounds," I said.

Ellie only nodded.

"There's something else going on here." I sat back in my chair and stared up, trying to divine the truth in the patchwork mould on the kitchen ceiling. "We're not seeing it all."

Ellie glanced away from the window, just for a second. "I don't think we're seeing anything."

Later we found out some more of what was happening. We went to bed, doors opened in the night, footsteps creaked old floorboards. And through the dark the sound of lovemaking drew us all to another, more terrible death.

III: The Colour of Mourning

I had not made love to anyone since Jayne's death. It was months before she died that we last indulged, a bitter, tearful experience when she held a sheet of polythene between our chests and stomachs to prevent her diseased skin touching my own. It did not make for the most romantic of occasions, and afterward she cried herself to sleep as I sat holding her hand and staring into the dark.

After her death I came to the manor, the others came along to find something or escape from something else, and there were secretive noises in the night. The manor was large enough for us to have a room each, but in the darkness doors would open and close again, and every morning the atmosphere at breakfast was different.

My door had never opened and I had opened no doors. There was a lingering guilt over Jayne's death, a sense that I would be betraying her love if I went with someone else. A greater cause of my loneliness was my inherent lack of confidence, a certainty that no one here would be interested in me: I was quiet, introspective, and uninteresting, a fledgling bird devoid of any hope of taking wing with any particular talent. No one would want me.

But none of this could prevent the sense of isolation, subtle jealousy and yearning I felt each time I heard footsteps in the dark. I never heard anything else – the walls were too thick for that, the building too solid – but my imagination filled in the missing parts. Usually, Ellie was the star. And there lay another problem – lusting after a woman I did not even like very much.

The night it all changed for us was the first time I heard someone making love in the manor. The voice was androgynous in its ecstasy, a high keening, dropping off into a prolonged sigh before rising again. I sat up in bed, trying to shake off the remnants of dreams that clung like seaweed to a drowned corpse. Jayne had been there, of course, and something in the snow, and another something that was Jayne and the snow combined. I recalled wallowing in the sharp whiteness and feeling my skin sliced by ice edges, watching the snow grow pink around me, then white again as Jayne came and spread her cleansing touch across the devastation.

The cry came once more, wanton and unhindered by any sense of decorum.

Who? I thought. *Obviously Hayden, but who was he with? Rosalie? Cynical, paranoid, terrified Rosalie?*

Or Ellie?

I hoped Rosalie.

I sat back against the headboard, unable to lie down and ignore the sound. The curtains hung open – I had no reason to close them – and the moonlight revealed that it was snowing once again. I wondered what was out there watching the sleeping manor, listening to the crazy sounds of lust emanating from a building still spattered with the blood and memory of those who had died so recently. I wondered whether the things out there had any understanding of human emotion – the highs, the lows, the tenacious spirit that could sometimes survive even the most downheartening, devastating events – and what they made of the sound they could hear now. Perhaps they thought they were screams of pain. Ecstasy and thoughtless agony often sounded the same.

The sound continued, rising and falling. Added to it now the noise of something thumping rhythmically against a wall.

I thought of the times before Jayne had been ill, before the great decline had really begun, when most of the population still thought humankind could clean up what it had dirtied and repair what it had torn asunder. We'd been married for several years, our love as deep as ever, our lust still refreshing and invigorating. Car seats, cinemas, woodland, even a telephone box, all had been visited by us at some stage, laughing like adolescents, moaning and sighing together, content in familiarity.

And as I sat there remembering my dead wife, something strange happened. I could not identify exactly when the realization hit me, but I was suddenly sure of one thing: the voice I was listening to was Jayne's. She was moaning as someone else in the house made love to her. She had come in from outside, that cold unreal Jayne I had seen so recently, and she had gone to Hayden's room, and now I was being betrayed by someone I had never betrayed, ever.

I shook my head, knowing it was nonsense but certain also that the voice was hers. I was so sure that I stood, dressed and opened my bedroom door without considering the impossibility of what was happening. Reality was controlled by the darkness, not by whatever light I could attempt to throw upon it. I may as well have had my eyes closed.

The landing was lit by several shaded candles in wall brackets, their soft light barely reaching the floor, flickering as breezes came from nowhere. Where the light did touch it showed old carpet, worn by time and faded by countless unknown footfalls. The walls hung with shredded paper, damp and torn like dead skin, the lath and plaster beneath pitted and crumbled. The air was thick with age, heavy with must, redolent with faint hints of hauntings. Where my feet fell I could sense the floor dipping slightly beneath me, though whether this was actuality or a runover from my dream I was unsure.

I could have been walking on snow.

I moved toward Hayden's room and the volume of the sighing and crying increased. I paused one door away, my heart thumping not with exertion but with the thought that Jayne was a dozen steps from me, making love with Hayden, a man I hardly really knew.

Jayne's dead, I told myself, and she cried out once, loud, as she came. Another voice then, sighing and straining, and this one was Jayne as well.

Someone touched my elbow. I gasped and spun around, too shocked to scream. Ellie was there in her night-shirt, bare legs hidden in shadow. She had a strange look in her eye. It may have been the subdued lighting. I went to ask her what she was doing here, but then I realized it was probably the same as me. She'd stayed downstairs last night, unwilling to share a watch duty, insistent that we should all sleep.

I went to tell her that Jayne was in there with Hayden, then I realized how stupid this would sound, how foolish it actually *was*.

At least, I thought, *it's not Ellie in there. Rosalie it must be. At least not Ellie. Certainly not Jayne.*

And Jayne cried out again.

Goosebumps speckled my skin and brought it to life. The hairs on my neck stood to attention, my spine tingled.

"Hayden having a nice time?" someone whispered, and Rosalie stepped up behind Ellie.

I closed my eyes, listening to Jayne's cries. She had once screamed like that in a park, and the keeper had chased us out with his waving torch and throaty shout, the light splaying across our nakedness as we laughed and struggled to gather our clothes around us as we ran.

"Doesn't sound like Hayden to me," Ellie said.

The three of us stood outside Hayden's door for a while, listening to the sounds of lovemaking from within – the cries, the moving bed, the thud of wood against the wall. I felt like an intruder, however much I realized something was very wrong with all of this. Hayden was on his own in there. As we each tried to figure out what we were really hearing, the sounds from within changed. There was not one cry, not two, but many, overlying each other, increasing and expanding until the voice became that of a crowd. The light in the corridor seemed to dim as the crying increased, though it may have been my imagination.

I struggled to make out Jayne's voice and there was a hint of something familiar, a whisper in the cacophony that was so slight as to be little more than an echo of a memory. But still, to me, it was real.

Ellie knelt and peered through the keyhole, and I noticed for the first time that she was carrying her shotgun. She stood quickly and backed away from the door, her mouth opening, eyes widening. "It's Hayden," she said aghast, and then she fired at the door handle and lock.

The explosion tore through the sounds of ecstasy and left them in shreds. They echoed away like streamers in the wind, to be replaced by the lonely moan of a man's voice, pleading not to stop, it was so wonderful so pure so alive . . .

The door swung open. None of us entered the room. We could not move.

Hayden was on his back on the bed, surrounded by the whites from outside. I had seen them as shadows against the snow, little more than pale phantoms, but here in the room they stood out bright and definite. There were several of them; I could not make out an exact number because they squirmed and twisted against each other, and against Hayden. Diaphanous limbs stretched out and wavered in the air, arms or wings or tentacles, tapping at the bed and the wall and the ceiling, leaving spots of ice like ink on blotting paper wherever they touched.

I could see no real faces but I knew that the things were looking at me.

Their crying and sighing had ceased, but Hayden's continued. He moved quickly and violently, thrusting into the malleable shape that still straddled him, not yet noticing our intrusion even though the shotgun blast still rang in my ears. He continued his penetration, but slowly the white lifted itself away until Hayden's cock flopped back wetly onto his stomach.

He raised his head and looked straight at us between his knees, looked *through* one of the things where it flipped itself easily across the bed. The air stank of sex and something else, something cold and old and rotten, frozen forever and only now experiencing a hint of thaw.

"Oh please . . ." he said, though whether he spoke to us or the constantly shifting shapes I could not tell.

I tried to focus but the whites were minutely out of phase with my vision, shifting to and fro too quickly for me to concentrate. I thought I saw a face, but it may have been a false splay of shadows thrown as a shape turned and sprang to the floor. I searched for something I knew – an arm kinked slightly from an old break; a breast with a mole near the nipple; a smile turned wryly down at the edges – and I realized I was looking for Jayne. Even in all this mess, I thought she may be here. *I'll be with you again*, she had said.

I almost called her name, but Ellie lifted the shotgun and shattered the moment once more. It barked out once, loud, and everything happened so quickly. One instant the white things were there, smothering Hayden and touching him with their fluid limbs. The next, the room was empty of all but us humans, moth-eaten curtains fluttering slightly, window invitingly open. And Hayden's face had disappeared into a red mist.

After the shotgun blast there was only the wet sound of Hayden's brains and skull fragments pattering down onto the bedding. His hard-on still glinted in the weak candlelight. His hands each clasped a fistful of blanket. One leg tipped and rested on the sheets clumped around him. His skin was pale, almost white.

Almost.

Rosalie leaned against the wall, dry heaving. Her dress was wet and heavy with puke and the stink of it had found a home in my nostrils. Ellie was busy reloading the shotgun, mumbling and cursing, trying to look anywhere but at the carnage of Hayden's body.

I could not tear my eyes away. I'd never seen anything like this. Brand and Boris and Charley, yes, their torn and tattered corpses had been terrible to behold, but here . . . I had seen the instant a rounded, functional person had turned into a shattered lump of meat. I'd seen the red splash of Hayden's head as it came apart and hit the wall, big bits ricocheting, the smaller, wetter pieces sticking to the old wallpaper and drawing their dreadful art for all to see. Every detail stood out and demanded my attention, as if the shot had cleared the air and brought light. It seemed red-tinged, the atmosphere itself stained with violence.

Hayden's right hand clasped onto the blanket, opening and closing very slightly, very slowly.

Doesn't feel so cold. Maybe there's a thaw on the way, I thought distractedly, trying perhaps to withdraw somewhere banal and comfortable and familiar . . .

There was a splash of sperm across his stomach. Blood from his ruined head was running down his neck and chest and mixing with it, dribbling soft and pink onto the bed.

Ten seconds ago he was alive. Now he was dead. Extinguished, just like that.

Where is he? I thought. *Where has he gone?*

"Hayden?" I said.

"He's dead!" Ellie hissed, a little too harshly.

"I can see that." But his hand still moved. Slowly. Slightly.

Something was happening at the window. The curtains were still now, but there was a definite sense of movement in the darkness beyond. I caught it from the corner of my eye as I stared at Hayden.

"Rosalie, go get some boards," Ellie whispered.

"You killed Hayden!" Rosalie spat. She coughed up the remnants of her last meal, and they hung on her chin like wet boils. "You blew his head off! You shot him! What the hell, what's going on, what's happening here. I don't know, I don't know . . ."

"The things are coming back in," Ellie said. She shouldered the gun, leaned through the door and fired at the window. Stray shot plucked at the curtains. There was a cessation of noise from outside, then a rustling, slipping, sliding. It sounded like something flopping around in snow. "Go and get the boards, you two."

Rosalie stumbled noisily along the corridor toward the staircase.

"You killed him," I said lamely.

"He was fucking them," Ellie shouted. Then, quieter: "I didn't mean to . . ." She looked at the body on the bed, only briefly but long enough for me to see her eyes narrow and her lips squeeze tight. "He was fucking them. His fault."

"What were they? What the hell, I've never seen any animals like them."

Ellie grabbed my biceps and squeezed hard, eliciting an unconscious yelp. She had fingers like steel nails. "They aren't animals," she said. "They aren't people. Help me with the door."

Her tone invited no response. She aimed the gun at the open window for as long as she could while I pulled the door shut. The shotgun blast had blown the handle away, and I could not see how we would be able to keep it shut should the whites return. We stood that way for a while, me hunkered down with two fingers through a jagged hole in the door to try to keep it closed, Ellie standing slightly back, aiming the gun at the pocked wood. I wondered whether I'd end up getting shot if the whites chose this moment to climb back into the room and launch themselves at the door . . .

Banging and cursing marked Rosalie's return. She carried several snapped floorboards, the hammer and nails. I held the boards up, Rosalie nailed, both of us now in Ellie's line of fire. Again I wondered about Ellie and guns, about her history. I was glad when the job was done.

We stepped back from the door and stood there silently, three relative strangers trying to understand and come to terms with what we had seen. But without understanding, coming to terms was impossible. I felt a tear run down my cheek, then another. A sense of breathless panic settled around me, clasping me in cool hands and sending my heart racing.

"What do we do?" I said. "How do we keep those things out?"

"They won't get through the boarded windows," Rosalie said confidently, doubt so evident in her voice.

I remembered how quickly they had moved, how lithe and alert they had been to virtually dodge the blast from Ellie's shotgun.

I held my breath; the others were doing the same.

Noises. Clambering and a soft whistling at first, then light thuds as something ran around the walls of the room, across the ceiling, bounding from the floor and the furniture. Then tearing, slurping, cracking, as the whites fed on what was left of Hayden.

"Let's go down," Ellie suggested. We were already backing away.

Jayne may be in danger, I thought, recalling her waving to me as she walked naked through the snow. If she was out there, and these things were out there as well, she would be at risk. She may not know, she may be too trusting, she may let them take advantage of her, abuse and molest her—

Hayden had been enjoying it. He was not being raped; if anything, he was doing the raping. Even as he died he'd been spurting ignorant bliss across his stomach.

And Jayne was dead. I repeated this over and over, whispering it, not caring if the others heard, certain that they would take no notice. Jayne was dead. Jayne was dead.

I suddenly knew for certain that the whites could smash in at any time, dodge Ellie's clumsy shooting and tear us to shreds in seconds. They could do it, but they did not. They scratched and tapped at windows, clambered around the house, but they did not break in. Not yet.

They were playing with us. Whether they needed us for food, fun, or revenge, it was nothing but a game.

Ellie was smashing up the kitchen.

She kicked open cupboard doors, swept the contents of shelves onto the floor with the barrel of the shotgun, sifted through them with her feet, then did the same to the next cupboard. At first I thought it was blind rage, fear, dread; then I saw that she was searching for something.

"What?" I asked. "What are you doing?"

"Just a hunch."

"What sort of hunch? Ellie, we should be watching out—"

"There's something moving out there," Rosalie said. She was looking through the slit in the boarded window. There was a band of moonlight across her eyes.

"Here!" Ellie said triumphantly. She knelt and rooted around in the mess on the floor, shoving jars and cans aside, delving into a splash of spilled rice to find a small bottle. "Bastard. The bastard. Oh God, the bastard's been doing it all along."

"There's something out there in the snow," Rosalie said again, louder this time. "It's coming to the manor. It's . . ." Her voice trailed off and I saw her stiffen, her mouth slightly open.

"Rosalie?" I moved towards her, but she glanced at me and waved me away.

"It's okay," she said. "It's nothing."

"Look." Ellie slammed a bottle down on the table and stood back for us to see.

"A bottle."

Ellie nodded. She looked at me and tilted her head. Waiting for me to see, expecting me to realize what she was trying to say.

"A bottle from Hayden's food cupboard," I said.

She nodded again.

I looked at Rosalie. She was still frozen at the window, hands pressed flat to her thighs, eyes wide and full of the moon. "Rosie?" She only shook her head. Nothing wrong, the gesture said, but it did not look like that. It looked like everything was wrong but she was too afraid to tell us. I went to move her out of the way, look for myself, see what had stolen her tongue.

"Poison," Ellie revealed. I paused, glanced at the bottle on the table. Ellie picked it up and held it in front of a candle, shook it, turned it this way and that. "Poison. Hayden's been cooking for us ever since we've been here. And he's always had this bottle. And a couple of times lately, he's added a little extra to certain meals."

"Brand," I nodded, aghast. "And Boris. But why? They were outside, they were killed by those things—"

"Torn up by those things," Ellie corrected. "Killed in here. Then dragged out."

"By Hayden?"

She shrugged. "Why not? He was fucking the whites."

"But why would he want to . . . Why did he have something against Boris and Brand? And Charley? An accident, like he said?"

"I guess he gave her a helping hand," Ellie mused, sitting at the table and rubbing her temples. "They both saw something outside. Boris and Brand, they'd both seen things in the snow. They made it known, they told us all about it, and Hayden heard as well. Maybe he felt threatened. Maybe he thought we'd steal his little sex mates." She stared down at the table, at the rings burnt there over the years by hot mugs, the scratches made by endless cutlery. "Maybe they told him to do it."

"Oh, come on!" I felt my eyes go wide like those of a rabbit caught in car headlights.

Ellie shrugged, stood and rested the gun on her shoulder. "Whatever, we've got to protect ourselves. They may be in soon, you saw them up there. They're intelligent. They're—"

"Animals!" I shouted. "They're animals! How could they tell Hayden anything? How could they get in?"

Ellie looked at me, weighing her reply.

"They're white animals, like you said!"

Ellie shook her head. "They're new. They're unique. They're a part of the change."

New. Unique. The words instilled very little hope in me, and Ellie's next comment did more to scare me than anything that had happened up to now.

"They were using Hayden to get rid of us. Now he's gone . . . well, they've no reason not to do it themselves."

As if on cue, something started to brush up against the outside wall of the house.

"Rosalie!" I shouted. "Step back!"

"It's alright," she said dreamily, "it's only the wind. Nothing there. Nothing to worry about." The sound continued, like soap on sandpaper. It came from beyond the boarded windows but it also seemed to filter through from elsewhere, surrounding us like an audio enemy.

"Ellie," I said, "what can we do?" She seemed to have taken charge so easily that I deferred to her without thinking, assuming she would have a plan with a certainty which was painfully cut down.

"I have no idea." She nursed the shotgun in the crook of her elbow like a baby substitute, and I realized I didn't know her half as well as I thought. Did she have children? I wondered. Where were her family? Where had this level of self-control come from?

"Rosalie," I said carefully, "what are you looking at?" Rosalie was staring through the slit at a moonlit scene none of us could see. Her expression had dropped from scared to melancholy, and I saw a tear trickle down her cheek. She was no longer her old cynical, bitter self. It was as if all her fears had come true and she was content with the fact. "Rosie!" I called again, quietly but firmly.

Rosalie turned to look at us. Reality hit her, but it could not hide the tears. "But he's dead," she said, half question, half statement.

Before I could ask whom she was talking about, something hit the
house.

The sound of smashing glass came from everywhere: behind the
boards across the kitchen windows; out in the corridor; muffled
crashes from elsewhere in the dark manor. Rosalie stepped back
from the slit just as a long, shimmering white limb came in, glassy
nails scratching for her face but ripping the air instead.

Ellie stepped forward, thrust the shotgun through the slit and
pulled the trigger. There was no cry of pain, no scream, but the limb
withdrew.

Something began to batter against the ruined kitchen window,
the vibration travelling through the hastily nailed boards, nail heads
emerging slowly from the gouged wood after each impact. Ellie fired
again, though I could not see what she was shooting at. As she turned
to reload she avoided my questioning glance.

"They're coming in!" I shouted.

"Can it!" Ellie said bitterly. She stepped back as a sliver of timber
broke away from the edge of one of the boards, clattering to the floor
stained with frost. She shouldered the gun and fired twice through
the widening gap. White things began to worm their way between
the boards, fingers perhaps, but long and thin and more flexible than
any I had ever seen. They twisted and felt blindly across the wood . . .
and then wrapped themselves around the exposed nails.

They began to pull.

The nails squealed as they were withdrawn from the wood, one
by one.

I hefted the hammer and went at the nails, hitting each of them
only once, aiming for those surrounded by cool white digits. As
each nail went back in the things around them drew back and
squirmed out of sight behind the boards, only to reappear elsewhere.
I hammered until my arm ached, resting my left hand against the
vibrating timber. Not once did I catch a white digit beneath the
hammer, even when I aimed for them specifically. I began to giggle
and the sound frightened me. It was the voice of a madman, the
utterance of someone looking for his lost mind, and I found that
funnier than ever. Every time I hit another nail it reminded me more
and more of an old fairground game. Pop the gophers on the head.
I wondered what the prize would be tonight.

"What the hell do we do?" I shouted.

Rosalie had stepped away from the windows and now leaned
against the kitchen worktop, eyes wide, mouth working slowly in

some unknown mantra. I glanced at her between hammer blows and saw her chest rising and falling at an almost impossible speed. She was slipping into shock.

"Where?" I shouted to Ellie over my shoulder.

"The hallway."

"Why?"

"Why not?"

I had no real answer, so I nodded and indicated with a jerk of my head that the other two should go first. Ellie shoved Rosalie ahead of her and stood waiting for me.

I continued bashing with the hammer, but now I had fresh targets. Not only were the slim white limbs nudging aside the boards and working at the nails, but they were also coming through the ventilation bricks at skirting level in the kitchen. They would gain no hold there, I knew; they could never pull their whole body through there. But still I found their presence abhorrent and terrifying, and every third hammer strike was directed at these white monstrosities trying to twist around my ankles.

And at the third missed strike, I knew what they were doing. It was then, also, that I had some true inkling of their intelligence and wiliness. Two digits trapped my leg between them – they were cold and hard, even through my jeans – and they jerked so hard that I felt my skin tearing in their grasp.

I went down and the hammer skittered across the kitchen floor. At the same instant a twisting forest of the things appeared between the boards above me, and in seconds the timber had started to snap and splinter as the onslaught intensified, the attackers now seemingly aware of my predicament. Shards of wood and glass and ice showered down on me, all of them sharp and cutting. And then, looking up, I saw one of the whites appear in the gap above me, framed by broken wood, its own limbs joined by others in their efforts to widen the gap and come in to tear me apart.

Jayne stared down at me. Her face was there but the thing was not her; it was as if her image were projected there, cast onto the pure whiteness of my attacker by memory or circumstance, put there because it knew what the sight would do to me.

I went weak, not because I thought Jayne was there – I knew that I was being fooled – but because her false visage inspired a flood of warm memories through my stunned bones, hitting cold muscles and sending me into a white-hot agony of paused circulation, blood pooling at my extremities, consciousness retreating into the warmer parts of my brain, all thought of escape and salvation and the other three survivors erased by the plain whiteness that invaded from outside, sweeping in through the rent in the wall and promising me a quick, painful death, but only if I no longer struggled, only if I submitted—

The explosion blew away everything but the pain. The thing above me had been so intent upon its imminent kill that it must have missed Ellic, leaning in the kitchen door and shouldering the shotgun.

The thing blew apart. I closed my eyes as I saw it fold up before me, and when I opened them again there was nothing there, not even a shower of dust in the air, no sprinkle of blood, no splash of insides. Whatever it had been it left nothing behind in death.

"Come on!" Ellie hissed, grabbing me under one arm and hauling me across the kitchen floor. I kicked with my feet to help her then finally managed to stand, albeit shakily.

There was now a gaping hole in the boards across the kitchen windows. Weak candlelight bled out and illuminated the falling snow and the shadows behind it. I expected the hole to be filled again in seconds and this time they would pour in, each of them a mimic of Jayne in some terrifying fashion.

"Shut the door," Ellie said calmly. I did so and Rosalie was there with a hammer and nails. We'd run out of broken floorboards, so we simply nailed the door into the frame. It was clumsy and would no doubt prove ineffectual, but it may give us a few more seconds.

But for what? What good would time do us now, other than to extend our agony?

"Now where?" I asked hopelessly. "Now what?" There were sounds all around us; soft thuds from behind the kitchen door, and louder noises from further away. Breaking glass; cracking wood; a gentle rustling, more horrible because they could not be identified. As far as I could see, we really had nowhere to go.

"Upstairs," Ellie said. "The attic. The hatch is outside my room, it's got a loft ladder, as far as I know it's the only way up. Maybe we could hold them off until . . ."

"Until they go home for tea," Rosalie whispered. I said nothing. There was no use in verbalizing the hopelessness we felt at the moment, because we could see it in each other's eyes. The snow had been here for weeks and maybe now it would be here forever. Along with whatever strangeness it contained.

Ellie checked the bag of cartridges and handed them to me. "Hand these to me," she said. "Six shots left. Then we have to beat them up."

It was dark inside the manor, even though dawn must now be breaking outside. I thanked God that at least we had some candles left . . . but that got me thinking about God and how He would let this happen, launch these things against us, torture us with the promise of certain death and yet give us these false splashes of hope. I'd spent most of my life thinking that God was indifferent, a passive force holding the big picture together while we acted out our own foolish little plays within it. Now, if He did exist, He could only be a cruel God indeed. And I'd rather there be nothing than a God who found pleasure or entertainment in the discomfort of His creations.

Maybe Rosalie had been right. She had seen God staring down with blood in his eyes.

As we stumbled out into the main hallway I began to cry, gasping out my fears and my grief, and Ellie held me up and whispered into my ear. "Prove Him wrong if you have to. Prove Him wrong. Help me to survive, and prove Him wrong."

I heard Jayne beyond the main front doors, calling my name into the snowbanks, her voice muffled and bland. I paused, confused, and then I even smelled her; apple-blossom shampoo; the sweet scent of her breath. For a few seconds Jayne was there with me and I could all but hold her hand. None of the last few weeks had happened. We were here on a holiday, but there was something wrong and she was in danger outside. I went to open the doors to her, ask her in and help her, assuage whatever fears she had.

I would have reached the doors and opened them if it were not for Ellie striking me on the shoulder with the stock of the shotgun.

"There's nothing out there but those things!" she shouted. I blinked rapidly as reality settled down around me but it was like wrapping paper, only disguising the truth I thought I knew, not dismissing it completely.

The onslaught increased.

Ellie ran up the stairs, shotgun held out before her. I glanced around once, listening to the sounds coming from near and far, all of them noises of siege, each of them promising pain at any second. Rosalie stood at the foot of the stairs doing likewise. Her face was pale and drawn and corpse-like.

"I can't believe Hayden," she said. "He was doing it with them. I can't believe . . . does Ellie really think he . . . ?"

"I can't believe a second of any of this," I said. "I hear my dead wife." As if ashamed of the admission I lowered my eyes as I walked by Rosalie. "Come on," I said. "We can hold out in the attic."

"I don't think so." Her voice was so sure, so full of conviction, that I thought she was all right. Ironic that a statement of doom should inspire such a feeling, but it was as close to the truth as anything.

I thought Rosalie was all right.

It was only as I reached the top of the stairs that I realized she had not followed me.

I looked out over the ornate old banister, down into the hallway where shadows played and cast false impressions on eyes I could barely trust anyway. At first I thought I was seeing things because Rosalie was not stupid; Rosalie was cynical and bitter, but never stupid. She would not do such a thing.

She stood by the open front doors. How I had not heard her unbolting and opening them I do not know, but there she was, a stark shadow against white fluttering snow, dim daylight parting around her and pouring in. Other things came in too, the whites, slinking across the floor and leaving paw prints of frost wherever they came. Rosalie stood with arms held wide in a welcoming embrace.

She said something as the whites launched at her. I could not hear the individual words but I sensed the tone; she was happy. As if she were greeting someone she had not seen for a very long time.

And then they hit her and took her apart in seconds.

"Run!" I shouted, sprinting along the corridor, chasing Ellie's shadow. In seconds I was right behind her, pushing at her shoulders as if this would make her move faster. "Run! Run! Run!"

She glanced back as she ran. "Where's Rosalie?"

"She opened the door." It was all I needed to say. Ellie turned away and concentrated on negotiating a corner in the corridor.

From behind me I heard the things bursting in all around. Those that had slunk past Rosalie must have broken into rooms from the inside even as others came in from outside, helping each other, crashing through our pathetic barricades by force of co-operation.

I noticed how cold it had become. Frost clung to the walls and the old carpet beneath our feet crunched with each footfall. Candles threw erratic shadows at icicle-encrusted ceilings. I felt ice under my fingernails.

Jayne's voice called out behind me and I slowed, but then I ran on once more, desperate to fight what I so wanted to believe. She'd said we would be together again and now she was calling me . . . but she was dead, she was dead. Still she called. Still I ran. And then she started to cry because I was not going to her, and I imagined her naked out there in the snow with white things everywhere. I stopped and turned around.

Ellie grabbed my shoulder, spun me and slapped me across the face. It brought tears to my eyes, but it also brought me back to shady reality. "We're here," she said. "Stay with us." Then she looked over my shoulder. Her eyes widened. She brought the gun up so quickly that it smacked into my ribs, and the explosion in the confined corridor felt like a hammer pummelling my ears.

I turned and saw what she had seen. It was like a drift of snow moving down the corridor toward us, rolling across the walls and ceiling, pouring along the floor. Ellie's shot had blown a hole through it, but the whites quickly regrouped and moved forward once more. Long, fine tendrils felt out before them, freezing the corridor seconds before the things passed by. There were no faces or eyes or mouths, but if I looked long enough I could see Jayne rolling naked in there with them, her mouth wide, arms holding whites to her, into her. If I really listened I was sure I would hear her sighs as she fucked them. They had passed from luring to mocking now that we were trapped, but still . . .

They stopped. The silence was a withheld chuckle.

"Why don't they rush us?" I whispered. Ellie had already pulled down the loft ladder and was waiting to climb up. She reached out and pulled me back, indicating with a nod of her head that I should go first. I reached out for the gun, wanting to give her a chance, but she elbowed me away without taking her eyes off the advancing white mass. "Why don't they . . .?"

She fired again. The shot tore a hole, but another thing soon filled that hole and stretched out toward us. "I'll shoot you if you stand in my way any more," she said.

I believed her. I handed her two cartridges and scurried up the ladder, trying not to see Jayne where she rolled and writhed, trying not to hear her sighs of ecstasy as the whites did things to her that only I knew she liked.

The instant I made it through the hatch the sounds changed. I heard Ellie squeal as the things rushed, the metallic clack as she slammed the gun shut again, two explosions in quick succession, a wet sound as whites ripped apart. Their charge sounded like a steam train: wood cracked and split, the floorboards were smashed up beneath icy feet, ceilings collapsed. I could not see, but I felt the corridor shattering as they came at Ellie, as if it were suddenly too small to house them all and they were ploughing their own way through the manor.

Ellie came up the ladder fast, throwing the shotgun through before hauling herself up after it. I saw a flash of white before she slammed the hatch down and locked it behind her.

"There's no way they can't get up here," I said. "They'll be here in seconds."

Ellie struck a match and lit a pathetic stub of candle. "Last one." She was panting. In the weak light she looked pale and worn out. "Let's see what they decide," she said.

We were in one of four attics in the manor roof. This one was boarded but bare, empty of everything except spiders and dust. Ellie shivered and cried, mumbling about her dead husband Jack frozen in the car. Maybe she heard him. Maybe she'd seen him down there. I found with a twinge of guilt that I could not care less.

"They herded us, didn't they?" I said. I was breathless and aching, but it was similar to the feeling after a good workout; enervated, not exhausted.

Ellie shrugged, then nodded. She moved over to me and took the last couple of cartridges from the bag on my belt. As she broke the gun and removed the spent shells her shoulders hitched. She gasped and dropped the gun.

"What? Ellie?" But she was not hearing me. She stared into old shadows which had not been bathed in light for years, seeing some unknown truths there, her mouth falling open into an expression so unfamiliar on her face that it took me some seconds to place it – a smile. Whatever she saw, whatever she heard, it was something she was happy with.

I almost let her go. In the space of a second, all possibilities flashed across my mind. We were going to die, there was no escape, they would take us singly or all in one go, they would starve us out, the snow would never melt, the whites would change and grow and evolve beneath us, we could do nothing, whatever they were they had won already, they had won when humankind brought the ruin down upon itself . . .

Then I leaned over and slapped Ellie across the face. Her head snapped around and she lost her balance, falling onto all fours over the gun.

I heard Jayne's footsteps as she prowled the corridors searching for me, calling my name with increasing exasperation. Her voice was changing from sing-song, to monotone, to panicked. The whites were down there with her, the white animals, all animals, searching and stalking her tender naked body through the freezing manor. I had to help her. I knew what it would mean but at least then we would be together, at least then her last promise to me would have been fulfilled.

Ellie's moan brought me back and for a second I hated her for that. I had been with Jayne and now I was here in some dark, filthy attic with a hundred creatures below trying to find a way to tear me apart. I hated her and I could not help it one little bit.

I moved to one of the sloping roof-lights and stared out. I looked for Jayne across the snowscape, but the whites now had other things on their mind. Fooling me was not a priority.

"What do we do?" I asked Ellie, sure even now that she would have an idea, a plan. "How many shots have you got left?"

She looked at me. The candle was too weak to light up her eyes. "Enough." Before I even realized what she was doing she had flipped the shotgun over, wrapped her mouth around the twin barrels, reached down, curved her thumb through the trigger guard and blasted her brains into the air.

It's been over an hour since Ellie killed herself and left me on my own.

In that time snow has been blown into the attic to cover her body from view. Elsewhere it's merely a sprinkling, but Ellie is little more than a white hump on the floor now, the mess of her head a pink splash across the ever-whitening boards.

At first the noise from downstairs was terrific. The whites raged and ran and screamed, and I curled into a ball and tried to prepare myself for them to smash through the hatch and take me apart. I even considered the shotgun . . . there's one shot left . . . but Ellie was brave, Ellie was strong. I don't have that strength.

Besides, there's Jayne to think of. She's down there now, I know, because I have not heard a sound for ten minutes. Outside it is snowing heavier than I've ever seen, it must be ten feet deep, and there is no movement whatsoever. Inside, below the hatch and throughout the manor, in rooms sealed and broken open, the whites must be waiting. Here and there, Jayne will be waiting with them. For me. So that I can be with her again.

Soon I will open the hatch, make my way downstairs and out through the front doors. I hope, Jayne, that you will meet me there.

2000

THE MAMMOTH BOOK OF

BEST NEW HORROR

The year's best horror stories
by such masters of dark suspense as:
Ramsey Campbell, Dennis Etchison, Christopher Fowler,
Mick Garris, Kim Newman, Iain Sinclair,
Michael Marshall Smith and many others

EDITED BY
STEPHEN JONES

"Top horror book of the year, a must for every fan."
— Kirkus Reviews

The Other Side of Midnight
Anno Dracula, 1981

Kim Newman

REMEMBER WHEN I SAID earlier that *Best New Horror 2* was the only book I have ever had censored by a publisher? Well, that's not strictly true.

After having been recently ripped-off by a British small press imprint to the tune of several thousand pounds, I decided that my editorial commentary for *The Mammoth Book of Best New Horror Volume Twelve* would be about integrity in publishing. Over the previous few years I had noticed that problems with publishers had been increasing as new technologies were steadily introduced, and I wanted to give a warning to new and upcoming writers. I felt that I was addressing a genuine concern in the horror field.

It therefore came as somewhat of a surprise when my agent informed me that my editor at the time was deeply upset about the piece and was "reluctant" to run it. Despite various attempts, I never did discover what she found objectionable about the editorial, yet I was forced to replace it with a hastily written rebuttal to (American) accusations on the Internet that I was including too many British writers in the series.

However, the whole baffling incident got me thinking. Obviously something in my piece had struck a nerve with my publisher and, for any writer, that is exactly the kind of response you hope to achieve with any kind of critical essay. So perhaps I had something worthwhile to say, after all . . .?

The original editorial eventually saw print a few years later in the World Horror Convention souvenir book and is available on my website, where it continues to attract positive comments.

But the problems with this volume did not end there. The publisher originally wanted to use a hilariously inappropriate image from an old Guy N. Smith novel on the cover that depicted a wormy corpse rising from the grave. After I strenuously complained, I was allowed to choose something more subtle from Les Edwards. Regrettably, the final image was cropped, but it was still a huge improvement over the initial choice.

Even with an abridged editorial, the Introduction came in at seventy-two pages, and the Necrology ran to forty-one. The book, which once again won the British Fantasy Award for Best Anthology, was dedicated to the memory of two old friends and colleagues, R. Chetwynd-Hayes and Richard Laymon.

The twenty-two stories were a nicely balanced selection that included Iain Sinclair's second contribution to the series and a story by Hollywood film director Mick Garris.

As I had done with Terry Lamsley and Steve Rasnic Tem in earlier volumes, I top-and-tailed the contents with two stories by the same author. This time the honour went to Kim Newman, whose fiction had been appearing regularly in the series since the very first volume.

Although "Red Reign" (in *Best New Horror 4*) is arguably his most influential story and became the basis of the hugely successful series of *Anno Dracula* vampire novels, it has been widely anthologized over the years. So I have therefore chosen another tale set in the same alternate universe. One that skilfully combines Kim's ability to mix real people with imaginary characters and his encyclopaedic knowledge of movie history . . .

I

AT MIDNIGHT, 1980 flew away across the Pacific and 1981 crept in from the East. A muted cheer rose from the pretty folk around the barbecue pit, barely an echo of the raucous welcome to a new decade that erupted at the height of the last Paradise Cove New Year party.

Of this company, only Geneviève clung to the old – the proper – manner of reckoning decades, centuries and (when they came) millennia. The passing of time was important to her; born in 1416, she'd let more time pass than most. Even among vampires, she was an elder. Five minutes ago – last year, last decade – she'd started to explain her position to a greying California boy, an ex-activist they called "the Dude". His eyes glazed over with more than the weed he'd been toking throughout the party, indeed since Jefferson Airplane went Starship. She quite liked the Dude's eyes, in any condition.

"It's as simple as this," she reiterated, hearing the French in her accent ("eet's", "seemple", "ziss") that only came out when she was tipsy ("teep-see") or trying for effect. "Since there was no Year Nothing, the first decade ended with the end of Year Ten AD; the first century with the end of 100 AD; the first millennium with the end of 1000 AD. Now, at this moment, a new decade is to begin. 1981 is the first year of the 1980s, as 1990 will be the last."

Momentarily, the Dude looked as if he understood, but he was just concentrating to make out her accented words. She saw insight spark in his mind, a vertiginous leap that made him want to back away from her. He held out his twisted, tufted joint. It might have been the one he'd rolled and started in 1968, replenished on and off ever since.

"Man, if you start questioning time," he said, "what have you got left? Physical matter? Maybe you question that next, and the mojo won't work any more. You'll think holes between molecules and sink through the surface of the Earth. Drawn by gravity. Heavy things should be left alone. Fundamental things, like the ground you walk on, the air you breathe. You do breathe, don't you, man? Suddenly, it hits me I don't know if you do."

"Yes, I breathe," she said. "When I turned, I didn't die. That's not common."

She proved her ability to inhale by taking a toke from the joint. She didn't get a high like his; for that, she'd have to sample his blood as it channelled the intoxicants from his alveoli to his brain. She had the mellow buzz of him, from saliva on the roach as much as from the dope smoke. It made her thirsty.

Because it was just after midnight on New Year's Eve, she kissed him. He enjoyed it, non-committally. Tasting straggles of tobacco in his beard and the film of a cocktail – white Russian – on his teeth and tongue, she sampled the ease of him, the defiant crusade of his back-burnered life. She understood now precisely what the expression "ex-activist" meant. If she let herself drink, his blood would be relaxing.

Breaking the kiss, she saw more sparks in his eyes, where her face was not reflected. Her lips were sometimes like razors, even more than her fang-teeth. She'd cut him slightly, just for a taste, not even thinking, and left some of herself on his tongue. She swallowed: mostly spit, but with tiny ribbons of blood from his gums.

French kissing was the kindest form of vampirism. From the minute exchange of fluid, she could draw a surprising sustenance.

For her, just now, it was enough. It took the edge off her red thirst.

"Keep on breathing, man," said the Dude, reclaiming his joint, smiling broadly, drifting back towards the rest of the party, enjoying the unreeling connection between them. "And don't question time. Let it pass."

Licking her lips daintily, she watched him amble. He wasn't convinced 1980 had been the last year of the old decade and not the first of the new. Rather, he wasn't convinced that it mattered. Like a lot of Southern Californians, he'd settled on a time that suited him and stayed in it. Many vampires did the same thing, though Geneviève thought it a waste of longevity. In her more pompous moments, she felt the whole point was to embrace change while carrying on what was of value from the past.

When she was born and when she was turned, time was reckoned by the Julian Calendar, with its annual error of eleven minutes and fourteen seconds. Thinking of it, she still regretted the ten days – the 5 to the 14 of October, 1582 – Pope Gregory XIII had stolen from her, from the world, to make his sums add up. England and Scotland, ten days behind Rome, held out against the Gregorian Calendar until 1752. Other countries stubbornly stuck with Julian dating until well into the twentieth century; Russia had not chimed in until 1918, Greece until 1923. Before the modern era, those ten-day shifts made diary-keeping a complex business for a necessarily much-travelled creature. In his 1885 journal, maintained while travelling on the continent and later excerpted by Bram Stoker, Jonathan Harker refers to May 4 as the eve of St George's Day, which would have been April 22 back home in England. The leap-frogged weeks had been far much more jarring than the time-zone-hopping she sometimes went through as an air passenger.

The Paradise Cove Trailer Park Colony had been her home for all of four years, an eyeblink which made her a senior resident among the constitutionally impermanent peoples of Malibu. Here, ancient history was Sonny and Cher and *Leave It to Beaver*, anything on the "golden oldies" station or in off-prime time re-run.

Geneviève – fully, Geneviève Sandrine de l'Isle Dieudonné, though she went by Gené Dee for convenience – remembered with a hazy vividity that she had once looked at the Atlantic and *not known* what lay between France and China. She was older than the name "America"; had she not turned, she'd probably have been dead before Columbus brought back the news. In all those years, ten days shouldn't matter, but supposedly significant dates made her aware of that fold in time, that wrench which pulled the future hungrily closer, which had swallowed one of her birthdays. By her internal calendar, the decade would not fully turn for nearly two weeks. This was a limbo between unarguable decades. She should have been used to limbos by now. For her, Paradise Cove was the latest of a long string of pockets out of time and space, cosy coffins shallowly buried away from the rush of the world.

She was the only one of her kind at the party; if she took "her kind" to mean vampires – there were others in her current profession, private investigation, even other in-comers from far enough out of state to be considered foreign parts. Born in Northern France under the rule of an English king, she'd seen enough history to recognize the irrelevance of nationality. To be Breton in 1416 was to be neither French nor English, or both at the same time. Much later, during the Revolution, France had scrapped the calendar again, ducking out of the 1790s, even renaming the months. In the long term, the experiment was not a success. That was the last time she – Citizen Dieudonné – had really lived in her native land; the gory business soured her not only on her own nationality, but humanity in general. Too many eras earned names like "the Terror". Vampires were supposed to be obscenely bloodthirsty and she wasn't blind to the excesses of her kind, but the warm drank just as deeply from open wounds and usually made more of a mess of it.

From the sandy patio beside her chrome-finished airstream trailer, she looked beyond the gaggle of folks about the pit, joking over franks impaled on skewers. The Dude was mixing a pitcher of White Russians with his bowling buddies, resuming a months-long argument over the precise wording of the opening narration/ song of *Branded*. An eight-track in an open-top car played "Hotel California", The Eagles' upbeat but ominous song about a vampire and her victims. Some were dancing on the sand, shoes in a pile that would be hard to sort out later. White rolls of surf crashed on the breakers, waves edged delicately up to the beach.

Out there was the Pacific Ocean and the curve of the Earth, and beyond the blue horizon, as another shivery song went, was a rising sun. Dawn didn't worry her; at her age, as long as she dressed carefully – sunglasses, a floppy hat, long sleeves – she wouldn't even catch a severe tan, let alone frazzle up into dust and essential salts like some *nosferatu* of the Dracula bloodline. She had grown out of the dark. To her owl eyes, it was no place to hide, which meant she had to be careful where she looked on party nights like this. She liked living by the sea: its depths were still impenetrable to her, still a mystery.

"Hey, Gidget," came a rough voice, "need a nip?"

It was one of the surfers, a shaggy bear of a man she had never heard called anything but Moondoggie. He wore frayed shorts, flip-flops and an old blue shirt, and probably had done since the 1950s. He was a legendary veteran of tubes and pipes and waves long gone. He seemed young to her, though his friends called him an old man.

His offer was generous. She had fed off him before, when the need was strong. With his blood came a salt rush, the sense of being enclosed by a curl of wave as his board torpedoed across the surface of the water.

Just now, she didn't need it. She still had the taste of the Dude. Smiling, she waved him away. As an elder, she didn't have the red thirst so badly. Since Charles, she had fed much less. That wasn't how it was with many vampires, especially those of the Dracula line. Some *nosferatu* got thirstier and thirstier with passing ages, and were finally consumed by their own raging red needs. Those were the ones who got to be called monsters. Beside them, she was a minnow.

Moondoggie tugged at his open collar, scratching below his salt-and-pepper beard. The LAPD had wanted to hang a murder rap on him two years ago, when a runaway turned up dead in his beach hut. She had investigated the situation, clearing his name. He would always be grateful to his "Gidget", which she learned was a contraction of "Girl Midget". Never tall, she had turned – frozen – at sixteen. Recently, after centuries of being treated almost as a child, she was most often taken for a woman in her twenties. That was: by people who didn't know she wasn't warm, wasn't entirely living. She'd have examined her face for the beginnings of lines, but looking glasses were no use to her.

Shots were fired, in the distance. She looked at the rise of the cliffs and saw the big houses, decks lit by fairy light UFO constellations, seeming to float above the beach, heavy with heavy hitters. Firing up into the sky was a Malibu New Year tradition among the rich. Reputedly started by the film director John Milius, a famous surf and gun nut, it was a stupid, dangerous thing to do. Gravity and momentum meant bullets came down somewhere, and not always into the water. In the light of New Year's Day, she found spent shells in the sand, or pocked holes in driftwood. One year, someone's head would be under a slug. Milius had made her cry with *Big Wednesday*, though. Movies with coming-of-age, end-of-an-era romanticism crawled inside her heart and melted her. She would have to tell Milius it got worse and worse with centuries.

So, the 1980s?

Some thought her overly formal for always using the full form, but she'd lived through decades called "the eighties" before. For the past hundred years, "the eighties" had meant the Anni Draculae, the 1880s, when the Transylvanian Count came to London and changed the world. Among other things, the founding of his brief Empire had drawn her out of the shadow of eternal evening into something approaching the light. That brought her together with Charles, the warm man with whom she had spent seventy-five years, until his death in 1959, the warm man who had shown her that she, a vampire, could still love, that she had turned without dying inside.

She wasn't unique, but she was rare. Most vampires lost more than they gained when they turned; they died and came back as different people, caricatures of their former selves, compelled by an inner drive to be extreme. Creatures like that were one of the reasons why she was here, at the far Western edge of a continent where "her kind" were still comparatively rare.

Other vampires had nests in the Greater Los Angeles area: Don Drago Robles, a landowner before the incorporation of the State into the Union, had quietly waited for the city to close around his *hacienda*, and was rising as a political figure with a growing constituency, a Californian answer to Baron Meinster's European Transylvania Movement; and a few long-lived movie or music people, the sort with reflections in silver and voices that registered on recording equipment, had Spanish-style castles along Sunset Boulevard, like eternal child rock God Timmy Valentine or silent movie star David Henry Reid. More, small sharks mostly, swam through Angelino sprawl, battening on marginal people to leech them dry of dreams as much as blood, or – in that ghastly new thing – selling squirts of their own blood ("drac") to sad addicts ("dhampires") who wanted to be a vampire for the night but didn't have the heart to turn all the way.

She should be grateful to the rogues; much of her business came from people who got mixed up with bad egg vampires. Her reputation for extricating victims from predators was like gold with distressed parents or cast-aside partners. Sometimes, she worked as a deprogrammer, helping kids out of all manner of cults. They grew beliefs stranger than Catholicism, or even vampirism, out here among the orange groves: the Moonies, the Esoteric Order of Dagon,

Immortology, Psychoplasmics. Another snatch of song: *the Voice said Daddy there's a million pigeons, waiting to be hooked on new religions*.

As always, she stuck it out until the party died. All the hours of the night rolled away and the rim of the horizon turned from navy blue to lovely turquoise. January cold gathered, driving those warmer folks who were still sensible from their barbecues and beach-towels to their beds.

Marty Burns, sometime sit-com star and current inhabitant of a major career slump, was passed out face down on the chilling sands in front of her trailer space. She found a blanket to throw over him. He murmured in liquor-and-pills lassitude, and she tucked the blanket comfortably around his neck. Marty was hilarious in person, even when completely off his face, but *Salt & Pepper*, the star-making show he was squandering residuals from, was puzzlingly free of actual humour. The dead people on the laugh-track audibly split sides at jokes deader than they were. The year was begun with a moderate good deed, though purging the kid's system and dragging him to A-A might have been a more lasting solution to whatever was inside him, chewing away.

She would sleep later, in the morning, locked in her sleek trailer, a big metal coffin equipped with everything she needed. Of all her homes over the years, this was the one she cherished the most. The trailer was chromed everywhere it could be, and customized with steel shutters that bolted over the windows and the never-used sun roof. Economy of space had forced her to limit her possessions – so few after so long – to those that really meant the most to her: ugly jewellery from her mediaeval girlhood, some of Charles' books and letters, a Dansette gramophone with an eclectic collection of sides, her beloved answering machine, a tacky Mexican crucifix with light-up eyes that she kept on show just to prove she wasn't one of *those* vampires, a rubber duck with a story attached, two decent formal dresses and four pairs of Victorian shoes (custom-cobbled for her tiny feet) which had outlasted everything made this century and would do for decades more. On the road, she could kink herself double and rest in the trunk of her automobile, a pillar-box red 1958 Plymouth Fury, but the trailer was more comfortable.

She wandered towards the sea-line, across the disturbed sands of the beach. There had been dancing earlier, grown-ups who had been in Frankie and Annette movies trying to fit their old moves to current music. *Le freak, c'est chic*.

She trod on a hot pebble that turned out to be a bullet, and saluted Big John up on his A-list Hollywood deck. Milius had written *Dracula* for Francis Ford Coppola, from the Bram Stoker novel she was left out of. Not wanting to have the Count brought back to mind, she'd avoided the movie, though her vampire journalist friend Kate Reed, also not mentioned in Stoker's fiction, had worked on it as technical advisor. She hadn't heard from Kate in too long; Geneviève believed she was behind the Iron Curtain, on the trail of the Transylvania Movement, that odd faction of the Baron Meinster's which wanted Dracula's estates as a homeland for vampires. God, if that ever happened, she would get round to re-applying for American citizenship; they were accepting *nosferatu* now, which they hadn't been in 1922 when she last looked into it. Meinster was one of those Dracula wannabes who couldn't quite carry off the opera cloak and ruffle shirt, with his prissy little fangs and his naked need to be the new King of the Cats.

Wavelets lapped at her bare toes. Her nails sparkled under water. The 1970s music hadn't been much, not after the 1960s. Glam rock. The Bee Gees. The Carpenters. She had liked Robert Altman's films and *Close Encounters*, but didn't see what all the fuss was about *Star Wars*. Watergate. An oil crisis. The Bicentennial Summer. The Iran hostage crisis. No Woodstock. No Swinging London. No one like Kennedy. Nothing like the Moon Landing.

If she were to fill a diary page for every decade, the 1970s would have to be heavily padded. She'd been to some parties and helped some people, settled into the slow, pastel, dusty ice-cream world of Southern California, a little to one side of the swift stream of human history. She wasn't even much bothered by memories, the curse of the long-lived.

Not bad, not good, not anything.

She wasn't over Charles, never would be really. He was a constant, silent presence in her heart, an ache and a support and a joy. He was a memory she would never let slip. And Dracula, finally destroyed soon after Charles' death, still cast a long cloak-shadow over her life. Like Bram Stoker, she wondered what her life, what the world, would have been like if Vlad Tepes had never turned or been defeated before his rise to power.

Might-have-beens and the dead. Bad company.

John Lennon was truly dead, too. Less than a month ago, in New York, he had taken a silver bullet through the heart, a cruel full stop for the 1970s, for what was left of the 1960s. Annie Wilkes,

Lennon's killer, said she was the musician's biggest fan, but that he
had to die for breaking up the Beatles. Geneviève didn't know how
long Lennon had been a vampire, but she sadly recognized in the
dirge "Imagine" that copy-of-a-copy voidishness characteristic of
creatives who turned to prolong their artistic lives but found the
essential thing that made them who they were, that powered their
talent, gone and that the best they could hope for was a kind of
rarefied self-plagiarism. Mad Annie might have done John a favour,
making him immortal again. Currently the most famous vampire-
slayer in the world, she was a heroine to the bedrock strata of warm
America that would never accept *nosferatu* as even kissing cousins to
humanity.

What, she wondered as the sun touched the sky, would this new
decade bring?

II

COUNT DRACULA

a screenplay

by Herman J. Mankiewicz and Orson Welles

based on the novel by Bram Stoker

Nov 30, 1939

Fade In

Ext. Transylvania — Faint Dawn — 1885

Window, very small in the distance, illuminated. All
around this an almost totally black screen. Now, as
the camera moves slowly towards this window, which
is almost a postage stamp in the frame, other forms
appear; spiked battlements, vast granite walls,
and now, looming up against the still-nighted sky,
enormous iron grillwork.

Camera travels up what is now shown to be a gateway
of gigantic proportions and holds on the top of
it — a huge initial "D" showing darker and darker
against the dawn sky. Through this and beyond we see
the gothic-tale mountaintop of Dracula's estate, the

great castle a silhouette at its summit, the little window a distant accent in the darkness.

Dissolve

(A series of setups, each closer to the great window, all telling something of:)

2. The Literally Incredible Domain of Vlad, Count Dracula

Its right flank resting for forty miles along the Borgo Pass, the estate truly extends in all directions farther than the eye can see. An ocean of sharp tree-tops, with occasionally a deep rift where there is a chasm. Here and there are silver threads where the rivers wind in deep gorges through the forests. Designed by nature to be almost completely vertical and jagged – it was, as will develop, primordial forested mountain when Dracula acquired and changed its face – it is now broken and shorn, with its fair share of carved peaks and winding paths, all man-made.

Castle Dracula itself – an enormous pile, compounded of several demolished and rebuilt structures, of varying architecture, with broken battlements and many towers – dominates the scene, from the very peak of the mountain. It sits on the edge of a very terrible precipice.

Dissolve

3. The Village

In the shadows, literally the shadows, of the mountain. As we move by, we see that the peasant doors and windows are shuttered and locked, with crucifixes and obscene clusters of garlic as further protection and sealing. Eyes peep out, timid, at us. The camera moves like a band of men, purposeful, cautious, intrepid, curious.

Dissolve

4. Forest of Stakes

Past which we move. The sward is wild with mountain
weeds, the stakes tilted at a variety of dutch
angles, the execution field unused and not seriously
tended for a long time.

                                        Dissolve

5. What Was Once a Good-Sized Prison Stockade

All that now remains, with one exception, are the
individual plots, surrounded by thorn fences, on
which the hostages were kept, free and yet safe from
each other and the landscape at large. (Bones in
several of the plots indicate that here there were
once human cattle, kept for blood.)

                                        Dissolve

6. A Wolf Pit

In the f.g., a great shaggy dire wolf, bound by a
silver chain, is outlined against the fawn murk.
He raises himself slowly, with more thought than
an animal should display, and looks out across the
estates of Count Dracula, to the distant light
glowing in the castle on the mountain. The wolf
howls, a child of the night, making sweet music.

                                        Dissolve

7. A Trench Below the Walls

A slow-scuttling armadillo. A crawling giant beetle.
Reflected in the muddy water -- the lighted window.

                                        Dissolve

8. The Moat

Angled spears sag. An old notebook floats on the
surface of the water - its pages covered in shorthand
scribble. As it moves across the frame, it discloses
again the reflection of the window in the castle,
closer than before.

                                        Dissolve

9. A Drawbridge

Over the wide moat, now stagnant and choked with
weeds. We move across it and through a huge rounded
archway into a formal courtyard, perhaps thirty
feet wide and one hundred yards deep, which extends
right up to the very wall of the castle. Let's see
Toland keep all of it in focus. The landscaping
surrounding it has been sloppy and casual for
centuries, but this particular courtyard has been
kept up in perfect shape. As the camera makes its
way through it, towards the lighted window of the
castle, there are revealed rare and exotic blooms
of all kinds: *mariphasa lupino lumino*, strange
orchid, *audriensis junior*, *triffidus celestus*.
The dominating note is one of almost exaggerated
wildness, sprouting sharp and desperate – rot,
rot, rot. The Hall of the Mountain King, the night
the last troll died. Some of the plants lash out,
defensively.

                                          Dissolve

10. The Window

Camera moves in until the frame of the window fills
the frame of the screen. Suddenly the light within
goes out. This stops the action of the camera and
cuts the music (Bernard Herrmann) which has been
accompanying the sequence. In the glass panes
of the window we see reflected the stark, dreary
mountainscape of the Dracula estate behind and the
dawn sky.

                                          Dissolve

11. Int. Corridor in Castle Dracula – Faint Dawn – 1885

Ornate mirrors line both walls of the corridor,
reflecting arches into infinity. A bulky shadow figure –
Dracula – proceeds slowly, heavy with years, through
the corridor. He pauses to look into the mirror, and

has no reflection, no reflections, to infinity. It seems
at last that he is simply not there.

Dissolve

12. Int. Dracula's Crypt - Faint Dawn - 1885

A very long shot of Dracula's enormous catafalque,
silhouetted against the enormous window.

                                                    Dissolve

13. Int. Dracula's Crypt - Faint Dawn - 1885

An eye. An incredible one. Big impossible drops of
bloody tears, the reflections of figures coming closer,
cutting implements raised. The jingling of sleigh bells
in the musical score now makes an ironic reference to
Indian temple bells - the music freezes --

                    DRACULA'S OLD VOICE
                    Rose's blood!

The camera pulls back to show the eye in the face
of the old Dracula, bloated with blood but his
stolen youth lost again, grey skin parchmented like
a mummy, fissures cracking open in the wrinkles
around his eyes, fangteeth too large for his mouth,
pouching his cheeks and stretching his lips, the
nose an improbable bulb. A flash - the descent of a
guillotine-like kukri knife, which has been raised
above Dracula's neck - across the screen. The head
rolls off the neck and bounds down two carpeted steps
leading to the catafalque, the camera following. The
head falls off the last step onto the marble floor
where it cracks, snaky tendrils of blood glittering
in the first ray of the morning sun. This ray cuts an
angular pattern across the floor, suddenly crossed
with a thousand cruciform bars of light as a dusty
curtain is wrested from the window.

14. The Foot of Dracula's Catafalque

The camera very close. Outlined against the
uncurtained window we can see a form - the form of a

man, as he raises a bowie knife over his head. The
camera moves down along the catafalque as the knife
descends into Dracula's heart, and rests on the
severed head. Its lips are still moving. The voice, a
whisper from the grave

> DRACULA'S OLD VOICE
> Rose's blood!

In the sunlight, a harsh shadow cross falling upon
it, the head lap-dissolves into a fanged, eyeless
skull.

Fade Out

III

COUNT DRACULA   Cast and Credits, as of January, 1940.

Production Company: Mercury Productions. Distributor: R.K.O. Radio
Pictures. Executive Producer: George J. Schaefer. Producer: Orson
Welles. Director: Orson Welles. Script: Herman J. Mankiewicz, Orson
Welles. From the novel by Bram Stoker. Director of Photography: Gregg
Toland. Editors: Mark Robson, Robert Wise. Art Director: Van Nest
Polglase. Special Effects: Vernon L. Walker. Music/Musical Director:
Bernard Herrmann.

Orson Welles (Dracula), Joseph Cotten (Jedediah Renfield), Everett
Sloane (Van Helsing), Dorothy Comingore (Mina Murray), Robert Coote
(Artie Holmwood), William Alland (Jon Harker), Agnes Moorehead
(Mrs Westenra), Lucille Ball (Lucy), George Couloris (Dr Walter Parkes
Seward), Paul Stewart (Raymond, Asylum Attendant), Alan Ladd
(Quincey P. Morris), Fortunio Bonanova (Inn-Keeper at Bistritz), Vladimir
Sokoloff (Szgany Chieftain), Dolores Del Rio, Ruth Warrick, Rita
Cansino (Vampire Brides), Gus Schilling (Skipper of the *Demeter*).

IV

"Mademoiselle Dieudonné," intoned the voice on her answering
machine, halfway between a growl and a purr, "this is Orson Welles."

The voice was deeper even than in the 1930s, when he was a radio
star. Geneviève had been in America over Halloween, 1938, when
Welles and the Mercury Theatre of the Air broadcast their you-are-

there dramatization of H.G. Wells' "The Flowering of the Strange Orchid" and convinced half the Eastern seaboard that the country was disappearing under a writhing plague of vampire blossoms. She remembered also the whisper of "who *knows* what evil *lurks* in the hearts of *men*?", followed by the triumphant declaration "the *Shadow* knows!" and the low chuckle which rose by terrifying lurches to a fiendish, maniacal shriek of insane laughter.

When she had first met the man himself, in Rome in 1959, the voice hadn't disappointed. Now, even on cheap tape and through the tinny, tiny amplifier, it was a call to the soul. Even hawking brandy or frozen peas, the voice was a powerful instrument. That Welles had to compete with Welles imitators for gigs as a commercial pitchman was one of the tragedies of the modern age. Then again, she suspected he drew a deal of sly enjoyment from his long-running role as a ruined titan. As an actor, his greatest role was always himself. Even leaving a message on a machine, he invested phrases with the weight – a quality he had more than a sufficiency of – of a Shakespearean deathbed speech.

"There is a small matter upon which I should like your opinion, in your capacities as a private detective and a member of the undead community. If you would call on me, I should be most grateful."

She thought about it. Welles was as famous for being broke as for living well. It was quite likely he wouldn't even come through with her modest rate of hundred dollars a day, let alone expenses. And gifts of rare wine or Cuban cigars weren't much use to her, though she supposed she could redeem them for cash.

Still, she was mildly bored with finding lost children or bail-jumpers. And no one ever accused Welles of being boring. He had left the message while she was resting through the hours of the day. This was the first of the ten or so days between the Gregorian 1980s and the Julian 1980s. She could afford to give a flawed genius – his own expression – that much time.

She would do it.

In leaving a message, Welles had given her a pause to think. She heard heavy breaths as he let the tape run on, his big man's lungs working. Then, confident that he had won her over, he cut in with address details, somewhere in Beverly Hills.

"I do so look forward to seeing you again. Until then, remember . . . *the weed of crime bears bitter fruit!*"

It was one of his old radio catchphrases.

He did the laugh, the King Laugh, the Shadow Laugh. It properly chilled her bones, but made her giggle too.

V

She discovered Orson Welles at the centre of attention, on the cracked bottom of a drained pool behind a rented bungalow. Three nude vampire girls waved objects – a luminous skull, a Macbethian blooded dagger, a fully-articulated monster bat puppet – at him, darting swiftly about his bulky figure, nipping at his head with their Halloween props. The former Boy Wonder was on his knees, enormous Russian shirt open to the waist, enormous (and putty) nose glistening under the lights, enormous spade-beard flecked with red syrup. A man with a hand-held camera, the sort of thing she'd seen used to make home movies, circled the odd quartet, not minding if the vampires got between him and his director-star.

A few other people were around the pool, holding up lights. No sound equipment, though: this was being shot silent. Geneviève hung back, by the bungalow, keeping out of the way of the work. She had been on film sets before, at Cinecittà and in Hollywood, and knew this crew would be deemed skeletal for a student short. If anyone else were directing, she'd have supposed he was shooting make-up tests or a rehearsal. But with Welles, she knew that this was the real film. It might end up with the dialogue out of sync, but it would be extraordinary.

Welles was rumbling through a soliloquy.

It took her a moment to realize what the undead girls were doing, then she had to swallow astonished laughter. They were nude not for the titillation of an eventual audience, for they wouldn't be seen. Non-reflecting *nosferatu* would be completely invisible when the footage was processed. The girls were naked because clothes would show up on film, though some elders – Dracula had been one – so violated the laws of optics that they robbed any costume they wore of its reflection also, sucking even that into their black hearts. In the final film, Welles would seem to be persecuted by malignly animated objects – the skull, the dagger and the bat. Now, he tore at his garments and hair like Lear, careful to leave his nose alone, and called out to the angry heavens. The girls flitted, slender and deathly white, not feeling the cold, faces blank, hands busy.

This was the cheapest special effect imaginable.

Welles fell forward on his face, lay still for a couple of beats and hefted himself upright, out of character, calling "cut". His nose was mashed.

A dark woman with a clipboard emerged from shadows to confer with the master. She wore a white fur coat and a matching hat. The vampire girls put the props down and stood back, nakedness unnoticed by the crew members. One took a cloak-like robe from a chair and settled it over her slim shoulders. She climbed out of the pool.

Geneviève had not announced herself. The vampire girl fixed her eye. She radiated a sense of being fed up with the supposed glamour of show business.

"Turning was supposed to help my career," she said. "I was going to stay pretty forever and be a star. Instead, I lost my image. I had good credits. I was up for the last season of *Charlie's Angels*. I'd have been the blonde."

"There's always the theatre," Geneviève suggested.

"That's not being a star," the girl said.

She was obviously a new-born, impatient with an eternity she didn't yet understand. She wanted all her presents *now*, and no nonsense about paying dues or waiting her turn. She had cropped blonde hair, very pale, almost translucent skin stretched over bird-delicate bones and a tight, hard, cute little face, with sharp angles and glinting teeth, small reddish eyes. Her upper arm was marked by parallel claw-marks, not yet healed, like sergeant's stripes. Geneviève stored away the detail.

"Who's that up there, Nico?" shouted one of the other girls.

Nico? Not the famous one, Geneviève supposed.

"Who?" the girl asked, out loud. "Famous?"

Nico – indeed, not the famous one – had picked the thought out of Geneviève's mind. That was a common elder talent, but unusual in a new-born. If she lasted, this girl might do well. She'd have to pick a new name though, to avoid confusion with the singer of "All Tomorrow's Parties".

"Another one of us," the starlet said, to the girl in the pool. "An invisible."

"I'm not here for a part," Geneviève explained. "I'm here to see Mr Welles."

Nico looked at her askew. Why would a vampire who wasn't an actress be here? Tumblers worked in the new-born's mind. It worked both ways: Nico could pick words up, but she also sent them out. The girls in the pool were named Mink and Vampi (please!), and often hung with Nico.

"You're old, aren't you?"

Geneviève nodded. Nico's transparent face showed eagerness.

"Does it come back? Your face in the mirror?"

"Mine hasn't."

Her face fell, a long way. She was a loss to the profession. Her feelings were all on the surface, projected to the back stalls.

"Different bloodlines have different qualities," Geneviève said, trying to be encouraging.

"So I heard."

Nico wasn't interested in faint hopes. She wanted instant cures.

"Is that Mademoiselle Dieudonné?" roared the familiar voice.

"Yes, Orson, it's me," she said.

Nico reacted, calculating. She was thinking that Geneviève might be an important person.

"Then that's a wrap for the evening. Thank you, people. Submit your expenses to Oja, and be back here tomorrow night, at midnight sharp. You were all stupendous."

Oja was the woman with the clipboard: Oja Kodar, Welles' companion and collaborator. She was from Yugoslavia, another refugee washed up on this California shore.

Welles seemed to float out of the swimming pool, easily hauling his enormous girth up the ladder by the strength of his own meaty arms. She was surprised at how light he was on his feet.

He pulled off his putty nose and hugged her.

"Geneviève, Geneviève, you are welcome."

The rest of the crew came up, one by one, carrying bits of equipment.

"I thought I'd get Van Helsing's mad scene in the can," explained Welles.

"Neat trick with the girls."

The twinkle in his eye was almost Santa Clausian. He gestured hypnotically.

"Elementary movie magic," he said. "Georges Méliès could have managed it in 1897."

"Has it ever been done before? I don't recall seeing a film with the device."

"As a matter of fact, I think it's an invention of my own. There are still tricks to be teased out of the cinema. Even after so many years – a single breath for you, my dear – the talkies are not quite perfected. My little vampires may have careers as puppeteers, animators. You'd never see their hands. I should shoot a short film, for children."

"You've been working on this for a long time?"

"I had the idea at about seven o'clock this evening," he said, with a modest chuckle. "This is Hollywood, my dear, and you can get anything with a phone call. I got my vampires by ordering out, like pizza."

Geneviève guessed the invisible girls were hookers, a traditional career option for those who couldn't make a showing in the movies. Some studio execs paid good money to be roughed up by girls they'd pass over with contempt at cattle calls. And vampires, properly trained, could venture into areas of pain and pleasure a warm girl would find uncomfortable, unappetising or unhealthy.

She noticed Nico had latched on to a young, male assistant and was alternately flirting with him and wheedling at him for some favour. Welles was right: she could have a career as a puppet-mistress.

"Come through into the house, Geneviève," said Welles. "We must talk."

The crew and the girls bundled together. Oja, as production manager, arranged for them to pool up in several cars and be returned to their homes or – in the case of Nico, Mink and Vampi – to a new club where there were hours to be spent before the dawn. Gary, the cameraman, wanted to get the film to the lab and hurried off on his own to an all-night facility. Many movie people kept vampire hours without being undead.

There was an after-buzz in the air. Geneviève wondered if it was genius, or had some of the crew been sniffing drac to keep going. She had heard it was better than speed. She assumed she would be immune to it; even as a blood-drinker – like all of her kind, she had turned by drinking vampire blood – she found the idea of dosing her system with another vampire's powdered blood, diluted with the Devil knew what, disgusting.

Welles went ahead of her, into the nondescript bungalow, turning on lights as he went. She looked back for a moment at the cast-off nose by the pool.

Van Helsing's mad scene?

She knew the subject of Welles's current project. He had mentioned to her that had always wanted to make *Dracula*. Now, it seemed, he was acting on the impulse. It shouldn't have, but it frightened her a little. She was in two minds about how often that story should be told.

VI

Orson Welles arrived in Hollywood in 1939, having negotiated a two-picture deal as producer-director-writer-actor with George Schaefer of RKO Pictures. Drawing on an entourage of colleagues from the New York theatre and radio, he established Mercury Productions as a filmmaking entity. Before embarking on *Citizen Kane* (1941) and *The Magnificent Ambersons* (1942), Welles developed other properties: Nicholas Blake's just-published anti-fascist thriller *The Smiler with a Knife* (1939), Conrad's *Heart of Darkness* (1902) and Stoker's *Dracula* (1897). Like the Conrad, *Dracula* was a novel Welles had already done for the *Mercury Theatre on the Air* radio series (July 11, 1938). A script was prepared (by Welles, Herman Mankiewicz and, uncredited, John Houseman), sets were designed, the film cast, and tests - the extent of which have never been revealed - shot, but the project was dropped.

The reasons for the abandonment of *Count Dracula* remain obscure. It has been speculated that RKO were nervous about Welles's stated intention to film most of the story with a first-person camera, adopting the viewpoints of the various characters as Stoker does in his might-have-been fictional history. Houseman, in his memoir *Run-Through* (1972), alleges that Welles' enthusiasm for this device was at least partly due to the fact that it would keep the fearless vampire slayers - Harker, Van Helsing, Quincey, Holmwood - mostly off screen, while Dracula, object of their attention, would always be in view. Houseman, long estranged from Welles at the time of writing, needlessly adds that Welles would have played Dracula. He toyed with the idea of playing Harker as well, before deciding William Alland could do it if kept to the shadows and occasionally dubbed by Welles. The rapidly-changing political situation in Europe, already forcing the Roosevelt administration to reassess its policies about vampirism and the very real Count Dracula, may have prompted certain factions to bring pressure to bear on RKO that such a film was "inadvisable" for 1940.

In an interview with Peter Bogdanovich, published in *This is Orson Welles* (1992) but held well before Francis Ford Coppola's controversial *Dracula* (1979), Welles said: "*Dracula* would make a marvellous movie. In fact, nobody has ever made it; they've never paid any attention to the book, which is the most hair-raising, marvellous book in the world. It's told by four people, and must be done with four narrations, as we did on the radio. There's one scene in London where he throws a heavy bag into the corner of a cellar and it's full of screaming babies! They can go that far out now."

–Jonathan Gates, "Welles' Lost Draculas",
Video Watchdog No. 23 May-July 1994

VII

Welles did not so much live in the bungalow as occupy it. She recognized the signs of high-end, temporary tenancy. Pieces of extremely valuable antique furniture, imported from Spain, stood among ugly, functional, modern sticks that had come with the let. The den, largest space in the building, was made aesthetically bearable by a hanging she put at sixteenth-century, nailed up over the open fireplace like a curtain. The tapestry depicted a knight trotting in full armour through forest greenery, with black-faced, red-eyed-and-tongued devils peeping from behind tall, straight trees. The piece was marred by a bad burn that had caught at one corner and spread evil fingers upwards. All around were stacks of books, square-bound antique volumes and bright modern paperbacks, and rickety towers of film cans.

Geneviève wondered why Welles would have cases of good sherry and boxes of potato chips stacked together in a corner, then realized he must have been part-paid in goods for his commercial work. He offered her sherry and she surprised him by accepting.

"I do sometimes drink wine, Orson. Dracula wasn't speaking for us all."

He arched an eyebrow and made a flourish of pouring sherry into a paper cup.

"My glassware hasn't arrived from Madrid," he apologised.

She sipped the stuff, which she couldn't really taste, and sat on a straight-backed gothic chair. It gave her a memory-flash, of hours spent in churches when she was a warm girl. She wanted to fidget.

Welles plumped himself down with a Falstaffian rumble and strain on a low couch that had a velvet curtain draped over it. He was broad enough in the beam to make it seem like a throne.

Oja joined them and silently hovered. Her hair was covered by a bright headscarf.

A pause.

Welles grinned, expansively. Geneviève realized he was protracting the moment, relishing a role. She even knew who he was doing, Sydney Greenstreet in *The Maltese Falcon*. The ambiguous mastermind enjoying himself by matching wits with the perplexed private eye. If Hollywood ever remade *Falcon*, which would be a sacrilege, Welles would be in the ring for Gutman. Too many of his acting jobs were like that, replacing another big personality in an inferior retread of something already got right.

"I'll be wondering why you asked me here tonight," she prompted.

"Yes," he said, amused.

"It'll be a long story."

"I'm rather afraid so."

"There are hours before dawn."

"Indeed."

Welles was comfortable now. She understood he had been switching off from the shoot, coming down not only from his on-screen character but from his position as backyard God.

"You know I've been playing with *Dracula* for years? I wanted to make it at RKO in '40, did a script, designed sets, cast everybody. Then it was dropped."

She nodded.

"We even shot some scenes. I'd love to steal in some night and rescue the footage from the vaults. Maybe for use in the current project. But the studio has the rights. Imagine if paintings belonged to whoever mixed the paints and wove the canvas. I'll have to abase myself, as usual. The children who inherited RKO after Hughes ran it aground barely know who I am, but they'll enjoy the spectacle of my contrition, my pleading, my total dejection. I may even get my way in the end."

"Hasn't *Dracula* been made? I understand that Francis . . ."

"I haven't seen that. It doesn't matter to me or the world. I didn't do the first stage productions of *Macbeth* or *Caesar*, merely the best. The same goes for the Stoker. A marvellous piece, you know."

"Funnily enough, I have read it," she put in.

"Of course you have."

"And I met Dracula."

Welles raised his eyes, as if that were news to him. Was this all about picking her brains? She had spent all of fifteen minutes in the Royal Presence, nearly a hundred years ago, but was quizzed about that (admittedly dramatic) occasion more than the entire rest of her five hundred and sixty-five years. She'd seen the Count again, after his true death – as had Welles, she remembered – and been at his last funeral, seen his ashes scattered. She supposed she had wanted to be sure he was really finally dead.

"I've started *Dracula* several times. It seems like a cursed property. This time, maybe, I'll finish it. I believe it has to be done."

Oja laid hands on his shoulders and squeezed. There was an almost imperial quality to Welles, but he was an emperor in exile, booted off his throne and cast out, retaining only the most loyal and long-suffering of his attendants.

"Does the name Alucard mean anything to you?" he asked. "John Alucard?"

"This may come as a shock to you, Orson, but 'Alucard' is 'Dracula' spelled backwards."

He gave out a good-humoured version of his Shadow laugh.

"I had noticed. He is a vampire, of course."

"Central and Eastern European *nosferatu* love anagrams as much as they love changing their names," she explained. "It's a real quirk. My late friend Carmilla Karnstein ran through at least half a dozen scramblings of her name before running out. Millarca, Marcilla, Allimarc . . ."

"My name used to be Olga Palinkas," put in Oja. "Until Orson thought up 'Oja Kodar' for me, to sound Hungarian."

"The promising sculptor 'Vladimir Zagdrov' is my darling Oja too. You are right about the undead predilection for *noms de plumes*, alter egos, secret identities, anagrams and palindromes and acrostics. Just like actors. A hold-over from the Byzantine mindset, I believe. It says something about the way the creatures think. Tricky but obvious, as it were. The back-spelling might also be a compensation: a reflection on parchment for those who have none in the glass."

"This Alucard? Who is he?"

"That's the exact question I'd like answered," said Welles. "And you, my dear Mademoiselle Dieudonné, are the person I should like to provide that answer."

"Alucard says he's an independent producer," said Oja. "With deals all over town."

"But no credits," said Welles.

Geneviève could imagine.

"He has money, though," said Welles. "No credits, but a line of credit. Cold cash and the Yankee Dollar banish all doubt. That seems unarguable."

"Seems?"

"Sharp little word, isn't it. Seems and is, syllables on either side of a chasm of meaning. This Mr Alucard, a *nosferatu*, wishes to finance my *Dracula*. He has offered me a deal the likes of which I haven't had since RKO and *Kane*. An unlimited budget, major studio facilities, right of final cut, control over everything from casting to publicity. The only condition he imposes is that I must make this subject. He wants not my *Don Quixote* or my *Around the World in 80 Days*, but my *Dracula* only."

"The Coppola," – a glare from Welles made her rephrase – "that other film, with Brando as the Count? That broke even in the end, didn't it? Made back its budget. *Dracula* is a box-office subject. There's probably room for another version. Not to mention sequels, a spin-off TV series and imitations. Your Mr Alucard makes sense. Especially if he has deep pockets and no credits. Being attached to a good, to a *great*, film would do him no harm. Perhaps he wants the acclaim?"

Welles rolled the idea around his head.

"No," he concluded, almost sadly. "Gené, I have never been accused of lack of ego. My largeness of spirit, my sense of self-worth, is part of my act, as it were. The armour I must needs haul on to do my daily battles. But I am not blind to my situation. No producer in his right mind would bankroll me to such an extent, would offer me such a deal. Not even these kids, this Spielberg and that Lucas, could get such a sweetheart deal. I am as responsible for that as anyone. The studios of today may be owned by oil companies and hotel magnates, but there's a race memory of that contract I signed when I was twenty-four and of how it all went wrong, for me and for everyone. When I was kicked off the lot in 1943, RKO took out ads in the trades announcing their new motto, 'showmanship, not genius'! Hollywood doesn't want to have me around. I remind the town of its mistakes, its crimes."

"Alucard is an independent producer, you say. Perhaps he's a fan?"

"I don't think he's seen any of my pictures."

"Do you think this is a cruel prank?"

Welles shrugged, raising huge hands. Oja was more guarded, more worried. Geneviève wondered whether she was the one who had insisted on calling in an investigator.

"The first cheques have cleared," said Welles. "The rent is paid on this place."

"You are familiar with the expression . . ."

"The one about equine dentistry? Yes."

"But it bothers you? The mystery?"

"The Mystery of Mr Alucard. That is so. If it blows up in my face, I can stand that. I've come to that pass before and I shall venture there again. But I should like some presentiment, either way. I want you to make some discreet inquiries about our Mr Alucard. At the very least, I'd like to know his real name and where he comes from. He seems very American at the moment, but I don't think that was always the case. Most of all, I want to know what he is up to. Can you help me, Mademoiselle Dieudonné?"

VIII

"You know, Gené," said Jack Martin wistfully, contemplating the melting ice in his empty glass through the wisps of cigarette smoke that always haloed his head, "none of this matters. It's not important. Writing. It's a trivial pursuit, hardly worth the effort, inconsequential on any cosmic level. It's just blood and sweat and guts and bone hauled out of our bodies and fed through a typewriter to slosh all over the platen. It's just the sick soul of America turning sour in the sunshine. Nobody really reads what I've written. In this town, they don't know Flannery O'Connor or Ray Bradbury, let alone Jack Martin. Nothing will be remembered. We'll all die and it'll be over. The sands will close over our civilization and the sun will turn into a huge red fireball and burn even you from the face of the earth."

"That's several million years away, Jack," she reminded him.

He didn't seem convinced. Martin was a writer. In high school, he'd won a national competition for an essay entitled "It's Great to Be Alive". Now in his grumbling forties, the sensitive but creepy short stories that were his most personal work were published in small science fiction and men's magazines, and put out in expensive limited editions by fan publishers who went out of business owing him money. He had made a living as a screenwriter for ten years without ever seeing anything written under his own name get made. He had a problem with happy endings.

However, he knew what was going on in "the Industry" and was her first port of call when a case got her mixed up with the movies. He lived in a tar-paper shack on Beverly Glen Boulevard, wedged between multi-million dollar estates, and told everybody that at least it was earthquake-proof.

Martin rattled the ice. She ordered him another Coca-Cola. He stubbed out one cigarette and lit another.

The girl behind the hotel bar, dressed as a magician, sloshed ice into another glass and reached for a small chromed hose. She squirted coke into the glass, covering the ice.

Martin held up his original glass.

"Wouldn't it be wonderful if you could slip the girl a buck and have her fill up *this* glass, not go through all the fuss of getting a fresh one and charging you all over again. There should be infinite refills. Imagine that, a utopian dream, Gené. It's what America needs. A *bottomless* coke!"

"It's not policy, sir," said the girl. With the coke came a quilted paper napkin, an unhappy edge of lemon and a plastic stirrer.

Martin looked at the bar-girl's legs. She was wearing black fishnets, high-heeled pumps, a tight white waistcoat, a tail coat and top-hat.

The writer sampled his new, bottomed, coke. The girl went to cope with other morning customers.

"I'll bet she's an actress," he said. "I think she does porno."

Geneviève raised an eyebrow.

"Most X-rated films are better directed than the slop that comes out of the majors," Martin insisted. "I could show you a reel of something by Gerard Damiano or Jack Horner that you'd swear was Bergman or Don Siegel. Except for the screwing."

Martin wrote "scripts" for adult movies, under well-guarded pseudonyms to protect his Writer's Guild membership. The Guild didn't have any moral position on porno, but members weren't supposed to take jobs which involved turning out a full-length feature script in two afternoons for three hundred dollars. Martin claimed to have invented Jamie Gillis' catchphrase, "suck it, bitch!"

"What can you tell me about John Alucard?"

"The name is . . ."

"Besides that his name is 'Dracula' written backwards."

"He's from New York. Well, that's where he was last. I heard he ran with that art crowd. You know, Warhol and Jack Smith. He's got a first-look deal at United Artists, and something cooking with Fox. There's going to be a story in the trades that he's set up an independent production company with Griffin Mill, Julia Phillips and Don Simpson."

"But he's never made a movie?"

"The word is that he's never *seen* a movie. That doesn't stop him calling himself a producer. Say, are you working for him? If you could mention that I was available. Mention my rewrite on *Can't Stop the Music*. No, don't. Say about that TV thing that didn't happen. I can get you sample scripts by sun-down."

Martin was gripping her upper arm.

"I've never met Alucard, Jack. I'm checking into him for a client."

"Still, if you get the chance, Gené. You know what it would mean to me. I'm fending off bill-collectors and Sharkko Press still hasn't come through for the *Tenebrous Twilight* limiteds. A development deal, even a rewrite or a polish, could get me through winter and spring. Buy me time to get down to Ensenada and finish some stories."

She would have to promise. She had learned more than the bare facts. The light in Jack Martin's eyes told her something about John Alucard. He had some sort of magic effect, but she didn't know whether he was a conjurer or a wizard.

Now, she would have to build on that.

IX

Short of forcing her way into Alucard's office and asking outright whether he was planning on leaving Orson Welles in the lurch, there wasn't much more she could do. After Martin, she made a few phone calls to industry contacts, looked over recent back numbers of *Variety* and the *Hollywood Reporter* and hit a couple of showbiz watering holes, hoping to soak up gossip.

Now, Geneviève was driving back along the Pacific Coast Highway to Paradise Cove. The sun was down and a heavy, unstarred darkness hung over the sea. The Plymouth, which she sometimes suspected of having a mind of its own, handled gently, taking the blind curves at speed. She twiddled the radio past a lot of disco, and found a station pumping out two-tone. That was good, that was new, that was a culture still alive.

" . . . *mirror in the bathroom, recompense*
all my crimes of self-defence . . ."

She wondered about what she had learned.

It wasn't like the old days, when the studios were tight little fiefdoms and a stringer for Louella Parsons would know everything going on in town and all the current scandal. Most movies weren't even made in Hollywood any more, and the studios were way down on the lists of interests owned by multi-national corporations with other primary concerns. The buzz was that United Artists might well be changing its name to TransAmerica Pictures.

General word confirmed most of what Martin had told her, and turned up surprisingly few extra details. Besides the Welles deal, financed off his own line of credit with no studio production coin as yet involved, John Alucard had projects in development all over town, with high-end talent attached. He was supposed to be in bed with Michael Cimino, still hot off *The Deer Hunter*, on *The Lincoln County Wars*, a Western about the vampire outlaw Billy the Kid and a massacre of settlers in Roswell, New Mexico, in the 1870s. With the Mill-Simpson-Phillips set-up, he was helping the long in-development Anne Rice project, *Interview with the Mummy*, which Elaine May was supposed to be making with Cher and Ryan O'Neal, unless it was Nancy Walker, with Diana Ross and Mark Spitz.

In an interview in the *Reporter*, Alucard said "The pursuit of making money is the only reason to make movies. We have no obligation to make history. We have no obligation to make art. We have no obligation to make a statement. Our obligation is to make money." A lot of execs, and not a few directors and writers, found his a refreshing and invigorating stance, though Geneviève had the impression Alucard was parroting someone else's grand theory. If he truly believed what he said, and was not just laying down something the studios' corporate owners wanted to hear, then John Alucard did not sound like someone who would happily want to be in business with Orson Welles. Apart from anything else, his manifesto was a 1980s rewrite, at five times the length with in-built repetition to get through to the admass morons at the back of the hall, of "showmanship, not genius".

The only thing she couldn't find out was what his projects really were. Besides Welles' *Dracula*, which wasn't mentioned by anyone she had talked with, and the long-gestating shows he was working with senior production partners, he had half-a-dozen other irons in the fire. Directors and stars were attached, budgets set, start dates announced, but no titles ever got mentioned, and the descriptions in the trades – "intense drama", "romantic comedy" – were hardly helpful. That was interesting and unusual. John Alucard was making a splash, waves radiating outwards, but surely he would have eventually to say what the pictures were. Or had that become the least important part of the package? An agent at CAA told her that for men like Alucard, the art was in the deal not on the screen.

That did worry her.

Could it be that there wasn't actually a pot of gold at the end of this rainbow? The man was a vampire, but was he also a phantom? No photographs existed, of course. Everyone had a second-hand description, always couched as a casting suggestion: a young Louis Jourdan, a smart Jack Palance, a rough trade David Niven. It was agreed that the man was European, a long time ago. No one had any idea how long he had been a vampire, even. He could be a new-born fresh-killed and risen last year, or a centuried elder who had changed his face a dozen times. His name always drew the same reaction: excitement, enthusiasm, fear. There was a sense that John Alucard was getting things on the road, and that it'd be a smart career move to get close, to be ready to haul out of the station with him.

She cruised across sandy tarmac into the trailer park. The seafood restaurant was doing a little New Year's Day business. She would be thirsty soon.

Someone sat on the stairs of her trailer, leaning back against her door, hands loose in his lap, legs in chinos, cowboy boots.

Someone dead.

X

Throughout Welles's career, *Dracula* remained an idée fixée. The Welles-Mankiewicz script was RKO property and the studio resisted Welles's offer to buy it back. They set their asking price at the notional but substantial sum accountants reckoned had been lost on the double debacle of *Ambersons* and the unfinished South American project, *It's All True*.

When Schaefer, Welles's patron, was removed from his position as Vice-President in Charge of Production and replaced by Charles Koerner, there was serious talk of putting the script into production through producer Val Lewton's unit, which had established a reputation for low-budget supernatural dramas with *Cat People* (1942). Lewton got as far as having DeWitt Bodeen and then Curt Siodmak take runs at further drafts, scaling the script down to fit a straitjacket budget. Jacques Tourneur was attached to direct, though editor Mark Robson was considered when Tourneur was promoted to A pictures. Stock players were assigned supporting roles: Tom Conway (Dr Seward), Kent Smith (Jonathan Harker), Henry Daniell (Van Helsing), Jean Brooks (Lucy), Alan Napier (Arthur Holmwood), Skelton Knaggs (Renfield), Elizabeth Russell (Countess Marya Dolingen), Sir Lancelot (a calypso-singing coachman). Simone Simon, star of *Cat People*, was set for Mina, very much the focus of Lewton's take on the story, but the project fell through because RKO were unable to secure their first and only choice of star, Boris Karloff, who was committed to *Arsenic and Old Lace* on Broadway.

In 1944, RKO sold the Welles-Mankiewicz script, along with a parcel of set designs, to 20th Century-Fox. Studio head Darryl F. Zanuck offered Welles the *role* of Dracula, promising Joan Fontaine and Olivia de Havilland for Mina and Lucy, suggesting Tyrone Power (Jonathan), George Sanders (Arthur), John Carradine (Quincey) and Laird Cregar (Van Helsing). This *Dracula* would have been a follow-up to Fox's successful Welles-Fontaine *Jane Eyre* (1943) and Welles might have committed if Zanuck had again assigned weak-willed Robert Stevenson, allowing Welles to direct in everything but credit. However, on a project this "important", Zanuck would consider only two directors; John Ford had no interest - sparing us John Wayne, Victor McLaglen, Ward Bond and John Agar as brawling, boozing fearless vampire slayers - so it inevitably fell to Henry King, a specialist in molasses-slow historical subjects like *Lloyd's of London* (1936) and *Brigham Young* (1940). King, a plodder who had a brief flash of genius in a few later films with Gregory Peck, had his own, highly-developed, chocolate box style and *gravitas*, and was not a congenial director for Welles, whose mercurial temperament was unsuited to methods he considered conservative and dreary. The film still might have been made, since Welles was as ever in need of money, but Zanuck went cold on Dracula at the end of the War when the Count was moving into his Italian exile.

Fox wound up backing *Prince of Foxes* (1949), directed by King, with Power and Welles topping the cast, shot on location in Europe. A lavish bore, enlivened briefly by Welles's committed Cesare Borgia, this suggests what the Zanuck *Dracula* might have been like. Welles used much of his earnings from the long shoot to pour into film projects made in bits and pieces over several years: the completed *Othello* (1952), the unfinished *Don Quixote* (begun 1955) and, rarely mentioned until now, yet another *Dracula*. *El conde Dràcula*, a French-Italian-Mexican-American-Irish-Liechtensteinian-British-Yugoslav-Moroccan-Iranian co-production, was shot in snippets, the earliest dating from 1949, the latest from 1972.

Each major part was taken by several actors, or single actors over a span of years. In the controversial edit supervised by the Spaniard Jesus Franco - a second unit director on Welles's *Chimes at Midnight* (1966) - and premiered at Cannes in 1997, the cast is as follows: Akim Tamiroff (Van Helsing), Micheál MacLiammóir (Jonathan), Paola Mori (Mina), Michael Redgrave (Arthur), Patty McCormick (Lucy), Hilton Edwards (Dr Seward), Mischa Auer (Renfield). The vampire brides are played by Jeanne Moreau,

Suzanne Cloutier and Katina Paxinou, shot in different years on different continents. There is no sight of Francisco Reiguera, Welles"s Quixote, cast as a skeletal Dracula, and the Count is present only as a substantial shadow voiced (as are several other characters) by Welles himself. Much of the film runs silent, and a crucial framing story, explaining the multi-narrator device, was either never filmed or shot and lost. Jonathan's panicky exploration of his castle prison, filled with steam like the Turkish bath in *Othello*, is the most remarkable, purely Expressionist scene Welles ever shot. But the final ascent to Castle Dracula, with Tamiroff dodging patently *papier-mâché* falling boulders and wobbly zooms into and out of stray details hardly seems the work of anyone other than a fumbling amateur.

In no sense "a real film", *El conde Dràcula* is a scrapbook of images from the novel and Welles's imagination. He told Henry Jaglom that he considered the project a private exercise, to keep the subject in his mind, a series of sketches for a painting he would execute later. As Francis Coppola would in 1977, while his multi-million-dollar *Dracula* was bogged down in production problems in Romania, Welles often made comparisons with the Sistine Chapel. While Coppola invoked Michelangelo with some desperation as the vast machine of his movie seemed to be collapsing around him, Welles always resorted playfully to the metaphor, daring the interviewer with a wave and a wink and a deep chuckle to suggest the Pope probably did turn up every day wanting to know when the great artist would be finished and how much it was going to cost.

In 1973, Welles assembled some *El conde Dràcula* footage, along with documentary material about the real Count Dracula and the scandals that followed his true death in 1959: the alleged, much-disputed will that deeded much of his vast fortune to English housewife Vivian Nicholson, who claimed she had encountered Dracula while on a school holiday in the early 1950s; the autobiography Clifford Irving sold for a record-breaking advance in 1971, only to have the book exposed as an arrant fake written by Irving in collaboration with Fred Saberhagen; the squabbles among sundry vampire elders, notably Baron Meinster and Princess Asa Vajda, as to who should claim the Count's unofficial title as ruler of their kind, King of the Cats. Welles called this playful, essay-like film - constructed around the skeleton of footage shot by Calvin Floyd for his own documentary, *In Search of Dracula* (1971) - *When Are You Going to Finish el conde Dràcula?*, though it was exhibited in most territories as *D is for Dracula*. On the evening Premier Conuococu withdrew the Romanian Cavalry needed for Coppola's assault on Castle Dracula in order to pursue the vampire banditti of the Transylvania Movement in the next valley, Francis Ford Coppola held a private screening of *D is for Dracula* and cabled Welles that there was a curse on anyone who dared invoke the dread name.

Gates, *ibid.*

XI

The someone on her steps was *truly* dead. In his left chest, over his punctured heart, a star-shaped blotch was black in the moonlight.

Geneviève felt no residue. The intangible thing – immortal soul, psychic energy, battery power – which kept mind and body together, in *nosferatu* or the warm, was gone.

Broken is the golden bowl, the spirit flown forever.

She found she was crying. She touched her cheek and looked at the thick, salt, red tears, then smeared them away on her handkerchief.

It was Moondoggie. In repose, his face looked old, the lines his smile had made appealing turned to slack wrinkles.

She took a moment with him, remembering the taste of the living man, that he was the only one who called her "Gidget", his inability to put in words what it was about surfing that made him devote his life to it (he'd been in pre-med once, long, long ago – when there was a crack-up or a near-drowning, the doctor he might have been would surface and take over), and the rush of the seas that came with his blood.

That man was gone. Besides sorrow at the waste, she was angry. And afraid.

It was easy to see how it had happened. The killer had come close, face to face, and stuck Moondoggie through the heart. The wound was round, not a slit. The weapon was probably a wooden stake or a sharpened metal pole. The angle of the wound was upwards, so the killer was shorter than the rangy surfer. Stuck through, Moondoggie had been carefully propped up on her doorstep. She was being sent a message.

Moondoggie was a warm man, but he'd been killed as if he were like her, a vampire.

He was not cold yet. The killing was recent.

Geneviève turned in a half-circle, looking out across the beach.

Like most vampires, she had above average night vision for a human being – without sun glare bleaching everything bone-white, she saw better than by day – but no hawk-like power of distinguishing far-off tiny objects or magical X-ray sight.

It was likely that the assassin was nearby, watching to see that the message was received. Counting on the popular belief that vampires did have unnatural eyesight, she moved slowly enough that anyone in concealment might think she was looking directly at them, that they had been seen.

A movement.

The trick worked. A couple of hundred yards off, beyond the trailer park, out on the beach, something – someone – moved, clambering upright from a hollow depression in the dry sand.

As the probable murderer stood, Geneviève saw a blonde pony-tail whipping. It was a girl, mid-to-late teens, in halter-top and denim shorts, with a wispy gauze neck-scarf and – suggestive detail – running shoes and knee-pads. She was undersized but athletic. Another girl midget: no wonder she'd been able to get close enough to Moondoggie, genial connoisseur of young bodies, to stab him in the heart.

She assumed the girl would bolt. Geneviève was fast enough to run her down, but the killer ought to panic. In California, what people knew about vampires was scrambled with fantasy and science fiction.

For once, Geneviève was tempted to live up to her image. She wanted to rip out the silly girl's throat.

(and drink)

She took a few long steps, flashing forwards across the beach.

The girl stood her ground, waiting.

Geneviève had pause. The stake wasn't in the dead man's chest. The girl still had it. Her right hand was out of sight, behind her back.

Closer, she saw the killer's face in the moonlight. Doll-pretty, with an upturned nose and the faintest fading traces of freckles. She was frowning with concentration now, but probably had a winning smile, perfect teeth. She should be a cheerleader, not an assassin.

This wasn't a vampire, but Geneviève knew she was no warm creampuff, either. She had killed a strong man twice her weight with a single thrust and was prepared for a charging *nosferatu*.

Geneviève stood still, twenty yards from the girl.

The killer produced her stake. It was stained.

"Meet Simon Sharp," she said. She had a clear, casual voice. Geneviève found her flippancy terrifying.

"You killed a man," Geneviève said, trying to get through to her, past the madness.

"Not a man, a viper. One of you, undead vermin."

"He was alive."

"You'd snacked on him, Frenchie. He would have turned."

"It doesn't work like that."

"That's not what I hear, not what I *know*."

From her icy eyes, this teenager was a fanatic. There could be no reasoning with her.

Geneviève would have to take her down, hold her until the police got here.

Whose side would the cops take? A vampire or a prom queen? Geneviève had fairly good relations with the local law, who were more uneasy about her as a private detective than as a vampire, but this might stretch things.

The girl smiled. She did look awfully cute.

Geneviève knew the mad bitch could probably get away with it. At least once. She had the whole Tuesday Weld thing going for her, pretty poison.

"You've been warned, not spared," said the girl. "My A plan was to skewer you on sight, but the Overlooker thinks this is better strategy. It's some English kick, like cricket. Go figure."

The Overlooker?

"It'd be peachiest all around if you left the state, Frenchie. The country, even. Preferably, the planet. Next time we meet, it won't be a warning. You'll get a formal introduction to the delightful Simon. *Capisce?*"

"Who are you?"

"The Slayer," said the girl, gesturing with her stake. "Barbie, the Vampire Slayer."

Despite herself, despite everything, Geneviève had to laugh.

That annoyed Barbie.

Geneviève reminded herself that this silly girl, playing dress-up-and-be-a-heroine, was a real live murderess.

She laughed more calculatedly.

Barbie wanted to kill her, but made no move. Whoever this Overlooker – bloody silly title – was, his or her creature didn't want to exceed the brief given her.

(Some English kick, like cricket.)

Geneviève darted at the girl, nails out. Barbie had good reactions. She pivoted to one side and launched a kick. A cleated shoe just missed Geneviève's midriff but raked her side, painfully. She jammed her palm-heel at Barbie's chin, and caught her solidly, shutting her mouth with a click.

Simon Sharp went flying. That made Geneviève less inhibited about close fighting.

Barbie was strong, trained and smart. She might have the brain of a flea, but her instincts were panther-like and she went all out for a kill. But Geneviève was still alive after five hundred and fifty years as a vampire.

Barbie tried the oldest move in girly martial arts and yanked her opponent's hair, cutting her hand open. Geneviève's hair was fine but stronger and sharper than it looked, like pampas grass. The burst of hot blood was a distraction, sparking lizardy synapses in Geneviève's brain, momentarily blurring her thoughts. She threw Barbie away, skittering her across the sand on her can in an undignified tangle.

Mistake.

Barbie pulled out something that looked like a mace spray and squirted at Geneviève's face.

Geneviève backed away from the cloud, but got a whiff of the mist. Garlic, holy water and silver salts. Garlic and holy water didn't bother her – more mumbo-jumbo, ineffective against someone not of Dracula's bloodline – but silver was deadly to all *nosferatu*. This spray might not kill her, but it could scar her for a couple of centuries, or even life. It was vanity, she supposed, but she had got used to people telling her she was pretty.

She scuttled away, backwards, across the sand. The cloud dissipated in the air. She saw the droplets, shining under the moon, falling with exaggerated slowness, pattering onto the beach.

When the spray was gone, so was Barbie the Vampire Slayer.

XII

" . . . and, uh, this is exactly where you found Mr Griffin, miss?" asked the LAPD homicide detective.

Geneviève was distracted. Even just after dawn, the sun was fatiguing her. In early daylight, on a gurney, Moondoggie – whose name turned out to have been Jeff Griffin – looked colder and emptier, another of the numberless dead stranded in her past while she went on and on and on.

"Miss Dew-dun-ee?"

"Dieudonné," she corrected, absent-mindedly.

"Ah yes, Dieudonné. Accent *grave* over the e. That's French, isn't it? I have a French car. My wife says . . ."

"Yes, this is where I found the body," she answered, catching up.

"Ah. There's just one thing I don't understand."

She paid attention to the crumpled little man. He had curly hair, a gravel voice and a raincoat. He was working on the first cigar of the day. One of his eyes was glass, and aimed off to the side.

"And what might that be, Lieutenant?"

"This girl you mentioned, this . . ." he consulted his note-book, or pretended to, "this 'Barbie'. Why would she hang around after the murder? Why did she have to make sure you found the body?"

"She implied that she was under orders, working for this Overlooker."

The detective touched his eyebrow as if to tuck his smelly cigar behind his ear like a pen, and made great play of thinking hard, trying to work through the story he had been told. He was obviously used to people lying to him, and equally obviously unused to dealing with vampires. He stood between her and the sun, as she inched into the shrinking shadow of her trailer.

She wanted to get a hat and dark glasses but police tape still barred her door.

"'Overlooker', yes. I've got a note of that, miss. Funny expression, isn't it? Gives the impression the 'Overlooker' is supposed *not* to see something, that the whole job is about, ah, overlooking. Not like my profession, miss. Or yours either, I figure. You're a PI, like on TV?"

"With fewer car chases and shoot-outs."

The detective laughed. He was a funny little duck. She realized he used his likeability as a psychological weapon, to get close to people he wanted to nail. She couldn't mistake the situation: she was in the ring for the killing, and her story about Barbie the Slayer didn't sound straight in daylight. What sane professional assassin gives a name, even a partial name, to a witness?

"A vampire private eye?" the detective scratched his head.

"It makes sense. I don't mind staying up all night. And I've got a wealth of varied experience."

"Have you solved any big cases? Really big ones?"

Without thinking, she told a truth. "In 1888, I halfway found out who Jack the Ripper was."

The detective was impressed.

"I thought no one knew how that panned out. Scotland Yard still have it open. What with you folk living longer and longer, it's not safe to close unsolved files. The guy who took the rap died, didn't he? These days, the theorists say it couldn't have been him."

"I said I halfway found out."

She had a discomfiting memory flash, of her and Charles in an office in Whitechapel in 1888, stumbling over the last clue, all the pieces falling into place. The problem was that solving the mystery hadn't meant sorting everything out, and the case had continued to spiral out of control. There was a message there.

"That wouldn't good enough for my captain, I'm afraid, miss. He has to answer to Police Chief Exley, and Chief Exley insists on a clearance and conviction rate. I can't just catch them, I have to prove they did it. I have to go to the courts. You'd be surprised how many guilty parties walk free. Especially the rich ones, with fancy lawyers. In this town, it's hard to get a conviction against a rich man."

"This girl looked like a high-school kid."

"Even worse, miss. Probably has rich folks."

"I've no idea about that."

"And pretty is as good as being rich. Better. Juries like pretty girls as much as lawyers like rich men."

There was a shout from the beach. One of the uniformed cops who had been combing the sand held up a plastic evidence bag. Inside was Barbie's bloody stake.

"Simon Sharp," Geneviève said. The detective's eyebrows rose. "That's what she called it. What kind of person gives a pet-name to a murder weapon?"

"You think you've heard everything in this business and then something else comes along and knocks you flat. Miss, if you don't mind me asking, I know it's awkward for some women, but, um, well, how old are you?"

"I was born in 1416," she said.

"That's five hundred and, um, sixty-five."

"Thereabouts."

The detective shook his head again and whistled.

"Tell me, does it get easier? Everything?"

"Sadly, no."

"You said you had – uh, how did you put it? – 'a wealth of varied experience'. Is that like getting cleverer every year? Knowing more and more of the answers?"

"Would that it did, Lieutenant. Sometimes I think it just means having more and more questions."

He chuckled. "Ain't that the truth."

"Can I get into my trailer now?" she asked, indicating the climbing sun.

"We were keeping you out?" he asked, knowing perfectly well he was. "That's dreadful, with your condition and everything. Of course you can go inside, miss. We'll be able to find you here, if there are any more questions that come up? It's a trailer, isn't it? You're not planning on hitching it up to your car and driving off, say, out of state?"

"No, Lieutenant."

"That's good to know."

He gallantly tore the police tape from her door. She had her keys out. Her skin tingled, and the glare off the sea turned everything into blobby, indistinct shapes.

"Just one more thing," said the detective, hand on her door.

The keys were hot in her fingers.

"Yes," she said, a little sharply.

"You're on a case, aren't you? Like on TV?"

"I'm working on several investigations. May I make a bet with you, Lieutenant? For a dime?"

The detective was surprised by that. But he fished around in his raincoat pocket and, after examining several tissues and a book of matches, came up with a coin and a smile.

"I bet I know what you're going to ask me next," she said. "You're going to ask me who I'm working for?"

He was theatrically astonished.

"That's just incredible, miss. Is it some kind of vampire mind-reading power? Or are you like Sherlock Holmes, picking up tiny hints from little clues, like the stains on the cigar-band or the dog not howling in the night?"

"Just a lucky guess," she said. Her cheeks were really burning, now.

"Well, see if I can luckily guess your answer. Client confidentiality privilege, like a lawyer or a doctor, eh?"

"See. You have hidden powers too, Lieutenant."

"Well, Miss Dieudonné, I do what I can, I do what I can. Any idea what I'm going to say next?"

"No."

His smile froze slightly and she saw ice in his real eye.

"Don't leave town, miss."

XIII

On rising, she found Jack Martin had left a message on her machine. He had something for her on "Mr A". Geneviève listened to the brief message twice, thinking it over.

She had spent only a few hours asking about John Alucard, and someone had got killed. A connection? It would be weird if there wasn't. Then again, as the detective reminded her, she'd been around for a long time. In her years, she'd ticked off a great many people, not a few as long-lived as she was herself. Also, this was Southern California, La-La Land, where the nuts came from: folk didn't necessarily need a reason to take against you, or to have you killed.

Could this Overlooker be another Manson? Crazy Charlie was a vampire-hater too, and used teenage girls as assassins. Everyone remembered the death of Sharon Tate, but the Manson Family had also destroyed a vampire elder, Count von Krolock, up on La Cienaga Drive, and painted bat-symbols on the walls with his old blood. Barbie the Slayer was cutie-pie where the Family chicks had been skaggy, but that could be a 1980s thing as opposed to a 1960s one.

Geneviève knew she could take care of herself, but the people who talked to her might be in danger. She must mention it to Martin, who wasn't long on survival skills. He could at least scurry down to Mexico for a couple of months. In the meantime, she was still trying to earn her fifty dollars a day, so she returned Martin's call. The number he had left was (typically) a bar, and the growling man who picked up had a message for her, giving an address in the valley where she could find Martin.

This late in the afternoon, the sun low in the sky. She loved the long winter nights.

In a twist-tied plastic bag buried among the cleaning products and rags under her sink unit was a gun, a ladylike palm-sized automatic. She considered fishing it out and transferring it to the Plymouth Fury, but resisted the impulse. No sense in escalating. As yet, even the Overlooker didn't want her dead.

That was not quite a comfort.

XIV

The address was an anonymous house in an anonymous neighbourhood out in the diaspora-like sprawl of ranchos and villas and vistas, but there were more cars and vans outside than a single family would need. Either there was a party on or this was a suburban commune. She parked on the street and watched for a moment. The lights from the windows and the patio were a few candles brighter than they needed to be. Cables snaked out of a side-door and round to the backyard.

She got out of the Plymouth and followed the hose-thick cables, passing through a cultivated arbour into a typical yard-space, with an oval pool, currently covered by a heavy canvas sheet that was damp where it rested on water, and a white wooden gazebo, made up with strands of dead ivy and at the centre of several beams of light. There were a lot of people around but this was no party. She should have guessed: it was another film set. She saw lights on stands and a camera crew, plus the usual assortment of hangers-on, gophers, rubberneckers, fluffers, runners and extras.

This was more like a "proper" movie set than the scene she had found at Welles's bungalow, but she knew from the naked people in the gazebo that this was a far less proper movie. Again, she should have guessed. This was a Jack Martin lead, after all.

"Are you here for 'Vampire Bitch, Number Three'?"

The long-haired, chubby kid addressing her wore a tie-dyed T-shirt and a fisherman's waistcoat, pockets stuffed with goodies. He carried a clipboard.

Geneviève shook her head. She didn't know whether to be flattered or offended. Then again, in this town, everyone thought everyone else was an actor or actress. They were usually more or less right.

She didn't like the sound of the part. If she had a reflection that caught on film and were going to prostitute herself for a skinflick, she would at least hold out for 'Vampire Bitch, Number One'.

"The part's taken, I'm afraid," said the kid, not exactly dashing her dreams of stardom. "We got Seka at the last minute."

He nodded towards the gazebo, where three warm girls in pancake make-up hissed at a hairy young man, undoing his Victorian cravat and waistcoat.

"I'm here to see Jack Martin," she said.

"Who?"

"The writer?"

She remembered Martin used pseudonyms for this kind of work, and spun off a description: "Salt-and-pepper beard, *Midnight Cowboy* jacket with the fringes cut off, smokes a lot, doesn't believe in positive thinking."

The kid knew who she meant. "That's 'Mr Stroker'. Come this way. He's in the kitchen, doing rewrites. Are you sure you're not here for a part? You'd make a groovy vampire chick."

She thanked him for the compliment, and followed his lead through a mess of equipment to the kitchen, torn between staring at what was going on between the three girls and one guy in the gazebo and keeping her eyes clear. About half the crew were of the madly ogling variety, while the others were jaded enough to stick to their jobs and look at their watches as the shoot edged towards golden time.

"Vampire Bitch Number Two, put more tongue in it," shouted an intense bearded man whose megaphone and beret marked him as the director. "I want to see fangs, Samantha. You've got a jones for that throbbing vein, you've got a real lust for blood. Don't slobber. That's in bad taste. Just nip nicely. That's it. That's colossal. That's the cream."

"What is the name of this picture?" Geneviève asked.

"*Debbie Does Dracula*," said the kid. "It's going to be a four-boner classic. Best thing Boris Adrian has ever shot. He goes for production values, not just screwing. It's got real crossover potential, as a 'couples' movie. Uh-oh, there's a gusher."

"Spurt higher, Ronny," shouted the director, Boris Adrian. "I need the arc to be highlit. Thank you, that's perfect. Seka, Samantha, Désirée, you can writhe in it if you like. That's outstanding. Now, collapse in exhaustion, Ronny. That's perfect. Cut, and print."

The guy in the gazebo collapsed in real exhaustion, and the girls called for assistants to wipe them off. Some of the crew applauded and congratulated the actors on their performances, which she supposed was fair enough. One of the "Vampire Bitches" had trouble with her false fang-teeth.

The director got off his shooting-stick and sat with his actors, talking motivation.

The kid held a screen door open and showed her into the kitchen. Martin sat at a tiny table, cigarette in his mouth, hammering away at a manual typewriter. Another clipboard kid, a wide girl with a frizz of hair and Smiley badges fastening her overall straps, stood over him.

"Gené, excuse me," said Martin. "I'll be through in a moment."

Martin tore through three pages, working the carriage return like a gunslinger fanning a Colt, and passed them up to the girl, who couldn't read as fast as he wrote.

"There's your Carfax Abbey scene," Martin said, delivering the last page.

The girl kissed his forehead and left the kitchen.

"She's in love with me."

"The assistant?"

"She's the producer, actually. Debbie W. Griffith. Had a monster hit distributing *Throat Sprockets* in Europe. You should see that. It's the first real adult film for the vampire market. Plays at midnight matinees."

"She's 'D.W. Griffith', and you're . . .?"

Martin grinned, "Meet 'Bram Stroker'."

"And why am I here?"

Martin looked around, to make sure he wasn't overheard, and whispered "This is it, this is his. Debbie's a front. This is *un film de* John Alucard."

"It's not Orson Welles."

"But it's a start."

A dark girl, kimono loose, walked through the kitchen, carrying a couple of live white rats in one hand, muttering to herself about "the Master". Martin tried to say hello, but she breezed past, deeply into her role, eyes drifting. She lingered a moment on Geneviève, but wafted out onto the patio and was given a mildly sarcastic round of applause.

"That's Kelly Nicholls," said Martin. "She plays Renfield. In this version, it's not *flies* she eats, not in the usual sense. This picture has a great cast: Dirk Diggler as Dracula, Annette Haven as Mina, Holly Body as Lucy, John Leslie as Van Helsing."

"Why didn't you tell me about this yesterday?"

"I didn't know then."

"But you're the screenwriter. You can't have been hired and written the whole thing to be shot this afternoon."

"I'm the re-writer. Even for the adult industry, their first pass at the script blew dead cats. It was called *Dracula Sucks*, and boy did it ever. They couldn't lick it, as it were. It's the subject, *Dracula*. You know what they say about the curse, the way it struck down Coppola in Romania. I've spent the day doing a page-one rewrite."

Someone shouted "Quiet on set," and Martin motioned Geneviève to come outside with him, to watch the shooting.

"The next scene is Dracula's entrance. He hauls the three vampire bitches – pardon the expression – off Jonathan and, ah, well, you can imagine, *satiates* them, before tossing them baby in a bag."

"I was just offered a role in the scene. I passed."

Martin *harrumphed*. Unsure about this whole thing, she began to follow.

A movement in an alcove distracted her. A pleasant-faced warm young man sat in there, hunched over a sideboard. He wore evening dress trousers and a bat-winged black cloak but nothing else. His hair was black and smoothed back, with a prominent widow's peak painted on his forehead. For a supposed vampire, he had a decent tan.

He had a rolled up ten-dollar bill stuck in his nose.

A line of red dust was on the sideboard. He bent over and snuffed it up. She had heard of drac, but never seen it.

The effect on the young man was instant. His eyes shone like bloodied marbles. Fang-teeth shot out like switchblades.

"Yeah, that's it," he said. "Instant vamp!"

He flowed upright, unbending from the alcove, and slid across the floor on bare feet. He wasn't warm, wasn't a vampire, but something in-between – a dhampire – that wouldn't last more than an hour.

"Where's Dracula?" shouted Boris Adrian. "Has he got the fangs on yet?"

"I am Dracula," intoned the youth, as much to himself, convincing himself. "I *am* Dracula!"

As he pushed past her, Geneviève noticed the actor's trousers were held together at the fly and down the sides by strips of velcro. She could imagine why.

She felt obscurely threatened. Drac – manufactured from vampire blood – was extremely expensive and highly addictive. In her own veins flowed the raw material of many a valuable fangs-on instant vamp fugue. In New York, where the craze came from, vampires had been kidnapped and slowly bled empty to make the foul stuff.

Geneviève followed the dhampire star. He reached out his arms like a wingspread, cloak billowing, and walked across the covered swimming pool, almost flying, as if weightless, skipping over sagging puddles and, without toppling or using his hands, made it over the far edge. He stood at poolside and let the cloak settle on his shoulders.

"I'm ready," he hissed through fangs.

The three fake vampire girls in the gazebo huddled together, a little afraid. They weren't looking at Dracula's face, his hypnotic eyes and fierce fangs, but at his trousers. Geneviève realized there were other properties of drac that she hadn't read about in the newspapers.

The long-haired kid who had spoken to her was working a pulley. A shiny cardboard full moon rose above the gazebo. Other assistants held bats on fishing lines. Boris Adrian nodded approval at the atmosphere.

"Well, Count, go to it," the director ordered. "Action."

The camera began to roll as Dracula strode up to the gazebo, cloak rippling. The girls writhed over the prone guy, Jonathan Harker, and awaited the coming of their dark prince.

"This man is mine," said Dracula, in a Californian drawl that owed nothing to Transylvania. "As you all are mine, you vampire bitches, you horny vampire bitches."

Martin silently recited the lines along with the actor, eyes alight with innocent glee.

"You never love," said the least-fanged of the girls, who had short blonde hair, "you yourself have never loved."

"That is not true, as you know well and as I shall prove to all three of you. In succession, and together. Now."

The rip of velcro preceded a gasp from the whole crew. Dirk Diggler's famous organ was blood-red and angry. She wondered if he could stab a person with it and suck their blood, or was that just a rumour like the Tijuana werewolf show Martin spent his vacations trying to track down.

The "vampire bitches" huddled in apparently real terror.

"Whatever he's taking, I want some of it," breathed Martin.

XV

Later, in an empty all-night diner, Martin was still excited about *Debbie Does Dracula*. Not really sexually, though she didn't underestimate his prurience, but mostly high on having his words read out, caught on film. Even as "Bram Stroker", he had pride in his work.

"It's a stop-gap till the real projects come through," he said, waving a deadly cigarette. "But it's cash in hand, Gené. Cash in hand. I don't have to hock the typewriter. Debbie wants me for the sequel they're making next week, *Taste the Cum of Dracula*, with Vanessa Del Rio as Marya Zaleska. But I may pass. I've got something set up at Universal, near as damn it. A remake of *Buck Privates*, with Belushi and Dan Aykroyd. It's between me and this one other guy, Lionel Fenn, and Fenn's a drac-head from the East with a burn-out date stamped on his forehead. I tell you, Gené, it's adios to "Bram Stroker" and "William Forkner" and "Charles Dickings". You'll be my date for the premiere, won't you? You pretty up good, don't you? When the name Jack Martin means something in this town, I want to direct."

He was tripping on dreams. She brought him down again.

"Why would John Alucard be in bed with Boris Adrian?" she asked.

"And Debbie Griffith," he said. "I don't know. There's an invisible barrier between adult and legit. It's like a parallel world. The adult industry has its own stars and genres and awards shows. No one ever crosses. Oh, some of the girls do bit-parts. Kelly was in *The Toolbox Murders*, with Cameron Mitchell."

"I missed that one."

"I didn't. She was the chickie in the bath, who gets it with a nail-gun. Anyway, that was a fluke. You hear stories that Stallone made a skin-flick once, and that some on-the-skids directors take paying gigs under pseudonyms."

"Like 'Bram Stroker'?"

Martin nodded, in his flow. "But it's not an apprenticeship, not really. Coppola shot nudies, but that was different. Just skin, no sex. Tame now. Nostalgia bait. You've got to trust me, Gené, don't tell anyone, and I mean not anyone, that I'm 'Bram Stroker'. It's a crucial time for me, a knife-edge between the big ring and the wash-out ward. I really need this *Buck Privates* deal. If it comes to it, I want to hire you to scare off Fenn. You do hauntings, don't you?"

She waved away his panic, her fingers drifting through his nicotine cloud.

"Maybe Alucard wants to raise cash quickly?" she suggested.

"Could be. Though the way Debbie tells it, he isn't just a sleeping partner. He originated the whole idea, got her and Boris together, borrowed Dirk from Jack Horner, even – and I didn't tell you this – supplied the bloody nose candy that gave Dracula's performance the added *frisson*."

It was sounding familiar.

"Did he write the script?" she asked. "The first script?"

"Certainly, no writer did. It might be Mr A. There was no name on the title page."

"It's not a porno movie he wants, not primarily," she said. "It's a Dracula movie. Another one. Yet another one."

Martin called for a coffee refill. The ancient, slightly mouldy character who was the sole staff of the Nighthawks Diner shambled over, coffee sloshing in the glass jug.

"Look at this guy," Martin said. "You'd swear he was a god-damned reanimated corpse. No offence, Gené, but you know what I mean. Maybe he's a dhamp. I hear they zombie out after a while, after they've burned their bat-cells."

Deaf to the discussion, the shambler sloshed coffee in Martin's mug. Here, in Jack Martin Heaven, there were infinite refills. He exhaled contented plumes of smoke.

"Jack, I have to warn you. This case might be getting dangerous. A friend of mine was killed yesterday night, as a warning. And the police like me for it. I can't prove anything, but it might be that asking about Alucard isn't good for your health. Still, keep your ears open. I know about two John Alucard productions now, and I'd like to collect the set. I have a feeling he's a one-note musician, but I want that confirmed."

"You think he only makes Dracula movies?"

"I think he only makes Dracula."

She didn't know what she meant by that, but it sounded horribly right.

XVI

There was night enough left after Martin had peeled off home to check in with the client. Geneviève knew Welles would still be holding court at four in the morning.

He was running footage.

"Come in, come in," he boomed.

Most of the crew she had met the night before were strewn on cushions or rugs in the den, along with a few newcomers, movie brats and law professors and a very old, very grave black man in a bright orange dashiki. Gary, the cameraman, was working the projector.

They were screening the scene she had seen shot, projecting the picture onto the tapestry over the fireplace. Van Helsing tormented by vampire symbols. It was strange to see Welles' huge, bearded face, the luminous skull, the flapping bat and the dripping dagger slide across the stiff, formal image of the mediaeval forest scene.

Clearly, Welles was in mid-performance, almost holding a dialogue with his screen self, and wouldn't detach himself from the show so she could report her preliminary findings to him.

She found herself drifting into the yard. There were people there, too. Nico, the vampire starlet, had just finished feeding, and lay on her back, looking up at the stars, licking blood from her lips and chin. She was a messy eater. A too-pretty young man staggered upright, shaking his head to dispel dizziness. His clothes were Rodeo Drive, but last year's in a town where last week was another era. She didn't have to sample Nico's broadcast thoughts to put him down as a rich kid who had found a new craze to blow his trust fund money on, and her crawling skin told her it wasn't a sports car.

"Your turn," he said to Nico, nagging.

She kept to the shadows. Nico had seen her but her partner was too preoccupied to notice anyone. The smear on his neck gave Geneviève a little prick of thirst.

Nico sat up with great weariness, the moment of repletion spoiled. She took a tiny paring knife from her clutch-purse. It glinted, silvered. The boy sat eagerly beside her and rolled up the left sleeve of her loose muslin blouse, exposing her upper arm. Geneviève saw the row of striped scars she had noticed last night. Carefully, the vampire girl opened a scar and let her blood trickle. The boy fixed his mouth over the wound. She held his hair in her fist.

"Remember, lick," she said. "Don't suck. You won't be able to take a full fangs-on."

His throat pulsed, as he swallowed.

With a roar, the boy let the girl go. He had the eyes and the fangs, even more than Dirk Diggler's Dracula. He moved fast, a temporary new-born high on all the extra senses and the sheer sense of power.

The dhampire put on wraparound mirror shades, ran razor-nailed hands through his gelled hair and stalked off to haunt the La-La night. Within a couple of hours, he would be a real live boy again. By that time, he could have got himself into all manner of scrapes.

Nico squeezed shut her wound. Geneviève caught her pain. The silver knife would be dangerous if it flaked in the cut. For a vampire, silver rot was like bad gangrene.

"It's not my place to say anything," began Geneviève.

"Then don't," said Nico, though she clearly received what Geneviève was thinking. "You're an elder. You can't know what it's like."

She had a flash that this new-born would never be old. What a pity.

"It's a simple exchange," said the girl. "Blood for blood. A gallon for a scratch. The economy is in our favour. Just like the President says."

Geneviève joined Nico at the edge of the property.

"This vampire trip really isn't working for me," said Nico. "That boy, Julian, will be warm again in the morning, mortal and with a reflection. And when he wants to, he'll be a vampire. If I'm not here, there are others. You can score drac on Hollywood Boulevard for twenty-five dollars a suck. Vile stuff, powdered, not from the tap, but it works."

Geneviève tidied Nico's hair. The girl lay on her lap, sobbing silently. She hadn't just lost blood.

This happened when you became an elder. You were mother and sister to the whole world of the undead.

The girl's despair passed. Her eyes were bright, with Julian's blood.

"Let's hunt, elder, like you did in Transylvania."

"I'm from France. I've never even been to Romania."

Now she mentioned it, that was odd. She'd been almost everywhere else. Without consciously thinking of it, she must have been avoiding the supposed homeland of the *nosferatu*. Kate Reed had told her she wasn't missing much, unless you enjoyed political corruption and paprika.

"There are human cattle out there," said Nico. "I know all the clubs. X is playing at the Roxy, if you like West Coast punk. And the doorman at After Hours always lets us in, vampire girls. There are so few of us. We go to the head of the line. Powers of fascination."

"Human cattle" was a real new-born expression. This close to dawn, Geneviève was thinking of her cosy trailer and shutting out the sun, but Nico was a race-the-sun girl, staying out until it was practically light, bleeding her last as the red circle rose in the sky.

She wondered if she should stick close to the girl, keep her out of trouble. Why? She couldn't protect everyone. She barely knew Nico, probably had nothing in common with her.

She remembered Moondoggie. And all the other dead, the ones she hadn't been able to help, hadn't tried to help, hadn't known about in time. The old gumshoe had told her she should get into her current business because there were girls like this, vampire girls, that only she could understand.

This girl really was none of her business.

"What's that?" said Nico, head darting. There was a noise from beyond the fence at the end of the garden.

Dominating the next property was a three-storey wooden mansion, California cheesecake. Nico might have called it old. Now Geneviève's attention was drawn to it, her night-eyes saw how strange the place was. A rusted-out pick-up truck was on cinderblocks in the yard, with a pile of ragged auto tyres next to it. The windshield was smashed out, and dried streaks – which any vampire would have scented as human blood, even after ten years – marked the hood.

"Who lives there?" Geneviève asked.

"In-bred backwoods brood," said Nico. "Orson says they struck it rich down in Texas, and moved to Beverly Hills. You know, swimming pools, movie stars . . ."

"Oil?"

"Chilli sauce recipe. Have you heard of Sawyer's Sauce?" Geneviève hadn't. "I guess not. I've not taken solid foods since I turned, though if I don't feed for a night or two I get this terrible phantom craving for those really shitty White Castle burgers. I suppose that if you don't get to the market, you don't know the brand-names."

"The Sawyers brought Texas style with them," Geneviève observed. "That truck's a period piece."

The back-porch was hung with mobiles of bones and nail-impaled alarm clocks. She saw a napping chicken, stuffed inside a canary cage.

"What's that noise?" Nico asked.

There was a wasp-like buzzing, muted. Geneviève scented burning gas. Her teeth were on edge.

"Power tool," she said. "Funny time of the night for warm folks to be doing carpentry."

"I don't think they're all entirely warm. I saw some gross Grandpaw peeping out the other night, face like dried leather, licking livery lips. If he isn't undead, he's certainly nothing like alive."

There was a stench in the air. Spoiled meat.

"Come on, let's snoop around," said Nico, springing up. She vaulted over the low fence dividing the properties and crept across the yard like a four-legged crab.

Geneviève thought that was unwise, but followed, standing upright and keeping to shadows.

This really was none of her business.

Nico was on the porch now, looking at the mobiles. Geneviève wasn't sure whether it was primitive art or voodoo. Some of the stick-and-bone dangles were roughly man-shaped.

"Come away," she said.

"Not just yet."

Nico examined the back door. It hung open, an impenetrable dark beyond. The buzzing was still coming from inside the ramshackle house.

Geneviève *knew* sudden death was near, walking like a man.

She called to Nico, more urgently.

Something small and fast came, not from inside the house but from the flatbed of the abandoned truck. The shape cartwheeled across the yard to the porch and collided purposefully with Nico. A length of wood pierced the vampire girl's thin chest. A look, more of surprise than pain or horror, froze on her face.

Geneviève felt the thrust in her own heart, then the silence in her mind. Nico was gone, in an instant.

"How do you like your stake, ma'am?"

It was Barbie. Only someone truly witless would think stake puns the height of repartee.

This time, Geneviève wouldn't let her get away.

"Just the time of night for a little viper-on-a-spit," said the Slayer, lifting Nico's deadweight so that her legs dangled. "This really should be you, Frenchie. By the way, I don't think you've met Simon's brother, Sidney. Frenchie, Sidney. Sidney, hellbitch creature of the night fit only to be impaled and left to rot in the light of the sun. That's the formalities out of the way."

She threw Nico away, sliding the dead girl off Sidney the Stake. The new-born, mould already on her startled face, flopped off the porch and fell to the yard.

Geneviève was still shocked by the passing, almost turned to ice. Nico had been in her mind, just barely and with tiny fingers, and her death was a wrench. She thought her skull might be leaking.

"They don't cotton much to trespassers down Texas way," said Barbie, in a bad cowboy accent. "Nor in Beverly Hills, neither."

Geneviève doubted the Sawyers knew Barbie was here.

"Next time, the Overlooker says I can do you too. I'm wishing and hoping and praying you ignore the warning. You'd look so fine on the end of a pole, Frenchie."

An engine revved, like a signal. Barbie was bounding away, with deer-like elegance.

Geneviève followed.

She rounded the corner of the Sawyer house and saw Barbie climbing into a sleek black Jaguar. In the driver's seat was a man wearing a tweed hunting jacket with matching bondage hood. He glanced backwards as he drove off.

The sports car had vanity plates. OVRLKER1.

Gravel flew as the car sped off down the drive.

"What's all this consarned ruckus?" shouted someone, from the house.

Geneviève turned and saw an American Gothic family group on the porch. Blotch-faced teenage boy, bosomy but slack-eyed girl in a polka-dot dress, stern patriarch in a dusty black suit, and hulking elder son in a stained apron and crude leather mask. Only the elder generation was missing, and Geneviève was sure they were up in rocking chairs on the third storey, peeking through the slatted blinds.

"That a dead'n?" asked the patriarch, nodding at Nico.

She conceded that it was.

"*True* dead'n?"

"Yes," she said, throat catching.

"What a shame and a waste," said Mr Sawyer, in a tone that made Geneviève think he wasn't referring to a life but to flesh and blood that was highly saleable.

"Shall I call the Sheriff, Paw?" asked the girl.

Mr Sawyer nodded, gravely.

Geneviève knew what was coming next.

XVII

" . . . there's just one thing I don't understand, miss."

"Lieutenant, if there were "just one thing" I didn't understand, I'd be a very happy old lady. At the moment, I can't think of 'just one thing' I do understand."

The detective smiled craggily.

"You're a vampire, miss. Like this dead girl, this, ah, Nico. That's right, isn't it?"

She admitted it. Orson Welles had lent her a crow-black umbrella which she was using as a parasol.

"And this Barbie, who again nobody else saw, was, ah, a living person?"

"Warm."

"Warm, yes. That's the expression. That's what you call us."

"It's not offensive."

"That's not how I take it, miss. No, what I'm wondering is: aren't vampires supposed to be faster than a warm person, harder to catch hold of in a tussle?"

"Nico was a new-born, and weakened. She'd lost some blood."

"That's one for the books."

"Not any more."

The detective scratched his head, lit cigar-end dangerously near his hair. "So I hear. It's called 'drac' on the streets. I have friends on the Narco Squad. They say it's worse than heroin, and it's not illegal yet."

"Where is this going, Lieutenant?"

He shut his notebook and pinned her with his eye.

"You could have, ah, *taken* Miss Nico? If you got into a fight with her?"

"I didn't."

"But you could have."

"I could have killed the Kennedys and Sanford White, but I didn't."

"Those are closed cases, as far as I'm concerned. This is open."

"I gave you the number-plate."

"Yes, miss. OVRLKER1. A Jaguar."

"Even if it's a fake plate, there can't be that many English sports cars in Los Angeles."

"There are, ah, one thousand, seven hundred and twenty-two registered Jaguars. Luxury vehicles are popular in this city, in some parts of it. Not all the same model."

"I don't know the model. I don't follow cars. I just know it was a Jaguar. It had the cat on the bonnet, the hood."

"Bonnet? That's the English expression, isn't it?"

"I lived in England for a long time."

With an Englishman. The detective's sharpness reminded her of Charles, with a witness or a suspect.

Suspect.

He had rattled the number of Jaguars in Greater Los Angeles off the top of his head, with no glance at the prop notebook. Gears were turning in his head.

"It was a black car," she said. "That should make it easier to find."

"Most automobiles look black at night. Even red ones."

"Not to me, Lieutenant."

Uniforms were off, grilling the Sawyers. Someone was even talking with Welles, who had let slip that Geneviève was working for him. Since the client had himself blown confidentiality, she was in an awkward position; Welles still didn't want it known what exactly she was doing for him.

"I think we can let you go now, miss," said the detective.

She had been on the point of presenting him her wrists for the cuffs.

"There isn't 'just one more thing' you want to ask?"

"No. I'm done. Unless there's anything you want to say?"

She didn't think so.

"Then you can go. Thank you, miss."

She turned away, knowing it would come, like a hand on her shoulder or around her heart.

"There is one thing, though. Not a question. More like a circumstance, something that has to be raised. I'm afraid I owe you an apology."

She turned back.

"It's just that I had to check you out, you know. Run you through the books. As a witness, yesterday. Purely routine."

Her umbrella seemed heavier.

"I may have got you in trouble with the state licensing board. They had all your details correctly, but it seems that every time anyone looked at your licence renewal application, they misread the date. As a European, you don't write an open four. It's easy to mistake a four for a nine. They thought you were born in 1916. Wondered when you'd be retiring, in fact. Had you down as a game old girl."

"Lieutenant, I am a game old girl."

"They didn't pull your licence, exactly. This is really embarrassing and I'm truly sorry to have been the cause of it, but they want to, ah, review your circumstances. There aren't any other vampires licensed as private investigators in the State of California, and there's no decision on whether a legally dead person can hold a licence."

"I never died. I'm not legally dead."

"They're trying to get your paperwork from, ah, France."

She looked up at the sky, momentarily hoping to burn out her eyes. Even if her original records existed, they'd be so old as to be protected historical documents. Photostats would not be coming over the wire from her homeland.

"Again, miss, I'm truly sorry."

She just wanted to get inside her trailer and sleep the day away.

"Do you have your licence with you?"

"In the car," she said, dully.

"I'm afraid I'm going to have to ask you to surrender it," said the detective. "And that until the legalities are settled, you cease to operate as a private investigator in the State of California."

XVIII

At sunset, she woke to another limbo, with one of her rare headaches. She was used to knowing what she was doing tonight, and the next night, if not specifically then at least generally. Now, she wasn't sure what she *could* do.

Geneviève wasn't a detective any more, not legally. Welles had not paid her off, but if she continued working on John Alucard for him she'd be breaking the law. Not a particularly important one, in her opinion . . . but vampires lived in such a twilight world that it was best to pay taxes on time and not park in tow-away zones. After all, this was what happened when she drew attention to herself.

She had two other ongoing investigations, neither promising. She should make contact with her clients, a law firm and an Orange County mother, and explain the situation. In both cases, she hadn't turned up any results and so would not in all conscience be able to charge a fee. She didn't even have that much Welles could use.

Money would start to be a problem around Valentine's Day. The licensing board might have sorted it out by then.

(In some alternate universe.)

She should call Beth Davenport, her lawyer, to start filing appeals and lodging complaints. That would cost, but anything else was just giving up.

Two people were truly dead. That bothered her too.

She sat at her tiny desk, by a slatted window, considering her telephone. She had forgotten to switch her answering machine on before turning in, and any calls that might have come today were lost. She had never done that before.

Should she re-record her outgoing message, stating that she was (temporarily?) out of business? The longer she was off the bus, the harder it would be to get back.

On TV, suspended cops, disbarred private eyes and innocent men on the run never dropped the case. And this was Southern California, where the TV came from.

She decided to compromise. She wouldn't work Alucard, which was what Welles had been paying her for. But, as a concerned – indeed, involved – citizen, no law said she couldn't use her talents unpaid to go after the Slayer.

Since this was a police case, word of her status should have filtered down to her LAPD contacts but might not yet have reached outlying agencies. She called Officer Baker, a contact in the Highway Patrol, and wheedled a little to get him to run a licence plate for her.

OVRLKER1.

The call-back came within minutes, excellent service she admitted was well worth a supper and cocktails one of these nights. Baker teased her awhile about that, then came over.

Amazingly, the plate *was* for a Jaguar. The car was registered in the name of Ernest Ralph Gorse, to an address in a town up the coast, Shadow Bay. The only other forthcoming details were that Gorse was a British subject – not citizen, of course – and held down a job as a high school librarian.

The Overlooker? A school librarian and a cheerleader might seem different species, but they swam in the same tank.

She thanked Baker and rang off.

If it was that easy, she could let the cops handle it. The Lieutenant was certainly sharp enough to run a Gorse down and scout around to see if a Barbie popped up. Even if the detective hadn't believed her, he would have been obliged to run the plate, to puncture her story. Now, he was obliged to check it out.

But wasn't it all too easy?

Since when did librarians drive Jaguars?

It had the air of a trap.

She was where the Lieutenant must have been seven hours ago. She wouldn't put the crumpled detective on her list of favourite people, but didn't want to hear he'd run into another of the Sharp Brothers. Apart from the loss of a fine public servant who was doubtless also an exemplary husband, it was quite likely that if the cop sizing her up for two murders showed up dead she would be even more suitable for framing.

Shadow Bay wasn't more than an hour away.

XIX

Welles' final Dracula project came together in 1981, just as the movies were gripped by a big vampire craze. Controversial and slow-building, and shut out of all but technical Oscars, Coppola's *Dracula* proved there was a substantial audience for vampire subjects. The next half-decade would see Werner Herzog's *Renfield, Jeder fur Sich und die Vampir Gegen Alle*, a retelling of the story from the point of the fly-eating lunatic (Klaus Kinski); of Tony Scott's *The Hunger*, with Catherine Deneuve and David Bowie as New York art patrons Miriam and John Blaylock, at the centre of a famous murder case defended by Alan Dershowitz (Ron Silver); of John Landis's *Scream, Blacula, Scream*, with Eddie Murphy as Dracula's African get Prince Mamuwalde, searching for his lost bride (Vanity) in New York - best remembered for a plagiarism lawsuit by screenwriter Pat Hobby that forced Paramount to open its books to the auditors; of Richard Attenborough's bloated, mammoth, Oscar-scooping *Varney*, with Anthony Hopkins as Sir Francis Varney, the vampire Viceroy overthrown by the Second

Indian Mutiny; of Brian DePalma's remake of *Scarface*, an explicit attack on the Transylvania Movement, with Al Pacino as Tony Sylvana, a Ceausescu cast-out rising in the booming drac trade and finally taken down by a Vatican army led by James Woods.

Slightly ahead of all this activity, Welles began shooting quietly, without publicity, working at his own pace, underwritten by the last of his many mysterious benefactors. His final script combined elements from Stoker's fiction with historical fact made public by the researches of Raymond McNally and Radu Florescu - associates as far back as *D is for Dracula* - and concentrated on the last days of the Count, abandoned in his castle, awaiting his executioners, remembering the betrayals and crimes of his lengthy, weighty life. This was the project Welles called *The Other Side of Midnight*. From sequences filmed as early as the 1972, the director culled footage of Peter Bogdanovich as Renfield, while he opted to play not the stick insect vampire but the corpulent slayer, finally gifting the world with his definitive Professor Van Helsing. If asked by the trade press, he made great play of having offered the role of Dracula to Warren Beatty, Steve McQueen or Robert DeNiro, but this was a conjurer's distraction, for he had fixed on his Count for some years and was now finally able to fit him for his cape and fangs. Welles' final Dracula was to be John Huston.

Gates, *ibid*

XX

She parked on the street but took the trouble to check out the Shadow Bay High teachers' parking lot. Two cars: a black Jaguar (OVERLKR1) and a beat-up silver Peugeot ("I have a French car"). Geneviève checked the Peugeot and found LAPD ID on display. The interior was a mess. She caught the after-whiff of cigars.

The school was as unexceptional as the town, with that faintly unreal movie-set feel that came from newness. The oldest building in sight was put up in 1965. To her, places like this felt temporary.

A helpful map by the front steps of the main building told her where the library was, across a grassy quadrangle. The school grounds were dark. The kids wouldn't be back from their Christmas vacation. And no evening classes. She had checked Gorse's address first, and found no one home.

A single light was on in the library, like the cover of a gothic romance paperback.

Cautious, she crossed the quad. Slumped in the doorway of the library was a raincoated bundle. Her heart plunging, she knelt and found the Lieutenant insensible but still alive. He had been bitten badly and bled. The ragged tear in his throat showed he'd been taken the old-fashioned way – a strong grip from behind, a rending fang-bite, then sucking and swallowing. Non-consensual vampirism, a felony in anyone's books, without the exercise of powers of fascination to cloud the issue. It was hard to mesmerize someone with one eye, though some vampires worked with whispers and could even put the 'fluence on a blind person.

There was another vampire in Shadow Bay. By the look of the leavings, one of the bad 'uns. Perhaps that explained Barbie's prejudice. It was always a mistake to extrapolate a general rule from a test sample of one.

She clamped a hand over the wound, feeling the weak pulse, pressing the edges together. Whoever had bitten the detective hadn't even had the consideration to shut off the faucet after glutting themselves. The smears of blood on his coat and shirt collar overrode her civilized impulses: her mouth became sharp-fanged and full of saliva. That was a good thing. A physical adaption of her turning was that her spittle had antiseptic properties. Vampires of her bloodline were evolved for gentle, repeated feedings. After biting and drinking, a full-tongued lick sealed the wound.

Angling her mouth awkwardly and holding up the Lieutenant's lolling head to expose his neck, she stuck out her tongue and slathered saliva over the long tear. She tried to ignore the euphoric if cigar-flavoured buzz of his blood. She had a connection to his clear, canny mind.

He had never thought her guilty. Until now.

"Makes a pretty picture, Frenchie," said a familiar girlish voice. "Classic Bloodsucker 101, viper and victim. Didn't your father-in-darkness warn you about snacking between meals? You won't be able to get into your party dresses if you bloat up. Where's the fun in that?"

Geneviève knew Barbie wasn't going to accept her explanation. For once, she understood why.

The wound had been left open for her.

"I've been framed," she said, around bloody fangs.

Barbie giggled, a teen vision in a red ra-ra skirt, white ankle socks, mutton-chop short-sleeved top and faux metallic choker. She had sparkle glitter on her cheeks and an Alice band with artificial antennae that ended in bobbling stars.

She held up her stake and said "Scissors cut paper."

Geneviève took out her gun and pointed it. "Stone blunts scissors."

"Hey, no fair," whined Barbie.

Geneviève set the wounded man aside as carefully as possible and stood up. She kept the gun trained on the Slayer's heart.

"Where does it say vampires have to do kung-fu fighting? Everyone else in this country carries a gun, why not me?"

For a moment, she almost felt sorry for Barbie the Slayer. Her forehead crinkled into a frown, her lower lip jutted like a sulky five-year-old's and tears of frustration started in her eyes. She had a lot to learn about life. If Geneviève got her wish, the girl would complete her education in Tehachapi Womens' Prison.

A silver knife slipped close to her neck.

"Paper wraps stone," suaved a British voice.

XXI

"Barbie doesn't know, does she? That you're *nosferatu?*"

Ernest Ralph Gorse, high school librarian, was an epitome of tweedy middle-aged stuffiness, so stage English that he made Alistair Cooke sound like a Dead End Kid. He arched an elegant eyebrow, made an elaborate business of cleaning his granny glasses with his top-pocket hankie, and gave out a little I'm-so-wicked moué that let his curly fangs peep out from beneath his stiff upper lip.

"No, 'fraid not. Lovely to look at, delightful to know but frightfully thick, that's our little Barbara."

The Overlooker – "yes," he had admitted, "bloody silly name, means nothing, just sounds 'cool' if you're a twit" – had sent Barbie the Slayer off with the drained detective, to call at the hospital ER and the Sheriff's office. Geneviève was left in the library, in the custody of Gorse. He had made her sit in a chair, and kept well beyond her arms' length.

"You bit the Lieutenant?" she stated.

Gorse raised a finger to his lips and tutted.

"Shush now, old thing, mustn't tell, don't speak it aloud. Jolly bad show to give away the game and all that rot. Would you care for some instant coffee? Ghastly muck, but I'm mildly addicted to it. It's what comes of being cast up on these heathen shores."

The Overlooker pottered around his desk, which was piled high with unread and probably unreadable books. He poured water from an electric kettle into an oversized green ceramic apple. She declined his offer with a headshake. He quaffed from his apple-for-the-teacher mug, and let out an exaggerated *ahh* of satisfaction.

"That takes the edge off. Washes down *cop au nicotin* very nicely."

"Why hasn't she noticed?"

Gorse chuckled. "Everything poor Barbara knows about the tribes of *nosferatu* comes from me. Of course, a lot of it I made up. I'm very creative, you know. It's always been one of my skills. Charm and persuasion, that's the ticket. The lovely featherhead hangs on my every word. She thinks all vampires are gruesome creatures of the night, demons beyond hope of redemption, frothing beasts fit only to be put down like mad dogs. I'm well aware of the irony, old thing. Some cold evenings, the hilarity becomes almost too much to handle. Oh, the stories I've spun for her, the wild things she'll believe. I've told her she's the Chosen One, the only girl in the world who can shoulder the burden of the crusade against the forces of Evil. Teenage girls adore that I'm-a-secret-Princess twaddle, you know. Especially the Yanks. I copped a lot of it from *Star Wars*. Bloody awful film, but very revealing about the state of the national mind."

Gorse was enjoying the chance to explain things. Bottling up his cleverness had been a trial for him. She thought it was the only reason she was still alive for this performance.

"But what's the point?"

"Originally, expedience. I've been 'passing' since I came to America. I'm not like you, sadly. I can't flutter my lashes and have pretty girls offer their necks for the taking. I really am one of those hunt-and-kill, rend-and-drain sort of *nosferatu*. I tried the other way, but courtship dances just bored me rigid and I thought, well, why not? Why not just rip open the odd throat.

"So, after a few months here in picturesque Shadow Bay, empties were piling up like junk mail. Then the stroke of genius came to me. I could hide behind a Vampire Slayer and since there were none in sight I made one up. I checked the academic records to find the dimmest dolly bird in school, and recruited her for the Cause. I killed her lunk of a boyfriend – captain of football team, would you believe it? – and a selection of snack-size teenagers. Then, I revealed to Barbara that her destiny was to be the Slayer.

"Together, we tracked and destroyed that first dread fiend – the school secretary who was nagging me about getting my employment records from Jolly Old England, as it happens – and staked the bloodlusting bitch. However, it seems she spawned before we got to her, and ever since we've been doing away with her murderous brood. You'll be glad to know I've managed to rid this town almost completely of real estate agents. When the roll is called up yonder, that must count in the plus column, though it's my long-term plan not to be there."

Actually, Gorse was worse than the vampires he had made up. He'd had a choice, and *decided* to be Evil. He worked hard on fussy geniality, modelling his accent and speech patterns on *Masterpiece Theatre*, but there was ice inside him, a complete vacuum.

"So, you have things working your way in Shadow Bay?" she said. "You have your little puppet theatre to play with. Why come after me?"

Gorse was wondering whether to tell her more. He pulled a half-hunter watch from his waistcoat pocket and pondered. She wondered if she could work her trick of fascination on him. Clearly, he loved to talk, was bored with dissimulation, had a real need to be appreciated. The sensible thing would have been to get this over with, but Gorse had to tell her how brilliant he was. Everything up to now had been his own story; now, there was more important stuff and he was wary of going on.

"Still time for one more story," he said. "One more *ghost* story."

Click. She had him.

He was an instinctive killer, probably a sociopath from birth, but she was his elder. The silver-bladed letter-opener was never far from his fingers. She would have to judge when to jump.

"It's a lonely life, isn't it? Ours, I mean. Wandering through the years, wearing out your clothes, lost in a world you never made? There was a golden age for us once, in London when Dracula was on the throne. 1888 and all that. You, famous girl, did your best to put a stop to it, turned us all back into nomads and parasites when we might have been masters of the universe. Some of us want it that way again, my darling. We've been getting together lately, sort of a pressure group. Not like those Transylvania fools who want to go back to the castles and the mountains, but like Him, battening onto a new, vital world, making a place for ourselves. An exalted place. He's still our inspiration, old thing. Let's say I did it for Dracula."

That wasn't enough, but it was all she was going to get now.

People were outside, coming in.

"Time flies, old thing. I'll have to make this quick."

Gorse took his silver pig-sticker and stood over her. He thrust. Faster than any eye could catch, her hands locked around his wrist.

"Swift filly, eh?"

She concentrated. He was strong but she was old. The knife-point dimpled her blouse. He tipped back her chair and put a knee on her stomach, pinning her down.

The silver touch was white hot.

She turned his arm and forced it upwards. The knife slid under his spectacles and the point stuck in his left eye.

Gorse screamed and she was free of him. He raged and roared, fangs erupting from his mouth, two-inch barbs bursting from his fingertips. Bony spars, the beginnings of wings, sprouted through his jacket around the collar and pierced his leather elbow-patches.

The doors opened and people came in. Barbie and two crucifix-waving Sheriff's Deputies.

The Slayer saw (and recognized?) the vampire and rushed across the room, stake out. Gorse caught the girl and snapped her neck, then dropped her in a dead tangle.

"Look what you made me do!" he said to Geneviève, voice distorted by the teeth but echoing from the cavern that was his reshaped mouth. "She's *broken* now. It'll take ages to make another. I hadn't even got to the full initiation rites. There would have been bleeding and I was making up something about Tantric sex. It would have been a real giggle, and you've spoiled it."

His eye congealed, frothing grey deadness in his face.

She motioned for the deputies to stay back. They wisely kept their distance.

"Just remember," said Gorse, directly to her. "You can't stop Him. He's coming back. And then, oh my best beloved, you will be as sorry a girl as ever drew a sorry breath. He is not one for forgiveness, if you get my drift."

Gorse's jacket shredded and wings unfurled. He flapped into the air, rising above the first tier of bookshelves, hovering at the mezzanine level. His old school tie dangled like a dead snake.

The deputies tried shooting at him. She supposed she would have too.

He crashed through a tall set of windows and flew off, vast shadow blotting out the moon and falling on the bay.

The deputies holstered their guns and looked at her. She wondered for about two minutes whether she should stick with her honesty policy.

Letting a bird flutter in her voice, she said "That man . . . he was a v-v-vampire."

Then she did a pretty fair imitation of a silly girl fainting. One deputy checked her heartbeat while she was "out", and was satisfied that she was warm. The other went to call for back-up.

Through a crack in her eyelids, she studied "her" deputy. His hands might have lingered a little too long on her chest for strict medical purposes. The thought that he was the type to cop a feel from a helpless girl just about made it all right to get him into trouble by slipping silently out of the library while he was checking out the dead Slayer.

She made it undetected back to her car.

XXII

In her trailer, after another day of lassitude, she watched the early evening bulletin on Channel 6. Anchor-persons Karen White and Lew Landers had details of the vampire killing in Shadow Bay. Because the primary victim was a cute teenage girl, it was top story. The wounding of a decorated LAPD veteran – the Lieutenant was still alive, but off the case – also rated a flagged mention.

The newscast split-screened a toothpaste commercial photograph of "Barbara Dahl Winters", smiling under a prom queen tiara, and an "artist's impression" of Gorse in giant bat-form, with blood tastefully dripping from his fangs. Ernest "Gory" Gorse turned out to be a fugitive from Scotland Yard, with a record of petty convictions before he turned and a couple of likely murders since. Considering a mug shot from his warm days, Karen said the killer looked like such a nice fellow, even scowling over numbers, and Lew commented that you couldn't judge a book by its cover.

Geneviève continued paying attention, well into the next item – about a scary candlelight vigil by hooded supporters of Annie Wilkes – and only turned the sound on her portable TV set down when she was sure her name was not going to come up in connection with the Shadow Bay story.

Gorse implied she was targeted because of her well-known involvement in the overthrow of Count Dracula, nearly a century ago. But that didn't explain why he had waited until now to give her a hard time. She also gathered from what he had let slip in flirtatious hints that he wasn't the top of the totem pole, that he was working with or perhaps for someone else.

Gorse had said: "You can't stop Him. He's coming back."

Him? He?

Only one vampire inspired that sort of *quondam rex que futurus* talk. Before he finally died, put out of his misery, Count Dracula had used himself up completely. Geneviève was sure of that. He had outlived his era, several times over, and been confronted with his own irrelevance. His true death was just a formality.

And He was not coming back.

A woodcut image of Dracula appeared on television. She turned the sound up.

The newscast had reached the entertainment round-up, which in this town came before major wars on other continents. A fluffy-haired woman in front of the Hollywood sign was talking about the latest studio craze, Dracula pictures. A race was on between Universal and Paramount to get their biopics of the Count to the screens. At Universal, director Joel Schumacher and writer-producer Jane Wagner had cast John Travolta and Lily Tomlin in *St George's Fire*; at MGM, producer Steven Spielberg and director Tobe Hooper had Peter Coyote and Karen Allen in *Vampirgeist*. There was no mention of Orson Welles – or, unsurprisingly, Boris Adrian – but another familiar name came up.

John Alucard.

"Hollywood deal-makers have often been characterized as bloodsuckers," said the reporter, "but John Alucard is the first actually to be one. Uniquely, this vampire executive is involved in *both* these competing projects, as a packager of the Universal production and as associate producer of the MGM film. Clearly, in a field where there are too few experts to go around, John Alucard is in demand. Unfortunately, Mr A – as Steven Spielberg calls him – is unable because of his image impairment to grant interviews for broadcast media, but he has issued a statement to the effect that he feels there is room for far more than two versions of the story he characterizes as 'the most important of the last two centuries'. He goes on to say 'there can be no definitive Dracula, but we hope we shall be able to conjure a different Dracula for every person'. For decades, Hollywood stayed away from this hot subject but, with the Francis Coppola epic of a few years ago cropping up on Best of All Time lists, it seems we are due, like the Londoners of 1885, for a veritable *invasion* of Draculas. This is Kimberley Wells, for Channel 6 KDHB *Update News*, at the Hollywood sign."

She switched the television off. The whole world, and Orson Welles, knew now what John Alucard was doing, but the other part of her original commission – who he was and where he came from – was still a mystery. He had come from the East, with a long line of credit. A source had told her he had skipped New York ahead of an investigation into insider-trading or junk bonds, but she might choose to put that down to typical Los Angeles cattiness. Another whisper had him living another life up in Silicon Valley as a consultant on something hush-hush President Reagan's people were calling the Strategic Defense Initiative, supposedly Buck Rogers stuff. Alucard could also be a Romanian shoe-salesman with a line in great patter who had quit his dull job and changed his name the night he learned his turning vampire wasn't going to take in the long run and set out to become the new Irving Thalberg before he rotted away to dirt.

There must be a connection between the movie-making mystery man and the high school librarian. Alucard and Gorse. Two vampires in California. She had started asking around about one of them, and the other had sent a puppet to warn her off.

John Alucard could not *be* Count Dracula.

Not yet, at least.

XXIII

On her way up into the Hollywood Hills, to consult the only real magician she knew, she decided to call on Jack Martin, to see if he wanted to come along on the trip. The movie mage would interest him.

The door of Martin's shack hung open.

Her heart skipped. Loose manuscript pages were drifting out of Martin's home, catching on the breeze, and scuttling along Beverly Glen Boulevard, sticking on the manicured hedges of the million-dollar estates, brushing across the white-painted faces of lawn jockeys who had been coal-black until Sidney Poitier made a fuss.

She knocked on the door, which popped a hinge and hung free.

"Jack?"

Had Gorse got to him?

She ventured inside, prepared to find walls dripping red and a ruined corpse lying in a nest of torn-up screenplays.

Martin lay on a beat-up sofa, mouth open, snoring slightly. He was no more battered than usual. A Mexican wrestling magazine was open on his round tummy.

"Jack?"

He came awake, blearily.

"It's you," he said, cold.

His tone was like a silver knife.

"What's the matter?"

"As if you didn't know. You're not good to be around, Gené. Not good at all. You don't see it, but you're a wrecker."

She backed away.

"Someone tipped off the Writers Guild about the porno. My ticket got yanked, my dues were not accepted. I'm off the list. I'm off all the lists. All possible lists. I didn't get *Buck Privates*. They went with Lionel Fenn."

"There'll be other projects," she said.

"I'll be lucky to get *Buck's Privates*."

Martin had been drinking, but didn't need to get drunk to be in this despair hole. It was where he went sometimes, a mental space like Ensenada, where he slunk to wallow, to soak up the misery he turned into prose. This time, she had an idea he wasn't coming back; he was going lower than ever, and would end up a beachcomber on a nighted seashore, picking broken skulls out of bloody seaweed, trailing bare feet through ink-black surf, becoming the exile king of his own dark country.

"It just took a phone call, Gené. To smash everything. To smash me. I wasn't even worth killing. That hurts. You, they'll kill. I don't want you to be near me when it happens."

"Does this mean our premiere date is off?"

She shouldn't have said that. Martin began crying, softly. It was a shocking scene, upsetting to her on a level she had thought she had escaped from. He wasn't just depressed, he was scared.

"Go away, Gené," he said.

XXIV

This was not a jaunt any more. Jack Martin was as lost to her as Moondoggie, as her licence.

How could things change so fast? It wasn't the second week of January, wasn't the Julian 1980s, but everything that had seemed certain last year, last decade, was up for debate or thrown away.

There was a cruelty at work. Beyond Gorse.

She parked the Plymouth and walked across a lawn to a ranch-style bungalow. A cabalist firmament of star-signs decorated the mailbox.

The mage was a trim, fiftyish man, handsome but small, less a fallen angel than a fallen cherub. He wore ceremonial robes to receive her into his *sanctum sanctorum*, an arrangement of literal shrines to movie stars of the 1920s and '30s: Theda Bara, Norma Desmond,

Clara Bow, Lina Lamont, Jean Harlow, Blanche Hudson, Myrna Loy. His all-seeing amulet contained a long-lashed black-and-white eye, taken from a still of Rudolph Valentino. His boots were black leather motorcycle gear, with polished chrome buckles and studs.

As a boy, the mage – Kenneth Anger to mortals of this plane – had appeared as the Prince in the 1935 Max Reinhardt film of *A Midsummer Night's Dream*. In later life, he had become a film-maker, but for himself not the studios (his "underground" trilogy consisted of *Scorpio Rising*, *Lucifer Rising* and *Dracula Rising*), and achieved a certain notoriety for compiling *Hollywood Babylon*, a collection of scurrilous but not necessarily true stories about the scamy private lives of the glamour gods and goddesses of the screen. A disciple of Aleister Crowley and Adrian Marcato, he was a genuine movie magician.

He was working on a sequel to *Hollywood Babylon*, which had been forthcoming for some years. It was called *Transylvania Babylon*, and contained all the gossip, scandal and lurid factoid speculation that had ever circulated about the elder members of the vampire community. Nine months ago, the manuscript and all his research material had been stolen by a couple of acid-heads in the employ of a pair of New Orleans-based vampire elders who were the focus of several fascinating, enlightening and perversely amusing chapters. Geneviève had recovered the materials, though the book was still not published, as Anger had to negotiate his way through a maze of injunctions and magical threats before he could get the thing in print.

She hesitated on the steps that led down to his slightly sunken *sanctum*. Incense burned before the framed pictures, swirling up to the low stucco ceiling.

"Do you have to be invited?" he asked. "Enter freely, spirit of dark."

"I was just being polite," she admitted.

The mage was a little disappointed. He arranged himself on a pile of harem cushions and indicated a patch of Turkish carpet where she might sit.

There was a very old bloodstain on the weave.

"Don't mind that," he said. "It's from a thirteen-year-old movie extra deflowered by Charlie Chaplin at the very height of the Roaring Twenties."

She decided not to tell him it wasn't hymenal blood (though it was human).

"I have cast spells of protection, as a precaution. It was respectful of you to warn me this interview might have consequences."

Over the centuries, Geneviève had grown out of thinking of herself as a supernatural creature, and was always a little surprised to run into people who still saw her that way. It wasn't that they might not be right, it was just unusual and unfashionable. The world had monsters, but she still didn't know if there was magic.

"One man who helped me says his career has been ruined because of it," she said, the wound still fresh. "Another, who was just my friend, died."

"My career is beyond ruination," said the mage. "And death means nothing. As you know, it's a passing thing. The lead-up, however, can be highly unpleasant, I understand. I think I'd opt to skip that experience, if at all possible."

She didn't blame him.

"I've seen some of your films and looked at your writings," she said. "It seems to me that you believe motion pictures are rituals."

"Well put. Yes, all real films are invocations, summonings. Most are made by people who don't realize that. But I do. When I call a film *Invocation of My Demon Brother*, I mean it exactly as it sounds. It's not enough to plop a camera in front of a ceremony. Then you only get religious television, God help you. It's in the lighting, the cutting, the music. Reality must be banished, channels opened to the Beyond. At screenings, there are always manifestations. Audiences might not realize on a conscious level what is happening, but they always know. Always. The amount of ectoplasm poured into the auditorium by drag queens alone at a West Hollywood revival of a Joan Crawford picture would be enough to embody a minor djinn in the shape of the Bitch Goddess, with a turban and razor cheekbones and shoulder pads out to here."

She found the image appealing, but also frightening.

"If you were to make a dozen films about, say, the Devil, would the Prince of Darkness appear?"

The mage was amused. "What an improbable notion? But it has some substance. If you made twelve ordinary films about the Devil, he might seem more real to people, become more of a figure in the culture, get talked about and put on magazine covers. But, let's face it, the same thing happens if you make one ordinary film about a shark. It's the thirteenth film that makes the difference, that might work the trick."

"That would be your film? The one made by a director who understands the ritual?"

"Sadly, no. A great tragedy of magick is that the most effective must be worked without conscious thought, without intent. To become a master image, you must pass beyond the mathematics and become a dreamer. My film, of the Devil you say, would be but a tentative summoning, attracting the notice of a spirit of the beyond. Fully to call His Satanic Majesty to Earth would require a work of surpassing genius, mounted by a director with no other intention but to make a wonderful illusion, a von Sternberg or a Frank Borzage. That thirteenth film, a *Shanghai Gesture* or a *History is Made at Night*, would be the perfect ritual. And its goaty hero could leave his cloven hoof-print in the cement outside Grauman's Chinese."

XXV

In January 1981, Welles began filming *The Other Side of Midnight* on the old Miracle Pictures lot, his first studio-shot - though independently-financed - picture since *Touch of Evil* in 1958, and his first "right of final cut" contract since *Citizen Kane*. The ins and outs of the deal have been assessed in entire books by Peter Bart and David J. Skal, but it seems that Welles, after a career of searching, had found a genuine "angel", a backer with the financial muscle to give him the budget and crew he needed to make a film that was truly his vision but also the self-effacing trust to let him have total artistic control of the result.

There were nay-saying voices and the industry was already beginning to wonder whether still in-progress runaway budget auteur movies like Michael Cimino's *The Lincoln County Wars* or Coppola's *Dracula* follow-up *One From the Heart* were such a great idea, but Welles himself denounced those runaways as examples of fuzzy thinking. As with his very first *Dracula* movie script and *Kane*, *The Other Side of Midnight* was meticulously pre-planned and pre-costed. Forty years on from *Kane*, Welles must have known this would be his last serious chance. A Boy Wonder no longer, the pressure was on him to produce a "mature masterpiece", a career book-end to the work that had topped so many Best of All Time lists and eclipsed all his other achievements. He must certainly have been aware of the legion of cineastes whose expectations of a film that would eclipse the flashy brilliance of the Coppola version were sky-rocketing. It may be that so many of Welles' other projects were left unfinished deliberately, because their creator knew they could never compete with the imagined masterpieces that were expected of him. With *Midnight*, he had to show all his cards and take the consequences.

The Other Side of Midnight occupied an unprecedented three adjacent sound-stages, where Ken Adam's sets for Bistritz and Borgo Pass and the exteriors and interiors of Castle Dracula were constructed. John Huston shaved his beard and let his moustache sprout, preparing for the acting role of his career, cast apparently because Welles admired him as the Los Angeles predator-patriarch Noah Cross (*Chinatown*, 1974). It has been rumoured that the seventy-four-year-old Huston went so far as to have transfusions of vampire blood and took to hunting the Hollywood night with packs of new-born vampire brats, piqued because he couldn't display trophies of his "kills". Other casting was announced, a canny mix of A-list stars who would have worked for scale just to be in a Welles film, long-time associates who couldn't bear to be left out of the adventure and fresh talent. Besides Welles (Van Helsing), the film would star Jack Nicholson (Jonathan Harker), Richard Gere (Arthur Holmwood), Shelley Duvall (Mina), Susan Sarandon (Lucy), Cameron Mitchell (Renfield), Dennis Hopper (Quincey), Jason Robards (Dr Seward), Joseph Cotten (Mr Hawkins), George Couloris (Mr Swales) and Jeanne Moreau (Peasant Woman). The three vampire brides were Anjelica Huston, Marie-France Pisier and then-unknown Kathleen Turner. John Williams was writing the score, Gary Graver remained Welles' preferred cinematographer, Rick Baker promised astounding and innovative special make-up effects and George Lucas's ILM contracted for the optical effects.

There were other vampire movies in pre-production, other *Dracula* movies, but Hollywood was really only interested in the Welles version.

Finally, it would happen.

Gates, *ibid*

XXVI

Geneviève parked the Plymouth near Bronson Caverns, in sight of the Hollywood Sign, and looked out over Los Angeles, transformed by distance into a carpet of Christmas lights. MGM used to boast "more stars than there were in the Heavens", and there they were, twinkling individually, a fallen constellation. Car lights on the freeways were like glowing platelets flowing through neon veins. From up here, you couldn't see the hookers on Hollywood Boulevard, the endless limbo motels and real estate developments, the lost, lonely and desperate. You couldn't hear the laugh track, or the screams.

It came down to magic. And whether she believed in it.

Clearly, Kenneth Anger did. He had devoted his life to rituals. A great many of them, she had to admit, had worked. And so did John Alucard and Ernest Gorse, vampires who thought themselves magical beings. Dracula had been another of the breed, thanking Satan for eternal night-life.

She just didn't know.

Maybe she was still undecided because she had never slipped into the blackness of death. Kate Reed, her Victorian friend, had done the proper thing. Kate's father-in-darkness, Harris, had drunk her blood and given of his own, then let her die and come back, turned. Chandagnac, Geneviève's mediaeval father-in-darkness, had worked on her for months. She had transformed slowly, coming alive by night, shaking off the warm girl she had been.

In the last century, since Dracula came out of his castle, there had been a lot of work done on the subject. It was no longer possible to disbelieve in vampires. With the *nosferatu* in the open, vampirism had to be incorporated into the prevalent belief systems and this was a scientific age. These days, everyone generally accepted the "explanation" that the condition was a blood-borne mutation, an evolutionary quirk adapting a strain of humankind for survival. But, as geneticists probed ever further, mysteries deepened: vampires retained the DNA pattern they were born with as warm humans, and yet they were *different* creatures. And, despite a lot of cracked theorizing, no one had ever convincingly adjusted the laws of optics to account for the business with mirrors.

If there were vampires, there could be magic.

And Alucard's ritual – the mage's thirteen movies – might work. He could come back, worse than ever.

Dracula.

She looked up, from the city-lights to the stars.

Was the Count out there, on some intangible plane, waiting to be summoned? Reinvigorated by a spell in the beyond, thirsting for blood, vengeance, power? What might he have learned in Hell, that he could bring to the Earth?

She hated to think.

XXVII

She drove through the studio gates shortly before dawn, waved on by the uniformed guard. She was accepted as a part of Orson's army, somehow granted an invisible arm-band by her association with the genius.

The Miracle Pictures lot was alive again. "If it's a good picture, it's a Miracle!" had run the self-mocking, double-edged slogan, all the more apt as the so-called fifth-wheel major declined from mounting Technicolor spectacles like the 1939 version of *The Duelling Cavalier*, with Errol Flynn and Fedora, to financing drive-in dodos like *Machete Maidens of Mora Tau*, with nobody and her uncle. In recent years, the fifty-year-old sound stages had mostly gone unused as Miracle shot their product in the Philippines or Canada. The standing sets seen in so many vintage movies had been torn down to make way for bland office buildings where scripts were "developed" rather than shot. There wasn't even a studio tour.

Now, it was different.

Orson Welles was in power and legions swarmed at his command, occupying every department, beavering away in the service of his vision. They were everywhere: gaffers, extras, carpenters, managers, accountants, make-up men, effects technicians, grips, key grips, boys, best boys, designers, draughtsmen, teamsters, caterers, guards, advisors, actors, writers, planners, plotters, doers, movers, shakers.

Once Welles had said this was the best train-set a boy could have. It was very different from three naked girls in an empty swimming pool.

She found herself on Stage 1, the Transylvanian village set. Faces she recognized were on the crew: Jack Nicholson, tearing through his lines with exaggerated expressions; Oja Kodar, handing down decisions from above; Debbie W. Griffith (in another life, she presumed), behind the craft services table; Dennis Hopper, in a cowboy hat and sunglasses.

The stage was crowded with on-lookers. Among the movie critics and TV reporters were other directors – she spotted Spielberg, DePalma and a shifty Coppola – intent on kibbitzing on the master, demonstrating support for the abused genius or suppressing poisonous envy. Burt Reynolds, Gene Hackman and Jane Fonda were dressed up as villagers, rendered unrecognizable by make-up, so desperate to be in this movie that they were willing to be unbilled extras.

Somewhere up there, in a platform under the roof, sat the big baby. The visionary who would give birth to his Dracula. The unwitting magician who might, this time, conjure more than even he had bargained for.

She scanned the rafters, a hundred feet or more above the studio floor. Riggers crawled like pirates among the lights. Someone abseiled down into the village square.

She was sorry Martin wasn't here. This was his dream.

A dangerous dream.

XXVIII

THE OTHER SIDE OF MIDNIGHT

a script by Orson Welles

based on *Dracula*, by Bram Stoker

revised final, January 6, 1981

1: An ominous chord introduces an extreme CU of a crucifix, held in a knotted fist. It is sunset, we hear sounds of village life. We see only the midsection of the VILLAGE WOMAN holding the crucifix. She pulls tight the rosary-like string from which the cross hangs, as if it were a strangling chord. A scream is heard off camera, coming from some distance. The WOMAN whirls around abruptly to the left, in the direction of the sound. Almost at once the camera pans in this direction too, and we follow a line of PEASANT CHILDREN, strung out hand in hand and dancing, towards the INN, of the Transylvanian Village of Bistritz. We close on a leaded window and pass through – the set opening up to let in the camera – to find JONATHAN HARKER, a young Englishman with a tigerish smile, in the centre of a tableau Breughel interior, surrounded by peasant activity, children, animals, etc. He is framed by dangling bulbs of garlic, and the VILLAGE WOMAN's crucifix is echoed by one that hangs on the wall. Everyone, including the animals, is frozen, shocked. The scream is still echoing from the low wooden beams.

> HARKER
> What did I say?

The INN-KEEPER crosses himself. The peasants mutter.

> HARKER
> Was it the place? Was it [relishing each syllable]
> Castle Dra-cu-la?

More muttering and crossing. HARKER shrugs and
continues with his meal. Without a cut, the camera
pans around the cramped interior, to find MINA,
HARKER's new wife, in the doorway. She is huge-
eyed and tremulous, more impressed by "native
superstitions" than her husband, but with an inner
steel core which will become apparent as JONATHAN's
outward bluff crumbles. Zither and fiddle music
conveys the bustle of this border community.

> MINA
> Jonathan dear, come on. The coach.

JONATHAN flashes a smile, showing teeth that wouldn't
shame a vampire. MINA doesn't see the beginnings of his
viperish second face, but smiles indulgently, hesitant.
JONATHAN pushes away his plate and stands, displacing
children and animals. He joins MINA and they leave,
followed by our snake-like camera, which almost jostles
them as they emerge into the twilight. Some of the
crowd hold aloft flaming torches, which make shadow-
featured flickering masks of the worn peasant faces.
JONATHAN, hefting a heavy bag, and MINA, fluttering at
every distraction, walk across the village square to
a waiting COACH. Standing in their path, a crow-black
figure centre-frame, is the VILLAGE WOMAN, eyes wet with
fear, crucifix shining. She bars the HARKERS' way, like
the Ancient Mariner, and extends the crucifix.

> VILLAGE WOMAN
> If you must go, wear this. Wear it for your
> mother's sake. It will protect you.

JONATHAN bristles, but MINA defuses the situation by
taking the cross.

> MINA
> Thank you. Thank you very much.

The WOMAN crosses herself, kisses MINA's cheek, and departs. JONATHAN gives an eyebrows-raised grimace, and MINA shrugs, placatory.

> COACHMAN
> All aboard for Borgo Pass, Visaria
> and Klausenburg.

We get into the coach with the HARKERS, who displace a fat MERCHANT and his "secretary" ZITA, and the camera gets comfortable opposite them. They exchange looks, and MINA holds JONATHAN's hand. The Coach lurches and moves off – it is vital that the camera remain fixed on the HARKERS to cover the progress from one sound stage to the next, with the illusion of travel maintained by the projection of reflected Transylvanian mountain road scenery onto the window. We have time to notice that the MERCHANT and ZITA are wary of the HARKERS; he is middle-aged and balding, and she is a flashy blonde. The coach stops.

> COACHMAN (v.o.)
> Borgo Pass.

> JONATHAN
> Mina, here's our stop.

> MERCHANT
> Here?

> MINA (proud)
> A carriage is meeting us here, at midnight.
> A nobleman's.

> MERCHANT
> Whose carriage?

> JONATHAN
> Count Dracula's.

JONATHAN, who knows the effect it will have, says the name with defiance and mad eyes. The MERCHANT is

terror-struck, and ZITA hisses like a cat, shrinking
against him. The HARKERS, and the camera, get out of
the coach, which hurries off, the COACHMAN whipping
the horses to make a quick getaway. We are alone in
a mountain pass, high above the Carpathians. Night-
sounds: wolves, the wind, bats. The full moon seems
for a moment to have eyes, DRACULA's hooded eyes.

> JONATHAN (pointing)
> You can see the castle.
> MINA
> It looks so . . . desolate, lonely.

> JONATHAN
> No wonder the Count wants to move to London. He
> must be raging with cabin fever, probably ready
> to tear his family apart and chew their bones.
> Like Sawney Beane.

> MINA
> The Count has a family?

> JONATHAN (delighted)
> Three wives. Like a Sultan. Imagine how that'll
> go down in Piccadilly.

Silently, with no hoof or wheel-sounds, a carriage
appears, the DRIVER a black, faceless shape. The
HARKERS climb in, but this time the camera rises
to the top of the coach, where the DRIVER has
vanished. We hover as the carriage moves off,
a LARGE BAT flapping purposefully over the lead
horses, and trundles along a narrow, vertiginous
mountain road towards the castle. We swoop ahead
of the carriage, becoming the eyes of the BAT, and
take a flying detour from the road, allowing us a
false perspective view of the miniature landscape
to either side of the full-side road and carriage,
passing beyond the thick rows of pines to a whited
scrape in the hillside that the HARKERS do not see,
an apparent chalk quarry which we realize consists
of a strew of complete human skeletons, in agonized
postures, skulls and rib-cages broken, the remains

of thousands and thousands of murdered men, women,
children and babies. Here and there, skeletons
of armoured horses and creatures between wolf or
lion and man. This gruesome landscape passes under
us and we close on CASTLE DRACULA, a miniature
constructed to allow our nimble camera to close
on the highest tower and pass down a stone spiral
stairway that affords covert access to the next
stage . . .

. . . and the resting chamber of DRACULA and his
BRIDES. We stalk through a curtain of cobweb,
which parts unharmed, and observe as the three
shroud-clad BRIDES rise from their boxes, flitting
about before us. Two are dark and feral, one is
blonde and waif-like. We have become DRACULA
and stalk through the corridors of his castle,
brassbound oaken doors opening before us.
Footsteps do not echo and we pass mirrors that
reveal nothing — reversed sets under glass, so
as not to catch our crew — but a spindle-fingered,
almost animate shadow is cast, impossibly long
arms reaching out, pointed head with bat-flared
ears momentarily sharp against a tapestry. We move
faster and faster through the CASTLE, coming out
into the great HALLWAY at the very top of a wide
staircase. Very small, at the bottom of the steps,
stand JONATHAN and MINA, beside their luggage.
Sedately, we fix on them and move downwards, our
cloaked shadow contracting. As we near the couple,
we see their faces: JONATHAN awe-struck, almost
in love at first sight, ready to become our slave;
MINA horrified, afraid for her husband, but almost
on the point of pity. The music, which has passed
from lusty human strings to ethereal theremin
themes, swells, conveying the ancient, corrupt,
magical soul of DRACULA. We pause on the steps,
six feet above the HARKERS, then leap forwards as
MINA holds up the crucifix, whose blinding light
fills the frame. The music climaxes, a sacred
choral theme battling the eerie theremin.

```
2: CU on the ancient face, points of red in the eyes,
hair and moustaches shocks of pure white, pulling
back to show the whole stick-thin frame wrapped in
unrelieved black.
```

                        THE COUNT
            I . . . am . . . Dracula.

XXIX

Welles had re-written the first scenes – the first shot – of the film to make full use of a new gadget called a Louma crane, which gave the camera enormous mobility and suppleness. Combined with breakaway sets and dark passages between stages, the device meant that he could open *The Other Side of Midnight* with a single tracking shot longer and more elaborate than the one he had pulled off in *Touch of Evil*.

Geneviève found Welles and his cinematographer on the road to Borgo Pass, a full-sized mock-up dirt track complete with wheel-ruts and milestones. The night-black carriage, as yet not equipped with a team of horses, stood on its marks, the crest of Dracula on its polished doors. To either side were forests, the nearest trees half life-size and those beyond getting smaller and smaller as they stretched out to the studio backdrop of a Carpathian night. Up ahead was Dracula's castle, a nine-foot-tall edifice, currently being sprayed by a technician who looked like a colossal man, griming and fogging the battlements.

The two men were debating a potentially thorny moment in the shot, when the camera would be detached from the coach and picked up by an aerial rig. Hanging from the ceiling was a contraption that looked like a Wright Brothers-Georges Méliès collaboration, a man-shaped flying frame with a camera hooked onto it, and a dauntless operator inside.

She hated to think what all this was costing.

Welles saw her, and grinned broadly.

"Gené, Gené," he welcomed. "You must look at this cunning bit of business. Even if I do say so myself, it's an absolute stroke of genius. A simple solution to a complex problem. When *Midnight* comes out, they'll all wonder how I did it."

He chuckled.

"Orson," she said, "we have to talk. I've found some things out. As you asked. About Mr Alucard."

He took that aboard. He must have a thousand and one mammoth and tiny matters to see to, but one more could be accommodated. That was part of his skill as a director, being a master strategist as well as a visionary artist.

She almost hated to tell him.

"Where can we talk in private?" she asked.

"In the coach," he said, standing aside to let her step up.

XXX

The prop coach, as detailed inside as out, creaked a lot as Welles shifted his weight. She wondered if the springs could take it.

She had laid out the whole thing.

She still didn't know who John Alucard was, though she supposed him some self-styled last disciple of the King Vampire, but she told Welles what she thought he was up to.

"He doesn't want a conjurer," Welles concluded, "but a sorcerer, a magician."

Geneviève remembered Welles had played Faustus on stage.

"Alucard needs a genius, Orson," she said, trying to be a comfort.

Welles' great brows were knit in a frown that made his nose seem like a baby's button. This was too great a thing to get even his mind around.

He asked the forty-thousand-dollar question: "and do you believe it will work? This conjuring of Dracula?"

She dodged it. "John Alucard does."

"Of that I have no doubt, no doubt at all," rumbled Welles. "The colossal conceit of it, the enormity of the conception, boggles belief. All this, after so long, all this can be mine, a real chance to, as the young people so aptly say, do my thing. And it's part of a Black Mass. A film to raise the Devil Himself. No mere charlatan could devise such a warped, intricate scheme."

With that, she had to agree.

"If Alucard is wrong, if magic doesn't work, then there's no harm in taking his money and making my movie. That would truly be beating the Devil."

"But if he's right . . ."

"Then I, Orson Welles, would not merely be Faustus, nor even Prometheus, I would be Pandora, unloosing all the ills of the world to reign anew. I would be the father-in-darkness of a veritable Bright Lucifer."

"It could be worse. You could be cloning Hitler."

Welles shook his head.

"And it's my decision," he said, wearily. Then he laughed, so loud that the interior of the prop carriage shook as with a thunderbolt from Zeus.

She didn't envy the genius his choice. After such great beginnings, no artist of the twentieth Century had been thwarted so consistently and so often. Everything he had made, even *Kane*, was compromised as soon as it left his mind and ventured into the marketplace. Dozens of unfinished or unmade films, unstaged theatrical productions, projects stolen away and botched by lesser talents, often with Welles still around as a cameo player to see the potential squandered. And here, at the end of his career, was the chance to claw everything back, to make good on his promise, to be a Boy Wonder again, to prove at last that he was the King of his World.

And against that, a touch of brimstone. Something she didn't even necessarily believe.

Great tears emerged from Welles' clear eyes and trickled into his beard. Tears of laughter.

There was a tap at the coach door.

"All ready on the set now, Mr Welles," said an assistant.

"This shot, Gené," said Welles, ruminating, "will be a marvel, one for the books. And it'll come in under budget. A whole reel, a quarter-of-an-hour, will be in the can by the end of the day. Months of planning, construction, drafting and setting up. Everything I've learned about the movies since 1939. It'll all be there."

Had she the heart to plead with him to stop?

"Mr Welles," prompted the assistant.

Suddenly firm, decided, Welles said, "We take the shot."

XXXI

On the first take, the sliding walls of the Bistritz Inn jammed, after only twenty seconds of exposure. The next take went perfectly, snaking through three stages, with over a hundred performers in addition to the principals and twice that many technicians focusing on fulfilling the vision of one great man. After lunch, at the pleading of Jack Nicholson – who thought he could do better – Welles put the whole show on again. This time, there were wobbles as the flying camera went momentarily out of control, plunging towards the toy forest, before the operator (pilot?) regained balance and completed the stunt with a remarkable save.

Two good takes. The spontaneous chaos might even work for the shot.

Geneviève had spent the day just watching, in awe.

If it came to a choice between a world without this film and a world with Dracula, she didn't know which way she would vote. Welles, in action, was a much younger man, a charmer and a tyrant, a cheerleader and a patriarch. He was everywhere, flirting in French with Jeanne Moreau, the peasant woman, and hauling ropes with the effects men. Dracula wasn't in the shot, except as a subjective camera and a shadow-puppet, but John Huston was on stage for every moment, when he could have been in resting his trailer, just amazed by what Welles was doing, a veteran as impressed as parvenus like Spielberg and DePalma, who were taking notes like train-spotters in locomotive heaven.

Still unsure about the outcome of it all, she left without talking to Welles.

Driving up to Malibu, she came down from the excitement.

In a few days, it would be the Julian 1980s. And she should start working to get her licence back. Considering everything, she should angle to get paid by Welles, who must have enough of John Alucard's money to settle her bill.

When she pulled into Paradise Cove, it was full dark. She took a moment after parking the car to listen to the surf, an eternal sound, pre and post-human.

She got out of the car and walked towards her trailer. As she fished around in her bag for her keys, she sensed something that made quills of her hair.

As if in slow motion, her trailer exploded.

A burst of flame in the sleeping section, spurted through the shutters, tearing them off their frames, and then a second, larger fireball expanded from the inside as the gas cylinders in the kitchen caught, rending the chromed walls apart, wrecking the integrity of the vessel.

The light hit her a split-second before the noise.

Then the blast lifted her off her feet and threw her back, across the sandy lot.

Everything she owned rained around her in flames.

XXXII

After a single day's shooting, Orson Welles abandoned *The Other Side of Midnight*. Between 1981 and his death in 1985, he made no further films and did no more work on such protracted projects as *Don Quixote*. He made no public statement about the reasons for his walking away from the film, which was abandoned after John Huston, Steven Spielberg and Brian DePalma in succession refused to take over the direction.

Most biographers have interpreted this wilful scuppering of what seemed to be an ideal, indeed impossibly perfect, set-up as a final symptom of the insecure, self-destructive streak that had always co-existed with genius in the heart of Orson Welles. Those closest to him, notably Oja Kodar, have argued vehemently against this interpretation and maintained that there were pressing reasons for Welles's actions, albeit reasons which have yet to come to light or even be tentatively suggested.

As for the exposed film, two full reels of one extended shot, it has never been developed and, due to a financing quirk, remains sealed up, inaccessible, in the vaults of a bank in Timisoara, Romania. More than one cineaste has expressed a willingness to part happily with his immortal soul for a single screening of those reels. Until those reels, like Rosebud itself, can be discovered and understood, the mystery of Orson Welles's last, lost *Dracula* will remain.

Gates, *ibid*

XXXIII

"Do you know what's the funny side of the whole kit and kaboodle?" said Ernest Gorse. "I didn't even think it would work. Johnny Alucard has big ideas and he is certainly making something of himself on the coast, but this Elvis Lives nonsense is potty. Then again, you never know with the dear old Count. He's been dead before."

She was too wrung out to try to get up yet.

Gorse, in a tweed ulster and fisherman's hat, leaned on her car, scratching the finish with the claws of his left hand. His face was demonized by the firelight.

Everything she owned.

That's what it had cost her.

"And, who knows, maybe Fatty wasn't the genius?" suggested Gorse. "Maybe it was Boris Adrian. Alucard backed all those

Dracula pictures equally. Perhaps you haven't thwarted him after all. Perhaps He really is coming back."

All the fight was out of her. Gorse must be enjoying this.

"You should leave the city, maybe the state," he said. "There is nothing here for you, old thing. Be thankful we've left you the motor. Nice roadboat, by the way, but it's not a Jag, is it? Consider the long lines, all the chrome, the ostentatious muscle. D'you think the Yanks are trying to prove something? Don't trouble yourself to answer. It was a rhetorical question."

She pushed herself up on her knees.

Gorse had a gun. "Paper wraps stone," he said. "With silver foil."

She got to her feet, not brushing the sand from her clothes. There was ash in her hair. People had come out of the other trailers, fascinated and horrified. Her trailer was a burning shell.

That annoyed her, gave her a spark.

With a swiftness Gorse couldn't match, she took his gun away from him. She broke his wrist and tore off his hat too. He was surprised in a heart-dead British sort of way, raising his eyebrows as far as they would go. His quizzical, ironic expression begged to be scraped off his face, but it would just grow back crooked.

"Jolly well done," he said, going limp. "Really super little move. Didn't see it coming at all."

She could have thrown him into the fire, but just gave his gun to one of the on-lookers, the Dude, with instructions that he was to be turned over to the police when they showed up.

"Watch him, he's a murderer," she said. Gorse looked hurt. "A common murderer," she elaborated.

The Dude understood and held the gun properly. People gathered round the shrinking vampire, holding him fast. He was no threat any more: he was cut, wrapped and blunted.

There were sirens. In situations like this, there were always sirens.

She kissed the Dude goodbye, got into the Plymouth, and drove North, away from Hollywood, along the winding coast road, without a look back. She wasn't sure whether she was lost or free.

2001

BEST NEW HORROR

POPPY Z. BRITE
CHRISTOPHER FOWLER
GLEN HIRSHBERG
GRAHAM JOYCE
TANITH LEE
THOMAS LIGOTTI
AND MANY OTHERS

"A formidable lineup
of must-read creepers
whose merits are
indisputable."
Publishers Weekly

Edited by Stephen Jones

Cleopatra Brimstone

Elizabeth Hand

I HAD HOPED THAT by now I had made my point regarding
the covers. However, when *The Mammoth Book of Best New Horror
13* came out with blobby lettering and what looked like a DayGlo
skull on the front, I knew that nobody was listening to my opinions
anymore.

The Introduction jumped to eighty-one pages, while the Necrology
held at around forty. This still pushed the book to nearly 600 pages.
There was only one subject the world was talking about in 2001:
what should have been remembered as the year made famous by
Arthur C. Clarke's classic science fiction novel was forever scarred
by the terrorist attacks of September 11 on New York's World Trade
Center and Washington's Pentagon Building.

The world has never been the same since, and I used the
editorial comment to look at what effect 9/11 had on the publishing
industry and specifically our own genre. As I said at the time: "For
the foreseeable future the world has new monsters to fear, new
bogeymen to keep us awake at night." In the intervening years,
those very real fears have sadly remained with us and, if anything,
grown.

The volume contained a bumper crop of twenty-three stories, with
a pair of authors represented by two stories each. However, at the
time I was not actually aware of that, as one of them misrepresented
themselves to me by submitting their second contribution under a
pseudonym. The other was Chico Kidd, who opened and closed the
anthology with two swashbuckling adventures featuring a Portuguese
sea captain named Luís Da Silva.

Elizabeth Hand has been writing smart and exotic fiction since
her first story was published in *The Twilight Zone* magazine in 1988.
Born in America, she splits her time between her home in coastal
Maine and London's Camden Town district, which just happens to

be the setting for her International Horror Guild Award-winning story "Cleopatra Brimstone".

HER EARLIEST MEMORY was of wings. Luminous red and blue, yellow and green and orange; a black so rich it appeared liquid, edible. They moved above her and the sunlight made them glow as though they were themselves made of light, fragments of another, brighter world falling to earth about her crib. Her tiny hands stretched upwards to grasp them but could not: they were too elusive, too radiant, too much of the air.

Could they ever have been real?

For years she thought she must have dreamed them. But one afternoon when she was ten she went into the attic, searching for old clothes to wear to a Halloween party. In a corner beneath a cobwebbed window she found a box of her baby things. Yellow-stained bibs and tiny fuzzy jumpers blued from bleaching, a much-nibbled stuffed dog that she had no memory of whatsoever.

And at the very bottom of the carton, something else. Wings flattened and twisted out of shape, wires bent and strings frayed: a mobile. Six plastic butterflies, colours faded and their wings giving off a musty smell, no longer eidolons of Eden but crude representations of monarch, zebra swallowtail, red admiral, sulphur, an unnaturally elongated hairskipper and *Agrias narcissus*. Except for the *narcissus*, all were common New World species that any child might see in a suburban garden. They hung limply from their wires, antennae long since broken off; when she touched one wing it felt cold and stiff as metal.

The afternoon had been overcast, tending to rain. But as she held the mobile to the window, a shaft of sun broke through the darkness to ignite the plastic wings, blood-red, ivy-green, the pure burning yellow of an August field. In that instant it was as though her entire being was burned away, skin hair lips fingers all ash; and nothing remained but the butterflies and her awareness of them, orange and black fluid filling her mouth, the edges of her eyes scored by wings.

As a girl she had always worn glasses. A mild childhood astigmatism worsened when she was thirteen: she started bumping into things, and found it increasingly difficult to concentrate on the entomological textbooks and journals that she read voraciously. Growing pains, her mother thought; but after two months, Janie's clumsiness and concomitant headaches became so severe that her mother admitted that this was perhaps something more serious, and took her to the family physician.

"Janie's fine," Dr Gordon announced after peering into her ears and eyes. "She needs to see the ophthalmologist, that's all. Sometimes our eyes change when we hit puberty." He gave her mother the name of an eye doctor nearby.

Her mother was relieved, and so was Jane – she had overheard her parents talking the night before her appointment, and the words *CAT scan* and *brain tumour* figured in their hushed conversation. Actually, Jane had been more concerned about another odd physical manifestation, one which no one but herself seemed to have noticed. She had started menstruating several months earlier: nothing unusual in that. Everything she had read about it mentioned the usual things – mood swings, growth spurts, acne, pubic hair.

But nothing was said about eyebrows. Janie first noticed something strange about hers when she got her period for the second time. She had retreated to the bathtub, where she spent a good half-hour reading an article in *Nature* about Oriental Ladybug swarms. When she finished the article, she got out of the tub, dressed and brushed her teeth, then spent a minute frowning at the mirror.

Something was different about her face. She turned sideways, squinting. Had her chin broken out? No; but something had changed. Her hair colour? Her teeth? She leaned over the sink until she was almost nose-to-nose with her reflection.

That was when she saw that her eyebrows had undergone a growth spurt of their own. At the inner edge of each eyebrow, above the bridge of her nose, three hairs had grown remarkably long. They furled back towards her temple, entwined in a sort of loose braid. She had not noticed them sooner because she seldom looked in a mirror, and also because the odd hairs did not arch above the eyebrows, but instead blended in with them, the way a bittersweet vine twines around a branch. Still, they seemed bizarre enough that she wanted no one, not even her parents, to notice. She found her mother's eyebrow tweezers, neatly plucked the six hairs and flushed them down the toilet. They did not grow back.

At the optometrist's, Jane opted for heavy tortoise-shell frames rather than contacts. The optometrist, and her mother, thought she was crazy, but it was a very deliberate choice. Janie was not one of those homely B-movie adolescent girls, driven to science as a last resort. She had always been a tomboy, skinny as a rail, with long slanted violet-blue eyes; a small rosy mouth; long, straight black hair that ran like oil between her fingers; skin so pale it had the periwinkle shimmer of skim milk.

When she hit puberty, all of these conspired to beauty. And Jane hated it. Hated the attention, hated being looked at, hated that other girls hated her. She was quiet, not shy but impatient to focus on her schoolwork, and this was mistaken for arrogance by her peers. All through high school she had few friends. She learned early the perils of befriending boys, even earnest boys who professed an interest in genetic mutations and intricate computer simulations of hive activity. Janie could trust them not to touch her, but she couldn't trust them not to fall in love. As a result of having none of the usual distractions of high school – sex, social life, mindless employment – she received an Intel/Westinghouse Science Scholarship for a computer-generated schematic of possible mutations in a small population of viceroy butterflies exposed to genetically-engineered crops. She graduated in her junior year, took her scholarship money, and ran.

She had been accepted at Stanford and MIT, but chose to attend a small, highly prestigious women's college in a big city several hundred miles away. Her parents were apprehensive about her being on her own at the tender age of seventeen, but the college, with its elegant, cloister-like buildings and lushly wooded grounds, put them at ease. That and the dean's assurances that the neighbourhood was completely safe, as long as students were sensible about not walking alone at night. Thus mollified, and at Janie's urging – she was desperate to move away from home – her father signed a very large cheque for the first semester's tuition. That September she started school.

She studied entomology, spending her first year examining the genitalia of male and female Scarce Wormwood Shark Moths, a species found on the Siberian steppes. Her hours in the zoology lab were rapturous, hunched over a microscope with a pair of tweezers so minute they were themselves like some delicate portion of her specimen's physiognomy. She would remove the butterflies' genitalia, tiny and geometrically precise as diatoms, and dip them first into glycerine, which acted as a preservative, and next into a mixture of water and alcohol. Then she observed them under the microscope. Her glasses interfered with this work – they bumped into the microscope's viewing lens – and so she switched to wearing contact lenses. In retrospect, she thought that this was probably a mistake.

At Argus College she still had no close friends, but neither was she the solitary creature she had been at home. She respected her fellow students, and grew to appreciate the company of women. She could go for days at a time seeing no men besides her professors or the commuters driving past the school's wrought-iron gates.

And she was not the school's only beauty. Argus College specialized in young women like Jane: elegant, diffident girls who studied the burial customs of Mongol women or the mating habits of rare antipodean birds; girls who composed concertos for violin and gamela orchestra, or wrote computer programs that charted the progress of potentially dangerous celestial objects through the Oort Cloud. Within this educational greenhouse, Janie was not so much orchid as sturdy milkweed blossom. She thrived.

Her first three years at Argus passed in a bright-winged blur with her butterflies. Summers were given to museum internships, where she spent months cleaning and mounting specimens in solitary delight. In her senior year Janie received permission to design her own thesis project, involving her beloved Shark Moths. She was given a corner in a dusty anteroom off the Zoology Lab, and there she set up her microscope and laptop. There was no window in her corner, indeed there was no window in the anteroom at all, though the adjoining Lab was pleasantly old-fashioned, with high arched windows set between Victorian cabinetry displaying *lepidoptera*, neon-carapaced beetles, unusual tree fungi and (she found these slightly tragic) numerous exotic finches, their brilliant plumage dimmed to dusty hues. Since she often worked late into the night, she requested and received her own set of keys. Most evenings she could be found beneath the glare of the small halogen lamp, entering data into her computer, scanning images of genetic mutations involving female Shark Moths exposed to dioxin, corresponding with other researchers in Melbourne and Kyoto, Siberia and London.

The rape occurred around ten o'clock one Friday night in early March. She had locked the door to her office, leaving her laptop behind, and started to walk to the subway station a few blocks away. It was a cold clear night, the yellow glow of the crime lights giving dead grass and leafless trees an eerie autumn shimmer. She hurried across the campus, seeing no one, then hesitated at Seventh Street. It was a longer walk, but safer, if she went down Seventh Street and then over to Michigan Avenue. The shortcut was much quicker, but

Argus authorities and the local police discouraged students from taking it after dark. Jane stood for a moment, looking across the road to where the desolate park lay; then, staring resolutely straight ahead and walking briskly, she crossed Seventh and took the shortcut.

A crumbling sidewalk passed through a weedy expanse of vacant lot, strewn with broken bottles and the spindly forms of half a dozen dusty-limbed oak trees. Where the grass ended, a narrow road skirted a block of abandoned row houses, intermittently lit by crime lights. Most of the lights had been vandalized, and one had been knocked down in a car accident – the car's fender was still there, twisted around the lamp-post. Jane picked her way carefully among shards of shattered glass, reached the sidewalk in front of the boarded-up houses and began to walk more quickly, towards the brightly-lit Michigan Avenue intersection where the subway waited.

She never saw him. He was *there*, she knew that; knew he had a face, and clothing; but afterwards she could recall none of it. Not the feel of him, not his smell; only the knife he held – awkwardly, she realized later, she probably could have wrested it from him – and the few words he spoke to her. He said nothing at first, just grabbed her and pulled her into an alley between the row houses, his fingers covering her mouth, the heel of his hand pressing against her windpipe so that she gagged. He pushed her onto the dead leaves and wads of matted windblown newspaper, yanked her pants down, ripped open her jacket and then tore her shirt open. She heard one of the buttons strike brick and roll away.

She thought desperately of what she had read once, in a Rape Awareness brochure: not to struggle, not to fight, not to do anything that might cause her attacker to kill her.

Janie did not fight. Instead, she divided into three parts. One part knelt nearby and prayed the way she had done as a child, not intently but automatically, trying to get through the strings of words as quickly as possible. The second part submitted blindly and silently to the man in the alley. And the third hovered above the other two, her hands wafting slowly up and down to keep her aloft as she watched.

"Try to get away," the man whispered. She could not see him or feel him though his hands were there. "Try to get away."

She remembered that she ought not to struggle, but from the noise she made and the way he tugged at her realized that was what aroused him. She did not want to anger him; she made a small sound deep in her throat and tried to push him from her chest. Almost immediately he groaned, and seconds later rolled off her. Only his hand lingered for a moment upon her cheek. Then he stumbled to his feet – she could hear him fumbling with his zipper – and fled.

The praying girl and the girl in the air also disappeared then. Only Janie was left, yanking her ruined clothes around her as she lurched from the alley and began to run, screaming and staggering back and forth across the road, towards the subway.

The police came, an ambulance. She was taken first to the police station and then to the City General Hospital, a hellish place, starkly-lit, with endless underground corridors that led into darkened rooms where solitary figures lay on narrow beds like gurneys. Her pubic hair was combed and stray hairs placed into sterile envelopes; semen samples were taken, and she was advised to be tested for HIV and other diseases. She spent the entire night in the hospital, waiting and undergoing various examinations. She refused to give the police or hospital staff her parents' phone number, or anyone else's. Just before dawn they finally released her, with an envelope full of brochures from the local Rape Crisis Centre, *New Hope for Women, Planned Parenthood*, and a business card from the police detective who was overseeing her case. The detective drove her to her apartment in his squad car; when he stopped in front of her building, she was suddenly terrified that he would know where she lived, that he would come back, that he had been her assailant.

But, of course, he had not been. He walked her to the door and waited for her to go inside. "Call your parents," he said right before he left.

"I will."

She pulled aside the bamboo window shade, watching until the squad car pulled away. Then she threw out the brochures she'd received, flung off her clothes and stuffed them into the trash. She showered and changed, packed a bag full of clothes and another of books. Then she called a cab. When it arrived, she directed it to the Argus campus, where she retrieved her laptop and her research on Tiger Moths, then had the cab bring her to Union Station.

She bought a train ticket home. Only after she arrived and told her parents what had happened did she finally start to cry. Even then, she could not remember what the man had looked like.

She lived at home for three months. Her parents insisted that she get psychiatric counselling and join a therapy group for rape survivors. She did so, reluctantly, but stopped attending after three weeks. The rape was something that had happened to her, but it was over.

"It was fifteen minutes out of my life," she said once at group. "That's all. It's not the rest of my life."

This didn't go over very well. Other women thought she was in denial; the therapist thought Jane would suffer later if she did not confront her fears now.

"But I'm not afraid," said Jane.

"Why not?" demanded a woman whose eyebrows had fallen out.

Because lightning doesn't strike twice, Jane thought grimly, but she said nothing. That was the last time she attended group.

That night her father had a phone call. He took the phone and sat at the dining table, listening; after a moment stood and walked into his study, giving a quick backward glance at his daughter before closing the door behind him. Jane felt as though her chest had suddenly frozen: but after some minutes she heard her father's laugh: he was not, after all, talking to the police detective. When after half-an-hour he returned, he gave Janie another quick look, more thoughtful this time.

"That was Andrew." Andrew was a doctor friend of his, an Englishman. "He and Fred are going to Provence for three months. They were wondering if you might want to housesit for them."

"In *London*?" Jane's mother shook her head. "I don't think—"

"I said we'd think about it."

"*I'll* think about it," Janie corrected him. She stared at both her parents, absently ran a finger along one eyebrow. "Just let me think about it."

And she went to bed.

She went to London. She already had a passport, from visiting Andrew with her parents when she was in high school. Before she left there were countless arguments with her mother and father, and phone calls back and forth to Andrew. He assured them that the flat was secure, there was a very nice reliable older woman who lived upstairs, that it would be a good idea for Janie to get out on her own again.

"So you don't get gun-shy," he said to her one night on the phone. He was a doctor, after all: a homeopath not an allopath, which Janie found reassuring. "It's important for you to get on with your life. You won't be able to get a real job here as a visitor, but I'll see what I can do."

It was on the plane to Heathrow that she made a discovery. She had splashed water onto her face, and was beginning to comb her hair when she blinked and stared into the mirror.

Above her eyebrows, the long hairs had grown back. They followed the contours of her brow, sweeping back towards her temples; still entwined, still difficult to make out unless she drew her face close to her reflection and tilted her head just so. Tentatively she touched one braided strand. It was stiff yet oddly pliant; but as she ran her finger along its length a sudden *surge* flowed through her. Not an electrical shock: more like the thrill of pain when a dentist's drill touches a nerve, or an elbow rams against a stone. She gasped; but immediately the pain was gone. Instead there was a thrumming behind her forehead, a spreading warmth that trickled into her throat like sweet syrup. She opened her mouth, her gasp turning into an uncontrollable yawn, the yawn into a spike of such profound physical ecstasy that she grabbed the edge of the sink and thrust forward, striking her head against the mirror. She was dimly aware of someone knocking at the lavatory door as she clutched the sink and, shuddering, climaxed.

"Hello?" someone called softly. "Hello, is this occupied?"

"Right out," Janie gasped. She caught her breath, still trembling; ran a hand across her face, her fingers halting before they could touch the hairs above her eyebrows. There was the faintest tingling, a temblor of sensation that faded as she grabbed her cosmetic bag, pulled the door open and stumbled back into the cabin.

Andrew and Fred lived in an old Georgian row house just north of Camden Town, overlooking the Regent's Canal. Their flat occupied the first floor and basement; there was a hexagonal solarium out back, with glass walls and heated stone floor, and beyond that a stepped terrace leading down to the canal. The bedroom had an old wooden four-poster piled high with duvets and down pillows, and French doors that also opened onto the terrace. Andrew showed her how to operate the elaborate sliding security doors that unfolded from the walls, and gave her the keys to the barred window guards.

"You're completely safe here," he said, smiling. "Tomorrow we'll introduce you to Kendra upstairs, and show you how to get around. Camden market's just up that way, and *that* way—"

He stepped out onto the terrace, pointing to where the canal coiled and disappeared beneath an arched stone bridge. "—that way's the Regent's Park Zoo. I've given you a membership—"

"Oh! Thank you!" Janie looked around delighted. "This is *wonderful.*"

"It is." Andrew put an arm around her and drew her close. "You're going to have a wonderful time, Janie. I thought you'd like the Zoo – there's a new exhibit there, 'The World Within' or words to that effect – it's about insects. I thought perhaps you might want to volunteer there – they have an active docent program, and you're so knowledgeable about that sort of thing."

"Sure. It sounds great – really great." She grinned and smoothed her hair back from her face, the wind sending up the rank scent of stagnant water from the canal, the sweetly poisonous smell of hawthorn blossom. As she stood gazing down past the potted geraniums and Fred's rosemary trees, the hairs upon her brow trembled, and she laughed out loud, giddily, with anticipation.

Fred and Andrew left two days later. It was enough time for Janie to get over her jet lag and begin to get barely acclimatized to the city, and to its smell. London had an acrid scent: damp ashes, the softer underlying fetor of rot that oozed from ancient bricks and stone buildings, the thick vegetative smell of the canal, sharpened with urine and spilled beer. So many thousands of people descended on Camden Town on the weekend that the tube station was restricted to incoming passengers, and the canal path became almost impassable. Even late on a week night she could hear voices from the other side of the canal, harsh London voices echoing beneath the bridges or shouting to be heard above the din of the Northern Line trains passing overhead.

Those first days Janie did not venture far from the flat. She unpacked her clothes, which did not take much time, and then unpacked her collecting box, which did. The sturdy wooden case had come through the overseas flight and Customs seemingly unscathed, but Janie found herself holding her breath as she undid the metal hinges, afraid of what she'd find inside.

"*Oh!*" she exclaimed. Relief, not chagrin: nothing had been damaged. The small glass vials of ethyl alcohol and gel shellac were intact, and the pillboxes where she kept the tiny #2 pins she used for mounting. Fighting her own eagerness she carefully removed packets of stiff archival paper, a block of Styrofoam covered with pinholes; two bottles of clear Maybelline nail polish and a small container of Elmer's Glue; more pillboxes, empty, and empty gelatine capsules for very small specimens; and last of all a small glass-fronted display box, framed in mahogany and holding her most precious specimen: a hybrid *Celerio harmuthi Kordesch*, the male crossbreed of a Spurge and an Elephant Hawkmoth. As long as the first joint of her thumb, it had the hawkmoth's typically streamlined wings but exquisitely delicate colouring, fuchsia bands shading to a soft rich brown, its thorax thick and seemingly feathered. Only a handful of these hybrid moths had ever existed, bred by the Prague entomologist Jan Pokorny in 1961; a few years afterward, both the Spurge Hawkmoth and the Elephant Hawkmoth had become extinct.

Janie had found this one for sale on the Internet three months ago. It was a former museum specimen and cost a fortune; she had a few bad nights, worrying whether it had actually been a legal purchase. Now she held the display box in her cupped palms and gazed at it raptly. Behind her eyes she felt a prickle, like sleep or unshed tears; then a slow thrumming warmth crept from her brows, spreading to her temples, down her neck and through her breasts, spreading like a stain. She swallowed, leaned back against the sofa and let the display box rest back within the larger case; slid first one hand then the other beneath her sweater and began to stroke her nipples. When some time later she came it was with stabbing force and a thunderous sensation above her eyes, as though she had struck her forehead against the floor.

She had not: gasping, she pushed the hair from her face, zipped her jeans and reflexively leaned forward, to make certain the hawkmoth in its glass box was safe.

Over the following days she made a few brief forays to the newsagent and greengrocer, trying to eke out the supplies Fred and Andrew had left in the kitchen. She sat in the solarium, her bare feet warm against the heated stone floor, and drank camomile tea or claret, staring down to where the ceaseless stream of people passed along the canal path, and watching the narrow boats as they plied their way slowly between Camden Lock and Little Venice, two miles to the west in Paddington. By the following Wednesday she felt brave enough, and bored enough, to leave her refuge and visit the zoo.

It was a short walk along the canal, dodging bicyclists who jingled their bells impatiently when she forgot to stay on the proper side of the path. She passed beneath several arching bridges, their undersides pleated with slime and moss. Drunks sprawled against the stones and stared at her blearily or challengingly by turns; well-dressed couples walked dogs, and there were excited knots of children, tugging their parents on to the zoo.

Fred had walked here with Janie, to show her the way. But it all looked unfamiliar now. She kept a few strides behind a family, her head down, trying not to look as though she was following them; and felt a pulse of relief when they reached a twisting stair with an arrowed sign at its top.

REGENT'S PARK ZOO

There was an old church across the street, its yellow stone walls overgrown with ivy; and down and around the corner a long stretch of hedges with high iron walls fronting them, and at last a huge set of gates, crammed with children and vendors selling balloons and banners and London guidebooks. Janie lifted her head and walked quickly past the family that had led her here, showed her membership card at the entrance, and went inside.

She wasted no time on the seals or tigers or monkeys, but went straight to the newly-renovated structure where a multicoloured banner flapped in the late-morning breeze.

AN ALTERNATE UNIVERSE: SECRETS OF THE INSECT WORLD

Inside, crowds of schoolchildren and harassed-looking adults formed a ragged queue that trailed through a brightly-lit corridor, its walls covered with huge glossy colour photos and computer-enhanced images of hissing cockroaches, hellgrammites, morpho butterflies, death-watch beetles, polyphemous moths. Janie dutifully joined the queue, but when the corridor opened into a vast sun-lit atrium she strode off on her own, leaving the children and teachers to gape at monarchs in butterfly cages and an interactive display of honeybees dancing. Instead she found a relatively quiet display at the far end of the exhibition space, a floor-to-ceiling cylinder of transparent net, perhaps six feet in diameter. Inside, buckthorn bushes and blooming hawthorn vied for sunlight with a slender beech sapling, and dozens of butterflies flitted upwards through the new yellow leaves, or sat with wings outstretched upon the beech tree. They were a type of Pieridae, the butterflies known as whites; though these were not white at all. The females had creamy yellow-green wings, very pale, their wingspans perhaps an inch and a half. The males were the same size; when they were at rest their flattened wings were a dull, rather sulphurous colour. But when the males lit into the air their wings revealed vivid, spectral yellow undersides. Janie caught her breath in delight, her neck prickling with that same atavistic joy she'd felt as a child in the attic.

"Wow," she breathed, and pressed up against the netting. It felt like wings against her face, soft, webbed; but as she stared at the insects inside her brow began to ache as with migraine. She shoved her glasses onto her nose, closed her eyes and drew a long breath; then took a step away from the cage. After a minute she opened her eyes. The headache had diminished to a dull throb; when she hesitantly touched one eyebrow, she could feel the entwined hairs there, stiff as wire. They were vibrating, but at her touch the vibrations like the headache dulled. She stared at the floor, the tiles sticky with contraband juice and gum; then looked up once again at the cage. There was a display sign off to one side; she walked over to it, slowly, and read.

CLEOPATRA BRIMSTONE
Gonepteryx rhamni cleopatra

This popular and subtly coloured species has a range which extends throughout the Northern Hemisphere, with the exception of Arctic regions and several remote islands. In Europe, the brimstone is a harbinger of spring, often emerging from its winter hibernation under dead leaves to revel in the countryside while there is still snow upon the ground.

"I must ask you please not to touch the cages."

Janie turned to see a man, perhaps fifty, standing a few feet away. A net was jammed under his arm; in his hand he held a clear plastic jar with several butterflies at the bottom, apparently dead.

"Oh. Sorry," said Jane. The man edged past her. He set his jar on the floor, opened a small door at the base of the cylindrical cage, and deftly angled the net inside. Butterflies lifted in a yellow-green blur from leaves and branches; the man swept the net carefully across the bottom of the cage, then withdrew it. Three dead butterflies, like scraps of coloured paper, drifted from the net into the open jar.

"Housecleaning," he said, and once more thrust his arm into the cage. He was slender and wiry, not much taller than she was, his face hawkish and burnt brown from the sun, his thick straight hair iron-streaked and pulled back into a long braid. He wore black jeans and a dark-blue hooded jersey, with an ID badge clipped to the collar.

"You work here," said Janie. The man glanced at her, his arm still in the cage; she could see him sizing her up. After a moment he glanced away again. A few minutes later he emptied the net for the last time, closed the cage and the jar, and stepped over to a waste bin, pulling bits of dead leaves from the net and dropping them into the container.

"I'm one of the curatorial staff. You American?"

Janie nodded. "Yeah. Actually, I – I wanted to see about volunteering here."

"Lifewatch desk at the main entrance." The man cocked his head towards the door. "They can get you signed up and registered, see what's available."

"No – I mean, I want to volunteer here. With the insects—"

"Butterfly collector, are you?" The man smiled, his tone mocking. He had hazel eyes, deep-set; his thin mouth made the smile seem perhaps more cruel than intended. "We get a lot of those."

Janie flushed. "No. I am not a *collector*," she said coldly, adjusting her glasses. "I'm doing a thesis on dioxin genital mutation in *Cucullia artemisia*." She didn't add that it was an undergraduate thesis. "I've been doing independent research for seven years now." She hesitated, thinking of her Intel scholarship, and added, "I've received several grants for my work."

The man regarded her appraisingly. "Are you studying here, then?"

"Yes," she lied again. "At Oxford. I'm on sabbatical right now. But I live near here, and so I thought I might—"

She shrugged, opening her hands; looked over at him and smiled tentatively. "Make myself useful?"

The man waited a moment, nodded. "Well. Do you have a few minutes now? I've got to do something with these, but if you want you can come with me and wait, and then we can see what we can do. Maybe circumvent some paperwork."

He turned and started across the room. He had a graceful, bouncing gait, like a gymnast or circus acrobat: impatient with the ground beneath him. "Shouldn't take long," he called over his shoulder as Janie hurried to catch up.

She followed him through a door marked AUTHORIZED PERSONS ONLY, into the exhibit laboratory, a reassuringly familiar place with its display cases and smells of shellac and camphor, acetone and ethyl alcohol. There were more cages here, but smaller ones, sheltering live specimens – pupating butterflies and moths, stick insects, leaf insects, dung beetles. The man dropped his net onto a desk, took the jar to a long table against one wall, blindingly lit by long fluorescent tubes. There were scores of bottles here, some empty, others filled with paper and tiny inert figures.

"Have a seat," said the man, gesturing at two folding chairs. He settled into one, grabbed an empty jar and a roll of absorbent paper.

"I'm David Bierce. So where're you staying? Camden Town?"

"Janie Kendall. Yes—"

"The High Street?"

Janie sat in the other chair, pulling it a few inches away from him. The questions made her uneasy, but she only nodded, lying again, and said, "Closer, actually. Off Gloucester Road. With friends."

"Mm." Bierce tore off a piece of absorbent paper, leaned across to a stainless steel sink and dampened the paper. Then he dropped it into the empty jar. He paused, turned to her and gestured at the table, smiling. "Care to join in?"

Janie shrugged. "Sure—"

She pulled her chair closer, found another empty jar and did as Bierce had, dampening a piece of paper towel and dropping it inside. Then she took the jar containing the dead brimstones and carefully shook one onto the counter. It was a female, its colouring more muted than the males'; she scooped it up very gently, careful not to disturb the scales like dull green glitter upon its wings, dropped it into the jar and replaced the top.

"Very nice." Bierce nodded, raising his eyebrows. "You seem to know what you're doing. Work with other insects? Soft-bodied ones?"

"Sometimes. Mostly moths, though. And butterflies."

"Right." He inclined his head to a recessed shelf. "How would you label that, then? Go ahead."

On the shelf she found a notepad and a case of Rapidograph pens. She began to write, conscious of Bierce staring at her. "We usually just put all this into the computer, of course, and print it out," he said. "I just want to see the benefits of an American education in the sciences."

Janie fought the urge to look at him. Instead she wrote out the information, making her printing as tiny as possible.

Gonepteryx rhamni cleopatra
UNITED KINGDOM: LONDON
Regent's Park Zoo

Lat/Long unknown
21.IV.2001
D. Bierce
Net/caged specimen

She handed it to Bierce. "I don't know the proper co-ordinates for London."

Bierce scrutinized the paper. "It's actually the Royal Zoological Park," he said. He looked at her, then smiled. "But you'll do."

"Great!" She grinned, the first time she'd really felt happy since arriving here. "When do you want me to start?"

"How about Monday?"

Janie hesitated: this was only Friday. "I could come in tomorrow—"

"I don't work on the weekend, and you'll need to be trained. Also they have to process the paperwork. Right—"

He stood and went to a desk, pulling open drawers until he found a clipboard holding sheaves of triplicate forms. "Here. Fill all this out, leave it with me and I'll pass it on to Carolyn – she's the head volunteer co-ordinator. They usually want to interview you, but I'll tell them we've done all that already."

"What time should I come in Monday?"

"Come at nine. Everything opens at ten, that way you'll avoid the crowds. Use the staff entrance, someone there will have an ID waiting for you to pick up when you sign in—"

She nodded and began filling out the forms.

"All right then." David Bierce leaned against the desk and again fixed her with that sly, almost taunting gaze. "Know how to find your way home?"

Janie lifted her chin defiantly. "Yes."

"Enjoying London? Going to go out tonight and do Camden Town with all the yobs?"

"Maybe. I haven't been out much yet."

"Mm. Beautiful American girl, they'll eat you alive. Just kidding." He straightened, started across the room towards the door. "I'll see you Monday then."

He held the door for her. "You really should check out the clubs. You're too young not to see the city by night." He smiled, the fluorescent light slanting sideways into his hazel eyes and making them suddenly glow icy blue. "Bye then."

"Bye," said Janie, and hurried quickly from the lab towards home.

*   *   *

That night, for the first time, she went out. She told herself she would have gone anyway, no matter what Bierce had said. She had no idea where the clubs were; Andrew had pointed out the Electric Ballroom to her, right across from the tube station, but he'd also warned her that was where the tourists flocked on weekends.

"They do a Disco thing on Saturday nights – Saturday Night Fever, everyone gets all done up in vintage clothes. Quite a fashion show," he'd said, smiling and shaking his head.

Janie had no interest in that. She ate a quick supper, Vindaloo from the take-away down the street from the flat; then dressed. She hadn't brought a huge number of clothes – at home she'd never bothered much with clothes at all, making do with thrift-shop finds and whatever her mother gave her for Christmas. But now she found herself sitting on the edge of the four-poster, staring with pursed lips at the sparse contents of two bureau drawers. Finally she pulled out a pair of black corduroy jeans and a black turtleneck and pulled on her sneakers. She removed her glasses, for the first time in weeks inserted her contact lenses. Then she shrugged into her old navy peacoat and left.

It was after ten o'clock. On the canal path, throngs of people stood, drinking from pints of canned lager. She made her way through them, ignoring catcalls and whispered invitations, stepping to avoid where kids lay making out against the brick wall that ran alongside the path, or pissing in the bushes. The bridge over the canal at Camden Lock was clogged with several dozen kids in mohawks or varicoloured hair, shouting at each other above the din of a boom box and swigging from bottles of Spanish champagne.

A boy with a champagne bottle leered, lunging at her.

"'Ere, sweetheart, 'ep youseff—"

Janie ducked, and he careered against the ledge, his arm striking brick and the bottle shattering in a starburst of black and gold.

"Fucking cunt!" he shrieked after her. "Fucking bloody *cunt!*"

People glanced at her, but Janie kept her head down, making a quick turn into the vast cobbled courtyard of Camden Market. The place had a desolate air: the vendors would not arrive until early next morning, and now only stray cats and bits of windblown trash moved in the shadows. In the surrounding buildings people spilled out onto balconies, drinking and calling back and forth, their voices hollow and their long shadows twisting across the ill-lit central courtyard. Janie hurried to the far end, but there found only brick walls, closed-up shop doors and a young woman huddled within the folds of a filthy sleeping bag.

"*Couldya – couldya—*" the woman murmured.

Janie turned and followed the wall until she found a door leading into a short passage. She entered it, hoping she was going in the direction of Camden High Street. She felt like Alice trying to find her way through the garden in Wonderland: arched doorways led not into the street but headshops and blindingly lit piercing parlours, open for business; other doors opened onto enclosed courtyards, dark, smelling of piss and marijuana. Finally from the corner of her eye she glimpsed what looked like the end of the passage, headlights piercing through the gloom like landing lights. Doggedly she made her way towards them.

"Ay watchowt watchowt," someone yelled as she emerged from the passage onto the sidewalk, and ran the last few steps to the curb.

She was on the High Street – rather, in that block or two of curving no-man's-land where it turned into Chalk Farm Road. The sidewalks were still crowded, but everyone was heading towards Camden Lock and not away from it. Janie waited for the light to change and raced across the street, to where a cobblestoned alley snaked off between a shop selling leather underwear and another advertising "Fine French Country Furniture".

For several minutes she stood there. She watched the crowds heading towards Camden Town, the steady stream of minicabs and taxis and buses heading up Chalk Farm Road towards Hampstead. Overhead dull orange clouds moved across a night sky the colour of charred wood; there was the steady low thunder of jets circling after takeoff at Heathrow. At last she tugged her collar up around her neck, letting her hair fall in loose waves down her back, shoved her hands into her coat pockets and turned to walk purposefully down the alley.

Before her the cobblestone path turned sharply to the right. She couldn't see what was beyond, but she could hear voices: a girl laughing, a man's sibilant retort. A moment later the alley spilled out onto a cul-de-sac. A couple stood a few yards away, before a doorway with a small copper awning above it. The young woman glanced sideways at Janie, quickly looked away again. A silhouette filled the doorway; the young man pulled out a wallet. His hand disappeared within the silhouette, re-emerged; and the couple walked inside. Janie waited until the shadowy figure withdrew. She looked over her shoulder, then approached the building.

There was a heavy metal door, black, with graffiti scratched into it and pale blurred spots where painted graffiti had been effaced. The door was set back several feet into a brick recess; there was a grilled metal slot at the top that could be slid back, so that one could peer out into the courtyard. To the right of the door, on the brick wall within the recess, was a small brass plaque with a single word on it.

HIVE

There was no doorbell or any other way to signal that you wanted to enter. Janie stood, wondering what was inside; feeling a small tingling unease that was less fear than the knowledge that even if she were to confront the figure who'd let that other couple inside, she herself would certainly be turned away.

With a *skreek* of metal on stone the door suddenly shot open. Janie looked up, into the sharp, raggedly handsome face of a tall, still youngish man with very short blond hair, a line of gleaming gold beads like drops of sweat piercing the edge of his left jaw.

"Good evening," he said, glancing past her to the alley. He wore a black sleeveless T-shirt with a small golden bee embroidered upon the breast. His bare arms were muscular, striated with long sweeping scars: black, red, white. "Are you waiting for Hannah?"

"No." Quickly Janie pulled out a handful of five-pound notes. "Just me tonight."

"That'll be twenty then." The man held his hand out, still gazing at the alley; when Janie slipped the notes to him he looked down and flashed her a vulpine smile. "Enjoy yourself." She darted past him into the building.

Abruptly it was as though some darker night had fallen. Thunderously so, since the enfolding blackness was slashed with music so loud it was itself like light: Janie hesitated, closing her eyes, and white flashes streaked across her eyelids like sleet, pulsing in time to the music. She opened her eyes, giving them a chance to adjust to the darkness, and tried to get a sense of where she was. A few feet away a blurry greyish lozenge sharpened into the window of a coat-check room. Janie walked past it, towards the source of the music. Immediately the floor slanted steeply beneath her feet. She steadied herself with one hand against the wall, following the incline until it opened onto a cavernous dance floor.

She gazed inside, disappointed. It looked like any other club, crowded, strobe-lit, turquoise smoke and silver glitter coiling between hundreds of whirling bodies clad in candy pink, sky-blue, neon red, rain-slicker yellow. Baby colours, Janie thought. There was a boy who was almost naked, except for shorts, a transparent water bottle strapped to his chest and long tubes snaking into his mouth. Another boy had hair the colour of lime Jell-O, his face corrugated with glitter and sweat; he swayed near the edge of the dance floor, turned to stare at Janie and then beamed, beckoning her to join him.

Janie gave him a quick smile, shaking her head; when the boy opened his arms to her in mock pleading she shouted "No!"

But she continued to smile, though she felt as though her head would crack like an egg from the throbbing music. Shoving her hands into her pockets she skirted the dance floor, pushed her way to the bar and bought a drink, something pink with no ice in a plastic cup. It smelled like Gatorade and lighter fluid. She gulped it down, then carried the cup held before her like a torch as she continued on her circuit of the room. There was nothing else of interest; just long queues for the lavatories and another bar, numerous doors and stairwells where kids clustered, drinking and smoking. Now and then beeps and whistles like birdsong or insect cries came through the stuttering electronic din, whoops and trilling laughter from the dancers. But mostly they moved in near-silence, eyes rolled ceiling-ward, bodies exploding into Catherine wheels of flesh and plastic and nylon, but all without a word.

It gave Janie a headache – a *real* headache, the back of her skull bruised, tender to the touch. She dropped her plastic cup and started looking for a way out. She could see past the dance floor to where she had entered, but it seemed as though another hundred people had arrived in the few minutes since then: kids were standing six-deep at both bars, and the action on the floor had spread, amoeba-like, towards the corridors angling back up toward the street.

"Sorry—"

A fat woman in an Arsenal jersey jostled her as she hurried by, leaving a smear of oily sweat on Janie's wrist. Janie grimaced and wiped her hand on the bottom of her coat. She gave one last look at the dance floor, but nothing had changed within the intricate lattice of dancers and smoke, braids of glow-lights and spotlit faces surging up and down, up and down, while more dancers fought their way to the centre.

"Shit." She turned and strode off, heading to where the huge room curved off into relative emptiness. Here, scores of tables were scattered, some overturned, others stacked against the wall. A few people sat, talking; a girl lay curled on the floor, her head pillowed on a Barbie knapsack. Janie crossed to the wall, and found first a door that led to a bare brick wall, then a second door that held a broom closet. The next was dark-red, metal, official-looking: the kind of door that Janie associated with school fire drills.

A fire door. It would lead outside, or into a hall that would lead there. Without hesitating she pushed it open and entered. A short corridor lit by EXIT signs stretched ahead of her, with another door at the end. She hurried towards it, already reaching reflexively for the keys to the flat, pushed the door-bar and stepped inside.

For an instant she thought she had somehow stumbled into a hospital emergency room. There was the glitter of halogen light on steel, distorted reflections thrown back at her from curved glass surfaces; the abrasive odour of isopropyl alcohol and the fainter tinny scent of blood, like metal in the mouth.

And bodies: everywhere, bodies, splayed on gurneys or suspended from gleaming metal hooks, laced with black electrical cord and pinned upright onto smooth rubber mats. She stared open-mouthed, neither appalled nor frightened but fascinated by the conundrum before her: how did *that* hand fit *there*, and whose leg was *that*? She inched backward, pressing herself against the door and trying to stay in the shadows – just inches ahead of her ribbons of luminous bluish light streamed from lamps hung high overhead. The chiaroscuro of pallid bodies and black furniture, shiny with sweat and here and there red-streaked, or brown; the mere sight of so many bodies, real bodies – flesh spilling over the edge of tabletops, too much hair or none at all, eyes squeezed shut in ecstasy or terror and mouths open to reveal stained teeth, pale gums – the sheer *fluidity* of it all enthralled her. She felt as she had, once, pulling aside a rotted log to disclose the ant's-nest beneath, masses of minute fleeing bodies, soldiers carrying eggs and larvae in their jaws, tunnels spiralling into the centre of another world. Her brow tingled, warmth flushed her from brow to breast . . .

Another world, that's what she had found then; and discovered again now.

"*Out.*"

Janie sucked her breath in sharply. Fingers dug into her shoulder, yanked her back through the metal door so roughly that she cut her wrist against it.

"No lurkers, what the fuck—"

A man flung her against the wall. She gasped, turned to run but he grabbed her shoulder again. "Christ, a fucking girl."

He sounded angry but relieved. She looked up: a huge man, more fat than muscle. He wore very tight leather briefs and the same black sleeveless shirt with a golden bee embroidered upon it. "How the hell'd you get in like *that*?" he demanded, cocking a thumb at her.

She shook her head, then realized he meant her clothes. "I was just trying to find my way out."

"Well you found your way in. In like fucking Flynn." He laughed: he had gold-capped teeth, and gold wires threading the tip of his tongue. "You want to join the party, you know the rules. No exceptions."

Before she could reply he turned and was gone, the door thudding softly behind him. She waited, heart pounding, then reached and pushed the bar on the door.

Locked. She was out, not in; she was nowhere at all. For a long time she stood there, trying to hear anything from the other side of the door, waiting to see if anyone would come back looking for her. At last she turned, and began to find her way home.

Next morning she woke early, to the sound of delivery trucks in the street and children on the canal path, laughing and squabbling on their way to the zoo. She sat up with a pang, remembering David Bierce and her volunteer job; then recalled this was Saturday not Monday.

"Wow," she said aloud. The extra days seemed like a gift.

For a few minutes she lay in Fred and Andrew's great four-poster, staring abstractedly at where she had rested her mounted specimens atop the wainscoting – the hybrid hawkmoth; a beautiful Honduran owl butterfly, *Caligo atreus*; a mourning cloak she had caught and mounted herself years ago. She thought of the club last night, mentally retracing her steps to the hidden back room; thought of the man who had thrown her out, the interplay of light and shadow upon the bodies pinned to mats and tables. She had slept in her clothes; now she rolled out of bed and pulled her sneakers on, forgoing breakfast but stuffing her pocket with ten and twenty pound notes before she left.

It was a clear cool morning, with a high pale-blue sky and the young leaves of nettles and hawthorn still glistening with dew. Someone had thrown a shopping cart from the nearby Sainsbury's into the canal; it edged sideways up out of the shallow water, like a frozen shipwreck. A boy stood a few yards down from it, fishing, an absent, placid expression on his face.

She crossed over the bridge to the canal path and headed for the High Street. With every step she took the day grew older, noisier, trains rattling on the bridge behind her and voices harsh as gulls rising from the other side of the brick wall that separated the canal path from the street.

At Camden Lock she had to fight her way through the market. There were tens of thousands of tourists, swarming from the maze of shops to pick their way between scores of vendors selling old and new clothes, bootleg CDs, cheap silver jewellery, kilims, feather boas, handcuffs, cell-phones, mass-produced furniture and puppets from Indonesia, Morocco, Guyana, Wales. The fug of burning incense and cheap candles choked her; she hurried to where a young woman was turning samosas in a vat of sputtering oil and dug into her pocket for a handful of change, standing so that the smells of hot grease and scorched chickpea batter cancelled out patchouli and Caribbean Nights.

"Two, please," Janie shouted.

She ate and almost immediately felt better; then walked a few steps to where a spike-haired girl sat behind a table covered with cheap clothes made of ripstock fabric in Jell-O shades.

"Everything five pounds," the girl announced. She stood, smiling helpfully as Janie began to sort through pairs of hugely baggy pants. They were cross-seamed with Velcro and deep zippered pockets. Janie held up a pair, frowning as the legs billowed, lavender and green, in the wind.

"It's so you can make them into shorts," the girl explained. She stepped around the table and took the pants from Janie, deftly tugging at the legs so that they detached. "See? Or a skirt." The girl replaced the pants, picked up another pair, screaming orange with black trim, and a matching windbreaker. "This colour would look nice on you."

"Okay." Janie paid for them, waited for the girl to put the clothes in a plastic bag. "Thanks."

"Bye now."

She went out into High Street. Shopkeepers stood guard over the tables spilling out from their storefronts, heaped with leather clothes and souvenir T-shirts: MIND THE GAP, LONDON UNDERGROUND, shirts emblazoned with the Cat in the Hat toking on a cheroot. THE CAT IN THE HAT SMOKES BLACK. Every three or four feet someone had set up a boom-box, deafening sound-bites of salsa, techno, "The Hustle", Bob Marley, "Anarchy in the UK", Radiohead. On the corner of Inverness and High Street a few punks squatted in a doorway, looking over the postcards they'd bought. A sign in the smoked-glass window said ALL HAIRCUTS TEN POUNDS, MEN WOMEN CHILDREN.

"Sorry," one of the punks said, as Janie stepped over them and into the shop.

The barber was sitting in an old-fashioned chair, his back to her, reading The *Sun*. At the sound of her footsteps he turned, smiling automatically. "Can I help you?"

"Yes please. I'd like my hair cut. All of it."

He nodded, gesturing to the chair. "Please."

Janie had thought she might have to convince him that she was serious. She had beautiful hair, well below her shoulders – the kind of hair people would kill for, she'd been hearing that her whole life. But the barber just hummed and chopped it off, the *snick snick* of his shears interspersed with kindly questions about whether she was enjoying her visit and his account of a vacation to Disney World ten years earlier.

"Dear, do we want it shaved or buzz-cut?"

In the mirror a huge-eyed creature gazed at Janie, like a tarsier or one of the owlish caligo moths. She stared at it, entranced, then nodded.

"Shaved. Please."

When he was finished she got out of the chair, dazed, and ran her hand across her scalp. It was smooth and cool as an apple. There were a few tiny nicks that stung beneath her fingers. She paid the barber, tipping him two pounds. He smiled and held the door open for her.

"Now when you want a touch-up, you come see us, dear. Only five pounds for a touch-up."

She went next to find new shoes. There were more shoe shops in Camden Town than she had ever seen anywhere in her life; she checked out four of them on one block before deciding on a discounted pair of twenty-hole black Doc Martens. They were no longer fashionable, but they had blunted steel caps on the toes. She bought them, giving the salesgirl her old sneakers to toss into the waste bin. When she went back onto the street it was like walking in wet cement – the shoes were so heavy, the leather so stiff that she ducked back into the shoe shop and bought a pair of heavy wool socks and put them on. She returned outside, hesitating on the front step before crossing the street and heading in the direction of Chalk Farm Road. There was a shop here that Fred had shown her before he left.

"Now, that's where you get your fetish gear, Janie," he said, pointing to a shop window painted matte black. THE PLACE, it said in red letters, with two linked circles beneath. Fred had grinned and rapped his knuckles against the glass as they walked by. "I've never been in, you'll have to tell me what it's like." They'd both laughed at the thought.

Now Janie walked slowly, the wind chill against her bare skull. When she could make out the shop, sun glinting off the crimson letters and a sad-eyed dog tied to a post out front, she began to hurry, her new boots making a hollow thump as she pushed through the door.

There was a security gate inside, a thin, sallow young man with dreadlocks nodding at her silently as she approached.

"You'll have to check that." He pointed at the bag with her new clothes in it. She handed it to him, reading the warning posted behind the counter.

SHOPLIFTERS WILL BE BEATEN,
FLAYED, SPANKED, BIRCHED, BLED
AND THEN PROSECUTED
TO THE FULL EXTENT OF THE LAW

The shop was well lit. It smelled strongly of new leather and coconut oil and pine-scented disinfectant. She seemed to be the only customer this early in the day, although she counted seven employees, manning cash registers, unpacking cartons, watching to make sure she didn't try to nick anything. A CD of dance music played, and the phone rang constantly.

She spent a good half-hour just walking through the place, impressed by the range of merchandise. Electrified wands to deliver shocks, things like meat cleavers made of stainless steel with rubber tips. Velcro dog collars, Velcro hoods, black rubber balls and balls in neon shades; a mat embedded with three-inch spikes that could be conveniently rolled up and came with its own lightweight carrying case. As she wandered about more customers arrived, some of them greeting the clerks by name, others furtive, making a quick circuit of the shelves before darting outside again.

At last Janie knew what she wanted. A set of wristcuffs and one of anklecuffs, both of very heavy black leather with stainless steel hardware; four adjustable nylon leashes, also black, with clips on either end that could be fastened to cuffs or looped around a post; a few spare S-clips.

"That it?"

Janie nodded, and the register clerk began scanning her purchases. She felt almost guilty, buying so few things, not taking advantage of the vast Meccano glory of all those shelves full of gleaming, sombre contrivances.

"There you go." He handed her the receipt, then inclined his head at her. "Nice touch, that—"

He pointed at her eyebrows. Janie drew her hand up, felt the long pliant hairs uncoiling like baby ferns. "Thanks," she murmured. She retrieved her bag and went home to wait for evening.

It was nearly midnight when she left the flat. She had slept for most of the afternoon, a deep but restless sleep, with anxious dreams of flight, falling, her hands encased in metal gloves, a shadowy figure crouching above her. She woke in the dark, heart pounding, terrified for a moment that she had slept all the way through till Sunday night.

But of course she had not. She showered, then dressed in a tight, low-cut black shirt and pulled on her new nylon pants and heavy boots. She seldom wore makeup, but tonight after putting in her contacts she carefully outlined her eyes with black, then chose a very pale lavender lipstick. She surveyed herself in the mirror critically. With her white skin, huge violet eyes and hairless skull, she resembled one of the Balinese puppets for sale in the market – beautiful but vacant, faintly ominous. She grabbed her keys and money, pulled on her windbreaker, and headed out.

When she reached the alley that led to the club, she entered it, walked about halfway, and stopped. After glancing back and forth to make sure no one was coming, she detached the legs from her nylon pants, stuffing them into a pocket, then adjusted the Velcro tabs so that the pants became a very short orange and black skirt. Her long legs were sheathed in black tights. She bent to tighten the laces on her metal-toed boots and hurried to the club entrance.

Tonight there was a line of people waiting to get in. Janie took her place, fastidiously avoiding looking at any of the others. They waited for thirty minutes, Janie shivering in her thin nylon windbreaker, before the door opened and the same gaunt blond man appeared to take their money. Janie felt her heart beat faster when it was her turn, wondering if he would recognize her. But he only scanned the courtyard, and, when the last of them darted inside, closed the door with a booming *clang*.

Inside all was as it had been, only far more crowded. Janie bought a drink, orange squash, no alcohol. It was horribly sweet, with a bitter, curdled aftertaste. Still, it had cost two pounds: she drank it all. She had just started on her way down to the dance floor when someone came up from behind to tap her shoulder, shouting into her ear.

"Wanna?"

It was a tall, broad-shouldered boy a few years older than she was, perhaps twenty-four, with a lean ruddy face, loose shoulder-length blond hair streaked green, and deep-set, very dark blue eyes. He swayed dreamily, gazing at the dance floor and hardly looking at her at all.

"Sure," Janie shouted back. He looped an arm around her shoulder, pulling her with him; his striped V-necked shirt smelled of talc and sweat. They danced for a long time, Janie moving with calculated abandon, the boy heaving and leaping as though a dog was biting at his shins.

"You're beautiful," he shouted. There was an almost imperceptible instant of silence as the DJ changed tracks. "What's your name?"

"Cleopatra Brimstone."

The shattering music grew deafening once more. The boy grinned. "Well, Cleopatra. Want something to drink?"

Janie nodded in time with the beat, so fast her head spun. He took her hand and she raced to keep up with him, threading their way toward the bar.

"Actually," she yelled, pausing so that he stopped short and bumped up against her. "I think I'd rather go outside. Want to come?"

He stared at her, half-smiling, and shrugged. "Aw right. Let me get a drink first—"

They went outside. In the alley the wind sent eddies of dead leaves and newspaper flying up into their faces. Janie laughed, and pressed herself against the boy's side. He grinned down at her, finished his drink, and tossed the can aside; then put his arm around her. "Do you want to go get a drink, then?" he asked.

They stumbled out onto the sidewalk, turned and began walking. People filled the High Street, lines snaking out from the entrances of pubs and restaurants. A blue glow surrounded the streetlights, and clouds of small white moths beat themselves against the globes; vapour and banners of grey smoke hung above the punks blocking the sidewalk by Camden Lock. Janie and the boy dipped down into the street. He pointed to a pub occupying the corner a few blocks up, a large old green-painted building with baskets of flowers hanging beneath its windows and a large sign swinging back and forth in the wind: THE END OF THE WORLD.

"In there, then?"

Janie shook her head. "I live right here, by the canal. We could go to my place if you want. We could have a few drinks there."

The boy glanced down at her. "Aw right," he said – very quickly, so she wouldn't change her mind. "That'd be awright."

It was quieter on the back street leading to the flat. An old drunk huddled in a doorway, cadging change; Janie looked away from him and got out her keys, while the boy stood restlessly, giving the drunk a belligerent look.

"Here we are," she announced, pushing the door open. "Home again, home again."

"Nice place." The boy followed her, gazing around admiringly. "You live here alone?"

"Yup." After she spoke Janie had a flash of unease, admitting that. But the boy only ambled into the kitchen, running a hand along the antique French farmhouse cupboard and nodding.

"You're American, right? Studying here?"

"Uh huh. What would you like to drink? Brandy?"

He made a face, then laughed. "Aw right! You got expensive taste. Goes with the name, I'd guess." Janie looked puzzled, and he went on, "Cleopatra – fancy name for a girl."

"Fancier for a boy," Janie retorted, and he laughed again.

She got the brandy, stood in the living room unlacing her boots. "Why don't we go in there?" she said, gesturing towards the bedroom. "It's kind of cold out here."

The boy ran a hand across his head, his blonde hair streaming through his fingers. "Yeah, aw right." He looked around. "Um, that the toilet there?" Janie nodded. "Right back, then . . ."

She went into the bedroom, set the brandy and two glasses on a night table and took off her windbreaker. On another table, several tall candles, creamy white and thick as her wrist, were set into ornate brass holders. She lit these – the room filled with the sweet scent of beeswax – and sat on the floor, leaning against the bed. A few minutes later the toilet flushed and the boy reappeared. His hands and face were damp, redder than they had been. He smiled and sank onto the floor beside her. Janie handed him a glass of brandy.

"Cheers," he said, and drank it all in one gulp.

"Cheers," said Janie. She took a sip from hers, then refilled his glass. He drank again, more slowly this time. The candles threw a soft yellow haze over the four-poster bed with its green velvet duvet, the mounds of pillows, forest-green, crimson, saffron yellow. They sat without speaking for several minutes. Then the boy set his glass on the floor. He turned to face Janie, extending one arm around her shoulder and drawing his face near hers.

"Well then," he said.

His mouth tasted acrid, nicotine and cheap gin beneath the blunter taste of brandy. His hand sliding under her shirt was cold; Janie felt goose pimples rising across her breast, her nipple shrinking beneath his touch. He pressed against her, his cock already hard, and reached down to unzip his jeans.

"Wait," Janie murmured. "Let's get on the bed . . ."

She slid from his grasp and onto the bed, crawling to the heaps of pillows and feeling beneath one until she found what she had placed there earlier. "Let's have a little fun first."

"*This* is fun," the boy said, a bit plaintively. But he slung himself onto the bed beside her, pulling off his shoes and letting them fall to the floor with a thud. "What you got there?"

Smiling, Janie turned and held up the wrist cuffs. The boy looked at them, then at her, grinning. "Oh ho. Been in the back room, then—"

Janie arched her shoulders and unbuttoned her shirt. He reached for one of the cuffs, but she shook her head. "No. Not me, yet."

"Ladies first."

"Gentleman's pleasure."

The boy's grin widened. "Won't argue with that."

She took his hand and pulled him, gently, to the middle of the bed. "Lie on your back," she whispered.

He did, watching as she removed first his shirt and then his jeans and underwear. His cock lay nudged against his thigh, not quite hard; when she brushed her fingers against it he moaned softly, took her hand and tried to press it against him.

"No," she whispered. "Not yet. Give me your hand."

She placed the cuffs around each wrist, and his ankles; fastened the nylon leash to each one and then began tying the bonds around each bedpost. It took longer than she had expected; it was difficult to get the bonds taut enough that the boy could not move. He lay there watchfully, his eyes glimmering in the candlelight as he craned his head to stare at her, his breath shallow, quickening.

"There." She sat back upon her haunches, staring at him. His cock was hard now, the hair on his chest and groin tawny in the half-light. He gazed back at her, his tongue pale as he licked his lips. "Try to get away," she whispered.

He moved slightly, his arms and legs a white X against a deep green field. "Can't," he said hoarsely.

She pulled her shirt off, then her nylon skirt. She had nothing on beneath. She leaned forward, letting her fingers trail from the cleft in his throat to his chest, cupping her palm atop his nipple and then sliding her hand down to his thigh. The flesh was warm, the little hairs soft and moist. Her own breath quickened; sudden heat flooded her, a honeyed liquid in her mouth. Above her brow the long hairs stiffened and furled straight out to either side: when she lifted her head to the candlelight she could see them from the corner of her eyes, twin barbs black and glistening like wire.

"You're so sexy." The boy's voice was hoarse. "God, you're—"

She placed her hand over his mouth. "Try to get away," she said, commandingly this time. "*Try to get away.*"

His torso writhed, the duvet bunching up around him in dark folds. She raked her fingernails down his chest and he cried out, moaning "Fuck me, god, fuck me . . ."

"Try to get away."

She stroked his cock, her fingers barely grazing its swollen head. With a moan he came, struggling helplessly to thrust his groin towards her. At the same moment Janie gasped, a fiery rush arrowing down from her brow to her breasts, her cunt. She rocked forward, crying out, her head brushing against the boy's side as she sprawled back across the bed. For a minute she lay there, the room around her seeming to pulse and swirl into myriad crystalline shapes, each bearing within it the same line of candles, the long curve of the boy's thigh swelling up into the hollow of his hip. She drew breath shakily, the flush of heat fading from her brow; then pushed herself up until she was sitting beside him. His eyes were shut. A thread of saliva traced the furrow between mouth and chin. Without thinking she drew her face down to his, and kissed his cheek.

Immediately he began to grow smaller. Janie reared back, smacking into one of the bedposts, and stared at the figure in front of her, shaking her head.

"No," she whispered. "No, no."

He was shrinking: so fast it was like watching water dissolve into dry sand. Man-size, child-size, large dog, small. His eyes flew open and for a fraction of a second stared horrified into her own. His hands and feet slipped like mercury from his bonds, wriggling until they met his torso and were absorbed into it. Janie's fingers kneaded the duvet; six inches away the boy was no larger than her hand, then smaller, smaller still. She blinked, for a heart-shredding instant thought he had disappeared completely.

Then she saw something crawling between folds of velvet. The length of her middle finger, its thorax black, yellow-striped, its lower wings elongated into frilled arabesques like those of a festoon, deep yellow, charcoal black, with indigo eye spots, its upper wings a chiaroscuro of black and white stripes.

Bhutanitis lidderdalii. A native of the eastern Himalayas, rarely glimpsed: it lived among the crowns of trees in mountain valleys, its caterpillars feeding on lianas. Janie held her breath, watching as its wings beat feebly. Without warning it lifted into the air. Janie cried out, falling onto her knees as she sprawled across the bed, cupping it quickly but carefully between her hands.

"Beautiful, beautiful," she crooned. She stepped from the bed, not daring to pause and examine it, and hurried into the kitchen. In the cupboard she found an empty jar, set it down and gingerly angled the lid from it, holding one hand with the butterfly against her breast. She swore, feeling its wings fluttering against her fingers, then quickly brought her hand to the jar's mouth, dropped the butterfly inside and screwed the lid back in place. It fluttered helplessly inside; she could see where the scales had already been scraped from its wing. Still swearing she ran back into the bedroom, putting the lights on and dragging her collection box from under the bed. She grabbed a vial of ethyl alcohol, went back into the kitchen and tore a bit of paper towel from the rack. She opened the vial, poured a few drops of ethyl alcohol onto the paper, opened the jar and gently tilted it onto its side. She slipped the paper inside, very slowly tipping the jar upright once more, until the paper had settled on the bottom, the butterfly on top of it. Its wings beat frantically for a few moments, then stopped. Its proboscis uncoiled, finer than a hair. Slowly Janie drew her own hand to her brow and ran it along the length of the antennae there. She sat there staring at it until the sun leaked through the wooden shutters in the kitchen window. The butterfly did not move again.

The next day passed in a metallic grey haze, the only colour the saturated blues and yellows of the *lidderdalii*'s wings, burned upon Janie's eyes as though she had looked into the sun. When she finally roused herself, she felt a spasm of panic at sight of the boy's clothes on the bedroom floor.

"Shit." She ran her hand across her head, was momentarily startled to recall she had no hair. "Now what?"

She stood there for a few minutes, thinking; then gathered the clothes – striped V-neck sweater, jeans, socks, jockey shorts, Timberlake knockoff shoes – and dumped them into a plastic Sainsbury's bag. There was a wallet in the jeans pocket. She opened it, gazed impassively at a driver's licence – KENNETH REED, WOLVERHAMPTON – and a few five-pound notes. She pocketed the money, took the licence into the bathroom and burned it, letting the ashes drop into the toilet. Then she went outside.

It was early Sunday morning, no one about except for a young mother pushing a baby in a stroller. In the neighbouring doorway the same drunk old man sprawled surrounded by empty bottles and rubbish. He stared blearily up at Janie as she approached.

"Here," she said. She bent and dropped the five-pound notes into his scabby hand.

"God bless you, darlin'." He coughed, his eyes focusing on neither Janie nor the notes. "God bless you."

She turned and walked briskly back toward the canal path. There were few waste bins in Camden Town, and so each day trash accumulated in rank heaps along the path, beneath streetlights, in vacant alleys. Street cleaners and sweeping machines then daily cleared it all away again: like elves, Janie thought. As she walked along the canal path she dropped the shoes in one pile of rubbish, tossed the sweater alongside a single high-heeled shoe in the market, stuffed the underwear and socks into a collapsing cardboard box filled with rotting lettuce, and left the jeans beside a stack of papers outside an unopened newsagent's shop. The wallet she tied into the Sainsbury's bag and dropped into an overflowing trash bag outside of Boots. Then she retraced her steps, stopping in front of a shop window filled with tatty polyester lingerie in large sizes and boldly artificial-looking wigs: pink afros, platinum blond falls, black-and-white Cruella De Vil tresses.

The door was propped open; Schubert lieder played softly on 3 2. Janie stuck her head in and looked around, saw a beefy man behind the register, cashing out. He had orange lipstick smeared around his mouth and delicate silver fish hanging from his ears.

"We're not open yet. Eleven on Sunday," he said without looking up.

"I'm just looking." Janie sidled over to a glass shelf where four wigs sat on styrofoam heads. One had very glossy black hair in a chin-length flapper bob. Janie tried it on, eyeing herself in a grimy mirror. "How much is this one?"

"Fifteen. But we're not—"

"Here. Thanks!" Janie stuck a twenty-pound note on the counter and ran from the shop. When she reached the corner she slowed, pirouetted to catch her reflection in a shop window. She stared at herself, grinning, then walked the rest of the way home, exhilarated and faintly dizzy.

Monday morning she went to the zoo to begin her volunteer work. She had mounted the *Bhutanitis lidderdalii*, on a piece of styrofoam with a piece of paper on it, to keep the butterfly's legs from becoming embedded in the styrofoam. She'd softened it first, putting it into a jar with damp paper, removed it and placed it on the mounting platform, neatly spearing its thorax – a little to the right – with a #2 pin. She propped it carefully on the wainscoting beside the hawkmoth, and left.

She arrived and found her ID badge waiting for her at the staff entrance. It was a clear morning, warmer than it had been for a week; the long hairs on her brow vibrated as though they were wires that had been plucked. Beneath the wig her shaved head felt hot and moist, the first new hairs starting to prickle across her scalp. Her nose itched where her glasses pressed against it. Janie walked, smiling, past the gibbons howling in their habitat and the pygmy hippos floating calmly in their pool, their eyes shut, green bubbles breaking around them like little fish. In front of the Insect Zoo a uniformed woman was unloading sacks of meal from a golf cart.

"Morning," Janie called cheerfully, and went inside.

She found David Bierce standing in front of a temperature gauge beside a glass cage holding the hissing cockroaches.

"Something happened last night, the damn things got too cold." He glanced over, handed her a clipboard and began to remove the top of the gauge. "I called Operations but they're at their fucking morning meeting. Fucking computers –"

He stuck his hand inside the control box and flicked angrily at the gauge. "You know anything about computers?"

"Not this kind." Janie brought her face up to the cage's glass front. Inside were half a dozen glossy roaches, five inches long and the colour of pale maple syrup. They lay, unmoving, near a glass Petri dish filled with what looked like damp brown sugar. "Are they dead?"

"Those things? They're fucking immortal. You could stamp on one and it wouldn't die. Believe me, I've done it." He continued to fiddle with the gauge, finally sighed and replaced the lid. "Well, let's let the boys over in Ops handle it. Come on, I'll get you started."

He gave her a brief tour of the lab, opening drawers full of dissecting instruments, mounting platforms, pins; showing her where the food for the various insects was kept in a series of small refrigerators. Sugar syrup, cornstarch, plastic containers full of smaller insects, grubs and mealworms, tiny grey beetles. "Mostly we just keep on top of replacing the ones that die," David explained, "that and making sure the plants don't develop the wrong kind of fungus. Nature takes her course and we just goose her along when she needs it. School groups are here constantly, but the docents handle that. You're more than welcome to talk to them, if that's the sort of thing you want to do."

He turned from where he'd been washing empty jars at a small sink, dried his hands and walked over to sit on top of a desk. "It's not terribly glamorous work here." He reached down for a styrofoam cup of coffee and sipped from it, gazing at her coolly. "We're none of us working on our PhDs anymore."

Janie shrugged. "That's all right."

"It's not even all that interesting. I mean, it can be very repetitive. Tedious."

"I don't mind." A sudden pang of anxiety made Janie's voice break. She could feel her face growing hot, and quickly looked away. "Really," she said sullenly.

"Suit yourself. Coffee's over there; you'll probably have to clean yourself a cup, though." He cocked his head, staring at her curiously, then said, "Did you do something different with your hair?"

She nodded once, brushing the edge of her bangs with a finger. "Yeah."

"Nice. Very Louise Brooks." He hopped from the desk and crossed to a computer set up in the corner. "You can use my computer if you need to, I'll give you the password later."

Janie nodded, her flush fading into relief. "How many people work here?"

"Actually, we're short-staffed here right now – no money for hiring and our grant's run out. It's pretty much just me, and whoever Carolyn sends over from the docents. Sweet little bluehairs mostly, they don't much like bugs. So it's providential you turned up, *Jane.*"

He said her name mockingly, gave her a crooked grin. "You said you have experience mounting? Well, I try to save as many of the dead specimens as I can, and when there's any slow days, which there never are, I mount them and use them for the workshops I do with the schools that come in. What would be nice would be if we had enough specimens that I could give some to the teachers, to take back to their classrooms. We have a nice website and we might be able to work up some interactive programs. No schools are scheduled today, Monday's usually slow here. So if you could work on some of *those*—" He gestured to where several dozen cardboard boxes and glass jars were strewn across a countertop. "—that would be really brilliant," he ended, and turned to his computer screen.

She spent the morning mounting insects. Few were interesting or unusual: a number of brown hairstreaks, some Camberwell Beauties, three hissing cockroaches, several brimstones. But there was a single *Acherontia atropos*, the Death's head hawkmoth, the pattern of grey and brown and pale yellow scales on the back of its thorax forming the image of a human skull. Its proboscis was unfurled, the twin points sharp enough to pierce a finger: Janie touched it gingerly, wincing delightedly as a pinprick of blood appeared on her fingertip.

"You bring lunch?"

She looked away from the bright magnifying light she'd been using and blinked in surprise. "Lunch?"

David Bierce laughed. "Enjoying yourself? Well, that's good, makes the day go faster. Yes, lunch!" He rubbed his hands together, the harsh light making him look gnome-like, his sharp features malevolent and leering. "They have some decent fish and chips at the stall over by the cats. Come on, I'll treat you. Your first day."

They sat at a picnic table beside the food booth and ate. David pulled a bottle of ale from his knapsack and shared it with Janie. Overhead scattered clouds like smoke moved swiftly southwards. An Indian woman with three small boys sat at another table, the boys tossing fries at seagulls that swept down, shrieking, and made the smallest boy wail.

"Rain later," David said, staring at the sky. "Too bad." He sprinkled vinegar on his fried haddock and looked at Janie. "So did you go out over the weekend?"

She stared at the table and smiled. "Yeah, I did. It was fun."

"Where'd you go? The Electric Ballroom?"

"God, no. This other place." She glanced at his hand resting on the table beside her. He had long fingers, the knuckles slightly enlarged; but the back of his hand was smooth, the same soft brown as the *Acherontia*'s wingtips. Her brows prickled, warmth trickling from them like water. When she lifted her head she could smell him, some kind of musky soap, salt; the bittersweet ale on his breath.

"Yeah? Where? I haven't been out in months, I'd be lost in Camden Town these days."

"I dunno. The Hive?"

She couldn't imagine he would have heard of it – far too old. But he swivelled on the bench, his eyebrows arching with feigned shock. "You went to *Hive*? And they let you in?"

"Yes," Janie stammered. "I mean, I didn't know – it was just a dance club. I just – danced."

"Did you." David Bierce's gaze sharpened, his hazel eyes catching the sun and sending back an icy emerald glitter. "Did you."

She picked up the bottle of ale and began to peel the label from it. "Yes."

"Have a boyfriend, then?"

She shook her head, rolled a fragment of label into a tiny pill. "No."

"Stop that." His hand closed over hers. He drew it away from the bottle, letting it rest against the table edge. She swallowed: he kept his hand on top of hers, pressing it against the metal edge until she felt her scored palm begin to ache. Her eyes closed: she could feel herself floating, and see a dozen feet below her own form, slender, the wig beetle-black upon her skull, her wrist like a bent stalk. Abruptly his hand slid away and beneath the table, brushing her leg as he stooped to retrieve his knapsack.

"Time to get back to work," he said lightly, sliding from the bench and slinging his bag over his shoulder. The breeze lifted his long greying hair as he turned away. "I'll see you back there."

Overhead the gulls screamed and flapped, dropping bits of fried fish on the sidewalk. She stared at the table in front of her, the cardboard trays that held the remnants of lunch, and watched as a yellow jacket landed on a fleck of grease, its golden thorax swollen with moisture as it began to feed.

She did not return to Hive that night. Instead she wore a patchwork dress over her jeans and Doc Martens, stuffed the wig inside a drawer and headed to a small bar on Inverness Street. The fair day had turned to rain, black puddles like molten metal capturing the amber glow of traffic signals and streetlights.

There were only a handful of tables at Bar Ganza. Most of the customers stood on the sidewalk outside, drinking and shouting to be heard above the sound of wailing Spanish love songs. Janie fought her way inside, got a glass of red wine and miraculously found an empty stool alongside the wall. She climbed onto it, wrapped her long legs around the pedestal, and sipped her wine.

"Hey. Nice hair." A man in his early thirties, his own head shaven, sidled up to Janie's stool. He held a cigarette, smoking it with quick, nervous gestures as he stared at her. He thrust his cigarette towards the ceiling, indicating a booming speaker. "You like the music?"

"Not particularly."

"Hey, you're American? Me too. Chicago. Good bud of mine, works for Citibank, he told me about this place. Food's not bad. Tapas. Baby octopus. You like octopus?"

Janie's eyes narrowed. The man wore expensive-looking corduroy trousers, a rumpled jacket of nubby charcoal-coloured linen. "No," she said, but didn't turn away.

"Me neither. Like eating great big slimy bugs. Geoff Lanning—"

He stuck his hand out. She touched it, lightly, and smiled. "Nice to meet you, Geoff."

For the next half-hour or so she pretended to listen to him, nodding and smiling brilliantly whenever he looked up at her. The bar grew louder and more crowded, and people began eyeing Janie's stool covetously.

"I think I'd better hand over this seat," she announced, hopping down and elbowing her way to the door. "Before they eat me."

Geoff Lanning hurried after her. "Hey, you want to get dinner? The Camden Brasserie's just up here—"

"No thanks." She hesitated on the curb, gazing demurely at her Doc Martens. "But would you like to come in for a drink?"

He was very impressed by her apartment. "Man, this place'd probably go for a half mil, easy! That's three quarters of a million American." He opened and closed cupboards, ran a hand lovingly across the slate sink. "Nice hardwood floors, high speed access – you never told me what you do."

Janie laughed. "As little as possible. Here—"

She handed him a brandy snifter, let her finger trace the back of his wrist. "You look like kind of an adventurous sort of guy."

"Hey, big adventure, that's me." He lifted his glass to her. "What exactly did you have in mind? Big game hunting?"

"Mmm. Maybe."

It was more of a struggle this time, not for Geoff Lanning but for Janie. He lay complacently in his bonds, his stocky torso wriggling obediently when Janie commanded. Her head ached from the cheap wine at Bar Ganza; the long hairs above her eyes lay sleek against her skull, and did not move at all until she closed her eyes, and, unbidden, the image of David Bierce's hand covering hers appeared.

"Try to get away," she whispered.

"Whoa, Nellie," Geoff Lanning gasped.

"Try to get away," she repeated, her voice hoarser.

"Oh." The man whimpered softly. "Jesus Christ, what – oh my God, *what—*"

Quickly she bent and kissed his fingertips, saw where the leather cuff had bitten into his pudgy wrist. This time she was prepared when with a keening sound he began to twist upon the bed, his arms and legs shrivelling and then coiling in upon themselves, his shaved head withdrawing into his tiny torso like a snail within its shell.

But she was not prepared for the creature that remained, its feathery antennae a trembling echo of her own, its extraordinarily elongated hind spurs nearly four inches long.

"*Oh,*" she gasped.

She didn't dare touch it until it took to the air: the slender spurs fragile as icicles, scarlet, their saffron tips curling like Christmas ribbon, its large delicate wings saffron with slate-blue and scarlet eye-spots, and spanning nearly six inches. A Madagascan Moon Moth, one of the loveliest and rarest silk moths, and almost impossible to find as an intact specimen.

"What do I do with you, what do I do?" she crooned as it spread its wings and lifted from the bed. It flew in short sweeping arcs; she scrambled to blow out the candles before it could near them. She pulled on her kimono and left the lights off, closed the bedroom door and hurried into the kitchen, looking for a flashlight. She found nothing, but recalled Andrew telling her there was a large torch in the basement.

She hadn't been down there since her initial tour of the flat. It was brightly lit, with long neat cabinets against both walls, a floor-to-ceiling wine rack filled with bottles of claret and vintage burgundy, compact washer and dryer, small refrigerator, buckets and brooms waiting for the cleaning lady's weekly visit. She found the flashlight sitting on top of the refrigerator, a container of extra batteries beside it. She switched it on and off a few times, then glanced down at the refrigerator and absently opened it.

Seeing all that wine had made her think the little refrigerator might be filled with beer. Instead it held only a long plastic box, with a red lid and a red biohazard sticker on the side. Janie put the flashlight down and stooped, carefully removing the box and setting it on the floor. A label with Andrew's neat architectural handwriting was on the top.

DR ANDREW FILDERMAN
ST MARTIN'S HOSPICE

"Huh," she said, and opened it.

Inside there was a small red biohazard waste container, and scores of plastic bags filled with disposable hypodermics, ampoules, and suppositories. All contained morphine at varying dosages. Janie stared, marvelling, then opened one of the bags. She shook half-a-dozen morphine ampoules into her palm, carefully re-closed the bag, put it back into the box and returned the box to the refrigerator. Then she grabbed the flashlight and ran upstairs.

It took her a while to capture the moon moth. First she had to find a killing jar large enough, and then she had to very carefully lure it inside, so that its frail wing spurs wouldn't be damaged. She did this by positioning the jar on its side and placing a gooseneck lamp directly behind it, so that the bare bulb shone through the glass. After about fifteen minutes, the moth landed on top of the jar, its tiny legs slipping as it struggled on the smooth curved surface. Another few minutes and it had crawled inside, nestled on the wad of tissues Janie had set there, moist with ethyl alcohol. She screwed the lid on tightly, left the jar on its side, and waited for it to die.

Over the next week she acquired three more specimens. *Papilio demetrius*, a Japanese swallowtail with elegant orange eyespots on a velvety black ground; a scarce copper, not scarce at all, really, but with lovely pumpkin-coloured wings; and *Graphium agamemnon*, a Malaysian species with vivid green spots and chrome-yellow strips on its sombre brown wings. She'd ventured away from Camden Town, capturing the swallowtail in a private room in an SM club in Islington and the *Graphium agamemnon* in a parked car behind a noisy pub in Crouch End. The scarce copper came from a vacant lot near the Tottenham Court Road tube station very late one night, where the wreckage of a chain-link fence stood in for her bedposts. She found the morphine to be useful, although she had to wait until immediately after the man ejaculated before pressing the ampoule against his throat, aiming for the carotid artery. This way the butterflies emerged already sedated, and in minutes died with no damage to their wings. Leftover clothing was easily disposed of, but she had to be more careful with wallets, stuffing them deep within rubbish bins, when she could, or burying them in her own trash bags and then watching as the waste trucks came by on their rounds.

In South Kensington she discovered an entomological supply store. There she bought more mounting supplies, and inquired casually as to whether the owner might be interested in purchasing some specimens.

He shrugged. "Depends. What you got?"

"Well, right now I have only one *Argema mittrei*." Janie adjusted her glasses and glanced around the shop. A lot of morphos, an Atlas moth: nothing too unusual. "But I might be getting another, in which case . . ."

"Moon moth, eh? How'd you come by that, I wonder?" The man raised his eyebrows, and Janie flushed. "Don't worry, I'm not going to turn you in. Christ, I'd go out of business. Well, obviously I can't display those in the shop, but if you want to part with one, let me know. I'm always scouting for my customers."

She began volunteering three days a week at the insect zoo. One Wednesday, the night after she'd gotten a gorgeous *Urania leilus*, its wings sadly damaged by rain, she arrived to see David Bierce reading that morning's *Camden New Journal*. He peered above the newspaper and frowned.

"You still going out alone at night?"

She froze, her mouth dry; turned and hurried over to the coffee-maker. "Why?" she said, fighting to keep her tone even.

"Because there's an article about some of the clubs around here. Apparently a few people have gone missing."

"Really?" Janie got her coffee, wiping up a spill with the side of her hand. "What happened?"

"Nobody knows. Two blokes reported gone, family frantic, sort of thing. Probably just runaways. Camden Town eats them alive, kids." He handed the paper to Janie. "Although one of them was last seen near Highbury Fields, some sex club there."

She scanned the article. There was no mention of any suspects. And no bodies had been found, although foul play was suspected. ("*Ken would never have gone away without notifying us or his employer . . .*")

Anyone with any information was urged to contact the police.

"I don't go to sex clubs," Janie said flatly. "Plus those are both guys."

"Mmm." David leaned back in his chair, regarding her coolly. "You're the one hitting Hive your first weekend in London."

"It's a *dance* club!" Janie retorted. She laughed, rolled the newspaper into a tube and batted him gently on the shoulder. "Don't worry. I'll be careful."

David continued to stare at her, hazel eyes glittering. "Who says it's you I'm worried about?"

She smiled, her mouth tight as she turned and began cleaning bottles in the sink.

It was a raw day, more late November than mid-May. Only two school groups were scheduled; otherwise the usual stream of visitors was reduced to a handful of elderly women who shook their heads over the cockroaches and gave barely a glance to the butterflies before shuffling on to another building. David Bierce paced restlessly through the lab on his way to clean the cages and make more complaints to the Operations Division. Janie cleaned and mounted two stag beetles, their spiny legs pricking her fingertips as she tried to force the pins through their glossy chestnut-coloured shells. Afterwards she busied herself with straightening the clutter of cabinets and drawers stuffed with requisition forms and microscopes, computer parts and dissection kits

It was well past two when David reappeared, his anorak slick with rain, his hair tucked beneath the hood. "Come on," he announced, standing impatiently by the open door. "Let's go to lunch."

Janie looked up from the computer where she'd been updating a specimen list. "I'm really not very hungry," she said, giving him an apologetic smile. "You go ahead."

"Oh, for Christ's sake." David let the door slam shut as he crossed to her, his sneakers leaving wet smears on the tiled floor. "That can wait till tomorrow. Come on, there's not a fucking thing here that needs doing."

"But—" She gazed up at him. The hood slid from his head; his grey-streaked hair hung loose to his shoulders, and the sheen of rain on his sharp cheekbones made him look carved from oiled wood. "What if somebody comes?"

"A very nice docent named Mrs Eleanor Feltwell is out there, *even as we speak*, in the unlikely event that we have a single visitor."

He stooped so that his head was beside hers, scowling as he stared at the computer screen. A lock of his hair fell to brush against her neck. Beneath the wig her scalp burned, as though stung by tiny ants; she breathed in the warm acrid smell of his sweat and something else, a sharper scent, like crushed oak-mast or fresh-sawn wood. Above her brows the antennae suddenly quivered. Sweetness coated her tongue like burnt syrup. With a rush of panic she turned her head so he wouldn't see her face.

"I – I should finish this—"

"Oh, just *fuck* it, Jane! It's not like we're *paying* you. Come on, now, there's a good girl—"

He took her hand and pulled her to her feet, Janie still looking away. The bangs of her cheap wig scraped her forehead and she batted at them feebly. "Get your things. What, don't you ever take days off in the States?"

"All right, all right." She turned and gathered her black vinyl raincoat and knapsack, pulled on the coat and waited for him by the door. "Jeez, you must be hungry," she said crossly.

"No. Just fucking bored out of my skull. Have you been to Ruby in the Dust? No? I'll take you then, let's go—"

The restaurant was down the High Street, a small, cheerfully claptrap place, dim in the grey afternoon, its small wooden tables scattered with abandoned newspapers and overflowing ashtrays. David Bierce ordered a steak and a pint. Janie had a small salad, nasturtium blossoms strewn across pale green lettuce, and a glass of red wine. She lacked an appetite lately, living on vitamin-enhanced, fruity bottled drinks from the health food store and baklava from a Greek bakery near the tube station.

"So." David Bierce stabbed a piece of steak, peering at her sideways. "Don't tell me you really haven't been here before."

"I haven't!" Despite her unease at being with him, she laughed, and caught her reflection in the wall-length mirror. A thin plain young woman in shapeless Peruvian sweater and jeans, bad haircut and ugly glasses. Gazing at herself she felt suddenly stronger, invisible. She tilted her head and smiled at Bierce. "The food's good."

"So you don't have someone taking you out to dinner every night? Cooking for you? I thought you American girls all had adoring men at your feet. Adoring slaves," he added dryly. "Or slave girls, I suppose. If that's your thing."

"No." She stared at her salad, shook her head demurely and took a sip of wine. It made her feel even more invulnerable. "No, I—"

"Boyfriend back home, right?" He finished his pint, flagged the waiter to order another and turned back to Janie. "Well, that's nice. That's very nice – for him," he added, and gave a short harsh laugh.

The waiter brought another pint, and more wine for Janie. "Oh really, I better—"

"Just drink it, Jane." Under the table, she felt a sharp pressure on her foot. She wasn't wearing her Doc Martens today but a pair of red plastic jellies. David Bierce had planted his heel firmly atop her toes; she sucked in her breath in shock and pain, the bones of her foot crackling as she tried to pull it from beneath him. Her antennae rippled, then stiffened, and heat burst like a seed inside her.

"Go ahead," he said softly, pushing the wineglass towards her. "Just a sip, that's right—"

She grabbed the glass, spilling wine on her sweater as she gulped at it. The vicious pressure on her foot subsided, but as the wine ran down her throat she could feel the heat thrusting her into the air, currents rushing beneath her as the girl at the table below set down her wineglass with trembling fingers.

"There." David Bierce smiled, leaning forward to gently cup her hand between his. "Now this is better than working. Right, Jane?"

He walked her home along the canal path. Janie tried to dissuade him, but he'd had a third pint by then; it didn't seem to make him drunk but coldly obdurate, and she finally gave in. The rain had turned to a fine drizzle, the canal's usually murky water silvered and softly gleaming in the twilight. They passed few other people, and Janie found herself wishing someone else would appear, so that she'd have an excuse to move closer to David Bierce. He kept close to the canal itself, several feet from Janie, when the breeze lifted she could catch his oaky scent again, rising above the dank reek of stagnant water and decaying hawthorn blossom.

They crossed over the bridge to approach her flat by the street. At the front sidewalk Janie stopped, smiled shyly and said, "Thanks. That was nice."

David nodded. "Glad I finally got you out of your cage." He lifted his head to gaze appraisingly at the row house. "Christ, this where you're staying? You split the rent with someone?"

"No." She hesitated: she couldn't remember what she had told him about her living arrangements. But before she could blurt something out he stepped past her to the front door, peeking into the window and bobbing impatiently up and down.

"Mind if I have a look? Professional entomologists don't often get the chance to see how the quality live."

Janie hesitated, her stomach clenching; decided it would be safer to have him in rather than continue to put him off.

"All right," she said reluctantly, and opened the door.

"Mmmm. Nice, nice, very nice." He swept around the living room, spinning on his heel and making a show of admiring the elaborate moulding, the tribal rugs, the fireplace mantel with its thick ecclesiastical candles and ormolu mirror. "Goodness, all this for a wee thing like you? You're a clever cat, landing on your feet here, Lady Jane."

She blushed. He bounded past her on his way into the bedroom, touching her shoulder; she had to close her eyes as a fiery wave surged through her and her antennae trembled.

"*Wow*," he exclaimed.

Slowly she followed him into the bedroom. He stood in front of the wall where her specimens were balanced in a neat line across the wainscoting. His eyes were wide, his mouth open in genuine astonishment.

"Are these *yours*?" he marvelled, his gaze fixed on the butterflies. "You didn't actually catch them—?"

She shrugged.

"These are incredible!" He picked up the *Graphium agamemnon* and tilted it to the pewter-coloured light falling through the French doors. "Did you mount them, too?"

She nodded, crossing to stand beside him. "Yeah. You can tell, with that one—" She pointed at the *Urania leilus* in its oak-framed box. "It got rained on."

David Bierce replaced the *Graphium agamemnon* and began to read the labels on the others.

Papilio demetrius
UNITED KINGDOM: LONDON
Highbury Fields, Islington
7.V.2001
J. Kendall

Isopa katinka
UNITED KINGDOM: LONDON
Finsbury Park
09.V.2001
J. Kendall

Argema mittrei
UNITED KINGDOM: LONDON
Camden Town
13.IV.2001
J Kendall

He shook his head. "You screwed up, though – you wrote 'London' for all of them." He turned to her, grinning wryly. "Can't think of the last time I saw a moon moth in Camden Town."

She forced a laugh. "Oh – right."

"And, I mean, you can't have actually *caught* them—"

He held up the *Isopa katinka*, a butter-yellow Emperor moth, its peacock's-eyes russet and jet-black. "I haven't seen any of these around lately. Not even in Finsbury."

Janie made a little grimace of apology. "Yeah. I meant, that's where I found them – where I bought them."

"Mmmm." He set the moth back on its ledge. "You'll have to share your sources with me. I can never find things like these in North London."

He turned and headed out of the bedroom. Janie hurriedly straightened the specimens, her hands shaking now as well, and followed him.

"Well, Lady Jane." For the first time he looked at her without his usual mocking arrogance, his green-flecked eyes bemused, almost regretful. "I think we managed to salvage something from the day."

He turned, gazing one last time at the flat's glazed walls and highly-waxed floors, the imported cabinetry and jewel-toned carpets. "I was going to say, when I walked you home, that you needed someone to take care of you. But it looks like you've managed that on your own."

Janie stared at her feet. He took a step toward her, the fragrance of oak-mast and honey filling her nostrils, crushed acorns, new fern. She grew dizzy, her hand lifting to find him; but he only reached to graze her cheek with his finger.

"Night then, Janie," he said softly, and walked back out into the misty evening.

When he was gone she raced to the windows and pulled all the velvet curtains, then tore the wig from her head and threw it onto the couch along with her glasses. Her heart was pounding, her face slick with sweat – from fear or rage or disappointment, she didn't know. She yanked off her sweater and jeans, left them on the living room floor and stomped into the bathroom. She stood in the shower for twenty minutes, head upturned as the water sluiced the smells of bracken and leaf-mould from her skin.

Finally she got out. She dried herself, let the towel drop, and went into the kitchen. Abruptly she was famished. She tore open cupboards and drawers until she found a half-full jar of lavender honey from Provence. She opened it, the top spinning off into the sink, and frantically spooned honey into her mouth with her fingers. When she was finished she grabbed a jar of lemon curd and ate most of that, until she felt as though she might be sick. She stuck her head into the sink, letting water run from the faucet into her mouth, and at last walked, surfeited, into the bedroom.

She dressed, feeling warm and drowsy, almost dreamlike; pulling on red-and-yellow striped stockings, her nylon skirt, a tight red T-shirt. No bra, no panties. She put in her contacts, then examined herself in the mirror. Her hair had begun to grow back, a scant velvety stubble, bluish in the dim light. She drew a sweeping black line across each eyelid, on a whim took the liner and extended the curve of each antenna until they touched her temples. She painted her lips black as well and went to find her black vinyl raincoat.

It was early when she went out, far too early for any of the clubs to be open. The rain had stopped, but a thick greasy fog covered everything, coating windshields and shop-windows, making Janie's face feel as though it were encased in a clammy shell. For hours she wandered Camden Town, huge violet eyes turning to stare back at the men who watched her, dismissing each of them. Once she thought she saw David Bierce, coming out of Ruby in the Dust; but when she stopped to watch him cross the street it was not David but someone else. Much younger, his long dark hair in a thick braid, his feet clad in knee-high boots. He crossed the High Street, heading towards the tube station. Janie hesitated, then darted after him.

He went to the Electric Ballroom. Fifteen or so people stood out front, talking quietly. The man she'd followed joined the line, standing by himself. Janie waited across the street, until the door opened and the little crowd began to shuffle inside. After the long-haired young man had entered she counted to one hundred, crossed the street, paid her cover, and went inside.

The club had three levels; she finally tracked him down on the uppermost one. Even on a rainy Wednesday night it was crowded, the sound system blaring Idris Mohammed and Jimmie Cliff. He was standing alone near the bar, drinking bottled water.

"Hi!" she shouted, swaying up to him with her best First Day of School Smile. "Want to dance?"

He was older than she'd thought – thirtyish, still not as old as Bierce. He stared at her, puzzled, then shrugged. "Sure."

They danced, passing the water bottle between them. "What's your name?" he shouted.

"Cleopatra Brimstone."

"You're kidding!" he yelled back. The song ended in a bleat of feedback, and they walked, panting, back to the bar.

"What, you know another Cleopatra?" Janie asked teasingly.

"No. It's just a crazy name, that's all." He smiled. He was handsomer than David Bierce, his features softer, more rounded, his eyes dark brown, his manner a bit reticent. "I'm Thomas Raybourne. Tom."

He bought another bottle of Pellegrino and one for Janie. She drank it quickly, trying to get his measure. When she finished she set the empty bottle on the floor and fanned herself with her hand.

"It's hot in here." Her throat hurt from shouting over the music. "I think I'm going to take a walk. Feel like coming?"

He hesitated, glancing around the club. "I was supposed to meet a friend here . . ." he began, frowning. "But—"

"Oh." Disappointment filled her, spiking into desperation. "Well, that's okay. I guess."

"Oh, what the hell." He smiled: he had nice eyes, a more stolid, reassuring gaze than Bierce. "I can always come back."

Outside she turned right, in the direction of the canal. "I live pretty close by. Feel like coming in for a drink?"

He shrugged again. "I don't drink, actually."

"Something to eat then? It's not far – just along the canal path a few blocks past Camden Lock—"

"Yeah, sure."

They made desultory conversation. "You should be careful," he said as they crossed the bridge. "Did you read about those people who've gone missing in Camden Town?"

Janie nodded but said nothing. She felt anxious and clumsy – as though she'd drunk too much, although she'd had nothing since the two glasses of wine with David Bierce. Her companion also seemed ill at ease; he kept glancing back, as though looking for someone on the canal path behind them.

"I should have tried to call," he explained ruefully. "But I forgot to recharge my mobile."

"You could call from my place."

"No, that's all right."

She could tell from his tone that he was figuring how he could leave, gracefully, as soon as possible.

Inside the flat he settled on the couch, picked up a copy of *Time Out* and flipped through it, pretending to read. Janie went immediately into the kitchen and poured herself a glass of brandy. She downed it, poured a second one, and joined him on the couch.

"So." She kicked off her Doc Martens, drew her stockinged foot slowly up his leg, from calf to thigh. "Where you from?"

He was passive, so passive she wondered if he would get aroused at all. But after a while they were lying on the couch, both their shirts on the floor, his pants unzipped and his cock stiff, pressing against her bare belly.

"Let's go in there," Janie whispered hoarsely. She took his hand and led him into the bedroom.

She only bothered lighting a single candle, before lying beside him on the bed. His eyes were half-closed, his breathing shallow. When she ran a fingernail around one nipple he made a small surprised sound, then quickly turned and pinned her to the bed.

"Wait! Slow down," Janie said, and wriggled from beneath him. For the last week she'd left the bonds attached to the bedposts, hiding them beneath the covers when not in use. Now she grabbed one of the wristcuffs and pulled it free. Before he could see what she was doing it was around his wrist.

"Hey!"

She dove for the foot of the bed, his leg narrowly missing her as it thrashed against the covers. It was more difficult to get this in place, but she made a great show of giggling and stroking his thigh, which seemed to calm him. The other leg was next, and finally she leapt from the bed and darted to the headboard, slipping from his grasp when he tried to grab her shoulder.

"This is not consensual," he said. She couldn't tell if he was serious or not.

"What about this, then?" she murmured, sliding down between his legs and cupping his erect penis between her hands. "This seems to be enjoying itself."

He groaned softly, shutting his eyes. "Try to get away," she said. "Try to get away."

He tried to lunge upward, his body arcing so violently that she drew back in alarm. The bonds held; he arched again, and again, but now she remained beside him, her hands on his cock, his breath coming faster and fainter and her own breath keeping pace with it, her heart pounding and the tingling above her eyes almost unbearable.

"Try to get away," she gasped. "Try to get away—"

When he came he cried out, his voice harsh, as though in pain, and Janie cried out as well, squeezing her eyes shut as spasms shook her from head to groin. Quickly her head dipped to kiss his chest; then she shuddered and drew back, watching.

His voice rose again, ended suddenly in a shrill wail, as his limbs knotted and shrivelled like burning rope. She had a final glimpse of him, a homunculus sprouting too many legs. Then on the bed before her a perfectly formed *Papilio krishna* swallowtail crawled across the rumpled duvet, its wings twitching to display glittering green scales amidst spectral washes of violet and crimson and gold.

"Oh, you're beautiful, beautiful," she whispered.

From across the room echoed a sound: soft, the rustle of her kimono falling from its hook as the door swung open. She snatched her hand from the butterfly and stared, through the door to the living room.

In her haste to get Thomas Raybourne inside she had forgotten to latch the front door. She scrambled to her feet, naked, staring wildly at the shadow looming in front of her, its features taking shape as it approached the candle, brown and black, light glinting across his face.

It was David Bierce. The scent of oak and bracken swelled, suffocating, fragrant, cut by the bitter odour of ethyl alcohol. He forced her gently onto the bed, heat piercing her breast and thighs, her antennae bursting out like flame from her brow and wings exploding everywhere around her as she struggled fruitlessly.

"Now. Try to get away," he said.

2002

· THE MAMMOTH BOOK OF ·

BEST NEW HORROR

The Year's Best Horror
Stories by Such Masters
of Dark Suspense as:

RAMSEY CAMPBELL
NEIL GAIMAN
GRAHAM JOYCE
CAITLÍN R. KIERNAN
PAUL McAULEY
CHINA MIÉVILLE
KIM NEWMAN
JEFF VANDERMEER
and many others

EDITED BY
STEPHEN JONES

"One of horror's best!"
— Publishers Weekly

20th Century Ghost

Joe Hill

AFTER THE PSYCHEDELIC SKULL of the previous year, things had to change. If there was any chance that the series would once again have a cover design that did justice to the contents, then I realized that I would actually have to do it myself.

Consequently, Michael Marshall Smith and I got together and presented Robinson with a selection of variant cover designs, all featuring the same painting by Les Edwards. I would have been happy with any of them, and we eventually went with the one the publisher preferred.

We also added a number to the spine for the first time – something I had been asking for over the years as regular readers couldn't remember which editions they had.

It was another almost-600 page volume, with an eighty-four-page Introduction and a fifty-six page Necrology. In my editorial I discussed a controversial online posting by Paula Guran in which she rightly criticised standards in the horror community. I may not have agreed with everything she said, but her piece raised many pertinent questions.

The British Fantasy Award-winning anthology was dedicated to my father, who had died unexpectedly while I was away earlier in the year attending a convention in America.

If it had been any other volume, from among the twenty stories I could have unhesitatingly selected Don Tumasonis' International Horror Guild Award-winning "The Prospect Cards" (one of two stories he had in the book), Glen Hirshberg's moving "The Two Sams", or even Graham Joyce's evocative "The Coventry Boy" for this present compilation.

But in the end, there was only one obvious choice. And here's the story behind the story: I had actually finished compiling the book and had already delivered it to the publisher when a writer I had never heard of before contacted me by e-mail. He enquired if he could send me a story that had been published the previous year in a small literary magazine in America. I initially explained how the book was now closed for submissions and had actually been handed in. However, as I have always considered part of the job of editing – in fact, the most exciting and rewarding part – is finding and developing new talent, I quickly reconsidered and told him to send it to me anyway. The least I could do was read it.

I did this some time over the next couple of days – and I was totally blown away by the depth of the narrative and the maturity of the prose. I immediately contacted him and said that I would buy the story out of my own share of what remained of the publisher's advance, and somehow we would squeeze it into the book.

I'm glad that we did. The story was "20th Century Ghost". The author was Joe Hill. And it was not until a few years later that I learned that he had quite a famous father – a certain writer by the name of . . . Stephen King.

THE BEST TIME TO SEE HER is when the place is almost full.

There is the well-known story of the man who wanders in for a late show, and finds the vast six-hundred seat theatre almost deserted. Halfway through the movie, he glances around and discovers her sitting next to him, in a chair that only moments before had been empty. Her witness stares at her. She turns her head and stares back. She has a nosebleed. Her eyes are wide, stricken. My head hurts, *she whispers.* I have to step out for a moment. Will you tell me what I miss? *It is in this instant that the person looking at her realizes she is as insubstantial as the shifting blue ray of light cast by the projector. It is possible to see the next seat over through her body. As she rises from her chair she fades away.*

Then there is the story about the group of friends who go in to the Rosebud together on a Thursday night. One of the bunch sits down next to a woman by herself, a woman in blue. When the movie doesn't start right away, the person who sat down beside her decides to make conversation. What's playing tomorrow? *He asks her.* The theatre is dark tomorrow, *she whispers. This is the last show. Shortly after the movie begins she vanishes. On the drive home, the man who spoke to her is killed in a car accident.*

These, and many of the other best-known legends of the Rosebud, are false . . . the ghost stories of people who have seen too many horror movies and who think they know exactly how a ghost story should be.

Alec Sheldon, who was one of the first to see Imogene Gilchrist, owns the Rosebud, and at seventy-three still operates the projector most nights. He can always tell, after talking to someone for just a few moments, whether or not they really saw her, but what he knows he keeps to himself, and he never publicly discredits anyone's story ... that would be bad for business.

He knows, though, that anyone who says they could see right through her didn't see her at all. Some of the put-on artists talk about blood pouring from her nose, her ears, her eyes; they say she gave them a pleading look, and asked for them to find somebody, to bring help. But she doesn't bleed that way, and when she wants to talk it isn't to tell someone to bring a doctor. A lot of the pretenders begin their stories by saying, you'll never believe what I just saw. *They're right. He won't, although he will listen to all that they have to say, with a patient, even encouraging smile.*

The ones who have seen her don't come looking for Alec to tell him about it. More often than not he finds them, comes across them wandering the lobby on unsteady legs; they've had a bad shock, they don't feel well. They need to sit down a while. They don't ever say, you won't believe what I just saw. *The experience is still too immediate. The idea that they might not be believed doesn't occur to them until later. Often they are in a state that might be described as subdued, even submissive. When he thinks about the effect she has on those who encounter her, he thinks of Steven Greenberg coming out of* The Birds *one cool Sunday afternoon in 1963. Steven was just twelve then, and it would be another twelve years before he went and got so famous; he was at that time not a golden boy, but just a boy.*

Alec was in the alley behind the Rosebud, having a smoke, when he heard the fire door into the theatre clang open behind him. He turned to see a lanky kid leaning in the doorway – just leaning there, not going in or out. The boy squinted into the harsh white sunshine, with the confused, wondering look of a small child who has just been shaken out of a deep sleep. Alec could see past him into a darkness filled with the shrill sounds of thousands of squeaking sparrows. Beneath that, he could hear a few in the audience stirring restlessly, beginning to complain.

Hey kid, in or out? *Alec said.* You're lettin' the light in.

The kid – Alec didn't know his name then – turned his head and stared back into the theatre for a long, searching moment. Then he stepped out and the door settled shut behind him, closing gently on its pneumatic hinge. And still he didn't go anywhere, didn't say anything. The Rosebud had been showing The Birds *for two weeks, and although Alec had seen others walk out before it was over, none of the early exits had been twelve-year-old boys. It was the sort of film most boys of that age waited all year to see, but who knew? Maybe the kid had a weak stomach.*

I left my Coke in the theatre, *the kid said, his voice distant, almost toneless.* I still had a lot of it left.

You want to go back in and look for it?

And the kid lifted his eyes and gave Alec a bright look of alarm, and then Alec knew. No.

Alec finished his cigarette, pitched it.

I sat with the dead lady, *the kid blurted.*

Alec nodded.

She talked to me.

What did she say?

He looked at the kid again, and found him staring back with eyes that were now wide and round with disbelief.

I need someone to talk to she said. When I get excited about a movie I need to talk.

Alec knows when she talks to someone she always wants to talk about the movies. She usually addresses herself to men, although sometimes she will sit and talk with a woman – Lois Weisel most notably. Alec has been working on a theory of what it is that causes her to show herself. He has been keeping notes in a yellow legal pad. He has a list of who she appeared to and in what movie and when (Leland King, Harold and Maude, *'72; Joel Harlowe,* Eraserhead, *'76; Hal Lash,* Blood Simple, *'84; and all the others). He has, over the years, developed clear ideas about what conditions are most likely to produce her, although the specifics of his theory are constantly being revised.*

As a young man, thoughts of her were always on his mind, or simmering just beneath the surface; she was his first and most strongly felt obsession. Then for a while he was better – when the theatre was a success, and he was an important businessman in the community, chamber of commerce, town planning board. In those days he could go weeks without thinking about her; and then someone would see her, or pretend to have seen her, and stir the whole thing up again.

But following his divorce – she kept the house, he moved into the one-bedroom under the theatre – and not long after the eight-screen Cineplex opened just outside of town, he began to obsess again, less about her than about the theatre itself (is there any difference, though? Not really, he supposes, thoughts of one always circling around to thoughts of the other). He never imagined he would be so old and owe so much money. He has a hard time sleeping, his head is so full of ideas – wild, desperate ideas – about how to keep the theatre from failing. He keeps himself awake thinking about income, staff, saleable assets. And when he can't think about money anymore, he tries to picture where he will go if the theatre closes. He envisions an old folks' home, mattresses that reek of Ben Gay, hunched geezers with their dentures out, sitting in a musty common room watching daytime sitcoms; he sees a place where he will passively fade away, like wallpaper that gets too much sunlight and slowly loses its colour.

This is bad. What is more terrible is when he tries to imagine what will happen to her if the Rosebud closes. He sees the theatre stripped of its seats, an echoing empty space, drifts of dust in the corners, petrified wads of gum stuck fast to the cement. Local teens have broken in to drink and screw; he sees scattered liquor bottles, ignorant graffiti on the walls, a single, grotesque, used condom on the floor in front of the stage. He sees the lonely and violated place where she will fade away.

Or won't fade . . . the worst thought of all.

Alec saw her – spoke to her – for the first time when he was fifteen, six days after he learned his older brother had been killed in the South Pacific. President Truman had sent a letter expressing his condolences. It was a form letter, but the signature on the bottom – that was really his. Alec hadn't cried yet. He knew, years later, that he spent that week in a state of shock; that he had lost the person he loved most in the world and it had badly traumatized him. But in 1945 no one used the word trauma to talk about emotions, and the only kind of shock anyone discussed was "shell-".

He told his mother he was going to school in the mornings. He wasn't going to school. He was shuffling around downtown looking for trouble. He shoplifted candy-bars from the American Luncheonette and ate them out at the empty shoe factory – the place closed down, all the men off in France, or the Pacific. With sugar zipping in his blood, he launched rocks through the windows, trying out his fastball.

He wandered through the alley behind the Rosebud and looked at the door into the theatre and saw that it wasn't firmly shut. The side facing the alley was a smooth metal surface, no door handle, but he was able to pry it open with his fingernails. He came in on the 3:30 p.m. show, the place crowded, mostly kids under the age of ten and their mothers. The fire door was halfway up the theatre, recessed into the wall, set in shadow. No one saw him come in. He slouched up the aisle and found a seat in the back.

"Jimmy Stewart went to the Pacific," his brother had told him while he was home on leave, before he shipped out. They were throwing the ball around out back. "Mr Smith is probably carpet-bombing the red fuck out of Tokyo right this instant. How's that for a crazy thought?" Alec's brother Ray was a self-described film freak. He and Alec went to every single movie that opened during his month-long leave: *Bataan*, *The Fighting Seabees*, *Going My Way*.

Alec waited through an episode of a serial concerning the latest adventures of a singing cowboy with long eyelashes and a mouth so dark his lips were black. It failed to interest him. He picked his nose and wondered how to get a Coke with no money. The feature started.

At first Alec couldn't figure out what the hell kind of movie it was, although right off he had the sinking feeling it was going to be a musical. First the members of an orchestra filed onto a stage against a bland blue backdrop. Then a starched shirt came out and started telling the audience all about the brand-new kind of entertainment they were about to see. When he started blithering about Walt Disney and his artists, Alec began to slide downwards in his seat, his head sinking between his shoulders. The orchestra surged into big dramatic blasts of strings and horns. In another moment his worst fears were realized. It wasn't just a musical; it was also a *cartoon*. Of course it was a cartoon, he should have known – the place crammed with little kids and their mothers – a 3.30 show in the middle of the week that led off with an episode of *The Lipstick Kid*, singing sissy of the high plains.

After a while he lifted his head and peeked at the screen through his fingers, watched some abstract animation for a while: silver raindrops falling against a background of roiling smoke, rays of molten light shimmering across an ashen sky. Eventually he straightened up to watch in a more comfortable position. He was not quite sure what he was feeling. He was bored, but interested too, almost a little mesmerized. It would have been hard not to watch. The visuals came at him in a steady hypnotic assault: ribs of red light, whirling stars, kingdoms of cloud glowing in the crimson light of a setting sun.

The little kids were shifting around in their seats. He heard a little girl whisper loudly, "Mom, when is there going to be *Mickey*?" For the kids it was like being in school. But by the time the movie hit the next segment, the orchestra shifting from Bach to Tchaikovsky, he was sitting all the way up, even leaning forward slightly, his forearms resting on his knees. He watched fairies flitting through a dark forest, touching flowers and spider-webs with enchanted wands and spreading sheets of glittering, incandescent dew. He felt a kind of baffled wonder watching them fly around, a curious feeling of yearning. He had the sudden idea he could sit there and watch forever.

"I could sit in this theatre forever," whispered someone beside him. It was a girl's voice. "Just sit here and watch and never leave."

He didn't know there was someone sitting beside him, and jumped to hear a voice so close. He thought – no, he knew – that when he sat down the seats on either side of him were empty. He turned his head.

She was only a few years older than him, couldn't have been more than twenty, and his first thought was that she was very close to being a fox; his heart beat a little faster to have such a girl speaking to him. He was already thinking *don't blow it*. She wasn't looking at him. She was staring up at the movie, and smiling in a way that seemed to express both admiration and a child's dazed wonder. He wanted desperately to say something smooth, but his voice was trapped in his throat.

She leaned towards him without glancing away from the screen, her left hand just touching the side of his arm on the armrest.

"I'm sorry to bother you," she whispered. "When I get excited about a movie I want to talk. I can't help it."

In the next moment he became aware of two things, more or less simultaneously. The first was that her hand against his arm was cold. He could feel the deadly chill of it through his sweater, a cold so palpable it startled him a little. The second thing he noticed was a single teardrop of blood on her upper lip, under her left nostril.

"You have a nosebleed," he said, in a voice that was too loud. He immediately wished he hadn't said it. You only had one opportunity to impress a fox like this. He should have found something for her to wipe her nose with, and handed it to her, murmured something real Sinatra: *you're bleeding, here*. He pushed his hands into his pockets, feeling for something she could wipe her nose with. He didn't have anything.

But she didn't seem to have heard him, didn't seem the slightest bit aware he had spoken. She absent-mindedly brushed the back of one hand under her nose, and left a dark smear of blood over her upper lip . . . and Alec froze with his hands in his pockets, staring at her. It was the first he knew there was something wrong about the girl sitting next to him, something slightly *off* about the scene playing out between them. He instinctively drew himself up and slightly away from her without even knowing he was doing it.

She laughed at something in the movie, her voice soft, breathless. Then she leaned towards him and whispered, "This is all wrong for kids. Harry Parcells loves this theatre but he plays all the wrong movies, Harry Parcells who runs the place?"

There was a fresh runner of blood leaking from her left nostril and blood on her lips, but by then Alec's attention had turned to something else. They were sitting directly under the projector beam, and there were moths and other insects whirring through the blue column of light above. A white moth had landed on her face. It was crawling up her cheek. She didn't notice, and Alec didn't mention it to her. There wasn't enough air in his chest to speak.

She whispered, "He thinks just because it's a cartoon they'll like it. It's funny he could be so crazy for movies and know so little about them. He won't run the place much longer."

She glanced at him and smiled. She had blood staining her teeth. Alec couldn't get up. A second moth, ivory white, landed just inside the delicate cup of her ear.

"Your brother Ray would have loved this," she said.

"Get away," Alec whispered hoarsely.

"You belong here, Alec," she said. "You belong here with me."

He moved at last, shoved himself up out of his seat. The first moth was crawling into her hair. He thought he heard himself moan, just faintly. He started to move away from her. She was staring at him. He backed a few feet down the aisle and bumped into some kid's legs, and the kid yelped. He glanced away from her for an instant, down at a fattish boy in a striped T-shirt who was glaring back at him, *watch where you're going meathead.*

Alec looked at her again and now she was slumped very low in her seat. Her head rested on her left shoulder. Her legs hung lewdly open. There were thick strings of blood, dried and crusted, running from her nostrils, bracketing her thin-lipped mouth. Her eyes were rolled back in her head. In her lap was an overturned carton of popcorn.

Alec thought he was going to scream. He didn't scream. She was perfectly motionless. He looked from her to the kid he had almost tripped over. The fat kid glanced casually in the direction of the dead girl, showed no reaction. He turned his gaze back to Alec, his eyes questioning, one corner of his mouth turned up in a derisive sneer.

"Sir," said a woman, the fat kid's mother. "Can you move, *please?* We're trying to watch the movie."

Alec threw another look towards the dead girl, only the chair where she had been was empty, the seat folded up. He started to retreat, bumping into knees, almost falling over once, grabbing someone for support. Then suddenly the room erupted into cheers, applause. His heart throbbed. He cried out, looked wildly around. It was Mickey, up there on the screen in droopy red robes – Mickey had arrived at last.

He backed up the aisle, swatted through the padded leather doors into the lobby. He flinched at the late afternoon brightness, narrowed his eyes to squints. He felt dangerously sick. Then someone was holding his shoulder, turning him, walking him across the room, over to the staircase up to balcony-level. Alec sat down on the bottom step, sat down hard.

"Take a minute," someone said. "Don't get up. Catch your breath. Do you think you're going to throw up?"

Alec shook his head.

"Because if you think you're going to throw up, hold on 'till I can get you a bag. It isn't so easy to get stains out of this carpet. Also when people smell vomit they don't want popcorn."

Whoever it was lingered beside him for another moment, then without a word turned and shuffled away. He returned maybe a minute later.

"Here. On the house. Drink it slow. The fizz will help with your stomach."

Alec took a wax cup sweating beads of cold water, found the straw with his mouth, sipped icy cola bubbly with carbonation. He looked up. The man standing over him was tall and slope-shouldered, with a sagging roll around the middle. His hair was cropped to a dark bristle and his eyes, behind his absurdly thick glasses, were small and pale and uneasy. He wore his slacks too high, the waistband up around his navel.

Alec said, "There's a dead girl in there." He didn't recognize his own voice.

The colour drained out of the big man's face and he cast an unhappy glance back at the doors into the theatre. "She's never been in a matinee before. I thought only night shows, I thought – for God's sake, it's a kid's movie. What's she trying to do to me?"

Alec opened his mouth, didn't even know what he was going to say, something about the dead girl, but what came out instead was: "It's not really a kid's film."

The big man shot him a look of mild annoyance. "Sure it is. It's Walt Disney."

Alec stared at him for a long moment, then said, "You must be Harry Parcells."

"Yeah. How'd you know?"

"Lucky guesser," Alec said. "Thanks for the Coke."

Alec followed Harry Parcells behind the concessions counter, through a door and out onto a landing at the bottom of some stairs.

Harry opened a door to the right and let them into a small, cluttered office. The floor was crowded with steel film cans. Fading film posters covered the walls, overlapping in places: *Boys Town*, *David Copperfield*, *Gone with the Wind*.

"Sorry she scared you," Harry said, collapsing into the office chair behind his desk. "You sure you're all right? You look kind of peaked."

"Who is she?"

"Something blew out in her brain," he said, and pointed a finger at his left temple, as if pretending to hold a gun to his head. "Four years ago. During *The Wizard of Oz*. The very first show. It was the most terrible thing. She used to come in all the time. She was my steadiest customer. We used to talk, kid around with each other—" his voice wandered off, confused and distraught. He squeezed his plump hands together on the desktop in front of him, said finally, "Now she's trying to bankrupt me."

"You've seen her." It wasn't a question.

Harry nodded. "A few months after she passed away. She told me I don't belong here. I don't know why she wants to scare me away when we used to get along so great. Did she tell you to go away?"

"Why is she here?" Alec said. His voice was still hoarse, and it was a strange kind of question to ask. For a while, Harry just peered at him through his thick glasses with what seemed to be total incomprehension.

Then he shook his head and said, "She's unhappy. She died before the end of *The Wizard* and she's still miserable about it. I understand. That was a good movie. I'd feel robbed too."

"Hello?" someone shouted from the lobby. "Anyone there?"

"Just a minute," Harry called out. He gave Alec a pained look. "My concession stand girl told me she was quitting yesterday. No notice or anything."

"Was it the ghost?"

"Heck no. One of her paste-on nails fell into someone's food so I told her not to wear them anymore. No one wants to get a fingernail in a mouthful of popcorn. She told me a lot of boys she knows come in here and if she can't wear her nails she wasn't going to work for me no more so now I got to do everything myself." He said this as he was coming around the desk. He had something in one hand, a newspaper clipping. "This will tell you about her." And then he gave Alec a look – it wasn't a glare exactly, but there was at least a measure of dull warning in it – and he added: "Don't run off on me. We still have to talk."

He went out, Alec staring after him, wondering what that last funny look was about. He glanced down at the clipping. It was an obituary – her obituary. The paper was creased, the edges worn, the ink faded; it looked as if it had been handled often. Her name was Imogene Gilchrist, she had died at nineteen, she worked at Water Street Stationery. She was survived by her parents, Colm and Mary. Friends and family spoke of her pretty laugh, her infectious sense of humour. They talked about how she loved the movies. She saw all the movies, saw them on opening day, first show. She could recite the entire cast from almost any picture you cared to name, it was like a party trick – she even knew the names of actors who had had just one line. She was president of the drama club in high school, acted in all the plays, built sets, arranged lighting. "I always thought she'd be a movie star," said her drama professor. "She had those looks and that laugh. All she needed was someone to point a camera at her and she would have been famous."

When Alec finished reading he looked around. The office was still empty. He looked back down at the obituary, rubbing the corner of the clipping between thumb and forefinger. He felt sick at the unfairness of it, and for a moment there was a pressure at the back of his eyeballs, a tingling, and he had the ridiculous idea he might start crying. He felt ill to live in a world where a nineteen-year-old girl full of laughter and life could be struck down like that, for no reason. The intensity of what he was feeling didn't really make sense, considering he had never known her when she was alive; didn't make sense until he thought about Ray, thought about Harry Truman's letter to his mom, the words *died with bravery, defending freedom, America is proud of him.* He thought about how Ray had taken him to *The Fighting Seabees,* right here in this theatre, and they sat together with their feet up on the seats in front of them, their shoulders touching. "Look at John Wayne," Ray said. "They oughta have one bomber to carry him, and another one to carry his balls." The stinging in his eyes was so intense he couldn't stand it, and it hurt to breathe. He rubbed at his wet nose, and focused intently on crying as soundlessly as possible.

He wiped his face with the tail of his shirt, put the obituary on Harry Parcells' desk, looked around. He glanced at the posters, and the stacks of steel cans. There was a curl of film in the corner of the room, just eight or so frames – he wondered where it had come from – and he picked it up for a closer look. He saw a girl closing her eyes and lifting her face, in a series of little increments, to kiss the man holding her in a tight embrace; giving herself to him. Alec

wanted to be kissed that way sometime. It gave him a curious thrill
to be holding an actual piece of a movie. On impulse he stuck it into
his pocket.

He wandered out of the office and back onto the landing at the
bottom of the stairwell. He peered into the lobby. He expected to see
Harry behind the concession stand, serving a customer, but there
was no one there. Alec hesitated, wondering where he might have
gone. While he was thinking it over, he became aware of a gentle
whirring sound coming from the top of the stairs. He looked up
them, and it clicked – the projector. Harry was changing reels.

Alec climbed the steps and entered the projection room, a dark
compartment with a low ceiling. A pair of square windows looked
into the theatre below. The projector itself was pointed through one of
them, a big machine made of brushed stainless steel, with the words
VITAPHONE stamped on the case. Harry stood on the far side of
it, leaning forward, peering out the same window through which the
projector was casting its beam. He heard Alec at the door, shot him a
brief look. Alec expected to be ordered away, but Harry said nothing,
only nodded and returned to his silent watch over the theatre.

Alec made his way to the Vitaphone, picking his way carefully
through the dark. There was a window to the left of the projector that
looked down into the theatre. Alec stared at it for a long moment, not
sure if he dared, and then put his face close to the glass and peered
into the darkened room beneath.

The theatre was lit a deep midnight blue by the image on the
screen: the conductor again, the orchestra in silhouette. The
announcer was introducing the next piece. Alec lowered his gaze and
scanned the rows of seats. It wasn't much trouble to find where he
had been sitting, an empty cluster of seats close to the back, on the
right. He half-expected to see her there, slid down in her chair, face
tilted up towards the ceiling and blood all down it – her eyes turned
perhaps to stare up at *him*. The thought of seeing her filled him with
both dread and a strange nervous exhilaration, and when he realized
she wasn't there, he was a little surprised by his own disappointment.

Music began: at first the wavering skirl of violins, rising and falling
in swoops, and then a series of menacing bursts from the brass
section, sounds of an almost military nature. Alec's gaze rose once
more to the screen – rose and held there. He felt a chill race through
him. His forearms prickled with gooseflesh. On the screen the dead
were rising from their graves, an army of white and watery spectres
pouring out of the ground and into the night above. A square-

shouldered demon, squatting on a mountain-top, beckoned them. They came to him, their ripped white shrouds fluttering around their gaunt bodies, their faces anguished, sorrowing. Alec caught his breath and held it, watched with a feeling rising in him of mingled shock and wonder.

The demon split a crack in the mountain, opened Hell. Fires leaped, the Damned jumped and danced, and Alec knew what he was seeing was about the war. It was about his brother dead for no reason in the South Pacific, *America is proud of him,* it was about bodies damaged beyond repair, bodies sloshing this way and that while they rolled in the surf at the edge of a beach somewhere in the far east, getting soggy, bloating. It was about Imogene Gilchrist, who loved the movies and died with her legs spread open and her brain swelled full of blood and she was nineteen, her parents were Colm and Mary. It was about young people, young healthy bodies, punched full of holes and the life pouring out in arterial gouts, not a single dream realized, not a single ambition achieved. It was about young people who loved and were loved in return, going away, and not coming back, and the pathetic little remembrances that marked their departure, *my prayers are with you today, Harry Truman,* and *I always thought she'd be a movie star.*

A church bell rang somewhere, a long way off. Alec looked up. It was part of the film. The dead were fading away. The churlish and square-shouldered demon covered himself with his vast black wings, hiding his face from the coming of dawn. A line of robed men moved across the land below, carrying softly glowing torches. The music moved in gentle pulses. The sky was a cold, shimmering blue, light rising in it, the glow of sunrise spreading through the branches of birch trees and northern pine. Alec watched with a feeling in him like religious awe until was over.

"I liked *Dumbo* better," Harry said.

He flipped a switch on the wall, and a bare light bulb came on, filling the projection room with harsh white light. The last of the film squiggled through the Vitaphone and came out at the other end, where it was being collected on one of the reels. The trailing end whirled around and around and went *slap, slap, slap.* Harry turned the projector off, looked at Alec over the top of the machine.

"You look better. You got your colour back."

"What did you want to talk about?" Alec remembered the vague look of warning Harry gave him when he told him not to go anywhere, and the thought occurred to him now that maybe Harry knew he had slipped in without buying a ticket, that maybe they were about to have a problem.

But Harry said, "I'm prepared to offer you a refund or two free passes to the show of your choice. Best I can do."

Alec stared. It was a long time before he could reply.

"For what?"

"For what? To shut up about it. You know what it would do to this place if it got out about her? I got reasons to think people don't want to pay money to sit in the dark with a chatty dead girl."

Alec shook his head. It surprised him that Harry thought it would keep people away, if it got out that the Rosebud was haunted. Alec had an idea it would have the opposite effect. People were happy to pay for the opportunity to experience a little terror in the dark – if they weren't there wouldn't be any business in horror pictures. And then he remembered what Imogene Gilchrist had said to him about Harry Parcells: *he won't run the place much longer.*

"So what do you want?" Harry asked. "You want passes?"

Alec shook his head.

"Refund then."

"No."

Harry froze with his hand on his wallet, flashed Alec a surprised, hostile look. "What do you want then?"

"How about a job? You need someone to sell popcorn. I promise not to wear my paste-on nails to work."

Harry stared at him for a long moment without any reply, then slowly removed his hand from his back pocket.

"Can you work weekends?" he asked.

In October, Alec hears that Steven Greenberg is back in New Hampshire, shooting exteriors for his new movie on the grounds of Phillips Exeter Academy – something with Tom Hanks and Haley Joel Osment, a misunderstood teacher inspiring troubled kid-geniuses. Alec doesn't need to know any more than that to know it smells like Steven might be on his way to winning another Oscar. Alec, though, preferred the earlier work, Steven's fantasies and suspense thrillers.

He considers driving down to have a look, wonders if he could talk his way onto the set – Oh yes, I knew Steven when he was a boy – wonders if he might even be allowed to speak with Steven himself. But he soon dismisses the idea. There must be hundreds of people in this part of New England who could claim to have known Steven back in the day, and it isn't as if they were ever close. They only really had that one conversation, the day Steven saw her. Nothing before; nothing much after.

So it is a surprise when one Friday afternoon close to the end of the month Alec takes a call from Steven's personal assistant, a cheerful, efficient-sounding woman named Marcia. She wants Alec to know that Steven was hoping to see him, and if he can drop in – is Sunday morning all right? – there will be a set pass waiting for him at Main Building, on the grounds of the Academy. They'll expect to see him around 10.00 a.m., she says in her bright chirp of a voice, before ringing off. It is not until well after the conversation has ended, that Alec realizes he has received not an invitation, but a summons.

A goateed P.A. meets Alec at Main and walks him out to where they're filming. Alec stands with thirty or so others, and watches from a distance, while Hanks and Osment stroll together across a green quad littered with fallen leaves, Hanks nodding pensively while Osment talks and gestures. In front of them is a dolly, with two men and their camera equipment sitting on it, and two men pulling it. Steven and a small group of others stand off to the side, Steven observing the shot on a video monitor. Alec has never been on a movie set before, and he watches the work of professional make-believe with great pleasure.

After he has what he wants, and has talked with Hanks for a few minutes about the shot, Steven starts over towards the crowd where Alec is standing. There is a shy, searching look on his face. Then he sees Alec and opens his mouth in a gap-toothed grin, lifts one hand in a wave, looks for a moment very much the lanky boy again. He asks Alec if he wants to walk to craft services with him, for a chilli dog and a soda.

On the walk Steven seems anxious, jiggling the change in his pockets and shooting sideways looks at Alec. Alec knows he wants to talk about Imogene, but can't figure how to broach the subject. When at last he begins to talk, it's about his memories of the Rosebud. He talks about how he loved the place, talks about all the great pictures he saw for the first time there. Alec smiles and nods, but is secretly a little astounded at the depths of Steven's self-deception. Steven never went back after The Birds. He didn't see any of the movies he says he saw there.

At last, Steven stammers, What's going to happen to the place after you retire? Not that you should retire! I just mean – do you think you'll run the place much longer?

Not much longer, Alec replies – it's the truth – but says no more. He is concerned not to degrade himself asking for a handout – although the thought is in him that this is in fact why he came. That ever since receiving Steven's invitation to visit the set he had been fantasizing that they would talk about the Rosebud, and that Steven, who is so wealthy, and who loves movies so much, might be persuaded to throw Alec a life preserver.

The old movie houses are national treasures, *Steven says.* I own a couple, believe it or not. I run them as revival joints. I'd love to do something like that with the Rosebud someday. That's a dream of mine you know.

Here is his chance, the opportunity Alec was not willing to admit he was hoping for. But instead of telling him that the Rosebud is in desperate straits, sure to close, Alec changes the subject . . . ultimately lacks the stomach to do what must be done.

What's your next project? *Alec asks.*

After this? I was considering a remake, *Steven says, and gives him another of those shifty sideways looks from the corners of his eyes.* You'd never guess what. *Then, suddenly, he reaches out, touches Alec's arm.* Being back in New Hampshire has really stirred some things up for me. I had a dream about our old friend, would you believe it?

Our old – *Alec starts, then realizes who he means.*

I had a dream the place was closed. There was a chain on the front doors, and boards in the windows. I dreamed I heard a girl crying inside, *Steven says, and grins nervously.* Isn't that the funniest thing?

Alec drives home with a cool sweat on his face, ill at ease. He doesn't know why he didn't say anything, why he couldn't *say anything; Greenberg was practically begging to give him some money. Alec thinks bitterly that he has become a very foolish and useless old man.*

At the theatre there are nine messages on Alec's machine. The first is from Lois Weisel, who Alec has not heard from in years. Her voice is brittle. She says, Hi Alec, Lois Weisel at B.U. *As if he could have forgotten her. Lois saw Imogene in* Midnight Cowboy. *Now she teaches documentary film-making to graduate students. Alec knows these two things are not unconnected, just as it is no accident Steven Greenberg became what he became.* Will you give me a call? I wanted to talk to you about – I just – will you call me? *Then she laughs, a strange, frightened kind of laugh, and says,* This is crazy. *She exhales heavily.* I just wanted to find out if something was happening to the Rosebud. Something bad. So – call me.

The next message is from Dana Lewellyn who saw her in The Wild Bunch. *The message after that is from Shane Leonard, who saw Imogene in* American Graffiti. *Darren Campbell, who saw her in* Reservoir Dogs. *Some of them talk about the dream, a dream identical to the one Steven Greenberg described, boarded over windows, chain on the door, girl crying. Some only say they want to talk. By the time the answering machine tape has played its way to the end, Alec is sitting on the floor of his office, his hands balled into fists – an old man weeping helplessly.*

Perhaps twenty people have seen Imogene in the last twenty-five years, and nearly half of them have left messages for Alec to call. The other half will get in touch with him over the next few days, to ask about the Rosebud, to talk about their dream. Alec will speak with almost everyone living who has ever seen her, all of those Imogene felt compelled to speak to: a drama professor, the manager of a video rental store, a retired financier who in his youth wrote angry, comical film reviews for The Lansdowne Record, and others. A whole congregation of people who flocked to the Rosebud instead of church on Sundays, those whose prayers were written by Paddy Chayefsky and whose hymnals were composed by John Williams and whose intensity of faith is a call Imogene is helpless to resist. Alec himself.

Steven's accountant handles the fine details of the fund-raiser to save the Rosebud. The place is closed for three weeks to refurbish. New seats, state-of-the-art sound. A dozen artisans put up scaffolding and work with little paintbrushes to restore the crumbling plaster moulding on the ceiling. Steven adds personnel to run the day-to-day operations. He has bought a controlling interest, and the place is really his now, although Alec has agreed to stay on to manage things for a little while.

Lois Weisel drives up three times a week to film a documentary about the renovation, using her grad students in various capacities, as electricians, sound people, grunts. Steven wants a gala reopening to celebrate the Rosebud's past. When Alec hears what he wants to show first – a double feature of The Wizard of Oz and The Birds – his forearms prickle with gooseflesh; but he makes no argument.

On reopening night, the place is crowded like it hasn't been since Titanic. The local news is there to film people walking inside in their best suits. Of course, Steven is there, which is why all the excitement . . . although Alec thinks he would have a sell-out even without Steven, that people would have come just to see the results of the renovation. Alec and Steven pose for photographs, the two of them standing under the marquee in their tuxedoes, shaking hands. Steven's tuxedo is Armani, bought for the occasion. Alec got married in his.

Steven leans into him, pressing a shoulder against his chest. What are you going to do with yourself?

Before Steven's money, Alec would have sat behind the counter handing out tickets, and then gone up himself to start the projector. But Steven hired someone to sell tickets and run the projector. Alec says, Guess I'm going to sit and watch the movie.

Save me a seat, Steven says. I might not get in until The Birds, though. I have some more press to do out here.

Lois Weisel has a camera set up at the front of the theatre, turned to point at the audience, and loaded with high-speed film for shooting in the dark. She films the crowd at different times, recording their reactions to The Wizard of Oz. *This was to be the conclusion of her documentary – a packed house enjoying a twentieth-century classic in this lovingly restored old movie palace – but her movie wasn't going to end like she thought it would.*

In the first shots on Lois' reel it is possible to see Alec sitting in the back left of the theatre, his face turned up towards the screen, his glasses flashing blue in the darkness. The seat to the left of him, on the aisle, is empty, the only empty seat in the house. Sometimes he can be seen eating popcorn. Other times he is just sitting there watching, his mouth open slightly, an almost worshipful look on his face.

Then in one shot he has turned sideways to face the seat to his left. He has been joined by a woman in blue. He is leaning over her. They are unmistakably kissing. No one around them pays them any mind. The Wizard of Oz *is ending. We know this because we can hear Judy Garland, reciting the same five words over and over in a soft, yearning voice, saying – well, you know what she is saying. They are only the loveliest five words ever said in all of film.*

In the shot immediately following this one, the house lights are up, and there is a crowd of people gathered around Alec's body, slumped heavily in his seat. Steven Greenberg is in the aisle, yelping hysterically for someone to bring a doctor. A child is crying. The rest of the crowd generates a low rustling buzz of excited conversation. But never mind this shot. The footage that came just before it is much more interesting.

It is only a few seconds long, this shot of Alec and his unidentified companion – a few hundred frames of film – but it is the shot that will make Lois Weisel's reputation, not to mention a large sum of money. It will appear on television shows about unexplained phenomena, it will be watched and re-watched at gatherings of those fascinated with the supernatural. It will be studied, written about, debunked, confirmed, and celebrated. Let's see it again.

He leans over her. She turns her face up to his, and closes her eyes and she is very young and she is giving herself to him completely. Alec has removed his glasses. He is touching her lightly at the waist. This is the way people dream of being kissed, a movie star kiss. Watching them, one almost wishes the moment would never end. And over all this, Dorothy's small, brave voice fills the darkened theatre. She is saying something about home. She is saying something everyone knows.

2003

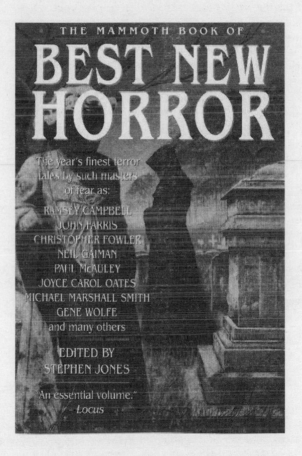

THE MAMMOTH BOOK OF

BEST NEW
HORROR

The year's finest terror
tales by such masters
of fear as:

RAMSEY CAMPBELL
JOHN FARRIS
CHRISTOPHER FOWLER
NEIL GAIMAN
PAUL McAULEY
JOYCE CAROL OATES
MICHAEL MARSHALL SMITH
GENE WOLFE
and many others

EDITED BY
STEPHEN JONES

"An essential volume."
— *Locus*

The White Hands

Mark Samuels

MICHAEL MARSHALL SMITH and I once again designed the cover of *The Mammoth Book of Best New Horror Volume Fifteen* around one of Les Edwards' atmospheric paintings, and the book looked even better than the previous edition.

As new publishing technologies such as print-on-demand, e-books and the Internet expanded, so did the amount of horror material available each year. As a result, the Introduction grew to ninety-two pages (or nearly 33,000 words). Even the Necrology increased to sixty-two pages to accommodate tributes to the ever-growing number of veteran writers, actors and others who were now reaching the end of their lives (the book was dedicated to the memory of another old friend and colleague, pulp writer Hugh B. Cave).

It was therefore no surprise that my editorial explained that there was just too much material now being produced in our genre every year for me to even attempt to cover everything in future. The publishers of the book on both sides of the Atlantic were already making noises about how the non-fiction content had grown over recent years (this volume was more than 630 pages long), and it was taking me ever longer to compile all this supplementary information as well as working my way through the ever-growing submission pile.

The twenty-five stories also reflected the changes that were happening in the horror field. Now, alongside such established names as Ramsey Campbell, Christopher Fowler, Michael Marshall Smith, John Farris, Gene Wolfe, Steve Rasnic Tem, Joyce Carol Oates, Neil Gaiman and Paul J. McAuley, a new generation of authors were starting to dominate the contents for the first time – Steve Nagy, Dale Bailey, Jay Lake, Scott Emerson Bull, Charles Coleman Finlay, Christopher Barzak and Mike O'Driscoll all represented a "new wave" of smart and talented writers who were using the horror genre to tell their stories of contemporary unease.

Another name that could be added to that list is British writer
Mark Samuels. However, whereas these other newcomers were
intent on pushing the boundaries of contemporary horror, Samuels'
first collection of stories hearkened back to the classic writings of
Arthur Machen and M. R. James. The collection's title story, "The
White Hands", is a masterful slice of Gothic horror in the grand
tradition, and it appeared for the first time in its full version in the
fifteenth edition of *Best New Horror*.

YOU MAY REMEMBER Alfred Muswell, whom devotees of the
weird tale will know as the author of numerous articles on the subject
of literary ghost stories. He died in obscurity just over a year ago.

Muswell had been an Oxford don for a time, but left the cloisters
of the University after an academic scandal. A former student (now
a journalist) wrote of him in a privately published memoir:

> *Muswell attempted single-handedly to alter the academic criteria of*
> *excellence in literature. He sought to eradicate what he termed the*
> *"tyranny of materialism and realism" from his teaching. He would*
> *loom over us in his black robes at lectures and tutorials, tearing*
> *prescribed and classic books to shreds with his gloved hands, urging*
> *us to read instead work by the likes of Sheridan Le Fanu, Vernon Lee,*
> *M. R. James and Lilith Blake. Muswell was a familiar sight amongst*
> *the squares and courtyards of the colleges at night and would stalk*
> *abroad like some bookish revenant. He had a very plump face and a*
> *pair of circular spectacles. His eyes peered into the darkness with an*
> *indefinable expression that could be somewhat disturbing.*

You will recall that Muswell's eccentric theories about literature
enjoyed a brief but notorious vogue in the 1950s. In a series of
essays in the short-lived American fantasy magazine *The Necrophile*,
he championed the supernatural tale. This was at a time when other
academics and critics were turning away from the genre in disgust,
following the illiterate excesses of pulp magazines such as *Weird
Tales*. Muswell argued that the anthropocentric concerns of realism
had the effect of stifling the much more profound study of infinity.
Contemplation of the infinite, he contended, was the faculty that
separated man from beast. Realism, in his view, was the literature of
the prosaic. It was the quest for the hidden mysteries, he contended,

which formed the proper subject of all great literature. Muswell also believed that literature, in its highest form, should unravel the secrets of life and death. This latter concept was never fully explained by him but he hinted that its attainment would involve some actual alteration in the structure of reality itself. This, perhaps inevitably, led to him being dismissed in academic circles as a foolish mystic.

After his quiet expulsion from Oxford, Muswell retreated to the lofty heights of Highgate. From here, the London village that had harboured Samuel Taylor Coleridge during the final phase of his struggle against opium addiction, Muswell continued his literary crusade. A series of photographs reproduced in the fourth issue of *The Necrophile* show Muswell wandering through the leafy streets of Highgate clad in his black three-piece suit, cigarette jammed between lips, plump and be-spectacled. In one of his gloved hands is a book of ghost stories by the writer he most admired, Lilith Blake. This Victorian author is perhaps best known for her collection of short stories, *The Reunion and Others*. Then, as now, fabulously rare, this book was printed in an edition of only one hundred copies. Amongst the cognoscenti, it has acquired legendary status. Muswell was undoubtedly the greatest authority on her life and works. He alone possessed the little that remained of her extant correspondence, as well as diaries, photographs and other personal effects.

In moving to Highgate, Muswell was perhaps most influenced by the fact that Blake had been resident in the village for all of the twenty-two years of her brief life. Her mortal remains were interred in the old West Cemetery in Swains Lane.

I first met Alfred Muswell after writing a letter to him requesting information about Lilith Blake for an article I was planning on supernatural writers of the late-nineteenth and early twentieth centuries. After an exchange of correspondence he suggested that we should meet one afternoon in the reading room of the Highgate Literary and Scientific Institution. From there he would escort me to his rooms, which, apparently, were difficult to find without help, being hidden in the maze of narrow brick passageways beyond Pond Square.

It was a very cold, clear winter afternoon when I alighted at the Underground station in Highgate and made my way up Southwood Lane towards its village. Snow had fallen since the night before and the lane was almost deserted. Only the sound of my footsteps crunching in the brittle snow broke the silence. When I reached the village I paused for a while to take in my surroundings. The

Georgian houses were cloaked in white and glittered in the freezing sunshine. A sharp wind blew chilly gusts across the sagging roofs and chimney pots. One or two residents, clad in greatcoats and well muffled, plodded warily along.

I accosted one of these pedestrians and was directed by him towards the Institute. This was a whitewashed structure, two floors high, facing the square on the corner of Swains Lane. I could see the glow of a coal fire within and a plump man reading in an easy chair through one of the ground floor windows. It was Alfred Muswell.

After dusting the snowflakes from my clothes, I made my way inside and introduced myself to him. He struggled out of his chair, stood upright like a hermit crab quitting its shell, and threw out a gloved hand for me to grasp. He was dressed in his habitual black suit, a cigarette drooping from his bottom lip. His eyes peered at me intensely from behind those round glasses. His hair had thinned and grown white since the photographs in *The Necrophile*. The loss of hair was mainly around the crown, giving him a somewhat monkish appearance.

I hung up my duffel coat and scarf and sat down in the chair facing him.

"We can sit here undisturbed for a few more minutes at least," he said, "the other members are in the library attending some lecture about that charlatan, James Joyce."

I nodded as if in agreement, but my attention was fixed on Muswell's leather gloves. He seemed always to wear them. He had worn a similar pair in *The Necrophile* photographs. I noticed the apparent emaciation of the hands and long fingers that the gloves concealed. His right hand fidgeted constantly with his cigarette while the fingers of his left coiled and uncoiled repeatedly. It was almost as if he were uncomfortable with the appendages.

"I'm very pleased to talk with a fellow devotee of Lilith Blake's tales," he said, in his odd, strained voice.

"Oh, I wouldn't describe myself as a devotee. Her work is striking, of course, but my own preferences are for Blackwood and Machen. Blake seems to me to lack balance. Her world is one of unremitting gloom and decay."

Muswell snorted at my comment. He exhaled a great breath of cigarette smoke in my direction and said:

"Unremitting gloom and decay? Rather say that she makes desolation glorious! I believe that De Quincey once wrote 'Holy was the grave. Saintly its darkness. Pure its corruption.' Words that describe Lilith Blake's work perfectly. Machen indeed! That red-faced old coot with his deluded Anglo-Catholic rubbish! The man was a drunken clown obsessed by sin. And Blackwood? Pantheistic rot that belongs to the Stone Age. The man wrote mainly for money and he wrote too much. No, no. Believe me, if you want the truth beyond the frontier of appearances it is to Lilith Blake you must turn. She never compromises. Her stories are infinitely more than mere accounts of supernatural phenomena . . ."

His voice had reached a peak of shrillness and it was all I could do not to squirm in my chair. Then he seemed to regain his composure and drew a handkerchief across his brow.

"You must excuse me. I have allowed my convictions to ruin my manners. I so seldom engage in debate these days that when I do I become overexcited." He allowed himself to calm down and was about to speak again when a side door opened and a group of people bustled into the room. They were chatting about the Joyce lecture that had evidently just finished. Muswell got to his feet and made for his hat and overcoat. I followed him.

Outside, in the cold afternoon air, he looked back over his shoulder and crumpled up his face in a gesture of disgust.

"How I detest those fools," he intoned.

We trudged through the snow, across the square and into a series of passageways. Tall buildings with dusty windows pressed upon us from both sides and, after a number of twists and turns, we reached the building that contained Muswell's rooms. They were in the basement and we walked down some well-worn steps outside, leaving the daylight above us.

He opened the front door and I followed him inside.

Muswell flicked on the light switch and a single bulb suspended from the ceiling and reaching halfway towards the bare floor revealed the meagre room. On each of the walls were long bookcases stuffed with volumes. There was an armchair and footstool in one corner along with a small, circular table on which a pile of books teetered precariously. A dangerous-looking Calor gas fire stood in the opposite corner. Muswell brought another chair (with a canvas back and seat) from an adjoining room and invited me to sit down. Soon afterwards he hauled a large trunk from the same room. It was extremely old and bore the monogram "L. B." on its side. He unlocked the trunk with some ceremony, and then sat down, lighting yet another cigarette, his eyes fixed on my face.

I took a notebook from my pocket and, drawing sheaves of manuscripts from the trunk, began to scan them. It seemed dark stuff, and rather strange, but just what I needed for the article. And there was a mountain of it to get through. Muswell, meanwhile, made a melancholy remark, apropos of nothing, the significance of which I did not appreciate until much later.

"Loneliness," he said, "can drive a man into mental regions of extreme strangeness."

I nodded absently. I had found a small box and, on opening it, my excitement mounted. It contained a sepia-coloured photographic portrait of Lilith Blake, dated 1890. It was the first I had seen of her, and must have been taken just before her death. Her beauty was quite astonishing.

Muswell leaned forward. He seemed to be watching my reaction with redoubled interest.

Lilith Blake's raven-black and luxuriant hair curled down to her shoulders. Her face was oval, finished with a small pointed chin. The eyes, wide apart and piercing, seemed to gaze across the vastness of the time which separated us. Her throat was long and pale, her forehead rounded and stray curls of hair framed the temples. The fleshy lips were slightly parted and her small, sharp teeth gleamed whitely. Around her neck hung a string of pearls and she wore a jet-black, velvet dress. The most delicate and lovely white hands I had ever seen were folded across her bosom. Although the alabaster skin of her face and neck was extremely pale, her hands were paler. They were whiter than the purest snow. It was as if daylight had never touched them. The length of her graceful fingers astonished me.

I must have sat there for some time in silent contemplation of that intoxicating image. Muswell, becoming impatient, finally broke my reverie in a most violent and unnecessary manner. He snatched the photograph from me and held it in the air while he spoke, his voice rising to a feverish pitch:

"Here is the hopeless despair of one haunted by the night. One who had gone down willingly into the grave with a black ecstasy in her heart instead of fear!"

I could only sit there in stunned silence. To me, Muswell seemed close to a complete nervous breakdown.

Later, Muswell must have helped me to sort through the various papers in the trunk. I remember little of the detail. I do know that by the time I finally left his rooms and found my way back to the square through the snow, I had realized that my research into Blake's work would be of the utmost importance to my academic career. Muswell had treasure in his keeping, a literary gold mine, and, given the right handling, it could make my name.

After that, my days were not my own. Try as I might, I could not expunge the vision of Blake from my mind. Her face haunted my thoughts, beckoning me onwards in my quest to discover the true meaning of her work. The correspondence between Muswell and myself grew voluminous as I sought to arrange a time when I would be enabled to draw further on his collection. For a while he seemed to distrust my mounting interest, but at last he accepted my enthusiasm as genuine. He welcomed me as a kindred spirit. By a happy chance, I even managed to rent a room in his building.

And so, during the course of the winter months, I shut myself away with Muswell, poring over Blake's letters and personal effects. I cannot deny that the handling of those things began to feel almost sacrilegious. But as I read the letters, diaries and notebooks I could see that Muswell had spoken only the truth when he described Blake as supreme in the field of supernatural literature.

He would scuttle around his library like a spider, climbing stepladders and hauling out volumes from the shelves, passing them down through the gloomy space to me. He would mark certain passages that he believed furthered a greater understanding of Blake's life and work. Outside, the frequent snow showers filled the gap between his basement window and the pavement above with icy whiteness. My research was progressing well; my notebook filling up with useful quotations and annotations, but somehow I felt that I was failing to reach the essence of Lilith; the most potent aspect of her vision was eluding my understanding. It was becoming agonizing to be so close to her, and yet to feel that her most secret and beautiful mysteries were buried from my view.

"I believe," Muswell once said, "that mental isolation is the essence of weird fiction. Isolation when confronted with disease, with madness, with horror and with death. These are the reverberations of the infinity that torments us. It is Blake who delineates these echoes of doom for us. She alone exposes our inescapable, blind stumbling towards eternal annihilation. She alone shows our souls screaming in the darkness with none to heed our cries. Ironic, isn't it, that such a beautiful young woman should possess an imagination so dark and riddled with nightmare?"

Muswell took a deep drag of his cigarette, and, in contemplating his words, seemed to gaze through everything into a limitless void.

Sometimes, when Muswell was away, I would have the collection to myself. Blake's personal letters became as sacred relics to me. Her framed photograph attained a special significance, and I was often unable to prevent myself from running my fingers around the outline of her lovely face.

As time passed, and my research into Lilith Blake's oeuvre began to yield ever more fascinating results, I felt that I was now ready to posthumously afford her the attention that she so richly deserved. Whereas previously I had planned to merely include references to her work in my lengthy article on supernatural fiction during the late nineteenth and early twentieth centuries, I now realized that she had to be accorded a complete critical book of her own, such was the importance of the literary legacy I had stumbled across by associating with Muswell. It seemed obvious to me that the man had little real idea of the prime importance of the materials in his possession and that his reclusive lifestyle had led him to regard anything relating to this dead and beautiful creature as his own personal property. His understanding was hopelessly confused by the unsubstantiated assertion that he made of the importance of the "work behind the works", which I took to mean some obscure mystical interpretation he had formulated from his own muddled, ageing brain.

One afternoon he came across me working on my proposed book and took an apparent polite interest in my writing, but mingled in with that interest was an infuriating sarcasm. I voiced my contention that Blake deserved a much higher place in the literary pantheon. The only reasonable explanation for the failure of her work to achieve this was, I had discovered, the almost total lack of contemporary interest in it. I could trace neither extant reviews of *The Reunion and Others* in neither any of the literary journals nor mention of her in society columns of the time. At this statement he actually laughed out loud. Holding one of his cigarettes between those thin, gloved fingers he waved it in the air dismissively, and said:

"I should have thought that you would have found the silence surrounding her person and work suggestive, as I did. Do not mistake silence for indifference. Any imbecile might make that erroneous conclusion and indeed many have done so in the past. Lilith Blake was no Count Stenbock, merely awaiting rediscovery. She was *deliberately* not mentioned; her work was specifically excluded from consideration. How much do you think was paid simply to ensure she had a fitting tomb in Highgate Cemetery? But pray continue, tell me more of your article and I shall try to take into consideration your youthful naiveté."

As I continued to expand on my theories I saw clearly that he began to smirk in a most offensive fashion. Why, it was as if he were humouring me! My face flushed and I stood up, my back rigid with tension. I was close to breaking point and could not tolerate this old fool's patronizing attitude any longer. Muswell took a step backwards and bowed, rather ornately, in some idiotic gentlemanly gesture. But as he did so, he almost lost his footing, as if a bout of dizziness had overcome him. I was momentarily startled by the action and he took the opportunity to make his exit. But before he did so he uttered some departing words:

"If you knew what I know my friend, and perhaps you soon will, then you would find this literary criticism as horribly amusing as I do. But I am extremely tired and will leave you to your work."

It seemed obvious to me at that point that Muswell was simply not fit to act as the trustee for Lilith Blake's estate. Moreover, his theatrics and lack of appreciation for my insights indicated progressive mental deterioration. I would somehow have to wrest control over the estate from his enfeebled grasp, for the sake of Blake's reputation.

The opportunity came more quickly than I could have dared hope.

One evening in February Muswell returned from one of his infrequent appointments looking particularly exhausted. I had noticed the creeping fatigue in his movements for a number of weeks. In addition to an almost constant sense of distraction he had also lost a considerable amount of weight. His subsequent confession did not, in any case, come as a shock.

"The game is up for me," he said, "I am wasting away. The doctor says I will not last much longer. I am glad that the moment of my assignation with Blake draws near. You must ensure that I am buried with her."

Muswell contemplated me from across the room, the light of the dim electric bulb reflected off the lenses of his spectacles, veiling the eyes behind. He continued:

"There are secrets which I have hidden from you, but I will reveal them now. I have come to learn that there are those who, though dead, lie in their coffins beyond the grip of decay. The power of eternal visions preserves them: there they lie, softly dead and dreaming. Lilith Blake is one of these and I shall be another. You will be our guardian in this world. You will ensure that our bodies are not disturbed. Once dead, we must not be awakened from the eternal dream. It is for the protection of Lilith and myself that I have allowed you to share in my thoughts and her literary legacy. Everything will make sense once you have read her final works."

He climbed up the steepest stepladder to the twilight of the room's ceiling and took a metal box from the top of one of the bookcases. He unlocked it and drew an old writing book bound in crumpled black leather from within. The title page was written in Lilith Blake's distinctive longhand style. I could see that it bore the title *The White Hands and Other Tales*.

"This volume," he said, handing it to me, "contains the final stories. They establish the truth of all that I have told you. The book must now be published. I want to be vindicated after I die. This book will prove, in the most shocking way, the supremacy of the horror tale over all other forms of literature. As I intimated to you once before, these stories are not accounts of supernatural phenomena but supernatural phenomena in themselves.

"Understand this: Blake was dead when these stories were conceived. But she still dreams and transmitted these images from her tomb to me so that I might transcribe them for her. When you read them you will know that I am not insane. All will become clear to you. You will understand how, at the point of death, the eternal dream is begun. It allows dissolution of the body to be held at bay for as long as one continues the dreaming."

I realized that Muswell's illness had deeply affected his mind. In order to bring him back to some awareness of reality I said:

"You say that Blake telepathically dictated the stories and you transcribed them? Then how is it that the handwriting is hers and not your own?"

Muswell smiled painfully, paused, and then, for the first and last time, took off his gloves. The hands were Lilith Blake's, the same pale, attenuated forms I recognized from her photograph.

"I asked for a sign that I was not mad," said Muswell, "and it was given to me."

Four weeks later Muswell died.

The doctor's certificate listed the cause of death as heart failure. I had been careful, and as he was already ill, there was little reason for the authorities to suspect anything.

Frankly, I had never countenanced the idea of fulfilling any of Muswell's requests and I arranged for his body to be cremated and interred at Marylebone and St Pancras Cemetery, amongst a plain of small, indistinguishable graves and headstones. He would not rest at Highgate Cemetery alongside Lilith Blake.

The ceremony was a simple one and beside myself there were no other mourners in attendance. Muswell's expulsion from Oxford had ensured that that his old colleagues were wary of keeping in touch with him and there were no surviving members of his family who chose to pay their last respects. The urn containing his ashes was interred in an unmarked plot and the priest who presided over the affair muttered his way through the rites in a mechanical, indifferent fashion. As the ceremony concluded and I made my way across that dull sepulchral plain, under a grey and miserable sky, I had a sense of finality. Muswell was gone forever and had found that oblivion he seemed so anxious to avoid.

It was a few days later that I made my first visit to Lilith Blake's vault. She had been interred in the old West section of Highgate Cemetery and I was unable to gain access alone. There were only official tours of the place available and I attended one, but afterwards I paid the guide to conduct me privately to Blake's vault. We had to negotiate our way through a tangle of overgrown pathways and crumbling gravestones. The vault was located in a near inaccessible portion of the hillside cemetery and as we proceeded through the undergrowth, with thick brambles catching on our trousers, the guide told me that he had only once before visited this vault. This was in the company of another man whose description led me to conclude had been Muswell himself. The guide mentioned that this particular area was a source of some curiosity to the various guides, volunteers and conservationists who worked here. Although wildlife flourished in other parts of the cemetery, here it was conspicuous by its absence. Even the birds seemed to avoid the place.

I remember distinctly that the sun had just set and that we reached the tomb in the twilight. The sycamores around us only added to the gloom. Then I caught sight of an arched roof covered with ivy just ahead, and the guide told me that we had reached our destination. As we approached it and the structure came fully into view I felt a mounting sense of anticipation. Some of the masonry had crumbled away but it was still an impressive example of High Victorian Gothic architecture. The corners of its square exterior were adorned with towers and each side boasted a miniature portico. On one of the sides, almost obliterated by neglect and decay, was a memorial stone, bearing the epitaph·

LILITH BLAKE
BORN 25 DECEMBER 1874
DIED 1 NOVEMBER 1896

"It is getting late," the guide whispered to me, "we must get back."

I saw his face in the gloom and he had a restless expression. His words had broken in on the strange silence that enveloped the area. I nodded absently, but made my way around to the front of the vault and the rusty trellis gates blocking the entrance to a stairway that led down to her coffin. Peering through the gates I could see the flight of stairs, covered by lichen, but darkness obscured its lower depths. The guide was at my elbow now and tugging my jacket sleeve.

"Come on, come on," he moaned, "I could get in real trouble for doing this."

There was something down there. I had the unnerving sensation that I was, in turn, being scrutinized by some presence in that perpetual darkness. It was almost as if it were trying to communicate with me, and images began to form in my mind, flashes of distorted scenes, of corpses that did not rot, of dreams that things no longer human might dream.

Then the guide got a grip of my arm and began forcibly dragging me away. I stumbled along with him as if in a trance, but the hallucinations seemed to fade the further away we got from the vault and by the time we reached the main gate, I had regained my mental faculties. Thereafter the guide refused any request that I made for him to again take me to the vault and my attempts to persuade his colleagues were met with the same response. In the end I was no longer even granted access to the cemetery on official tours. I later learned that my connection with Muswell had been discovered and that he had caused much trouble to the cemetery authorities in the past with his demands for unsupervised access. On one occasion there were even threats of legal action for trespassing.

As indicated, Muswell had informed me that I was to be his literary executor and thus his collection of Blakeiana was left in my control. I also gained possession of his rooms. So I turned again to the study of Blake's work, hoping therein to further my understanding of the enigma that had taken control of my life. I had still to read *The White Hands and Other Tales* and had been put off doing so by Muswell's insistence that this would enlighten me. I still held to the view that his mystical interpretation was fallacious and the thought that this book might be what he actually claimed it to be was almost detestable to me. I wanted desperately to believe that Muswell had written the book himself, rather than as a conduit for Blake. And yet, even if I dismissed the fact of his peculiar hands, so like Blake's own, even if I put that down to some self-inflicted mutilation due to his long-disordered mental state, not to mention the book's comparatively recent age, still there remained the experience at the vault to undermine my certainty. And so it was to *The White Hands and Other Tales* I turned, hoping there to determine matters once and for all.

I had only managed to read the title story. Frankly, the book was too hideous for anyone but a lunatic to read in its entirety. The tale was like an incantation. The further one progressed the more incomprehensible and sinister the words became. They were sometimes reversed and increasingly obscene. The words in that book conjured visions of eternal desolation. The little that I had read had already damaged my own mind. I became obsessed with the idea of her lying in her coffin, dreaming and waiting for me to liberate her.

During the nights of sleeplessness her voice would call across the dark. When I was able to sleep strange dreams came to me. I would be walking among pale shades in an overgrown and crumbling necropolis. The moonlight seemed abnormally bright and even filtered down to the catacombs where I would follow the shrouded form of Lilith Blake. The world of the dead seemed to be replacing my own.

For weeks, I drew down the blinds in Muswell's library, shutting out the daylight, lost in my speculations.

As time passed I began to wonder just why Muswell had been so insistent that he must be interred with Blake at all costs? My experiences at her vault and the strange hallucinations that I had suffered; might they not have been authentic after all? Could it be that Muswell had actually divined some other mode of existence beyond death, which I too had gleaned only dimly? I did not reach this conclusion lightly. I had explored many avenues of philosophical enquiry before coming back again and again to the conclusion that I might have to rely on Muswell's own interpretation. The critical book on Blake that I proposed to write floundered lost in its own limitations. For, incredible as it seemed, the only explanation that lay before me was that the corpse itself did harbour some form of unnatural sentience, and that close contact with it brought final understanding of the mystery.

I sought to solve a riddle beyond life and death yet feared the answer. The image that held the solution to the enigma that tormented me was the corpse of Lilith Blake. I had to see it in the flesh.

I decided that I would arrange for the body to be exhumed and brought to me here in Muswell's – *my* – rooms. It took me weeks to make the necessary contacts and raise the money required. How difficult it can be to get something done, even something so seemingly simple! How tedious the search for the sordid haunts of the necessary types, the hints dropped in endless conversations with untrustworthy strangers in dirty public houses. How venal, how mercenary is the world at large. During the nights of sleeplessness Lilith Blake's voice would sometimes seem to call to me across the darkness. When I was able to sleep I encountered beautiful dreams, where I would be walking among pale shades in an overgrown and crumbling necropolis. The moonlight seemed abnormally bright and even filtered down to the catacombs where I would find Lilith's shrouded form.

At last terms were agreed. Two labourers were hired to undertake the job, and on the appointed night I waited in my rooms. Outside, the rain was falling heavily and in my mind's eye, as I sat anxiously in the armchair smoking cigarette after cigarette, I saw the deed done; the two simpletons, clad in their raincoats and with crowbars and pickaxes, climbing over the high wall which ran along Swains Lane, stumbling through the storm and the overgrown grounds past stone angels and ruined monuments, down worn steps to the circular avenue, deep in the earth, but open to the mottled grey-and-black sky. Wet leaves must have choked the passageways. I could see the rain sweeping over the hillside cemetery as they levered open the door to her vault, their coats floundering in the wind. The memory of Lilith Blake's face rose before me through the hours that passed. I seemed to see it in every object that caught my gaze. I had left the blind up and watched the rain beating at the window above me, the water streaming down the small Georgian panes. I began to feel like an outcast of the universe.

As I waited, I thought I saw a pair of eyes staring back at me in the clock on the mantelpiece. I thought too that I saw two huge and thin white spiders crawling across the books on the shelves.

At last there were three loud knocks on the door and I came to in my chair, my heart pounding in my chest. I opened the door to the still-pouring rain, and there at last, shadowy in the night, were my two grave-robbers. They were smiling unpleasantly, their hair plastered down over their worm-white faces. I pulled the wad of bank notes from my pocket and stuffed them into the nearest one's grasp.

They lugged the coffin inside and set it down in the middle of the room.

And then they left me alone with the thing. For a while, the sodden coffin dripped silently onto the rug, the dark pools forming at its foot spreading slowly outwards, sinking gradually into the worn and faded pile. Although its wooden boards were decrepit and disfigured with dank patches of greenish mould, the lid remained securely battened down by a phalanx of rusty nails. I had prepared for this moment carefully; I had all the tools I needed ready in the adjoining room, but something, a sudden sense of foreboding, made me hesitate foolishly. At last, with a massive effort of will, I fetched the claw hammer and chisel, and knelt beside the coffin. Once I had prised the lid upwards and then down again, leaving the rusted nail-tops proud, I drew them out one by one. It seemed to take forever – levering each one up and out and dropping it onto the slowly growing pile at my feet. My lips were dry and I could barely grip the tools in my slippery hands. The shadows of the rain still trickling down the window were thrown over the room and across the coffin by the orange glow of the street lamp outside.

Very slowly, I lifted the lid.

Resting in the coffin was a figure clothed in a muslin shroud that was discoloured with age. Those long hands and attenuated fingers were folded across its bosom. Lilith Blake's raven-black hair seemed to have grown whilst she had slept in the vault and it reached down to her waist. Her head was lost in shadow, so I bent closer to examine it. There was no trace of decay in the features, which were those in the photograph and yet it now had a horrible aspect, quite unlike that decomposition I might have anticipated. The skin was puffy and white, resembling paint applied on a tailor's dummy. Those fleshy lips that so attracted me in the photograph were now repulsive. They were lustreless and drew back from her yellowed, sharp little teeth. The eyes were closed and even the lashes seemed longer, as if they too had grown, and they reminded me of the limbs of a spider. As I gazed at the face and fought back my repulsion, I had again the sensation that I had experienced at the vault.

Consciousness seemed to mingle with dreams. The two states were becoming one and I saw visions of some hellish ecstasy. At first I again glimpsed corpses that did not rot, as if a million graves had been opened, illuminated by the phosphoric radiance of suspended decay. But these gave way to wilder nightmares that I could glimpse only dimly, as if through a billowing vapour; nightmares that to see clearly would result in my mind being destroyed. And I could not help being reminded of the notion that what we term sanity is only a measure of success in concealing underlying madness.

Then I came back to myself and saw Lilith Blake appearing to awaken. As she slowly opened her eyes, the spell was broken, and I looked into them with mounting horror. They were blank and repugnant, no longer belonging in a human face; the eyes of a thing that had seen sights no living creature could see. Then one of her hands reached up and her long fingers clutched feebly against my throat as if trying to scratch, or perhaps caress, me.

With the touch of those clammy hands I managed to summon up enough self-control to close the lid and begin replacing the coffin nails, fighting against the impulses that were driving me to gaze again upon the awakened apparition. Then, during a lull in the rain, I burned the coffin and its deathly contents in the back yard. As I watched the fire build I thought that I heard a shrieking, like a curse being invoked in the sinister and incomprehensible language of Blake's tale. But the noise was soon lost in the roar of the flames.

It was only after many days that I discovered that the touch of Lilith Blake's long white fingers had produced marks that, once visible, remained permanently impressed upon my throat.

I travelled abroad for some months afterwards, seeking southern climes bathed in warm sunshine and blessed with short nights. But my thoughts gradually returned to *The White Hands and Other Tales*. I wondered if it might be possible to achieve control over it, to read it in its entirety and use it to attain my goal. Finally, its lure proved decisive. I convinced myself that I had already borne the darkest horrors, that this would have proved a meet preparation for its mysteries, however obscenely they were clothed. And so, returning once more to Highgate, I began the task of transcribing and interpreting the occult language of the book, delving far into its deep mysteries. Surely I could mould the dreams to my own will and overcome the nightmare. Once achieved, I would dwell forever, in Paradise . . .

Text of a letter written by John Harrington whilst under confinement in Maudsley Psychiatric Hospital:

My dearest wife Lilith,

I do not know why you have not written or come to see me.

The gentlemen looking after me here are very kind but will not allow any mirrors.

I know there is something awful about my face. Everyone is scared to look at it.

They have taken your book away. They say it is gibberish. But I know all the secrets now.

Sometimes I laugh and laugh.

But I like the white hands that crawl around my bed at night like two spiders.

They laugh with me.

Please write or come.

With all my heart,

—John

2004

THE MAMMOTH BOOK OF

BEST NEW HORROR

The Year's Best Macabre
Fiction by Such Masters
of Terror as:

POPPY Z. BRITE
RAMSEY CAMPBELL
NEIL GAIMAN
STEPHEN GALLAGHER
TIM LEBBON
TANITH LEE
KIM NEWMAN
MICHAEL SHEA
MICHAEL MARSHALL SMITH
LISA TUTTLE

EDITED BY STEPHEN JONES

"The must-have annual anthology for horror fans"
— *Time Out*

My Death

Lisa Tuttle

LES EDWARDS' RED-EYED bat that graced the cover of *The Mammoth Book of Best New Horror Volume Sixteen* is, in my opinion, one of the strongest images we have ever used on the book.

This was another 600-plus page edition. As I promised my editor, I managed to get the Introduction down to just eighty pages, and the Necrology was also reduced to fifty-one. What some readers do not seem to understand is that the books' non-fiction elements do not take anything away from the fiction content. Each year I have a set amount of money to pay for the stories, and I include all the other material at no extra cost from my editorial budget. If the extraneous matter not in there, the number of stories in each book would remain exactly the same.

For the editorial, I discussed some American opposition to the current copyright law, and how some smaller publishers blatantly ignored international copyright protection when they reprinted works by deceased authors.

Volume Sixteen was dedicated to another one of these, my old friend John Brosnan, who died at far too young an age.

This volume included twenty-one tales, topped-and-tailed by two very different stories from Neil Gaiman. However, the stand-out for me was Lisa Tuttle's remarkable mythological novella "My Death", which was originally published as a separate book by PS Publishing.

I have known Lisa, a Texan who has lived in Britain since 1980, for many years, and admired and championed her horror fiction ever since her first collection of stories, *A Nest of Nightmares*, appeared in 1986. As the following World Fantasy Award- and International Horror Guild Award-nominated novella proves, her talent to disturb the reader has only grown over the intervening years, and it is to be regretted that she does not publish more often in our particular genre.

why must I write?
you would not care for this,
but She draws the veil aside,

unbinds my eyes,
commands,
write, write or die.
— H.D., *Hermetic Definition*

... a typical death island where the familiar
Death-goddess sings as she spins.
— Robert Graves, *The Greek Myths*

I

AS I TRAVELLED, I watched the landscape – lochs and hillsides, the trees still winter-bare, etched against a soft, grey sky – and all the time my empty hand moved on my lap, tracing the pattern the branches made, smoothing the lines of the hills.

That drawing could be a way of not thinking and a barrier against feeling I didn't need a psychotherapist to tell me. Once upon a time I would have whiled away the journey by making up stories, but since Allan's death, this escape had failed me.

I had been a writer all my life – professionally, thirty years – but the urge to make up stories went back even further. Whether they were for my own private entertainment or printed out and hand-bound as presents for family, whether they appeared in fanzines or between hardcovers, one thousand words long or one hundred thousand, sold barely two hundred copies or hovered at the bottom of (one) bestseller list, whether they won glowing reviews or were uniformly ignored, my stories were me, they were what I did. Publishers might fail me, readers lose interest, but that a story itself let me down was something that had never occurred before.

Strange that I could still take pleasure in sketching, because that was so completely associated with my life with Allan that the reminder ought to have been too painful. He had been a keen amateur artist, a weekend watercolourist, and, following his relaxed example, I'd tried my hand on our first holiday together and liked the results. It became something we could do together, another shared interest. I had not painted or sketched since childhood, having decided very early in life that I must devote myself to the one thing I was good at in order to succeed. Anything else seemed like a waste of time.

Allan had never seen life in those terms; he came from a different world. He was English, middle-class, ten years older than me. My parents were self-made, first-generation Americans who knew and thought little about what their parents had left behind, whereas his could trace their ancestry back to the Middle Ages, and while they were nothing so vulgar as rich, they had never had to worry about money. Allan had gone to a "progressive" school where the importance of being well-rounded was emphasized and little attention given to the practicalities of earning a living. And so he was athletic – he could play cricket and football, swim, shoot, and sail – and musical, and artistic, and handy – a good plain cook, he could put up a garden shed or any large item of flat-packed furniture by himself – and prodigiously well-read. But, as he sometimes said with a sigh, his skills were many, useful, and entertaining, but not the sort to attract financial reward.

We'd been living modestly but comfortably mainly on his investments, augmented by my erratic writing income, until the collapse of the stock market. Before we'd done more than consider ways we might live even more modestly, Allan had died from a massive heart attack.

I had no debts – even the mortgage was paid off – but my writing income had dried to the merest trickle, and the past year and a half had eaten away at my savings. Something had to change – which was why I was on my way to Edinburgh to meet my agent.

I hadn't seen Selwyn in several years. At least, not on business: he had come up to Scotland for Allan's funeral. When he'd sent me an e-mail to say he would be in Edinburgh on business, and was it possible I'd be free for lunch, I'd known it was an opportunity I had to take. I'd written nothing to speak of since Allan's death, one year and five months ago. I still didn't know if I would ever want to write again, but I had to make some money, and I wasn't trained or qualified to do anything else. The prospect of embarking, in my fifties, on a new, low-paid career as a cleaner or carer was too grim to contemplate.

I'd hoped having a deadline would focus my mind, but by the time I arrived at Waverley Station the only thing I felt sure of was that, as stories had failed me, my next book would have to be non-fiction.

I arrived with time to spare and, as it wasn't raining and was, for February, remarkably mild, I took a stroll up to the National Gallery.

Access to art was one thing I really missed in my remote country home. I had lots of books, but reproductions just weren't the same as being able to wander around a spacious gallery staring at the original paintings.

It was hard to relax and concentrate on the pictures that day; my mind was jittering around, desperate for an idea. And then all of a sudden, there *she* was.

I knew her, standing there, an imposing female figure in a dark purple robe, crowned with a gold filigreed tiara in her reddish-gold hair, one slim white arm held up commandingly, her pale face stern and angular, not entirely beautiful, but unique, arresting, and as intimately familiar to me as were the fleshy, naked-looking pink and grey swine who scattered and bolted in terror before her. I also knew the pile of stones behind her, and the grove of trees, and, in the middle distance, the sly, crouching figure of her nemesis hiding behind a rock as he watched and waited.

"Circe", 1928, by W. E. Logan.

It was like coming across an old friend in an unfamiliar place. As a college student, I'd had a poster-print of this same painting hanging on the wall of my dormitory room. Later, it had accompanied me to adorn various apartments in New York, Seattle, New Orleans, and Austin, but, despite my affection for it, I'd never bothered to have it framed, and by the time I left for London it was too frayed and torn and stained to move again.

For ten eventful, formative years this picture had been part of my life. I had gazed up at her and Circe had looked down on me through times of heartbreak and exultation, in boredom and in ecstasy. I much preferred the powerful enchantress who would turn men into pigs to the dreamier, more passive maidens beloved of my contemporaries. The walls of my friends' rooms featured reproductions of Pre-Raphaelite beauties: poor, drowned Ophelia, Mariana waiting patiently at her window, Isabella moping over her pot of basil. I preferred Circe's more angular and determined features, her lively, impatient stare: *Cast out that swine!* she advised. *All men are pigs. You don't need them. Live alone, like me, and make magic.*

I gazed with wonder at the original painting. It was so much more vivid and alive than the rather dull tones of the reproduction. Although I'd visited the National Gallery of Scotland many times, I could not remember having seen it here before. Now I noticed details in it that I didn't recall from the reproduction: the distinct shape of oak-leaf, and a scattering of acorns on the ground; a line of alders in the distance – alders, the tree of resurrection and concealment – and above, in a patch of blue sky, hovered a tiny bird, Circe's namesake, the female falcon.

My fascination with this painting when I was younger was mostly to do with the subject matter: I liked pictures that told a story, and the stories I liked best were from ancient mythology. I had been sadly disappointed by all the other paintings by W. E. Logan that I had managed to track down: they were either landscapes (mostly of the South of France) or dull portraits of middle-class Glaswegians.

"Circe", which marked a total departure in style and approach, had also been W. E. Logan's last completed painting. His model was a young art student called Helen Elizabeth Ralston – an American who had gone to Glasgow to study art. Shortly after Logan completed his study of her as the enchantress, she had fallen – or leaped – from the high window of a flat in the west-end of Glasgow. Although badly injured, she survived. Logan had left his wife and children to devote himself to Helen. He paid for her operations and the medical care she needed, and during the long hours he spent sitting at her bedside, he'd made up a story about a little girl who had walked out of a high window and discovered a world of adventure in the clouds high above the city. As he talked, he sketched, creating a sharp-nosed determined little girl menaced and befriended by weird, amorphous cloud-shapes, and then he put the pictures in order, and wrote up the text to create *Hermine in Cloud-Land,* his first book and a popular seller in Britain throughout the 1930s.

The real Helen Ralston was not only Logan's muse and inspiration, but went on to become a successful writer herself. She'd written the cult classic *In Troy,* that amazing, poetic cry of a book, which throughout my twenties had been practically my Bible.

And yet I'd had no idea, when I'd huddled on my bed and lost myself in the mythic story and compelling, almost ritualistic phrases of *In Troy,* that its author was staring down at me from the wall. I'd only discovered that in the early 1980s, when I was living in London and *In Troy* was reprinted as one of those green-backed Virago Classics, with a detail from W. E. Logan's "Circe" on the cover. Angela Carter had written the appreciative introduction to the reprint, and it was there that I had learned of Helen Elizabeth Ralston's relationship with W. E. (Willy) Logan.

Feeling suddenly much livelier, I left the gallery and went down Princes Street to the big bookshop there. I couldn't find *In Troy* or anything else by Helen Ralston in the fiction section. Browsing through the essays and criticism I eventually found a book called *A Late Flowering* by some American academic, which devoted a chapter to the books of Helen Ralston. Willy Logan was better represented. Under "L" in the fiction section was a whole row of his novels, the uniform edition from Canongate. The only book I'd read of his was one based on Celtic mythology, which had been published, with an amazing George Barr cover, in the Ballantine Adult Fantasy line around about 1968. I remembered nothing at all about it now, not even the title.

After a little hesitation I decided to try *In Circe's Snare* for its suggestive title, and I also bought *Second Chance at Life* by Brian Ross, a big fat biography of Logan, recently published. And then I noticed the time and knew I had to run.

II

Selwyn was waiting for me at the restaurant. He stood up, beaming, and came over to give me a close, warm hug.

"My dear. You're looking very well."

I'd been feeling flushed and sweaty, but his appreciative gaze made me feel better. He'd always had the knack of that. Selwyn was an attractive man, even if these days he had to rely on expensive, well-cut clothes to disguise his expanding middle. His hair, no longer long and shaggy, nevertheless was still thick and only slightly sprinkled with grey. When young, he'd worn little round Lennon-type glasses; now, contact lenses made his brown eyes even more liquid, and his eyelashes were as enviably thick and black as I remembered.

"Let's order quickly, and then we can talk," he said after I was settled. "I've already ordered wine, if white's all right with you; if not—"

"It's fine. What do you recommend?"

"Everything is good here; the crab cakes are sensational."

"That sounds good." I was relieved not to have to bother with the menu, being a little out of practice with restaurants. "Crab cakes with a green salad."

Smoothly he summoned the waiter and swiftly sent him away again, and then those brown eyes, gentle yet disconcertingly sharp, were focused on me again. "So. How *are* you? Really."

"Fine. I'm fine. I mean – I'm not, not really, but, you know, life goes on. I'm okay."

"Writing again?"

I took a deep breath and shook my head.

His eyebrows went up. "But – your novel. You were writing a novel."

He meant a year-and-a-half ago.

"It wasn't any good."

"Please. You're much too close to it. You need another perspective. Send it to me, whatever you've got, and I'll give you my thoughts on it. I'll be honest, I promise."

I trusted Selwyn's opinion more than most, but I'd never liked anyone reading my rough drafts – sometimes I could scarcely bear to read them through myself. This one was permeated by Allan, and the happy, hopeful person who had written it was gone.

"There's no point," I said. "I'm not going to finish it. Even if you liked it, even if there's something good in it – too much has changed. I can't get back into that frame of mind; I don't even want to try. I need to get on and write the *next* book."

"All right. That sounds good to me. So what might the next book be?"

To my relief, the waiter arrived with our drinks. When the wine had been poured, I raised my glass to his and said, "To the next book!"

"To the next book," he agreed. We clinked glasses and sipped, and then he waited for me to explain.

Finally I said, "It's going to be non-fiction."

My last non-fiction book had been published nearly fifteen years ago and had been neither a howling success nor a disaster. There had been good reviews, and the first printing had sold out. Unfortunately for me, there was never a second printing, nor the expected paperback sale. The publisher was taken over in mid-process, and my editor was among the many staff members to be "rationalized" and let go. My book got lost in the shuffle, and by the time I'd come up with an idea for another, the fashion had changed, no one was really interested, and my brave new career as an author of popular non-fiction had fizzled out. All that was a very long time ago: I didn't see why I shouldn't be allowed to start again.

Selwyn nodded. When he spoke, I could tell that his thoughts had been following the same track as mine. "It was the publisher's fault that you didn't do a lot better last time. That was a good book, and it always had the potential to be a steady seller on the backlist. I don't know why they didn't stick with it, but it was nothing to do with you – you did a great job with it, and it could have, *should* have, launched a whole new career for you." He paused to take a drink of wine and then looked at me inquiringly. "What sort of non-fiction?"

"Biography?"

"Perfect. With your understanding of characters, your ability to bring them to life in fiction – yes, you'd do very well, writing a life."

Even though I knew it was his job to build me up and promote me, I couldn't help feeling pleased. I responded to his praise like a parched plant to water.

"Really?"

"Absolutely." He beamed. "There's always a demand for good biographies, so selling it shouldn't be tough. I don't know how much I could get you up-front, that would depend – they can be expensive projects, you know, take a long time to write, and there's travel, research . . . of course, there are grants, too—" he broke off suddenly and cocked his head at me. "Now, tell me, do you have a particular subject in mind? Because *who* it is could make a big difference."

"Helen Ralston." Until I spoke, I hadn't really known.

Plenty of well-read people would have responded, quite reasonably, with a blank stare or a puzzled shake of the head. Helen Ralston was hardly a household name, now or ever. Her fame, such as it was, rested entirely on one book. *In Troy* had been published by a small press in the 1930s and developed a kind of underground reputation, read by few but admired by those discerning readers who made the effort. In the 1960s it was published again – in America for the first time – and there was even a mass-market paperback, which is what I'd read in college. It was revived from obscurity once again by Virago in the 1980s, but, from the results of my bookstore visit before lunch, I was pretty sure it was out of print again.

Selwyn knew all this as well as I did. Not only was he a voracious reader, but before becoming an agent he'd been a book-dealer, twentieth-century first editions his specialty.

"I sold my first edition of *In Troy* to Carmen Callil," he said.

I was horrified. "Not to set from?" Reprints like the Virago Classics are photo-offset from other editions, a process that destroys the original book.

He shook his head. "No. She already had a copy of the 1964 Peter Owen edition. She wanted the first for herself. I let her have it for sixty quid. These days, I doubt you could get a first edition for under three hundred."

It always amazed me that people could remember how much they'd paid for things in the past. Such specifics eluded me. I could only remember emotionally, comparatively: something had cost *a lot* or *not much*.

"I should talk to Carmen," I said. "She probably met Helen Ralston when she decided to publish her."

"Probably." He had a thoughtful look on his face. "Didn't we talk about *In Troy* once before? When I was selling *Isis*. *In Troy* had some influence on your book, didn't it?"

I ducked my head in agreement, slightly embarrassed. *Isis* was either my first or my second novel, depending on whether you judged by date of composition or actual publication. Either way, I'd written it a lifetime ago. I could hardly recall the young woman I had been when I'd started it, and by now my attitude toward that novel – once so important to me – was clear-eyed, critical, fond but distant. "Yes, it was my model. Almost too much influence, it had – I didn't realize how deeply I'd absorbed *In Troy* until my second or third revision of *Isis*. Then I had to cut out great tranches of poetic prose because it was too much like hers, and wasn't really *me* at all."

I recalled how I'd been pierced, at the age of nineteen, by the insights and language of *In Troy*. It felt at times like I was reading my own story, only written so much better than I could ever hope to match. It was such an amazingly personal book, I felt it had been written for me alone. If Helen of Troy was Helen Ralston's mythic equivalent for the purposes of her novel, then she was mine. Somehow, the author's affair with her teacher in Scotland was exactly the same as mine, fifty years later in upstate New York. Details of time, space, location and even personal identity were insignificant set in the balance with the eternal truths, the great rhythms of birth and death and change.

I had a genuine, Proustian rush then, the undeniable certainty that time could be conquered. All at once, sitting at a table in an Edinburgh restaurant, the taste of wine sharp and fresh on my tongue, I felt myself still curled in the basket chair in that long-ago dorm room in upstate New York, the smell of a joss-stick from my room-mate's side of the room competing with the clove, orange, and cinnamon scent of the cup of Constant Comment tea I sipped while I read, the sound of Joni Mitchell on the stereo as Helen Ralston's words blazed up at me, changing me and my world forever with the universe-destroying, universe-creating revelation that time is an illusion.

"I was *meant* to write this book," I said to my agent, with all the passion and conviction of the teenager I had been thirty-two years ago.

He didn't grin, but I caught the spark of amusement in his eyes, and it made me scowl with self-doubt. "You think I'm crazy?"

"No. No." He leaned across the table and put his hand firmly on mine. "I think you sound like your old self again."

Our food arrived and we talked about other things.

The crab cakes were, indeed, superb. They were served with a crunchy potato gallette and a delicious mixture of seared red peppers and Spanish onion. My salad included rocket, watercress, baby spinach, and some other tasty and exotic leaves I couldn't identify, all tossed in a subtle, herby balsamic dressing. When I exclaimed at it, Selewyn grinned and shook his head.

"You should get out more. That's a standard restaurant salad."

My nearest restaurant was a twenty-mile drive away, and didn't suit my budget.

"I don't get out much, but I'd make this for myself, if I could get rocket in the Co-Op."

"The Co-Op?" His delivery brought to mind Dame Edith Evans uttering the immortal question – "A handbag?" – in *The Importance of Being Earnest*.

"Does the Co-Op still exist? And you *shop* there?"

"When I must."

"Oh, my dear. When *are* you moving back to civilization?"

"I don't consider that civilization resides in consumer convenience, actually."

"No." He sounded unconvinced. "But what do you *do* out in the country? I mean, what's the great appeal?" Selwyn was such a complete urbanite, he couldn't imagine any use for countryside except to provide a quiet chill-out zone at the weekend.

"I do the same things I'd do anywhere else."

"You'd shop at the Co-Op?"

I laughed. "Well, no. But I can write anywhere."

"Of course you can. And when you're not writing, in the city, there's art galleries, theatres, bookstores . . . what is it you like about the country?"

"The hills, the sea, peace and quiet, going for walks, going sailing. . ."

He was nodding. "I remember, I remember. I grilled you on this before, when you told me you were going to marry your former editor and leave London. I couldn't understand it. *Not* the part about marrying Allan – who was a better man than the publishing world deserved – but why leave London?"

I sighed a little. "We'd decided to down-shift. Allan hated his job; I was fed up in general . . . we figured out we could sell our flats and buy a boat, spend more time together and have a better quality of life on less money there."

"It still suits you?"

I pushed a strip of red pepper around on my plate. That life had been planned for, and suited, two people. After Allan's death I'd taken the advice of my closest friends not to rush into anything or do anything too drastic, so I hadn't moved, or made any major changes to my life. What was the point, anyway? Nothing I could do would change the only thing that really mattered.

"I couldn't afford to move back to London."

"There are other places. Don't tell the folks down south I said so, but I actually prefer Edinburgh. Or Glasgow."

"I guess you haven't checked out property prices since devolution."

"But surely if you sold your farm—"

"It's not a farm, Selwyn, it's a farm *cottage*. A dinky toy. Somebody else owns the farm and the nice big farmhouse and all the land and lets us share the farm track."

"Still, it must be worth something. Think about it. Once you start writing this book you won't want to have the hassle of moving, but you will want to be near a good library."

I thought of myself in a library, surrounded by stacks of books. The idea of having a project, things to look up, real work to do again, was incredibly seductive. "The first thing is to put together a proposal, something I can show around. Just a few basic facts, the reason Helen Ralston is of interest, the stance you're going to take, why she's well overdue for a biography—" he broke off. "There hasn't already been one, has there?"

"Not that I know of."

"Mmm. Better check the more obscure university press catalogues . . . you can do that online. And ask around, just in case somebody is already working on her. It would be good to know."

My heart gave a jolt. "If there was . . . couldn't I still write mine?"

"The trouble is, publishers are always ready to commission a new life of Dickens or Churchill, but nobody wants to publish two 'first' biographies in the same year – probably not even in the same decade."

Until a couple of hours ago, I hadn't given Helen Ralston more than a passing thought in years. I'd had no notion of writing her biography before lunch, and yet now it was the one thing I most wanted to do. I couldn't bear the idea of giving it up.

"How will I find out if somebody else is already doing one?"

"Don't look so tragic! If someone *has* got a commission, it may be some boring old academic who's going to take ten years, and you could get yours out first. Anyway, don't worry about it. Just have a scout around. If there's going to be a biography coming out next year, well, much better to find out now, before you've invested a lot of time and energy in it."

Forewarned wasn't necessarily forearmed, I thought. I didn't put much stock in the theory of minimizing pain that way. If I'd known in advance that Allan would die of a heart attack at the age of sixty it wouldn't have hurt any less when it happened, and it wouldn't have stopped me loving him. I did know, when I married him, that his father had died of a heart attack at sixty, and even without that genetic factor, the statistical chances were that I'd outlive him by a couple of decades. I came of sturdy peasant stock, and the women in my family were long-lived.

"How do I scout around? I mean, who do I talk to?"

"You could start with her."

"Her? You mean Helen Ralston?"

He was surprised by my surprise. "She is still alive."

"Is she? She'd be awfully old."

"Ninety-six or ninety-seven. Not impossible. I don't remember seeing an obituary of her in the last few years."

"Me either. I'm sure I would have noticed. Well. I guess they might still have an address for her at Virago. And there's a biography of Willy Logan, quite new, that should have something." I patted the heavy square shape of it in the bag slung across the side of my chair.

"Dessert? No? Coffee?" He summoned the waiter and, when he'd gone away again, turned back to me. "By the way, I know someone who owns one of Helen Ralston's paintings."

"'By the way'?"

He smiled. "Really, I just remembered. And he lives here in Edinburgh. An old friend. I should probably call in on him while I'm here – are you free for the rest of this afternoon, or do you have to rush off?"

"I'm free. Do you mean it? I'd love to see it!"

I felt a little stunned by this sudden unexpected bonus. While Selwyn got out his phone and made the call I tried to imagine what a Helen Ralston painting would look like. Although I knew she'd been an art student, I thought of her always as a writer, and I'd never seen so much as a description of one of her paintings. That it should have fallen into my lap like this, before I'd even started work, did not strike me as odd or unusual. Everyone who writes or researches knows that this sort of serendipity – the chance discovery, the perfectly timed meeting, the amazing coincidence – is far from rare. The fact that this first one had come along so soon, before I was definitely committed to the project, just confirmed my feeling: I was *meant* to write this book.

III

Selwyn's friend lived a short cab ride away in an area known as The Colonies. This was a collection of quaint, tidy little cottages set in eleven parallel terraces, built, he told me, in 1861 to provide affordable housing for respectable artisans and their families, and now much in demand among singles and young professional couples for their central location and old-fashioned charm.

The sight of these neat little houses set out like a model village in narrow, cobbled streets roused the long-dormant American tourist in me, and before I could crush her down again I was gushing, "Ooh, they're so *cute!*"

The big black cab had to stop on the corner to let us out, as it clearly would not be able to turn around if it went any further.

"They're just adorable!" I became more excited as I noticed the window boxes and trim green lawns. In its day, this had been inexpensive housing, but that hadn't translated into an ugly utilitarianism. The houses were small – I couldn't imagine how they'd ever been thought suitable for the large families people had in the old days – but their proportions were appealing to the eye, and they didn't look cramped. "What a great place to live – so quiet and pretty, like a village, but right in the middle of the city. You could walk everywhere from here, or bike, you wouldn't even need a car."

Selwyn was looking amused. "I'll get Alistair to let you know as soon as one comes on the market. They're very much in demand, but with advance notice maybe you could put in a pre-emptive bid."

"I didn't mean *I* wanted to live here—" but as I spoke, I thought again. Why shouldn't it be me living the life I'd suddenly glimpsed, in a small, neat, pretty house or a flat within an ancient city? I still loved the country, but after all, there were trains and buses for whenever

I wanted a day out, and these days I was feeling distinctly more starved of culture than I was of fresh air and wide open spaces.

"Well," I said, changing tack, "If you can re-launch my career, I will definitely think about re-launching my life."

He draped an arm loosely about my shoulders and led me gently down the street. "*We* – the operative word is *we* – are going to re-launch your career, big-time. Turn in at the green gate."

The house where Selwyn's friend lived was divided into two residences, top and bottom. His was upstairs, the front door reached by a rather elegant sweeping curve of stairs.

A thin, neat, very clean-looking old man opened the door to us. This was Alistair Reid. He had a long nose and slightly protuberant bright blue eyes in a reddish, taut-skinned face. His cheeks were as shiny as apples – I imagined him buffing them every morning – and his sleeked back hair was cream-coloured.

"I've just put the kettle on," he said, leading us into his sitting room. "Indian, or China?"

He was looking at me. I looked at Selwyn.

"China, if you've got it."

"I should hardly make the offer if I hadn't got it," the old man said reprovingly. But despite his tone there was a twinkle in his eye, so I guessed it was meant to be a joke. "Please, make yourselves at home. I'll not be long," he said as he left us.

I looked around the room, which was light and airy and beautifully furnished. It was clear even to my untutored eye that the delicate writing table beside the window, the glass-fronted bookcase in the corner, and the dark chest beside the door were all very old, finely made, unique pieces that were undoubtedly very expensive. Even the couch where Selwyn and I perched had a solidity and individuality about it that suggested it had not been mass-produced.

The pale walls were hung with paintings. I got up and went to look at them. One wall displayed a series of watercolour landscapes, the usual Scottish scenes of mountains, water, cloud-streaked skies and island-dotted seas. They were attractive enough, yet rather bland; more accomplished than my own attempts, but nothing special.

Beside the bookcase were two still-lifes in oils: one, very realistic and very dark, looked old; I guessed it could be two or three hundred years old. It depicted a large dead fish lying on a marble slab with a bundle of herbs and, incongruously, a single yellow flower. The other painting was much more modern in style, an arrangement of a blue bowl, dull silver spoon, and bright yellow lemon on a surface in front of a window, partly visible behind a blue and white striped curtain.

The largest painting in the room had a whole wall to itself. It was the portrait of a young woman. She had smartly bobbed hair and wore a long single strand of pearls against a dark green tunic. I stared at this picture for some time before noticing that it was signed in the lower left-hand corner with the initials W. E. L.

Alistair Reid came in with a tray, which he set down on a small table near the couch. I went back to take a seat and saw, with some dismay, that besides the tea he'd brought a plate of thinly sliced, liberally buttered white bread and another plate piled high with small, iced cakes.

"Store-bought, I'm afraid," he said in his soft, lilting voice. "But I can recommend them. They're really rather nice. Or would you rather have sandwiches? I wasn't sure. It won't take me a moment to make them if you'd like. Ham, or cheese, or anchovy paste, or tomato."

"Thank you, Alistair, you're more than kind, but we've just had lunch," Selwyn said. He turned to me. "You know the old joke, that in Glasgow unexpected afternoon visitors are greeted with the cry of 'You'll be wanting your tea, then,' whereas in Edinburgh, no matter the time, it's always, 'You'll have had your tea, then.'" He shot a grin in the old man's direction. "Well, I should have warned you, but Alistair has devoted his *life* to disproving that calumny on the hospitable souls of native Edinburghers."

"Oh, go on, I know you've a sweet tooth," Alistair said, not quite smiling.

"Well, I think I might just manage a fancy or two," said Selwyn.

I took a slice of bread and butter and eventually allowed a cake to be pressed upon me, glad that we'd skipped dessert. The tea was light and delicate, flavoured with jasmine blossoms.

Alistair leaned towards me. "I believe when I came in I saw you admiring the portrait of my mother?"

"That was your mother? Painted by W. E. Logan?"

He nodded, eyelids drooping a little. "Long before I was born, of course. Her father commissioned it in 1926. It was quite possibly the last portrait W. E. Logan ever painted, apart from some studies of Helen Ralston, of course." He gestured towards the watercolour landscapes. "And those are my mother's."

"Your mother was an artist, too?"

He shook his head. "Oh, no. My mother painted purely for her own enjoyment. I have them on display because they remind me of her and because of where they were painted. It's where we always took our summer holidays, on the west-coast, in Argyll."

"That's where I'm from!"

"Really? I'd have guessed you're from much further west." A teasing smile flickered about his thin lips.

I felt a little weary and tried not to show it. No matter how long I lived in Britain – and it was now nearly a quarter of a century – I could never pass for native. As soon as I opened my mouth I was a foreigner, always required to account for my past. Yet I didn't want to be unkind or rude, and it wasn't fair to take offence where none was intended. Scots, unlike some other Europeans, were generally fond of Americans.

"I was born in Texas," I said. "Later I lived in New York, and then London. I've been living in Argyll for just over ten years. It's a tiny little place called Mealdarroch, not far from—"

"But that's exactly where we stayed!" he exclaimed. "It was always Mealdarroch, or Ardfern." Looking delighted, he turned to Selwyn. "My dear, how marvellous! You never said you were bringing someone from Mealdarroch! My favourite spot in the universe!" He turned back to me. "You sail, of course."

"We – I – have a boat. My husband loved to sail. Since he died, I haven't felt like taking her out on my own."

"Oh, my dear, I am so sorry." His sharp blue eyes were suddenly gentle.

I looked down at my teacup, into the light gold liquid, and thought of how one might recreate that colour in a watercolour wash. After a moment I could face him again, quite calm.

"I was looking at your pictures trying to guess which one was by Helen Ralston. But if the watercolours are your mother's, and the portrait by Logan—"

His eyes widened. "Oh, that's not hanging in here! I could hardly have it on display to all and sundry – far too risky!"

I thought at first he was speaking of *risk* before I realized he meant the painting itself was *risqué* – did he mean it was a nude figure? But nudes had been common currency in fine art for a long time and surely were acceptable even in buttoned-down Calvinist Scotland?

Alistair turned to Selwyn. "Didn't you explain?"

"I thought she'd better see for herself."

I tried to imagine it. Had Helen Ralston turned the tables on the male-dominated art world and depicted her lover in the altogether?

Willy Logan and his little willy? And if it wasn't so little, or dangling
. . ? The erect penis was taboo even today.

"May I see it?"

"But of course. Drink up your tea. Sure you won't have another
fancy cake? No? Selwyn? Oh, go on, dear boy, no one cares about
your figure now!"

We went out by the door we had come in, back into the tiny
entrance-way, where a steep, narrow staircase rose to the left.

"Go halfway up the stair," Alistair instructed. "It's too narrow for
more than one person at a time. You'll see it hanging on the wall just
at the turn of the stair."

It certainly was narrow and steep. Maybe that was the reason for
the inclusion of the little half-landing, to give the intrepid climber a
space to pause and make a ninety-degree turn before mounting to
the floor above.

The picture hung on the wall that faced the second flight of stairs.
It was about eight inches by ten inches, or the size of a standard sheet
of paper torn from an artist's pad. I saw a watercolour landscape, not
so very different from the pictures hanging in the room downstairs.

Then there was a click from the hall below, and the shaded bulb
above my head blazed, illuminating the picture.

I gazed at the painted image of an island, a rocky island rendered
loosely in shades of brown and green and grey and greyish pink. I
remained unimpressed, and baffled by Alistair's attitude towards this
uninspired daub. *Risky?*

And then, all at once, as if another light had been switched on,
I saw the hidden picture. Within the contours of the island was a
woman. A woman, naked, on her back, her knees up and legs splayed
open, her face hidden by a forearm flung across it and by the long
hair – greenish, greyish – that flowed around her like the sea.

The centre of the painting, what drew the eye and commanded
the attention, was the woman's vulva: all the life of the painting
was concentrated there. A slash of pink, startling against the mossy
greens and browns, seemed to touch a nerve in my own groin.

One immediate, furious thought rose in my mind: *How could she
expose herself like that?*

Somehow I knew this was a self-portrait, that the artist would not
have exploited another woman in this way. Yet she had not flinched
from depicting *herself* as naked, passive, open, sexually receptive
– no, sexually voracious, demanding to be looked at, to be taken,
explored, used, filled . . .

Well, why not? I was all in favour of female autonomy, in the freedom of women to act out of their own desires, whatever they were. After all, I still called myself a feminist, and I had come of age during the 1960s, a member of the post-Pill, pre-AIDS, sexually liberated generation who believed in letting it all hang out, and a woman's right to choose.

And yet – and yet—

Whatever theory I held, the sight of this picture made me cringe away in revulsion, even fear. As if this was something I should not have seen, something that should not have been revealed. It was deeper than reason; I simply felt there was something wrong and *dangerous* in this painting.

Then, like a cloud passing across the sun, the atmosphere changed again. Outlines blurred, colours became drab, and abruptly the painting was only the depiction of an island in the sea.

But I knew now what was hidden in those rocky outlines, and I didn't trust it to stay hidden. I turned away immediately and saw the two men standing at the bottom of the stairs, looking up at me.

There was a sudden rush of blood to my head: my cheeks burned. They knew what I'd been looking at; they'd seen it, too. And then, far worse than the embarrassment, came a clutch of fear, because I was a woman, and my only way out was blocked by two men.

The moment passed. The old man went back into the other room, and I was looking down at Selwyn, whom I'd known for twenty years.

I hated the fact that I was blushing, but I'd look even more of a fool if I hovered there on the landing waiting for the red to fade, so I went down. Unostentatiously polite as ever, he turned away, allowing me to follow him into the sitting room where Alistair waited for us.

Selwyn cleared his throat. "Well—"

"Sit down," said the old man. "You'll want to hear the story. First, let me fetch down the picture. There's something written on the back that you should see."

In uneasy silence, we sat down. The silence was uneasy on my part, anyway, as I struggled to understand my own reaction. I was not a prude, and although hardcore porn made me uncomfortable, mere nudity didn't. I had no problem, usually, with images of healthy female bodies and I'd seen beaver shots before, far more graphic than Helen Ralston's *trompe-l'œil* depiction.

In the nineteenth century Gustave Courbet had painted a detailed, close-up, highly realistic view of a woman's pubic area, calling it "The Origin of the World". At the time, this was a deeply shocking thing to have done, and although Courbet was a well-respected artist, the painting could not be shown. Now, of course, it could be seen by anyone who cared to call up a reproduction on the internet, purchased in museum shops all over the world as a post card or poster, and for all I knew it was available on T-shirts and mouse-mats, too.

Courbet's realistic depiction was far more graphic than Ralston's impressionistic watercolour, and it might be argued that, as a male artist, he was objectifying women, serving her sexual parts up on canvas for the viewing pleasure of his fellow men, whereas Ralston had been exploring her own feelings about herself with, possibly, no intention of ever having it on public display. The question I should be asking myself was why, when Courbet's picture did not disturb me, hers *did*.

Alistair returned, carrying the picture. He handed it to me, face down, and I took it, gingerly, awkwardly, into my lap.

"I had it mounted with a bit cut away at the back so you can still see what she wrote," he explained.

I looked down and had my first sight of Helen Ralston's bold, clear handwriting:

> *My Death*
> *April 14, 1929*
> *This, like all I own or produce, is for*
> *My Beloved Willy*
> *HER*

I shivered and made to pass it to Selwyn, but he demurred: he'd seen it before. So I went on holding it in my lap, feeling it slowly burning a hole in me, and looked at Alistair.

"Why 'My Death'? Did she mean . . . sexuality equates with death?"

He spread his hands. "Much more than that, I'm sure. The two of them used certain words almost as if they were a special code, and capital-D Death was one of them. And consider the painting: the woman is also an island. A particular island, from your part of the world," he added with a nod at me. "In fact, I must have sailed past it many times myself on our family holidays, although I don't think we ever landed there. According to Willy Logan in his memoirs, the moment she set eyes upon the island she declared, 'I've seen my death.' Whether 'my death' meant the same as capital-D Death to them, I couldn't say, but clearly it wasn't perceived as a threat or I'm sure they would have sailed away, rather than dropping anchor and going ashore, full of excitement, to explore."

I knew that in the Tarot the Death card did not signify physical demise, but rather meant a sudden, dramatic change of fortune. And sometimes people had to dare death in order to regain their lives. I wondered if Helen Ralston had been a precursor of Sylvia Plath, if she was another Lady Lazarus, making death her life's art. First, out of a window into the air; the second time, on a rocky island . . .

"What happened? Did something happen there?"

"Logan went blind," Selwyn told me.

I had known, of course, that Logan had lost his sight – the transformation of a rather dull, society painter into the blind poetic visionary was the most famous thing about him. But I didn't know how it had happened. "On the island? Some sort of accident?"

"No accident," said Alistair crisply. "Haven't you read *Touched by the Goddess?* You must read Logan's memoirs. His explanation . . . well, it's hardly satisfactory, but it's all we have. No one will ever know what *really* happened."

Had Logan intervened somehow, I wondered. Had the Death waiting for Helen been made to give her up, but taken Logan's sight in exchange? It was clear that Alistair wasn't going to tell – if he knew.

"How did you come to have the painting?" Selwyn asked.

"You know I was an art and antiques dealer back in the 1970s and '80s. Torquil Logan – Willy's youngest son – was on the fringe of the trade himself, and that was how we knew each other. When the old man died, although his literary agent was the executor of his estate, it was the sons and daughters who did all the donkey work of clearing out his things and deciding what should be sold, or given away, shipped to the library that was to have the official collection, or whatever. Torquil got in touch with me when he came across 'My Death' – it was in an envelope at the back of a file of old letters and probably had not been seen in fifty years.

"He knew what it was, straight away. Well, of course: it was described in *Touched by the Goddess* right down to the inscription on the back, and invested with huge significance as the last work of art he ever looked at, the final gift from his mistress/muse, and even as a sort of premonition of what was about to happen to him, his blinding by the goddess.

"And Torquil didn't know what to do with it. *He* didn't want it; in fact, he told me, he felt a sort of revulsion about the very thought of having it in his house. He couldn't ask his mother – she was in poor health and quite devastated by the loss of her husband; he didn't want to take any risks by even reminding her in any way of the existence of Helen Ralston. He'd considered leaving it in the envelope and slipping it into one of the boxes destined for the library – it would be safe enough in a university collection, he thought, and yet the idea of students looking at it and writing about it in their theses made him feel queasy, just as did the thought of it going into a public auction, to be numbered and listed and described in a catalogue."

Alistair paused and took a deep breath. Then he went on. "I offered to take care of it for him. I promised there'd be no publicity. In fact, I said, if the price was right, I'd be happy to buy it for myself, not to sell on. Torq knew, because we'd talked about it, just how important Willy Logan's books had been to me. Especially as a young man. That mystical strand of his, the idea that the old gods are still alive in the land and can be brought back to life through us, *in* us – I can't quite explain how deeply that affected me, but the idea of owning something that had belonged to him, which had been so deeply, personally meaningful, was irresistible.

"And Torquil said I could have it. In fact, he said he would like to *give* it to me. He didn't want payment; it didn't seem right to sell it. I protested, but he wouldn't hear of it. In fact, he mailed it to me that same day, by ordinary post, in a padded envelope, but otherwise unprotected – when I think how easily it could have been lost or damaged . . ."

We all stared at the thing in my lap. Unable to bear it any longer, I lifted the framed painting like a tray and held it out to Alistair. When he didn't respond, I glared at him, but still he made no move to take it away.

"I could never sell it," he said quietly. "I've respected Torquil's feelings about that. And yet, I've never felt right about owning it. It came to me by chance." He paused. His tongue appeared at the corner of his mouth and ran quickly around his lips. "I'd like you to have it."

"Me!" I felt the same unexpectedly sexual shock I'd had on first recognizing the hidden meaning of the picture I now held. "Oh, no, I couldn't. It's not right."

"Selwyn tells me you're writing a biography of Helen Ralston. I've felt for some time that the painting should go back to her, but I didn't know how to approach her. It seemed too difficult, and potentially too disturbing. How would she feel to learn that a male stranger had this very personal thing? Yet she might want it back. And it *is* hers, by rights, since Willy's death. It might come more easily from another woman, and, as her biographer, you'll be in on lots of intimate secrets; she'll have to accept that . . ."

"I don't know that she'll even accept me as her biographer. I can't. I don't even know if she's still alive." I couldn't seem to stop shaking my head.

"Of course she will. Of course she is. And if she doesn't want it, or you can't find her, and you don't feel you can keep it yourself, well, you could always mail it back to me in a plain brown envelope. Please."

And although I really didn't want to do it, in the end I found it impossible not to agree.

I'd booked a room for the night at Jury's hotel, which was located just behind the train station. I'd planned, when I'd booked, to take myself out for a nice dinner and to see a movie, but by the time I'd parted from Selwyn, very late in the afternoon, the only thing I wanted was to find out more about Helen Ralston.

I hit another bookshop, where I determined that *In Troy* was definitely out of print, and so was that old-fashioned children's classic *Hermine in Cloud-Land*. "But you can find loads of second-hand copies on the Internet," a helpful clerk assured me.

"Thanks, I'll do that when I get home," I said, and paid for a copy of *Touched by the Goddess*. I bought a selection of interesting-looking gourmet salads from Marks and Spencer – ah, the luxuries of city life! – and settled into my hotel room to read everything in the big fat biography of Willy Logan that had anything to do with Helen Ralston.

IV

She was the girl from faraway, the girl from another land, and she swept into the dreich damp grey streets of Glasgow like a warm wind, smelling of exotic spices and a hint of dangerous mystery. She claimed to be half-Greek and half-Irish, with a mother who told fortunes and a father possessed of the second sight. She herself, according to at least one bewildered classmate, was subject to "fits" when she would go rigid and begin to prophesy in a voice manifestly not her own – afterwards, she appeared exhausted and claimed to remember nothing.

In appearance, she made a most unlikely *femme fatale*. She was small and skinny, with sharp features, including a prominent nose, and her eyes, although large and lustrous, were disturbingly deep-set. Logan's portrait glamorized her; the few photographs taken of Helen Ralston in the late 1920s reveal an odd shrunken figure who appeared prematurely old.

Helen Elizabeth Ralston was a new student on the rolls of The Glasgow School of Art in September 1927; prior to that she had studied at Syracuse University, New York. Her reasons for departing New York for Glasgow are unknown. She had no Scottish connections whatsoever, and was far from wealthy. Although her tuition fees were paid in advance, she clearly found it a struggle to pay for supplies and other necessities of life. A fellow student, Mabel Scott Smith, who recalls buying her dinner more than once, made it a practice to bring along an extra bun for Helen at tea time: "She would pretend she'd forgotten, or that she wasn't hungry, but the truth was, she didn't have a penny to spare. Everybody knew she was broke, even though you thought Americans must all be rich. She went around with a portfolio of drawings, trying to sell to the papers, but she never had a hope. She was good, but so were plenty others, and times were hard. It was even worse in Glasgow than in other places; you couldn't make money from pretty pictures there, not then."

The budding friendship between Mabel and Helen came to an abrupt end when the American student moved out of her shared lodgings and into a West End flat paid for by W. E. Logan. Mabel Smith: "It wasn't the sex – we art school girls had quite a liberal attitude towards that! – but that she would let herself be *kept* and by a married man! I lost my respect for Mr Logan, too."

Logan noticed the "young-old" quality of Helen Ralston's face during his first class with her, and invited her to sit for him on Saturday afternoon. He singled out several students like this every year; there was nothing unusual, or improper, in his attentions. But from her first sitting it was clear that Helen would be different. Fixing her large, hypnotic eyes upon him, she began to speak and immediately held him spell-bound by her stories.

These were probably mostly a retelling of myths and legends from many different cultures, Russian fairy tales mingled with Greek myths, and Celtic motifs interwoven with material stolen from the Arabian Nights. To Logan they were pure magic, igniting in him the passion for myth that would dominate his life.

In his autobiography Logan writes of certain "magical" moments in his early childhood. Apart from that, however, there is no evidence that he experienced any significant mystical or spiritual leanings before meeting Helen Ralston.

Despite the stories she told him about her background, Helen Elizabeth Ralston had neither Greek nor Irish blood. Her parents, Ben and Sadie Rudinski, were Polish Jews who arrived in New York around 1890. By the time their last child, Helen, was born in Brooklyn in 1907, the family fortunes were thriving. Helen's artistic ambitions were encouraged, and she was both educated and indulged. As America prepared to go to war in 1917, the Rudinskis changed their name to Ralston – around this time, Helen adopted Elizabeth as a middle name and began signing her drawings with the initials HER.

Helen did well at school and was accepted into the undergraduate liberal arts program at Syracuse University. Her grades from her freshman year were good, and she participated in the drama society (painting sets and making costumes rather than acting) and contributed to the student newspaper and seemed in general to have settled. But instead of returning as expected for a second year, Helen Elizabeth Ralston applied to the Glasgow School of Art, and embarked on a new life in Great Britain.

Logan wrote later that she made this great change in her life on the prompting of a dream. He also believed that her parents were dead, that she was an only child, and that she had been self-supporting since the age of thirteen. It is impossible to know for certain when the relationship between them altered and they became lovers, as Logan is uncharacteristically reticent about this in his memoirs. But by January 1928 he had begun to paint "Circe", and by March she was living in the flat for which he paid the rent, and to which he was a frequent visitor.

After January, although she did not formally withdraw from the School, Helen attended fewer and fewer classes, until, by March, the other students scarcely saw her at all, unless she was in Logan's company. Their relationship was certainly gossiped about, but Logan's reputation was such that some thought him above suspicion. He was a respectable family man, with several children and a beautiful, gentle wife from a well-to-do Edinburgh background. The American student was such an odd creature it was hard to credit that the great W. E. Logan was seriously attracted to her.

He had often taken a paternal interest in his students, male and female, and had even been known to make small financial contributions to help support those who were talented but poor. Helen Ralston clearly fell into that category. Brian Ross, Logan's biographer, suggested that Logan's natural innocence combined with generosity and good intentions might have got him into trouble. He thought that Helen had fallen in love with the great man, who had been interested in her only as a model. When "Circe" was finished, and it became clear that he would no longer be spending so much time alone in the studio with her, she had thrown herself out of the window in despair, and only then had he become aware of her true feelings for him.

I shut Ross's book in disgust. In the whole history of human relationships, how many men had ever rented an expensive flat for an unrelated female without expecting sexual favours in return? If she'd been one-sidedly in love with him, her suicide attempt would have been his signal to run like hell, not to abandon wife and children to nurse her back to health. Logan's sacrifice only made sense if he was deeply in love with her, and her leap had shocked him into recognizing his responsibilities.

I was willing to believe that it had been one-sided – on *his* part. She might have stopped going to art school to avoid him, even though her poverty had forced her into accepting his financial support, and she might have hoped that, once he no longer needed her to model for "Circe" she would have nothing more to do with him. Only he wouldn't let her go maybe he'd turned up that August day not to say goodbye, but to tell her he was going to leave his wife and children to live with her. I imagined her backing away from him, evading his hands, his lips, his unwanted declarations of undying devotion until, in a last, desperate squirm out of his arms, she'd fallen out of the window.

I frowned as I considered this. What sort of window was it? How did a conscious, healthy adult fall out of a window? I found it hard to visualize from Ross's description – he said she was "sitting on the window ledge." Sideways, or with her back to the air? It was August, and hot, so naturally enough the windows were open. Did she lean too far back and lose her balance, or did she deliberately swivel around and jump?

I picked up *Touched by the Goddess* and paged through it looking for references to Hermine, which was his name for Helen. There was no index. One reference leaped out at me:

Truth then flying out the window, Hermine went after it. She caught it, although she nearly died in the attempt, and so restored me to the way of truth, and life.

Well, that was a lot of help. Logan was concerned with myth, as he saw it, a deeper truth than mere facts could provide.

I turned back to Ross again. It seemed that, however briefly, an attempted murder charge had been considered, on the grounds of Logan's distraught "confession" to a policeman at the hospital to which Helen had been taken. Undoubtedly, he'd been filled with feelings of guilt, but was it the guilt of a violent seducer, or that of a man who felt torn between two women, or simply what anyone close to an attempted suicide might feel? Even his actual words at the time were unclear. And, as Ross pointed out, suicide was a crime, so Logan might have been trying to save Helen from prosecution and/or deportation for attempted self-murder by suggesting it was really his fault.

More than one story could be told about what had happened in that room in Glasgow, a room with an open window, four storeys up, on a warm August day in 1928. There had been only two witnesses, who were also the protagonists, or the protagonist and the antagonist, the two people in the room, Willy Logan and Helen Ralston.

Ross wrote far more clearly and simply than Logan in his attempt to establish the truth, but, as far as I could see, he was no less biased, and no more reliable, because there was only one story he wanted to tell, and that was Willy Logan's. Helen's experience, her interpretation, her story, was nowhere in his book.

I went back to the beginning and made my way carefully through the acknowledgments. This ran to over two pages of names of all the people who had helped him in some way, and Helen Ralston's name was not included. If she was dead, I thought, he might have quoted from one of her books or letters – surely she had written about her relationship with Logan at some point, to someone? Some of the passages from *In Troy* could well have been pertinent. His restraint made me think he must have been refused permission to quote, with possibly the threat of legal action if he said anything about her that could be deemed offensive . . . the libel laws in Britain were pretty fierce, and if the old lady had a taste for litigation that would have tied his hands.

I read swiftly through the pages that dealt with Logan's desertion of his family, his devoted vigils beside Helen's hospital bed, the loss of his job scarcely registering on him, her surgery, the creation of little Hermine and her adventures, then Helen's convalescence in the West End flat, now *their* home, until, in the spring of 1929, although she still had to walk with a cane, Helen was deemed well enough to travel, and Logan took her on a sailing holiday up the west coast. In the fresh air away from the city they would rest and sketch and grow strong, Willy wrote in a letter to his son Torquil, adding:

I hope you know how much I love you, darling boy, and that I don't stay away out of crossness or dislike or any wrong reason, but only because Helen needs me so much more than the rest of you do. She has been very ill, you know, but finally is getting better. I hope soon she will be well enough to meet you. I have written and drawn a funny little story for her which I think you will like, too. It is to be published as a book in September, and I have told the publishers to be sure to send you your very own copy . . .

On their first day out, they spotted a small island. In Logan's description, Helen went "rigid", her face paled, and her large, shiny eyes seemed to become even larger, a trio of symptoms which had always heralded her prophesying fits. This time all she said was, "I've seen my death. My death is there."

Logan never explained why, in that case, he didn't just sail as far away from the island as he could. To him, it was self-evidently necessary to go where Helen had foreseen her own death. In his novel *In Circe's Snare* (1948) Logan has Odysseus declare, "Every man must seek his own death."

"And every woman, too," Circe chimed in quickly. "If, that is, she wishes to be more than just a woman."

On the charts the island bears the name of *Eilean nan Achlan*. At the time, this probably meant nothing to Logan, but later, when he began his study of Gaelic, he would have found that it bears the meaning "the isle of lamentation".

Modern archaeologists believe that Achlan was an important funerary site in pre-Christian Scotland. Not only the name points to this conclusion, but the many cairns, including one large chambered tomb, still awaiting serious excavation today, believed to have been in use for a period of several hundred years. There was a tradition for a long time on the west coast of interring the dead on uninhabited islands reserved for that purpose. More often these islands were located in lakes or inland lochs, but Achlan's position in the straits of Jura, relatively near to the mainland shore, would have made it equally accessible and therefore suitable for this purpose.

Because it was late in the day, they did not attempt to land just then, but dropped anchor and spent the night on board in view of the little island. While the light was good they both made watercolour sketches of it. What Logan thought of his own painting – the last he would ever produce – or what became of it is not recorded. But, as Logan recalled in *Touched by the Goddess,* Helen's swiftly rendered landscape was "technically remarkably assured, and quite surprising; the most remarkable piece of work I ever saw her produce." He expressed his belief that already "The Goddess was working through her." On the back of the little sketch she wrote the title "My Death," the date – April 14 1929 – and a dedication to her lover.

Reading this, I was quite certain that Brian Ross had never set eyes on the painting he seemed to describe. The passage was footnoted; I looked it up and read, "The current whereabouts of this painting is unknown. Personal correspondence with Torquil Logan."

I looked across the room where the painting now lay in a plain brown envelope. Alistair would have been happy to give me the frame, but I thought it would be too much to cart around. After all, I didn't intend to hang it, but just return it to the woman who had painted it.

The morning of April 15 1929 dawned calm and fine. The sun was shining, the air warm for April, and quite still: perfect weather for exploring the island. Helen stripped off her clothes, wrapped them in a Sou'wester to make a waterproof bundle she could carry on top of her head, and slipped over the side of the boat while Willy was still blinking sleep from his eyes. She gave a sudden sharp hiss as the salt water hit her scarred back and legs: the sight of those raw, red wounds against her pale flesh seemed to reproach Willy, and although the water was not very deep he felt obliged to follow her lead and strip completely rather than just removing shoes and trousers as he would have preferred.

Naked as Adam and Eve they emerged from the sea to set foot on their new Eden. As they travelled inland, the two noticed signs of ancient human activity everywhere: burial mounds, standing stones, and slabs covered with the obsessively repeated cup and ring markings that appear throughout the west of Scotland and Ireland, their ancient significance long forgotten. Eventually they came upon the ruins of some old building, and a well. Although it was more likely to have been either an enclosure for sheep, or an early Christian hermit's cell, Logan decided their find was a "shrine" or "temple", and proclaimed this the *omphalos* of the island where they would rest, and drink the good fresh water, and give thanks to the Goddess.

In later years, Willy Logan would connect the Gaelic *Achlan* with the ancient Greek *Aeaea* "wailing", the name of the "typical death island" that was the home of the enchantress Circe.

After their pagan prayers, they made love within the boundaries of the shrine. According to his much later account, this act was at Helen's urging and was the first sexual intercourse they'd had since her fall. Yet all did not go as planned. Reading between the lines, it appears that Willy was unable to sustain an erection. Determined to please his mistress, he had to use "other means". Oral sex is fairly obviously implied. He brought his lover to orgasm – his surprise suggests that this, too, may have been a first – and almost immediately after that, darkness fell. His lover's transformed, contorted face was the last thing he ever saw.

An annihilating blow, for an artist to lose his sight, and this event became the centre of the myth that Willy Logan was to create of his life. Although it was a moment of terror, in his writing he would describe it in terms more of awe than of fear, and of discovery and re-birth rather than of death and loss.

"The Goddess is come!" he cried (or so he claims, in his autobiography). "Oh, how she dazzles!" Then: "Where is She? Where is the sun? Is it night?" So suddenly, orgasmically, W. E. Logan had been plunged into perpetual night, yet spiritually, he might have said "I was blind, but now can see."

With *Touched by the Goddess* open beside *Second Chance at Life*, it was easy to see how closely Ross followed Logan's own account. Yet although he did not accept every detail uncritically, he did no more than provide a slightly ironic commentary as counterpoint to Logan's "facts". No matter how I struggled and searched, I could find no other voice, no other view, but Logan's. Helen's absence was glaring. In Logan's own autobiography, Helen was less an individual than an idea, and in Ross's book she was scarcely even that.

Yet she had certainly been there on the island; and if Logan wanted to blame her for his blindness (I was shocked by his choosing to quote, without irony, a sixteenth-century Arabian scholar who declared that any man who looked into a woman's vagina would go blind), he had also to recognize that she had saved him.

While Willy wept and raved about the Goddess, Helen managed to get him back onto the boat, which she then sailed, single-handed, into Crinan Harbour. (And where, I wondered, had the girl from New York learned to sail?)

Fortunately for them, a doctor from Glasgow was staying with his wife in the Crinan Hotel – and the wife turned out to be some sort of second-cousin to Logan's mother. They immediately offered to cut short their holiday and drive Logan and Helen to Glasgow, where he could be seen by specialists.

By the time they reached Glasgow, Logan was almost supernaturally calm. He had accepted his blindness, he was convinced it was permanent and that nothing could be done about it. But his wish to go home with Helen was overruled. A bed was found for him at the Western Infirmary and arrangements were made for a battery of tests and examinations by a variety of specialists as soon as possible.

In the meantime, all were agreed, he must rest. Once she'd seen him settled in, Helen Ralston went to the nearest post office to dispatch a telegram to Mrs William Logan, whom she knew to be staying with the children and her parents in Edinburgh.

> WILLY BLIND PLEASE COME AT ONCE
> GLASGOW WESTERN INFIRMARY

She did not sign the telegram. As soon as it was sent, she went to the flat she'd shared with Willy and packed her bags. She left Glasgow that night, on a train bound for London, and never saw or directly communicated with Willy Logan again.

What would make someone who had painted a sexually explicit portrait of herself, dedicating it to her beloved, abandon that same man, blind and helpless, only twenty-four hours later? Brian Ross did not speculate or comment. I wondered who she went to in London.

I checked the index for further references to Helen Ralston. There were only a few, and every one of them concerned something Logan had written later about their brief time together (most of them clustered in the chapter about the writing of *Touched by the Goddess* in 1956). You'd never know from this book that Helen Ralston had ever done or been anything of the slightest importance in the world except to be, for a little while, Logan's chief muse and model. None of her books were listed in the "Selected Bibliography" at the end, not even *In Troy*.

I became all the more determined to tell Helen Ralston's story.

V

I didn't sleep well that night – I rarely do, away from home. I had brief, disturbing dreams. The one that frightened me most, making me wake with a gasp and a pounding heart, was about "My Death". I dreamed that when I got home and took the picture out to look at it, I found it was just an ordinary watercolour sketch of island, sea and sky, no more unusual or accomplished than one of my own.

I don't know why that should have been so terrifying – especially considering how upsetting I'd found the hidden picture – but when

I woke, heart pounding like a drum, it was impossible to put it out of my mind. I had to get up and look at the picture again to be sure I hadn't imagined the whole thing.

At first sight it was an island, but as I waited, staring through sleep-blurred eyes, the outlines underwent the same, subtle shift I'd seen before, and I was looking down at a woman lying with her legs splayed open. This time the sight was not so disturbing, maybe because I'd been expecting it, maybe because this time I was alone, half-asleep, naked myself, and feeling a certain amount of indignant sisterly support for a fellow writer who'd practically been written out of history.

I put the picture away, oddly comforted, and went back to bed, reflecting on the oddness of dreams.

In the jumbled, fragmented memories I carry from my childhood there are probably nearly as many dreams as images from waking life. I thought of one that might have been my earliest remembered nightmare. I was probably about four years old – I don't think I'd started school yet – when I woke up screaming. The image I retained of the dream, the thing that had frightened me so, was an ugly, clown-like doll made of soft red- and cream-coloured rubber. When you squeezed it, bulbous eyes popped out on stalks and the mouth opened in a gaping scream. As I recall it now, it was disturbingly ugly, not really an appropriate toy for a very young child, but it had been mine when I was younger, at least until I'd bitten its nose off, at which point it had been taken away from me. At the time when I had the dream I hadn't seen it for a year or more – I don't think I consciously remembered it until its sudden looming appearance in a dream had frightened me awake.

When I told my mother about the dream, she was puzzled.

"But what's scary about that? You were never scared of that doll."

I shook my head, meaning that the doll I'd owned – and barely remembered – had never scared me. "But it was very scary," I said, meaning that the reappearance of it in my dream had been terrifying.

My mother looked at me, baffled. "But it's *not* scary," she said gently. I'm sure she was trying to make me feel better and thought this reasonable statement would help. She was absolutely amazed when it had the opposite result, and I burst into tears.

Of course she had no idea why, and of course I couldn't explain. Now I think – and of course I could be wrong – that what upset me was that I'd just realized that my mother and I were separate people. We didn't share the same dreams or nightmares. I was alone in the universe, like everybody else. In some confused way, *that* was what the doll had been telling me. Once it had loved me enough to let me eat its nose; now it would make me wake up screaming.

VI

As soon as I was home and through the back door, sorrow was on me like an untrained, wet and smelly dog.

My kitchen smelled of untreated damp and ancient cooking – an unappetising combination of mould, old vegetables and fried onions. The creeping patch of black mould had returned to the ceiling in the corner nearest the back door, and the pile of newspapers meant for recycling was weeks old. There were crumbs on the table along with a pile of unanswered mail and three dirty cups, a bath-towel draped across one of the chairs, and an odd sock on the floor. When I'd left, the general dirt and untidiness had been invisibly familiar, but now I saw it as a stranger might, and was dismayed. The very thought of all that needed to be done made me tired.

I couldn't cope with it now. Without even pausing to make a cup of tea, I dumped my bag in the bedroom and escaped upstairs to the loft-conversion that was my office. There it was untidy, but not noticeably unclean, and the air was filled with the friendly familiar smell of old books. I picked my way through the stacks on the floor to my desk, where I switched on the computer and went straight to my e-mail inbox.

Selwyn, bless him, was already on the case, but along with the rousing words of his faith in my ability to write a "splendid, uniquely insightful biography" of Helen Ralston, his e-mail carried disquieting news. He'd found an article – "Masks and Identity in Three American Novels" – published three years earlier in an academic journal. The author, Lilith Fischler, Tulane University, was said to be working on a book about Helen Elizabeth Ralston.

> This should certainly be taken with a grain of salt (he wrote) – academics are required to be always working on some project or other, and very few of these putative books ever appear in print. And if it does exist it is more likely to be a critical study than a biography. But why don't you ask her and find out?

The prospect scared me right out of the office and back downstairs, where I began to clean the kitchen. As I scrubbed and washed and tidied, I brooded about what to do.

I must write to her, of course. But what should I say? How much should I tell her? How could I get her on my side?

My usual inclination when writing to strangers is to keep the letter short and formal, but I knew that this could backfire. I could come across as cold when I only meant to be unobtrusive, and, in an e-mail, particularly, it was treacherously easy to be misunderstood. What if Lilith Fischler read my formality as arrogance? I didn't want to alienate her; with a little effort maybe she'd be glad to help. Writing this letter required almost as much care as composing a book proposal to send to an unknown editor.

I considered my approach very carefully, balancing and polishing phrases as I scrubbed the kitchen surfaces. By the time I had the room spruced up, the letter was ready in my head. I ate a sandwich, and went upstairs to write to the address Selwyn had provided.

Next I went looking for my copy of *In Troy*. It wasn't on the shelf where I'd remembered it, so I searched all the bookcases, and then, very carefully, investigated every stack and corner of my office. I didn't remember lending it to anyone, so it was probably in one of the boxes in the loft, where the only way to find a particular book was to crouch down with a flashlight in the dark, and dig.

Instead, I went online to see what I could find out about Helen Ralston.

My first trawl didn't net much, but I was able to find copies of her second and fifth novels, as well as one of the many reprints of *Hermine in Cloud Land* available to order. Two first editions of *In Troy* were listed: the dealer in London was asking $452.82 while one in San Francisco offered a lovingly-described "very fine" copy for a mere $320.00. There were also lots of the Virago edition about, with the cheapest offered at $2.00. On a whim, I added that to my order.

Before I logged off I checked my e-mail again and found that Lilith Fischler had already replied.

My efforts had paid off. Her reply was as transparently open and friendly as I had struggled to make mine seem, and she told me exactly what I had been hoping to hear. She was *not* writing a biography, only a critical study of *In Troy*. Her essay would be appearing in an anthology to be published by Wesleyan University Press next year – she'd be happy to send me a copy as a file attachment. More importantly, she knew how to get in touch with Helen Ralston:

She was happy to talk about her writing, but not so much about her early life, and especially not about the relationship with

W. E. Logan. But she sent very clear and interesting answers to everything else. I don't know if she will be quite as energetic and coherent now, since she had a stroke last year. Her daughter, Clarissa Breen, wrote to me that she was recovering well, but couldn't live on her own any more. They sold the flat in London, and Helen is now living with Clarissa in Glasgow. I'm sure she wouldn't mind me giving you the phone number . . .

At nine o'clock the next morning, I rang the number Lilith Fischler had given me and asked the woman who answered if I could speak to Helen Ralston.

"May I ask who's calling?"

I gave my name, adding quickly, "She doesn't know me; I'm a writer. I wanted to talk to her about her work."

"Hold on a minute, I'll just get her."

Much more than a minute passed before the phone was picked up again, and I heard the same woman's voice saying, "I'm sorry, she doesn't want to speak on the phone; can you come here?"

I was so startled I could hardly speak at first. I'd assumed that this invitation would come much later, if at all. I finally managed to say, "Of course. If you'll give me directions. But I'm quite a distance away – in Argyll, on the west coast. It'll take me a couple of hours to drive to Glasgow."

"Ah. Well, tomorrow would be better, then. She's at her best in the mornings; she flags a bit around midday."

"I could come tomorrow. Whatever time suits you."

"Nine o'clock?"

"I'll be there."

"Thank you," she said warmly, surprising me. "I know mother is looking forward to meeting you. She doesn't have much excitement in her life these days – it was a real blow to her to have to leave London. The mention of your name perked her right up."

"That's nice," I said, surprised that my name should mean anything to Helen Ralston. "Can you tell me how to get to your house?"

"Do you know Glasgow at all? Well, it's not difficult, if you come in on the Great Western Road . . ."

VII

Helen Ralston lived with her daughter in an ordinary two-storey, semi-detached house in a quiet neighbourhood on the north-western edge of the city. The drive through Argyll, along the narrow, loch-hugging road, switching back upon itself again and again as it crossed a land divided and defined by water, up into the mountains and then down again, went more swiftly than I'd dared to hope, without any of the delays that could be caused by log-lorries, farm vehicles, and road works, and I was parking on the street in front of the house at five minutes after nine o'clock the following morning. I got out of the car stiffly, feeling numb and a little dazed by the speed of it all. That so soon after I decided I wanted to write about Helen Ralston I should be meeting her seemed little short of miraculous.

Her picture "My Death" was in the boot of the car, well wrapped, ready to be handed back to its rightful owner, yet now that I was here in front of her house, I hesitated. Remembering my first, visceral reaction to it, I could not expect that the artist's reaction would be the ordinary one of someone to whom a piece of lost property has been returned. What if she was angry that I'd seen it? I decided to wait and see, try to find out her likely response before admitting that I had it.

That settled, I opened the side door to take out my bag and hesitated again at the sight of my new tape recorder, bought yesterday in the Woolworth's in Oban.

I was unprepared for this interview in more ways than one.

Yesterday, I had discovered that my cassette recorder, which had seen me through more than ten years of occasional interviewing, was no longer working. I'd driven off to Oban immediately to buy one, only to find that the electronics shop I'd remembered had closed down – driven out of business, I guessed, by the stacks of cut-price VCRs, DVD players, printers, personal stereos, and telephones on sale in the aisles of Tesco. Alas for me, Tesco did not sell cassette recorders – players, yes, but nothing with a recording function. The closest equivalent I'd been able to find after searching every store in town was a toy for young children. It was the size of a school lunch-box and made of bright red and yellow plastic, with a bright blue microphone attached to it by a curly yellow cord. But it worked, and so I'd bought it.

Now, though, I knew I couldn't possibly arrive for my first meeting with Helen Elizabeth Ralston clutching this children's toy. In any case, she hadn't agreed to an interview; I hadn't even spoken to her yet. I couldn't remember if I'd told her daughter that I was planning to write a biography, but I was pretty sure I'd said only that I admired her mother's work and wanted to talk to her about it. Best if this first meeting should be informal, relaxed, a friendly conversation. Questions "for the record" could come later.

With some relief, I left the childish machine in the car and locked the door behind me. Now my dissatisfaction with the few questions I'd been able to formulate no longer mattered, no more than the fact that I could barely remember anything about *In Troy* (I'd spent a fruitless hour searching the loft for it) and hadn't yet even seen any of her other books. We were just going to talk.

From the first moment I saw her, I knew I would like Clarissa Breen. Sometimes it happens like that: you seem to recognize someone you've never set eyes on before and feel drawn to them, as if you're both members of the same, far-flung family. I don't know why it should be, but those instantaneous feelings are nearly always right.

I smiled at her, and she smiled back, and from the warmth and interest in her grey eyes I knew she felt the same about me.

She was a slight, trim woman who appeared to be about my own age, her light brown hair in a short, feathery cut. The only faintly whispered echo of Circe's features were in her deep-set, luminous eyes; her own face was softer, wider, friendlier, her chin and nose less prominent, and she had a lovely, long smiling mouth.

As I liked her, so I also felt immediately at home in her house. I liked the dramatic mauve colour of the entrance hall, the atmospheric black and white photographs hanging on the wall opposite the stairs, the scent of fresh coffee and something baking that wafted through from the back of the house.

The room to which she led me was a combination of kitchen and living room. At one end, a wicker couch was set into a window recess, grouped together with a glass-topped table and a couple of arm chairs. My eyes were briefly distracted by the green of the garden beyond the window, where birds hopped and hovered around a bird-table, and then I caught sight of the shrivelled, white-haired figure hunched in a chair, and my heart gave a great, frightened leap.

"Mum, here's someone come to see you."

Feeling horribly self-conscious, more awkward than I had since the first few interviews I'd done for a student newspaper, I went forward on legs that felt like sticks of wood. Bending down to her, speaking in a voice that struck my own ears as harsh and unnatural, I introduced myself and began to explain my interest. I hadn't got very far before she interrupted.

"I know who you are," she said sharply, blinking watery blue eyes. "I was wondering when you'd finally get here."

Although I felt intimidated, I said, "I left home before seven. I think I made pretty good time."

The old lady made an impatient, huffing sound and stretched out an arm. "That's not what I meant. Never mind. I suppose we should say how do you do."

Awkward still, and wishing that my heart would stop racing, I took her skinny, age-spotted hand gently in mine. "I'm very pleased to meet you. Thank you so much for letting me come."

"You're younger than I thought you'd be. I suppose you think you're old."

I smiled uncertainly. "I think I'm middle-aged, although that's right only if I live to a hundred."

She made a little sound, half-sniff, half-grunt. "Well, sit down," she said. "I suppose you'll want to ask me questions about my life?"

Clarissa came over with a tray. "Coffee all right for you? Mum, do you want anything else?" She turned to me. "I'll be in my office, down the hall, first door on the right – just come and knock if you need anything, but I'm sure Mum will look after you."

I felt sorry to see her go.

"Like her?"

Helen's question startled me. "She seems very nice."

"She is. She's a wonderful daughter, but, more than that, I think we'd be friends even if we weren't related."

"That must be nice, to feel like that. To have that sort of relationship." I waited tensely for the inevitable next question, but it didn't come.

"Yes. It is."

I took a sip of coffee, then put the cup down and rummaged in my bag for notepad and pen. "I thought . . . do you mind if I take a few notes? Or, or would you rather we just talked, and I could record a more formal interview later?"

"It's up to you. Why ask me? Surely you've done this sort of thing before." She sounded disapproving, and I didn't blame her. I didn't understand myself what had thrown me into such a flutter, as if I were a kid again, the novice reporter speechless before her first visiting celebrity. I'd interviewed more than a hundred people, most of them more famous than Helen Elizabeth Ralston. But this was different, not only because this wasn't an assignment – there was no newspaper behind me, I didn't even have a contract for a book – but because it was *her*. She mattered so much; I wanted her to like me; I wanted to be friends with the author of *In Troy*.

And I knew that if I wanted to prove myself to her, I was going about it in exactly the wrong way.

"I want you to be comfortable," I said, as firmly as I could. "I did think that we might start by chatting – I'll bring a recorder next time – and if there's anything you don't want to talk about . . ."

"I'll let you know."

"Okay, then." I took a deep breath and took the plunge. "What made you, an American, decide to come to Glasgow to study art?"

She peered at me. "Right to the heart of it? All right, let's get this over with. It was for W. E. Logan."

"You knew his work?"

"I had seen one painting, a landscape. One of my teachers, the head of the art department at Syracuse, owned it. He had met Logan and some other Scottish painters on a visit to the South of France a few years earlier, and been very impressed by his work . . . although not, I think, quite as greatly impressed by it as I was. I don't know, young people, they're so wild, so ready to fly off at the slightest encouragement, don't you think?" She shot me a little, conspiratorial smile. "Well, I was, anyway. I must have been searching for a mentor, as young people often do. At any rate, soon after seeing this picture, which I convinced myself was a masterpiece, I wrote off to the artist, Mr Logan, in far-away Scotland, and I sent him some of my sketches, and I asked for his comments and advice.

"And his advice – now, you may find this hard to believe, but I still have the letter; I've kept it all these years, and I'll let you see it later – his response was to praise my work to the skies and tell me that the next step was to find the right teacher and embark on a proper course of study. Despite my living so far away – had he even noticed where the letter came from? – the school that he recommended was his own, where he could be my teacher. At that age, and in my impressionable state of mind, a suggestion from W. E. Logan had the force of a command."

She paused to pick up a glass of water from the table and take a small sip.

I was astonished. How was it that Logan's biographer hadn't known this? And why had Logan himself tried to cover it up, with his little fantasy about Helen's prophetic dreams? "I'd love to see your sketches from that time."

"They're gone."

"Oh, no! What happened?"

She lifted her narrow shoulders. "I don't know what became of them. They're long gone. I didn't take them with me when I left Glasgow. I suppose Willy – or his wife – might have destroyed them."

It was on the tip of my tongue to tell her about the painting in the car. "Maybe not all of them."

She shrugged. "They're nothing to me now. And they weren't then, or I would have kept them, wouldn't I."

"Like you kept W. E. Logan's letter to you."

"Letters. There were several, tucked inside my diary. I took that with me to Paris."

"*Paris?* You left Glasgow for Paris? Why?"

Her smile this time included her eyes, which narrowed so much they nearly disappeared. "Why Paris?" she repeated slowly. "My dear, it was 1929. I was an artist, I was an American, cut loose, without much money but free – where would *you* have gone?"

I met her eyes and smiled back. "Paris," I agreed. "Of all the places and times I wish I could see for myself – Paris, in the '20s."

"Well, then. You understand."

"Tell me – what was it like? What did you do there? Did you know anyone?"

She raised her eyebrows and looked away. "So many questions! My, my. Where to begin?" She reached with a hand that trembled slightly for her water glass. I waited until she had taken another tiny sip and put the glass back down before I repeated, "Did you know anyone in Paris when you arrived?"

"No. Not personally. But I knew a few names, and it was not hard, then, to fall in with the expatriate crowd. There were certain cafes and hotels where they gathered. And, as a young woman, unaccompanied, reasonably attractive, it was easy to make new friends."

VIII

For the next hour Helen Ralston kept me entranced and fascinated with anecdotes from her years in Paris. She name-dropped without restraint. I could hardly believe my luck, to be sitting in the same room, talking to someone who had actually attended some of Gertrude Stein's famous salons. Picasso and Hemingway were both, by then, *much* too grand to be known – she said – she'd seen them around, though. And she'd been friendly with Djuna Barnes and

Man Ray and Marcel Duchamp and Brancusi, Caresse and Harry Crosby, Anais Nin and Henry Miller, and she'd taken tea with Sylvia Beach and James Joyce and his Norah . . . so many evocative names.

At one point I remember thinking *She's a living time machine* and at another I could have cursed myself for not having brought in the tape recorder, however idiotic it looked. How could I remember all the details? Would she be willing to relate all these stories again another day? It occurred to me that maybe there wouldn't *be* another interview – not that she'd be unwilling to talk to me again, but simply because she could drop dead at any minute. At her age, especially, you couldn't count on anything.

I wanted her to go on talking forever, to soak up as much of her remembered experiences as I possibly could, but after a couple of hours it was clear she was running out of energy. The pauses for tiny sips of water became more frequent, and her face seemed to sag, and she stumbled often over simple words. Even aware of this, I was too selfish to let her stop; it was only when Clarissa came in and exclaimed at the sight of her mother's obvious exhaustion that Helen finally fell silent.

"Time for a break," said Clarissa.

I jumped up guiltily. "I'm sorry, I've just been so fascinated—"

"I'm all right, I'm all right," Helen said, flapping a hand at her daughter. "Don't *fuss.*"

"You're tired—"

"Yes, of course I'm tired – what's wrong with that? It means I'll sleep. I'll have my rest now, and eat later."

I chewed my lip, watching as Clarissa helped her mother rise from the chair.

"I'm fine, I'm fine, don't fuss me."

"I'll just come upstairs and see you into bed. Excuse us," Clarissa said as she and her mother moved slowly across the room.

When they had gone out, I wandered aimlessly around the room, gazing out the window at the birds and then looking around at the pictures on the walls – they were highly detailed drawings of plants, like illustrations from an old-fashioned botany book. I had noticed a bookcase in one corner, and now gravitated towards it. A few familiar spines caught my attention immediately – *Nightwood, The Rings of Saturn, Hallucinating Foucault, Possession* – all dear friends which I had at home – and then the breath caught in my throat at the sight of a familiar pink and blue spine, the letters of my own name written there above the title. I had to put my hand on it and draw it out, and yes, it was one of my own short story collections.

I was still holding it, bemused and pleased, when Clarissa came back in.

"Out like a light," she said.

"I'm sorry—"

"Oh, that's all right, she loved it! But she can't take much excitement, that's all. Sad when talking about the past is the most excitement you can know." She noticed the book in my hands then and gave me a different sort of smile. "I liked your stories. I didn't think I would – I don't read sci-fi or fantasy – but yours aren't really sci-fi, are they? They're more like myths. I especially liked that one where the mother is born again – what's it called? – where she becomes a little baby, and her son has to look after her."

"Thank you." Always nice to meet a reader, but I couldn't help the quick stab of disappointment. "I thought maybe this belonged to Helen."

"Of course it does. She has all your books. That's just the only one I've read – but now I'll be sure to read the others," she said quickly.

"Helen Ralston has read all my books?" This was better than winning an award.

"Of course. Why do you suppose she was so excited to meet you? Didn't she tell you?"

"The conversation didn't go in that direction."

Clarissa shrugged and rolled her eyes. "Well. Would you like another coffee? There's a pastry in the oven. Mum has a sweet tooth, and normally I take a break and join her about now." As she spoke, we had been drifting together towards the kitchen area, where she now took a cinnamon plait from the oven.

"What sort of work do you do?" I asked.

"Writing – but not like yours or Mum's. It's mostly catalogue copy and travel brochures. I used to work in marketing. This is handy because I can do it from home."

We settled in against the counter, sipping coffee and nibbling the warm, sweet soft pastry while we traded information about our lives, laying the foundations for a friendship. After about a quarter of an hour, her eyes strayed to the clock on the stove, and although I wanted nothing more than to go on talking to Clarissa, I knew I was interrupting her work, so I said, "I should be going."

"You're welcome to stay," she said, hesitating slightly. "If you wanted to wait and say goodbye to Mum when she wakes up . . . only I don't think she'll have the energy for much more than that."

"No, that's all right, as long as I can come back – how about the day after tomorrow? If that's not too soon?"

"That should be fine. I'll call you if there's any problem. I've got your number."

As soon as I got back to the car, I remembered "My Death" still in the boot. I thought of taking it up to the house and handing it over to Clarissa, just to get the problem off my hands, but then decided that wasn't fair. I'd make a point of mentioning it to Helen next time. I felt I could count on getting a fairly rational response, although whether she'd be happy to have this strange painting back in her possession again, I didn't know.

Before starting on the long drive home, I went shopping. I bought myself a neat, unobtrusive mini-cassette recorder and spent some more time in the bookshops of Glasgow, this time concentrating on memoirs and histories of Paris in the 1920s and 1930s, searching for and finding Helen Ralston's name in index after index.

The next day, two of the books I had ordered – *Hermine in Cloud-Land* and *The Second Wife* – arrived in the post, so the time passed pleasurably in reading. I was not very impressed by Willy Logan's first book. The pictures were charming, but by comparison the text strained after charm and achieved only a kind of dated, fey whimsicality. I didn't care for it and, having met the original of Hermine, I didn't think that she would have either.

The Second Wife, Helen Ralston's fifth novel, was a revelation: understated, subtle, psychologically complex, ambiguous, and faintly sinister . . . it was just the sort of novel I aspired to write myself, and reading it now, at this fallow period of my life, stirred a creative envy in me. For the first time in ages I wished I was at work on a novel and, although I knew I wasn't anywhere near ready to start one, I could believe that one day I would be, that the roads of fiction weren't forever closed to me. Maybe, after I'd finished with Helen Ralston, I'd be inspired by her example to write fiction again.

That night, the unseasonably dry, mild weather broke, and a gale began to blow. I lay awake listening to the keening wind, the rain flung like shot against the windows, and worried. I hated driving in bad weather; I was nervous enough about the narrow, twisting roads in this country when they were dry and the visibility was good – had it been anyone else I was going to meet, I would have phoned to suggest rescheduling. But at Helen Ralston's age, any day might be her last. I felt I had to go.

By six o'clock in the morning the winds had died; but the rain had settled in, falling heavily and relentlessly from the laden sky. A few hours of that, and the road I lived on would be flooded, impassable. I made a thermos of coffee and a peanut butter sandwich to take in the car along with my heavy-weather gear, a flashlight, and the shoulder bag holding *The Second Wife,* notebook, new tape recorder, extra batteries and tapes, and drove off without giving myself time to reconsider. "My Death" was still in its wrappings in the boot, awaiting delivery.

I was tense and cautious, and although the rain had scarcely lessened by the time I reached the outskirts of Glasgow and the traffic reports on Radio Scotland warned of problems on other roads, my way was clear. Drawing up in front of Clarissa Breen's house I felt the happy relief of the traveller who has, against all odds, battled safely home again.

"Home is the sailor, home from the sea," I murmured to myself as I hurried up the walkway. Clarissa, opening the door to my knock, looked surprised and pleased.

"I thought we'd be getting a call from you to say you weren't going to risk it – this rain is dreadful!" she exclaimed, letting me in.

There was the same smell of coffee and something sweet baking, and the black and white photographs displayed against the mauve walls of the entrance hall looked as familiar as if I'd been coming in through that front door for months. I sighed happily. "Oh, the roads weren't bad, really. How are you? How's Helen?"

I had not spoken loudly, but my voice must have carried to the back of the house, because the old woman shouted, "Waiting for you so we can get started!"

"Very bright today," said Clarissa, behind me, and murmured closer to my ear, "A little over-excited."

"Tears before bed-time?"

"Let's hope not."

"What are you *talking* about out there? She's *my* visitor, Clarissa! Let her come through, don't you keep her gossiping!"

We exchanged a glance, and I was split between enjoying our conspiracy and guilt over betraying Helen, and then I went on ahead into the big, bright, room.

"Hello, Helen. It's good to see you again. How are you?"

"Not getting any younger," she said crisply. Her eyes were sparkling; she looked pleased with herself. "You see, Clarissa, didn't I say she would come? I knew she wouldn't be scared of rain!"

"I couldn't live in Scotland if I were."

I was soon settled into a chair beside Helen, with a cup of fresh, strong, hot coffee close at hand and my unobtrusive little tape recorder pointing in her direction.

"I thought we might talk a bit about your childhood," I said. I had decided to be organized and chronological about my investigations, even though, after reading *The Second Wife,* I longed to talk about that.

A small sigh escaped her, and I felt I'd disappointed her in some way. "Very well. Ask your questions."

"Well . . . do you want to start by telling me your earliest memory?"

She looked vague. "I can try. Mostly what I remember are *things,* not events, so it's hard to put a time to them. The first house where I lived, where I was born – we were there until I was about eleven – all my memories are there. I could close my eyes now and take you on a tour of that house, describing every room, all the furniture, every nook and cranny, not just how it looked from every perspective, but the texture of the rugs and the painted walls and the bathroom tiles, the smells and tastes as well – but that would be far too boring."

I felt my heart beat faster in sympathy. In fact, this was exactly how I felt about my own first childhood home, which remained more clear in my memory, more *real,* than anywhere I had lived since. Those first ten years of life, in which I had so exhaustively explored my surroundings, had given me a depth of useless knowledge, made me an expert in the geography and furnishings of the house at 4534 Waring Street, Houston, Texas, between the years 1952 and 1963. I supposed that other people – unless, like my first husband, they'd moved house every year or two – carried around with them a similarly useless mental floor-plan and inventory – but until now I'd never heard anyone else talk about it.

"I remember, there was coloured glass in the window, a fanlight, above the front door, and when the sun shone through it made a pattern of magical, shimmering colours against the wall. I remember trying to touch the colours, to catch them, and feeling frustrated that they slipped through my fingers – I was too young to understand.

"And there was a wonderful old, dark wood chest that I was always trying to get into. It didn't matter how many times I saw inside, that it was only blankets and linens and so on, I would still imagine it was hiding some treasure. That was one of my fancies . . . my dreams and my fancies, now, I remember some of them as clearly as the things that were real. Perhaps my earliest memory was a dream.

"I had a toy. It might have been my first toy, maybe my only one – children didn't have so many toys in those days, you know, we made do with bits and pieces, cast-off things our elders had no use for, a wooden spoon with a face for a doll, but this was a ready-made toy, it had been manufactured for no other purpose but play. It was a doll made of rubber, an ugly little thing really I suppose, but it was my baby and I loved it dearly. Sometimes I'd put my finger into its mouth to let it suck – because its mouth would open if you squeezed it, and close again when the pressure was released – and sometimes I'd take its whole head into my mouth and suck on it – not very motherly behaviour, but I wasn't much more than a baby myself, and perhaps I resented having been weaned – at any rate, I wanted something to suck. Once I bit off a piece of its nose – something about the colour and the texture of it convinced me it would taste nice, but of course it didn't; it tasted of rubber, nasty, although the sensation of chewing it, feeling it slide through my teeth and then catch, again and again, was intriguing enough that I was in no hurry to spit it out. After I'd chewed a hole in it, of course the doll no longer worked properly, the mouth wouldn't open and shut like before, but that didn't bother me, I still loved it and carried it around with me everywhere until one day I suppose I must have dropped it when I was out, and my mother didn't pick it up, and so I lost my baby, my treasure, my first child, you might say."

She looked at me as if expecting some comment, but I could not respond. I felt almost giddy with *déjà vu* – only this wasn't merely *déjà vu*, but something much stronger and stranger, and it had cut the ground right out from under me. I didn't know what to think about what I was hearing; could it be coincidence? Lots of children in the past century must have owned rubber dolls and sucked and chewed them to destruction. She hadn't even described it very well – my doll had been a sort of clown, but hers presumably was a baby.

When I said nothing, she went on.

"I don't remember when I lost it, how it happened, when I noticed, if I was upset, and I don't know how long after that it was that he came back to me in a dream."

I noticed the switch from "it" to "he", and saw my own long-lost clown doll in my mind's eye.

"It wasn't a detailed dream, it was just him. He had come back. But instead of being glad to see him, I was frightened, and I screamed and woke myself up. I woke the whole house up with my screaming.

"When I told my mother about it I began to cry. She thought I was unhappy because I missed my doll. She didn't understand. To have the doll back was the last thing I wanted. I was terrified in case I did by some chance find it again, because I knew . . . I knew it would be like the dream. He would have changed. He wouldn't be my baby anymore. What the dream had shown me was the familiar become strange, how frightening the ordinary can be. You understand?"

I stared back as if hypnotized and just managed to nod my head. But I didn't understand. How could this person – a stranger, and of another generation – have had the very same dream as me? Even her interpretation, although different from my own, rang true, so that I thought yes, that was the real reason my dream had scared me.

As I still said nothing, after another little pause, Helen went on talking about her childhood. I hardly listened. I was in a welter, all confused, of frightening emotions as I tried to make sense of this impossible connection between us. I could not accept that it was mere coincidence, that *both* of us had shared the same experience as children – an experience that had given rise to the same dream, which had been significant enough for both of us to remember it all our lives. There had to be a reason for it; some link, an explanation . . .

And suddenly I remembered what I had, of course, known all along. That dream of mine, that highly significant, personal memory, was no secret. I had written about it. I had put it into a short story that anyone could read – I knew that both Clarissa and Helen had read it, because it was in the volume I'd found in their bookcase.

But what did Helen mean by telling me back my own story as if it were one of her own memories? Was it a joke? A tease? A veiled compliment?

At any rate, unless she was genuinely senile, confused enough that she couldn't sort out her own experiences from things she'd only read about, she must have expected me to recognize what she was doing, and comment on it. I recalled her suggestive pauses, the way she had looked at me and awaited a response, and I almost groaned aloud.

What an idiot she must think me!

Maybe she was feeling foolish herself, knowing her joke had misfired, thinking, perhaps, that my dream was not real, but something I'd made up, a passing notion that meant so little to me that I'd forgotten it and took her "memory" at face value.

I couldn't say anything now – she'd reached high school in her recollections, and it would be far too rude to interrupt her to say that I'd belatedly got her joke – I'd have to wait until she gave me an opening.

Maybe it was because I was concentrating so hard on not missing my chance to speak, but I could not get involved in what she was telling me. It seemed remote and unreal, second-hand, as if she was just retelling a tale she had memorized. Maybe that was my fault: perhaps she felt it was her duty, to get things right and in the proper sequence, and had prepared this potted history for me. But I missed the lively, spontaneous jumble of impressions that had come bubbling up the day before when she'd talked about her years in Paris.

We had soon reached the point where the young Helen Ralston made her dramatic, life-changing decision to leave America and go to study art in Glasgow.

"But you know all that," she said briskly. "And I've told you about Paris . . ."

"Wait, wait." I held up a hand. "Slow down and back up. You *didn't* tell me about your time in Glasgow – not at all. I sort of understand why you went, but not really—"

"What do you mean 'not really'? I told you, it was because of his letters. I suppose I fell in love with him. Well, it wouldn't be the first time such a thing has happened. I still have those letters, you know! I can show you."

"I'm not doubting you," I said quickly. "But what happened after you got to Glasgow – you haven't told me any of that."

She gave me a long, hooded look – very like a bird of prey considering whether it was worthwhile to pounce – before she spoke. "But you know, don't you." It was hardly a question.

"I've read one side of the story. I'd really like to hear yours."

"I don't know why. I'm sure you can imagine it well enough. Why is it people are only interested in women because of their connections to some man, some famous man?"

"That's not true."

She wasn't listening to me. "The letters I've had from people wanting to know *the truth*! That's what they say, but it isn't the truth they want at all, just gossip. Did Helen Ralston try to kill herself because Willy Logan wouldn't stay with her, or was she trying to get away from him? Or was it nothing to do with him at all, and he only happened to be there? Something happened – it happened more than seventy years ago – does it matter *why* it happened?"

"It matters to me – *your* story is the one I want to hear."

Her eyes flickered. "Then why keep asking about Logan?"

"I'm not – I don't mean to. I want to know what happened to you. How you felt about things. Everything. Your childhood, your youth, the time you spent in Glasgow and Paris, and everything else. I know you weren't with Logan for long. Not even two years. Out of ninety-six years, that's not much. But it is a part of your life – the things that happened to you in your early twenties—"

"The truth."

I shut up.

She leaned forward, fixing me with her deep-set, faded blue eyes, her hands like claws clutching the chair arms. "The truth is that I don't know why Helen Ralston jumped out of that window – or if she was pushed. It happened to someone else. I don't remember anything about it."

I knew that serious accidents could sometimes result in memory loss, but I thought of the way she had given me back my own dream as if it were her own, and I wasn't sure I believed her.

"Okay. But you mentioned a diary—"

"Yes, and I'll let you see it. You can see all of them, in due course."

"Thank you. That will be very helpful. And we'll leave that day in August. But – would you mind talking about something else that happened before you left Glasgow and W. E. Logan?"

She shrugged her shoulders slightly. "What is it you want to know?"

"About the island. Achlan. I wonder if you could tell me about that."

There was a sharp click, and we both looked at the tape recorder, which had switched itself off.

"It's okay," I said, reaching for it. "I've got another cassette in my bag."

"I'd like something to drink. My mouth is so dry."

I stood up. "Shall I get you some more water? Or something else?"

"Why don't you go fetch Clarissa, and we'll take our break now."

It was too early; we'd had barely an hour together, and I knew that after the break she'd be bound to go for a nap. My disappointment must have shown, because she gave a small, thin-lipped smile. "Oh, don't worry. We'll get back to the island. I promise you, we'll get back to Achlan."

Clarissa did not seem surprised when I knocked at her door.

"She was up at six this morning, rummaging through her papers, sorting things out, making notes, muttering to herself. Getting ready for you. Nearly bit my head off when I dared suggest you might not come today, because of the weather. 'Of course she'll come! She has to come!'."

Strangely, a shiver ran through me at the idea of the two of them talking about me in my absence, although there was surely nothing odd or sinister in it.

"Such a shame, when you've come such a long way for such a short visit . . . tell you what, why don't you stay for lunch today, and talk to Mum again later on?"

"That would be wonderful – if she's up for it."

"I'm sure she'll tell you if she's not." Clarissa grinned.

Over fresh coffee – decaffeinated for Helen – and slices of apple tart, talk about Helen's life went on, leapfrogging a couple of decades to London during the Blitz and the brief war-time love-affair with Robbie, a much younger fighter pilot. He was Clarissa's father, although he'd not lived to see his only child. I was surprised to learn that Clarissa was sixty – I told her honestly that she looked much younger – but she'd been born during the war, to a grieving single mother.

"I named her after *Mrs Dalloway*," Helen informed me. "I was reading that book during my confinement – in fact, I read it three times. It was the only escape I had, a window into the world before the War, London before the bombs fell, before . . ." she trailed off, blinking rapidly, and her daughter stroked her hand.

Helen's memories of the war years in London were vivid, her descriptions of that time of fear, tedium, deprivation, and passion full of the circumstantial detail I'd missed when she had talked about her earlier life. People said that when you got older the past seemed more immediate and was easier to recall than more recent years, but in every life there must also be periods you would rather forget, and others that you kept fresh by constantly reviewing. Obviously Helen had not wanted to lose a single, precious moment from her short time with Clarissa's father – from the way that Clarissa listened and smiled and chimed in, it was clear she'd heard it all before – but the affair with Willy Logan was different. Maybe it had been too unhappy, maybe her feelings and her actions then didn't suit her older self-image. I could well imagine her not wanting to remember what a reckless and troubled young girl she had been, whether she had seduced or been seduced by her teacher. In my experience, such an affair at such an age was too intense and life-shaping to be forgotten, but if anything could wipe the slate clean, I thought, it had to be a near-death experience.

Although Helen announced her intention that we should carry on talking, her energy was clearly flagging, so I chimed in with her daughter to insist that she have a lie down.

"I'll stay," I promised her. "Clarissa's invited me for lunch. I'll read while you're resting. We can talk all afternoon if you're up to it. I've brought plenty of cassettes."

Helen accepted this. "Come upstairs with me. I'll give you something to read. I'll show you those letters."

Clarissa went back to her work while I went slowly upstairs after Helen.

"I've kept diaries," she told me after she had paused to catch her breath at the top of the stairs. "And there's an autobiographical novel. I never wanted it published, before, but now, maybe . . . You could let me know what you think."

Her room was a dim, narrow space – an ordinary bedroom whose dimensions had been shrunk by the addition of bookshelves on every wall. There was one window, shaded and curtained. The shelves were deep, double-stacked with books, notebooks, and box-files. The other furnishings were a single bed, a small wardrobe, a bedside table, and something that might have been either a writing desk or a dressing table, but it was so cluttered with a mix of toiletries, papers, medicines, notebooks, tissues, books and pens that it seemed unlikely it was used for either purpose now.

"My memories," said Helen. "We got rid of a lot when I moved up from London, but I had to keep my favourite books and all my papers." With a heavy sigh, she sank down onto the bed. Then, with a groan, she struggled to rise again. "My diaries. I was going to show you . . ."

I put a hand on her shoulder, pushing her gently down again. "I'll get it. Tell me where to look."

"Thank you, dear. If you don't mind . . ." She lay back, putting her head down on the pillow with a sigh of relief. "They're on my work-table. Desk. The whole lot. You're not ready to read them all, not yet, but you could look at one now, I think. Well, why not? Let me think. Which one? Hmmm."

Her eyes closed. I watched her uncertainly, feeling a mixture of affection, amusement, and exasperation as I realized she was falling asleep. I opened my mouth to call her back, but just then she gave a tiny, stuttering snore.

I turned to look at the table and saw the pile of notebooks she must have meant. She had been intending to give me one to read. I picked up the one on top, a hardbound black and red book with lined pages. There was nothing marked on the cover to indicate its contents. I opened it to the first page, a fly-leaf where she had written her name and the year, 1981. Oh, far too late.

I put the notebook down carefully to one side and reached for the next in the stack. This one was much more battered and obviously old. It had a blue and white marbled cover with a square in the centre of the front cover where it said COMPOSITIONS. I'd had one just like it in high school in the late 1960s and had used it to record my most intimate feelings, all the daily emotional upheavals, the first stirrings of sexual interest – to my misery, unreciprocated. How I'd poured my heart out, the protestations of my elaborate and undying love for the golden Yale – sometimes, long ago as it was now, I could still remember the particular bittersweet flavour of that feeling, the ache of unrequited love. And then, in the same year – things happened so rapidly in youth – there had been the mutual attraction between me and Andy, and the pain of being unloved had been assuaged by passionate love-making in the back of borrowed cars. My descriptions of what we'd done must have verged on the pornographic – even now, the idea of someone else reading about my first love affair horrified me. I suppose it was the thought of the contents of my own, so similar-looking diary, that made me set this one aside without even opening it to check the date.

As I did so, I dislodged a stack of photographs lying on top of the next notebook; they slithered in a watery rush down the side of the notebook-tower.

Shooting a quick, nervous glance at the figure in the bed behind me, making sure that she still slept, I gathered them up. They were all old, black and white snapshots of people, most of them posed in some outdoor location. They were identified on the backs with pencilled dates, names, or initials.

London 1941 Robbie

I recognized Helen, skirted and hatted amid pigeons at the base of some statue, holding on to the arm of a uniformed young man. As I peered into the distant grey shadows of his face, my heart gave a jolt: in the curve of his mouth and the line of his jaw I thought I could see a resemblance to Allan. The likeness to Clarissa was obvious, and it dawned on me that this was why I'd felt so immediately drawn to her. Her father looked a bit like Allan, and she reminded me of him, too.

I glanced quickly through the other pictures, usually able to pick out Helen by her distinctive looks. Some of the other figures were also familiar: Djuna Barnes, Peggy Guggenheim, James Joyce. I caught my breath. In an English garden Helen Ralston stood, beaming triumphantly beside a tall, shy, elegant, faintly bemused-looking woman. There was no need for me to turn over the photo to check the name written on the back – Virginia Woolf was unmistakable.

Brilliant! My heart pounded with excitement. I wondered if she'd let me use these pictures in my book and immediately knew the answer. Of course she would – why else had she sorted them out, if not to give to me? With so many well-known names to toss into my proposal, I felt the biography was a done deal. *Helen Elizabeth Ralston, The Forgotten Modernist.* As I gathered the pictures up and stacked them neatly again my eyes turned greedily to the pile of old journals.

The one now on top was a slightly odd size, narrower than the contemporary standard, bound in some stiff black cloth, and as I reached out to touch it I somehow *knew* that this was one of her earliest notebooks, from her Paris years.

Without even pausing to question my right to do so, I picked the book up and opened it.

There was no date on the first page and, as I flipped through, I got the impression that it was one continuous narrative, for it wasn't broken down into entries like a diary. It seemed to be told in the first person, and there were long passages of description, but also conversations, set off with single quotes and dashes. Maybe this was the autobiographical novel she had mentioned?

Helen's handwriting was small, neat and angular, but despite its regularity it was not easy to read – especially not in the dim light of her bedroom. I flipped ahead a few pages and moved a little closer to the covered window, trying to find something I could make sense of. I saw that, despite the cramped and careful handwriting, she used her notebooks the same way I did, writing on only one side of the page. (I wondered if she had continued this profligacy during the war, with paper rationing.) The blank sides weren't wasted; for me they provided a space for notes, second thoughts, later comments, trial runs at complicated sentences, reminders, lists of interesting words and of books I wanted to read, occasionally quotations from the books I was reading, or ideas for stories, and as I flipped through the book, concentrating now on the "other" pages, I could tell that Helen worked just like me.

These pages were easier to read since there was less on them. I managed to puzzle out a few quotations: there were lines from Baudelaire – his French followed by her rough translation – a paragraph from *The Golden Bowl* and two from *The Great Gatsby*. A list of British and American authors might have been one of my own "must read" lists, with the difference being that all of them were still alive in 1929. I wondered if she was reminding herself of books to look for, or people she wanted to meet.

The next list was something else. I read it again and again, trying to make some other sense of it than the personal meaning it had for me at first glance:

Yale
Andy
Ira
Mark
John
Jimmy
Patrick
John
Chas
Allan

Nine masculine forenames, one of them repeated twice. The names of the ten men I had loved.

How could Helen Ralston have known that?

She couldn't; it wasn't possible; not *all* of them. My husbands were a matter of public record, and plenty of people knew that I'd lived with a man called Mark for three years. Although my affair with Ira was ostensibly secret, I had dedicated my first book to him, and, invited to contribute to a magazine feature called "The First Time," I hadn't bothered to disguise Andy with a pseudonym. But Yale? Or the fact that I'd been involved with two different men called John? And *nobody* knew about Chas.

Could it be coincidence? Another writer, drawing up a list of names for characters, stumbling so precisely on those most meaningful to me?

I couldn't believe it.

I saw stars and jags of light in front of my eyes as I carefully replaced that notebook with the others.

Somehow, I got out of that stuffy little room, filled with the sound of an old woman's shallow breathing, without bumping into anything or falling over, and made my way down the stairs. I was halfway to the front door, driven by terror, before I remembered that my bag with all my things, including my car keys, was still in the kitchen.

Although I desperately wanted to sneak away, I couldn't. I went back to the big room to fetch my things, and then, after a moment of concentrating on my breathing, knocked at Clarissa's door.

The sight of me took the smile off her face. "What's wrong? Is it Mum?"

"Your mother's fine, she was sleeping when I left her. I'm afraid I've got to go – something's come up—" Unable to think of a convincing lie, I patted my shoulder bag as if indicating the presence of a mobile phone.

Clarissa's expression relaxed, but still she frowned. "Oh, dear. I hope it's not anything—"

"Oh, no, no."

"You're so pale."

I tried to laugh. "Really? Well, it's nothing terrible, just – kind of crossed wires, complicated to explain, but I have to be back there this afternoon. So – if you'll apologise to your mother?"

"Sure. You'll come again?"

"Oh, of course." I turned away from her as I spoke. "I'll phone in the next few days to arrange a time . . ." I felt like crying. I had liked her so much, and now I wondered if her seeming friendliness was part of some Byzantine plot, if she'd somehow been helping her mother to gather information about me, if they were stalkers, or planning something . . . but what? And why?

I stopped at the Little Chef in Dumbarton, not because I was hungry, but because I realized I was in no fit state to drive. I needed to stop and think.

The café was soothingly anonymous and, so late on a weekday morning, almost empty. I ordered the all-day breakfast and coffee – although I felt jittery enough already – and got out my pen and notebook to write down the list again.

It was a list I thought only I could have made. These weren't the only lovers I'd had in my life – in fact, two fiancés were missing – but they were, to me, the most significant. Yale hadn't even been my lover, except in fantasy, and I wasn't sure there was anyone now alive who knew how I'd felt about him. I'd never told *anyone* about my two-week fling with the man I'd called Chas – which wasn't even his real name! Only I had called him Chas, the personal nickname adding another layer of secrecy and fantasy to the forbidden passion.

I wondered, as I dug into my eggs and bacon, if I'd ever written down this list of names I knew so well. Perhaps, one lonely night, on a piece of paper, or in a notebook that had later gone missing . . .? That might explain *how* she knew it, although not why she would have been driven to copy it down on a blank page in one of her old notebooks. Was it possible that she'd become obsessed with me? That she, or her daughter, had been spying on me for some strange psychological reasons of their own, eventually manoeuvring me into the idea of the biography. . .

No, no, that just wasn't possible. There had been no outside influence I had suggested Helen Ralston's name to Selwyn, not vice versa. Even if Alistair Reid and "My Death" could have been a plant, no one could have influenced, or predicted, the chain of thoughts that had led to my decision. If I'd had some other idea on the journey to Edinburgh, or if I'd decided to go shopping instead of look at pictures . . .

Another possibility, which I thought of as I pushed my varifocal specs up on my nose and frowned in a futile attempt to make out the headlines on a newspaper at the other side of the room, was that I hadn't seen what I thought I'd seen. It was not unheard of for me to misread a word or two even in the best conditions, and in the dim light of Helen's bedroom I might have read Dale as Yale, Ivo as Ira, and been fooled by that into imagining a list of perfectly ordinary male names was something uniquely personal to me.

I'd written too many stories about people with weird obsessions. It did not follow that just because Helen had read my stories, that she was obsessed with me.

IX

By the time I'd finished eating I'd convinced myself there was a wholly rational, non-threatening explanation for it all. Yet some fearful, pre-rational doubt must have remained, because although I wrote a note to Helen, apologising for rushing off as I had done and promising to be in touch again soon, I did not suggest a date for our next meeting, and I was in no hurry to arrange anything.

For the next two weeks I didn't write or think about writing. Instead, I cleaned house. I had a major clear-out, giving my own piles and stacks of stale belongings the same treatment I'd forced myself to apply to Allan's things a year earlier. I burned and recycled box-load after box-load of paper, made donations to the charity shops in Oban, and invited a Glasgow bookseller to come up and make me an offer. It wasn't easy, getting rid of so much stuff – I had to steel myself to it. But this was the obvious and necessary first step towards a major life-change. If I was going to be moving, I didn't want to be laden down with clutter, paying to shift box after box of stale memories, books, clothes and other stuff I had not used in years.

The rain had been short-lived; the weather that spring was magnificent. It was the warmest, driest March I could remember since I'd moved to Scotland, and I took a break from my chores indoors to work outside, sanding down and repainting the window-frames, clearing and cutting back the normally wild and overgrown garden, getting everything ready for the change that I felt sure was coming, although I did nothing to make it happen.

And then it was April, with blue skies, fresh winds, and a warm and welcoming sun that seemed to say it was already summer. One morning the telephone rang, and it was Clarissa Breen.

A great wash of guilt made me hunch down in my chair, as if she could see me, and my cheeks began to burn. "I'm sorry I haven't been in touch, I was meaning to call," I said, and came to a sudden halt, unable to think of an excuse for my silence.

"That's okay. Mum was pleased to get your note. I did wonder . . . is everything all right?"

I couldn't remember what I had said, or hinted, about my reason for rushing out of the house. "Yes, yes, I'm fine. Everything's fine. I've just been busy, you know."

"That's good. Look, I don't want to bother you if you're busy—"

"No, no, I didn't mean – it's good to hear from you. I'm glad you called."

"I just wanted to let you know – there's no pressure, and I'll understand if you're busy – but we're going to be in your part of the world this weekend."

This news was so unexpected that I didn't know how to respond. "Do you need a place to stay?"

"Oh, no! That's not why – I didn't mean – only, if you'd like to meet for coffee, or a meal, some time. We'll be staying at the Crinan Hotel."

"That's great – of course I want to see you! You must come here for dinner one night. How long are you staying? Have you made a lot of plans?" All at once I was eager to see them again.

"Just for the weekend. Three nights. I really can't take any more time off right now, but Mum has been so desperate to get back up there lately, and with the weather being so fine, for once, and the forecast good – well, the time seemed right I haven't made any plans yet; there's just one thing Mum really wants to do. I thought I'd ask at the hotel after we arrive. They might know someone who could take us out sailing one day."

"I'll take you out." I didn't even stop to think, although my heart was pounding so hard, I knew this was no light promise. I'd already guessed where Helen would want me to take her.

"Really? You have a boat?"

"Yes. And I'm fully qualified to sail her, so you don't have to worry. I haven't been out since . . . I haven't been out yet this year, and the forecast is good, as you say. It'll be fun."

We arranged that I would meet them at their hotel at nine o'clock Saturday morning and go out for a sail. I would bring provisions for a picnic lunch.

After her call, I went straight out to the boatyard, to find out if *Daisy*, to whom I'd given no thought whatsoever in more than a year, was in any state to be taken out on the water in a mere two days' time.

Fortunately, the manager of the boatyard, Duncan MacInnes, who was the best friend Allan and I had made during our years in Scotland, had taken as good care of *Daisy* as if she'd been his own, doing everything Allan would have done (and a bit more) without needing to be told, or intruding on my grief.

With the arrival of spring and the approach of the Easter holidays, even our quiet little boatyard was all bustle and go as everything was made ready for the start of the tourist season

When I set eyes on *Daisy* she was back in the water after her long winter's sleep, barnacles scraped, rigging and sails repaired, the engine recently serviced, all neat and tidy and absolutely ship-shape, ready to go at a moment's notice.

I turned a look of wonder on Duncan. He stared at the boat, not at me, and rubbed his chin. "I thought, if you were interested, I could lease her out this season. There's always a demand for a sweet little boat like this one, and it can be a good way to make extra money."

"Thanks, but I think I'm going to want her for myself." After Allan's death I had thought once about selling *Daisy*, but she had been so intimately a part of our marriage that I had been unable to go through with it, even though keeping a boat, even one that you *do* use, is, as they say, a hole in the ocean for throwing money in.

Now he looked at me, still rubbing his chin. "Oh, aye, but we mostly do short leases anyway. One or two weeks at a time. You could book her for when you wanted her for yourself, and the rest of the time, you get paid. There's the upkeep, of course, but you could pay me a commission and I'd take care of that, and the expenses would all come out of the rental fees. I handle three other boats like that. All you have to do is say the word, and I'll add *Daisy* to the list."

As he spoke, I thought that perhaps he had mentioned this to me before, but I had been too deep in grief to take it in. I maybe hadn't understood, and he would have been too diffident to persist. I saw immediately now how sensible it was and how useful it would be to have another source of income. I told him so, and agreed to a meeting early the next week to agree the details and fill in the paperwork.

I went home and surprised myself by actually writing a book proposal. It was only three pages, and it hinted at more than it explained, but I thought it might pique an editor's interest. I sent it as an e-mail attachment to Selwyn without agonising further. The time for procrastinating and running away was over. I was going to write Helen Ralston's life.

X

Saturday morning was bright and dry, the sun warm and the winds westerly and not too stiff, a perfect day for a pleasant little sail down the coast. The sight of Helen and Clarissa waiting for me in the lobby when I entered the Crinan Hotel made my heart beat a little faster, partly with pleasure, partly with fear.

Helen Ralston fascinated me; she also frightened me.

If my feelings for Clarissa were uncomplicated, the emotions Helen aroused were anything but.

This time, I didn't run away. It would have been easy enough to go forward, smiling and falsely apologetic, to claim there was something wrong with my boat and offer to take them out for a drive instead. Clarissa, I knew, would be on my side – I sensed she wasn't thrilled with the prospect of taking a ninety-six-year-old woman onto the ocean in a small boat – and Helen's anger, annoyance, disappointment could all be weathered.

The whole sequence of events for a safe, dull, socially uncomfortable day flashed through my mind in a split-second. I had only to say the word to make it happen, but I did not.

I decided instead to confront my fear and the mystery at the heart of Helen Elizabeth Ralston, and when she announced that we were going to pay a visit to the isle of Achlan, although my heart gave a queasy lurch, I still did not back down.

"Oh, yes, *Eilean nan Achlan*. The island of lamentation. I have your painting of it – it's in the boot of the car. I brought it to give back to you."

The old woman looked at me with her hooded, hawk's eyes, unreadable. "I don't want it. You keep it. It's yours now."

Clarissa was frowning. I thought she would ask what we were talking about – I was eager to explain, ready to get the painting out of its wrappings and show it to her – but she was following her own train of thought.

"Mum, we can't go there. It's an uninhabited island. There's nowhere to land. You told me yourself how you had to swim ashore – I hope you don't imagine we're going swimming today!"

"*You'll* get us ashore, won't you?" Helen put her cold, claw-like hand on my arm and gave me an appealing, almost flirtatious look with tilted head.

I spoke over Helen's head to her daughter. "There's a dinghy on board, a little inflatable. We can go ashore in that."

"'There, you see?" Helen looked as triumphant as she had in that old photograph with Virginia Woolf. This was a woman who liked to have her way.

"I still think it sounds like too much trouble," Clarissa said, offering me another chance to back out. "It's up to you, of course."

I was as curious – and almost as eager – as Helen to visit Achlan .

"It's not far away, and it's somewhere I've always meant to go. We – Allan and I – always meant to go ashore and explore, but we never did. I think it was because it was so close, too close – once we were out in the boat we wanted more of a sail."

"Well, if you really don't mind," Clarissa sighed.

I looked at Helen. "I'd like to get a picture of you there, today. For my book."

"You mean *my* book, don't you?"

"That's what I said." I gave her a bland, mock-innocent smile, and she snorted delicately.

I could see she was happy. And why not? I felt happy, too. It was only Clarissa who looked a bit out of sorts.

"Do you sail?" I asked her.

She shook her head. "No, I'm sorry. Is that a problem?"

"No, of course not. I can sail *Daisy* single-handed."

Despite my long absence from her, she seemed to welcome me, and the old skills came rushing back. It was all very easy and smooth, pulling away from the dock and putting slowly out of the busy harbour until I was able to cut the noisy engine. I felt my own spirit crackle and lift like the crisp white sails as we went gliding through the Sound of Jura.

There are treacherous waters there, whirlpools and rocks of legendary fame, but I knew my way and was going nowhere near the local Scylla and Charybdis. I had only a short and easy sail ahead of me, never very far from shore. As I breathed in the fresh, salt air and eased *Daisy* along the familiar sea-lane, I imagined Allan close beside me, his hand resting lightly atop mine on the tiller. He had taught me to sail. I felt an unexpected ease in the thought. I still missed him badly, but the memory no longer crippled me with sorrow. I could take pleasure in the good memories, and there were many of them, so many aboard this little boat.

Helen murmured, "Allan would have loved this."

It was as if she'd spoken my own thought aloud. I whipped around to stare at her, deeply shocked, but she didn't even notice, staring out at the water.

I thought of the list in her journal, and I moistened dry lips to croak, "Who?"

She turned to give me one of her filmy, blue-eyed stares. "Your husband, dear."

"How did you . . . I didn't know you knew him."

"Oh, yes." She nodded. "I met him in London. This was years ago – before you were married to him. He worked for Collins at that time, I think. My agent introduced us at a party, I do remember that. I was very struck by him. A lovely young man, so kind, yet so witty. That combination is rare, you know. And he reminded me more than a little bit of – but never mind that."

This was plausible. Allan *had* worked for Collins in the 1970s, years before I had known him, and he'd been a stalwart of the publishing party scene. And it was not surprising that Helen Ralston should have been drawn to him, recalling the photograph of Clarissa's father.

"But – how did you know—"

"That he was a sailor? We talked about it, of course! He told me about his holidays with his family, when he was a child, and how he learned to sail in the very same place where I came on holiday with Logan."

What I'd meant was how had she known that the man she'd met once, thirty years ago, had been my husband, but I realized there was no point in asking her. She might have claimed that I'd told her, or maybe she'd read it on a book-jacket. Anyone might have told her; it wouldn't have taken much effort to find out.

Plausible though her story of meeting Allan was, I didn't believe it. Allan had a wonderful memory for the people he'd met over the years, and he knew how much I loved *In Troy.* If he had ever met its author, he would have told me.

I was sure that Helen was teasing, just as she had been with the story of "her" dream, and that I would find out why before too much longer.

Eilean nan Achlan came into view within a few minutes, but I waited until we were much closer before pointing it out. Clarissa shaded her eyes with a hand to look. Helen turned her head with no change of expression.

"Did you ever come back?" I asked her.

She shook her head. "Never. I didn't want to, until now."

I steered *Daisy* into the little bay at the south-westerly end of the island and after some finicky manoeuvring, hove to. I had judged it very well, I thought: the view from here was just about exactly what Helen Ralston had been looking at when she'd painted "My Death" more than seventy years before.

When I got a chance to rest after hauling in the sails and making everything tight, I looked at Helen to see how she was responding.

She was sitting very still, staring up at the gorse and bracken-covered hills. Feeling my gaze upon her, she turned to meet my eyes. "Thank you," she said quietly. Something about her look or her tone sent a shiver down my spine.

"You're welcome. Shall we go ashore?"

"Yes. Let's."

Clarissa fought one last-ditch effort, casting an uneasy eye on the little rubber dinghy. "You know, I really don't think that's such a good idea, Mum . . ."

"Then you can stay here."

"That's not what I meant."

"I know. You meant that I should sit down and shut up like a good little girl. I'm not your child, Clarissa."

"No, but you do act like one sometimes!"

"It's my right."

"Why won't you be sensible!"

The two women glared at each other, driven past endurance by the unfair role-reversal that aging forces upon parents and children. I felt sympathy for them both but gladly removed from it all. This was not a situation I would ever confront: I had two sisters, better qualified by geography and temperament to look after our parents (both still in good health) if the need arose, and I had no children. When I was as old and frail as Helen Ralston, assuming I made it that long, there would be no one left to care if I looked after myself properly or not. And unless I had the money to pay for it, there would certainly be no expedition like today's for the elderly me.

Although I thought Helen had every right to do what she wanted with what remained of her life – even if it hastened her death – I felt a terrible sad empathy for Clarissa. I thought we both had guessed the real reason for Helen's determination to visit the little death-island again, and I wondered how we would manage if the old woman simply refused to leave it.

Something like that must have been going through Clarissa's mind when she broke the stalemate with her mother and asked me, "Will I be able to get a signal on my mobile phone out here?"

I shrugged. "You can try. I've got a short-wave radio on board for emergencies."

The tension left her shoulders. "That's good to know. Shall we go?"

There were a few minor hair-raising moments still ahead, helping Helen into the dinghy, but we finally managed to make landfall on Achlan, and I was the only one who got even slightly wet.

"Shall we have our picnic on that big flat rock over there?" asked Clarissa. "It looks like a nice spot."

"We can rest and eat at the shrine," said Helen. "I'm not stopping now." She turned to me. "You can take my picture there, nowhere else."

"Do you remember how to get there? Is it far?" I looked at the thin, blue-veined, old woman's ankles above the sensible sturdy shoes, and recalled Willy Logan's description of the long, slow, torturous descent over rough, rocky ground, leaning heavily on his lover and suffering many stumbles and painful encounters with brambles, nettles, and rabbit holes that he was unable to avoid in his blindness.

"How far can it be?" Helen replied unhelpfully. "Anyway, we'll follow the water-course; that will take us to the source."

I followed the direction of her gaze and realized when I glimpsed the fresh water tumbling over rocks to spill into the bay that I had been hearing its roar, subtly different from the rumble of the waves, ever since we'd landed.

Following the stream might have been sensible, but it wasn't easy. Even so early in spring there was a riot of vegetation to slow our progress, wicked blackberry vines that snatched at our clothing and scored our flesh, roots and unseen rocks and hollows to trip us up. Clarissa and I led fairly sedentary lives and were not as fit as we might have been, but we were still relatively supple and capable of putting on the occasional burst of speed.

Helen, so much older, had fewer reserves. It must have been many years since she had walked for more than ten minutes at a stretch or over anything more taxing than a roughly pebbled drive. Within minutes, her breathing was sounding tortured, and I knew she must be in pain, pushing herself to her limit. Yet, no matter what we said, she would not consider giving up or turning back. A little rest was all she needed, she said, and then we could go on. And so, every three or four minutes, she would give a gasp and stop walking, her shoulders rising up and down as, for a full minute, she marshalled her resources to continue.

Of course we stayed with her, standing in harsh sunlight or in buzzing, leafy shade, during her frequent rest-stops, and then continuing to creep up the gentle slope of the island, plodding along like weary tortoises.

I recalled Helen Ralston's comment as a young woman that in this island she had seen her death and Willy Logan's conviction that "death" meant something else. But maybe he was wrong. Maybe death was just death, and Helen, now so near to the end of life, had finally come to meet it.

We crept along in silence except for the whine and tortured pant of Helen's breathing and the laughing bubbling rush of the stream, and the background sough of wind and sea. I kept my eyes fixed on the ground, mostly, on the look-out for hazards. The sounds, our unnaturally slow pace, my worries about what was going to happen all combined to affect my brain, and after awhile it seemed to me that the earth beneath my feet had become flesh, that I was treading upon a gigantic female body. This was bad enough, but there was something stranger to come, as it seemed I felt the footsteps upon my own, naked, supine body: that I was the land, and it was me. My body began to ache, but it seemed there was nothing to be done. I lost track of time, and my sense of myself as an individual became tenuous.

"Is that it?"

Clarissa's voice cut through the feverish dream or self-hypnosis or whatever it was that had possessed me, and I raised my head with a gasp, like someone who had been swimming for too long underwater, and looked around.

The stream had dwindled into a bubbling rill between two rocks. Nearby I saw a large tumble of stones, partly overgrown by brambles and weeds. Impossible to say now what it might once have been – a tomb, a sheep-fank, or a tumble-down cottage – but clearly they had been piled up deliberately by someone sometime in the past.

"Look at me. Now."

It was Helen's voice, but so different that I thought maybe I'd heard it only in my head. Yet at the same time I knew that she was speaking to me. I looked around and met her eyes. What happened then I can't describe, can barely remember. I think I saw something that I shouldn't have seen. But maybe it was nothing to do with sight, was purely a brain event. I flail around for an explanation, or at least a metaphor. It was like a lightning bolt, fairy-stroke, the touch of the goddess, death itself, birth.

The next thing I knew, I was lying on the ground, naked beneath the high, cloudy sky. I heard water sounds and the noise of someone weeping.

There was an awful, dull ache in my back. I opened my eyes and sat up slowly, painfully, wondering what had happened. I smelled sweat and blood and sex and crushed vegetation. I remembered looking at Helen, but if that had been seconds ago, or hours, or even longer, I had no idea. The other two women were gone. I was alone with a man – a naked man huddled a few feet away from me, beside the cairn he'd named a shrine, and weeping. I recognized him as Willy Logan.

Then I understood who I was.

I was Helen Ralston.

XI

Now, more than a year later, I am still Helen, as I will be, I suppose, until I die.

I avoid mirrors. It gives me a sickening, horrific jolt to see those alien, deep-set eyes glaring back at me out of another woman's face, even if the terror I feel is reflected in hers.

Of course I keep what I know to myself – I certainly have no desire to be locked up in an early twentieth-century loony bin – and, as time goes by, it has become somewhat easier. Memories of my other life and of that other world that I suppose to be the future are growing dimmer, harder to recall and to believe. That's why I decided to write this, before it is forever too late. The words in this book, which I intend to keep safe, will ensure that what happened once doesn't have to go on happening into an infinity of futures – unless I want it to. I will show it to myself when the time is right, seventy-three years from now.

The feeling of dislocation, of alienation and fear, which I had at first, has eased with the passage of time. The strangeness has faded like my impossible, disturbing memories, and the sense of being embarked upon a great adventure – a new life! – has become more powerful. After all, this is not such a bad time or place to be young and alive.

– Helen Elizabeth Ralston
Paris
September 22 1930

XII

The interview – my one and only interview with Helen – had not gone exactly as she described. For one thing, she'd been more disabled by her stroke than the story indicated, and the conversation between us had been painfully repetitious, slow and circular. She did mention a few famous names, people she had known in Paris and London in the 1930s, but her anecdotes had a way of petering out rather than coming to a point, and one story would frequently blend into another, so that an incident that took place in pre-war Paris would segue abruptly into something that had happened to her in post-war London. I felt sorry for her and rather frustrated as I realized I was unlikely to get much first-hand information from her for my book.

After about an hour, Clarissa took her mother upstairs to bed. When she came back down, she gave me the notebook.

"Mum wants you to have this," she said. "She wants you to read it."

I took the old, hardbound notebook with a feeling of great privilege and excitement. "What is it? Did she say?"

"She said it has the deepest, most important truth about her life."

"Wow."

We smiled at each other – the charge of sympathetic, affectionate sympathy between us was very real – and she invited me to stay and have a bite to eat. We spent maybe an hour over coffee and cake, talking, getting to know each other. I left, then, and after a detour to do some shopping at Braehead, drove home.

I remember the details of my arrival home – putting away the groceries, looking through the mail, heating up a Marks and Spencer Indian meal and then eating it while listening to *Front Row* on Radio 4 – as if they were incidents from a lost Eden of innocence. Afterwards, I brewed a pot of herbal tea and took it upstairs to my office. There, at my desk, I pushed the keyboard aside, set Helen Ralston's book where it had been and pulled the reading light forward and angled it down to cast a strong cone of light directly onto the page. I began to read and fell into the abyss.

It was after midnight when I finished reading, my neck and spine aching from the tense crouch I'd maintained for hours at my desk as I struggled to decipher her cramped, narrow writing. I was trembling with exhaustion, terror and bewilderment.

How was this possible? Could her story be true?

If it wasn't, how did she know so much about me? How was she able to write in my voice, including so many accurate details about my life and everything that had happened starting with the chain of events that had caused me to decide to write a biography of Helen Ralston up to our first meeting?

I didn't sleep that night.

At eight o'clock the next morning, so blank, cold, and numb that I could have said I was feeling nothing at all, I telephoned Clarissa Breen and asked to speak to Helen.

In a voice that wavered slightly, she told me her mother was dead.

"It happened not long after you left. Or maybe . . . maybe before." She took a deep breath. "She was sleeping when I left her to come downstairs to you. Normally, she'll sleep for about two hours. At lunchtime, I went upstairs to check on her. As soon as I went into her bedroom I knew. She was gone."

All my questions seemed suddenly insignificant, and the terror that had gripped me loosed its hold. I rushed to sympathize, uttering all the usual, insufficient phrases of sorrow and respect.

"Thank you. I was going to call you, later today. I wanted to thank you – for coming when you did and making Mum's last day so special. She was happy, you know, really thrilled to be meeting you. Not just because of the biography – of course it was great for her to know she hadn't been forgotten – but because it was *you*. She loved your work, you know. She'd been reading your stories since you were first published – she always felt there was a special connection between you."

I shivered convulsively and gripped the phone hard. "Did she *say* that?"

"Oh – it was obvious how she felt. Didn't I tell you, that's why I read that book of yours, because you were obviously so important to her. Anyway, I wanted you to know how much your coming meant to her. It was the first time I'd seen her happy and excited in – well, the last seven months were very hard for her. Since the stroke, and having to leave London, no longer able to live on her own. I–I really thought this was going to be the start of a new phase for her, I can't quite – I'm sorry . . ." she stumbled, then recovered herself. "I can't quite believe she's gone. But it was the best way, to go like that, suddenly and all at once, it's what she wanted – she hated the idea of another, even more crippling, stroke – so did I – of dwindling away in a hospital bed, dying by inches."

We talked for a few more minutes. Clarissa had a lot to do; she promised she'd let me know about the funeral.

I went to Glasgow for it the following week and took the notebook and the painting to give back. I found my chance after the cremation when we few mourners – most of them Clarissa's own friends and extended family – gathered in her house to eat the traditional cold food. I took the notebook out of my bag, but she shook her head and told me it was mine.

"Mum wanted you to have it. No, I mean it; she couldn't have been more clear about her wishes; she left instructions in her will. In fact, not just the notebook, but a painting as well. It's called "My Death", she said it's a watercolour, but I've never seen it – I'm sure Mum didn't keep any of her early works, she never mentioned it before, and in the will she didn't explain where it was or anything."

I launched into a rushed, stumbling explanation of how I'd come into possession of "My Death" until she stopped me with a hand on my shoulder. "That's all right. That's fine. I'm glad you've got it. It was what she wanted."

"I've got it in the car – I was going to give it back to you—"

"No, you must keep it."

"Well – would you like to see it? Just before I go. It's in the car."

She nodded slowly. "Yes. Yes I would. Thank you. I know Mum was an artist before she was a writer, but I've never seen anything she painted."

We left the house and walked down to the street where my car was parked. My heart began to pound unpleasantly as I took the wrapped parcel out of the boot, and I wondered if I should try to warn her, to prepare her in some way. But the words would not come, and so I unwrapped it in silence and laid it down, face up, inside the open boot of the car, and we looked down upon "My Death" in silence.

A watercolour landscape in tones of blue and brown and grey and green and pink, a rocky island in the sea. Tears blurred my vision and I looked away in time to see Clarissa dash her hand across her eyes and give a soft, shuddering sigh.

She turned away, and I put my arms around her.

"Thank you," she murmured, returning my hug.

I kissed her cheek. "Let's stay in touch."

2005

THE MAMMOTH BOOK OF

BEST NEW

HORROR

The Year's Top
Terror Tales by such
Masters of Horror as:

CLIVE BARKER
RAMSEY CAMPBELL
CAROL EMSHWILLER
GLEN HIRSHBERG
JOE HILL
TERRY LAMSLEY
BRIAN LUMLEY
CHINA MIÉVILLE
DAVID MORRELL
GAHAN WILSON

EDITED BY STEPHEN JONES

Haeckel's Tale

Clive Barker

HAVING HAD THREE SUCCESSIVE covers that I supervised and (obviously) liked, I guess it was only inevitable that I would eventually run into further conflict with my publisher. This came with the Les Edwards painting we chose for *The Mammoth Book of Best New Horror Volume Seventeen*.

What I loved about Les' original design was that the concept he had produced was far more subtle than it appeared at first glance, and the image itself contained its own subtexual narrative. In short, it perfectly complemented the type of fiction that I tried to select for the anthology series.

Unfortunately, my publisher disagreed, and said that no bookseller would take a mass-market volume with that image on the cover. (To be honest, they were probably correct.) I don't know what they expected from a volume of horror stories, but in the end we compromised with a painting of a creepy old lady holding a bloodied cleaver. Apparently that was acceptable to everybody!

Was I wrong? Well, that original painting of Les' that I wanted to use eventually appeared on the cover of the limited edition of this book in America. Suffice to say that this trade paperback edition features a completely different – if no less creepy – image.

Just as I was putting the finishing touches to this omnibus compilation, I also discovered that a Russian edition of Volume Seventeen was published in 2008 and had already gone into reprint.

I somehow managed to reduce the Introduction to seventy-eight pages, but the Necrology jumped to a record seventy. At least on a happier note, the dedication celebrated milestone birthdays for both Ramsey Campbell and Forrest J Ackerman.

For my end thought I questioned if books – as a physical item at least – would still be around in coming years. Or would the printed page eventually go the way of the vinyl record album? The jury is still out at the moment, but the recent resurrection of vinyl has at least given me hope.

This time around it was series stalwart Ramsey Campbell's turn to be represented with the first and last contributions amongst the twenty-two stories. Joe Hill was back with a Bram Stoker Award- and British Fantasy Award-winning tale entitled "Best New Horror" (and how could I *not* include a story called that?), as were Peter Atkins, Mark Samuels, Roberta Lannes, Gahan Wilson, Terry Lamsley and Brian Lumley, amongst others. *Rambo* creator David Morrell made his first appearance in the series, as did veteran SF author Carol Emshwiller and extraordinary newcomer Holly Philips.

However, none of their stories could match Clive Barker's "Haeckel's Tale" for gleeful grue. I had been introduced to Clive in the early 1980s by our mutual friend Ramsey Campbell, before the publication of his ground-breaking *Books of Blood* collections. We subsequently worked together on his movies *Hellraiser* and *Nightbreed*, as well as a number of literary projects before he moved to California in the early 1990s.

In recent years, Clive has become better known as the author of a number of bestselling fantasy novels, often illustrated with his own, distinctive, paintings. It was therefore a great pleasure to discover that he had returned to his horror roots with the erotic tale that follows, which was nominated for a Bram Stoker Award and adapted for the Showtime cable TV series *Masters of Horror* by another *Best New Horror* alumni, Mick Garris.

PURRUCKER DIED LAST week, after a long illness. I never much liked the man, but the news of his passing still saddened me. With him gone I am now the last of our little group; there's no one left with whom to talk over the old times. Not that I ever did; at least not with him. We followed such different paths, after Hamburg. He became a physicist, and lived mostly, I think, in Paris. I stayed here in Germany, and worked with Herman Helmholtz, mainly working in the area of mathematics, but occasionally offering my contribution to other disciplines. I do not think I will be remembered when I go. Herman was touched by greatness; I never was. But I found comfort in the cool shadow of his theories. He had a clear mind, a precise mind. He refused to let sentiment or superstition into his view of the world. I learned a good deal from that.

And yet now, as I think back over my life to my early twenties (I'm two years younger than the century, which turns in a month), it is not the times of intellectual triumph that I find myself remembering; it is not Helmholtz's analytical skills, or his gentle detachment.

In truth, it is little more than the slip of a story that's on my mind right now. But it refuses to go away, so I am setting it down here, as a way of clearing it from my mind.

In 1822, I was – along with Purrucker and another eight or so bright young men – the member of an informal club of aspirant intellectuals in Hamburg. We were all of us in that circle learning to be scientists, and being young had great ambition, both for ourselves and for the future of scientific endeavour. Every Sunday we gathered at a coffee-house on the Reeperbahn, and in a back room which we hired for the purpose, fell to debate on any subject that suited us, as long as we felt the exchanges in some manner advanced our comprehension of the world. We were pompous, no doubt, and very full of ourselves; but our ardour was quite genuine. It was an exciting time. Every week, it seemed, one of us would come to a meeting with some new idea.

It was an evening during the summer – which was, that year, oppressively hot, even at night – when Ernst Haeckel told us all the story I am about to relate. I remember the circumstances well. At least I think I do. Memory is less exact than it believes itself to be, yes? Well, it scarcely matters. What I remember may as well *be* the truth. After all, there's nobody left to disprove it. What happened was this: towards the end of the evening, when everyone had drunk enough beer to float the German fleet, and the keen edge of intellectual debate had been dulled somewhat (to be honest we were descending into gossip, as we inevitably did after midnight), Eisentrout, who later became a great surgeon, made casual mention of a man called Montesquino. The fellow's name was familiar to us all, though none of us had met him. He had come into the city a month before, and attracted a good deal of attention in society, because he claimed to be a necromancer. He could speak with and even raise the dead, he claimed, and was holding seances in the houses of the rich. He was charging the ladies of the city a small fortune for his services.

The mention of Montesquino's name brought a chorus of slurred opinions from around the room, every one of them unflattering. He was a contemptuous cheat and a sham. He should be sent back to France – from whence he'd come – but not before the skin had been flogged off his back for his impertinence.

The only voice in the room that was not raised against him was that of Ernst Haeckel, who in my opinion was the finest mind amongst us. He sat by the open window – hoping perhaps for some stir of a breeze off the Elbe on this smothering night – with his chin laid against his hand.

"What do you think of all this, Ernst?" I asked him.

"You don't want to know," he said softly.

"Yes we do. Of course we do."

Haeckel looked back at us. "Very well then," he said. "I'll tell you."

His face looked sickly in the candlelight, and I remember thinking – distinctly thinking – that I'd never seen such a look in his eyes as he had at that moment. Whatever thoughts had ventured into his head, they had muddied the clarity of his gaze. He looked fretful.

"Here's what I think," he said. "That we should be careful when we talk about necromancers."

"Careful?" said Purrucker, who was an argumentative man at the best of times, and even more volatile when drunk. "Why should we be *careful* of a little French prick who preys on our women? Good Lord, he's practically stealing from their purses!"

"How so?"

"Because he's telling them he can raise the dead!" Purrucker yelled, banging the table for emphasis.

"And how do we know he cannot?"

"Oh now Haeckel," I said, "you don't believe—"

"I believe the evidence of my eyes, Theodor," Haeckel said to me. "And I saw – once in my life – what I take to be proof that such crafts as this Montesquino professes are real."

The room erupted with laughter and protests. Haeckel sat them out, unmoving. At last, when all our din had subsided, he said: "Do you want to hear what I have to say or don't you?"

"Of *course* we want to hear," said Julius Linneman, who doted on Haeckel; almost girlishly, we used to think.

"Then listen," Haeckel said. "What I'm about to tell you is absolutely true, though by the time I get to the end of it you may not welcome me back into this room, because you may think I am a little crazy. More than a little perhaps."

The softness of his voice, and the haunted look in his eyes, had quieted everyone, even the volatile Purrucker. We all took seats, or lounged against the mantelpiece, and listened. After a moment of introspection, Haeckel began to tell his tale. And as best I remember it, this is what he told us.

"Ten years ago I was at Wittenberg, studying philosophy under Wilhem Hauser. He was a metaphysician, of course; monkish in his ways. He didn't care for the physical world; it didn't touch him, really. And he urged his students to live with the same asceticism as he himself practices. This was of course hard for us. We were very young, and full of appetite. But while I was in Wittenberg, and under his watchful eye, I really tried to live as close to his precepts as I could.

"In the spring of my second year under Hauser, I got word that my father – who lived in Luneburg – was seriously ill, and I had to leave my studies and return home. I was a student. I'd spent all my money on books and bread. I couldn't afford the carriage fare. So I had to walk. It was several days' journey, of course, across the empty heath, but I had my meditations to accompany, and I was happy enough. At least for the first half of the journey. Then, out of nowhere there came a terrible rainstorm. I was soaked to the skin, and despite my valiant attempts to put my concern for physical comfort out of my mind, I could not. I was cold and unhappy, and the rarifications of the metaphysical life were very far from my mind.

"On the fourth or fifth evening, sniffling and cursing, I gathered some twigs and made a fire against a little stone wall, hoping to dry myself out before I slept. While I was gathering moss to make a pillow for my head an old man, his face the very portrait of melancholy, appeared out of the gloom, and spoke to me like a prophet.

"'It would not be wise for you to sleep here tonight,' he said to me.

"I was in no mood to debate the issue with him. I was too fed up. 'I'm not going to move an inch,' I told him. 'This is an open road. I have very right to sleep here if I wish to.'

"'Of course you do,' the old man said to me. 'I didn't say the right was not yours. I simply said it wasn't wise.'

"I was a little ashamed of my sharpness, to be honest. 'I'm sorry,' I said to him. 'I'm cold and I'm tired and I'm hungry. I meant no insult.'

"The old man said that none was taken. His name, he said, was Walter Wolfram.

"I told him my name, and my situation. He listened, then offered to bring me back to his house, which he said was close by. There I might enjoy a proper fire and some hot potato soup. I did not refuse him, of course. But I did ask him, when I'd risen, why he thought it was unwise for me to sleep in that place.

"He gave me such a sorrowful look. A heart-breaking look, the meaning of which I did not comprehend. Then he said: 'You are a young man, and no doubt you do not fear the workings of the world. But please believe me when I tell you there are nights when it's not good to sleep next to a place where the dead are laid.'

"'The dead?' I replied, and looked back. In my exhausted state I had not seen what lay on the other side of the stone wall. Now, with the rain-clouds cleared and the moon climbing, I could see a large number of graves there, old and new intermingled. Usually such a sight would not have much disturbed me. Hauser had taught us to look coldly on death. It should not, he said, move a man more than the prospect of sunrise, for it is just as certain, and just as unremarkable. It was good advice when heard on a warm afternoon in a classroom in Wittenberg. But here – out in the middle of nowhere, with an old man murmuring his superstitions at my side – I was not so certain it made sense.

"Anyway, Wolfram took me home to his little house, which lay no more than half a mile from the necropolis. There was the fire, as he'd promised. And the soup, as he'd promised. But there also, much to my surprise and delight, wife, Elise.

"She could not have been more than twenty-two, and easily the most beautiful woman I had ever seen. Wittenberg had its share of beauties, of course. But I don't believe its streets ever boasted a woman as perfect as this. Chestnut hair, all the way down to her tiny waist. Full lips, full hips, full breasts. And such eyes! When they met mine they seemed to consume me.

"I did my best, for decency's sake, to conceal my admiration, but it was hard to do. I wanted to fall down on my knees and declare my undying devotion to her, there and then.

"If Walter noticed any of this, he made no sign. He was anxious about something, I began to realize. He constantly glanced up at the clock on the mantel, and looked towards the door.

"I was glad of his distraction, in truth. It allowed me to talk to Elise, who – though she was reticent at first – grew more animated as the evening proceeded. She kept plying me with wine, and I kept drinking it, until sometime before midnight I fell asleep, right there amongst the dishes I'd eaten from."

At this juncture, somebody in our little assembly – I think it may have been Purrucker – remarked that he hoped this wasn't going to be a story about disappointed love, because he really wasn't in the mood. To which Haeckel replied that the story had absolutely nothing to do with love in any shape or form. It was a simple enough reply, but it did the job: it silenced the man who'd interrupted, and it deepened our sense of foreboding.

The noise from the café had by now died almost completely; as had the sounds from the street outside. Hamburg had retired to bed. But we were held there, by the story, and by the look in Ernst Haeckel's eyes.

"I awoke a little while later," he went on, "but I was so weary and so heavy with wine, I barely opened my eyes. The door was ajar, and on the threshold stood a man in a dark cloak. He was having a whispered conversation with Walter. There was, I thought, an exchange of money; though I couldn't see clearly. Then the man departed. I got only the merest glimpse of his face, by the light thrown from the fire. It was not the face of a man I would like to quarrel with, I thought. Nor indeed even meet. Narrow eyes, sunk deep in fretful flesh. I was glad he was gone. As Walter closed the door I lay my head back down and almost closed my eyes, preferring that he not know I was awake. I can't tell you exactly why. I just knew that something was going on I was better not becoming involved with.

"Then, as I lay there, listening, I hear a baby crying. Walter called for Elise, instructing her to calm the infant down. I didn't hear her response. Rather, I heard it, I just couldn't make any sense of it. Her voice, which had been soft and sweet when I'd talked with her, now sounded strange. Through the slits of my eyes I could see that she'd gone to the window, and was staring out, her palms pressed flat against the glass.

"Again, Walter told her to attend to the child. Again, she gave him some guttural reply. This time she turned to him, and I saw that she was by no means the same woman as I'd conversed with. She seemed to be in the early stages of some kind of fit. Her colour was high, her eyes wild, her lips drawn back from her teeth.

"So much that had seemed, earlier, evidence of her beauty and vitality now looked more like a glimpse of the sickness that was consuming her. She'd glowed too brightly; like someone consumed by a fever, who in that hour when all is at risk seems to burn with a terrible vividness.

"One of her hands went down between her legs and she began to rub herself there, in a most disturbing manner. If you've ever been to a madhouse you've maybe seen some of the kind of behaviour she was exhibiting.

"'Patience,' Walter said to her, 'everything's being taken care of. Now go and look after the child.'

"Finally she conceded to his request, and off she went into the next room. Until I'd heard the infant crying I hadn't even realized they had a child, and it seemed odd to me that Elise had not made mention of it. Lying there, feigning sleep, I tried to work out what I should do next. Should I perhaps pretend to wake, and announce to my host that I would not after all be accepting his hospitality? I decided against this course. I would stay where I was. As long as they thought I was asleep they'd ignore me. Or so I hoped.

"The baby's crying had now subsided. Elise's presence had soothed it.

"'Make sure he's had enough before you put him down,' I heard Walter say to her. 'I don't want him waking and crying for you when you're gone.'

"From this I gathered that she was breast-feeding the child; which fact explained the lovely generosity of her breasts. They were plump with milk. And I must admit, even after the way Elise had looked when she was at the window, I felt a little spasm of envy for the child, suckling at those lovely breasts.

"Then I returned my thoughts to the business of trying to understand what was happening here. Who was the man who'd come to the front door? Elise's lover, perhaps? If so, why was Walter *paying* him? Was it possible that the old man had hired this fellow to satisfy his wife, because he was incapable of doing the job himself? Was Elise's twitching at the window simply erotic anticipation?

"At last, she came out of the infant's room, and very carefully closed the door. There was a whispered exchange between the husband and wife, which I caught no part of, but which set off a new round of questions in my head. Suppose they were conspiring to kill me? I will tell you, my neck felt very naked at that moment. . .

"But I needn't have worried. After a minute they finished their whispering and Elise left the house. Walter, for his part, went to sit by the fire. I heard him pour himself a drink, and down it noisily; then pour himself another. Plainly he was drowning his sorrows; or doing his best. He kept drinking, and muttering to himself while he drank. Presently, the muttering became tearful. Soon he was sobbing.

"I couldn't bear this any longer. I raised my head off the table, and I turned to him.

"'Herr Wolfram,' I said, '. . .what's going on here?'

"He had tears pouring down his face, running into his beard.

"'Oh my friend,' he said, shaking his head, 'I could not begin to explain. This is a night of unutterable sadness.'

"'Would you prefer that I left you to your tears?' I asked him.

"'*No*,' he said. 'No, I don't want you to go out there right now.'

"I wanted to know why, of course. Was there something he was afraid I'd see?

"I had risen from the table, and now went to him. 'The man who came to the door—'

"Walter's lip curled at my mention of him. 'Who is he?' I asked.

"'His name is Doctor Skal. He's an Englishman of my acquaintance.'

"I waited for further explanation. But when none was forthcoming, I said: 'And a friend of your wife's.'

"'No,' Walter said. 'It's not what you think it is.' He poured himself some more brandy, and drank again. 'You're supposing they're lovers. But they're not. Elise has not the slightest interest in the company of Doctor Skal, believe me. Nor indeed in any visitor to this house.'

"I assumed this remark was a little barb directed at me, and I began to defend myself, but Walter waved my protestations away.

"'Don't concern yourself,' he said, 'I took no offence at the looks you gave my wife. How could you not? She's a very beautiful woman, and I'd be surprised if a young man such as yourself *didn't* try to seduce her. At least in his heart. But let me tell you, my friend: you could never satisfy her.' He let this remark lie for a moment. Then he added: 'Neither, of course, could I. When I married her I was already too old to be a husband to her in the truest sense.'

"'But you have a baby,' I said to him.

"'The boy isn't mine,' Walter replied.

"'So you're raising this infant, even though he isn't yours?'

"'Yes.'

"'Where's the father?'

"'I'm afraid he's dead.'

"'Ah.' This all began to seem very tragic. Elise pregnant, the father dead, and Walter coming to the rescue, saving her from dishonour. That was the story constructed in my head. The only part I could not yet fit into this neat scheme was Doctor Skal, whose cloaked presence at the door had so unsettled me.

"'I know none of this is my business—' I said to Walter.

"'And better keep it that way,' he replied.

"'But I have one more question.'

"'Ask it.'

"'What kind of Doctor is this man Skal?'

"'Ah.' Walter set his glass down, and stared into the fire. It had not been fed in a while, and now was little more than a heap of glowing embers. 'The esteemed Doctor Skal is a necromancer. He deals in a science which I do not profess to understand.' He leaned a little closer to the fire, as though talking of the mysterious man had chilled him to the marrow. I felt something similar. I knew very little about the work of a necromancer, but I knew that they dealt with the dead.

"I thought of the graveyard, and of Walter's first words to me:

"*It would not be wise for you to sleep here tonight.*'

"Suddenly, I understood. I got to my feet, my barely sobered head throbbing. 'I know what's going on here,' I announced. 'You paid Skal so that Elise could speak to the dead! To the man who fathered her baby.' Walter continued to stare into the fire. I came close to him. 'That's it, isn't it? And now Skal's going to play some miserable trick on poor Elise to make her believe she's talking to a spirit.'

"'It's *not* a trick,' Walter said. For the first time during this grim exchange he looked up at me. 'What Skal does is real, I'm afraid to say. Which is why you should stay in here until it's over and done with. It's nothing you need ever—'

"He broke off at that moment, his thought unfinished, because we heard Elise's voice. It wasn't a word she uttered, it was a sob; and then another, and another, I knew whence they came, of course. Elise was at the graveyard with Skal. In the stillness of the night her voice carried easily.

"'Listen to her,' I said.

"'Better not,' Walter said.

"I ignored him, and went to the door, driven by a kind of morbid fascination. I didn't for a moment believe what Walter had said about the necromancer. Though much else that Hauser had taught me had become hard to believe tonight, I still believed in his teachings on the matter of life and death. The soul, he'd taught us, was certainly immortal. But once it was released from the constraints of flesh and blood, the body had no more significance than a piece of rotted meat. The man or woman who had animated it was gone, to be with those who had already left this life. There was, he insisted, no way to call that spirit back. And nor therefore – though Hauser had never extrapolated this far – was there any validity in the claims of those who said that they could commune with the dead.

"In short, Doctor Skal was a fake: this was my certain belief. And poor distracted Elise was his dupe. God knows what demands he was making of her, to have her sobbing that way! My imagination – having first dwelt on the woman's charms shamelessly, and then decided she was mad – now re-invented her a third time, as Skal's hapless victim. I knew from stories I'd heard in Hamburg what power charlatans like this wielded over vulnerable women. I'd heard of some necromancers who demanded that their seances be held with everyone as naked as Adam, for purity's sake! Others who had so battered the tender hearts of their victims with their ghoulishness that the women had swooned, and been violated in their swoon. I pictured all this happening to Elise. And the louder her sobs and cries became the more certain I was that my worst imaginings were true.

"At last I couldn't bear it any longer, and I stepped out into the darkness to get her.

"Herr Wolfram came after me, and caught hold of my arm. 'Come back into the house!' he demanded. 'For pity's sake, leave this alone *and come back into the house!*'

"Elise was shrieking now. I couldn't have gone back in if my life had depended upon it. I shook myself free of Wolfram's grip and started out for the graveyard. At first I thought he was going to leave me alone, but when I glanced back I saw that though he'd returned into the house he was now emerging again, cradling a musket in his arms. I thought at first he intended to threaten me with it, but instead he said:

"'Take it!' offering the weapon to me.

"'I don't intend to kill anybody!' I said, feeling very heroic and self-righteous now that I was on my way. 'I just want to get Elise out of this damn Englishman's hands.'

"'She won't come, believe me,' Walter said. 'Please take the musket! You're a good fellow. I don't want to see any harm come to you.'

"I ignored him and strode on. Though Walter's age made him wheeze, he did his best to keep up with me. He even managed to talk, though what he said – between my agitated state and his panting – wasn't always easy to grasp.

"'She has a sickness . . . she's had it all her life . . . what did I know? . . . I loved her . . . wanted her to be happy . . .'

"'She doesn't sound very happy right now,' I remarked.

"'It's not what you think . . . it is and it isn't . . . oh God, please come back to the house!'

"'I said no! I don't want her being molested by that man!'

"'You don't understand. We couldn't begin to please her. Neither of us.'

"'So you hire Skal to service her? Jesus!'

"I turned and pushed him hard in the chest, then I picked up my pace. Any last doubts I might have entertained about what was going on in the graveyard were forgotten. All this talk of necromancy was just a morbid veil drawn over the filthy truth of the matter. Poor Elise! Stuck with a broken-down husband, who knew no better way to please than to give her over to an Englishman for an occasional pleasuring. Of all things, an Englishman! As if the English knew anything about making love.

"As I ran, I envisaged what I'd do when I reached the graveyard. I imagined myself hopping over the wall and with a shout racing at Skal, and plucking him off my poor Elise. Then I'd beat him senseless. And when he was laid low, and I'd proved just how heroic a fellow I was, I'd go to the girl, take her in my arms, and show her what a good German does when he wants to make a woman happy.

"Oh, my head was spinning with ideas, right up until the moment that I emerged from the corner of the trees and came in sight of the necropolis . . ."

Here, after several minutes of headlong narration, Haeckel ceased speaking. It was not for dramatic effect, I think. He was simply preparing himself, mentally, for the final stretch of his story. I'm sure that none of us in that room doubted that what lay ahead would not be pleasant. From the beginning this had been a tale overshadowed by the prospect of some horror. None of us spoke; that I do remember. We sat there, in thrall to the persuasions of Haeckel's tale, waiting for him to begin again. We were like children.

After a minute or so, during which time he stared out of the window at the night sky (though seeing, I think, nothing of its beauty) he turned back to us and rewarded our patience.

"The moon was full and white," he said. "It showed me every detail.

"There were no great, noble tombs in this place, such as you'd see at the Ohlsdorf Cemetery; just coarsely carved headstones and wooden crosses. And in their midst, a kind of ceremony was going on. There were candles set in the grass, their flames steady in the still air. I suppose they made some kind of circle – perhaps ten feet across – in which the necromancer had performed his rituals. Now, however, with his work done, he had retired some distance from this place. He was sitting on a tombstone, smoking a long, Turkish pipe, and watching.

"The subject of his study, of course, was Elise. When I had first laid eyes on her I had guiltily imagined what she would look like stripped of her clothes. Now I had my answer. There she was, lit by the gold of the candle flames and the silver of the moon. Available to my eyes in all her glory.

"But oh God! What she was doing turned every single drop of pleasure I might have taken in her beauty to the bitterest gall.

"Those cries I'd heard – those sobs that had made my heart go out to her – they weren't provoked by the pawings of Doctor Skal, but by the touch of the dead. The dead, raised out of their dirt to pleasure her! She was squatting, and there between her legs was a face, pushed up out of the earth. A man recently buried, to judge by his condition, the flesh still moist on the bone, and the tongue – Jesus, the tongue! – still flicking between his bared teeth.

"If this had been all it would have been enough. But it was not all. The same grotesque genius that had inspired the cadaver between her legs into this resemblance of life, had also brought forth a crop of smaller parts – pieces of the whole, which had wormed their way out of the grave by some means or other. Bony pieces, held together with leathery sinew. A rib-cage, crawling around on its elbows; a head, propelled by a whiplash length of stripped spine; several hands, with some fleshless lengths of bone attached. There was a morbid bestiary of these things. And they were all upon her, or waiting their turn to be upon her.

"Nor did she for a moment protest their attentions. Quite the contrary. Having climbed off the corpse that was pleasuring her from below, she rolled over onto her back and invited a dozen of these pieces upon her, like a whore in a fever, and they came, oh God they came, as though they might have out of her the juices that would return them to wholesomeness.

"Walter, by now, had caught up with me.

"'I warned you,' he said.

"'You knew this was happening?'

"'Of course I knew. I'm afraid it's the only way she's satisfied.'

"'What is she?' I said to him.

"'A woman,' Walter replied.

"'No natural woman would endure *that*,' I said. 'Jesus! Jesus!'

"The sight before me was getting worse by the moment. Elise was up on her knees in the grave dirt now, and a second corpse – stripped of whatever garments he had been buried in – was coupling with her, his motion vigorous, his pleasure intense, to judge by the way he threw back his putrefying head. As for Elise, she was kneading her full tits, directing arcs of milk into the air so that it rained down on the vile menagerie cavorting before her. Her lovers were in ecstasy.

They clattered and scampered around in the torrents, as though they were being blessed.

"I took the musket from Walter.

"'Don't hurt her!' he begged. 'She's not to blame.'

"I ignored him, and made my way towards the yard, calling to the necromancer as I did so.

"'Skal! *Skal!*'

"He looked up from his meditations, whatever they were, and seeing the musket I was brandishing, immediately began to protest his innocence. His German wasn't good, but I didn't have any difficulty catching his general drift. He was just doing what he'd been paid to do, he said. He wasn't to blame.

"I clambered over the wall and approached him through the graves, instructing him to get to his feet. He got up, his hands raised in surrender. Plainly he was terrified that I was going to shoot him. But that wasn't my intention. I just wanted to stop this obscenity.

"'Whatever you did to start this, *undo it!*' I told him.

"He shook his head, his eyes wild. I thought perhaps he didn't understand so I repeated the instruction.

"Again, he shook his head. All his composure was gone. He looked like a shabby little cut-purse who'd just been caught in the act. I was right in front of him, and I jabbed the musket in his belly. If he didn't stop this, I told him, I'd shoot him.

"I might have done it too, but for Herr Wolfram, who had clambered over the wall and was approaching his wife, calling her name.

"'Elise . . . please, Elise . . . you should come home.'

"I've never in my life heard anything as absurd or as sad as that man calling to his wife. '*You should come home . . .*'

"Of course she didn't listen to him. Didn't *hear* him, probably, in the heat of what she was doing, and what was being done to her.

"But her *lovers* heard. One of the men who'd been raised up whole, and was waiting his turn at the woman, started shambling towards Walter, waving him away. It was a curious thing to see. The corpse trying to shoo the old man off. But Walter wouldn't go. He kept calling to Elise, the tears pouring down his face. Calling to her, calling to her—

"I yelled to him to stay away. He didn't listen to me. I suppose he thought if he got close enough he could maybe catch hold of her arm. But the corpse came at him, still waving its hands, still shooing, and when Walter wouldn't be shooed the thing simply knocked him down. I saw him flail for a moment, and then try to get back up. But the dead — or pieces of the dead — were everywhere in the grass around his feet. And once he was down, they were upon him.

"I told the Englishman to come with me, and I started off across the yard to help Walter. There was only one ball in the musket, so I didn't want to waste it firing from a distance, and maybe missing my target. Besides I wasn't sure what I was going to fire at. The closer I got to the circle in which Elise was crawling around — still being clawed and petted — the more of Skal's unholy handiwork I saw. Whatever spells he'd cast here, they seemed to have raised every last dead thing in the place. The ground was crawling with bits of this and that; fingers, pieces of dried up flesh with locks of hair attached; wormy fragments that were beyond recognition.

"By the time we reached Walter, he'd already lost the fight. The horrors he'd paid to have resurrected — ungrateful things — had torn him open in a hundred places. One of his eyes had been thumbed out, there was a gaping hole in his chest.

"His murderers were still working on him. I batted a few limbs off him with the musket, but there were so many it was only a matter of time, I knew, before they came after me. I turned around to Skal, intending to order him again to bring this abomination to a halt, but he was springing off between the graves. In a sudden surge of rage, I raised the musket and I fired. The felon went down, howling in the grass. I went to him. He was badly wounded, and in great pain, but I was in no mood to help him. He was responsible for all this. Wolfram dead, and Elise still crouching amongst her rotted admirers; all of this was Skal's fault. I had no sympathy for the man.

"'What does it take to make this stop?' I asked him. '*What are the words?*'

"His teeth were chattering. It was hard to make out what he was saying. Finally I understood.

"'When . . . the . . . sun . . . comes up . . .' he said to me.

"'You can't stop it any other way?'

"'No,' he said. 'No . . . other . . . way . . .'

"Then he died. You can imagine my despair. I could do nothing. There was no way to get to Elise without suffering the same fate as Walter. And anyway, she wouldn't have come. It was an hour from dawn, at least. All I could do was what I did: climb over the wall, and wait. The sounds were horrible. In some ways, worse than the sight. She must have been exhausted by now, but she kept going. Sighing sometimes, sobbing sometimes, moaning sometimes. Not —

let me make it perfectly clear – the despairing moan of a woman who understands that she is in the grip of the dead. This was the moan of a deeply pleasured woman; a woman in bliss.

"Just a few minutes before dawn, the sounds subsided. Only when they had died away completely did I look back over the wall. Elise had gone. Her lovers lay around in the ground, exhausted as perhaps only the dead can be. The clouds were lightening in the East. I suppose resurrected flesh has a fear of the light, because as the last stars crept away so did the dead. They crawled back into the earth, and covered themselves with the dirt that had been shovelled down upon their coffins . . ."

Haeckel's voice had become a whisper in these last minutes, and now it trailed away completely. We sat around not looking at one another, each of us deep in thought. If any of us had entertained the notion that Haeckel's tale was some invention, the force of his telling – the whiteness of his skin, the tears that had now and then appeared in his eyes – had thrust such doubts from us, at least for now.

It was Purrucker who spoke first, inevitably. "So you killed a man," he said. "I'm impressed."

Haeckel looked up at him. "I haven't finished my story," he said.

"Jesus . . ." I murmured, ". . . what else is there to tell?"

"If you remember, I'd left all my books, and some gifts I'd brought from Wittenberg for my father, at Herr Wolfram's house. So I made my way back there. I was in a kind of terrified trance, my mind still barely able to grasp what I'd seen.

"When I got to the house I heard somebody singing. A sweet lilting voice it was. I went to the door. My belongings were sitting there on the table where I'd left them. The room was empty. Praying that I'd go unheard, I entered. As I picked up my philosophy books and my father's gift the singing stopped.

"I retreated to the door but before I could reach the threshold Elise appeared, with her infant in her arms. The woman looked the worse for her philanderings, no question about that. There were scratches all over her face, and her arms, and on the plump breast at which the baby now sucked. But marked as she was, there was nothing but happiness in her eyes. She was sweetly content with her life at that moment.

"I thought perhaps she had no memory of what had happened to her. Maybe the necromancer had put her into some kind of trance, I reasoned; and now she'd woken from it the past was all forgotten.

"I started to explain to her. 'Walter . . .' I said.

"'You, I know—' she replied. 'He's dead.' She smiled at me; a May morning smile. 'He was old,' she said, matter-of-factly. 'But he was always kind to me. Old men are the best husbands. As long as you don't want children.'

"My gaze must have gone from her radiant face to the baby at her nipple, because she said:

"'Oh, this isn't Walter's boy.'

"As she spoke she tenderly teased the infant from her breast, and it looked my way. There it was: life-in-death, perfected. Its face was shiny pink, and its limbs fat from its mother's milk, but its sockets were deep as the grave, and its mouth wide, so that its teeth, which were not an infant's teeth, were bared in a perpetual grimace.

"The dead, it seemed, had given her more than pleasure.

"I dropped the books, and the gift for my father there on the doorstep. I stumbled back out into the daylight, and I ran – oh God in Heaven, I ran! – afraid to the very depths of my soul. I kept on running until I reached the road. Though I had no desire to venture past the graveyard again, I had no choice: it was the only route I knew, and I did not want to get lost, I wanted to be home. I wanted a church, an altar, piety, prayers.

"It was not a busy thoroughfare by any means, and if anyone had passed along it since day-break they'd decided to leave the necromancer's body where it lay beside the wall. But the crows were at his face, and foxes at his hands and feet. I crept by without disturbing their feast."

Again, Haeckel halted. This time, he expelled a long, long sigh. "And that, gentlemen, is why I advise you to be careful in your judgments of this man Montesquino."

He rose as he spoke, and went to the door. Of course we all had questions, but none of us spoke then, not then. We let him go. And for my part, gladly. I'd enough of these horrors for one night.

Make of all this what you will. I don't know to this day whether I believe the story or not (though I can't see any reason why Haeckel would have *invented* it. Just as he'd predicted, he was treated very differently after that night; kept at arm's length). The point is that the thing still haunts me; in part, I suppose, *because* I never made up my mind whether I thought it was a falsehood or not. I've sometimes wondered what part it played in the shaping of my life: if perhaps my cleaving to empiricism – my devotion to Helmholtz's methodologies

– was not in some way the consequence of this hour spent in the company of Haeckel's account.

Nor do I think I was alone in my preoccupation with what I heard.

Though I saw less and less of the other members of the group as the years went by, on those occasions when we did meet up the conversation would often drift round to that story, and our voices would drop to near-whispers, as though we were embarrassed to be confessing that we even remembered what Haeckel had said.

A couple of members of the group went to some lengths to pluck holes in what they'd heard, I remember; to expose it as nonsense. I think Eisentrout actually claimed he'd retraced Haeckel's journey from Wittenberg to Luneburg, and claimed there was no necropolis along the route. As for Haeckel himself, he treated these attacks upon his veracity with indifference. We had asked him to tell us what he thought of necromancers, and he'd told us. There was nothing more to say on the matter.

And in a way he was right. It was just a story told on a hot night, long ago, when I was still dreaming of what I would become.

And yet now, sitting here at the window, knowing I will never again be strong enough to step outside, and that soon I must join Purrucker and the others in the earth, I find the terror coming back to me; the terror of some convulsive place where death has a beautiful woman in its teeth, and she gives voice to bliss. I have, if you will, fled Haeckel's story over the years; hidden my head under the covers of reason. But here, at the end, I see that there is no asylum to be had from it; or rather, from the terrible suspicion that it contains a clue to the ruling principle of the world.

2006

THE MAMMOTH BOOK OF

BEST NEW
HORROR

The Year's Best
Supernatural Stories
by top authors such as:

MICHAEL BISHOP
RAMSEY CAMPBELL
CHRISTOPHER FOWLER
ELIZABETH HAND
GLEN HIRSHBERG
DAVID MORRELL
KIM NEWMAN
GEOFF RYMAN
DAVID J. SCHOW
GENE WOLFE

EDITED BY STEPHEN JONES

Devil's Smile

Glen Hirshberg

LES EDWARDS' COVER PAINTING for volume eighteen could easily depict one of the characters from Clive Barker's preceding tale. It was designed by Mike and myself on the understanding that only some of the cover would be reproduced in the foil technique, to give greater impact to the image.

Unfortunately, a mistake in the printing process resulted in the entire cover – including the spine and back cover, along with all the lettering – being rendered in the process. Although it did not quite work as envisaged, if you hold the book under a direct light source you can still get a sense of the subtle shades of Les' original work.

The Introduction was down again, to only seventy-two pages, and even the Necrology came in at a respectable sixty-two. This time I brought attention to the refusal of the judges of the 2006 International Horror Guild Award to nominate *any* anthology for an award that year. It was not that they decided to simply not to name a winner, but that they felt that there was not *one single volume* published in that year that was worthy of even a nomination. When I became involved in an open letter to the administrators condemning their decision, I started receiving threatening and insulting e-mails. My editor asked me to cut the piece, even though it would have made no difference to the overall length of the book.

As it turns out, the IHG Awards no longer exist, but at the time they did themselves – and the field they supposedly represented a major disservice by their actions, and the whole episode was a disheartening one for me personally.

After seventeen years, this was also the final American edition under the Carroll & Graf imprint. After the departure of its eponymous founders, successive publishing corporations had acquired the once-independent imprint until it was finally phased out in 2007.

The anthology once again won the British Fantasy Award, and the twenty-four stories featured the now usual mixture of old and new names, including young adult author John Gordon, science fiction writer Michael Bishop, and Geoff Ryman with a World Fantasy Award-nominated novella that involved Cambodian ghosts.

I was first introduced to Glen Hirshberg by Ellen Datlow at the 2001 World Fantasy Convention in Montreal, Canada. At her urging, I looked at his published fiction and quickly realized that he was a major new talent in our genre. His first story in *The Mammoth Book of Best New Horror* appeared in the thirteenth volume (with the infamous glowing skull on the cover). Since then, he has been represented by a remarkable six stories over a further seven volumes. He really is that good.

I could have chosen any one of them to appear in this book, but in the end I went for "Devil's Smile" – simply because it is the creepiest of all of them . . .

> "*In hollows of the liquid hills*
> *Where the long Blue Ridges run*
> *The flatter of no echo thrills*
> *For echo the seas have none;*
> *Nor aught that gives man back man's strain–*
> *The hope of his heart, the dream in his brain.*"
> —Herman Melville, "Pebbles"

TURNING IN HIS SADDLE, Selkirk peered behind him through the flurrying snow, trying to determine which piece of debris had lamed his horse. All along what had been the carriage road, bits of driftwood, splintered sections of hull and harpoon handle, discarded household goods – pans, candlesticks, broken-backed books, empty lanterns – and at least one section of long, bleached-white jaw lay half-buried in the sand. The jaw still had baleen attached, and bits of blown snow had stuck in it, which made it look more recently alive than it should have.

Selkirk rubbed his tired eyes against the grey December morning and hunched deeper into his inadequate long coat as the wind whistled off the whitecaps and sliced between the dunes. The straw hat he wore more out of habit than hope of protection did nothing to warm him, and stray blond curls kept whipping across his eyes. Easing himself from the horse, Selkirk dropped to the sand.

He should have conducted his business here months ago. His surveying route for the still-fledgling United States Lighthouse Service had taken him in a criss-crossing loop from the tip of the Cape all the way up into Maine and back. He'd passed within fifty miles of Cape Roby Light and its singular keeper twice this fall, and both times had continued on. Why? Because Amalia had told him the keeper's tale on the night he'd imagined she loved him? Or maybe he just hated coming back here even more than he thought he would. For all he knew, the keeper had long since moved on, dragging her memories behind her. She might even have died. So many did, around here. Setting his teeth against the wind, Selkirk wrapped his frozen fingers in his horse's bridle and led her the last down-sloping mile and a half into Winsett.

Entering from the east, he saw a scatter of stone and clapboard homes and boarding houses hunched against the dunes, their windows dark. None of them looked familiar. Like so many of the little whaling communities he'd visited during his survey, the town he'd known had simply drained away into the burgeoning, bloody industry centres at New Bedford and Nantuckett.

Selkirk had spent one miserable fall and winter here fourteen years ago, sent by his drunken father to learn candle-making from his drunken uncle. He'd accepted the nightly open-fisted beatings without comment, skulking afterward down to the Blubber Pike tavern to watch the whalers: the Portuguese swearing loudly at each other and the Negroes – so many Negroes, most of them recently freed, more than a few newly-escaped – clinging in clumps to the shadowy back tables and stealing fearful glances at every passing face, as though they expected at any moment to be spirited away.

Of course, there'd been his cousin, Amalia, for all the good that had ever done him. She'd just turned eighteen at the time, two years his senior. Despite her blond hair and startling fullness, the Winsett whalers had already learned to steer clear, but for some reason, she'd liked Selkirk. At least, she'd liked needling him about his outsized ears, his floppy hair, the crack in his voice he could not outgrow. Whatever the reason, she'd lured him away from the pub on several occasions to stare at the moon and drink beside him. And once, in a driving sleet, she'd led him on a midnight walk to Cape Roby Point. There, lurking uncomfortably close but never touching him, standing on the rocks with her dark eyes cocked like rifle sites at the rain, she'd told him the lighthouse keeper's story. At the end, without any explanation, she'd turned, opened her heavy coat and pulled him to her. He'd had no idea what she wanted him to do, and had wound up simply setting his ear against her slicked skin, all but tasting the water that rushed into the valley between her breasts, listening to her heart banging way down inside her.

After that, she'd stopped speaking to him entirely. He'd knocked on her door, chased her half out of the shop one morning and been stopped by a chop to the throat from his uncle, left notes he hoped she'd find peeking out from under the rug in the upstairs hallway. She'd responded to none of it, and hadn't even bothered to say goodbye when he left. And Selkirk had steered clear of all women for more than a decade afterward, except for the very occasional company he paid for near the docks where he slung cargo, until the Lighthouse Service offered him an unexpected escape.

Now, half-dragging his horse down the empty main street, Selkirk found he couldn't even remember which grim room the Blubber Pike had been. He passed no one. But at the western edge of the frozen, cracking main thoroughfare, less than a block from where his uncle had kept his establishment, he found a traveller's stable and entered.

The barn was lit by banks of horseshoe-shaped wall sconces – apparently, local whale oil or no, candles remained in ready supply – and a coal fire glowed in the open iron stove at the rear of the barn. A dark-haired stable lad with a clam-shaped birthmark covering his left cheek and part of his forehead appeared from one of the stables in the back, *tsked* over Selkirk's injured mount and said he'd send for the horse doctor as soon as he'd got the animal dried and warmed and fed.

"Still a horse doctor here?" Selkirk asked.

The boy nodded. He was almost as tall as Selkirk, and spoke with a Scottish burr. "Still good business. Got to keep the means of getting out healthy."

"Not many staying in town anymore, then?"

"Just the dead ones. Lot of those."

Selkirk paid the boy and thanked him, then wandered toward the stove and stood with his hands extended to the heat, which turned them purplish red. If he got about doing what should have been done years ago, he'd be gone by nightfall, providing his horse could take him. From his memory of the midnight walk with Amalia, Cape Roby Point couldn't be more than three miles away. Once at the lighthouse, if its long-time occupant did indeed still live there, he'd brook no romantic nonsense – neither his own, nor the keeper's. The property did not belong to her, was barely suitable for habitation, and its lack of both updated equipment and experienced, capable attendant posed an undue and unacceptable threat to any ship unlucky enough to hazard past. Not that many bothered anymore with this particular stretch of abandoned, storm-battered coast.

Out he went into the snow. In a matter of minutes, he'd left Winsett behind. Head down, he burrowed through the gusts. With neither buildings nor dunes to block it, the wind raked him with bits of shell and sand that clung to his cheeks like the tips of fingernails and then ripped free. When he looked up, he saw beach pocked with snow and snarls of seaweed, then the ocean thrashing about between the shore and the sandbar a hundred yards or so out.

An hour passed. More. The tamped-down path, barely discernible during Winsett's heyday, had sunk completely into the shifting earth. Selkirk stepped through stands of beach heather and sand bur, pricking himself repeatedly about the ankles. Eventually, he felt blood beneath one heavy sock, but he didn't peel the sock back, simply yanked out the most accessible spines and kept moving. Far out to sea, bright, yellow sun flickered in the depths of the cloud cover and vanished as suddenly as it had appeared. Devil's smile, as the Portuguese sailors called it. At the time, it hadn't occurred to Selkirk to ask why the light would be the devil, instead of the dark or the gathering storm. Stepping from the V between two leaning dunes, he saw the lighthouse.

He'd read the report from the initial Lighthouse Service survey three years ago, and more than once. That document mentioned rot in every beam, chips and cracks in the bricks that made up the conical tower, erosion all around the foundation. As far as Selkirk could see, the report had been kind. The building seemed to be crumbling to nothing before his eyes, bleeding into the pool of shore-water churning at the rocks beneath it.

Staring into the black tide racing up the sand to meet him, Selkirk caught a sea-salt tang on his tongue and found himself murmuring a prayer he hadn't planned for Amalia, who'd reportedly wandered into the dunes and vanished one winter night, six years after Selkirk left. Her father had written Selkirk's father that the girl had never had friends, hated him, hated Winsett, and was probably happier wherever she was now. Then he'd said, "*Here's what I hope: that she's alive. And that she's somewhere far from anywhere I will ever be.*"

On another night than the one they'd spent out here, somewhere closer to town but similarly deserted, he and Amalia once found themselves beset by gulls that swept out of the moonlight all together, by the hundreds, as though storming the mainland. Amalia had pitched stones at them, laughing as they shrieked and swirled nearer. Finally, she'd hit one in the head and killed it. Then she'd bent over the body, calling Selkirk to her. He'd expected her to cradle it or cry. Instead, she'd dipped her finger in its blood and painted a streak down Selkirk's face. Not her own.

Looking down now, Selkirk watched the tide reach the tips of his boots again. How much time had he wasted during his dock-working years imagining – hoping – that Amalia might be hidden behind some stack of crates or in a nearby alley, having sought him out after leaving Winsett?

Angry now, Selkirk picked his way between rocks to the foot of the tower. A surge of whitewater caught him off guard and pasted his trousers to his legs, and the wind promptly froze them with a gust.

Up close, the tower looked even worse. Most of the bricks had crumbled and whitened, the salt air creating blotchy lesions like leper spots all over them. The main building still stood straight enough, but even from below, with the wind whipping the murky winter light around, Selkirk could see filth filming the windows that surrounded the lantern room, and cracks in the glass.

The keeper's quarters squatted to the left of the light tower, and looked, if possible, even more dishevelled. Along the base, lime had taken hold, sprouting up the wooden walls like algae. Or maybe it was algae. This would not be somewhere the Service salvaged. Cape Roby Light would have to come down, or simply be abandoned to the sea.

Selkirk rapped hard on the heavy oak door of the tower. For answer, he got a blast of wind nearly powerful enough to tip him off the rocks. Grunting, he rapped harder. Behind him, the water gurgled, the way spermaceti oil sometimes did as it bubbled, and though he knew it wasn't possible, Selkirk would have sworn he could smell it, that faint but nauseating reek his uncle swore was imaginary, because that was the glory of spermaceti oil, the whole goddamn point: it had no significant odour. Every day of that dismal fall, though, Selkirk's nostrils had filled anyway. Blood, whale brain, desiccated fish. He began to pound.

Just before the door opened, he became aware of movement behind it, the slap of shoed feet descending stone steps. But he didn't stop knocking until the oak swung away from him, the light rushing not out from the lighthouse but in from the air.

He knew right away this was her, though he'd never actually seen her. Her black hair twisted over her shoulders and down her back in tangled strands like vines, just as Amalia had described. He'd expected a wild, white-haired, wind-ravaged thing, bent with age and the grief she could not shake. But of course, if Amalia's story had been accurate, this woman had been all of twenty during Selkirk's year here, and so barely over eighteen when she'd been widowed. She gazed at him now through royal blue eyes that seemed set into the darkness behind her like the last sunlit patches in a blackening sky.

"Mrs Marchant," he said. "I'm Robert Selkirk from the Lighthouse Service. May I come in?"

For a moment, he thought she might shut the door in his face. Instead, she hovered, both arms lifting slightly from her sides, as though she were considering taking wing. Her skirt was long, her blouse pale yellow, clinging to her square and powerful shoulders.

"Selkirk," she said. "From Winsett?"

Astonished, Selkirk started to raise his hand. Then he shook his head. "From the lighthouse service. But yes, I was nephew to the Winsett Selkirks."

"Well," she said, the Portuguese tilt to her words stirring memories of the Blubber Pike whalers, the smoke and the smell in there. Abruptly, she grinned. "Then you're welcome here."

"You may not feel that way in a few minutes, Mrs Marchant. I'm afraid I've come to . . ."

But she'd stepped away from the door, starting back up the stairs and beckoning him without turning around. Over her shoulder, he heard her say, "You must be frozen. I have tea."

In he went, and stood still in the entryway, listening to the whistling in the walls, feeling drafts rushing at him from all directions. If it weren't for the roof, the place would hardly qualify as a dwelling anymore, let alone a lifesaving beacon and refuge. He started after the woman up the twisting stairs.

Inside, too, the walls had begun to flake and mould, and the air flapped overhead, as though the whole place were full of nesting birds. Four steps from the platform surrounding the lantern room, just at the edge of the spill of yellow candlelight from up there, Selkirk slowed, then stopped. His gaze swung to his right and down toward his feet.

Sitting against the wall with her little porcelain ankles sticking out of the bottom of her habit and crossed at the ankle, sat a doll of a nun. From beneath the hood of the doll's black veil, disconcertingly blue eyes peered from under long lashes. A silver crucifix lay in the doll's lap, and miniature rosary beads trailed back down the steps, winking pale yellow and pink in the flickering light like seashells underwater. And in fact, they were bits of shell.

Glancing behind him, Selkirk spotted the other dolls he'd somehow missed. One for every other stair, on alternating walls. These were made mostly from shell, as far as he could tell. Two of them were standing, while a third sat with her legs folded underneath her and a stone tucked against her ear, as though she were listening. At the top of the steps, still another nun dangled from her curved, seashell hands on the decaying wooden banister. Not only were her eyes blue, but she was grinning like a little girl. Momentarily baffled to silence, Selkirk stumbled the rest of the way up to the lantern room. This time, he froze completely.

Even on this dark day, even through the dust and salt that caked the window glass inside and out, light flooded the chamber. None of it came from the big lamp, which of course lay unlit. Assuming it still worked at all. Across the platform, a pair of white wicker chairs sat side by side, aimed out to sea. Over their backs, the keeper had draped blankets of bright red wool, and beneath them lay a rug of similar red. And on the rug stood a house.

Like most of the dolls, it had been assembled entirely from shells and seaweed and sand. From its peaked roof, tassels of purple flowers hung like feathers, and all around the eves, gull feathers hung like the decorative flourishes on some outrageous society woman's hat. On the rug – clearly, it served as a yard – tiny nuns prowled like cats. Some lay on their backs with their arms folded across their crucifixes, soaking up the light. One was climbing the leg of one of the wicker chairs. And a group – at least five – stood at the base of the window, staring out to sea.

And that is what reminded Selkirk of his purpose, and brought him at least part way back to himself. He glanced around the rest of the room, noting half a dozen round wooden tables evenly spaced around the perimeter. On each, yellow beeswax candles blazed in their candlesticks, lending the air a misleading tint of yellow and promising more heat than actually existed here. Mostly, the tables held doll-making things. Tiny silver crosses, multi-coloured rocks, thousands of shells. The table directly to Selkirk's right had a single place setting laid out neatly upon it. Clean white plate, fork, spoon, one chipped teacup decorated with paintings of leaping silver fish.

Selkirk realized he was staring at a crude sort of living sundial. Each day, Mrs Marchant began with her tea and breakfast, proceeded around the platform to assemble and place her nuns, spent far too long sitting in one or the other of the wicker chairs and staring at the place where it had all happened, and eventually retired, to do it all over again when daybreak came. In spite of himself, he felt a surprisingly strong twinge of pity.

"That hat can't have helped you much," Mrs Marchant said, straightening from a bureau near her dining table where she apparently kept her tea things. The cup she brought matched the one on her breakfast table, flying fish, chips and all, and chattered lightly on its saucer as she handed it to him.

More grateful for its warmth than he realized, Selkirk rushed the cup to his mouth and winced as the hot liquid scalded his tongue. The woman stood a little too close to him. Loose strands of her hair almost tickled the back of his hand like the fringe on a shawl. Her blue eyes flicked over his face. Then she started laughing.

"What?" Selkirk took an uncertain half-step back.

"The fish," she said. When he stared, she laughed again and gestured at the cup. "When you drank, it looked like they were going to leap right into your teeth."

Selkirk glanced at the side of the cup, then back to the woman's laughing face. Judging by the layout and contents of this room, he couldn't imagine her venturing anywhere near town, but she clearly got outside to collect supplies. As a result, her skin had retained its dusky continental coloration. A beautiful creature, and no mistake.

"I am sorry," she said, meeting his eyes. "It's been a long time since anyone drank from my china but me. It's an unfamiliar sight. Come." She started around the left side of the platform. Selkirk watched, then took the opposite route, past the seaweed table, and met the woman in the centre of the seaward side of the platform, at the wicker chairs. Without waiting for him, she bent, lifted a tiny nun whose bandeau hid most of her face like a bandit's mask off the rug, and settled in the right-hand chair. The nun wound up tucked against her hip like a rabbit.

For whom, Selkirk wondered, was the left-hand chair meant, on ordinary days? The obvious answer chilled and also saddened him, and he saw no point in wasting further time.

"Mrs Marchant—"

"Manners, Mr Selkirk," the woman said, and for the second time smiled at him. "The sisters do not approve of being lectured to."

It took him a moment to understand she was teasing him. And not like Amalia had, or not exactly like. Teasing him hadn't made Amalia any happier. He sat.

"Mrs Marchant, I have bad news. Actually, it isn't really bad news, but it may feel that way at first. I know – that is, I really think I have a sense – of what this place must mean to you. I did live in town here once, and I do know your story. But it's not good for you, staying here. And there are more important considerations than you or your grief here, anyway, aren't there? There are the sailors still out there braving the seas, and . . ."

Mrs Marchant cocked her head, and her eyes trailed over his face so slowly that he almost thought he could feel them, faintly, like the moisture in the air but warmer.

"Would you remove your hat, Mr Selkirk?"

Was she teasing now? She wasn't smiling at the moment. Increasingly flustered, Selkirk settled the teacup on the floor at his feet and pulled his sopping hat from his head. Instantly, his poodle's ruff of curls spilled onto his forehead and over his ears.

Mrs Marchant sat very still. "I'd forgotten," she finally said. "Isn't that funny?"

"Ma'am?"

Sighing, she leaned back. "Men's hair by daylight." Then she winked at him, and whispered, "The nuns are scandalized."

"Mrs Marchant. The time has come. The Lighthouse Service – perhaps you've heard of it – needs to—"

"We had a dog, then," Mrs Marchant said, and her eyes swung toward the windows.

Selkirk closed his eyes, feeling the warmth of the tea unfurling in his guts, hearing the longing underneath the play in the keeper's voice. When he opened his eyes again, he found Mrs Marchant still staring toward the horizon.

"We named the dog Luis. For my father, who died at sea while my mother and I were on our way here from Lisbon. Charlie gave him to me."

After that, Selkirk hardly moved. It wasn't the story, which Amalia had told him, and which he hadn't forgotten. It was the way this woman said her husband's name.

"He didn't have to work, you know. Charlie. His family built half the boats that ever left this place. He said he just wanted to make certain his friends got home. Also, I think he liked living in the lighthouse. Especially alone with me. And my girls."

"Smart fellow," Selkirk murmured, realized to his amazement that he'd said it aloud, and blushed.

But the keeper simply nodded. "Yes. He was. Also reckless, in a way. No, that is wrong. He liked . . . playing at recklessness. In storms, he used to lash himself to the railing out there." She gestured toward the thin band of metal that encircled the platform outside the windows. "Then he would lean into the rain. He said it was like sailing without having to hunt. And without leaving me."

"Was he religious like you?" Selkirk hadn't meant to ask anything. And Mrs Marchant looked completely baffled. "The . . ." Selkirk muttered, and gestured at the rug, the house. Sand-convent. Whatever it was.

"Oh," she said. "It is a habit, only." Again, she grinned, but unlike Amalia, she waited until she was certain he'd got the joke. Then she went on. "While my father lived here, my mother and I earned extra money making dolls for the Sacred Heart of Mary. They gave them to poor girls. Poorer than we were."

The glow from Mrs Marchant's eyes intensified on his cheek, as though he'd leaned nearer to a candle flame. Somehow, the feeling annoyed him, made him nervous.

"But he did leave you," he said, more harshly than he intended. "Your husband."

Mrs Marchant's lips flattened slowly. "He meant to take me. The Kendall brothers – Kit was his best and oldest friend, and he'd known Kevin since the day Kevin was born – wanted us both to come sail with them, on the only beautiful January weekend I have ever experienced here. 1837. The air was so warm, Mr Selkirk, and the whales gone for the winter. I didn't realize until then that Charlie had never once, in his whole life, been to sea. I'd never known until that weekend that he wanted to go. Of course I said yes. Then Luis twisted his foreleg in the rocks out there, and I stayed to be with him. And I made Charlie go anyway. He was blonde like you. Did you know that?"

Shifting in his seat, Selkirk stared over the water. The sky hung heavy and low, its colour an unbroken blackish grey, so that he no longer had any idea what time it was. After noon, surely. If he failed to conclude his business here soon, he'd never make it out of Winsett before nightfall, horse or no. At his feet, the nuns watched the water.

"Mrs Marchant."

"He wasn't as tall as you are, of course. Happier, though."

Selkirk swung his head toward the woman. She took no notice.

"Of course, why wouldn't he be? He had so much luck in his short life. More than anyone deserves or has any right to expect. The Sacred Heart of Mary sisters always taught that it was bad luck to consort with the lucky. What do you make of that, Mr Selkirk?"

It took Selkirk several seconds to sort the question, and as he sat, Mrs Marchant stood abruptly and put her open palm on the window. For a crazy second, just because of the stillness of her posture and the oddly misdirected tilt of her head – toward land, away from the sea – Selkirk wondered if she were blind, like her dolls.

"I guess I've never been around enough luck to say," Selkirk finally said.

She'd been looking down the coast, but now she turned to him, beaming once more. "The sisters find you an honest man, sir. They invite you to more tea."

Returning to the bureau with his cup, she refilled it, then sat back down beside him. She'd left the nun she'd had before on the bureau, balancing in the centre of a white plate like a tiny ice skater.

"The morning after they set sail," she said, "Luis woke me up." In the window, her eyes reflected against the grey. "He'd gotten better all through the day, and he'd been out all night. He loved to be. I often didn't see him until I came outside to hang the wash or do the chores. But that day, he scratched and whined against the door. I thought he'd fallen or hurt himself again and hurried to let him in. But when I did, he raced straight past me up the stairs. I hurried after, and found him whimpering against the light there. I was so worried that I didn't even look at the window for the longest time. And when I did . . . "

All the while, Mrs Marchant had kept her hands pressed together in the folds of her dress, but now she opened them. Selkirk half-expected a nun to flap free of them on starfish wings, but they were empty. "So much whiteness, Mr Selkirk. And yet it was dark. You wouldn't think that would be possible, would you?"

"I've lived by the sea all my life," Selkirk said.

"Well, then. That's what it was like. A wall of white that shed no light at all. I couldn't even see the water. I had the lamp lit, of course, but all that did was emphasize the difference between *in here* and *out there*."

Selkirk stood. If he were Charlie Marchant, he thought, he would never have left the Convent, as he'd begun to think of the whole place. Not to go to sea. Not even to town. He found himself remembering the letters he'd sent Amalia during his dock-working years. Pathetic, clumsy things. She'd never responded to those, either. Maybe she'd been trying, in her way, to be kind.

"I've often wondered if Luis somehow sensed the ship coming," Mrs Marchant said. "We'd trained him to bark in the fog, in case a passing captain could hear but not see us. But maybe that day Luis was just barking at the whiteness.

"The sound was unmistakable when it came. I heard wood splintering. Sails collapsing. A mast smashing into the water. But there wasn't any screaming. And I thought . . ."

"You thought maybe the crew had escaped to the lifeboats," Selkirk said, when it was clear Mrs Marchant was not going to finish her sentence.

For the first time in several minutes, Mrs Marchant turned her gaze on him. Abruptly, that luminous smile crept over her lips. "You would make the most marvellous stuffed giraffe," she said.

Selkirk stiffened. Was he going to have to carry this poor, gently raving woman out of here? "Mrs Marchant, it's already late. We need to be starting for town soon."

If she understood what he meant, she gave no sign. "I knew what ship it was." She sank back into her wicker chair, the smile gone, and crossed her legs. "What other vessel would be out there in the middle of winter? I started screaming, pounding the glass. It didn't take me long to realize they wouldn't have gone to the rowboats. In all likelihood, they'd had no idea where they were. The Kendall boys were experienced seamen, excellent sailors, Mr Selkirk. But that fog had dropped straight out of the heart of the sky, or maybe it had risen from the dead sea bottom, and it was solid as stone.

"And then – as if it were the fogbank itself, and not Charlie's boat, that had run aground on the sandbar out there – all that whiteness just shattered. The whole wall cracked apart into whistling, flying fragments. Just like that, the blizzard blew in. How does that happen, Mr Selkirk? How does the sea change its mind like that?"

Selkirk didn't answer. But for the first time, he thought he understood why the sailors in the Blubber Pike referred to those teasing, far-off flickers of light the way they did.

"I rushed downstairs, thinking I'd get the rowboat and haul myself out there and save them. But the waves . . . they were snarling and snapping all over themselves, and I knew I'd have to wait. My tears were freezing on my face. I was wearing only a dressing gown, and the wind whipped right through me. The door to the lighthouse was banging because I hadn't shut it properly, and I was so full of fury and panic I was ready to start screaming again. I looked out to sea, and all but fell to my knees in gratitude.

"It was there, Mr Selkirk. I could see the ship. Some of it, anyway. Enough, perhaps. I could just make it out. The prow, part of the fore-deck, a stump of mast. I turned around and raced back inside for my clothes.

"Then I ran all the way to town. We never kept a horse here, Charlie didn't like them. The strangest thing was this sensation I kept having, this feeling that I'd gotten lost. It was impossible; that path out there was well-travelled in those days, and even now, you had no trouble, did you? But I couldn't feel my skin. Or . . . it was as though I had come out of it. There was snow and sand flying all around, wind in the dunes. So cold. My Charlie out there. I remember thinking, *This is what the Bruxsa feels like. This is why she torments travellers. This is why she feeds.* You know, at some point, I thought maybe I'd become her."

Pursing his lips, Selkirk stirred from the daze that had settled over him. "Brucka?"

"*Bruxsa.* It is like . . . a banshee? Do you know the word? A ghost, but not of anyone. A horrid thing all its own."

Was it his imagination, or had the dark outside deepened toward evening? If he didn't get this finished, neither one of them would make it out of here tonight. "Mrs Marchant, perhaps we could continue this on the way back to town."

Finally, as though he'd slapped her, Mrs Marchant blinked. "What?"

"Mrs Marchant, surely you understand the reason for my coming. We'll send for your things. You don't *have* to leave today, but wouldn't that be easiest? I'll walk with you. I'll make certain—"

"When I finally reached Winsett," Mrs Marchant said, her stare returning as that peculiar, distant smiled played across her mouth, "I went straight for the first lit window I saw. Selkirk's. The candle-maker. Your uncle."

Selkirk cringed, remembering those hard, overheated hands smashing against the side of his skull.

"He was so kind," she said, and his mouth quivered and fell open as she went on. "He rushed me inside. It was warm in his shop. At the time, it literally felt as though he'd saved my life. Returned me to my body. I sat by his fire, and he raced all over town through the blizzard and came back with whalers, sailing men. Charlie's father, and the Kendalls' older brother. There were fifteen of them, at least. Most set out immediately on horseback for the point. Your uncle wrapped me in two additional sweaters and an overcoat, and he walked all the way back out here with me, telling me it would be all right. By the time we reached the lighthouse, he said, the sailors would already have figured a way to get the boys off that sandbar and home."

To Selkirk, it seemed this woman had reached into his memories and daubed them with colours he knew couldn't have been there. His uncle had been kind to no one. His uncle had hardly spoken except to complete business. The very idea of his using his shop fire to warm somebody, risking himself to rouse the town to some wealthy playboy's rescue . . .

But of course, by the time Selkirk had come here, the town was well on its way to failing, and his aunt had died in some awful, silent way no one spoke about. Maybe his uncle had been different, before. Or maybe, he thought with a sick quivering deep in his stomach, he was just an old lecher, on top of being a drunk.

"By the time we got back here, it was nearly dusk," Mrs Marchant said. "The older Kendall and four of the sailors had already tried four different times to get the rowboat away from shore and into the waves. They were all tucked inside my house, now, trying to stave off pneumonia.

"'Tomorrow,' one of the sailors told me. 'Tomorrow, please God, if they can just hold on. We'll find a way to them.'

"And right then, Mr Selkirk. Right as the light went out of that awful day for good, the snow cleared. For one moment. And there they were."

A single tear crept from the lashes of her right eye. She was almost whispering, now. "It was like a gift. Like a glimpse of him in heaven. I raced back outside, called out, leapt up and down, we all did, but of course they couldn't hear, and weren't paying attention. They were scrambling all over the deck. I knew right away which was Charlie. He was in the bow, all bundled up in a hat that wasn't his and what looked like three or four coats. He looked like one of my nuns, Mr Selkirk." She grinned again. "The one with the bandeau that hides her face? I was holding her in my lap before. I made her in memory of this one moment."

Selkirk stared. Was the woman actually celebrating this story?

"I could also see the Kendall boys' hair as they worked amidships. So red, like twin suns burning off the overcast.

"'Bailing,' Charlie's father told me. 'The ship must be taking on water. They're trying to keep her where she is.'"

Again, Mrs Marchant's smile slid, but didn't vanish entirely. "I asked how long they could keep doing that. But what I really wondered was how long they'd already been at it. Those poor, beautiful boys.

"Our glimpse lasted two minutes. Maybe even less. I could see new clouds rising behind them. Like a sea-monster rearing right out of the waves. But at the last, just before the snow and the dark obliterated our sight of them, they all stopped as one, and turned around. I'm sorry, Mr Selkirk."

She didn't wipe her face, and there weren't any tears Selkirk could see. She simply sat in her chair, breathing softly. Selkirk watched her with some relief.

"I remember the older Kendall boy standing beside me," she finally said. "He was whispering. '*Aw, come on boys. Get your gear on.*' The Kendalls, you see . . . they'd removed their coats. And I finally realized what it meant, that I could see their hair. They hadn't bothered with their hats, even though they'd kept at the bailing. Remember, I've been around sailors all my life, Mr Selkirk. All the men in my family were sailors, long before they came to this country. My father had been whaling here when he sent for us. So I knew what I was seeing."

"And what was that?"

"The Kendalls had given up. Less than one hundred yards from shore, they'd given up. Or decided that they weren't going to make it through the night. Either rescue would come before dawn, or it would no longer matter. The ship would not hold. Or the cold would overwhelm them. So they were hastening the end, one way or another.

"But not Charlie. Not my Charlie. He didn't jump in the air. He just slumped against the railing. But I know he saw me, Mr Selkirk. I could feel him. Even under all those hats. I could always feel him. Then the snow came back. And night fell.

"The next time we saw them, they were in the rigging."

Silently, Selkirk gave up the idea of escaping Winsett until morning. The network of functioning lights and functional keepers the Service had been toiling so hard to establish could wait one more winter evening.

"This was midday, the second day. That storm was a freak of nature. Or perhaps not natural at all. How can that much wind blow a storm nowhere? It was as though the blizzard itself had locked jaws on those boys – on my boy – and would not let go. The men who weren't already wracked by coughs and fever made another five attempts with the rowboat, and never got more than fifteen feet from shore. The ice in the air was like arrows raining down.

"Not long after the last attempt, when almost everyone was indoors and I was rushing about making tea and caring for the sick and trying to shush Luis, who had been barking since dawn, I heard Charlie's father cry out and hurried outside.

"I'd never seen light like that, Mr Selkirk, and I haven't since. Neither snow nor wind had eased one bit, and the clouds hadn't lifted. But there was the ship again, and there were our boys. Up in the ropes, now. The Kendalls had their hats back on and their coats around them, tucked up tight together with their arms through the lines. Charlie had gone even higher, crouching by himself, looking down at the brothers or maybe the deck. I hoped they were talking to each other, or singing, anything to keep their spirits up and their breath in them. Because the ship . . . have you ever seen quicksand, Mr Selkirk? It was almost like that. This glimpse lasted a minute, maybe less. But in that time, the hull dropped what looked like another full foot underwater. And that was the only thing we saw move."

"I don't understand," Selkirk said. "The sandbar was right there. It's what they hit, right? Or the rocks right around it? Why not just climb down?"

"If they'd so much as put their feet in that water, after all they'd been exposed to, they would have frozen on the spot. All they could do was cling to the ropes.

"So they clung. The last healthy men came out behind Charlie's father and me to watch. And somehow, just the clear sight of the ship out there inspired us all. And the way the mast was tilting toward the surface got us all angry and active again.

"We got close once, just at dark. The snow hadn't cleared, but the wind had eased. It had been in our ears so long, I'm not sure we even realized it at first. The sickest men, including the older Kendall boy, had been run back to town on horseback, and we hoped other Winsett whalers might be rigging up a brig in the harbour to try reaching Charlie's ship from the sea-side, rather than from land, the moment the weather permitted. I kept thinking I'd heard new sounds out there, caught a glimpse of the mast of a rescue vessel. But of course it was too soon, and we couldn't really hear or see anything but the storm, anyway. And in the midst of another round of crazy, useless running about, Charlie's father grabbed my wrist and whirled me around to face the water and said, 'Stop. Listen.'

"And I understood finally that I heard nothing. Sweet, beautiful nothing. Right away I imagined that I should be able to hear Charlie and the Kendalls through the quiet. Before anyone could stop me, I was racing for the shore, my feet flying into the frozen water and my dress freezing against my legs, but I could hardly feel it. I was already so cold, so numb. We all were. I started screaming my husband's name. It was too shadowy and snowy to see. But I went right on screaming, and everyone else that was left with us held still.

"But I got no answer. If it weren't for the swirling around my feet, I might have thought even the water had had its voice sucked from it.

"And then."

Finally, for the first time, Mrs Marchant's voice broke. In a horrible way, Selkirk realized he envied her this experience. No single hour, let alone day, had ever impressed itself on him the way these days had on her, except perhaps for those few fleeting, sleet-drenched moments with Amalia. And those had cast an uglier, darker shadow.

When Mrs Marchant continued, the quaver had gone, as though she'd swallowed it. "It was to be the last time I heard his real voice, Mr Selkirk. I think I already knew that. And when I remember it now, I'm not even certain I really did hear it. How could I have? It was a croak, barely even a whisper. But it was Charlie's voice. I'd still swear to it, in spite of everything, even though he said just the one word. '*Hurry.*'

"The last two remaining men from Winsett needed no further encouragement. In an instant, they had the rowboat in the water. Charlie's dad and I shoved off while they pulled with all their might against the crush of the surf. For a minute, no more, they hung up in that same spot that had devilled all our efforts for the past thirty-six hours, caught in waves that beat them back and back. Then they just sprung free. All of a sudden, they were in open water, heaving with all their might toward the sandbar. We were too exhausted to clap or cheer. But my heart leapt so hard in my chest I thought it might break my ribs.

"As soon as they were twenty feet from shore, we lost sight of them, and later, they said all they saw was blackness and water and snow, so none of us knows how close they actually got. They were gone six, maybe seven minutes. Then, as if a dyke had collapsed, sound came rushing over us. The wind roared in and brought a new, hard sleet. There was a one last, terrible pause that none of us mistook for calm. The water had simply risen up, you see, Mr Selkirk. It lifted our rescue rowboat in one giant black wave and hurled it halfway up the beach. The two men in the boat got slammed to the sand. Fortunately – miraculously, really – the wave hadn't crested until it was nearly on top of the shore, so neither man drowned. One broke both wrists, the other his nose and teeth. Meanwhile, the water poured up the beach, soaked us all, and retreated as instantaneously as it had come."

For the first time, Selkirk realized that the story he was hearing no longer quite matched the one Amalia had told him. Even more startling, Amalia's had been less cruel. No rescues had been attempted because none had been possible. No real hope had ever emerged. The ship had simply slid off the sandbar, and all aboard had drowned.

"Waves don't just rise up," he said.

Mrs Marchant tilted her head. "No? My father used to come home from half a year at sea and tell us stories. Waves riding the ghost of a wind two years gone and two thousand leagues distant, roaming alone like great, rogue beasts, devouring everything they encounter. Not an uncommon occurrence on the open ocean."

"But this isn't the open ocean."

"And you think the ocean knows, or cares? Though I will admit to you, Mr Selkirk. At the time, it seemed like the sea just didn't want us out there.

"By now, the only two healthy people at Cape Roby Point were Charlie's father and me. And when that new sleet kept coming and coming . . . well. We didn't talk about it. We made our wounded rowers as comfortable as we could by the fire on the rugs inside. Then we set about washing bedding, setting out candles. I began making this little sister here—" as she spoke, she toed the doll with the white bandeau, which leaned against her feet "—to keep him company in his coffin. Although both of us knew, I'm sure, that we weren't even likely to get the bodies back.

"My God, the sounds of that night. I can still hear the sleet drumming on the roof. The wind coiling around the tower. All I could think about was Charlie out there, clinging to the ropes for hope of reaching me. I knew he would be gone by morning. Around two o'clock, Charlie's father fell asleep leaning against a wall, and I eased him into a chair and sank down on the floor beside him. I must have been so exhausted, so overwhelmed, that I slept, too, without meaning to, right there at his feet.

"And when I woke . . ."

The Kendalls, Selkirk thought, as he watched the woman purse her mouth and hold still. Had he known them? It seemed to him he'd at least known who they were. At that time, though, he'd had eyes only for Amalia. And after that, he'd kept to himself, and left everyone else alone.

"When I woke," Mrs Marchant murmured, "there was sunlight. I didn't wait to make sense of what I was seeing. I didn't think about what I'd find. I didn't wake Charlie's father, but he came roaring after me as I sprinted from the house.

"We didn't even know if our rowboat would float. We made straight for it anyway. I didn't look at the sandbar. Do you find that strange? I didn't want to see. Not yet. I looked at the dunes, and they were gold, Mr Selkirk. Even with the blown grass and seaweed strewn all over them, they looked newly born.

"The rowboat had landed on its side. The wood had begun to split all down one side, but Charlie's father thought it would hold. Anyway, it was all we had, our last chance. Without a word, we righted it and dragged it to the water, which was like glass. Absolutely flat, barely rolling over to touch the beach. Charlie's father wasn't waiting for me. He'd already got into the boat and begun to pull. But when I caught the back and dragged myself in, he held position just long enough, still not saying a single thing. Then he started rowing for all he was worth.

"For a few seconds longer, I kept my head down. I wanted to pray, but I couldn't. My mother was a Catholic, and we'd worked for the nuns. But somehow, making the dolls had turned God doll-like, for me. Does that make sense? I found it impossible to have faith in anything that took the face we made for it. I wanted some other face than the one I knew, then. So I closed my eyes and listened to the seagulls squealing around, skimming the surface for dead fish. Nothing came to me, except how badly I wanted Charlie back. Finally, I lifted my head.

"I didn't gasp, or cry out. I don't think I even felt anything.

"First off, there were only two of them. The highest was Charlie. He'd climbed almost to the very top of the main mast, which had tilted over so far that it couldn't have been more than twenty-five feet above the water. Even with that overcoat engulfing him and the hat pulled all the way down over his ears, I could tell by the arms and legs snarled in the rigging that it was him.

"'Is he moving, girl?' Charlie's father asked, and I realized he hadn't been able to bring himself to look, either. We lurched closer.

"Then I did gasp, Mr Selkirk. Just once. Because he *was* moving. Or I thought he was. He seemed to be settling . . . resettling . . . I can't explain it. He was winding his arms and legs through the ropes, like a child trying to fit into a hiding place as you come for him. As if he'd just come back there. Or maybe the movement was wind. Even now, I don't know.

"Charlie's father swore at me and snarled his question again. When I didn't answer, he turned around. 'Lord Jesus,' I heard him say. After that, he just put his head down and rowed. And I kept my eyes on Charlie, and the empty blue sky beyond him. Anywhere but down the mast, where the other Kendall boy hung.

"By his ankles, Mr Selkirk. His ankles, and nothing more. God only knows what held him there. The wind had torn his clothes right off him. He had his eyes and his mouth open. He looked so pale, so thin, nothing like he had in life. His body had red slashes all over it, as though the storm had literally tried to rip him open. Just a boy, Mr Selkirk. His fingertips all but dancing on the water.

"Charlie's father gave one last heave, and our little boat knocked against the last showing bit of the Kendalls' ship's hull. The masts above us groaned, and I thought the whole thing was going to crash down on top of us. Charlie's father tried to wedge an oar in the wood, get us in close, and finally he just rowed around the ship and ran us aground on the sandbar. I leapt out after him, thinking I should be the one to climb the mast. I was lighter, less likely to sink the whole thing once and for all. Our home, our lighthouse, was so close it seemed I could have waded over and grabbed it. I probably could have. I leaned back, looked up again, and this time I was certain I saw Charlie move.

"His father saw it, too, and he started screaming. He wasn't even making words, but I was. I had my arms wide open, and I was calling my husband. 'Come down. Come home, my love.' I saw his arms disentangle themselves, his legs slide free. The ship sagged beneath him. If he so much as touched that water, I thought, it would be too much. The cold would have him at the last. He halted, and his father stopped screaming, and I went silent. He hung there so long I thought he'd died after all, now that he'd heard our voices one last time. Then, hand over hand, so painfully slowly, like a spider crawling down a web, he began to edge upside-down over the ropes. He reached the Kendall boy's poor, naked body and bumped it with his hip. It swung out and back, out and back. Charlie never even looked, and he didn't slow or alter his path. He kept coming.

"I don't even remember how he got over the rail. As he reached the deck, he disappeared a moment from our sight. We were trying to figure how to get up there to him. Then he just climbed over the edge and fell to the sand at our feet. The momentum from his body gave the wreck a final push, and it slid off the sandbar into the water and sank, taking the Kendall boy's body with it.

"The effort of getting down had taken everything Charlie had. His eyes were closed. His breaths were shallow, and he didn't respond when we shook him. So Charlie's father lifted him and dropped him in the rowboat. I hopped in the bow with my back to the shore, and Charlie's father began to pull desperately for the mainland. I was sitting calf-deep in water, cradling my husband's head facedown in my lap. I stroked his cheeks, and they were so cold. Impossibly cold, and bristly, and hard. Like rock. All my thoughts, all my energy, all the heat I had I was willing into my fingers, and I was cooing like a dove. Charlie's father had his back to us, pulling for everything he was worth. He never turned around. And so he didn't . . ."

Once more, Mrs Marchant's voice trailed away. Out the filthy windows, in the grey that had definitely darkened into full-blown dusk now, Selkirk could see a single trail of yellow-red, right at the horizon, like the glimpse of eye underneath a cat's closed lid. Tomorrow the weather would clear. And he would be gone, on his way home. Maybe he would stay there this time. Find somebody he didn't have to pay to keep him company.

"It's a brave thing you've done, Mrs Marchant," he said, and before he could think about what he was doing, he slid forward and took her chilly hand in his. He meant nothing by it but comfort, and was surprised to discover the sweet, transitory sadness of another person's fingers curled in his. A devil's smile of a feeling, if ever there was one. "He was a good man, your husband. You have mourned him properly and well."

"Just a boy," she whispered.

"A good boy, then. And he loved you. You have paid him the tribute he deserved, and more. And now it's time to do him the honour of living again. Come back to town. I'll see you somewhere safe and warm. I'll see you there myself, if you'll let me."

Very slowly, without removing her fingers, Mrs Marchant raised her eyes to his, and her mouth came open. "You . . . you silly man. You think . . . But you said you knew the story."

Confused, Selkirk squeezed her hand. "I know it now."

"You believe I have stayed here, cut off from all that is good in the world, shut up with my nuns all these years like an abbess, for love? For grief?"

Now Selkirk let go, watching as Mrs Marchant's hand fluttered before settling in her lap like a blown leaf. "There's no crime in that, surely. But now—"

"I've always wondered how the rowboat flipped," she said, in a completely new, expressionless tone devoid of all her half-sung tones, as he stuttered to silence. "All the times I've gone through it and over it, and I can't get it straight. I can't see how it happened."

Unsure what to do with his hands, Selkirk finally settled them on his knees. "The rowboat?"

"Dead calm. No ghost wave this time. We were twenty yards from shore. Less. We could have hopped out and walked. I was still cooing. Still stroking my husband's cheeks. But I knew already. And I think his father knew, too. Charlie had died before we even got him in the boat. He wasn't breathing. Wasn't moving. He hadn't during the whole, silent trip back to shore. I turned toward land to see exactly how close we were. And just like that I was in the water.

"If you had three men and were trying, you couldn't flip a boat that quickly. One of the oars banged me on the head. I don't know if it was that or the cold that stunned me. But I couldn't think. For a second, I had no idea which way was up, even in three feet of water, and then my feet found bottom, and I stood and staggered toward shore. The oar had caught me right on the scalp, and a stream of blood kept pouring into my eyes. I wasn't thinking about Charlie. I wasn't thinking anything except that I needed to be out of the cold before I became it. I could feel it in my bloodstream. I got to the beach, collapsed in the sun, remembered where I was and what I'd been doing, and spun around.

"There was the boat, floating right-side up, as though it hadn't flipped it all. Oars neatly shipped, like arms folded across a chest. Water still as a lagoon beneath it. And neither my husband nor his father *anywhere*.

"I almost laughed. It was impossible. Ridiculous. So cruel. I didn't scream. I waited, scanning the water, ready to lunge in and save Charlie's dad if I could only see him. But there was nothing. No trace. I sat down and stared at the horizon and didn't weep. It seemed perfectly possible that I might freeze to death right there, complete the event. I even opened the throat of my dress, thinking of the Kendall boys shedding their coats that first day. That's what I was doing when Charlie crawled out of the water."

Selkirk stood up. "But you said—"

"He'd lost his hat. And his coat had come open. He crawled right up the beach, sidewise, like a crab. Just the way he had down the rigging. Of course, my arms opened to him, and the cold dove down my dress. I was laughing, Mr Selkirk. Weeping and laughing and cooing, and his head swung up, and I saw."

With a single, determined wriggle of her shoulders, Mrs Marchant went completely still. She didn't speak again for several minutes. Helpless, Selkirk sat back down.

"The only question I had in the end, Mr Selkirk, was when it had happened."

For no reason he could name, Selkirk experienced a flash of Amalia's cruel, haunted face, and tried for the thousandth time to imagine where she'd gone. Then he thought of the dead town behind him, the debris disappearing piece by piece and bone by bone into the dunes, his aunt's silent death. His uncle. He'd never made any effort to determine what had happened to his uncle after Amalia vanished.

"I still think about those boys, you know," Mrs Marchant murmured. "Every day. The one suspended in the ropes, exposed like that, all torn up. And the one that disappeared. Do you think he jumped to get away, Mr Selkirk? I think he might have. I would have."

"What on earth are you—"

"Even the dead's eyes reflect light," she said, turning her bright and living ones on him. "Did you know that? But Charlie's eyes . . . Of course, it wasn't really Charlie, but . . ."

Selkirk almost leapt to his feet again, wanted to, wished he could hurtle downstairs, flee into the dusk. And simultaneously he found that he couldn't.

"What do you mean?"

For answer, Mrs Marchant cocked her head at him, and the ghost of her smile hovered over her mouth and evaporated. "What do I mean? How do I know? Was it a ghost? Do you know how many hundreds of sailors have died within five miles of this point? Surely one or two of them might have been angry about it."

"Are you actually saying—"

"Or maybe that's silly. Maybe ghosts are like gods, no? Familiar faces we have clamped on what comes for us? Maybe it was the sea. I can't tell you. What I can tell you is that there was no Charlie in the face before me, Mr Selkirk. None. I had no doubt. No question.

My only hope was that whatever it was had come for him after he was gone, the way a hermit crab climbs inside a shell. Please God, whatever that is, let it be the wind and the cold that took him."

Staggering upright, Selkirk shook his head. "You said he was dead."

"So he was."

"You were mistaken."

"It killed the Kendall boy, Mr Selkirk. It crawled down and tore him to shreds. I'm fairly certain it killed its own father as well. Charlie's father, I mean. Luis took one look at him and vanished into the dunes. I never saw the dog again."

"Of course it was him. You're not yourself, Mrs Marchant. All these years alone . . . It spared you, didn't it? Didn't he?"

Mrs Marchant smiled one more time and broke down weeping, silently. "It had just eaten," she whispered. "Or whatever it is it does. Or maybe I had just lost my last loved ones, and stank of the sea, and appeared as dead to it as it did to me."

"Listen to me," Selkirk said, and on impulse he dropped to one knee and took her hands once more. God, but they were cold. So many years in this cold, with this weight on her shoulders. "That day was so full of tragedy. Whatever you think you . . ."

Very slowly, Selkirk stopped. His mind retreated down the stairs, out the lighthouse door to the mainland, over the disappearing path he'd walked between the dunes, and all the way back into Winsett. He saw anew the shuttered boarding houses and empty taverns, the grim smile of the stable-boy. He saw the street where his uncle's cabin had been. What had happened to his uncle? His aunt? *Amalia?* Where had they all gone? Just how long had it taken Winsett to die? His mind scrambled farther, out of town, up the track he had taken, between the discarded pots and decaying whale-bones toward the other silent, deserted towns all along this blasted section of the Cape.

"Mrs Marchant," he whispered, his hands tightening around hers, having finally understood why she had stayed. "Mrs Marchant, please. Where is Charlie now?"

She stood, then, and twined one gentle finger through the tops of his curls as she wiped at her tears. The gesture felt dispassionate, almost maternal, something a mother might do to a son who has just awoken. He looked up and found her gazing again not out to sea but over the dunes at the dark streaming inland.

"It's going to get even colder," she said. "I'll put the kettle on."

2007

THE MAMMOTH BOOK OF

BEST NEW
HORROR

Stephen Jones

The finest stories such terrifying

NEIL GAIMAN
RAMSEY CAMPBELL
CHRISTOPHER FOWLER
KIM NEWMAN
STEVEN ERIKSON
MICHAEL MARSHALL SMITH
and many others

One of the major bargains of this as of any other year *Time Out*

The Church on the Island

Simon Kurt Unsworth

AFTER THE PROBLEMS with the foil cover on volume eighteen, my publishers decided they wanted to take the look of the series in a new direction. I had no problem with them trying something different with the design, although I had obviously been more than happy with the way the books had looked when Michael Marshall Smith and I produced the covers.

What I was not expecting was a figure with his chest exploding and the authors' names spilling out in gouts of gore! When I complained that this kind of image did not actually represent the content of the book, I was told that the new American publisher, Running Press, had actually increased its order on the basis of it. During uncertain publishing times, that is the kind of argument you simply cannot disagree with.

After my disappointment at how some people in our field responded to protests at the IHG Award's decision to exclude anthologies from the previous year's nominations, I was even more taken aback at the vitriol that greeted my involvement in moving the 2007 World Horror Convention outside the United States for the first time. Held in Toronto, Canada, certain members of one particular online message board decided to wage a hate campaign against the event when they decided that the organizers were being too "professional". Although the convention was an unqualified success, it was not an example of one of the genre's finest moments.

Although the Introduction covered eighty pages and the Necrology dropped to fifty-one, this edition was up to over 600 pages again. This was because the book contained twenty-six stories, including a long novella by Kim Newman (the World Fantasy Award-nominated "Cold Snap").

The anthology once again won The British Fantasy Award, and along with plenty of familiar names, the Contents page included newcomers Gary McMahon, Simon Strantzas, Marc Lecard and Joel Knight for the first time.

Also making his debut in *The Mammoth Book of Best New Horror Volume Nineteen* was British writer Simon Kurt Unsworth. As I said earlier, one of the most rewarding elements of this job is discovering new talent. Whatever some people might think, editors are always looking out for new writers who they can nurture and develop. Otherwise any genre will stagnate and, eventually, die.

However, what was even more remarkable about the World Fantasy Award-nominated "The Church on the Island" was that it was Simon's first published story, although you would never guess it from the following . . .

CHARLOTTE PULLED HERSELF onto the beach and pushed her hair back off her face in a cascade of water. She took a couple of deep breaths, quietly pleased by the fact that she was not more affected by her swim. As she let her heart rate and breathing settle, she untied the string from around her waist and freed her plastic sandals; they had spent the swim bobbing along at her side, gently tapping her thighs every now and again as if to remind her of their existence. Now, she let them fall to the floor and slid her feet into them. Water squeezed under her feet and around her toes, spilling out onto the wet sand. Then, walking away from the sea, she let her eyes rise to the object of her visit: the little blue and white church.

Charlotte had seen the church the first time she had looked out from her hotel room window. Perhaps half a mile out from shore, nestling into the vibrant blue sea, was a tiny island. It seemed to be little more than an upthrust of grey rock from the ocean, its flanks covered in scrubby green foliage. Its lower slopes looked gentle, but there was a central outcrop of rock that appeared almost cubic, as though cut by some giant hand with a dull knife. This mass was settled on to the centre of the island as though the same hand that had cut it had placed it down, forcing it into the earth like a cake decoration into icing. Its sides were almost vertical and striated with dark fissures and it looked to be fifty or sixty feet tall, although Charlotte found it hard to judge this accurately and changed her mind every time she gazed at it.

The church was in front of the outcrop, tiny and colourful against the doleful grey of the rock face. Its walls were a startling white with blue edging, the roof a wash of the same blue. By squinting, Charlotte could just make out a door in the front of the building and a cross, set at the front of the roof. At night, the church was lit by a pale yellow light that flickered in time with the wind; Charlotte assumed that oil lamps hung around its exterior. The light made its walls shimmer and stand out starkly against the grey stone mass behind it. The mass itself loomed even more at night, rearing and blocking out the stars in the Greek darkness. It gave the impression of being man-made; the crags and fissures became the battlements of a castle, abandoned and decaying but resisting a final collapse with bleak force. It, too, appeared lit at its base by the same yellowing illumination. Charlotte never saw anyone light the lamps.

In fact, as hard and as often as she looked (and she spent long periods of time simply staring at the island, to Roger's irritation), she only ever saw one person at the church, and then only for a fleeting moment. A shadow framed in the doorway, seen in the corner of her eye as she turned away, that was gone by the time she turned back. It had to be a person, she told herself. Someone lights the lamps, and the church is well cared-for. Its sides (the two that she could see from her hotel balcony, at least) were the white of freshly painted stone or brick, and the blue roof and trim were neat and well-defined. The low wall that surrounded the church corralled ground that was clear of plants or noticeable litter. It was curiously entrancing, this little blue and white building with its domed roof and dark doorway, and Charlotte studied it for hours.

It was Roger that put the idea in her head. "Why don't you swim out there?" he asked on about the third day of their holiday. "If you see it up close, you might stop staring at it all the time."

Charlotte could hear the irritation in his voice, but also the joking tone. She knew he was simply trying to draw her attention back to him and their break together, but the idea took hold in her mind and would not let go. The next day, she said to him, "It's not that far, is it? And the sea's fairly calm around here."

"You're serious?" he asked.

"Of course," she said, and couldn't help adding, "it was your idea, after all."

Charlotte planned the Great Swim (as Roger had taken to sarcastically calling it) for the second week of their break. It gave her time to get used to swimming in the sea, to feel the way it pulled and pushed at her. It also gave her the opportunity to ask around about the little church, but no one seemed to know anything about it. The holiday company representative merely shrugged, and the locals looked at her blankly when she asked. One said, "It is just an old church," and looked at Charlotte as though she were mad, but it *wasn't*. It was not old, not to look at anyway. This apparent disinterest in the church, which made Roger more dismissive of her plan, only strengthened her resolve and by the morning of the swim, she was determined to reach it, to feel its stonework for herself.

The path from the beach to the church was steeper that it had looked from the mainland and Charlotte had to scramble and grasp at plants and roots to support her on her ascent. The climb was more tiring than the swim and she reached the top grateful that she had not needed to go further. Grit had worked its way into her sandals and her feet felt hot and scratched by the time she reached her destination and her hands were grimy and sore. When she placed her hands on the top of the low wall and felt the heat of the sun on the rock and saw the church, however, all her aches were forgotten.

Close to, the building was even prettier than she expected. She wanted to walk straight to it, to marvel at its simple beauty, but before she could she had to deal with Roger. Standing by the wall, she turned back towards the beach. Across the strip of blue sea (I swam that, she thought proudly), the wedge of golden sand gleamed in the late morning sun. She located Roger's tiny, frail form by finding the hut that sold fresh fruit and cold drinks and looking just in front of it, the way they had arranged. There, besides a family group, sat Roger. She raised one arm in greeting and saw him do the same in return. At least now he would not worry and might even start to relax a little. Ah, Roger, she thought, What are we going to do with you? Back home, his constant attentiveness was flattering. Here, its focus unbroken by time apart for work and without the diluting presence of other friends, it had become claustrophobic. She could not move, it seemed, without him asking if she was all right or if she wanted anything. The Great Swim had appealed, in part at least, because it gave her time away from him. He was neither a strong enough swimmer nor adventurous enough to want to do it with her, and although she felt a little guilty at taking advantage of his weakness, she revelled in the freedom that it gave her. She could not see their relationship continuing after they returned home and although this made her sad, it was a distant sadness rather than a raw grief.

Roger hopefully placated, Charlotte turned again to the church. The path up from the beach had brought her out directly facing the door, which hunched inside a shadowed patch surrounded by a neat blue border. There was a simple wooden step up to the door. Around it, the wall was plain, white-painted stonework. Instead of approaching, however (worried that she might find the door locked and that her little adventure would end too soon and in disappointment), Charlotte went around to the far side of the building.

As she came around the church's flank, Charlotte saw that one of her assumptions about the place had been wrong; she had expected that it was built on a little plateau (possibly man-made?) and entirely separate from the rocky outcrop that glowered behind it. It was not: the rear of the church was built up against the base of the natural cliff. Going closer, she saw that the mortar that joined the church's wall to the cliff was spread thickly so that no gaps remained. Under the skin of the paint, different-sized stones had been used to ensure that the wall fitted as snugly as possible; she could see the irregular lattice of them.

The wall itself was plain except for a single dark window of quartered glass set just below the roof. The window was low enough for Charlotte to be able to see through if she went close, as the building was only single-storey. Along from the window, a metal and glass lamp hung from a bracket, and she gave a little private cheer. Her assumption about the night-time lights had, at least, been correct. She resisted the temptation to look through the window for the same reason that she had not tried the door; she wanted to save the inside of the building for as long as possible. Instead, she turned away from the church to look at the land around it.

It was beautiful. What appeared to be scrub from half a mile's distance was actually a thickly-knotted tangle of plants and small trees. The air was heavy with the smell of jasmine and curcuma and other unidentifiable but equally rich scents. Butterflies chased each other around the branches and lazy bees drifted somnambulantly from flower to flower. Their buzzing came to Charlotte in a sleepy wave, rising and falling in pitch like the roll of the sea. Under it was the sound of crickets and grasshoppers, an insistent whirring that was at the same time both frantic and curiously relaxing.

The press of plants and insects, and the birds that darted and hovered in irregular patterns above it all, was held back by the stone wall surrounding the church. In places, the wall bulged and roots pushed their way between the rough stones. The only break in the stonework was a rusted iron gate. Past the gate, there was a gap in the flora and an earthen track that led away along the base of the cliff. Here, the dark green leaves and branches and the blooming flowers had been cut and pushed back so that they formed an archway over the gate and made living, breathing walls for the path.

Charlotte stood, breathing in the scented air and luxuriating in the quiet. If Roger were there, she thought, he'd be taking photographs, pointing out interesting creatures or sounds, asking if I was *okay*, if I *wanted anything*. Being there allowed her to just *be*, unfettered by expectation or implication or demand. It was the most relaxed she had felt for her entire holiday.

Finally, Charlotte walked back around to the front of the church. She intended to go and try the door, but instead she carried on walking, going to the right side of the building. It was, as she expected, the same as the other side, only in reverse. The window was dark and the lamp's brass fittings were shiny with age. There was another gate in the surrounding wall, also rusted (although, looking closely, she saw that the hinges were well-oiled and clean) and another path along the base of the cliff. She wondered if it was simply the end of the path that started around the other side and which travelled all the way around the base of the great ragged cube, and decided that it probably was. She smiled at the simplicity of it and its unrefined, functional beauty.

Through the window, Charlotte thought she could see a light inside the building. She went close, brushing away a thin layer of sand and dust from the glass and peering through into the interior of the church. What she saw disappointed her.

Other Greek Orthodox chapels that Charlotte had visited, both large and small, had been extensively decorated, with pictures of saints lining the lower part of the walls, scenes from the life of Jesus above them ("As a teaching aid," Roger had told her pompously in a church they had visited earlier in the week. "Remember, the peasants couldn't read and so the pictures could be used by the priests as illustrations to what they were saying." She had remained silent after he spoke, not trusting herself to say anything pleasant to him, so irritated was she at his thoughtless condescension). Icons, frequently of the Holy Mother and Child, lined the walls of these other churches, their silver and gold plate ("To protect the picture beneath" – more from Roger) shining in the light from the devotional candles that burned in trays of sand. The little blue and white church, however, had none of this. The walls were bare of pictures, painted or framed. There were no candles or chairs or tapestries here. Indeed, the only decoration seemed to be mirrors in ornate frames. There was one above the door, one behind the altar and one opposite her to the side of the window. The altar, which she expected to be bedecked with, at the very least, a delicately stitched altar cloth, was a simple table partly covered in what looked like a plain white strip of material. Two candles in simple silver candlesticks burned, one at each end. Behind the altar was an open doorway. Seeing the open doorway made Charlotte nod to herself; whilst it was, in other respects, odd, the church was at least conforming to some of what she knew about the Greek Orthodox Church, where Chapels had a narthex, a central area where worshipers gathered and a private area for the priests behind the altar. Presumably, this was what lay beyond the doorway.

Charlotte stepped back from the window, still confused. The inside of the church was so plain that it might belong to some dour Calvinist chapel and she wanted to know why this was so different from the exuberant stylings she had seen in other Greek churches. She went back around to the door, confident that she could enter: that candles were burning made her sure that there must be a priest there, and that the church should be unlocked. Before she entered, however, she went once more to the top of the path up from the beach. She was experiencing a little guilt about her feelings towards Roger and wanted to wave to him, show him some affection. It would make him feel good, and might stop him worrying. When she looked, however, she could not find him. There was the fruit and drink stall, there was the family, but Roger was nowhere to be seen. Maybe he had gone to get some shade, she thought. He was paranoid about becoming sunburnt or dehydrated, another little thing about him that irritated her. Maybe he'd got angry waiting for her and taken himself off for an early beer; in a funny way, she hoped that this was the case. It would be a spark of adventurousness, a small reminder of the Roger she first met and liked, who'd made her laugh and surprised her and paid attention to her.

Swallowing a surprisingly large hitch of disappointment, Charlotte turned back to the church. As the sun rose higher, the church's shadows were creeping back towards it like whipped dogs, and its white walls gleamed. The domed blue roof was bright in the sun and the reflections of the light off the white walls were so sharp that she had to narrow her eyes as she approached the door. Whilst she expected it to be open, there was still a part of her that wondered if it might resist her push, but she never had the chance to find out. Even as she reached for the handle, the door swung open to reveal an old man who looked at her silently.

The man was dressed in a simple black robe, tied at the waist with belt of rope. His beard was a pepper of white and grey and black and a white cloth was draped over the crown of his head. Under the cloth, Charlotte saw long hair that fell in ringlets past his shoulders. He wore sandals and his toenails were long and curled.

"Welcome to the Island of the Church of the Order of St John of Patmos. My name is Babbas," the man said, and bowed. He straightened up slowly and walked by Charlotte without another word. As he went, she caught an unpleasant whiff of sour body odour and another, sweeter smell that was, if anything, even less pleasant.

Babbas was fully eight inches shorter than she was and as he walked by, she could see the top of his head with its cloth covering. What she taken for white, she saw, was actually a dirty yellow. It was stained with countless greasy rings, all overlapping like cup stains on an unvarnished table. With a little jolt of disgust, Charlotte realized that the rings were marks from his hair, from where it pressed against the linen. She took an involuntary step back from him, shocked and surprised in equal measure. Why doesn't he wash? she thought, and took another step away. He stopped and turned to her.

"This is a small church, with few facilities," he said, as though reading her thoughts. "Come, I will show you around and explain what needs to be done." His English was excellent, but she could still detect an accent there. Greek, almost definitely. Babbas spoke slowly, as though thinking about each word before he uttered it, and she wondered if this was because he was speaking a language that was not his own. His eyes were a faded blue, circled by wrinkles and overhung by heavy, grey eyebrows. He looked at her intently and then span around again and walked on. His walk was not an old man's shuffle, precisely, but Charlotte saw that he did not pick his feet far up off the ground and his steps were not long.

"Each day, before sunset," Babbas said, walking around to the left of the church, "the lamps must be lit. There are six. One here, one on the other side of the church and four at points around the island. The path will take you there; it goes all the way around this rock and comes out on the other side of the church." Silently, Charlotte gave herself another cheer. One point for me, she thought, I already worked that out!

Babbas was looking speculatively along the path and Charlotte stopped next to him. She was pleased to find that the scents from the plants and flowers covered the old man's own odour.

"It looks beautiful, does it not?" asked Babbas, but did not wait for a response. "It is, now. But it can be a long walk around the inland, even in good weather. In winter, it is treacherous. The path becomes slippery when it is wet, and the wind can be harsh, but the work is vital. All four sides of this rock must be lit with light from a flame throughout every night. Each morning, the lamps must be extinguished and filled in preparation for being lit again that forthcoming night. This means that the morning walk is often the harder, as you must carry the oil with you in a can." He sighed.

Standing next to the old man gave Charlotte the opportunity to study him more closely. His face was deeply lined and his skin was the deep brown of someone who spent a great deal of time outdoors. Except for his dress, which seemed too simple, he acted as though he were in charge here. He must be the priest, she thought. Why else would he be here? Perhaps this parish isn't well off enough to afford to buy nice robes or icons for the church. I mean, it can't have many regular parishioners, can it? Even as she thought this, her eyes were taking in more details about him. His beard hung down to his chest and his hands were ridged with prominent veins. There was something else about him, though, something harder to identify. It took her a moment to recognize it, but when she did, Charlotte was a little surprised: he seemed sad.

The two of them stood in silence, looking down the path along the base of cliff for so long that it began to make Charlotte uncomfortable. She wanted to ask the man something, but did not know what. Besides, he did not give the impression of wanting to talk. True, he had started tell her about the church, but not in an especially welcoming way. It reminded her of the lectures she had attended at university, given by tutors who saw teaching as a chore.

"Come," said the priest suddenly, making Charlotte jump, "there is much to show you."

Babbas walked back towards the church, not looking at Charlotte as he went. She followed, halfway between amused and irritated by the man's brusque manner. As he walked into the church, however, she stopped.

"Wait a minute, please," Charlotte said, "I can't come in dressed like this, can I?" She gestured down at her bikini, her naked legs and belly and shoulders now prickling in the sun. She wished she had brought sunscreen and a sarong with her; she could have tied them in a waterproof bag and towed it along with her sandals.

"Why?" asked the old man.

"Don't I have to cover my shoulders and legs out of respect? I've had to do that for the other Greek churches I've been in."

The priest looked at Charlotte as though seeing her properly for the first time. He let his gaze drop from her face down her body and she began to wonder if she was safe here alone with him. Before she had time to pursue this thought, however, he raised his gaze to her face again and sighed, as though terribly tired.

"God made both skin and cloth and loves you equally in both," he said. "He is with you dressed and undressed. He is in your clothes, and so always sees you as naked. He is God and sees us all as naked all the time. What use are clothes to Him? Religion, churches and chapels and monasteries, often forget that God sees beyond the covers that we put around the world. They forget that the ceremonies they perform have function, have purpose beyond simply tradition or habit or worship. When ceremonies and rules become all-important, then God is forgotten. Here, the ceremonies are about a purpose. They have a function. They are not about simply the look or the sound or the history of things. You may enter this church of the Order of St John of Patmos dressed however you wish, as long as you respect the work that is done here and not just the ceremony that surrounds it." He stopped and sighed again, as though exhausted by his speech. Charlotte, unsure as to whether to be embarrassed by her lack of clothes or by the fact that she had asked about her lack of clothes and so drawn attention to it, simply nodded and followed him into the church.

The inside of the small building was not as plain as it had appeared from the outside. There was decoration of a sort, but it was delicate and subtle. A black strip was painted along the base of the walls, stretching about three inches up from the floor. The top of the back strip was irregular, dipping and rising as it went around the room. When Babbas closed the door behind her, Charlotte saw that it had been painted across the bottom of the door as well. Above the black strip, the walls were painted a light yellow. There were small streaks of orange in the yellow, along with tiny flecks of blue and green. The church was lit by the candles on its altar and by the sunlight coming in through the two windows. The mirrors on the walls (and there was one on each wall, she saw) caught the light and reflected it all around, catching the streaks of colour on the walls and making them dance in the corner of her eyes. It was like being at the centre of a vast, calm flame and it was magical in a way she had not expected. The air had a warmth that held her softly and she laughed in delight at it. The old man, hearing this, smiled for the first time and did not seem so bad.

"It is wonderful, is it not?" asked Babbas.

"It's beautiful," Charlotte answered, although this did not do justice to how beautiful or wonderful it was.

"The Order of St John of Patmos, here and elsewhere, is charged with the maintenance of the light of God, and we try to love the light wherever possible. It is not an easy life here on the island; there is only one delivery of food and equipment a week, and between these times, it can be lonely. These altar candles must always be aflame, as must other torches that we will come to soon. There must always be enough fuel, enough candles, enough torches, and this takes planning, so that the necessary items can be ordered at least a week in advance, to come in with the following week's delivery. But when it is hard and when the life I have had given to me seems tiring, I need simply stand in here and feel the beauty and power of God and His love, and I know that I am valued, that I am playing my part in the worship of the light over the darkness." He stopped talking and his face fell into sadness and tiredness once more. Charlotte wondered why Babbas was telling her these things, but dared not ask. Wasn't this what she had come here for, after all? And besides, it was interesting, listening to this old man. *Such single-mindedness*, she thought briefly. *I'm not sure I could do what he does, day in, day out.*

As if reading her thoughts again, Babbas said, "It is not always so. Sometimes, there are more here than just me. In past years, this place has housed four or five of the called at a time and we would split the daily tasks between us."

"Jesus, you mean there's just you by yourself?" exclaimed Charlotte, startled, and fast on the heels of this startlement, embarrassed at having sworn in church. Babbas seemed not to notice, however, but simply sighed again and turned away. He walked to the rear of the church, going behind the altar. He went to the doorway and stopped, calling back over his shoulder, "Come."

This time, Charlotte did not move. It was not just the peremptory way in which he had called her, although that was irritating to be sure. No, it was also that the idea of going behind the altar, of entering the place where only those who served God as priests or higher could go that made her uncomfortable. Whilst her own faith was, at best, questionable, she had been raised in a family that respected even if it did not believe. She found it hard to disagree with members of the clergy and even thinking critical or dismissive thoughts about the church's ceremonies or regulations made her feel guilty. She sometimes felt it was this inability as much as anything that stopped her from taking the final step and dismissing the teaching of the church as simple superstition, and that this was a weakness in her that she should try to overcome, but she did not. Hard though it was to admit it even to herself, she liked that the church had mysteries, and revealing them would be akin to stripping away layers of her upbringing and replacing them with something smaller and infinitely more miserable. Seeing behind the altar would solve one of those mysteries, and the thought of it made her sad. She could not articulate this, knowing it made little sense. Rather, she remained still and hoped that the old man would return, would show her something else instead of what lay in the private inner sanctum.

"Come, now!" said Babbas from the darkness, and he no longer sounded old or tired, but implacable. He loomed into the light briefly, waving her towards him and saying in the same tone of voice, "There is much to show you." Miserably, feeling far worse than when she thought of losing Roger, she followed him.

She had expected to find a small chamber beyond the doorway, but was surprised to find a long passage cut into rock, lit by candles set into carved recesses. These recesses were at head height and occurred every five or six feet along the passage. The smell of smoke and old flames was strong but under it, the same sickly, corrupt odour from before caught in Charlotte's nose. Babbas was already some distance down the passage, walking in that stooped half-shuffle that she had begun to recognize. Wondering what other surprises were in store, she hurried after him.

The slap of her sandals echoed around her as she walked, the sound coming at her from all angles. She saw as she passed that behind each candle, painted on the back of the recesses, were portraits of people. There were both men and women, all unsmiling and serious-looking. All were wearing a white cloth over their heads, and all had dates across the base of the portraits. In the flickering light of the candles, their eyes seemed to follow her and their lips pursed in disapproval. As much to break the silence and to draw her attention from their gaze as anything, Charlotte called ahead to the old man, "Who are the people in portraits?"

"The previous leaders of the Order here."

"But there are women," she said before she could stop herself. Babbas turned back to her. There was light from somewhere ahead and for a moment, he was simply a silhouette in the passage. He stretched his arms out, placing his palms against the walls. Leaning forward, he let his arms take his weight. His face came into the light and Charlotte saw his teeth, gleaming a terrible ivory. He stared at her and smiled, although there was no humour in it.

"This is not a branch of the Orthodox Church," he said, "and we have always known that God gave women the same role to play in the struggle between good and evil as men. He cares not whether it is a man or a woman who lights the candles and lamps and torches, as long as they are lit. Try to understand, this place has a function, a purpose, beyond simply mouthing words and performing ceremonies, the reason for whose existence most have forgotten. To these walls, men and women are called equally to play their role as God intended." He glared fiercely at Charlotte and then whirled about, his belt ends and the hem of his robe flailing around him. Charlotte, against her better, more rational, judgment, followed.

The passage opened out into a cave that took Charlotte's breath away. It looked as if the whole of the huge outcrop of rock in the island's centre had been hollowed out. Looking up, she saw a roof far above her that was ragged with gullies and peaks, like a sonar map of deep ocean floors. Here and there, chisel marks were visible and she realized that this must have been a natural opening in the rock, and that man had expanded what nature (God? She wondered fleetingly) had begun. The floor was inlaid with white marble and the walls painted the same yellow and orange as in the church, although there was no black stripe around the base of the walls. At either side of her, doorways were set into the wall, carved rectangles of darker air. The nearest one, she saw, opened into a small carved room that appeared to contain nothing but a bed. *He lives here as well!* she thought in surprise, and then her eyes were drawn to what lay in the centre of the cavern.

There was a large opening in the floor.

Charlotte walked to the opening, beckoned on by Babbas who had gone to stand at its edge. It was roughly square and at each corner was a burning torch set on top of a metal stand. Lamps burned around the walls, she noticed, and then she was looking into the hole.

It was pitch black. Charlotte stared down and immediately felt dizzy, as though she were having an attack of vertigo and, in truth, it was like looking down from a great height. The darkness in the hole seemed to start just feet below its rim, as if it was filled with inky water. Why doesn't the light go into it? she had time to think and then Babbas' hand was on her shoulder and he drew her gently away. He guided her back to where she had been standing, to where the floor was all around her, gleaming and white.

"There is the function of the Order of St John of Patmos," he said in a soft voice. "We keep the light burning that holds the darkness at bay, and it is what you have come here to do."

Charlotte stood, breathing deeply to overcome her dizziness. The old man stood looking at her kindly. His eyes glimmered with . . . what? Expectation? Hope? She could not tell and then the thing that he had said last of all lurched in her memory and the individual words connected, made a sentence, gained meaning.

"I'm not here to do anything!" she said loudly. "I just wanted to look around!"

"Of course you did not," said Babbas, and the sadness was there again in his voice, the sound of a teacher coaxing a particularly slow child. "You were called here, as I was before you and the others were before me. No one comes here to look; we come because God needs us."

"No," Charlotte said as emphatically as she could, "I wanted to see the church. Now I've seen it, I'll go. Thank you for showing it to me." She took a step back, moving towards the passageway. Babbas did not move, but simply said, "You may leave, if you wish, of course. I shall not stop you, but you will find that the world has already forgotten you."

Charlotte opened her mouth to say something, to say anything to counter the oddly threatening madness that was coming from the old man's mouth, but nothing came. She wanted to tell him that he was insane, that the place she had made for herself in the world was as secure as it had ever been, but instead, the thought of Roger popped unbidden into her mind. Or rather, the memory that Roger had been gone when she looked for him a second time. Could he have forgotten her? Gone back to their hotel room because she no longer existed for him? No, it was madness, she was real, she had a home, a job, a boyfriend.

"He has forgotten you," said Babbas, once more guessing at what she thinking, seeing her thoughts and fears reflected in her expression. "Already, the skin of the world is healing over the space you have left in it. In a few days, no trace of you will be left. Now, your place is here."

Charlotte stared at the old man and took another step back towards the passage. He was looking at her with that calm, lecturer's assurance again, confident in the absolute truth of what he was saying. She wanted to say, That's impossible, but she dared not speak. Saying anything would be an admittance of the fact that, just for a moment, she had wondered, and in her wondering, Babbas' words attained a sort of reality. But he couldn't be right, could he? It was an absurdity spouted by an old man driven mad by solitude and religious extremism. Wasn't it? How could he believe it? she asked herself, and in that moment, she realized that she did not want to leave yet. She had to persuade him of his folly, make him see that he was wrong. Frantically, she went through the things she could say that might puncture his reality and let hers in. Finally, she came across what she felt was the perfect argument.

"But I can't," she said, "I don't believe, and how can I have been called if I don't believe?"

Babbas did not reply and Charlotte thought, for the shortest time, that she's done it, had made him see his error. But then, the sad little smile never leaving his face, he said, "Believe in what? This church, this place? It is all around you, more solid than you own flesh can ever hope to be. God, perhaps? Well, he does not care, he exists outside of your beliefs or mine and He does not need your faith or mine to continue. Ah, but I see that it is not Him that you do not believe in, but the function of this place. You think, maybe, that all here is ceremony without purpose, or that the purpose itself has become obsolete, like the act of watering a dead plant?"

Babbas' smile widened into a grin that showed his teeth. Under his eyebrows, his eyes were lost in pools of flickering shadow. "This is no place of idle ceremony," he said. "Watch."

Babbas took hold of Charlotte's arm in a grip that was gentle but unyielding and pulled her to one corner of the pit in the floor. Nodding at her, he took hold of the torch and removed it from the bracket in the floor. Holding it high over his head like a lantern, he retreated to the far side of the cavern and stood in the entrance to the passage. With the torch above him, the light danced more frenziedly around him. The walls, their colours melting and merging, were flames about Charlotte's skin and felt herself try to retreat from them, wrapping her arms tightly around her stomach. She made to step away, but with his free hand, Babbas gestured to the pit by her feet. She looked down.

The surface of the darkness was writhing and bucking. Even as she gasped in surprise and fear, Charlotte imagined some great creature roiling and thrashing just below the surface of inky water. There were no reflections within the pit or the boiling darkness.

Charlotte never knew how long she watched the moving darkness for; it may have been one minute or one hour. She only knew that she was mesmerized by the rippling thing that moved before her. There was no light in it, but there *were* colours, things she could neither name nor even recognize, flashes and sparks and flows that moved and swirled and came and went. She felt herself become trapped in it, like a fly in amber, and it was only with an effort that she pulled herself away, brought her mind back in to herself.

The darkness in the corner of the pit nearest her had risen.

The black, moving thing had crept up and was lapping at the edge of the pit and tiny strands of it had slithered out onto the marble floor. It no longer looked like a liquid to Charlotte, but like some shadowed thing slowly reaching out tentacles, sending them questing across the marble floor. They reminded her of tree roots groping blindly through the earth for sustenance. Even as she watched, the first tendril had found a patch of shadow, cast by the holder that Babbas had removed the torch from. The tendril (or root? or feeler? she did not know how to explain what she was seeing) writhed furiously as it reached the shadow, thickening and pulsing. The shadow itself seemed to bulge and sway and then it was solid, more solid than it ought to be. She could not see the floor through it. More tendrils found other shadows, moving with a greedy hunger, and with them came a sound.

It was the noise of insects in the night-time, of unidentifiable slitherings and raspings, of rustling feet and creaking, ominous walls. Claws tickled across hard floors and breathing came, low and deep. There was the whisper of saliva slipping down teeth as yellow and huge as the bones of long-dead monsters, of hate given voice and pain that hummed in the blood.

Charlotte tried to scream as the noise slipped about her but the air became locked in her throat as she looked at her feet and saw that the questing tendrils had reached her. They caressed her gently and then the shadows between her toes thickened, became as impenetrable as velvet. When she tried to lift her foot to kick them away, she felt them cling with a warm tenacity that nuzzled gently at her instep and the back of her ankle. It was soft, like the touch of a lover, and it pulsed with a rhythm all of its own, and then she screamed.

Charlotte stumbled back as she screamed, and it seemed to her as she stumbled that her own shadow felt different, had a weight and a solidity that it had never had before. She felt it hold on to her knees and ankles, slipping across her skin like rough silk. She kicked out, knowing the irrationality of being frightened of your own shadow but kicking nonetheless, and then her back hit something else, something warm and she screamed even louder. The warm thing wrapped itself around her and she caught a flash of light at her side. She recognized the same sweet, sickly smell as she had caught before and then Babbas was saying in her ear, "It is alright. Do not panic."

The old man had the torch in front of Charlotte, its flaming head close to the floor. He swept it around in great arcs, forcing it into the shadows and using it as though he were driving an animal away. He was breathing hard, the air coming from his mouth in heavy puffs across her cheek. It was warm and moist and made her want to cringe. The heat of the torch flashed near her foot and she yelped in surprise and pain. She started to cry, helpless in his arms, tears of frustration and fear and anger rolling down her face. She closed her eyes and waited, useless, until the old man let her go.

"It is gone," he said simply. Charlotte heard the rattle of the torch being placed back onto its stand. Trembling, she opened her eyes.

The cavern was normal again or at least, as normal as it had been when she first saw it. The walls still seemed to move with a fluid, balletic grace around her, the light from the torches giving the colours life. Now, the vibrancy she felt was a blessing, something that pinned the contents of the pit down with its warmth and vitality.

"What was that?" she asked, hearing the idiocy of the question but having to ask anyway.

"Darkness," said Babbas. "There are places where darkness gets into the world, through pits and caverns and sunless spots. The Order of St John of Patmos is dedicated to finding these places and to keeping in them the light of God, to keeping the darkness at bay. It has been my job on this island for many years, and now it is yours."

Babbas went past Charlotte and stepped through one of the openings carved into the cavern's wall. Charlotte, terrified of being left alone near the pit, scurried after him. At the doorway, she stopped, peering through into the shadowed beyond. There was a flare of a match igniting and then the softer glow of a lantern spread around in tones of red and orange, revealing a small room.

The walls were lined with shelves, and the shelves bristled with leather-bound book, their spines black despite the light. The far wall was curtained off and in front of the curtains was a desk. Its scarred surface held an open journal and a pen.

"This is where the records are written," said Babbas, gesturing first at the open journal and then at the books lining the shelves.

"The activities of each day are listed, written in confirmation of their completion."

Charlotte, interested despite herself, said, "Are these the records for the whole order?"

"No, only this church. The Order has churches in other places and they keep their records as they see fit."

"How many other churches?"

"I do not know. People are called, and the order receives them. We do not move around. There are many places where darkness can escape into the world, and when the Order discovers them, it takes in light to combat it. That there is still darkness means that we have not found all of the places. Now, we must go. There are things to do."

Charlotte wanted to refuse, to tell him that she could not leave her life behind, but the sheer size and complexity of the loss she was facing meant that the words would not fit around it. No more saunas, she thought. No more work or going out at lunchtime with my friends. No more nights curled up on the sofa with a bottle of wine watching a movie. No more pizza or restaurants, no more telephone calls. No more life. I can't, she thought hopelessly, I can't do it. And yet, as she thought, she heard again that slithering, chitinous noise and remembered the darkness slipping across her foot like the warm kiss of some terrible, moistureless mouth, and she could not turn him down. Instead, she said, "Why can't you carry on?" A question, she knew, to avoid her own final acceptance.

"I'm dying," Babbas said. "I have something growing inside me and it is killing me. I cannot carry the oil for the lamps any more. I am slow. I have not yet, but one day I will slip and fall, or forget something, and then? It will escape. I can stay and teach you, but I cannot carry the responsibility any longer. It is why God called you." He removed the stained white cloth from his head and came towards her, holding it out in front of him reverently. She saw the marks of the old grease that stained it like tree-rings denoting age, and smelled the sickly scent of his decaying, dying flesh.

"We wear this, those of us who carry the burden," Babbas said. "It is, perhaps, our only symbolic act, the only thing we do that is devoid of true function. This is the mantle of light."

So saying, Babbas draped the cloth over Charlotte's hair so that it hung down, brushing her shoulders. It smelled old and sour. Babbas smiled at her and stepped back as the weight of centuries settled on Charlotte's head.

2008

The *New York Times* at
Special Bargain Rates

Stephen King

THE COVER THEY WANTED to put on the Twentieth Anniversary edition was even more awful than the previous one. I finally had to put my foot down. Again.

Thankfully, my latest editor at Robinson was sympathetic to my concerns and did everything he could to make sure that the final design of the book not only reflected the sophistication of the fiction it contained, but still met the needs of the marketing department. Disappointingly, the American publisher decided to ignore our wishes and went with the original design and lettering, resulting in the first totally different US cover for the series since Volume Three.

Although the previous edition had not been one of the largest ever produced, the publisher was still concerned about the overall length, and I was now contractually obligated not to allow the book to go above a certain word-length.

The Introduction still came in at seventy-seven pages and the Necrology at sixty, and the dedication continued to mark the passing of old friends and colleagues.

At least, after the controversial editorials of the previous two volumes, I contented myself with a look back over the series' twenty-year history.

I also managed to squeeze in twenty stories from a satisfying mixture of old names and relative newcomers to the genre.

However, there was one name that stood out above all the rest. After two decades, I was finally able to include a story by one of the world's most successful, popular and influential writers.

Stephen King truly is a household name, and "The *New York Times* at Special Bargain Rates" is a ghost story written in his inimitable style. He has done more to champion and popularize the horror genre over the past thirty-five years than any other author, and I can think of no better way to end this retrospective volume than with his contribution.

SHE'S FRESH OUT OF THE shower when the phone begins to ring, but although the house is still full of relatives – she can hear them downstairs, it seems they will never go away, it seems she never had so many – no one picks up. Nor does the answering machine, as James programmed it to do after the fifth ring.

Anne goes to the extension on the bed-table, wrapping a towel around herself, her wet hair thwacking unpleasantly on the back of her neck and bare shoulders. She picks it up, she says hello, and then he says her name. It's James. They had thirty years together, and one word is all she needs. He says *Annie* like no one else, always did.

For a moment she can't speak or even breathe. He has caught her on the exhale and her lungs feel as flat as sheets of paper. Then, as he says her name again (sounding uncharacteristically hesitant and unsure of himself), the strength slips from her legs. They turn to sand and she sits on the bed, the towel falling off her, her wet bottom dampening the sheet beneath her. If the bed hadn't been there, she would have gone to the floor.

Her teeth click together and that starts her breathing again. "James? Where *are* you? *What happened?*" In her normal voice, this might have come out sounding shrewish – a mother scolding her wayward eleven-year-old who's come late to the supper-table yet again – but now it emerges in a kind of horrified growl. The murmuring relatives below her are, after all, planning his funeral.

James chuckles. It is a bewildered sound. "Well, I tell you what," he says. "I don't exactly know where I am."

Her first confused thought is that he must have missed the plane in London, even though he called her from Heathrow not long before it took off. Then a clearer idea comes: although both the *Times* and the TV news say there were no survivors, there was at least one. Her husband crawled from the wreckage of the burning plane (and the burning apartment building the plane hit, don't forget that, twenty-four more dead on the ground and the number apt to rise before the world moved on to the next tragedy) and has been wandering around Brooklyn ever since, in a state of shock.

"Jimmy, are you all right? Are you . . . are you burned?" The truth of what that would mean occurs after the question, thumping down with the heavy weight of a dropped book on a bare foot, and she begins to cry. "Are you in the hospital?"

"Hush," he says, and at his old kindness – and at that old word, just one small piece of their marriage's furniture – she begins to cry harder. "Honey, hush."

"But I don't *understand!*"

"I'm all right," he says. "Most of us are."

"Most—? There are *others?*"

"Not the pilot," he says. "He's not so good. Or maybe it's the co-pilot. He keeps screaming, 'We're going down, there's no power, oh my God.' Also 'This isn't my fault, don't let them blame it on me.' He says that, too."

She's cold all over. "Who is this really? Why are you being so horrible? I just lost my husband, you asshole!"

"Honey—"

"Don't call me that!" There's a clear strand of mucus hanging from one of her nostrils. She wipes it away with the back of her hand and then flings it into the wherever, a thing she hasn't done since she was a child. "Listen, mister – I'm going to star-sixty-nine this call and the police will come and slam your *ass* . . . your ignorant, unfeeling ass . . ."

But she can go no further. It's his voice. There's no denying it. The way the call rang right through – no pick-up downstairs, no answering machine – suggests this call was just for her. And . . . *honey, hush.* Like in the old Carl Perkins song.

He has remained quiet, as if letting her work these things through for herself. But before she can speak again, there's a beep on the line.

"James? *Jimmy?* Are you still there?"

"Yeah, but I can't talk long. I was trying to call you when we went down, and I guess that's the only reason I was able to get through at all. Lots of others have been trying, we're lousy with cell phones, but no luck." That beep again. "Only now my phone's almost out of juice."

"Jimmy, did you know?" This idea has been the hardest and most terrible part for her – that he might have known, if only for an endless minute or two. Others might picture burned bodies or dismembered heads with grinning teeth; even light-fingered first responders filching wedding rings and diamond ear-clips, but what has robbed Annie Driscoll's sleep is the image of Jimmy looking out his window as the streets and cars and the brown apartment buildings of Brooklyn swell closer. The useless masks flopping down like the corpses of small yellow animals. The overhead bins popping open, carry-ons starting to fly, someone's Norelco razor rolling up the tilted aisle.

"Did you know you were going down?"

"Not really," he says. "Everything seemed all right until the very end – maybe the last thirty seconds. Although it's hard to keep track of time in situations like that, I always think."

Situations like that. And even more telling: *I always think.* As if he has been aboard half a dozen crashing 767s instead of just the one.

"In any case," he goes on, "I was just calling to say we'd be early, so be sure to get the FedEx man out of bed before I got there."

Her absurd attraction for the FedEx man has been a joke between them for years. She begins to cry again. His cell utters another of those beeps, as if scolding her for it.

"I think I died just a second or two before it rang the first time. I think that's why I was able to get through to you. But this thing's gonna give up the ghost pretty soon."

He chuckles as if this is funny. She supposes that in a way it is. She may see the humour in it herself, eventually. *Give me ten years or so, she thinks.*

Then, in that just-talking-to-myself voice she knows so well: "Why didn't I put the tiresome motherfucker on charge last night? Just forgot, that's all. Just forgot."

"James . . . honey . . . the plane crashed two days ago."

A pause. Mercifully with no beep to fill it. Then: "Really? Mrs Corey *said* time was funny here. Some of us agreed, some of us disagreed. I was a disagreer, but looks like she was right."

"Hearts?" Annie asks. She feels now as if she is floating outside and slightly above her plump damp middle-aged body, but she hasn't forgotten Jimmy's old habits. On a long flight he was always looking for a game. Cribbage or canasta would do, but hearts was his true love.

"Hearts," he agrees. The phone beeps, as if seconding that.

"Jimmy . . ." She hesitates long enough to ask herself if this is information she really wants, then plunges with that question still unanswered. "Where *are* you, exactly?"

"Looks like Grand Central Station," he says. "Only bigger. And emptier. As if it wasn't really Grand Central at all but only . . . mmm . . . a movie set of Grand Central. Do you know what I'm trying to say?"

"I . . . I think so . . ."

"There certainly aren't any trains . . . and we can't hear any in the distance . . . but there are doors going everywhere. Oh, and there's an escalator, but it's broken. All dusty, and some of the treads are gone." He pauses, and when he speaks again he does so in a lower voice, as if afraid of being overheard. "People are leaving. Some climbed the escalator – I saw them – but most are using the doors. I guess

I'll have to leave, too. For one thing, there's nothing to eat. There's a candy machine, but that's broken, too."

"Are you . . . honey, are you hungry?"

"A little. Mostly what I'd like is some water. I'd *kill* for a cold bottle of Dasani."

Annie looks guiltily down at her own legs, still beaded with water. She imagines him licking off those beads and is horrified to feel a sexual stirring.

"I'm all right, though," he adds hastily. "For now, anyway. But there's no sense staying here. Only . . ."

"What? What, Jimmy?"

"I don't know which door to use."

Another beep.

"I wish I knew which one Mrs Corey took. She's got my damn cards."

"Are you . . ." She wipes her face with the towel she wore out of the shower; then she was fresh, now she's all tears and snot. "Are you scared?"

"Scared?" he asks thoughtfully. "No. A little worried, that's all. Mostly about which door to use."

Find your way home, she almost says. *Find the right door and find your way home*. But if he did, would she want to see him? A ghost might be all right, but what if she opened the door on a smoking cinder with red eyes and the remains of jeans (he always travelled in jeans) melted into his legs? And what if Mrs Corey was with him, his baked deck of cards in one twisted hand?

Beep.

"I don't need to tell you to be careful about the FedEx man anymore," he says. "If you really want him, he's all yours."

She shocks herself by laughing.

"But I did want to say I love you—"

"Oh honey I love you t—"

"—and not to let the McCormack kid do the gutters this fall, he works hard but he's a risk-taker, last year he almost broke his fucking neck. And don't go to the bakery anymore on Sundays. Something's going to happen there, and I know it's going to be on a Sunday, but I don't know which Sunday. Time really *is* funny here."

The McCormack kid he's talking about must be the son of the guy who used to be their caretaker in Vermont . . . only they sold that place ten years ago, and the kid must be in his mid-twenties by now. And the bakery? She supposes he's talking about Zoltan's, but what on *Earth*—

Beep.

"Some of the people here were on the ground, I guess. That's very tough, because they don't have a clue how they got here. And the pilot keeps screaming. Or maybe it's the co-pilot. I think he's going to be here for quite a while. He just wanders around. He's very confused."

The beeps are coming closer together now.

"I have to go, Annie. I can't stay here, and the phone's going to shit the bed any second now, anyway." Once more in that I'm-scolding-myself voice (impossible to believe she will never hear it again after today; impossible *not* to believe), he mutters, "It would have been so simple just to . . . well, never mind. I love you, sweetheart."

"Wait! Don't go!"

"I c—"

"I love you, too! Don't go!"

But he already has. In her ear there is only black silence.

She sits there with the dead phone to her ear for a minute or more, then breaks the connection. The non-connection. When she opens the line again and gets a perfectly normal dial tone, she touches star-sixty-nine after all. According to the robot who answers her page, the last incoming call was at nine o'clock that morning. She knows who that one was: her sister Nell, calling from New Mexico. Nell called to tell Annie that her plane had been delayed and she wouldn't be in until tonight. Nell told her to be strong.

All the relatives who live at a distance – James', Annie's – flew in. Apparently they feel that James used up all the family's Destruction Points, at least for the time being.

There is no record of an incoming call at – she glances at the bedside clock and sees it's now 3.17 p.m. – at about ten past three, on the third afternoon of her widowhood.

Someone raps briefly on the door and her brother calls, "Anne? Annie?"

"Dressing!" she calls back. Her voice sounds like she's been crying, but unfortunately, no one in this house would find that strange. "Privacy, please!"

"You okay?" he calls through the door. "We thought we heard you talking. And Ellie thought she heard you call out."

"Fine!" she calls, then wipes her face again with the towel. "Down in a few!"

"Okay. Take your time." Pause. "We're here for you." Then he clumps away.

"Beep," she whispers, then covers her mouth to hold in laughter that is some emotion even more complicated than grief trying to find the only way out it has. "Beep, beep. Beep, beep, beep." She lies back on the bed, laughing, and above her cupped hands her eyes are large and awash with tears that overspill down her cheeks and run all the way to her ears. "Beep-fucking-beepity-beep."

She laughs for quite a while, then dresses and goes downstairs to be with her relatives, who have come to mingle their grief with hers. Only they feel apart from her, because he didn't call any of them. He called her. For better or worse, he called her.

During the autumn of that year, with the blackened remains of the apartment building the jet crashed into still closed off from the rest of the world by yellow police tape (although the taggers have been inside, one leaving a spray-painted message reading CRISPY CRITTERS LAND HERE), Annie receives the sort of e-blast computer-addicts like to send to a wide circle of acquaintances. This one comes from Gert Fisher, the town librarian in Tilton, Vermont. When Annie and James summered there, Annie used to volunteer at the library, and although the two women never got on especially well, Gert has included Annie in her quarterly updates ever since. They are usually not very interesting, but halfway through the weddings, funerals, and 4-H winners in this one, Annie comes across a bit of news that makes her catch her breath. Jason McCormack, the son of old Hughie McCormack, was killed in an accident on Labor Day. He fell from the roof of a summer cottage while cleaning the gutters and broke his neck.

"He was only doing a favour for his dad, who as you may remember had a stroke the year before last," Gert wrote before going on to how it rained on the library's end-of-summer lawn sale, and how disappointed they all were.

Gert doesn't say in her three-page compendium of breaking news, but Annie is quite sure Jason fell from the roof of what used to be their cottage. In fact, she is positive.

Five years after the death of her husband (and the death of Jason McCormack not long after), Annie remarries. And although they relocate to Boca Raton, she gets back to the old neighbourhood often. Craig, the new husband, is only semi-retired, and his business takes him to New York every three or four months. Annie almost always goes with him, because she still has family in Brooklyn and on Long Island. More than she knows what to do with, it sometimes seems. But she loves them with that exasperated affection that seems to belong, she thinks, only to people in their fifties and sixties. She never forgets how they drew together for her after James's plane went down, and made the best cushion for her that they could. So she wouldn't crash, too.

When she and Craig go back to New York, they fly. About this she never has a qualm, but she stops going to Zoltan's Family Bakery on Sundays when she's home, even though their raisin bagels are, she is sure, served in heaven's waiting room. She goes to Froger's instead. She is actually there, buying doughnuts (the doughnuts are at least passable), when she hears the blast. She hears it clearly even though Zoltan's is eleven blocks away. LP gas explosion. Four killed, including the woman who always passed Annie her bagels with the top of the bag rolled down, saying, "Keep it that way until you get home or you lose the freshness."

People stand on the sidewalks, looking east toward the sound of the explosion and the rising smoke, shading their eyes with their hands. Annie hurries past them, not looking. She doesn't want to see a plume of rising smoke after a big bang; she thinks of James enough as it is, especially on the nights when she can't sleep. When she gets home she can hear the phone ringing inside. Either everyone has gone down the block to where the local school is having a sidewalk art sale, or no one can hear that ringing phone. Except for her, that is. And by the time she gets her key turned in the lock, the ringing has stopped.

Sarah, the only one of her sisters who never married, *is* there, it turns out, but there is no need to ask her why she didn't answer the phone; Sarah Bernicke, the one-time disco queen, is in the kitchen with the Village People turned up, dancing around with the O-Cedar in one hand, looking like a chick in a TV ad. She missed the bakery explosion, too, although their building is even closer to Zoltan's than Froger's.

Annie checks the answering machine, but there's a big red zero in the MESSAGES WAITING window. That means nothing in itself, lots of people call without leaving a message, but—

Star-sixty-nine reports the last call at eight-forty last night. Annie dials it anyway, hoping against hope that somewhere outside the big room that looks like a Grand Central Station movie set he found a place to re-charge his phone. To him it might seem he last spoke to her yesterday. Or only minutes ago. *Time is funny here*, he said. She has dreamed of that call so many times it now almost seems like a dream itself, but she has never told anyone about it. Not Craig, not even her own mother, now almost ninety but alert and with a firmly held belief in the afterlife.

In the kitchen, the Village People advise that there is no need to feel down. There isn't, and she doesn't. She nevertheless holds the phone very tightly as the number she has star-sixty-nined rings once, then twice. Annie stands in the living room with the phone to her ear and her free hand touching the brooch above her left breast, as if touching the brooch could still the pounding heart beneath it. Then the ringing stops and a recorded voice offers to sell her The *New York Times* at special bargain rates that will not be repeated.

INDEX TO TWENTY YEARS OF *BEST NEW HORROR*

Index by Contributor

Index by Title

Note: There are no artist credits for the US cover of volume #3 or the covers for volume #4 and #9.

Contents of Previous
Omnibus Editions

In the early 1990s, Robinson Publishing's bargain imprint Magpie Books published two omnibus editions of Best New Horror *in budget trade paperback editions. The details of the contents are listed below.*

"The Same in Any Language"   RAMSEY CAMPBELL
"His Mouth Will Taste of Wormwood"   POPPY Z. BRITE
"One Life in an Hourglass"   CHARLES L. GRANT
"The Braille Encyclopedia"   GRANT MORRISON
"Those of Rhenea"   DAVID SUTTON
"Power Cut"   JOEL LANE
"Jane Doe 112"   HARLAN ELLISON
"Pelts"   F. PAUL WILSON
"On the Wing"   JEAN-DANIEL BREQUE
"Where Flies Are Born"   DOUGLAS CLEGG
"Inside the Walled City"   GARRY KILWORTH
"The Dead Love You"   JONATHAN CARROLL
"Chui Chai"   S.P. SOMTOW
"When They Gave Us Memory"   DENNIS ETCHISON
"Lord of the Land"   GENE WOLFE
"Mister Ice Cold"   GAHAN WILSON
"The Original Dr Shade"   KIM NEWMAN

THE GIANT BOOK OF TERROR (1994)
Edited by Stephen Jones and Ramsey Campbell
Cover by Luis Rey

Introduction   THE EDITORS
"The Miracle Mile"   ROBERT R. McCAMMON
"The Suicide Artist"   SCOTT EDELMAN
"Dancing on a Blade of Dreams"   ROBERTA LANNES
"The Departed"   CLIVE BARKER
"How to Get Ahead in New York"   POPPY Z. BRITE
"Love, Death and the Maiden"   ROGER JOHNSON
"They Take"   JOHN BRUNNER
"Colder Than Hell"   EDWARD BRYANT
"Replacements"   LISA TUTTLE
"Under the Pylon"   GRAHAM JOYCE
"The Medusa"   THOMAS LIGOTTI
"Under the Ice"   JOHN GORDON
"Guignoir"   NORMAN PARTRIDGE
"The Little Green Ones"   LES DANIELS
"The Bacchae"   ELIZABETH HAND
"Mirror Man"   STEVE RASNIC TEM
"Mothmusic"   SARAH ASH
"Did They Get You to Trade?"   KARL EDWARD WAGNER
"Night Shift Sister"   NICHOLAS ROYLE
"Norman Wisdom and the Angel of Death"   CHRISTOPHER FOWLER
"The Dark Land"   MICHAEL MARSHALL SMITH
"Aviatrix"   PETER ATKINS
"Snodgrass"   IAIN R. MacLEOD
"The Day of the Sharks"   KATE WILHELM
"Anima"   M. JOHN HARRISON
"Red Reign"   KIM NEWMAN
"Bright Lights, Big Zombie"   DOUGLAS E. WINTER
"The Ghost Village"   PETER STRAUB

STEPHEN JONES lives in London, England. He is the winner of three World Fantasy Awards, four Horror Writers Association Bram Stoker Awards and three International Horror Guild Awards as well as being twenty-times recipient of the British Fantasy Award and a Hugo Award nominee. A former television producer/director and genre movie publicist and consultant (the first three *Hellraiser* movies, *Night Life, Nightbreed, Split Second, Mind Ripper, Last Gasp* etc.), he is the co-editor of *Horror: 100 Best Books, Horror: Another 100 Best Books, The Best Horror from Fantasy Tales, Gaslight & Ghosts, Now We Are Sick, H.P. Lovecraft's Book of Horror, The Anthology of Fantasy & the Supernatural, Secret City: Strange Tales of London, Great Ghost Stories, Tales to Freeze the Blood: More Great Ghost Stories* and the *Dark Terrors, Dark Voices* and *Fantasy Tales* series. He has written *Coraline: A Visual Companion, Stardust: The Visual Companion, Creepshows: The Illustrated Stephen King Movie Guide, The Essential Monster Movie Guide, The Illustrated Vampire Movie Guide, The Illustrated Dinosaur Movie Guide, The Illustrated Frankenstein Movie Guide* and *The Illustrated Werewolf Movie Guide*, and compiled *The Mammoth Book of Best New Horror* series, *The Mammoth Book of Terror, The Mammoth Book of Vampires, The Mammoth Book of Zombies, The Mammoth Book of Werewolves, The Mammoth Book of Frankenstein, The Mammoth Book of Dracula, The Mammoth Book of Vampire Stories By Women, The Mammoth Book of New Terror, The Mammoth Book of Monsters, Shadows Over Innsmouth, Weird Shadows Over Innsmouth, Dark Detectives, Dancing with the Dark, Dark of the Night, White of the Moon, Keep Out the Night, By Moonlight Only, Don't Turn Out the Light, H. P. Lovecraft's Book of the Supernatural, Travellers in Darkness, Summer Chills, Exorcisms and Ecstasies* by Karl Edward Wagner, *The Vampire Stories of R. Chetwynd-Hayes, Phantoms and Fiends* and *Frights and Fancies* by R. Chetwynd-Hayes, *James Herbert: By Horror Haunted, Basil Copper: A Life in Books, Necronomicon: The Best Weird Tales of H. P. Lovecraft, The Complete Chronicles of Conan* by Robert E. Howard, *The Emperor of Dreams: The Lost Worlds of Clark Ashton Smith, Sea-Kings of Mars and Otherworldly Stories* by Leigh Brackett, *The Mark of the Beast and Other Fantastical Tales* by Rudyard Kipling, *Clive Barker's A–Z of Horror, Clive Barker's Shadows in Eden, Clive Barker's The Nightbreed Chronicles* and the *Hellraiser Chronicles*. A Guest of Honour at the 2002 World Fantasy Convention in Minneapolis, Minnesota, and the 2004 World Horror Convention in Phoenix, Arizona, he has been a guest lecturer at UCLA in California and London's Kingston University and St Mary's University College. You can visit his website at *www. stephenjoneseditor.com*